SIDNEY SHELDON

Three Complete Novels

SIDNEY SHELDON

Three Complete Novels

BLOODLINE
★
A STRANGER IN THE MIRROR
★
THE NAKED FACE

WINGS BOOKS
New York • Avenel, New Jersey

This omnibus was originally published in separate volumes under the titles:
The Naked Face, copyright © 1970 by Sheldon Literary Trust
A Stranger In The Mirror, copyright © 1976 by Sheldon Literary Trust
Bloodline, copyright © 1977 by Sidney Sheldon

This 1992 edition is published by Wings Books, distributed by Outlet Book Company, Inc., a Random House Company,
40 Engelhard Avenue, Avenel, New Jersey, 07001,
by arrangement with William Morrow & Company.

Random House
New York • Toronto • London • Sydney • Auckland

Printed and bound in the United States of America

Library of Congress Cataloging-in-Publication Data
Sheldon, Sidney.
Sidney Sheldon—three complete novels / Sidney Sheldon.
p.   cm.
Contents: Bloodline—A stranger in the mirror—The naked face.
ISBN 0-517-07773-6
I. Title.   II. Title: Three complete novels.
PS3569.H3927 A6   1992
813'.54—dc20   92-7599   CIP
8 7 6 5 4 3 2

CONTENTS

BLOODLINE

For Natalie
with love

ACKNOWLEDGMENTS

While this is a work of fiction, the backgrounds are authentic, and I wish to express my gratitude to those who so generously contributed to my research. If, in adapting their information to the requirements of a novel, I have found it necessary to expand or contract certain time elements, I take full responsibility. My deepest appreciation goes to

Dr. Margaret M. McCarron
Associate Medical Director
Los Angeles County,
 University of Southern California

Dean Brady, USC Pharmacy School

Dr. Gregory A. Thompson
Director, Drug Information Center
Los Angeles County,
 University of Southern California

Dr. Bernd W. Schulze
Drug Information Center
Los Angeles County,
 University of Southern California

Dr. Judy Flesh

Urs Jäggi, Hoffmann-La Roche & Co., A. G., Basel

Dr. Gunter Siebel, Schering A. G., Berlin

The Criminal Investigation Divisions
 of Scotland Yard, Zurich and Berlin

Charles Walford, Sotheby Parke Bernet, London

And to Jorja, who makes all things possible.

"The physician will carefully prepare a mixture of crocodile dung, lizard flesh, bat's blood and camel's spit . . ."

—from a papyrus listing 811 prescriptions used by the Egyptians in 1550 B.C.

Book One

He was seated in the dark, alone, behind the desk of Hajib Kafir, staring unseeingly out of the dusty office window at the timeless minarets of Istanbul. He was a man who was at home in a dozen capitals of the world, but Istanbul was one of his favorite cities. Not the tourist Istanbul of Beyoglu Street, or the gaudy Lalezab Bar of the Hilton, but the out-of-the-way places that only the Moslems knew: the *yalis,* and the small markets beyond the *souks,* and the Telli Baba, the cemetery where only one person was buried, and the people came to pray to him.

His waiting had the patience of a hunter, the quiet stillness of a man in control of his body and his emotions. He was Welsh, with the dark, stormy good looks of his ancestors. He had black hair and a strong face, and quick intelligent eyes that were a deep blue. He was over six feet tall, with the lean muscular body of a man who kept himself in good physical condition. The office was filled with the odors of Hajib Kafir, his sickly sweet tobacco, his acrid Turkish coffee, his fat, oily body. Rhys Williams was unaware of them. He was thinking about the telephone call he had received from Chamonix an hour earlier.

". . . A terrible accident! Believe me, Mr. Williams, we are all devastated. It happened so quickly that there was no chance to save him. Mr. Roffe was killed instantly . . ."

Sam Roffe, president of Roffe and Sons, the second largest

11

pharmaceutical company in the world, a multibillion-dollar dynasty that girdled the globe. It was impossible to think of Sam
Roffe as being dead. He had always been so vital, so full of life and
energy, a man on the move, living in airplanes that raced him to
company factories and offices all over the world, where he solved
problems others could not deal with, created new concepts,
pushed everyone to do more, to do better. Even though he had
married, and fathered a child, his only real interest had been the
business. Sam Roffe had been a brilliant and extraordinary man.
Who could replace him? Who was capable of running the enormous empire he had left? Sam Roffe had not chosen an heir
apparent. But then, he had not planned to die at fifty-two. He had
thought there would be plenty of time.

And now his time had run out.

The lights in the office suddenly flashed on and Rhys Williams
looked toward the doorway, momentarily blinded.

"Mr. Williams! I did not know anyone was here."

It was Sophie, one of the company secretaries, who was assigned
to Rhys Williams whenever he was in Istanbul. She was Turkish,
in her middle twenties, with an attractive face and a lithe, sensuous
body, rich with promise. She had let Rhys know in subtle, ancient
ways that she was available to bring him whatever pleasures he
wished, whenever he desired them, but Rhys was not interested.

Now she said, "I returned to finish some letters for Mr. Kafir."
She added softly, "Perhaps there is something I can do for you?"

As she moved closer to the desk, Rhys could sense the musky
smell of a wild animal in season.

"Where is Mr. Kafir?"

Sophie shook her head regretfully. "He has left for the day."
She smoothed the front of her dress with the palms of soft, clever
hands. "Can I help you in some way?" Her eyes were dark and
moist.

"Yes," Rhys said. "Find him."

She frowned. "I have no idea where he could—"

"Try the Kervansaray, or the Mermara." It would probably be
the former, where one of Hajib Kafir's mistresses worked as a belly
dancer. Although you never knew with Kafir, Rhys thought. He
might even be with his wife.

Sophie was apologetic. "I will try, but I am afraid I—"

"Explain to him that if he's not here in one hour, he no longer has a job."

The expression on her face changed. "I will see what I can do, Mr. Williams." She started toward the door.

"Turn out the lights."

Somehow, it was easier to sit in the dark with his thoughts. The image of Sam Roffe kept intruding. Mont Blanc should have been an easy climb this time of the year, early September. Sam had tried the climb before, but storms had kept him from reaching the peak.

"I'll plant the company flag up there this time," he had promised Rhys, jokingly.

And then the telephone call a short while ago as Rhys was checking out of the Pera Palace. He could hear the agitated voice on the telephone. ". . . They were doing a traverse over a glacier. . . . Mr. Roffe lost his footing and his rope broke. . . . He fell into a bottomless crevasse . . ."

Rhys could visualize Sam's body smashing against the unforgiving ice, hurtling downward into the crevasse. He forced his mind away from the scene. That was the past. There was the present to worry about now. The members of Sam Roffe's family had to be notified of his death, and they were scattered in various parts of the world. A press announcement had to be prepared. The news was going to travel through international financial circles like a shock wave. With the company in the midst of a financial crisis, it was vital that the impact of Sam Roffe's death be minimized as much as possible. That would be Rhys's job.

Rhys Williams had first met Sam Roffe nine years earlier. Rhys, then twenty-five, had been sales manager for a small drug firm. He was brilliant and innovative, and as the company had expanded, Rhys's reputation had quickly spread. He was offered a job at Roffe and Sons and when he turned it down, Sam Roffe bought the company Rhys worked for and sent for him. Even now he could recall the overwhelming power of Sam Roffe's presence at their first meeting.

"You belong here at Roffe and Sons," Sam Roffe had informed him. "That's why I bought that horse-and-buggy outfit you were with."

Rhys had found himself flattered and irritated at the same time. "Suppose I don't want to stay?"

Sam Roffe had smiled and said confidently, "You'll want to stay. You and I have something in common, Rhys. We're both ambitious. We want to own the world. I'm going to show you how."

The words were magic, a promised feast for the fierce hunger that burned in the young man, for he knew something that Sam Roffe did not: There was no Rhys Williams. He was a myth that had been created out of desperation and poverty and despair.

He had been born near the coalfields of Gwent and Carmarthen, the red scarred valleys of Wales where layers of sandstone and saucer-shaped beds of limestone and coal puckered the green earth. He grew up in a fabled land where the very names were poetry: Brecon and Pen-y Fan and Penderyn and Glyncorrwg and Maesteg. It was a land of legend, where the coal buried deep in the ground had been created 280 million years before, where the landscape was once covered with so many trees that a squirrel could travel from Brecon Beacons to the sea without ever touching the ground. But the industrial revolution had come along and the beautiful green trees were chopped down by the charcoal burners to feed the insatiable fires of the iron industry.

The young boy grew up with the heroes of another time and another world. Robert Farrer, burned at the stake by the Roman Catholic Church because he would not take a vow of celibacy and abandon his wife; King Hywel the Good, who brought the law to Wales in the tenth century; the fierce warrior Brychen who sired twelve sons and twenty-four daughters and savagely put down all attacks on his kingdom. It was a land of glorious histories in which the lad had been raised. But it was not all glory. Rhys's ancestors were miners, every one of them, and the young boy used to listen to the tales of hell that his father and his uncles recounted. They talked of the terrible times when there was no work, when the rich coalfields of Gwent and Carmarthen had been closed in a bitter fight between the companies and the miners, and the miners were debased by a poverty that eroded ambition and pride, that sapped a man's spirit and strength and finally made him surrender.

When the mines were open, it was another kind of hell. Most of

Rhys's family had died in the mines. Some had perished in the bowels of the earth, others had coughed their blackened lungs away. Few had lived past the age of thirty.

Rhys used to listen to his father and his aging young uncles discussing the past, the cave-ins and the cripplings and the strikes; talking of the good times and the bad, and to the young boy they seemed the same. All bad. The thought of spending his years in the darkness of the earth appalled Rhys. He knew he had to escape.

He ran away from home when he was twelve. He left the valleys of coal and went to the coast, to Sully Ranny Bay and Lavernock, where the rich tourists flocked, and the young boy fetched and carried and made himself useful, helping ladies down the steep cliffs to the beach, lugging heavy picnic baskets, driving a pony cart at Penarth, and working at the amusement park at Whitmore Bay.

He was only a few hours away from home, but the distance could not be measured. The people here were from another world. Rhys Williams had never imagined such beautiful people or such glorious finery. Each woman looked like a queen to him and the men were all elegant and splendid. This was the world where he belonged, and there was nothing he would not do to make it his.

By the time Rhys Williams was fourteen, he had saved enough money to pay for his passage to London. He spent the first three days simply walking around the huge city, staring at everything, hungrily drinking in the incredible sights and the sounds and the smells.

His first job was as a delivery boy at a draper's shop. There were two male clerks, superior beings both, and a female clerk, who made the young Welsh boy's heart sing every time he looked at her. The men treated Rhys as he was meant to be treated, like dirt. He was a curiosity. He dressed peculiarly, had abominable manners and spoke with an incomprehensible accent. They could not even pronounce his name. They called him Rice, and Rye, and Rise. "It's pronounced Reese," Rhys kept telling them.

The girl took pity on him. Her name was Gladys Simpkins and she shared a tiny flat in Tooting with three other girls. One day she allowed the young boy to walk her home after work and invited him in for a cup of tea. Young Rhys was overcome with nervousness. He had thought this was going to be his first sexual experience, but when he began to put his arm around Gladys, she stared at him a moment, then laughed. "I'm not giving none of that to you," she said. "But I'll give you some advice. If you want to make somethin' of yourself, get yourself some proper clothes and a bit of education and learn yourself some manners." She studied the thin, passionate young face and looked into Rhys's deep blue eyes, and said softly, "You're gonna be a bit of all right when you grow up."

If you want to make somethin' of yourself . . . That was the moment when the fictitious Rhys Williams was born. The real Rhys Williams was an uneducated, ignorant boy with no background, no breeding, no past, no future. But he had imagination, intelligence and a fiery ambition. It was enough. He started with the image of what he wanted to be, who he intended to be. When he looked in his mirror, he did not see the clumsy, grubby little boy with the funny accent; his mirror image was polished and suave and successful. Little by little, Rhys began to match himself to the image in his mind. He attended night school, and he spent his weekends in art galleries. He haunted public libraries and went to the theater, sitting in the gallery, studying the fine clothes of the men seated in the stalls. He scrimped on food, so that once a month he could go to a good restaurant, where he carefully copied the table manners of others. He observed and learned and remembered. He was like a sponge, erasing the past, soaking up the future.

In one short year Rhys had learned enough to realize that Gladys Simpkins, his princess, was a cheap Cockney girl who was already beneath his tastes. He quit the draper's shop and went to work as a clerk at a chemist's shop that was part of a large chain. He was almost sixteen now, but he looked older. He had filled out and was taller. Women were beginning to pay attention to his dark Welsh good looks and his quick, flattering tongue. He was an instant success in the shop. Female customers would wait until Rhys was available to take care of them. He dressed well and spoke correctly, and he knew he had come a long way from Gwent and Carmarthen, but when he looked in the mirror, he was still not satisfied. The journey he intended to make was still ahead of him.

Within two years Rhys Williams was made manager of the shop where he worked. The district manager of the chain said to Rhys, "This is just the beginning, Williams. Work hard and one day you'll be the superintendent of half a dozen stores."

Rhys almost laughed aloud. To think that that could be the height of anyone's ambition! Rhys had never stopped going to school. He was studying business administration and marketing and commercial law. He wanted more. His image in the mirror was at the top of the ladder; Rhys felt he was still at the bottom. His opportunity to move up came when a drug salesman walked in one day, watched Rhys charm several ladies into buying products they had no use for, and said, "You're wasting your time here, lad. You should be working in a bigger pond."

"What did you have in mind?" Rhys asked.

"Let me talk to my boss about you."

Two weeks later Rhys was working as a salesman at the small drug firm. He was one of fifty salesmen, but when Rhys looked in his special mirror, he knew that that was not true. His only competition was himself. He was getting closer to his image now, closer to the fictitious character he was creating. A man who was intelligent, cultured, sophisticated and charming. What he was trying to do was impossible. Everyone knew that one had to be born with those qualities; they could not be created. But Rhys did it. He became the image he had envisioned.

He traveled around the country, selling the firm's products, talking and listening. He would return to London full of practical suggestions, and he quickly began to move up the ladder.

Three years after he had joined the company, Rhys was made general sales manager. Under his skillful guidance the company began to expand.

And four years later, Sam Roffe had come into his life. He had recognized the hunger in Rhys.

"You're like me," Sam Roffe had said. "We want to own the world. I'm going to show you how." And he had.

Sam Roffe had been a brilliant mentor. Over the next nine years under Sam Roffe's tutelage, Rhys Williams had become invaluable to the company. As time went on, he was given more and more responsibility, reorganizing various divisions, troubleshooting in whatever part of the world he was needed, coordinating the different branches of Roffe and Sons, creating new concepts. In the end Rhys knew more about running the company than anyone except Sam Roffe himself. Rhys Williams was the logical successor to the presidency. One morning, when Rhys and Sam Roffe were returning from Caracas in a company jet, a luxurious converted Boeing 707-320, one of a fleet of eight planes, Sam Roffe had complimented Rhys on a lucrative deal that he had concluded with the Venezuelan government.

"There'll be a fat bonus in this for you, Rhys."

Rhys had replied quietly, "I don't want a bonus, Sam. I'd prefer some stock and a place on your board of directors."

He had earned it, and both men were aware of it. But Sam had said, "I'm sorry. I can't change the rules, even for you. Roffe and Sons is a privately held company. No one outside of the family can sit on the board or hold stock."

Rhys had known that, of course. He attended all board meetings, but not as a member. He was an outsider. Sam Roffe was the last male in the Roffe bloodline. The other Roffes, Sam's cousins, were females. The men they had married sat on the board of the company. Walther Gassner, who had married Anna Roffe; Ivo Palazzi, married to Simonetta Roffe; Charles Martel, married to Hélène Roffe. And Sir Alec Nichols, whose mother had been a Roffe.

So Rhys had been forced to make a decision. He knew that he deserved to be on the board, that one day he should be running the company. Present circumstances prevented it, but circumstances had a way of changing. Rhys had decided to stay, to wait and see what happened. Sam had taught him patience. And now Sam was dead.

The office lights blazed on again, and Hajib Kafir stood in the doorway. Kafir was the Turkish sales manager for Roffe and Sons. He was a short, swarthy man who wore diamonds and his fat belly like proud ornaments. He had the disheveled air of a man who had dressed hastily. So Sophie had not found him in a nightclub. Ah, well, Rhys thought. A side effect of Sam Roffe's death. Coitus interruptus.

"Rhys!" Kafir was exclaiming. "My dear fellow, forgive me! I had no idea you were still in Istanbul! You were on your way to catch a plane, and I had some urgent business to—"

"Sit down, Hajib. Listen carefully. I want you to send four cables in company code. They're going to different countries. I want them hand-delivered by our own messengers. Do you understand?"

"Of course," Kafir said, bewildered. "Perfectly."

Rhys glanced at the thin, gold Baume & Mercier watch on his wrist. "The New City Post Office will be closed. Send the cables from Yeni Posthane Cad. I want them on their way within thirty minutes." He handed Kafir a copy of the cable he had written out. "Anyone who discusses this will be instantly discharged."

Kafir glanced at the cable and his eyes widened. "My God!" he said. "Oh, my God!" He looked up at Rhys's dark face. "How—how did this terrible thing happen?"

"Sam Roffe died in an accident," Rhys said.

Now, for the first time, Rhys allowed his thoughts to go to what he had been pushing away from his consciousness, what he had been trying to avoid thinking about: Elizabeth Roffe, Sam's daughter. She was twenty-four now. When Rhys had first met her, she had been a fifteen-year-old girl with braces on her teeth, fiercely shy and overweight, a lonely rebel. Over the years Rhys had watched Elizabeth develop into a very special young woman, with her mother's beauty and her father's intelligence and spirit. She had become close to Sam. Rhys knew how deeply the news would affect her. He would have to tell her himself.

Two hours later, Rhys Williams was over the Mediterranean on a company jet, headed for New York.

Anna Roffe Gassner knew that she must not let herself scream
again or Walther would return and kill her. She crouched in a
corner of her bedroom, her body trembling uncontrollably, waiting for death. What had started out as a beautiful fairy tale had
ended in terror, unspeakable horror. It had taken her too long to
face the truth: the man she had married was a homicidal maniac.

Anna Roffe had never loved anyone before she met Walther
Gassner, including her mother, her father and herself. Anna had
been a frail, sickly child who suffered from fainting spells. She
could not remember a time when she had been free of hospitals or
nurses or specialists flown in from far-off places. Because her
father was Anton Roffe, of Roffe and Sons, the top medical experts
flew to Anna's bedside in Berlin. But when they had examined her
and tested her and finally departed, they knew no more than they
had known before. They could not diagnose her condition.

Anna was unable to go to school like other children, and in time
she had become withdrawn, creating a world of her own, full of
dreams and fantasies, where no one else was allowed to enter. She
painted her own pictures of life, because the colors of reality were
too harsh for her to accept. When Anna was eighteen, her dizziness
and fainting spells disappeared as mysteriously as they had
started. But they had marred her life. At an age when most girls

were getting engaged or married, Anna had never even been kissed by a boy. She insisted to herself that she did not mind. She was content to live her own dream life, apart from everything and everyone. In her middle twenties suitors came calling, for Anna Roffe was an heiress who bore one of the most prestigious names in the world, and many men were eager to share her fortune. She received proposals from a Swedish count, an Italian poet and half a dozen princes from indigent countries. Anna refused them all. On his daughter's thirtieth birthday, Anton Roffe moaned, "I'm going to die without leaving any grandchildren."

On her thirty-fifth birthday Anna had gone to Kitzbühel, in Austria, and there she had met Walther Gassner, a ski instructor thirteen years younger than she.

The first time Anna had seen Walther, the sight of him had literally taken her breath away. He was skiing down the *Hahnen-kamm*, the steep racing slope, and it was the most beautiful sight Anna had ever seen. She had moved closer to the bottom of the ski run to get a better look at him. He was like a young god, and Anna had been satisfied to do nothing but watch him. He had caught her staring at him.

"Aren't you skiing, *gnädiges Fräulein?*"

She had shaken her head, not trusting her voice, and he had smiled and said, "Then let me buy you lunch."

Anna had fled in a panic, like a schoolgirl. From then on, Walther Gassner had pursued her. Anna Roffe was not a fool. She was aware that she was neither pretty nor brilliant, that she was a plain woman, and that, aside from her name, she had seemingly very little to offer a man. But Anna knew that trapped within that ordinary facade was a beautiful, sensitive girl filled with love and poetry and music.

Perhaps because Anna was not beautiful, she had a deep reverence for beauty. She would go to the great museums and spend hours staring at the paintings and the statues. When she had seen Walther Gassner it was as though all the gods had come alive for her.

Anna was having breakfast on the terrace of the Tennerhof Hotel on the second day when Walther Gassner joined her. He did look like a young god. He had a regular, clean-cut profile, and his features were delicate, sensitive, strong. His face was deeply tanned and his teeth were white and even. He had blond hair and his eyes were a slate gray. Beneath his ski clothes Anna could see the movement of his biceps and thigh muscles, and she felt tremors going through her loins. She hid her hands in her lap so that he could not see the keratosis.

"I looked for you on the slopes yesterday afternoon," Walther said. Anna could not speak. "If you don't ski, I'd like to teach you." He smiled, and added, "No charge."

He had taken her to the *Hausberg*, the beginners slope, for her first lesson. It was immediately apparent to them both that Anna had no talent for skiing. She kept losing her balance and falling down, but she insisted on trying again and again because she was afraid that Walther would despise her if she failed. Instead, he had picked her up after her tenth fall and had said gently, "You were meant to do better things than this."

"What things?" Anna had asked, miserable.

"I'll tell you at dinner tonight."

They had dined that evening and breakfasted the next morning, and then had lunch and dinner again. Walther neglected his clients. He skipped skiing lessons in order to go into the village with Anna. He took her to the casino in Der Goldene Greif, and they went sleigh riding and shopping and hiking, and sat on the terrace of the hotel hour after hour, talking. For Anna, it was a time of magic.

Five days after they had met, Walther took her hands in his and said, "Anna, *liebchen*, I want to marry you."

He had spoiled it. He had taken her out of her wonderful fairyland and brought her back to the cruel reality of who and what she was. An unattractive, thirty-five-year-old virginal prize for fortune hunters.

She had tried to leave but Walther had stopped her. "We love each other, Anna. You can't run away from that."

She listened to him lying, listened to him saying, "I've never loved anyone before," and she made it easy for him because she wanted so desperately to believe him. She took him back to her room, and they sat there, talking, and as Walther told Anna the story of his life, she suddenly began to believe, thinking with wonder, It is really the story of my own life.

Like her, Walther had never had anyone to love. He had been

alienated from the world by his birth as a bastard, as Anna had been alienated by her illness. Like her, Walther had been filled with the need to give love. He had been brought up in an orphanage, and when he was thirteen and his extraordinary good looks were already apparent, the women in the orphanage had begun to use him, bringing him to their rooms at night, taking him to bed with them, teaching him how to please them. As a reward the young boy was given extra food and pieces of meat, and desserts made with real sugar. He received everything but love.

When Walther was old enough to run away from the orphanage, he found that the world outside was no different. Women wanted to use his good looks, to wear him as a badge; but it never went any deeper than that. They gave him gifts of money and clothes and jewelry, but never of themselves.

Walther was her soul mate, Anna realized, her doppelgänger. They were married in a quiet ceremony at the town hall.

Anna had expected her father to be overjoyed. Instead, he had flown into a rage. "You're a silly, vain fool," Anton Roffe screamed at her. "You've married a no-good fortune hunter. I've had him checked out. All his life he's lived off women, but he's never found anyone stupid enough to marry him before."

"Stop it!" Anna cried. "You don't understand him."

But Anton Roffe knew that he understood Walther Gassner only too well. He asked his new son-in-law to come to his office.

Walther looked around approvingly at the dark paneling and the old paintings hanging on the walls. "I like this place," Walther said.

"Yes. I'm sure it's better than the orphanage."

Walther looked up at him sharply, his eyes suddenly wary. "I beg your pardon?"

Anton said, "Let's cut out the *Scheiss*. You've made a mistake. My daughter has no money."

Walther's gray eyes seemed to turn to stone. "What are you trying to tell me?"

"I'm not trying to tell you anything. I'm telling you. You won't get anything from Anna because she hasn't got anything. If you had done your homework more thoroughly, you would have learned that Roffe and Sons is a close-held corporation. That means that none of its stock can be sold. We live comfortably, but that's it. There is no big fortune to be milked here." He fumbled in his pocket, drew out an envelope and threw it on the desk in front of Walther. "This will reimburse you for your trouble. I will expect you to be out of Berlin by six o'clock. I don't want Anna ever to hear from you again."

Walther said quietly, "Did it ever cross your mind that I might have married Anna because I fell in love with her?"

"No," Anton said acidly. "Did it ever cross yours?"

Walther looked at him a moment. "Let's see what my market price is." He tore open the envelope and counted the money. He looked up at Anton Roffe again. "I value myself at much higher than twenty thousand marks."

"It's all you're getting. Count yourself lucky."

"I do," Walther said. "If you want to know the truth, I think I am very lucky. Thank you." He put the money in his pocket with a careless gesture and a moment later was walking out the door.

Anton Roffe was relieved. He experienced a slight sense of guilt and distaste for what he had done and yet he knew it had been the only solution. Anna would be unhappy at being deserted by her groom, but it was better to have it happen now than later. He would try to see to it that she met some eligible men her own age, who would at least respect her if not love her. Someone who would be interested in her and not her money or her name. Someone who would not be bought for twenty thousand marks.

When Anton Roffe arrived home, Anna ran up to greet him, tears in her eyes. He took her in his arms and hugged her, and said, "Anna, *liebchen*, it's going to be all right. You'll get over him—"

And Anton looked over her shoulder, and standing in the doorway was Walther Gassner. Anna was holding up her finger, saying, "Look what Walther bought me! Isn't it the most beautiful ring you've ever seen? It cost twenty thousand marks."

In the end, Anna's parents were forced to accept Walther Gassner. As a wedding gift they bought them a lovely Schinkel manor house in Wannsee, with French furniture, mixed with antiques, comfortable couches and easy chairs, a Roentgen desk in the library, and bookcases lining the walls. The upstairs was furnished with elegant eighteenth-century pieces from Denmark and Sweden.

"It's too much," Walther told Anna. "I don't want anything

from them or from you. I want to be able to buy you beautiful things, *liebchen*." He gave her that boyish grin and said, "But I have no money."

"Of course you do," Anna replied. "Everything I have belongs to you."

Walther smiled at her sweetly and said, "Does it?"

At Anna's insistence—for Walther seemed reluctant to discuss money—she explained her financial situation to him. She had a trust fund that was enough for her to live on comfortably, but the bulk of her fortune was in shares of Roffe and Sons. The shares could not be sold without the unanimous approval of the board of directors.

"How much is your stock worth?" Walther asked.

Anna told him. Walther could not believe it. He made her repeat the sum.

"And you can't sell the stock?"

"No. My cousin Sam won't let it be sold. He holds the controlling shares. One day . . ."

Walther expressed an interest in working in the family business. Anton Roffe was against it.

"What can a ski bum contribute to Roffe and Sons?" he asked.

But in the end he gave in to his daughter, and Walther was given a job with the company in administration. He proved to be excellent at it and advanced rapidly. When Anna's father died two year's later, Walther Gassner was made a member of the board. Anna was so proud of him. He was always the perfect husband and lover. He was always bringing her flowers and little gifts, and he seemed content to stay at home with her in the evening, just the two of them. Anna's happiness was almost too much for her to bear. *Ach, danke, lieber Gott,* she would say silently.

Anna learned to cook, so that she could make Walther's favorite dishes. She made *choucroute,* a bed of crunchy sauerkraut and creamy mashed potatoes heaped with a smoked pork chop, a frankfurter and a Nuremberg sausage. She prepared fillet of pork cooked in beer and flavored with cumin, and served it with a fat baked apple, cored and peeled, the center filled with *airelles,* the little red berries.

"You're the best cook in the world, *liebchen,*" Walther would say, and Anna would blush with pride.

In the third year of their marriage, Anna became pregnant.

25

There was a great deal of pain during the first eight months of her pregnancy, but Anna bore that happily. It was something else that worried her.

It started one day after lunch. She had been knitting a sweater for Walther, daydreaming, and suddenly she heard Walther's voice, saying, "My God, Anna, what are you doing, sitting here in the dark?"

The afternoon had turned to dusk, and she looked down at the sweater in her lap and she had not touched it. Where had the day gone? Where had her mind been? After that, Anna had other similar experiences, and she began to wonder whether this sliding away into nothingness was a portent, an omen that she was going to die. She did not think she was afraid of death, but she could not bear the thought of leaving Walther.

Four weeks before the baby was due, Anna lapsed into one of her daydreams, missed a step and fell down an entire flight of stairs.

She awakened in the hospital.

Walther was seated on the edge of the bed, holding her hand. "You gave me a terrible scare."

In a sudden panic she thought, The baby! I can't feel the baby. She reached down. Her stomach was flat. "Where is my baby?"

And Walther had held her close and hugged her.

The doctor said, "You had twins, Mrs. Gassner."

Anna turned to Walther, and his eyes were filled with tears. "A boy and girl, *liebchen.*"

And she could have died right then of happiness. She felt a sudden, irresistible longing to have them in her arms. She had to see them, feel them, hold them.

"We'll talk about that when you're stronger," the doctor said. "Not until you're stronger."

They assured Anna that she was getting better every day, but she was becoming frightened. Something was happening to her that she did not understand. Walther would arrive and take her hand and say good-bye, and she would look at him in surprise and start to say, "But you just got here . . ." And then she would see the clock, and three or four hours would have passed.

She had no idea where they had gone.

She had a vague recollection that they had brought the children to her in the night and that she had fallen asleep. She could not remember too clearly, and she was afraid to ask. It did not matter. She would have them to herself when Walther took her home.

The wonderful day finally arrived. Anna left her hospital room in a wheelchair, even though she insisted she was strong enough to walk. She actually felt very weak, but she was so excited that nothing mattered except the fact that she was going to see her babies. Walther carried her into the house, and he started to take her upstairs to their bedroom.

"No, no!" she said. "Take me to the nursery."

"You must rest now, darling. You're not strong enough to—"

She did not listen to the rest of what he was saying. She slipped out of his arms and ran into the nursery.

The blinds were drawn and the room was dark and it took Anna's eyes a moment to adjust. She was filled with such excitement that it made her dizzy. She was afraid she was going to faint.

Walther had come in behind her. He was talking to her, trying to explain something, but whatever it was was unimportant.

For there they were. They were both asleep in their cribs, and Anna moved toward them softly, so as not to disturb them, and stood there, staring down at them. They were the most beautiful children she had ever seen. Even now, she could see that the boy would have Walther's handsome features and his thick blond hair. The girl was like an exquisite doll, with soft, golden hair and a small, triangular face.

Anna turned to Walther and said, her voice choked, "They're beautiful. I—I'm so happy."

"Come, Anna," Walther whispered. He put his arms around Anna, and held her close, and there was a fierce hunger in him, and she began to feel a stirring within her. They had not made love for such a long time. Walther was right. There would be plenty of time for the children later.

The boy she named Peter and the girl Birgitta. They were two beautiful miracles that she and Walther had made, and Anna would spend hour after hour in the nursery, playing with them, talking to them. Even though they could not understand her yet, she knew they could feel her love. Sometimes, in the middle of play, she would turn and Walther would be standing in the doorway, home from the office, and Anna would realize that somehow the whole day had slipped by.

"Come and join us," she would say. "We're playing a game."

"Have you fixed dinner yet?" Walther would ask, and she would suddenly feel guilty. She would resolve to pay more attention to Walther, and less to the children, but the next day the same thing would happen. The twins were like an irresistible magnet that drew her to them. Anna still loved Walther very much, and she tried to assuage her guilt by telling herself that the children were a part of him. Every night, as soon as Walther was asleep, Anna would slip out of bed and creep into the nursery, and sit and stare at the children until dawn started filtering into the room. Then she would turn and hurry back to bed before Walther awoke.

Once, in the middle of the night, Walther walked into the nursery and caught her. "What in God's name do you think you're doing?" he said.

"Nothing, darling. I was just—"

"Go back to bed!"

He had never spoken to her like that before.

At breakfast Walther said, "I think we should take a vacation. It will be good for us to get away."

"But, Walther, the children are too young to travel."

"I'm talking about the two of us."

She shook her head. "I couldn't leave them."

He took her hand and said, "I want you to forget about the children."

"Forget about the children?" There was shock in her voice.

He looked into her eyes and said, "Anna, remember how wonderful it was between us before you were pregnant? What good times we had? How much joy it was to be together, just the two of us, with no one else around to interfere?"

It was then that she understood. Walther was jealous of the children.

The weeks and months passed swiftly. Walther never went near the children now. On their birthdays Anna bought them lovely presents. Walther always managed to be out of town on business.

Anna could not go on deceiving herself forever. The truth was that Walther had no interest in the children at all. Anna felt that perhaps it was her fault, because she was *too* interested in them. *Obsessed* was the word Walther had used. He had asked her to consult a doctor about it, and she had gone only to please Walther. But the doctor was a fool. The moment he had started talking to her, Anna had shut him out, letting her mind drift, until she heard him say, "Our time is up, Mrs. Gassner. Will I see you next week?"

"Of course."

She never returned.

Anna felt that the problem was as much Walther's as hers. If her fault lay in loving the children too much, then his fault lay in not loving them enough.

Anna learned not to mention the children in Walther's presence, but she could hardly wait for him to leave for the office, so she could hurry into the nursery to be with her babies. Except that they were no longer babies. They had had their third birthday, and already Anna could see what they would look like as adults. Peter was tall for his age and his body was strong and athletic, like his father's. Anna would hold him on her lap and croon, "Ah, Peter, what are you going to do to the poor fräuleins? Be gentle with them, my darling son. They won't have a chance."

And Peter would smile shyly and hug her.

Then Anna would turn to Birgitta. Birgitta grew prettier each day. She looked like neither Anna nor Walther. She had spun-golden hair and skin as delicate as porcelain. Peter had his father's fiery temper and sometimes it would be necessary for Anna to spank him gently, but Birgitta had the disposition of an angel. When Walther was not around, Anna played records or read to them. Their favorite book was *101 Märchens*. They would insist that Anna read them the tales of ogres and goblins and witches over and over again, and at night, Anna would put them to bed, singing them a lullaby:

> *Schlaf, Kindlein, schlaf,*
> *Der Vater hüt't die Schaf . . .*

Anna had prayed that time would soften Walther's attitude, that he would change. He did change, but for the worse. He hated the children. In the beginning Anna had told herself that it was because Walther wanted all of her love for himself, that he was unwilling to share it with anyone else. But slowly she became aware that it had nothing to do with loving her. It had to do with hating her. Her father had been right. Walther had married her for her money. The children were a threat to him. He wanted to get rid of them. More and more he talked to Anna about selling the stock. "Sam has no right to stop us! We could take all that money and go away somewhere. Just the two of us."

She stared at him. "What about the children?"

His eyes were feverish. "No. Listen to me. For both our sakes we've got to get rid of them. We must."

It was then that Anna began to realize that he was insane. She was terrified. Walther had fired all the domestic help, and except for a cleaning woman who came in once a week, Anna and the children were alone with him, at his mercy. He needed help. Perhaps it was not too late to cure him. In the fifteenth century they gathered the insane and imprisoned them forever on houseboats, *Narrenschiffe*, the ships of fools, but today, with modern medicine, she felt there must be something they could do to help Walther.

Now, on this day in September, Anna sat huddled on the floor in her bedroom, where Walther had locked her, waiting for him to return. She knew what she had to do. For his sake, as well as hers and the children's. Anna rose unsteadily and walked over to the telephone. She hesitated for only an instant, then picked it up and began to dial 110, the police emergency number.

An alien voice in her ear said, *"Hallo. Hier is der Notruf der Polizei. Kann ich ihnen helfen?"*

"Ja, bitte!" Her voice was choked. *"Ich—"*

A hand came out of nowhere and tore the receiver from her, and slammed it down into the cradle.

Anna backed away. "Oh, please," she whimpered, "don't hurt me."

Walther was moving toward her, his eyes bright, his voice so soft that she could hardly make out the words. *"Liebchen,* I'm not going to hurt you. I love you, don't you know that?" He touched her, and she could feel her flesh crawl. "it's just that we don't want the police coming here, do we?" She shook her head from side to side, too filled with terror to speak. "It's the children that are causing the trouble, Anna. We're going to get rid of them. I—"

Downstairs the front doorbell rang. Walther stood there, hesitating. It rang again.

"Stay here," he ordered. "I'll be back."

Anna watched, petrified, as he walked out the bedroom door. He slammed it behind him and she could hear the click of the key as he locked it.

I'll be back, he had said.

Walther Gassner hurried down the stairs, walked to the front door and opened it. A man in a gray messenger's uniform stood there, holding a sealed manila envelope.

"I have a special delivery for Mr. and Mrs. Walther Gassner."

"Yes," Walther said. "I will take it."

He closed the door, looked at the envelope in his hand, then ripped it open. Slowly, he read the message inside.

DEEPLY REGRET TO INFORM YOU THAT SAM
ROFFE WAS KILLED IN A CLIMBING
ACCIDENT. PLEASE BE IN ZURICH
FRIDAY NOON FOR AN EMERGENCY
MEETING OF THE BOARD OF DIRECTORS.

It was signed "Rhys Williams."

Rome.
Monday, September 7.
Six p.m.

Ivo Palazzi stood in the middle of his bedroom, the blood streaming down his face. *"Mamma mia! Mi hai rovinato!"*

"I haven't begun to ruin you, you miserable *figlio de putana!"*
Donatella screamed at him.

They were both naked in the large bedroom of their apartment
in Via Montemignaio. Donatella had the most sensuous, exciting
body Ivo Palazzi had ever seen, and even now, as his life's blood
poured from his face, from the terrible scratches she had inflicted
on him, he felt a familiar stirring in his loins. *Dio,* she was beautiful. There was an innocent decadence about her that drove him
wild. She had the face of a leopard, high cheekbones and slant
eyes, full ripe lips, lips that nibbled him and sucked him and—but
he must not think of that now. He picked up a white cloth from
a chair to stanch the flow of blood, and too late he realized that it
was his shirt. Donatella was standing in the middle of their huge
double bed, yelling at him. "I hope you bleed to death! When I've
finished with you, you filthy whoremonger, there won't be enough
left for a *gattino* to shit on!"

For the hundredth time Ivo Palazzi wondered how he had gotten
himself into this impossible situation. He had always prided himself on being the happiest of men, and all his friends had agreed
with him. His *friends? Everybody!* Because Ivo had no enemies. In
his bachelor days he had been a happy-go-lucky Roman without a

care in the world, a Don Giovanni who was the envy of half the males in Italy. His philosophy was summed up in the phrase *Farsi onore con una donna*—"Honor oneself with a woman." It kept Ivo very busy. He was a true romantic. He kept falling in love, and each time he used his new love to help him forget his old love. Ivo adored women, and to him they were all beautiful, from the *putane* who plied their ancient trade along the Via Appia, to the high-fashion models strutting along the Via Condotti. The only girls Ivo did not care for were the Americans. They were too independent for his taste. Besides, what could one expect of a nation whose language was so unromantic that they would translate the name of Giuseppe Verdi to Joe Green?

Ivo always managed to have a dozen girls in various states of preparation. There were five stages. In stage one were the girls he had just met. They received daily phone calls, flowers, slim volumes of erotic poetry. In stage two were those to whom he sent little gifts of Gucci scarves and porcelain boxes filled with Perugina chocolates. Those in stage three received jewelry and clothes and were taken to dinner at El Toula, or Taverna Flavia. Those in stage four shared Ivo's bed and enjoyed his formidable skills as a lover. An assignation with Ivo was a production. His beautifully decorated little apartment on the Via Margutta would be filled with flowers, *garofani* or *papaveri*, the music would be opera, classical or rock, according to the chosen girl's taste. Ivo was a superb cook, and one of his specialties, appropriately enough, was *pollo alla cacciatora*, chicken of the hunter. After dinner, a bottle of chilled champagne to drink in bed . . . Ah, yes, Ivo loved stage four.

But stage five was probably the most delicate of them all. It consisted of a heartbreaking farewell speech, a generous parting gift and a tearful *arrivederci*.

But all that was in the past. Now Ivo Palazzi took a quick glance at his bleeding, scratched face in the mirror over his bed and was horrified. He looked as though he had been attacked by a mad threshing machine.

"Look at what you've done to me!" he cried. "*Cara*, I know you didn't mean it."

He moved over to the bed to take Donatella in his arms. Her soft arms flew around him and as he started to hug her, she buried her long fingernails in his naked back and clawed him like a wild animal. Ivo yelled with pain.

"Scream!" Donatella shouted. "If I had a knife, I'd cut your *cazzo* and ram it down your miserable throat."

"Please!" Ivo begged. "The children will hear you."

"Let them!" she shrieked. "It's time they found out what kind of monster their father is."

He took a step toward her. *"Carissima—"*

"Don't you touch me! I'd give my body to the first drunken syphilitic sailor I met on the streets before I'd ever let you come near me again."

Ivo drew himself up, his pride offended. "That is not the way I expect the mother of my children to talk to me."

"You want me to talk nice to you? You want me to stop treating you like the vermin you are?" Donatella's voice rose to a scream. *"Then give me what I want!"*

Ivo looked nervously toward the door. *"Carissima*—I can't. I don't have it."

"Then get it for me!" she cried. "You pronmised!"

She was beginning to get hysterical again, and Ivo decided the best thing for him to do was to get out of there quickly before the neighbors called the carabinieri again.

"It will take time to get a million dollars," he said soothingly. "But I'll—I'll find a way."

He hastily donned his undershorts and pants, and socks and shoes, while Donatella stormed around the room, her magnificent, firm breasts waving in the air, and Ivo thought to himself, My God, what a woman! How I adore her! He reached for his bloodstained shirt. There was no help for it. He put it on, feeling the cold stickiness against his back and chest. He took a last look in the mirror. Small pools of blood were still oozing from the deep gashes where Donatella had raked her fingernails across his face.

"Carissima," Ivo moaned, "how am I ever going to explain this to my wife?"

Ivo Palazzi's wife was Simonetta Roffe, an heiress of the Italian branch of the Roffe family. Ivo had been a young architect when he had met Simonetta. His firm had sent him to supervise some changes in the Roffe villa at Porto Ercole. The instant Simonetta had set eyes on Ivo, his bachelor days were numbered. Ivo had gotten to the fourth stage with her on the first night, and found himself married to her a short time later. Simonetta was as determined as she was lovely, and she knew what she wanted: she wanted Ivo Palazzi. Thus it was that Ivo found himself transformed from a carefree bachelor to the husband of a beautiful young heiress. He gave up his architectural aspirations with no regrets and joined Roffe and Sons, with a magnificent office in EUR, the section of Rome started with such high hopes by the late, ill-fated Duce.

Ivo was a success with the firm from the beginning. He was intelligent, learned quickly, and everyone adored him. It was impossible not to adore Ivo. He was always smiling, always charming. His friends envied him his wonderful disposition and wondered how he did it. The answer was simple. Ivo kept the dark side of his nature buried. In fact, he was a deeply emotional man, capable of great volatile hatreds, capable of killing.

Ivo's marriage with Simonetta thrived. At first, he had feared that marriage would prove to be a bondage that would strangle his manhood to death, but his fears proved to be unfounded. He simply put himself on an austerity program, reducing the number of his girl friends, and everything went on as before.

Simonetta's father bought them a beautiful home in Olgiata, a large private estate twenty-five kilometers north of Rome, guarded by closed gates and manned by uniformed guards.

Simonetta was a wonderful wife. She loved Ivo and treated him like a king, which was no more than he felt he deserved. There was just one tiny flaw in Simonetta. When she became jealous, she turned into a savage. She had once suspected Ivo of taking a female buyer on a trip to Brazil. He was righteously indignant at the accusation. Before the argument was over, their entire house was a shambles. Not one dish or piece of furniture was left intact, and much of it had been broken over Ivo's head. Simonetta had gone after him with a butcher knife, threatening to kill him and then herself, and it had taken all of Ivo's strength to wrest the knife from her. They had wound up fighting on the floor, and Ivo had finally torn off her clothes and made her forget her anger. But after that incident Ivo became very discreet. He had told the buyer he could not take any more trips with her, and he was careful never to let the faintest breath of suspicion touch him. He knew that he was the luckiest man in the world. Simonetta was young and beautiful and intelligent and rich. They enjoyed the same things and the same people. It was a perfect marriage, and Ivo sometimes found himself wondering, as he transferred a girl from stage two to stage three, and another from stage four to stage five, why he kept on being unfaithful. Then he would shrug philosophically and say to himself, Someone has to make these women happy.

Ivo and Simonetta had been married for three years when Ivo met Donatella Spolini on a business trip to Sicily. It was more of an explosion than a meeting, two planets coming together and colliding. Where Simonetta had the slender, sweet body of a young woman sculpted by Manzù, Donatella had the sensuous, ripe body of a Rubens. Her face was exquisite and her green, smoldering eyes set Ivo aflame. They were in bed one hour after they had met, and Ivo, who had always prided himself on his prowess as a lover, found that he was the pupil and Donatella the teacher. She made him rise to heights he had never achieved before, and her body did things to his that he had never dreamed possible. She was an endless cornucopia of pleasure, and as Ivo lay in bed, his eyes closed, savoring incredible sensations, he knew he would be a fool to let Donatella go.

And so Donatella had become Ivo's mistress. The only condition she imposed was that he had to get rid of all the other women in his life, except his wife. Ivo had happily agreed That had been eight years ago, and in all that time Ivo had never been unfaithful to either his wife or his mistress. Satisfying two hungry women would have been enough to exhaust an ordinary man, but in Ivo's case it was exactly the opposite. When he made love to Simonetta he thought about Donatella and her ripe full body, and he was filled with lust. And when he made love to Donatella, he thought of Simonetta's sweet young breasts and tiny *culo* and he performed like a wild man. No matter which woman he was with, he felt that he was cheating on the other. It added enormously to his pleasure.

Ivo bought Donatella a beautiful apartment in Via Montemignaio, and he was with her every moment that he could manage. He would arrange to be away on a sudden business trip and, instead of leaving, he would spend the time in bed with Donatella. He would stop by to see her on his way to the office, and he would spend his afternoon siestas with her. Once, when Ivo sailed to New York on the *QE 2* with Simonetta, he installed Donatella in a cabin one deck below. They were the five most stimulating days of Ivo's life.

On the evening that Simonetta announced to Ivo that she was pregnant, Ivo was filled with an indescribable joy. A week later, Donatella informed Ivo that *she* was pregnant, and Ivo's cup ranneth over. Why, he asked himself, are the gods so good to me? In all humility, Ivo sometimes felt that he did not deserve all the great pleasures that were being bestowed upon him.

In due course Simonetta gave birth to a girl and a week later Donatella gave birth to a boy. What more could any man ask? But the gods were not finished with Ivo. A short time later, Donatella informed Ivo that she was pregnant again, and the following week Simonetta also became pregnant. Nine months later, Donatella gave Ivo another son and Simonetta presented her husband with another daughter. Four months later, both women were pregnant again and this time they gave birth on the same day. Ivo frantically raced from the Salvator Mundi, where Simonetta was encouched, to the Clinica Santa Chiara where Ivo had taken Donatella. He sped from hospital to hospital, driving on the Raccordo Anulare, waving to the girls sitting in front of their little tents along the sides of the road, under pink umbrellas, waiting for customers. Ivo was driving too fast to see their faces, but he loved them all and wished them well.

Donatella gave birth to another boy and Simonetta to another girl.

Sometimes Ivo wished it had been the other way around. It was ironical that his wife had borne him daughters and his mistress had borne him sons, for he would have liked male heirs to carry on his name. Still, he was a contented man. He had three children with outdoor plumbing, and three children with indoor plumbing. He adored them and he was wonderful to them, remembering their birthdays, their saints' days, and their names. The girls were called

Isabella and Benedetta and Camilla. The boys were Francesco and Carlo and Luca.

As the children grew older, life began to get more complicated for Ivo. Including his wife, his mistress and his six children, Ivo had to cope with eight birthdays, eight saints' days, and two of every holiday. He made sure that the children's schools were well separated. The girls were sent to Saint Dominique, the French convent on the Via Cassia, and the boys to Massimo, the Jesuit school in EUR. Ivo met and charmed all their teachers, helped the children with their homework, played with them, fixed their broken toys. It taxed all of Ivo's ingenuity to handle two families and keep them apart, but he managed. He was truly an exemplary father, husband and lover. On Christmas Day he stayed home with Simonetta, Isabella, Benedetta and Camilla. On *Befana,* the sixth of January, Ivo dressed up as the *Befana,* the witch, and handed out presents and *carbone,* the black rock candy prized by children, to Francesco, Carlo and Luca.

Ivo's wife and his mistress were lovely, and his children were bright and beautiful, and he was proud of them all. Life was wonderful.

And then the gods shat in Ivo Palazzi's face.

As in the case of most major disasters, this one struck without any warning.

Ivo had made love to Simonetta that morning before breakfast, and then had gone directly to his office, where he did a profitable morning's work. At one o'clock he told his secretary—male, at Simonetta's insistence—that he would be at a meeting the rest of the afternoon.

Smiling at the thought of the pleasures that lay ahead of him, Ivo circled the construction that blocked the street along the Lungo Tevere, where they had been building a subway for the past seventeen years, crossed the bridge to the Corso Francia, and thirty minutes later was driving into his garage at Via Montemignaio. The instant Ivo opened the door of the apartment, he knew something was terribly wrong. Francesco, Carlo and Luca were clustered around Donatella, sobbing, and as Ivo walked toward Donatella, she looked at him with an expression of such hatred on her face that for a moment Ivo thought he must have entered the wrong apartment.

"*Stronzo!*" she screamed at him.

Ivo looked around him, bewildered. "*Carissima*—children—what's wrong? What have I done?"

Donatella rose to her feet. "Here's what you've done!" She threw a copy of the magazine *Oggi* in his face. "Look at it!"

Bewildered, Ivo reached down and picked up the magazine. Staring out from the cover was a photograph of himself, Simonetta and their three daughters. The caption read: "*Padre di Famiglia.*"

Dio! He had forgotten all about it. Months before, the magazine had asked permission to do a story about him and he had foolishly agreed. But Ivo had never dreamed that it would be given this prominence. He looked over at his sobbing mistress and children, and said, "I can explain this . . ."

"Their schoolmates have already explained it," Donatella shrieked. "My children came home crying because everybody at school is calling them bastards!"

"*Cara*, I—"

"My landlord and the neighbors treated us like we were lepers. We can't hold up our heads anymore. I have to get them out of here."

Ivo stared at her, shocked. "What are you talking about?"

"I'm leaving Rome, and I'm taking my sons with me."

"They're mine too," he shouted. "You can't do it."

"Try to stop me and I'll kill you!"

It was a nightmare. Ivo stood there, watching his three sons and his beloved mistress in hysterics, and he thought, This can't be happening to me.

But Donatella was not finished with him. "Before we go," she announced, "I want one million dollars. In cash."

It was so ridiculous that Ivo started to laugh. "A million—"

"Either that, or I telephone your wife."

That had happened six months earlier. Donatella had not carried out her threat—not yet—but Ivo knew she would. Each week she had increased the pressure. She would telephone him at his office and say, "I don't care how you get the money. Do it!"

There was only one way that Ivo could possibly obtain such a huge sum. He had to be able to sell the stock in Roffe and Sons. It was Sam Roffe who was blocking the sale, Sam who was jeopardizing Ivo's marriage, his future. He had to be stopped. If one knew the right people, anything could be done.

What hurt Ivo more than anything was that Donatella—his darling, passionate mistress—would not let him touch her. Ivo was permitted to visit the children every day, but the bedroom was off limits.

"After you give me the money," Donatella promised, "then I will let you make love to me."

It was out of desperation that Ivo telephoned Donatella one afternoon and said, "I'm coming right over. The money is arranged."

He would make love to her first and placate her later. It had not worked out that way. He had managed to undress her, and when they were both naked, he had told her the truth. "I don't have the money yet, *cara*, but one day soon—"

It was then that she had attacked him like a wild animal.

Ivo was thinking of these things now, as he drove away from Donatella's apartment (as he now thought of it) and turned north onto the crowded Via Cassia, toward his home at Olgiata. He glanced at his face in the rearview mirror. The bleeding had lessened, but the scratches were raw-looking and discolored. He looked down at his shirt, stained with blood. How was he going to explain to Simonetta the scratches on his face and his back? For one reckless moment Ivo actually considered telling her the truth, but dismissed the thought as quickly as it came into his head. He might—he just might—have been able to confess to Simonetta that in a moment of mental aberration he had gone to bed with a girl and gotten her pregnant, and he might—he just *might*—have gotten away with a whole skin. But *three children?* Over a period of *three years?* His life would not be worth a five-lire piece. There was no way he could avoid going home now, for they were expecting guests for dinner, and Simonetta would be waiting for him. Ivo was trapped. His marriage was finished. Only San Gennaro, the patron saint of miracles, could help him. Ivo's eye was caught by a sign at the side of the Via Cassia. He suddenly slammed on the brakes, turned off the highway and brought the car to a stop.

Thirty minutes later, Ivo drove through the gates of Olgiata. Ignoring the stares of the guards as they saw his torn-up face and bloodstained shirt, Ivo drove along the winding roads, came to the turn that led to his driveway, and pulled up in front of his house. He parked the car, opened the front door of the house and walked into the living room. Simonetta and Isabella, their eldest daughter, were in the room. A look of shock came over Simonetta's face as she saw her husband.

"Ivo! What happened?"

Ivo smiled awkwardly, trying to ignore the pain it cost, and admitted sheepishly, "I'm afraid I did something stupid, *cara*—"

Simonetta was moving closer, studying the scratches on his face, and Ivo could see her eyes begin to narrow. When she spoke, her voice was frosty. "Who scratched your face?"

"Tiberio," Ivo announced. From behind his back he produced a large, spitting, ugly gray cat that leaped out of his arms and raced off. "I bought it for Isabella, but the damned thing attacked me while I was trying to put it in its case."

"*Povero amore mio!*" Instantly, Simonetta was at his side. "*Angelo mio!* Come upstairs and lie down. I'll get the doctor. I'll get some iodine. I'll—"

"No, no! I'm fine," Ivo said bravely. He winced as she put her arms around him. "Careful! I'm afraid he's clawed my back, too."

"*Amore!* How you must be suffering!"

"No, really," Ivo said. "I feel good." And he meant it.

The front doorbell rang.

"I'll get it," Simonetta said.

"No, I'll get it," Ivo said quickly. "I—I'm expecting some important papers from the office."

He hurried to the front door and opened it.

"Signor Palazzi?"

"*Sì.*"

A messenger, dressed in a gray uniform, handed him an envelope. Inside was a teletype from Rhys Williams. Ivo read the message rapidly. He stood there for a long, long time.

Then he took a deep breath and went upstairs to get ready for his guests.

Buenos Aires.
Monday, September 7.
Three P.M.

The Buenos Aires autodrome on the dusty outskirts of Argentina's capital city was crammed with fifty thousand spectators who had come to watch the championship classic. It was a 115-lap race over the almost four-mile circuit. The race had been running for nearly five hours, under a hot, punishing sun, and out of a starting field of thirty cars only a handful remained. The crowd was seeing history being made. There had never been such a race before, and perhaps never would be again. All the names that had become legend were on the track this day: Chris Amon from New Zealand, and Brian Redman from Lancashire. There was the Italian Andrea de Adamici, in an Alfa Romeo Tipo 33, and Carlos Maco of Brazil, in a Mach Formula 1. The prize-winning Belgian Jacky Ickx was there, and Sweden's Reine Wisell in a BRM.

The track looked like a rainbow gone mad, filled with the swirling reds and greens and blacks and whites and golds of the Ferraris and Brabhams and McLaren M19-A's and Lotus Formula 3's.

As lap after grueling lap went by, the giants began to fall. Chris Amon was in fourth place when his throttles jammed open. He sideswiped Brian Redman's Cooper before he brought his own car under control by cutting the ignition, but both cars were finished. Reine Wisell was in first position, with Jacky Ickx close behind the BRM. On the far turn, the BRM gearbox disintegrated and the

42

battery and electrical equipment caught fire. The car started spinning, and Jacky Ickx's Ferrari was caught in the vortex.

The crowd was in a frenzy.

Three cars were outpacing the rest of the field. Jorje Amandaris
from Argentina, driving a Surtees; Nils Nilsson from Sweden in a
Matra; and a Ferrari 312 B-2, driven by Martel of France. They
were driving brilliantly, daring the straight track, challenging the
curves, moving up.

Jorje Amandaris was in the lead, and because he was one of
them, the Argentinians cheered him madly. Close behind Amandaris was Nils Nilsson, at the wheel of a red-and-white Matra, and
behind him the black-and-gold Ferrari, driven by Martel of
France.

The French car had gone almost unnoticed until the last five
minutes, when it had started gaining on the field. It had reached
tenth position, then seventh, then fifth. And was coming on
strong. The crowd was watching it now as the French driver
started moving up on number two, driven by Nilsson. The three
cars were travelling at speeds in excess of 180 miles an hour. That
was dangerous enough at carefully contoured racetracks like
Brands Hatch or Watkins Glen, but on the cruder Argentine track
it was suicide. A red-coated referee stood at the side of the track,
holding up a sign: "FIVE LAPS."

The French black-and-gold Ferrari attempted to pass Nilsson's
Matra on the outside, and Nilsson inched over, blocking the
French car's way. They were lapping a German car on the inside
track, moving up on it fast. Now it was opposite Nilsson's car. The
French car dropped back and edged over so that it was positioned
in the tight space behind the German car and Nilsson's Matra.
With a quick burst of acceleration the French driver made for the
narrow slot, forcing the two cars out of its way and shooting ahead
into the number-two spot. The crowd, which had been holding its
breath, roared its approval. It had been a brilliant, dangerous
maneuver.

It was Amandaris in the lead now, Martel second and Nilsson in
third position, with three laps remaining. Amandaris had seen the
move. The French driver is good, Amandaris told himself, but not
good enough to beat me. Amandaris intended to win this race.
Ahead of him he saw the sign being flashed—"TWO LAPS." The

race was almost over, and it was his. Out of the corner of his eye he could see the black-and-gold Ferrari trying to pull up alongside him. He got a glimpse of the driver's goggled, dirt-streaked face, tight and determined. Amandaris gave an inward sigh. He regretted what he was about to do, but he had no choice. Racing was not a game for sportsmen, it was a game for winners.

The two cars were approaching the north end of the oval, where there was a high banking turn, the most dangerous in the track, the scene of a dozen crashes. Amandaris shot another quick look at the French driver of the Ferrari and then tightened his grip on the wheel. As the two cars started to approach the curve, Amandaris imperceptibly lifted his foot from the accelerator, so that the Ferrari began to pull ahead. He saw the driver give him a quick, speculative look. Then the driver was abreast of him, falling into his trap. The crowd was screaming. Jorje Amandaris waited until the black-and-gold Ferrari was fully committed to pass him on the outside. At that moment Amandaris opened his throttles wide and started to move toward the right, cutting off the French driver's path to the straightaway, so that the only choice was to head up the embankment.

Amandaris saw the sudden, dismayed expression on the French driver's face and silently said, *¡Salud!* At that instant the driver of the French car turned the wheel directly into Amandaris' Surtees. Amandaris could not believe it. The Ferrari was on a crash course with him. They were only three feet apart and at that speed Amandaris had to make a split-second decision. *How could anyone have known that the French driver was completely loco?* In a swift, reflex action, Amandaris swung the wheel sharply to the left, trying to avoid the thousand pounds of metal hurtling at him, and braked hard, so that the French car missed him by a fraction of an inch, and shot past him toward the finish line. For a moment Jorje Amandaris' car fishtailed, then went out of control into a spin, flinging itself wildly across the track, rolling over and over until it burst into a tower of red and black flames.

But the crowd's attention was riveted on the French Ferrari, roaring across the finish line to victory. There were wild screams from the spectators as they ran toward the car, surrounding it, cheering. The driver slowly stood up and took off the racing goggles and helmet.

She had wheat-colored hair, cut short, and her face was sculpted with strong, firm features. There was a classic cold beauty about her. Her body was trembling, not with exhaustion, but with excitement, the memory of the moment when she had looked into Jorje Amandaris' eyes as she sent him to his death. Over the loudspeaker the announcer was excitedly yelling, "The winner is Hélène Roffe-Martel, from France, driving a Ferrari."

Two hours later, Hélène and her husband, Charles, were in their suite in the Ritz Hotel in downtown Buenos Aires, lying on the rug in front of the fireplace, and Hélène was naked on top of him in the classic position of *la Diligence de Lyon*, and Charles was saying, "Oh, Christ! Please don't do that to me! Please!"

And his begging increased her excitement and she began to put on more pressure, hurting him, watching the tears come to his eyes. I'm being punished for no reason, Charles thought. He dreaded to think what Hélène would do to him if she ever found out about the crime he had committed.

Charles Martel had married Hélène Roffe for her name and for her money. After the ceremony she had kept her name, along with his, and she had kept her money. By the time Charles found out he had made a bad bargain, it was too late.

Charles Martel was a junior attorney in a large Paris law firm when he first met Hélène Roffe. He had been asked to bring some documents into the conference room, where a meeting was taking place. In the room were the four senior partners in the firm and Hélène Roffe. Charles had heard of her. Everyone in Europe had. She was an heiress to the Roffe pharmaceutical fortune. She was wild and unconventional, and the newspapers and magazines adored her. She was a champion skier; flew her own Learjet, had led a mountain-climbing expedition in Nepal, raced cars and horses, and changed men as casually as she changed her wardrobe. Her photograph was constantly appearing in *Paris-Match* and *Jours de France*. She was in the law office now because the firm was handling her divorce. Her fourth or fifth—Charles Martel was not sure which, nor was he interested. The Roffes of the world were out of his reach.

Charles handed the papers to his superior, nervous, not because

Hélène Roffe was in the room—he hardly glanced at her—but because of the presence of the four senior partners. They represented Authority, and Charles Martel respected Authority. He was basically a retiring man, content to make a modest living, reside in a little apartment in Passy and tend to his small stamp collection.

Charles Martel was not a brilliant attorney, but he was a competent one, thorough and reliable. He had a stiff *petsec* dignity about him. He was in his early forties and his physical appearance, while not unattractive, was certainly far from prepossessing. Someone had once said that he had the personality of wet sand, and the description was not an unjust one. It was with a good deal of surprise, therefore, that the day after he had met Hélène Roffe, Charles Martel received a summons to go to the office of M. Michel Sachard, the senior partner, where he was told. "Hélène Roffe wishes you to assume personal charge of her divorce case. You will take over at once."

Charles Martel was stunned. He asked. "Why me, Monsieur Sachard?"

Sachard looked him in the eye and replied. "I can't imagine. See that you service her well."

Being in charge of Hélène's divorce action made it necessary for Charles to see her frequently. Too frequently, he felt. She would telephone him and invite him to dinner at her villa in Le Vésinet to discuss the case, and to the opera and to her house in Deauville. Charles kept trying to explain to her that it was a very simple case, that there would be no problem in obtaining the divorce, but Hélène—she insisted that he call her Hélène, to his acute embarrassment—told him she needed his constant reassurance. Later he was to think back on that with bitter amusement.

During the weeks that followed their first meeting, Charles began to suspect that Hélène Roffe was interested in him romantically. He could not believe it. He was a nobody, and she was a member of one of the great families, but Hélène left him in no doubt as to her intentions. "I'm going to marry you, Charles."

He had never thought of getting married. He was not comfortable with women. Besides, he did not love Hélène. He was not even certain he liked her. The fuss and attention that attended her wherever they went discomfited him. He was caught in the limelight of her celebrity and it was a role he was not accustomed to. He was also painfully aware of the contrast between them. Her flamboyance was an irritant to his conservative nature. She set fashion styles and was the epitome of glamour, while he—well, he was a simple, ordinary, middle-aged lawyer. He could not understand what Hélène Roffe saw in him. Nor could anyone else. Because of her well-publicized participation in dangerous sports that were normally the exclusive province of men, there were rumors that Hélène Roffe was an advocate of the women's liberation movement. In fact, she despised the movement, and had only contempt for its concept of equality. She saw no reason why men should be allowed to become the equal of women. Men were handy to have around, when required. They were not particularly intelligent, but they could be taught to fetch and light cigarettes, run errands, open doors and give satisfaction in bed. They made excellent pets, dressed and bathed themselves and were toilet-trained. An amusing species.

Hélène Roffe had had the playboys, the daredevils, the tycoons, the glamour boys. She had never had a Charles Martel. She knew exactly what he was: *Nothing*. A piece of blank clay. And that was precisely the challenge. She intended to take him over, mold him, see what she could make of him. Once Hélène Roffe made up her mind, Charles Martel never had a chance.

They were married in Neuilly and they honeymooned in Monte Carlo, where Charles lost his virginity and his illusions. He had planned on returning to the law firm.

"Don't be a fool," his bride said. "Do you think I want to be married to a law clerk? You'll go into the family business. One day you'll be running it. *We'll* be running it."

Hélène arranged for Charles to work in the Paris branch of Roffe and Sons. He reported to her on everything that went on and she guided him, helped him, gave him suggestions to make. Charles's advancement was rapid. He was soon in charge of the French operation, and a member of the board of directors. Hélène Roffe had changed him from an obscure lawyer to an executive of one of the largest corporations in the world. He should have been ecstatic. He was miserable. From the first moment of their marriage Charles found himself totally dominated by his wife. She chose his tailor, his shoemaker and his shirtmaker. She got him into the exclusive Jockey Club. Hélène treated Charles like a gigolo. His salary went directly to her, and she gave him an embarrassingly small allowance. If Charles needed any extra money, he had to ask Hélène for it. She made him account for every moment of his time, and he was at her constant beck and call. She seemed to enjoy humiliating him. She would telephone him at the office and order him to come home immediately with a jar of massage cream, or something equally stupid. When he arrived, she would be in the bedroom, naked, waiting for him. She was insatiable, an animal. Charles had lived with his mother until he was thirty-two, when she had died of cancer. She had been an invalid for as long as Charles could remember, and he had taken care of her. There had been no time to think about going out with girls or getting married. His mother had been a burden and when she died, Charles thought he would feel a sense of freedom. Instead, he felt a sense of loss. He had no interest in women or sex. He had, in a naive burst of candor, explained his feelings to Hélène when she had first mentioned marriage. "My—libido is not very strong," he had said.

Hélène had smiled. "Poor Charles. Don't worry about sex. I promise you, you'll like it."

He hated it. That only seemed to add to Hélène's pleasure. She would laugh at him for his weakness, and force him to do disgusting things that made Charles feel degraded and sick. The sex act itself was debasing enough. But Hélène was interested in experimenting. Charles never knew what to expect. Once, at the moment he was having an orgasm, she had put crushed ice on his testicles, and another time she had shoved an electric prod up his anus. Charles was terrified of Hélène. She made him feel that she was the male and he was the female. He tried to salvage his pride but, alas, he could find no area in which Hélène was not superior to him. She had a brilliant mind. She knew as much about the law as he did, and much more about business. She spent hour after hour discussing the company with him. She never tired of it. "Think of all that power, Charles! Roffe and Sons can make or break more than half the countries in the world. *I* should be running the company. My great-grandfather founded it. It's part of me."

After one of these outbursts Hélène would be sexually insatiable, and Charles was forced to satisfy her in ways that did not bear thinking about. He came to despise her. His one dream was to get away from her, to escape. But for that he needed money.

One day, over lunch, a friend of his, René Duchamps, told Charles about an opportunity to make a fortune.

"An uncle of mine who owned a large vineyard in Burgundy has just died. The vineyard is going to be put up for sale—ten thousand acres of first-class *Appellation d'origine contrôllée*. I have the inside track," René Duchamps continued, "because it's my family. I don't have enough to swing the deal by myself, but if you came in with me, we could double our money in one year. At least, come and look at it."

Because Charles could not bear to admit to his friend that he was penniless, he went to the rolling red slopes of Burgundy to view the land. He was deeply impressed.

René Duchamps said, "We'll each put in two million francs. In a year we'll each have four million."

Four million francs! It would mean freedom, escape. He could go away to some place where Hélène could never find him.

"I'll think about it," Charles promised his friend.

And he did. Day and night. It was the chance of a lifetime. But *how?* Charles knew that it would be impossible for him to try to borrow money without Hélène immediately learning about it. Everything was in her name, the houses, the paintings, the cars, the jewelry. The jewelry . . . those beautiful, useless ornaments she kept locked up in the safe in the bedroom. Gradually, the idea was born. If he could get hold of her jewelry, a little at a time, he could replace the pieces with copies and borrow money on the real jewelry. After he had made his killing in the vineyard, he would simply return her jewels. And have enough money to disappear forever.

Charles telephoned René Duchamps and said, his heart pounding with excitement, "I've decided to go in with you."

The first part of the plan filled Charles with terror. He had to get into the safe and steal Hélène's jewelry.

The anticipation of the terrible thing he was about to do made Charles so nervous that he was barely able to function. He went through each day like an automaton, neither seeing nor hearing what was happening around him. Every time Charles saw Hélène he began to sweat. His hands would tremble at odd times. Hélène was concerned about him, as she would have been concerned about any pet. She had the doctor examine Charles, but the doctor could find nothing wrong. "He seems a bit tense. A day or two in bed, perhaps."

Hélène looked long at Charles, lying in bed, naked, and smiled, "Thank you, doctor."

The moment the doctor left, Hélène began getting undressed. "I—I'm not feeling very strong." Charles protested.

"I am," Hélène replied.

He had never hated her more.

Charles's opportunity came the following week. Hélène was going to Garmisch-Partenkirchen to ski with some friends. She decided to leave Charles in Paris.

"I want you home every night," Hélène told him. "I'll telephone you."

Charles watched her speed away, at the wheel of her red Jensen, and the moment she was out of sight he hurried to the wall safe. He had watched her open it often, and he knew most of the combination. It took him an hour to figure out the rest of it. With trembling fingers he pulled the safe open. There, in velvet-lined boxes, sparkling like miniature stars, lay his freedom. He had already located a jeweler, one Pierre Richaud, who was a master at duplicating jewelry. Charles had begun a long, nervous explanation about why he wanted the jewels copied, but Richaud said, matter-of-factly, "Monsieur, I am making copies for everyone. No one with any sense wears real jewelry on the streets these days."

Charles gave him one piece at a time to work on, and when the copy was ready, he substituted it for the real piece. He borrowed money on the real jewelry from the Crédit Municipal, the state-owned pawnshop.

The operation took longer than Charles had anticipated. He could only get into the safe when Hélène was out of the house, and there were unforeseen delays in copying the pieces. But finally the day came when Charles was able to say to René Duchamps, "I'll have all the money for you tomorrow."

He had accomplished it. He was half-owner of a great vineyard. And Hélène had not the slightest suspicion of what he had done.

Charles had secretly begun to read up on the growing of vines.

And why not? Was he not a vintner now? He learned about the different vines: *cabernet sauvignon* was the principal vine used, but others were planted alongside it: *gros cabernet, merlot, malbec, petit verdot*. The desk drawers of Charles's office were filled with pamphlets on soil and vine pressing. He learned about fermentation and pruning and grafting. And that the worldwide demand for wine kept growing.

He met regularly with his partner. "It's going to be even better than I thought," René told Charles. "Prices for wine are skyrocketing. We should get three hundred thousand francs a *tonneau* for the first pressings."

More than Charles had dreamed! The grapes were red gold. Charles began to buy travel pamphlets on the South Sea Islands and Venezuela and Brazil. The very names had a magic about them. The only problem was that there were few places in the world where Roffe and Sons did not have offices, where Hélène could not find him. And if she found him, she would kill him. He knew that, with an absolute certainty. Unless he killed her first. It was one of his favorite fantasies. He murdered Hélène over and over again, in a thousand delicious ways.

Perversely, Charles now began to enjoy Hélène's abuse. All the time she was forcing him to do unspeakable things to her, he was thinking, I'll be gone soon, you *convasse*. I'll be rich on your money and there's nothing you can do about it.

And she would command, "Faster now," or "Harder," or "Don't stop!" and he would meekly obey her.

And smile inside.

In wine growing, Charles knew the crucial months were in the spring and summer, for the grapes were picked in September and they had to have a carefully balanced season of sun and rain. Too much sun would burn the flavor, just as too much rain would drown it. The month of June began splendidly. Charles checked the weather in Burgundy once, then twice a day. He was in a fever of impatience, only weeks away from the fulfillment of his dream. He had decided on Montego Bay. Roffe and Sons had no office in Jamaica. It would be easy to lose himself there. He would not go near Round Hill or Ocho Rios, where any of Hélène's friends might see him. He would buy a small house in the hills. Life was cheap on the island. He could afford servants, and fine food, and in his own small way live in luxury.

And so in those first days of June, Charles Martel was a very happy man. His present life was an ignominy, but he was not living in the present: he was living in the future, on a tropical, sun-bathed, wind-caressed island in the Caribbean.

The June weather seemed to get better each day. There was sun, and there was rain. Perfect for the tender little grapes. And as the grapes grew, so did Charles's fortune.

On the fifteenth day of June it began to drizzle in the Burgundy region. Then it began to rain harder. It rained day after day, and week after week, until Charles could no longer bring himself to check the weather reports.

René Duchamps telephoned. "If it stops by the middle of July, the crop can still be saved."

July turned out to be the rainiest month in the history of the French weather bureau. By the first of August, Charles Martel had lost every centime of the money he had stolen. He was filled with a fear such as he had never known.

"We're flying to Argentina next month," Hélène had informed Charles. "I've entered a car race there."

He had watched her speeding round the track in the Ferrari, and he could not help thinking: *If she crashes, I'm free.*

But she was Hélène Roffe-Martel. Life had cast her in the role of a winner, just as it had cast him in the role of a loser.

Winning the race had excited Hélène even more than usual. They had returned to their hotel suite in Buenos Aires, and she had made Charles get undressed and lie on the rug, on his stomach. When he saw what she had in her hand as she straddled him, he said, "Please, no!"

There was a knock on the door.

"*Merde!*" Hélène said. She waited, silent, but the knocking was repeated.

A voice called, "Señor Martel?"

"Stay here!" Hélène commanded. She got up, whipped a heavy silk robe around her slim, firm body, walked over to the door and pulled it open. A man in a gray messenger's uniform stood there, holding a sealed manila envelope.

"I have a special delivery for Señor and Señora Martel."

She took the envelope and closed the door.

She tore the envelope open and read the message inside, then slowly read it again.

"What is it?" Charles asked.

"Sam Roffe is dead," she said. She was smiling.

White's Club was situated at the top of St. James's Street, near Piccadilly. Built as a gambling club in the eighteenth century, White's was one of the oldest clubs in England, and the most exclusive. Members put their sons' names in for membership at birth, for there was a thirty-year waiting list.

The facade of White's was the epitome of discretion. The wide bow windows looking out on St. James's Street were meant to accommodate those within rather than to satisfy the curiosity of the outsiders passing by. A short flight of steps led to the entrance but, aside from members and their guests, few people ever got past the door. The rooms in the club were large and impressive, burnished with the dark rich patina of time. The furniture was old and comfortable—leather couches, newspaper racks, priceless antique tables and deep stuffed armchairs that had held the posteriors of half a dozen prime ministers. There was a backgammon room with a large, open fireplace behind a bronze-covered rail, and a formal curved staircase led to the dining room upstairs. The dining room ran across the entire breadth of the house, and contained one huge mahogany table which seated thirty persons, and five side tables. At any luncheon or dinner the room contained some of the most influential men in the world.

Sir Alec Nichols, Member of Parliament, was seated at one of the small corner tables, having lunch with a guest, Jon Swinton.

54

Sir Alec's father had been a baronet, and his father and grandfather before him. They had all belonged to White's. Sir Alec was a thin, pale man in his late forties, with a sensitive, aristocratic face and an engaging smile. He had just motored in from his country estate in Gloucestershire, and was dressed in a tweed sports jacket and slacks, with loafers. His guest wore a pinstripe suit with a loud checked shirt and a red tie, and seemed out of place in this quiet, rich atmosphere.

"They really do you proud here," Jon Swinton said, his mouth full, as he chewed the remains of a large veal chop on his plate.

Sir Alec nodded. "Yes. Things have changed since Voltaire said, 'The British have a hundred religions and only one sauce.' "

Jon Swinton looked up. "Who's Voltaire?"

Sir Alec said, embarrassed, "A—a French chap."

"Oh." Jon Swinton washed his food down with a swallow of wine. He laid down his knife and fork and wiped a napkin across his mouth. "Well, now, Sir Alec. Time for you and I to talk a little business."

Alec Nichols said softly, "I told you two weeks ago I'm working everything out, Mr. Swinton. I need a bit more time."

A waiter walked over to the table, balancing a high stack of wooden cigar boxes. He skillfully set them down on the table.

"Don't mind if I do," Jon Swinton said. He examined the labels on the boxes, whistled in admiration, pulled out several cigars which he put in his breast pocket, then lit one. Neither the waiter nor Sir Alec showed any reaction to this breach of manners. The waiter nodded to Sir Alec, and carried the cigars to another table.

"My employers have been very lenient with you, Sir Alec. Now, I'm afraid, they've got impatient." He picked up the burned match, leaned forward and dropped it into Sir Alec's glass of wine. "Between you and I, they're not nice people when they're upset. You don't want to get them down on you, you know what I mean?"

"I simply don't have the money right now."

Jon Swinton laughed loudly. "Come off it, chum. Your mom was a Roffe, right? You got a hundred-acre farm, a posh town house in Knightsbridge, a Rolls-Royce and a bloody Bentley. You're not exactly on the dole then, are you?"

Sir Alec looked around, pained, and said quietly, "None of them is a liquid asset. I can't—"

Swinton winked and said, "I'll bet that sweet little wife of yours, Vivian, is a liquid asset, eh? She's got a great pair of Bristols."

Sir Alec flushed. Vivian's name on this man's lips was a sacrilege. Alec thought of Vivian as he had left her that morning, still sweetly asleep. They had separate bedrooms, and one of Alec Nichols' great joys was to go into Vivian's room for one of his "visits." Sometimes, when Alec awakened early, he would walk into Vivian's bedroom while she was asleep and simply stare at her. Awake or asleep, she was the most beautiful girl he had ever seen. She slept in the nude, and her soft, curved body would be half exposed as she curled into the sheets. She was blond, with wide, pale-blue eyes and skin like cream. Vivian had been a minor actress when Sir Alec had first met her at a charity ball. He had been enchanted by her looks, but what had drawn him to her was her easy, outgoing personality. She was twenty years younger than Alec, and filled with a zest for living. Where Alec was shy and introverted, Vivian was gregarious and vivacious. Alec had been unable to get her out of his mind, but it had taken him two weeks to summon up nerve enough to telephone her. To his surprise and delight Vivian had accepted his invitation. Alec had taken her to a play at the Old Vic, and then to dinner at the Mirabelle. Vivian lived in a dreary little basement flat in Notting Hill, and when Alec had brought her home, she had said, "Would you like to come in then?" He had stayed the night, and it had changed his whole life. It was the first time that any woman had been able to bring him to a climax. He had never experienced anything like Vivian. She was velvet tongue and trailing golden hair and moist pulsing demanding depths that Alec explored until he was drained. He could become aroused simply thinking about her.

There was something else. She made him laugh, she made him come alive. She poked fun at Alec because he was shy and a bit stodgy, and he adored it. He was with her as often as Vivian would permit it. When Alec took Vivian to a party, she was always the center of attention. Alec was proud of that, but jealous of the young men gathered around her, and he could not help wondering how many of them she had been to bed with.

On the nights when Vivian could not see him because she had another engagement, Alec was frantic with jealousy. He would drive to her flat and park down the block to see what time she came home, and whom she was with. Alec knew that he was behaving like a fool, and yet he could not help himself. He was in the grip of something too strong to break.

He realized that Vivian was wrong for him, that it was out of the question for him to marry her. He was a baronet, a respected Member of Parliament, with a brilliant future. He was part of the Roffe dynasty, on the board of directors of the company. Vivian had no background to help her cope with Alec's world. Her mother and father had been second-rate music-hall artists, playing the provincial circuit. Vivian had had no education except for what she had picked up in the streets, or backstage. Alec knew that she was promiscuous and superficial. She was shrewd but not particularly intelligent. And yet Alec was obsessed with her. He fought it. He tried to stop seeing her, but it was no use. He was happy when he was with her, and he was miserable when he was without her. In the end he proposed to her because he had to, and when Vivian accepted, Sir Alec Nichols was ecstatic.

His new bride moved into the family house, a beautiful old Robert Adam house in Gloucestershire, a Georgian mansion with Delphic columns and a long sweeping driveway. It was set amid the green of a hundred acres of lush farmland, with its own private hunting, and running streams to fish. At the back of the house was a park that had been laid out by "Capability" Brown.

The interior of the house was stunning. The large front hall had a stone floor and walls of painted wood. There were pairs of old lanterns and marble-topped Adam giltwood tables and mahogany chairs. The library had original eighteenth-century built-in bookcases, and a pair of pedestal tables by Henry Holland, and chairs designed by Thomas Hope. The drawing room was a mixture of Hepplewhite and Chippendale, with a Wilton carpet, and a pair of Waterford glass chandeliers. There was a huge dining room that would seat forty guests, and a smoking room. On the second floor were six bedrooms, each with an Adam fireplace, and on the third floor were the servants' quarters.

Six weeks after she had moved into the house, Vivian said, "Let's get out of this place, Alec."

He looked at her, puzzled. "You mean you'd like to go up to London for a few days?"

"I mean I want to *move* back to London."

Alec looked out the window at the emerald-green meadows, where he had played as a child, and at the giant sycamore and oak trees, and he said hesitantly, "Vivian, it's so peaceful here. I—"

And she said, "I know, luv. That's what I can't stand—the fucking peace!"

They moved to London the following week.

Alec had an elegant four-story town house in Wilton Crescent, off Knightsbridge, with a lovely drawing room, a study, a large dining room, and at the back of the house, a picture window that overlooked a grotto, with a waterfall and statues and white benches set amid a beautiful formal garden. Upstairs were a magnificent master suite and four smaller bedrooms.

Vivian and Alec shared the master suite for two weeks, until one morning Vivian said, "I love you, Alec, but you do snore, you know." Alec had not known. "I really must sleep alone, luv. You don't mind, do you?"

Alec minded deeply. He loved the feel of her soft body in bed, warm against him. But deep inside, Alec knew that he did not excite Vivian sexually the way other men excited her. That was why she did not want him in her bed. So now he said, "Of course I understand, darling."

At Alec's insistence, Vivian kept the master suite, and he moved into one of the small guest bedrooms.

In the beginning, Vivian had gone to the House of Commons and sat in the Visitors' Gallery on days when Alec was to speak. He would look up at her and be filled with a deep, ineffable pride. She was undoubtedly the most beautiful woman there. And then came the day when Alec finished his speech and looked up for Vivian's approval, and saw only an empty seat.

Alec blamed himself for the fact that Vivian was restless. His friends were older than Vivian, too conservative for her. He encouraged her to invite her young companions to the house, and brought them together with his friends. The results were disastrous.

Alec kept telling himself that when Vivian had a child, she would settle down and change. But one day, somehow—and Alec could not bear to know how—she picked up a vaginal infection and had to have a hysterectomy. Alec had longed for a son. The news had shattered him, but Vivian was unperturbed.

"Don't worry, luv," she said, smiling. "They took out the nursery, but they left in the playpen."

He looked at her for a long moment, then turned and walked away.

Vivian loved to go on buying sprees. She spent money indiscriminately, recklessly, on clothes and jewelry and cars, and Alec did not have the heart to stop her. He told himself that she had grown up in poverty, hungry for beautiful things. He wanted to buy them for her. Unfortunately, he could not afford it. His salary was consumed by taxes. His fortune lay in his shares of stock in Roffe and Sons but those shares were restricted. He tried to explain that to Vivian but she was not interested. Business discussions bored her. And so Alec let her carry on.

He had first learned of her gambling when Tod Michaels, the owner of Tod's Club, a disreputable gambling place in Soho, had dropped in to see him.

"I have your wife's IOU's here for a thousand pounds, Sir Alec. She had a rotten run at roulette."

Alec had been shocked. He had paid off the IOU's and had had a confrontation with Vivian that evening. "We simply can't afford it," he had told her. "You're spending more than I'm making."

She had been very contrite. "I'm sorry, angel. Baby's been bad."

And she had walked over to him and put her arms around him and pressed her body against his, and he had forgotten his anger.

Alec had spent a memorable night in her bed. He was sure now that there would be no more problems.

Two weeks later Tod Michaels had come to visit Alec again. This time Vivian's IOU's were five thousand pounds. Alec was furious. "Why did you let her have credit?" he demanded.

"She's your wife, Sir Alec," Michaels had replied blandly. "How would it look if we refused her?"

"I'll—I'll have to get the money," Alec had said. "I don't have that much cash at the moment."

"Please! Consider it a loan. Pay it back when you can."

Alec had been greatly relieved. "That's very generous of you, Mr. Michaels."

It was not until a month later that Alec learned that Vivian had gambled away another twenty-five thousand pounds, and that Alec was being charged interest at the rate of 10 percent a week. He was horrified. There was no way he could raise that much cash. There was nothing that he could even sell. The houses, the beautiful antiques, the cars, all belonged to Roffe and Sons. His anger frightened Vivian enough so that she promised not to gamble anymore. But it was too late. Alec found himself in the hands of loan sharks. No matter how much Alec gave them, he could not manage to pay off the debt. It kept mounting each month, instead of getting smaller, and it had been going on for almost a year.

When Tod Michaels' hoodlums first began to press him for the money, Alec had threatened to go to the police commissioner. "I have connections in the highest quarters," Alec had said.

The man had grinned. "I got connections in the lowest."

Now Sir Alec found himself sitting here at White's with this dreadful man, having to contain his pride, and beg for a little more time.

"I've already paid them back more than the money I borrowed. They can't—"

Swinton replied, "That was just on the interest, Sir Alec. You still haven't paid the principal."

"It's extortion," Alec said.

Swinton's eyes darkened. "I'll give the boss your message." He started to rise.

Alec said quickly, "No! Sit down. Please."

Slowly Swinton sat down again. "Don't use words like that," he warned. "The last chap who talked like that had both his knees nailed to the floor."

Alec had read about it. The Kray brothers had invented the punishment for their victims. And the people Alec was dealing with were just as bad, just as ruthless. He could feel the bile rising in his throat. "I didn't mean that," Alec said. "It's just that I—I don't have any more cash."

Swinton flicked the ash from his cigar into Alec's glass of wine, and said, "You have a big bundle of stock in Roffe and Sons, don't you, Alec baby?"

"Yes," Alec replied, "but it's nonsalable and nontransferable.

60

It's no good to anyone unless Roffe and Sons goes public."

Swinton took a puff on his cigar. "And is it going public?"

"That's up to Sam Roffe. I've—I've been trying to persuade him."

"Try harder."

"Tell Mr. Michaels he'll get his money," Alec said. "But please stop hounding me."

Swinton stared. "Hounding you? Why, Sir Alec, you little cock-sucker, you'll know when we start hounding you. Your fucking stables will burn down, and you'll be eating roast horsemeat. Then your house will burn. And maybe your wife." He smiled, and Alec wished he had not. "Have you ever eaten cooked pussy?"

Alec had turned pale. "For God's sake—"

Swinton said soothingly, "I'm kidding. Tod Michaels's your friend. And friends help each other, right? We were talking about you at our meeting this morning. And do you know what the boss said? He said, 'Sir Alec's a good sort. If he hasn't got the money, I'm sure he'll think of some other way to take care of us.' "

Alec frowned. "What other way?"

"Well, now, it's not all that hard for a bright chap like you to work out, is it? You're running a big drug company, right? You make things like cocaine, for example. Just between you and I, who'd ever know if you happened to accidentally misplace a few shipments here and there?"

Alec stared at him. "You're insane," he said. "I—I couldn't do that."

"It's amazing what people can do when they have to," Swinton said genially. He rose to his feet. "You either have our money for us, or we'll tell you where to deliver the merchandise."

He ground his cigar out in Alec's butter plate. "Give my regards to Vivian, Sir Alec. Ta."

And Jon Swinton was gone.

Sir Alec sat there alone, unseeing, surrounded by all the familiar, comfortable things that were so much a part of his past life, that were now threatened. The only alien thing was the obscene wet cigar butt in the plate. How had he ever allowed them to come into his life? He had permitted himself to be maneuvered into a position where he was in the hands of the underworld. And now he knew that they wanted more than money from him. The money was merely the bait with which they had trapped him. They were after his connections with the drug company. They were going to try to force him to work with them. If it became known he was in their power, the Opposition would not hesitate to make capital of it. His own party would probably ask him to resign. It would be done tactfully and quietly. They would probably exert pressure on him to apply for the Chiltern Hundreds, a post that paid a nominal salary of a hundred pounds a year from the Crown. The one barrier to being an M.P. was that you could not be in receipt of pay from the Crown or the Government. So Alec would no longer be allowed to serve in Parliament. The reason could not be kept secret, of course. He would be in disgrace. Unless he could come up with a large sum of money. He had talked to Sam Roffe again and again, asking him to let the company go public, to let the shares of stock be marketed.

"Forget it," Sam had told him. "The minute we let outsiders in, we have a lot of strangers telling us how to run our business. Before you know it, they'll take over the board, and then the company. What's the difference to you, Alec? You have a big salary, an unlimited expense account. You don't *need* the money."

For a moment Alec had been tempted to tell Sam how desperately he needed it. But he knew it would do no good. Sam Roffe was a company man, a man without compassion. If he knew that Alec had in any way compromised Roffe and Sons, he would have dismissed him without a moment's hesitation. No, Sam Roffe was the last person to whom he could turn.

Alec was facing ruin.

The reception porter at White's walked toward Sir Alec's table with a man dressed in a messenger's uniform, carrying a sealed manila envelope.

"Excuse me, Sir Alec," the porter apologized, "but this man insists that he has instructions to deliver something to you personally."

"Thank you," Sir Alec said. The messenger handed him the envelope, and the porter led him back to the door.

Alec sat there a long time before he reached for the envelope and opened it. He read the message through three times, then he slowly crumpled the paper in his fist, and his eyes began to fill with tears.

The private Boeing 707-320 was making its final approach to Kennedy Airport, gliding out of the stacked-up traffic pattern. It had been a long, tedious flight and Rhys Williams was exhausted, but he had been unable to sleep during the night. He had ridden in this plane too often with Sam Roffe. His presence still filled it.

Elizabeth Roffe was expecting him. Rhys had sent her a cable from Istanbul, merely announcing that he would arrive the following day. He could have broken the news of her father's death over the telephone but she deserved more than that.

The plane was on the ground now, taxiing toward the terminal. Rhys carried very little luggage, and he was quickly ushered through Customs. Outside, the sky was gray and bleak, a foretaste of the winter to come. A limousine was waiting at the side entrance to drive him to Sam Roffe's Long Island estate, where Elizabeth would be waiting.

During the drive Rhys tried to rehearse the words that he would say to her, to try to soften the blow, but the moment Elizabeth opened the front door to greet him, the words flew out of his head. Each time Rhys saw Elizabeth, her beauty caught him by surprise. She had inherited her mother's looks, the same patrician features, midnight-black eyes framed by long heavy lashes. Her skin was white and soft, her hair a shiny black. Her figure was rich and firm. She was wearing an open-necked creamy silk blouse and a pleated gray-flannel skirt and fawn-colored pumps. There was no sign of the awkward little girl Rhys had first met nine years earlier. She had become a woman, intelligent and warm and completely unself-conscious about her beauty. She was smiling at him now, pleased to see him. She took his hand and said, "Come in, Rhys," and led him into the large oak-paneled library. "Did Sam fly in with you?"

There was no way to break it gently. Rhys took a deep breath and said, "Sam had a bad accident, Liz." He watched the color drain from her face. She waited for him to go on. "He was killed."

She stood there frozen. When she finally spoke, Rhys could barely hear her. "What—what happened?"

"We don't have any of the details yet. He was climbing Mont Blanc. A rope broke. He fell into a crevasse."

"Did they find—?"

She closed her eyes for a moment, then opened them.

"A bottomless crevasse."

Her face had turned white. Rhys felt a quick sense of alarm. "Are you all right?"

She smiled brightly, and said, "Of course. I'm fine, thank you. Would you like some tea or something to eat?"

He looked at her in surprise, and started to speak, and then he understood. She was in shock. She was rattling on, making no sense, her eyes unnaturally bright, her smile fixed.

"Sam was such a great athlete," Elizabeth was saying. "You've seen his trophies. He always won, didn't he? Did you know he climbed Mont Blanc before?"

"Liz—"

"Of course you did. You went with him once, didn't you, Rhys?"

Rhys let her talk, anesthetizing herself against the pain, trying to build an armor of words to ward off the moment when she would have to face her own anguish. For an instant, as he listened to her, he was reminded of the vulnerable little girl he had first known, too sensitive and shy to have any protection against brutal reality. She was dangerously wound up now, tense and brittle, and there was a fragility about her that worried Rhys.

"Let me call a doctor," he said. "He can give you something to—"

"Oh, no. I'm really quite all right. If you don't mind, I think I'll lie down for a while. I'm feeling a bit tired."

"Would you like me to stay?"

"Thank you. That won't be necessary."

She walked him to the door, and as he started to get into the car Elizabeth called, "Rhys!"

He turned.

"Thank you for coming."

Jesus Christ.

Long hours after Rhys Williams had gone, Elizabeth Roffe lay in her bed, staring at the ceiling, watching the shifting patterns painted by the pale September sun.

And the pain came. She had not taken a sedative, because she wanted the pain. She owed that to Sam. She would be able to bear it, because she was his daughter. And so she lay there, all day and all night, thinking of nothing, thinking of everything, remembering, feeling. She laughed, and she cried, and she supposed that she was in a state of hysteria. It did not matter. There was no one to hear her. In the middle of the night, she suddenly became ravenously hungry and went down into the kitchen and devoured a large sandwich and then threw it up. She felt no better. Nothing could ease the pain that filled her. She felt as though all her nerve ends were on fire. Her mind kept going back, back over the years with her father. Through her bedroom window she watched the sun rise. Sometime later, one of the servants knocked at the door, and Elizabeth sent her away. Once the phone rang, and her heart leaped and she reached for it, thinking. It's Sam! Then she remembered, and snatched her hand away.

He would never call her again. She would never hear his voice again. She would never see him again.

A bottomless crevasse.

Bottomless.

Elizabeth lay there, letting the past wash over her, remembering it all.

The birth of Elizabeth Rowane Roffe was a double tragedy. The minor tragedy was that Elizabeth's mother died on the delivery table. The major tragedy was that Elizabeth was born a girl.

For nine months, until she emerged from the darkness of her mother's womb, she was the most eagerly awaited child in the world, heir to a colossal empire, the multibillion-dollar giant, Roffe and Sons.

Sam Roffe's wife, Patricia, was a dark-haired woman of surpassing beauty. Many women had tried to marry Sam Roffe, for his position, his prestige, his wealth. Patricia had married him because she had fallen in love with him. It had proved to be the worst of reasons. Sam Roffe had been looking for a business arrangement, and Patricia had suited his requirements ideally. Sam had neither the time nor the temperament to be a family man. There was no room in his life for anything but Roffe and Sons. He was fanatically dedicated to the company, and he expected no less from those around him. Patricia's importance to him lay solely in the contribution she could make to the image of the company. By the time Patricia came to a realization of what kind of marriage she had made, it was too late. Sam gave her a role to play, and she played it beautifully. She was the perfect hostess, the perfect Mrs. Sam Roffe. She received no love from her husband and in time Patricia learned to give none. She served Sam, and was as much an employee of Roffe and Sons as the lowliest secretary. She was on call twenty-four hours a day, ready to fly wherever Sam needed her, capable of entertaining a small company of world leaders or serving a gourmet dinner to a hundred guests, on a day's notice, with crisp, heavily embroidered tablecloths, gleaming Baccarat crystal, heavy Georgian silverware. Patricia was one of Roffe and Sons' unlisted assets. She worked at keeping herself beautiful, and exercised and dieted like a Spartan. Her figure was perfect, and her clothes were designed for her by Norell in New York, Chanel in Paris, Hartnell in London, and young Sybil Connolly in Dublin. The jewelry Patricia wore was created for her by Jean Schlumberger in Bulgaria. Her life was busy and full and joyless and empty. Becoming pregnant had changed all that.

Sam Roffe was the last male heir of the Roffe dynasty, and Patricia knew how desperately he wanted a son. He was depending on her. And now she was the queen mother, busy with the baby within her, the young prince, who would one day inherit the kingdom. When they wheeled Patricia into the delivery room, Sam clasped her hand and said, "Thank you."

She was dead of an embolism thirty minutes later, and the only blessing about Patricia's death was that she died without knowing that she had failed her husband.

Sam Roffe took time off from his grueling schedule to bury his wife, and then turned his attention to the problem of what he should do with his infant daughter.

One week after Elizabeth was born, she was taken home and turned over to a nanny, the beginning of a long series of nannies. During the first five years of her life, Elizabeth saw very little of her father. He was barely more than a blur, a stranger who was always arriving or leaving. He traveled constantly and Elizabeth was a nuisance who had to be carted along, like a piece of extra luggage. One month Elizabeth would find herself living at their Long Island estate, with its bowling alley, tennis court, swimming pool and squash court. A few weeks later, her nanny would pack Elizabeth's clothes and she would be flown to their villa in Biarritz. It had fifty rooms and thirty acres of grounds and Elizabeth kept getting lost.

In addition, Sam Roffe owned a large duplex penthouse apartment on Beekman Place, and a villa on the Costa Smeralda in Sardinia. Elizabeth traveled to all these places, shunted from house to apartment to villa, and grew up amid all the lavish elegance. But always she felt like an outsider who had wandered by mistake into a beautiful birthday party given by unloving strangers.

As Elizabeth grew older, she came to know what it meant to be the daughter of Sam Roffe. Just as her mother had been an emotional victim of the company, so was Elizabeth. If she had no family life, it was because there was no family, only the paid surrogates and the distant figure of the man who had fathered her, who seemed to have no interest in her, only in the company. Patricia had been able to accept her situation, but for the child it was torment. Elizabeth felt unwanted and unloved, and did not know how to cope with her despair, and in the end she blamed herself for being unlovable. She tried desperately to win the affection of her father. When Elizabeth was old enough to go to school, she made things for him in class, childish drawings and watercolor paintings and lopsided ashtrays, and she would guard them fiercely, waiting for him to return from one of his trips, so that she could surprise him, please him, hear him say, *It's beautiful, Elizabeth. You're very talented.*

When he returned, Elizabeth would present her love offering, and her father would glance at it absently and nod, or shake his head. "You'll never be an artist, will you?"

Sometimes Elizabeth would awaken in the middle of the night, and walk down the long winding staircase of the Beekman Place apartment and through the large cavernous hall that led to her father's study. She would step into the empty room as if she were entering a shrine. This was *his* room, where he worked and signed important pieces of paper and ran the world. Elizabeth would walk over to his enormous leather-topped desk and slowly rub her hands across it. Then she would move behind the desk and sit in his leather chair. She felt closer to her father there. It was as though by being where he was, sitting where he sat, she could become a part of him. She would hold imaginary conversations with him, and he would listen, interested and caring as she poured out her problems. One night, as Elizabeth sat at his desk in the dark, the lights in the room suddenly came on. Her father was standing in the doorway. He looked at Elizabeth seated behind his desk, clad in a thin nightgown, and said, "What are you doing here alone in the dark?" And he scooped her up in his arms and carried her upstairs, to her bed, and Elizabeth had lain awake all night, thinking about how her father had held her.

After that, she went downstairs every night and sat in his office waiting for him to come and get her, but it never happened again.

No one discussed Elizabeth's mother with her, but there was a beautiful full-length portrait of Patricia Roffe hanging in the reception hall, and Elizabeth would stare at it by the hour. Then she would turn to her mirror. Ugly. They had put braces on her teeth, and she looked like a gargoyle. No wonder my father isn't interested in me, Elizabeth thought.

Overnight she developed an insatiable appetite, and began to gain weight. For she had arrived at a wonderful truth: if she were fat and ugly, no one would expect her to look like her mother.

When Elizabeth was twelve years old, she attended an exclusive private school on the East Side of Manhattan, in the upper seventies. She would arrive in a chauffeur-driven Rolls-Royce, walk into her classes and sit there, withdrawn and silent, ignoring everyone around her. She never volunteered to answer a question. And when she was called upon, she never seemed to know the answer. Her teachers soon got in the habit of ignoring her. They discussed Elizabeth among themselves and unanimously agreed that she was the most spoiled child they had ever seen. In a confidential year-end report to the headmistress, Elizabeth's homeroom teacher wrote:

> We have been able to make no progress with Elizabeth Roffe. She is aloof from her classmates and refuses to participate in any of the group activities. She has made no friends at school. Her grades are unsatisfactory, but it is difficult to tell if this is because she makes no effort, or because she is unable to handle the assignments. She is arrogant and egotistical. Were it not for the fact that her father is a major benefactor of this school, I would strongly recommend expelling her.

The report was light-years from the reality. The simple truth was that Elizabeth Roffe had no protective shield, no armor against the terrible loneliness that engulfed her. She was filled with such a deep sense of her own unworthiness that she was afraid to make friends, for fear they would discover that she was worthless, unlovable. She was not arrogant, she was almost pathologically shy. She felt that she did not belong in the same world that her father inhabited. She did not belong anywhere. She loathed being driven to school in the Rolls-Royce, because she knew she did not deserve it. In her classes she knew the answers to the questions the teachers asked, but she did not dare to speak out, to call attention to herself. She loved to read, and she would lie awake late at night in her bed, devouring books.

She daydreamed, and oh! what lovely fantasies. She was in Paris with her father, and they were driving through the Bois in a horse-drawn carriage, and he took her to his office, an enormous room something like Saint Patrick's cathedral, and people kept walking in with papers for him to sign, and he would wave them away and say, "Can't you see I'm busy now? I'm talking to my daughter, Elizabeth."

She and her father were skiing in Switzerland, moving down a steep slope side by side, with an icy wind whipping past them, and he suddenly fell and cried out with pain, because his leg was broken, and she said, "Don't worry, Papa! I'll take care of you." And she skied down to the hospital and said, "Quickly, my father's hurt," and a dozen men in white jackets brought him there in a shiny ambulance and she was at his bedside, feeding him (it was probably his arm that was broken, then, not his leg), and her mother walked into the room, alive somehow, and her father said, "I can't see you now, Patricia. Elizabeth and I are talking."

Or they would be in their beautiful villa in Sardinia, and the servants would be away, and Elizabeth would cook dinner for her father. He would eat two helpings of everything and say, "You're a much better cook than your mother was, Elizabeth."

The scenes with her father always ended in the same way. The doorbell would ring and a tall man, who towered over her father, would come in and beg Elizabeth to marry him, and her father would plead with her, "Please, Elizabeth, don't leave me. I need you."

And she would agree to stay.

Of all the homes in which Elizabeth grew up, the villa in Sardinia was her favorite. It was by no means the largest, but it was

70

the most colorful, the friendliest. Sardinia itself delighted Elizabeth. It was a dramatic, rockbound island, some 160 miles southwest of the Italian coast, a stunning panorama of mountains, sea and green farmland. Its enormous volcanic cliffs had been thrown up thousands of years ago from the primal sea, and the shoreline swept in a vast crescent as far as the eye could follow, the Tyrrhenian Sea framing the island in a blue border.

For Elizabeth the island had its own special odors, the smell of sea breezes and forests, the white and yellow *macchia*, the fabled flower that Napoleon had loved. There were the *corbeccola* bushes that grew six feet high and had a red fruit that tasted like strawberries, and the *guarcias*, the giant stone oaks whose bark was exported to the mainland to be used for making cork for wine bottles.

She loved to listen to the singing rocks, the mysterious giant boulders with holes through them. When the winds blew through the holes, the rocks emitted an eerie keening sound, like a dirge of lost souls.

And the winds blew. Elizabeth grew to know them all. The *mistrale* and the *ponente*, the *tramontana* and the *grecate* and the *levante*. Soft winds and fierce winds. And then there was the dreaded scirocco, the warm wind that blew in from the Sahara.

The Roffe villa was on the Costa Smeralda, above Porto Cervo, set high atop a cliff overlooking the sea, secluded by juniper trees and the wild-growing Sardinian olive trees with their bitter fruit. There was a breathtaking view of the harbor far below, and around it, sprinkled over the green hills, a jumble of stucco and stone houses thrown together in a crazy hodgepodge of colors resembling a child's crayon drawing.

The villa was stucco, with huge juniper beans inside. It was built on several levels, with large, comfortable rooms, each with its own fireplace and balcony. The living room and dining room had picture windows that gave a panoramic view of the island. A free-form staircase led to four bedrooms upstairs. The furniture blended perfectly with the surroundings. There were rustic refectory tables and benches, and soft easy chairs. Across the windows were fringed white wool draperies that had been hand-woven on the island, and the floors were laid with colorful *cerasarda* tiles from Sardinia and other tiles from Tuscany. In the bathrooms and bedrooms were native wool carpets, colored with vegetable dyes in the traditional way. The house was ablaze with paintings, a mixture of French Impressionists, Italian masters and Sardo primitives. In the hallway hung portraits of Samuel Roffe and Terenia Roffe, Elizabeth's great-great grandfather and grandmother.

The feature of the house that Elizabeth loved most was the tower room, under the sloping tile roof. It was reached by a narrow staircase from the second floor, and Sam Roffe used it as his study. It contained a large work desk and a comfortable padded swivel chair. The walls were lined with bookcases and maps, most of them pertaining to the Roffe empire. French doors led to a small balcony built over a sheer cliff, and the view from there was heart-stopping.

It was in this house, when she was thirteen years old, that Elizabeth discovered the origins of her family, and for the first time in her life that she felt she belonged, that she was part of something.

It began the day she found the Book. Elizabeth's father had driven to Olbia, and Elizabeth had wandered upstairs to the tower room. She was not interested in the books on the shelves, for she had long since learned that they were technical volumes on pharmacology and pharmacognosy, and on multinational corporations and international law. Dull and boring. Some of the manuscripts were rare, and these were kept in glass cases. There was a medical volume in Latin called *Circa Instans,* written in the Middle Ages, and another called *De Materia Medica.* It was because Elizabeth was studying Latin and was curious to see one of the old volumes that she opened the glass case to take it out. Behind it, tucked away out of sight, she saw another volume. Elizabeth picked it up. It was thick, bound in red leather, and had no title.

Intrigued, Elizabeth opened it. It was like opening the door to another world. It was a biography of her great-great grandfather, Samuel Roffe, in English, privately printed on vellum. There was no author given, and no date, but Elizabeth was sure that it was more than one hundred years old, for most of the pages were faded, and others were yellowed and flaking with age. But none of this was important. It was the story that mattered, a story that brought life to the portraits hanging on the wall downstairs. Elizabeth had seen the pictures of her great-great grandparents a hundred times: paintings of an old-fashioned man and woman, dressed in unfamiliar clothes. The man was not handsome, but there was great strength and intelligence in his face. He had fair hair, high Slavic cheekbones and keen, bright-blue eyes. The woman was a beauty. Dark hair, a flawless complexion and eyes as black as coal. She wore a white-silk dress with a tabard over the top, and a bodice made of brocade. Two strangers who meant nothing to Elizabeth.

But now, alone in the tower room, as Elizabeth opened the Book and began to read, Samuel and Terenia Roffe became alive. Elizabeth felt as though she had been transported back in time, that she was living in the ghetto of Krakow, in the year 1853, with Samuel and Terenia. As she read deeper and deeper into the Book, she learned that her great-great grandfather Samuel, the founder of Roffe and Sons, was a romantic and an adventurer.

And a murderer.

Samuel Roffe's earliest memory, Elizabeth read, was of his mother being killed in a pogrom in 1855 when Samuel was five years old. He had been hidden in the cellar of the small wooden house the Roffes shared with other families in the ghetto of Krakow. When the rioting was finally over, endless hours later, and the only sound left was the weeping of the survivors, Samuel cautiously left his hiding place and went out into the streets of the ghetto to look for his mother. It seemed to the young boy that the whole world was on fire. The entire sky was red from the blazing wooden buildings that burned on every side, and clouds of thick black smoke hung everywhere. Men and women were frantically searching for their families, or trying to save their businesses and homes and meager possessions. Krakow, in the mid-nineteenth century, had a fire department, but it was forbidden to the Jews. Here in the ghetto, at the edge of the city, they were forced to fight the holocaust by hand, with water drawn from their wells, and scores of people formed bucket brigades to drown the flames. Samuel saw death wherever he looked, mutilated bodies of men and women tossed aside like broken dolls; naked, raped women and children, bleeding and moaning for help.

Samuel found his mother lying in the street, half conscious, her face covered with blood. The young boy knelt down at her side, his heart pounding wildly. "Mama!"

She opened her eyes and saw him, and tried to speak, and Samuel knew that she was dying. He desperately wanted to save her, but he did not know how, and even as he gently wiped the blood away, it was already too late.

Later, Samuel stood there watching as the burial party carefully dug up the ground under his mother's body: for it was soaked in her blood, and according to the Scriptures, it had to be buried with her so that she could be returned to God whole.

It was at that moment that Samuel made up his mind that he wanted to become a doctor.

The Roffe family shared a three-story narrow wooden house with eight other families. Young Samuel lived in one small room with his father and his aunt Rachel, and in all his life he had never been in a room by himself or slept or eaten alone. He could not remember a single moment when he could not hear the sound of voices, but Samuel did not crave privacy, for he had no idea that it existed. He had always lived in a crowded maze.

Each evening Samuel and his relatives and friends were locked into the ghetto by the gentiles, as the Jews penned up their goats and cows and chickens.

At sundown the massive double wooden gates of the ghetto were closed and locked with a large iron key. At sunrise the gates were opened again, and the Jewish merchants were permitted to go into the city of Krakow to conduct business with the gentiles, but they were required to be back inside the ghetto walls before sunset.

Samuel's father had come from Russia, where he had fled from a pogrom in Kiev, and he had made his way to Krakow, where he had met his bride. Samuel's father was a stooped, gray-haired man, his face worn and wrinkled, a pushcart peddler who hawked his wares of notions and trinkets and utensils through the narrow winding streets of the ghetto. Young Samuel loved to roam the crowded, bustling, cobblestoned streets. He enjoyed the smell of fresh-baked bread mingled with the odors of drying fish and cheeses and ripening fruit and sawdust and leather. He liked to listen to the peddlers singing out their wares, and the housewives bargaining with them in outraged, grieved tones. The variety of goods that the peddlers sold was staggering: linens and laces, ticking and yarn, leather and meats and vegetables and needles and soft soap and plucked whole chickens and candies and buttons and syrups and shoes.

On Samuel's twelfth birthday his father took him into the city of Krakow for the first time. The idea of going through the forbidden gates and seeing Krakow itself, the home of the gentiles, filled the boy with an almost unbearable excitement.

At six o'clock in the morning Samuel, wearing his one good suit, stood in the dark next to his father in front of the huge closed gates to the city, surrounded by a noisy crowd of men with crude, homemade pushcarts, wagons or barrows. The air was cold and raw, and Samuel huddled into his threadbare sheep's-wool coat.

After what seemed hours, a bright-orange sun peeped over the eastern horizon and there was an expectant stir from the crowd. Moments later, the huge wooden gates began to swing open and the merchants started to pour through them like a stream of industrious ants, heading toward the city.

As they approached the wonderful, terrible city, Samuel's heart began to beat faster. Ahead he could see the fortifications towering over the Vistula. Samuel clung to his father more tightly. He was actually in Krakow, surrounded by the feared goyim, the people who locked them up every night. He stole quick, frightened glances at the faces of the passersby and he marveled at how different they looked. They did not wear *payves*, earlocks, and *bekeches*, the long black coats, and many of them were clean-shaven. Samuel and his father walked along the Plante toward the Rynek, the crowded marketplace, where they passed the enormous cloth hall, and the twin-towered Church of Saint Mary. Samuel had never seen such magnificence. The new world was filled with wonders. First of all, there was an exciting feeling of freedom and space that left Samuel breathless. The houses on the streets were all set apart, not jumbled together, and most of them had a small garden in front. Surely, Samuel thought, everyone in Krakow must be a millionaire.

Samuel accompanied his father to half a dozen different suppliers, where his father bought goods which he tossed into the cart. When the cart was filled, he and the boy headed back toward the ghetto.

"Can't we stay longer?" Samuel begged.

"No, son. We have to go home."

Samuel did not want to go home. He had been outside the gates for the first time in his life, and he was filled with an elation that was so strong it almost choked him. That people could live like *this*, free to walk wherever they pleased, free to do whatever they wanted . . . Why could he not have been born outside the gate? Instantly, he was ashamed of himself for having such disloyal thoughts.

That night when Samuel went to bed, he lay awake for a long time, thinking about Krakow and the beautiful houses with their flowers and green gardens. He had to find a way to get free. He wanted to talk to someone about the things he felt, but there was no one who would understand him.

Elizabeth put the Book down and sat back, closing her eyes, visualizing Samuel's loneliness, his excitement, his frustration.

It was at that moment that Elizabeth began to identify with him, to feel that she was a part of him, as he was a part of her. His blood ran in her veins. She had a wonderful, heady sense of belonging.

Elizabeth heard the sound of her father's car coming up the driveway, and she quickly put the Book away. She had no further chance to read it during her stay there, but when she returned to New York the Book was hidden at the bottom of her suitcase.

After the warm winter sunshine of Sardinia, New York seemed like Siberia. The streets were filled with snow and slush, and the wind blowing off the East River was frigid; but Elizabeth did not mind. She was living in Poland, in another century, sharing the adventures of her great-great grandfather. Every afternoon after school, Elizabeth would rush up to her room, lock the door and take out the Book. She had thought of discussing it with her father, but she was afraid to, for fear he would take it away from her.

In a wonderful, unexpected way, it was old Samuel who gave Elizabeth encouragement. It seemed to Elizabeth that they were so much alike. Samuel was a loner. He had no one to talk to. Like me, thought Elizabeth. And because they were almost the same age—even though a century apart—she could identify with him.

Samuel wanted to be a doctor.

Only three physicians were allowed to take care of the thousands of people crowded into the unsanitary, epidemic-ridden confines of the ghetto; and of the three, the most prosperous was Dr. Zeno Wal. His house stood among its poorer neighbors like a castle in the midst of a slum. It was three stories high, and through its windows could be seen freshly washed and starched white-lace curtains and glimpses of shining, polished furniture. Samuel could visualize the doctor inside, treating his patients, helping them, curing them: doing what Samuel longed to do. Surely, if someone like Dr. Wal took an interest in him, Samuel thought, he could help him become a doctor. But as far as Samuel was concerned, Dr. Wal was as inaccessible as any of the gentiles living in the city of Krakow, outside the forbidden wall.

From time to time Samuel would catch glimpses of the great Dr. Zeno Wal walking along the street, engaged in earnest conversation with a colleague. One day, as Samuel was passing the Wal house, the front door opened and the doctor came out with his daughter. She was about Samuel's age, and she was the most beautiful creature Samuel had ever seen. The moment Samuel looked at her, he knew she was going to be his wife. He did not know how he was going to manage that miracle, he only knew that he had to.

Every day after that, Samuel found an excuse to be near her house, hoping to get another glimpse of her.

One afternoon, as Samuel was walking by the Wal house on an errand, he heard piano music coming from inside, and he knew that *she* was playing. He had to see her. Looking around to make sure no one was observing him, Samuel walked to the side of the house. The music was coming from upstairs, directly above his head. Samuel stepped back and studied the wall. There were enough handholds for him to climb it, and without a moment's hesitation he started up. The second floor was higher than he had realized, and before he reached the window he was ten feet above the ground. He looked down and felt a momentary sense of dizziness. The music was louder now, and he felt as if she were playing for him. He grabbed another handhold and pulled himself up to the window. Slowly he raised his head so he could peer over the sill. He found himself looking into an exquisitely furnished parlor. The girl was seated before a gold-and-white piano, playing, and behind her in an armchair, reading a book, was Dr. Wal. Samuel had no eyes for him. He could only stare at the beautiful vision just a few feet away from him. He loved her! He would do something spectacular and daring so that she would fall in love with him. He would— So engrossed was Samuel in his daydream that he loosened his grip and began to fall into space. He let out a cry and saw two startled faces staring at him just before he plunged to the ground.

He woke up on an operating table in Dr. Wal's office, a spacious room outfitted with medical cabinets and an array of surgical equipment. Dr. Wal was holding an awful-smelling piece of cotton under Samuel's nose. Samuel choked and sat up.

"That's better," Dr. Wal said. "I should remove your brain but I doubt if you have one. What were you planning to steal, boy?"

"Nothing," Samuel replied indignantly.

"What's your name?"

"Samuel Roffe."

The doctor's fingers began to probe Samuel's right wrist, and the boy cried out with pain.

"Hm. You have a broken wrist, Samuel Roffe. Maybe we should let the police fix it."

Samuel groaned aloud. He was thinking about what would happen when the police brought him home in disgrace. His aunt Rachel's heart would be broken; his father would kill him. But, even more important, how could he ever hope to win Dr. Wal's daughter now? He was a criminal, a marked man. Samuel felt a sudden, agonizing jerk on his wrist, and he looked up at the doctor in shocked surprise.

"It's all right," Dr. Wal said. "I've set it." He went to work putting a splint on it. "Do you live around here, Samuel Roffe?"

"No, sir."

"Haven't I seen you hanging about?"

"Yes, sir."

"Why?"

Why? If Samuel told him the truth, Dr. Wal would laugh at him.

"I want to become a doctor," Samuel blurted out, unable to contain himself.

Dr. Wal was staring at him in disbelief. *"That's* why you climbed the wall of my house like a burglar?"

Samuel found himself telling his entire story. He told about his mother dying in the streets, and about his father, about his first visit to Krakow and his frustration at being locked inside the ghetto walls at night like an animal. He told how he felt about Dr. Wal's daughter. He told everything, and the doctor listened in silence. Even to Samuel's ears his story sounded ridiculous; and when he was finished, he whispered, "I—I'm sorry."

Dr. Wal looked at him for a long time, and then said, "I'm sorry, too. For you, and for me, and for all of us. Every man is a prisoner, and the greatest irony of all is to be the prisoner of another man."

Samuel looked up at him, puzzled. "I don't understand, sir."

The doctor sighed. "One day you will." He rose to his feet, walked over to his desk, selected a pipe and slowly and methodically filled it. "I'm afraid this is a very bad day for you, Samuel Roffe."

He put a match to the tobacco, blew it out and then turned to the boy. "Not because of your broken wrist. That will heal. But I'm going to have to do something to you that may not heal so quickly." Samuel was watching him, his eyes wide. Dr. Wal walked over to his side, and when he spoke his voice was gentle. "Very few people ever have a dream. You have two dreams. And I'm afraid I am going to have to break both of them."

"I don't—"

"Listen to me carefully, Samuel. You can never be a doctor— not in our world. Only three of us are allowed to practice medicine in the ghetto. There are dozens of skilled doctors here, waiting for one of us to retire or to die, so that they can take our place. There's no chance for you. None. You were born at the wrong time, in the wrong place. Do you understand me, boy?"

Samuel swallowed. "Yes, sir."

The doctor hesitated, then went on. "About your second dream—I'm afraid that one is just as impossible. There is no chance of your ever marrying Terenia."

"Why?" Samuel asked.

Dr. Wal stared at him. "*Why?* For the same reason you can't become a doctor. We live by the rules, by our traditions. My daughter will marry someone of her own class, someone who can afford to keep her in the same style in which she has been raised. She will marry a professional man, a lawyer or a doctor or a rabbi. You—well, you must put her out of your mind."

"But—"

The doctor was ushering him toward the door. "Have someone look at that splint in a few days. See that the bandage is kept clean."

"Yes, sir," Samuel said. "Thank you, Dr. Wal."

Dr. Wal studied the blond, intelligent-looking boy before him. "Good-bye, Samuel Roffe."

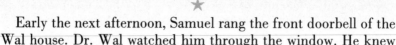
Early the next afternoon, Samuel rang the front doorbell of the Wal house. Dr. Wal watched him through the window. He knew that he should send him away.

"Send him in," Dr. Wal said to the maid.

After that, Samuel came to Dr. Wal's house two or three times a week. He ran errands for the doctor, and in exchange Dr. Wal let him watch as he treated patients or worked in his laboratory, concocting medicines. The boy observed and learned and remembered everything. He had a natural talent. Dr. Wal felt a growing sense of guilt, for he knew that in a way he was encouraging Samuel, encouraging him to be something he could never be; and yet he could not bring himself to turn the boy away.

Whether it was by accident or design, Terenia was almost always around when Samuel was there. Occasionally he would get a glimpse of her walking past the laboratory, or leaving the house, and once he bumped into her in the kitchen, and his heart began to pound so hard that he thought he would faint. She studied him for a long moment, a look of speculation in her eyes, then she nodded coolly and was gone. At least she had noticed him! That was the first step. The rest was only a matter of time. There was not the slightest doubt in Samuel's mind. It was fated. Terenia had become a major part of Samuel's dreams about the future. Where once he had dreamed for himself, he now dreamed for the two of them. Somehow he would get them both out of this terrible ghetto, this stinking, overcrowded prison. And he would become a great success. But now his success would not be for him alone, but for both of them.

Even though it was impossible.

Elizabeth fell asleep, reading about old Samuel. In the morning when she awakened, she carefully hid the Book and began to get dressed for school. She could not get Samuel off her mind. How did he marry Terenia? How did he get out of the ghetto? How did he become famous? Elizabeth was consumed by the Book, and she resented the intrusions that tore her away from it and forced her to return to the twentieth century.

One of the classes that Elizabeth had to attend was ballet, and she loathed it. She would stuff herself into her pink tutu, and stare at her image in the mirror and try to tell herself that her figure was voluptuous. But the truth was there for her to see. She was fat. She would never be a ballet dancer.

Shortly after Elizabeth's fourteenth birthday, Mme. Netturova, her dance teacher, announced that in two weeks the class would give its yearly dance recital in the auditorium, and that the students were to invite their parents. Elizabeth was in a state of panic. The mere thought of getting up on a stage in front of an audience filled her with dread. She could not go through with it.

A child was running across a street in front of a car. Elizabeth saw her, raced out and snatched the child from the jaws of death. Unfortunately, ladies and gentlemen, Elizabeth Roffe's toes were crushed by the wheels of the automobile, and she will not be able to dance at the recital this evening.

A careless maid left a bar of soap at the top of the stairs. Elizabeth slipped and fell down the long flight, breaking her hip. Nothing to worry about, the doctor said. It will heal in three weeks.

No such luck. On the day of the performance, Elizabeth was in perfect health, and a state of hysteria. Again, it was old Samuel who helped her. She remembered how frightened he had been, but he had gone back to face Dr. Wal. She would not do anything to disgrace Samuel. She would face up to her ordeal.

Elizabeth had not even mentioned the recital to her father. In the past she had often asked him to school meetings and parties which parents were requested to attend, but he had always been too busy.

On this evening, as Elizabeth was getting ready to leave for the dance recital, her father returned home. He had been out of town for ten days.

He passed her bedroom, saw her and said, "Good evening, Elizabeth." Then, "You've put on some weight."

She flushed and tried to pull in her stomach. "Yes, Father."

He started to say something, then changed his mind. "How's school coming along?"

"Fine, thank you."

"Any problems?"

"No, Father."

"Good."

It was a dialogue they had had a hundred times over the years, a meaningless litany that seemed to be their only form of communication. How's-school-coming-along-fine-thank-you-any-problems-no-Father-good. Two strangers discussing the weather, neither listening nor caring about the other's opinion. Well, one of us cares, Elizabeth thought.

But this time Sam Roffe stood there, watching his daughter, a thoughtful expression on his face. He was used to dealing with concrete problems and although he sensed that there was a problem here, he had no idea what it was, and if anyone had told him, Sam Roffe's answer would have been, "Don't be a fool. I've given Elizabeth everything."

As her father started to leave, Elizabeth heard herself say, "My—my—ballet class is giving a recital. I'm in it. You don't want to come, do you?"

And even as she said the words, she was filled with a sense of horror. She did not want him there to see her clumsiness. Why had she asked him? But she knew why. Because she was the only girl in the class whose parents would not be in that auditorium. It doesn't matter, anyway, she told herself, because he's going to say no. She shook her head, furious with herself, and turned away. And behind her, incredibly, she heard her father's voice saying, "I'd like that."

The auditorium was crowded with parents, relatives and friends, watching the students dance to the accompaniment of two grand pianos on either side of the stage. Mme. Netturova stood off to one side, counting the beat aloud as the children danced, calling the attention of the parents to herself.

A few of the children were remarkably graceful, and showed signs of real talent. The others went through their performances determined to substitute enthusiasm for ability. The mimeographed program announced three musical excerpts from *Coppélia*, *Cinderella* and, inevitably, *Swan Lake*. The *pièce de résistance* was to be the solos, when each child would have her moment of glory, alone.

Backstage, Elizabeth was in an agony of apprehension. She kept peering through the side curtain, and each time she saw her father sitting in the second row center, she thought what a fool she had been to ask him. So far during the show, Elizabeth had been able to lose herself in the background, hidden behind the other dancers. But now her solo was coming up. She felt gross in her tutu, like something in a circus. She was certain they would all laugh at her when she came out on the stage—and she had *invited* her father to watch her humiliation! Elizabeth's only consolation was that her solo lasted for only sixty seconds. Mme. Netturova was no fool. It would all be over so quickly that no one would even notice her. All Elizabeth's father had to do was to glance away for a minute, and her number would be finished.

Elizabeth watched the other girls as they danced, one by one, and they seemed to her like Markova, Maximova, Fonteyn. She was startled by a cold hand on her bare arm, and Mme. Netturova hissed, "On your toes, Elizabeth, you're next."

Elizabeth tried to say, "Yes, madame," but her throat was so dry that no words came out. The two pianists struck up the familiar theme of Elizabeth's solo. She stood there, frozen, incapable of moving, and Mme Netturova was whispering, "Get out there!" and Elizabeth felt a shove against her back, and she was out on the stage, half naked, in front of a hundred hostile strangers. She did not dare look at her father. All she wanted was to get this ordeal over with as quickly as possible and flee. What she had to do was simple, a few pliés and jetés and leaps. She began to execute the steps, keeping time to the music, trying to think herself thin and tall and lithe. As she finished, there was a smattering of polite applause from the audience. Elizabeth looked down at the second row, and there was her father, smiling proudly and applauding—applauding *her*, and something inside Elizabeth snapped. The music had stopped. But Elizabeth kept on dancing, doing pliés and jetés and battements and turns, carried away, transported beyond herself. The confused musicians began to pick up her beat, first one pianist, then the other, trying to keep up with her. Backstage, Mme. Netturova was signaling to Elizabeth wildly, her face filled with fury. But Elizabeth was blissfully unaware of her, transported beyond herself. The only thing that mattered to her was that she was onstage, dancing for her father.

"I am sure you understand, Mr. Roffe, that this school simply cannot tolerate that type of behavior." Mme. Netturova's voice was trembling with anger. "Your daughter ignored everyone else and took over, as though—as though she were some kind of *star*."

Elizabeth could feel her father turn to look at her, and she was afraid to meet his eyes. She knew that what she had done was unforgivable, but she had been unable to stop herself. For one moment on that stage she had tried to create something beautiful for her father, had tried to impress him, make him notice her, be proud of her. Love her.

Now she heard him say, "You're absolutely right, Madame Netturova. I will see to it that Elizabeth is suitably punished."

Mme. Netturova gave Elizabeth a look of triumph, and said, "Thank you, Mr. Roffe. I will leave it in your hands."

Elizabeth and her father were standing outside the school. He had not said one word to her since leaving Mme. Netturova's office. Elizabeth was trying to compose a speech of apology—but what could she say? How could she ever make her father understand why she had done what she had done? He was a stranger, and she was afraid of him. She had heard him vent his terrible anger on others for making mistakes, or for having disobeyed him. Now she stood there waiting for his wrath to fall upon her.

He turned to her and said, "Elizabeth, why don't we drop in at Rumpelmayer's and get a chocolate soda?"

And Elizabeth burst into tears.

She lay in her bed that night, wide awake, too stimulated to go to sleep. She kept re-playing the evening over and over in her mind. The excitement of it had been almost more than she could bear. Because this was no made-up daydream. It had happened, it was real. She could see herself and her father, seated at the table at Rumpelmayer's, surrounded by the large, colorful stuffed bears and elephants and lions and zebras. Elizabeth had ordered a banana split, which had turned out to be absolutely enormous, and her father had not criticized her. He was talking to her. Not how's-school-coming-along-fine-thank-you-any-problems-no-Father-good. But really *talking*. He told her about his recent trip to Tokyo, and how his host had served chocolate-covered grasshoppers and ants as a special treat for him, and how he had had to eat them in order not to lose face.

When Elizabeth had scooped up the last drop of the ice cream, her father suddenly said, "What made you do it, Liz?"

She knew that everything was going to be spoiled now, that he was going to reprimand her, tell her how disappointed he was in her.

She said, "I wanted to be better than everyone else." She could not bring herself to add, *For you.*

He looked at her for what seemed a long time, and then he laughed. "You certainly surprised the hell out of everybody." There was a note of pride in his voice.

Elizabeth felt the blood rushing to her cheeks, and she said, "You're not angry with me?"

There was a look in his eyes that she had never seen before. "For wanting to be the best? That's what the Roffes are all about." And he reached over and squeezed her hand.

Elizabeth's last thoughts as she drifted off to sleep were: My father likes me, he really likes me. From now on, we'll be together all the time. He'll take me on trips with him. We'll talk about things and we'll become good friends.

The following afternoon her father's secretary informed her that arrangements had been made to send Elizabeth away to a boarding school in Switzerland.

10

Elizabeth was enrolled in the International Château Lemand, a girls' school situated in the village of Sainte-Blaise, overlooking the Lake of Neuchâtel. The age of the girls ranged from fourteen to eighteen. It was one of the finest schools in the excellent Swiss educational system.

Elizabeth hated every minute of it.

She felt exiled. She had been sent away from home, and it was like some dire punishment for a crime she had not committed. On that one magic evening she had felt that she was on the verge of something wonderful, discovering her father, and her father discovering her, and their becoming friends. But now he was farther away than ever.

Elizabeth was able to keep track of her father in the newspapers and magazines. There were frequent stories and photographs of him meeting with a prime minister or a president, opening a new pharmaceutical plant in Bombay, mountain climbing, dining with the Shah of Iran. Elizabeth pasted all the stories in a scrapbook which she constantly pored over. She hid it next to the book of Samuel.

Elizabeth remained aloof from the other students. Some of the girls shared rooms with two or three others, but Elizabeth had asked for a room by herself. She wrote long letters to her father, then tore up the ones that revealed her feelings. From time to time she received a note from him, and there were gaily wrapped packages from expensive stores on her birthday, sent by his secretary. Elizabeth missed her father terribly.

She was going to join him at the villa in Sardinia for Christmas, and as the time drew nearer, the waiting became almost unbearable. She was sick with excitement. She made a list of resolutions for herself and carefully wrote them down:

> Do not be a pest.
> Be interesting.
> Do not complain about anything,
>   especially school.
> Do not let him know you are lonely.
> Do not interrupt while he is speaking.
> Be well groomed at all times, even at breakfast.
> Laugh a lot so that he can see how happy you are.

The notes were a prayer, a litany, her offering to the gods. If she did all these things, maybe—maybe—Elizabeth's resolutions merged into fantasies. She would make profound observations about the Third World and the nineteen developing nations, and her father would say, "I didn't know you were so interesting" (rule number two). "You're a very bright girl, Elizabeth." Then he would turn to his secretary and say, "I don't think Elizabeth needs to go back to school. Why don't I keep her here with me?"

A prayer, a litany.

A company Learjet picked Elizabeth up at Zurich and flew her to the airport at Olbia, where she was met by a limousine. Elizabeth sat in the back of the car, silent, forcing her knees together to keep them from trembling. No matter what happens, she thought fiercely, I won't let him see me cry. He mustn't know how much I've missed him.

The car drove up the long, winding mountain highway that led to the Costa Smeralda, then off onto the small road that wound to the top. This road had always frightened Elizabeth. It was very narrow and steep, with the mountain on one side and a terrifying abyss on the other.

The car pulled up in front of the house, and Elizabeth stepped out and began walking toward the house and then running, her legs carrying her as fast as they could. The front door opened and

Margherita, the Sardinian housekeeper, stood there smiling. "Hello, Miss Elizabeth."

"Where's my father?" Elizabeth asked.

"He had to go to Australia on some emergency. But he left a lot of pretty presents for you. It's going to be a lovely Christmas."

Elizabeth had brought the Book with her. She stood in the hallway of the villa, studying the painting of Samuel Roffe, and next to him, Terenia, feeling their presence, as though they had come to life. After a long time Elizabeth turned and climbed up the ladder to the tower room, taking the Book. She spent hours every day in the tower room, reading and rereading, and each time she felt closer to Samuel and Terenia, the century that separated them disappearing . . .

Over the next few years, Elizabeth read, Samuel spent long hours in Dr. Wal's laboratory, helping him mix ointments and medicines, learning how they worked. And always in the background was Terenia, haunting, beautiful. The very sight of her was enough to keep alive Samuel's dream that one day she would belong to him. Samuel got along well with Dr. Wal, but Terenia's mother was another story. She was a sharp-tongued virago, a snob, and she hated Samuel. He tried to keep out of her way.

Samuel was fascinated by the many drugs that could heal people. A papyrus had been found that listed 811 prescriptions used by the Egyptians in 1550 B.C. Life expectancy at birth then was fifteen years and Samuel could understand why when he read some of the prescriptions: crocodile dung, lizard flesh, bat's blood, camel's spit, lion's liver, toe of a frog, unicorn powder. The *Rx* sign on every prescription was the ancient prayer to Horae, the Egyptian god of healing. Even the word "chemistry" derived from the ancient name of Egypt, the land of Kahmi, or Chemi. The priest-physicians were called magi, Samuel learned.

The apothecary shops in the ghetto and in Krakow itself were primitive. Most of the bottles and jars were filled with untested and untried medicinal items, some useless, some harmful. Samuel became familiar with them all. There were castor oil, calomel, and rhubarb, iodine compounds and codeine and ipecac. You could purchase panaceas for whooping cough, colic and typhoid fever. Because no sanitary precautions were taken, it was common to find ointments and gargles filled with dead insects, roaches, rat droppings and bits of feathers and furs. The majority of patients who took the remedies died either of their diseases or from the remedies.

Several magazines were printed that were devoted to apothecary news, and Samuel read them all avidly. He discussed his theories with Dr. Wal.

"It stands to reason," Samuel said, his voice ringing with conviction, "that there must be a cure for every disease. Health is natural, disease is unnatural."

"Perhaps," Dr. Wal said, "but most of my patients won't even let me try the new medications on them." He added dryly, "And I think they're wise."

Samuel devoured Dr. Wal's sparse library on pharmacy. And when he had read and reread those books, he felt frustrated by the unanswered questions that lay between the covers.

Samuel was fired by the revolution that was taking place. Some scientists believed that it was possible to counteract the cause of diseases by building up a resistance that would destroy the illness. Dr. Wal tried it once. He took the blood of a patient with diphtheria and injected it into a horse. When the horse died, Dr. Wal gave up his experiments. But young Samuel was sure that Dr. Wal had been on the right track.

"You can't stop now," Samuel said. "I know it will work."

Dr. Wal shook his head. "That's because you're seventeen, Samuel. When you're my age, you won't be as sure of anything. Forget about it."

But Samuel was not convinced. He wanted to continue his experiments, but for that Samuel needed animals, and there were few available except for the stray cats and rats that he was able to catch. No matter how minute the doses that Samuel gave them, they died. They're too small, Samuel thought. I need a larger animal. A horse or a cow or a sheep. But where was he going to find one?

One late afternoon when Samuel arrived home, an ancient horse and cart stood in front of the house. On the side of the cart a crudely lettered sign read: "ROFFE & SON." Samuel stared at it unbelievingly, then raced into the house to find his father. "That—that horse out there," he said. "Where did you get it?"

His father smiled at him proudly. "I made a deal. We can cover more territory with a horse. Maybe in four or five years we can buy another horse. Think of it. We'll have *two* horses."

That was the extent of his father's ambition, owning two broken-down horses pulling carts through the dirty, crowded streets of the Krakow ghetto. It made Samuel want to weep.

That night when everyone was asleep, Samuel went out to the stable and examined the horse, which they had named Ferd. As horses went, this one was without question one of the lowest of the species. She was a very old horse, swaybacked and spavined. It was doubtful whether she could move much faster than Samuel's father. But none of that mattered. What was important was that Samuel now had his laboratory animal. He could do his experiments without having to worry about catching rats and stray cats. Of course, he would have to be careful. His father must never find out what he was doing. Samuel stroked the horse's head. "You're going into the drug business," he informed Ferd.

Samuel improvised his own laboratory, using a corner of the stable in which Ferd was kept.

He grew a culture of diphtheria germs in a dish of rich broth. When the broth turned cloudy, he removed some of it to another container and then weakened it, first by diluting the broth, then by heating it slightly. He filled a hypodermic needle with it and approached Ferd. "Remember what I told you?" Samuel whispered. "Well, this is your big day."

Samuel plunged the contents of the hypodermic into the loose skin of the horse's shoulder, as he had seen Dr. Wal do. Ferd turned to look at him reproachfully, and sprayed him with urine.

Samuel estimated that it would take about seventy-two hours for the culture to develop in Ferd. At the end of that time Samuel would give her a larger dose. Then another. If the antibody theory was right, each dose would build up a stronger blood resistance to the disease. Samuel would have his vaccine. Later, he would have to find a human being to test it on, of course, but that should not be difficult. A victim of the dread disease should be only too happy to try something that might save his life.

For the next two days Samuel spent almost every waking moment with Ferd.

"I've never seen anyone love an animal so much," his father said. "You can't keep away from her, can you?"

Samuel mumbled an inaudible reply. He felt a sense of guilt about what he was doing, but he knew what would happen if he even mentioned it to his father. However, there was no need for his father to know. All Samuel had to do was extract enough blood from Ferd to make up a vial or two of serum, and no one would ever be the wiser.

On the morning of the third and crucial day, Samuel was awakened by the sound of his father's voice from in front of the house. Samuel got out of bed, hurried to the window and looked out. His father was standing in the street with his cart, bellowing at the top of his lungs. There was no sign of Ferd. Samuel threw on some clothes and raced outside.

"Momser!" his father was yelling. "Cheater! Liar! Thief!"

Samuel pushed past the crowd that was beginning to gather around his father.

"Where's Ferd?" Samuel demanded.

"I'm glad you asked me," his father moaned. "She's dead. She died in the streets like a dog."

Samuel's heart sank.

"We're going along as nice as you please. I'm tending to business, not rushing her, you understand, not whipping her, or pushing her like some of the other peddlers I could name. And how does she show her appreciation? She drops dead. When I catch that *gonif* who sold her to me, I'll kill him!"

Samuel turned away, sick at heart. More than Ferd had passed away. Samuel's dreams had died. With Ferd went the escape from the ghetto, the freedom, the beautiful house for Terenia and their children.

But a greater disaster was to befall.

The day after Ferd died, Samuel learned that Dr. Wal and his wife had arranged for Terenia to marry a rabbi. Samuel could not believe it. Terenia belonged to *him!* Samuel raced over to the Wal house. He found Dr. and Mrs. Wal in the parlor. He walked up to them, took a deep breath and announced, "There's been a mistake, Terenia's mistake, Terenia's going to marry *me.*"

They stared at him in astonishment.

"I know I'm not good enough for her," Samuel hurried on, "but she won't be happy married to anyone but me. The rabbi's too old for—"

"*Nebbich!* Out! Out!" Terenia's mother was apoplectic.

Sixty seconds later Samuel found himself standing out in the street, forbidden ever to enter the Wal house again.

In the middle of the night Samuel had a long talk with God.

"What do you want from me? If I can't have Terenia, why did you make me love her? Haven't you any feelings?" He raised his voice in frustration and yelled, "Can you hear me?"

And the others in the crowded little house yelled back, "We can all hear you, Samuel. For God's sake, shut up and let us get some sleep!"

The following afternoon Dr. Wal sent for Samuel. He was ushered into the parlor, where Dr. and Mrs. Wal and Terenia were gathered.

"It seems we have a problem," Dr. Wal began. "Our daughter can be quite a stubborn young lady. For some reason she's taken a fancy to you. I cannot call it love, Samuel, because I don't believe that young girls know what love is. However, she has refused to marry Rabbi Rabinowitz. She thinks she wants to marry you."

Samuel sneaked a glance at Terenia, and she smiled at him and he almost burst with joy. It was short-lived.

Dr. Wall was going on. "You said that you love my daughter."

"Y—y—yes, sir," Samuel stammered. He tried it again, his voice stronger. "Yes, sir."

"Then let me ask you something, Samuel. Would you like Terenia to spend the rest of her life married to a peddler?"

Samuel instantly saw the trap, but there was no way out of it. He looked at Terenia again and said slowly, "No, sir."

"Ah. Then you see the problem. None of us wants Terenia to marry a peddler. And you're a peddler, Samuel."

"I won't always be, Dr. Wal." Samuel's voice was strong and sure.

"And what *will* you be?" Mrs. Wall snapped. "You come from

a family of peddlers, you'll remain a family of peddlers. I will not allow my daughter to marry one."

Samuel looked at the three of them, his mind filled with confusion. He had come here with trepidation and despair, had been lifted to the heights of joy, and now he had been plunged into a black abyss again. What did they want from him?

"We've agreed on a compromise," Dr. Wal said. "We're going to give you six months to prove that you're more than just a peddler. If, by the end of that time, you cannot offer Terenia the kind of life she is accustomed to, then she is going to marry Rabbi Rabinowitz."

Samuel stared at him, aghast. "Six months!"

No one could become a success in six months! No one, certainly, who lived in the ghetto of Krakow.

"Do you understand?" Dr. Wal asked.

"Yes, sir." Samuel understood only too well. He felt as if his stomach were filled with lead. He did not need a solution, he needed a miracle. The Wals would only be content with a son-in-law who was a doctor or a rabbi, or who was wealthy. Samuel quickly examined each possibility.

The law forbade him to become a doctor.

A rabbi? One had to start studying for the rabbinate by thirteen, and Samuel was almost eighteen now.

Wealthy? That was out of the question. If he worked twenty-four hours a day peddling his wares in the streets of the ghetto until he was ninety, he would still be a poor man. The Wals had set an impossible task for him. They had seemingly given in to Terenia by allowing her to postpone her marriage to the rabbi, while at the same time setting conditions that they knew would be impossible for Samuel to meet. Terenia was the only one who believed in him. She had confidence that he could find some kind of fame or fortune in six months. She's crazier than I am, Samuel thought in despair.

The six months began, and time flew. Samuel's days were spent as a peddler, helping his father. But the moment the shadows of the setting sun began to fall on the walls of the ghetto, Samuel would hurry home, gulp down a bite to eat, and then go to work in his laboratory. He made hundreds of batches of serums, and injected rabbits and cats and dogs and birds, and all the animals died. They're too small, Samuel thought desperately. I need a larger animal.

But he had none, and time was racing by.

Twice a week Samuel would go into Krakow to replenish the merchandise that he and his father sold from the cart. He would stand inside the locked gates at dawn, surrounded by the other peddlers, but he neither saw nor heard them. His mind was in another world.

As Samuel stood there one morning, daydreaming, a voice yelled, "You! Jew! Move on!"

Samuel looked up. The gates had been opened and his cart was blocking the way. One of the guards was angrily motioning for Samuel to move. There were always two guards on duty in front of the gate. They wore green uniforms and special insignia and were armed with pistols and heavy clubs. On a chain around his waist one of the guards carried a large key that opened and locked the gates. Alongside the ghetto ran a small river spanned by an old wooden bridge. Across the bridge was the police garrison where the ghetto guards were stationed. More than once, Samuel had witnessed a hapless Jew being dragged across the bridge. It was always a one-way trip. Jews were required to be back inside the ghetto by sundown, and any Jew caught outside the gates after dark was arrested and deported to a labor camp. It was the nightmare of every Jew that he might be caught outside the ghetto after sunset.

Both guards were supposed to remain on duty, patrolling in front of the gates, all night; but it was common knowledge inside the ghetto that after the Jews were locked in, one of the guards would slip away for a night of pleasure in the city. Just before dawn he would return to help his partner open the gates for the new day.

The two guards that were usually stationed there were named Paul and Aram. Paul was a pleasant man with a genial disposition. Aram was an entirely different matter. He was an animal, swarthy and stockily built, with powerful arms and a body like a beer keg. He was a Jew-baiter, and whenever he was on duty, all the Jews outside the gates made sure that they returned early, because nothing delighted Aram more than to lock a Jew out, club him senseless and drag him across the bridge to the dreaded police barracks.

It was Aram now who stood yelling at Samuel to move his cart. He hurriedly went through the gates and headed for the city, and he could feel Aram's eyes boring into his back.

Samuel's six-months grace period quickly dwindled to five months and then to four months, then three. There was not a day, not an hour, when Samuel was not thinking about a solution to his problem, or feverishly working in his tiny laboratory. He tried to speak to some of the wealthy merchants of the ghetto, but few had time for him, and those who had time offered him useless advice.

"You want to make money? Save your pennies, boy, and one day you'll have enough to buy a fine business like mine."

That was easy enough for them to say—most of them had been born into wealthy homes.

Samuel thought of taking Terenia and running away. But where? At the end of their journey would lie another ghetto, and he would still be a penniless *nebbich*. No, he loved Terenia too much to do that to her. That was the real trap in which he was caught.

Inexorably the clock ran on, and the three months became two, and then one. Samuel's only consolation during that time was that he was allowed to see his beloved Terenia three times a week, chaperoned, of course, and each time Samuel saw her, he loved her more deeply. It was a bittersweet feeling, for the more often he saw her, the closer he was coming to losing her. "You'll find a way," Terenia kept assuring him.

But now there were only three weeks left, and Samuel was no closer to a solution than when he had started.

Late one night Terenia came to see Samuel at the stable. She put her arms around him and said, "Let's run away, Samuel."

He had never loved her so much as he loved her at that moment. She was willing to disgrace herself, give up her mother and father, the wonderful life she lived, for him.

He held her close and said, "We can't. Wherever we went, I'd still be a peddler."

"I don't mind."

Samuel thought of her beautiful home with the spacious rooms and the servants, and he thought of the tiny squalid room he shared with his father and his aunt, and he said, "*I* would mind, Terenia."

And she turned and left.

The following morning Samuel met Isaac, a former schoolmate, walking down the street, leading a horse. It had one eye, suffered from acute colic, was spavined and deaf.

"Morning, Samuel."

"Morning, Isaac. I don't know where you're going with that poor horse, but you'd better hurry. It doesn't look like it's going to last much longer."

"It doesn't have to. I'm taking Lottie to a glue factory."

Samuel eyed the animal with a sudden, quickened interest. "I shouldn't think they'd give you much for her."

"I know. I just want a couple of florins to buy a cart."

Samuel's heart began to pump faster. "I think I can save you a trip. I'll trade you my cart for your horse."

It took less than five minutes to conclude the bargain.

Now all Samuel had to do was build another cart and explain to his father how he had lost the old one, and how he had come into possession of a horse that was on its last legs.

Samuel led Lottie to the barn where he had kept Ferd. On closer examination the horse was an even more discouraging sight. Samuel patted the animal and said, "Don't worry, Lottie, you're going to make medical history."

A few minutes later Samuel was at work on a new serum.

Because of the crowded and unsanitary conditions of the ghetto, epidemics were frequent. The latest plague was a fever that produced a choking cough, swollen glands and a painful death. The doctors did not know what caused it, or how to treat it. Isaac's father came down with the disease. When Samuel heard the news, he hurried over to see Isaac.

"The doctor has been here," the weeping boy told Samuel. "He said there's nothing to be done."

From upstairs they could hear the terrible sounds of a wracking cough that seemed to go on forever.

"I want you to do something for me," Samuel said. "Get me a handkerchief of your father's."

Isaac stared at him. *"What?"*

"One that he's used. And be careful how you handle it. It will be full of germs."

An hour later Samuel was back at the stable, carefully scraping the contents of the handerchief into a dish filled with broth.

He worked all that night and all the next day and the following day, injecting small doses of the substance into the patient Lottie, then larger doses, fighting against time, trying to save the life of Isaac's father.

Trying to save his own life.

In later years Samuel was never sure whether God was looking out for him or for the old horse, but Lottie survived the gradually increased doses, and Samuel had his first batch of antitoxin. His next task was to persuade Isaac's father to let him use it on him.

As it turned out, it needed no persuasion. When Samuel reached Isaac's house, it was filled with relatives, mourning the dying man upstairs.

"He only has a little time left," Isaac told Samuel.

"Can I see him?"

The two boys went upstairs. Isaac's father was in bed, his face flushed with fever. each racking cough sent his wasted frame into spasms that left him weaker. It was obvious that he was dying.

Samuel took a deep breath and said, "I want to talk to you and your mother."

Neither of them had any confidence in the little glass vial that Samuel had brought, but the alternative was death. They took a chance simply because there was nothing to lose.

Samuel injected Isaac's father with the serum. He waited at the bedside for three hours, and there was no change. The serum had no effect. If anything, the coughing spells seemed more frequent. Finally Samuel left, avoiding Isaac's eyes.

At dawn the next day Samuel had to go into Krakow to buy goods. He was in a fever of impatience to get back to see whether Isaac's father was still alive.

There were large crowds at all the markets, and it seemed to Samuel that it took forever to make his purchases. It was late afternoon by the time his cart was finally filled and he headed back toward the ghetto.

When Samuel was still two miles away from the gates, disaster struck. One of the wheels of the cart broke in half and the merchandise began to spill onto the sidewalk. Samuel was in a terrible dilemma. He had to find another wheel somewhere, and yet he did not dare leave the cart unguarded. A crowd had begun to gather, eyeing the spilled merchandise with avid eyes. Samuel saw a uniformed policeman approaching—a gentile—and he knew that he was lost. They would take everything away from him. The policeman pushed his way through the crowd and turned to the frightened boy. "Your cart needs a new wheel."

"Y—yes, sir."

"Do you know where to find one?"

"No, sir."

The policeman wrote something on a piece of paper. "Go there. Tell him what you need."

Samuel said, "I can't leave the cart."

"Yes, you can," the policeman said. He cast a stern eye over the crowd. "I'll be right here. Hurry!"

Samuel ran all the way. Following the directions on the piece of paper, he found himself in a blacksmith's shop, and when Samuel explained the situation, the blacksmith found a wheel that was the right size for the wagon. Samuel paid for the wheel out of the small bag of money he carried. He had half a dozen guldens left.

He raced back to his cart, rolling the wheel before him. The policeman was still there, and the crowd had dispersed. The merchandise was safe. With the policeman helping him, it took another half hour to get the wheel on and secure it. Once more he started back home. His thoughts were on Isaac's father. Would Samuel find him dead or alive? He did not think he could stand the suspense of not knowing a moment longer.

He was only a mile from the ghetto now. Samuel could see the high walls rising against the sky. And even as he watched, the sun set on the western horizon, and the unfamiliar streets were bathed in darkness. In the excitement of what had happened, Samuel had forgotten about the time. It was past sundown and he was outside the gates! He began to run, pushing the heavy cart ahead of him, his heart pounding until it felt ready to burst. The ghetto gates would be closed. Samuel recalled all the terrible stories he had heard about Jews who were locked out of the ghetto at night. He began running faster. There would probably be only one guard on duty now. If it were Paul, the friendly one, then Samuel might have a chance. If it were Aram—Samuel could not bear to think about it. The darkness was thickening now, closing in on him like a black fog, and a light rain began to fall. Samuel was nearing the ghetto walls, only two blocks away, and suddenly the huge gates loomed into view. They were locked.

Samuel had never seen them closed from the outside before. It was as though life had suddenly been turned inside out, and he shivered with terror. He was shut away from his family, from his world, from everything that was familiar. He slowed down, approaching the gates warily, looking for the guards. They were not in sight. Samuel was filled with a sudden wild hope. The guards had probably been called away on some emergency. Samuel would find a way to open the gates, or to scale the walls without being seen. As he reached the gates, the figure of a guard stepped out of the shadows.

"Keep coming," the guard commanded.

In the darkness Samuel could not see his face. But he recognized the voice. It was Aram.

"Closer. Come here."

Aram was watching Samuel approach, a thin grin on his face. The boy faltered.

"That's it," Aram called encouragingly. "Keep walking."

Slowly, Samuel moved toward the giant, his stomach churning, his head pounding. "Sir," Samuel said. "Please let me explain. I had an accident. My cart—"

Aram reached out with his hamlike fist, grabbed Samuel by the collar and lifted him into the air. "You dumb son-of-a-bitch of a Jew," he crooned softly. "Do you think I care why you're out? You're on the wrong side of the gates! Do you know what's going to happen to you now?"

The boy shook his head in terror.

"Let me tell you," Aram said. "We got a new edict last week. All Jews caught outside the gates after sundown are to be shipped to Silesia. Ten years at hard labor. How do you like that?"

Samuel could not believe it. "But I—I haven't done anything. I—"

With his right hand Aram hit Samuel hard across the mouth,

then let him drop heavily to the ground. "Let's go," Aram said.

"Wh—where?" Samuel asked. His voice was choked with terror.

"To the police barracks. In the morning you'll be shipped out with the rest of the scum. Get up."

Samuel lay there, unable to bring his mind into focus. "I—I have to go inside to say good-bye to my family."

Aram grinned. "They won't miss you."

"Please!" Samuel pleaded. "Let me—let me at least send them a message."

The smile died on Aram's face. He stood over Samuel menacingly. When he spoke his voice was soft. "I said get up, Jew shit. If I have to say it once more, I'll kick your balls in for you."

Slowly, Samuel rose to his feet. Aram took his arm with an iron grip and started walking him toward the police barracks. *Ten years of hard labor in Silesia!* No one ever returned from there. He looked up at the man holding his arm, pulling him toward the bridge that led to the barracks.

"Please don't do this," Samuel pleaded. "Let me go."

Aram squeezed his arm tighter, so that the blood seemed to stop flowing. "Keep begging," Aram said. "I love to hear a Jew beg. Have you heard about Silesia? You'll be just in time for the winter. But don't worry, it's nice and warm underground in the mines. And when your lungs get black with coal and you start coughing them up, they'll leave you out in the snow to die."

Ahead of them across the bridge, barely visible in the rain, was the stark building that served as the police barracks.

"Faster!" Aram said.

And suddenly Samuel knew that he could not let anyone do this to him. He thought of Terenia and his family and Isaac's father. No one would take his life from him. Somehow he had to escape, to save himself. They were crossing the narrow bridge now, the river running noisily below, swollen by the winter rains. There were only thirty yards left to go. Whatever was going to be done had to be done now. But how could he escape? Aram had a gun and even without it the enormous guard could have killed him easily. He was almost twice as big as Samuel and much more powerful. They had reached the other side of the bridge now, and the barracks lay just ahead of them.

"Hurry up," Aram growled, pulling Samuel along. "I've got other things to do."

They were so close to the building now that Samuel could hear the laughter of the guards coming from inside. Aram tightened his grip and started to drag the boy across the cobblestoned yard that led to the police station. There were only seconds left. Samuel reached into his pocket with his right hand and felt the bag with the half-dozen guldens in it. His fingers closed around it, and his blood began to course with excitement. Carefully, he pulled the bag out of his pocket with his free hand, loosened the drawstring and dropped the bag. It landed on the stones with a loud tinkle of coins.

Aram stopped suddenly. "What was that?"

"Nothing," Samuel replied quickly.

Aram looked into the boy's eyes and grinned. Holding Samuel tightly, he took a step back, looked down at the ground and saw the open bag of money.

"You won't need money where you're going," Aram said.

He reached down to pick up the sack, and Samuel reached down at the same time. Aram snatched the sack of money away from him. But it was not the sack that Samuel was after. His hand closed on one of the large cobblestones lying on the ground, and as Samuel straightened up, he smashed it into Aram's right eye with all his strength, turning it into a red jelly, and he kept pounding at him, again and again. He watched the guard's nose cave in, and then his mouth, until the face was nothing but a gout of red blood. And still Aram stood there on his feet, like some blind monster. Samuel looked at him sick with fear, unable to hit him again. Then, slowly, the giant body began to collapse. Samuel stared down at the dead guard, unable to believe what he had done. He heard the voices from the barracks and he became suddenly aware of the terrible danger he was in. If they caught him now, they would not send him to Silesia. They would flay him alive and hang him in the town square. The penalty for even *striking* a policeman was death. And Samuel had killed one of them. He must get away quickly. He could try to flee across the border, but then he would be a hunted fugitive for the rest of his life. There had to be another solution. He stared down at the faceless corpse and suddenly he knew what he had to do. He reached down and searched the guard's body until he found the large key that opened the gates. Then, overcoming his revulsion, Samuel grabbed Aram's boots and began pulling the guard toward the riverbank. The dead man seemed to weigh a ton. Samuel kept pulling, spurred by the sounds coming from the barracks. He reached the riverbank. He stopped a moment to regain his breath, then shoved the body over the edge of the steep embankment and watched it roll into the coursing waters below. One hand clung to the sides of the bank for what seemed an eternity, and then the body was slowly washed downstream, out of sight. Samuel stood there, hypnotized, filled with horror at what he had done. He picked up the rock he had used and threw it into the water. He was still in great danger. He turned and ran back across the bridge toward the huge, locked gates of the ghetto. There was no one around. With trembling fingers Samuel placed the giant key into the lock and turned it. He pulled against the great wooden gates. Nothing happened. They were too heavy for him to move. But on *that* night nothing was impossible to Samuel. He was filled with a strength that came from outside and he pulled the huge gates open. He shoved the cart inside, then closed the gates behind him, and ran toward his house, pushing the cart ahead of him. The tenants of the house were gathered in the living room, and when Samuel walked in, they stared at him as if he were a living ghost.

"They let you come back!"

"I—I don't understand," his father stammered. "We thought you—"

Quickly, Samuel explained what had happened, and their looks of concern turned to expressions of terror.

"Oh, my God!" groaned Samuel's father. "They'll murder us all!"

"Not if you listen to me," Samuel said. He explained his plan.

Fifteen minutes later Samuel and his father and two of their neighbors stood at the gates of the ghetto.

"Suppose the other guard comes back?" Samuel's father whispered.

Samuel said, "We have to take that chance. If he's there, I'll take all the blame."

Samuel pushed open the huge gates and slipped outside alone, expecting to be pounced upon at any moment. He put the huge key in the lock and turned it. The gates of the ghetto were now locked from the outside. Samuel tied the key around his waist, and walked a few yards to the left of the gates. A moment later a rope slithered down the wall like a thick snake. Samuel clung to it while on the other side his father and the others began to haul him up. When Samuel reached the top of the wall, he made a noose of one end of the rope, fastened it to a projecting spike and lowered himself to the ground. When he was safely down, he shook the rope loose.

"Oh, my God!" his father was mumbling. "What's going to happen at sunup?"

Samuel looked at him and replied, "We're going to be pounding on the gates, telling them to let us out."

At dawn the ghetto was swarming with uniformed police and soldiers. They had had to locate a special key to open the gates at sunrise for the merchants who were yelling to be let out. Paul, the second guard, had confessed to leaving his post and spending the night in Krakow, and he had been placed under arrest. But that still did not solve the mystery of Aram. Ordinarily the incident of a guard disappearing so close to the ghetto would have been a perfect excuse to start a pogram. But the police were baffled by the locked gate. Since the Jews were safely locked up on the *inside*, they obviously could not have harmed him. In the end they decided that Aram must have run off with one of his many girl friends. They thought he might have thrown away the heavy, cumbersome key, and they searched for it everywhere, but they could not find it. Nor would they because it was buried deep in the ground, under Samuel's house.

Exhausted physically and emotionally, Samuel had fallen into his bed and was asleep almost instantly. He was awakened by someone yelling and shaking him. Samuel's first thought was: *They've found Aram's body. They've come to get me.*

He opened his eyes. Isaac was standing there in a state of hysteria. "It's stopped," Isaac was screaming. "The coughing's stopped. It's a *bracha!* Come back to the house."

Isaac's father was sitting up in bed. The fever had miraculously disappeared, and the coughing had stopped.

As Samuel walked up to his bedside, the old man said, "I think

106

I could eat some chicken soup," and Samuel began to cry.

In one day he had taken a life and saved a life.

The news about Isaac's father swept through the ghetto. The families of dying men and women besieged the Roffe house, pleading with Samuel for some of his magic serum. It was impossible for him to keep up with the demand. He went to see Dr. Wal. The doctor had heard about what Samuel had done, but was skeptical.

"I'll have to see it with my own eyes," he said. "Make up a batch and I'll try it out on one of my patients."

There were dozens to choose from, and Dr. Wal selected the one he felt was closest to death. Within twenty-four hours the patient was on his way to recovery.

Dr. Wal went to the stable where Samuel had been working day and night, preparing serum, and said, "It works, Samuel. You've done it. What do you want for your dowry?"

And Samuel looked up at him and replied wearily, "Another horse."

That year, 1868, was the beginning of Roffe and Sons.

Samuel and Terenia were married, and Samuel's dowry was six horses and a small, well-equipped laboratory of his own. Samuel expanded his experiments. He began to distill drugs from herbs, and soon his neighbors began coming to the little laboratory to buy remedies for whatever ills bothered them. They were helped, and Samuel's reputation spread. To those who could not afford to pay, Samuel would say, "Don't worry about it. Take it anyway." And to Terenia, "Medicine is for healing, not for profit."

His business kept increasing, and soon he was able to say to Terenia, "I think it's time to open a small apothecary shop where we can sell ointments and powders and other things besides prescriptions."

The shop was a success from the beginning. The rich men who had refused to help Samuel before came to him now with offers of money.

"We'll be partners," they said. "We'll open a chain of shops."

Samuel discussed it with Terenia. "I'm afraid of partners. It's *our* business. I don't like the idea of strangers owning part of our lives."

Terenia agreed with him.

As the business grew and expanded into additional shops, the offers of money increased. Samuel continued to turn them all down.

When his father-in-law asked him why, Samuel replied, "Never let a friendly fox into your hen house. One day he's going to get hungry."

As the business flourished, so did the marriage of Samuel and Terenia. She bore him five sons—Abraham, Joseph, Anton, Jan and Pitor—and with the birth of each son Samuel opened a new apothecary shop, each one larger than the one before. In the beginning Samuel hired one man to work for him, then two, and soon he had more than two dozen employees.

One day Samuel received a visit from a government official. "We're lifting some of the restrictions on Jews," he told Samuel. "We would like you to open an apothecary shop in Krakow."

And Samuel did. Three years later he had prospered enough to erect his own building in downtown Krakow and to buy Terenia a beautiful house in the city. Samuel had finally achieved his dream of escaping from the ghetto.

But he had dreams far beyond Krakow.

As the boys grew older, Samuel hired tutors for them, and each of the boys learned a different language.

"He's gone crazy," Samuel's mother-in-law said. He's the laughingstock of the neighborhood, teaching Abraham and Jan English, Joseph German, Anton French and Pitor Italian. Who are they going to speak to? No one here speaks any of those barbaric languages. The boys won't even be able to talk to one another!"

Samuel merely smiled and said patiently, "It's part of their education." He knew to whom his sons would be talking.

By the time the boys reached their middle teens, they had traveled to different countries with their father. On each of his trips Samuel laid the groundwork for his future plans. When Abraham was twenty-one years old, Samuel called the family together and announced, "Abraham is going to America to live."

"America!" Terenia's mother shouted. "It's filled with savages! I will not let you do this to my grandson. The boy is staying here where he will be safe."

Safe. Samuel thought of the pogroms and Aram, and of his mother's murder.

"He's going abroad," Samuel declared. He turned to Abraham. "You'll open a factory in New York and be in charge of the business there."

Abraham said proudly, "Yes, Father."

Samuel turned to Joseph. "On your twenty-first birthday you will go to Berlin." Joseph nodded.

Anton said, "And I will go to France. Paris, I hope."

"Just watch yourself," Samuel growled. "Some of those gentiles are very beautiful."

He turned to Jan. "You will go to England."

Pitor, the youngest son, said eagerly, "And I'm going to Italy, Papa. How soon can I leave?"

Samuel laughed and replied, "Not tonight, Pitor. You'll have to wait until you're twenty-one."

And thus it worked out. Samuel accompanied his sons abroad and helped them establish offices and factories. Within the next seven years, there were branches of the Roffe family in five foreign countries. It was becoming a dynasty, and Samuel had his lawyer set it up so that, while each company was independent, it was at the same time responsible to the parent company.

"No strangers," Samuel kept warning the lawyer. "The stock must never leave the family."

"It won't," the lawyer assured him. "But if your sons can't sell their stock, Samuel, how are they going to get along? I'm sure you'll want them to live in comfort."

Samuel nodded. "We'll arrange for them to live in beautiful homes. They'll have generous salaries and expense accounts, but everything else must go back into the business. If they ever want to sell the stock, it must be unanimous. The majority of the stock will belong to my oldest son, and his heirs. We're going to be big. We're going to be bigger than the Rothschilds."

Over the years Samuel's prophecy became a reality. The business grew and prospered. Though the family was widely scattered, Samuel and Terenia saw to it that they remained as closely knit as possible. Their sons returned home for birthdays and high holidays. Their visits were more than festive occasions, however. The boys would closet themselves with their father and discuss business. They had their own private espionage system. Whenever one son in one country heard about a new drug development, he would dispatch couriers to report it to the others, and they would begin manufacturing it themselves, so that in this way they kept constantly ahead of their competitors.

As the wheel of the century turned, the boys married and had children and gave Samuel grandchildren. Abraham had gone to America on his twenty-first birthday, in the year 1891. He had married an American girl seven years later and in 1905 she gave birth to Samuel's first grandchild, Woodrow, who sired a son named Sam. Joseph had married a German girl, who bore him a son and a daughter. The son in his turn married a girl, who bore a daughter, Anna. Anna married a German, Walther Gassner. In France, Anton had married a French girl, by whom he had two sons. One son committed suicide. The other married and had one daughter, Hélène. She married several times but had no children. Jan, in London, had married an English girl. Their only daughter had married a baronet named Nichols and had a son whom they christened Alec. In Rome, Pitor had married an Italian girl. They had a son and a daughter. When the son, in his turn, married, his wife gave him a daughter, Simonetta, who fell in love with and married a young architect, Ivo Palazzi.

These then were the descendants of Samuel and Terenia Roffe.

Samuel lived long enough to see the winds of change that swept across the world. Marconi created wireless telegraphy and the Wright brothers launched the first aeroplane at Kitty Hawk. The Dreyfus affair captured the headlines and Admiral Peary reached the North Pole. Ford's Model T's were in mass production; there were electric lights and telephones. In medicine, the germs that caused tuberculosis and typhoid and malaria were isolated and tamed.

Roffe and Sons, a little less than half a century after it had been founded, was a multinational behemoth that circled the globe.

Samuel and his broken-down horse, Lottie, had created a dynasty.

When Elizabeth had finished reading the Book for perhaps the fifth time, she quietly returned it to its place in the glass case. She no longer needed it. She was a part of it, just as it was a part of her.

For the first time in her life, Elizabeth knew who she was, and where she had come from.

I t was on her fifteenth birthday in the second term of her first
year at school that Elizabeth first met Rhys Williams. He had
dropped in at the school to bring Elizabeth a birthday present
from her father.

"He wanted to come himself," Rhys explained, "but he
couldn't get away." Elizabeth tried to conceal her disappointment
but Rhys was quick to see it. There was something forlorn about
the young girl, a naked vulnerability, that touched him. On an
impulse he said, "Why don't you and I have dinner together?"

It was a terrible idea, Elizabeth thought. She could visualize the
two of them walking into a restaurant together: him, incredibly
good-looking and suave, and her, all braces and pudge. "Thank
you, no," Elizabeth said stiffly. "I—I have some studying to do."

But Rhys Williams refused to accept no for an answer. He
thought of the lonely birthdays he had spent by himself. He got
permission from the headmistress to take Elizabeth out for dinner.
They got into Rhys's car and started heading toward the airport.

"Neuchâtel is the other way," Elizabeth said.

Rhys looked at her and asked innocently, "Who said we were
going to Neuchâtel?"

"Where are we going?"

"Maxim's. It's the *only* place to celebrate a fifteenth birthday."

They flew to Paris in a private jet, and had a superb dinner. It
began with pâté de foie gras with truffles, lobster bisque, crisp duck
à l'orange and Maxim's special salad, and ended with champagne
and a birthday cake. Rhys drove Elizabeth down the Champs-
Élysées afterward, and they returned to Switzerland late that night.

It was the loveliest evening of Elizabeth's life. Somehow Rhys managed to make her feel interesting, and beautiful, and it was a heady experience. When Rhys dropped Elizabeth off at school, she said, "I don't know how to thank you. I—it's the nicest time I've ever had."

"Thank your father." Rhys grinned. "It was all his idea."

But Elizabeth knew that that was not true.

She decided that Rhys Williams was the most wonderful man she had ever met. And without doubt the most attractive. She got into her bed that night thinking about him. Then she rose and went to the small desk under the window. She took out a piece of paper and a pen, and wrote, "Mrs. Rhys Williams."

She stared at the words for a long time.

Rhys was twenty-four hours late for his date with a glamorous French actress, but he was not concerned. They wound up at Maxim's, and somehow Rhys could not help thinking that his evening there with Elizabeth had been more interesting.

She would be someone to reckon with, one day.

Elizabeth was never certain who was more responsible for the change that began in her—Samuel or Rhys Williams—but she began to take a new pride in herself. She lost the compulsion to eat constantly, and her body began to slim down. She began to enjoy sports and started to take an interest in school. She made an effort to socialize with the other girls. They could not believe it. They had often invited Elizabeth to their pajama parties, and she had always declined. Unexpectedly, she appeared at a pajama party one night.

The party was being held in a room shared by four girls, and when Elizabeth arrived, the room was crammed with at least two dozen students, all in pajamas or robes. One of the girls looked up in surprise and said, "Look who's here! We were betting you wouldn't come."

"I—I'm here."

The air was filled with the pungent sweet aroma of cigarette smoke. Elizabeth knew that many of the girls smoked marijuana, but she had never tried any. Her hostess, a French girl named Renée Tocar, walked up to Elizabeth, smoking a stubby brown cigarette. She took a deep puff, then held it out to Elizabeth. "You smoke?"

It was more of a statement than a question.

"Of course," Elizabeth lied. She took the cigarette, hesitated a moment, then put it between her lips and inhaled. She could feel her face going green, and her lungs rebelling, but she managed a smile and gasped, "Neat."

The moment Renée turned away, Elizabeth sank down onto a couch. She experienced a dizziness, but in a moment it passed Experimentally she took another puff. She began to feel curiously light-headed. Elizabeth had heard and read about the effects of marijuana. It was supposed to release inhibitions, take you out of yourself. She took another puff, deeper this time, and she began to feel a pleasant floating sensation, as if she were on another planet. She could see the girls in the room and hear them talking, but somehow they were all blurred, and the sounds were muted and far away. The lights seemed very bright, and she closed her eyes. The moment she did, she was floating off into space. It was a lovely feeling. She could watch herself drifting over the roof of the school, up and up, over the snowy Alps into a sea of fluffy white clouds. Someone was calling her name, calling her back to earth. Reluctantly, Elizabeth opened her eyes. Renée was leaning over her, a look of concern on her face.

"Are you all right, Roffe?"

Elizabeth gave her a slow, contented smile, and said fuzzily, "I'm just wonderful." And in her infinite, euphoric state, she confessed, "I've never smoked marijuana before."

Renée was staring at her, "Marijuana? That's a Gauloise."

On the other side of the village of Neuchâtel was a boys' school, and Elizabeth's classmates sneaked away for trysts at every opportunity. The girls talked about the boys constantly. They talked about their bodies and the size of their penises and what they allowed the boys to do to them, and what they did to the boys in turn. At times it seemed to Elizabeth that she was trapped in a school full of raving nymphomaniacs. Sex was an obsession with them. One of the private games at school was *frôlage*. A girl would completely strip, and lie in bed on her back while another girl stroked her from her breasts to her thighs. The payment was a pastry bought in the village. Ten minutes of *frôlage* earned one pastry. By the end of ten minutes the girl usually reached orgasm, but if she had not, the one administering the *frôlage* would continue and earn an additional pastry.

Another favorite sexual *divertissement* was to be found in the bathroom. The school had large, old-fashioned bathtubs, with flexible hand showers that could be removed from the hook on the side of the wall. The girls would sit in a tub, turn on the shower, and then with the warm water gushing out, they would push the head of the shower between their legs and rub it gently back and forth.

Elizabeth indulged in neither *frôlage* nor the shower head, but her sexual urges were beginning to get stronger and stronger. It was at about this time that she made a shattering discovery.

One of Elizabeth's teachers was a small, slim woman named Chantal Harriot. She was in her late twenties, almost a schoolgirl herself. She was attractive-looking, and when she smiled she became beautiful. She was the most sympathetic teacher Elizabeth had, and Elizabeth felt a strong bond with her. Whenever Elizabeth was unhappy, she would go to Mlle. Harriot and tell her her problems. Mlle. Harriot was an understanding listener. She would take Elizabeth's hand and stroke it, and give her soothing advice and a cup of hot chocolate and cookies, and Elizabeth always felt better immediately.

Mlle. Harriot taught French and also taught a class in fashion, in which she emphasized style and harmony of colors, and the proper accessories.

"Remember, girls," she would say, "the smartest clothes in the world will look terrible if you wear the wrong accessories." "Accessories" was Mlle. Harriot's watchword.

Whenever Elizabeth lay in the warm tub, she found that she was thinking of Mlle. Harriot, of the look on her face when they talked together, and of the way Mlle. Harriot caressed her hand, softly and tenderly.

When Elizabeth was in other classes, she would find her mind drifting toward Mlle. Harriot, and she would remember the times that the teacher had put her arms around her, consoling her, and had touched her breasts. At first Elizabeth had believed that the touches were accidental, but they had happened more and more often, and each time Mlle. Harriot would give Elizabeth a soft, questioning look as though waiting for some response. In her mind Elizabeth could see Mlle. Harriot, with her gently swelling breasts, and her long legs, and she would wonder what she looked like naked, in bed. It was then that the full realization stunned Elizabeth.

She was a lesbian.

She was not interested in boys, because she was interested in girls. Not the kind of silly little girls who were her classmates, but someone sensitive and understanding, like Mlle. Harriot. Elizabeth could visualize the two of them in bed together, holding and comforting each other.

Elizabeth had read and heard enough about lesbians to know how difficult life was for them. Society did not approve. Lesbianism was considered a crime against nature. But what was wrong, Elizabeth wondered, in loving someone tenderly and deeply? Did it matter whether it was a man or a woman? Was it not the love itself that was the important thing? Was it better to have a loveless heterosexual marriage than a loving homosexual one?

Elizabeth thought about how horrified her father was going to be when he learned the truth about her. Well, she would just have to face up to it. She would have to readjust her thinking about the future. She could never have a so-called normal life like other girls, with a husband and children. Wherever she went, she would always be an outcast, a rebel, living outside the mainstream of society. She and Mlle. Harriot—Chantal—would find a little apartment somewhere, or perhaps a small house. Elizabeth would decorate it beautifully in soft pastels, with all the proper accessories. There would be graceful French furniture and lovely paintings on the walls. Her father could help—no, she must not expect any help from her father. In all probability he would never even speak to her again.

Elizabeth thought about her wardrobe. She might be a lesbian, but she was determined not to dress like one. No tweeds or slacks, or tailored suits or vulgar mannish hats. They were the lepers' bells of emotionally crippled women. She would try to look as feminine as possible.

Elizabeth decided that she would learn to be a great cook so that she could prepare Mlle. Harriot's—Chantal's—favorite dishes.

She visualized the two of them sitting in their apartment, or small house, enjoying a candle-lit dinner that Elizabeth had prepared. First, there would be vichyssoise, followed by a lovely salad, then perhaps shrimp or lobster, or a Chateaubriand, with delicate ices for dessert. After dinner they would sit on the floor before a blazing fire in the hearth, watching the soft snowflakes fall outside. *Snowflakes.* So it would be winter. Elizabeth hastily revised the menu. Instead of a cold vichyssoise she would prepare a nice, hearty onion soup, and perhaps make a fondue. The dessert could be a soufflé. She would have to learn to time it so that it would not fall. *Then* the two of them would sit on the floor before a warming fire, and read poetry to each other. T. S. Eliot, perhaps. Or V. J. Rajadhon.

> Time is the enemy of love,
> The thief that shortens
> All our golden hours.
> I have never understood then
> Why lovers count their happiness
> In days and nights and years,
> While our love can only be measured
> In our joys and sighs and tears.

Ah, yes, Elizabeth could see the long years stretching out before the two of them, and the passage of time would begin to melt into a golden, warm glow.

She would fall asleep.

Elizabeth had been expecting it, and yet when it happened it caught her by surprise. She was awakened one night by the sound of someone entering her room and softly closing the door. Elizabeth's eyes flew open. She could see a shadow moving across the moon-dappled room toward her bed, and a ray of moonlight fell across Mlle. Harriot's—Chantal's face. Elizabeth's heart began to beat wildly.

Chantal whispered, "Elizabeth," and, standing there, slipped off her robe. She was wearing nothing underneath. Elizabeth's mouth went dry. She had thought of this moment so often, and now that it was actually happening, she was in a panic. In truth she was not sure exactly what she was supposed to do, or how. She did not want to make a fool of herself in front of the woman she loved.

"Look at me," Chantal commanded hoarsely. Elizabeth did. She let her eyes roam over the naked body. In the flesh Chantal Harriot was not quite what Elizabeth had envisioned. Her breasts looked a little like puckered apples, and they sagged a bit. She had a tiny potbelly, and her derrière seemed—this was the only word Elizabeth could think of—underslung.

But none of that was important. What mattered was what lay underneath, the soul of the woman, the courage and the daring to be different from everyone else, to defy the whole world and to want to share the rest of her life with Elizabeth.

"Move over, *mon petit ange,*" she was whispering.

Elizabeth did as she was told, and the teacher slipped into bed beside her. There was a strong, feral smell about her. She turned toward Elizabeth and put her arms around her, and said, "Oh, *chérie*, I have dreamed of this moment." And she kissed Elizabeth on the lips, forcing her tongue into Elizabeth's mouth, and making quick, groaning noises.

It was without doubt the most unpleasant sensation Elizabeth had ever experienced. She lay there in shock. Chantal's—Mlle. Harriot's—fingers were moving across Elizabeth's body, squeezing her breasts, slowly sliding down her stomach toward her thighs. And all the time her lips were on Elizabeth's, slobbering, like an animal.

This was it. This was the beautiful magic moment. *If we were one, you and I, together we would make a universe to shake the stars and move the heavens.*

Mlle. Harriot's hands were moving downward, caressing Elizabeth's thighs, starting to reach between her legs. Quickly, Elizabeth tried to conjure up the candle-lit diners and the soufflé and the evenings before the fireplace, and all the wonderful years the two of them would share together; but it was no use. Elizabeth's mind and flesh were repelled; she felt as though her body was being violated.

Mlle. Harriot moaned, "Oh, *chérie*, I want to fuck you."

And all Elizabeth could think of to say was, "There's a problem. One of us has the wrong accessories."

And she began to laugh and cry hysterically, weeping for the beautiful candlelit vision that had died, and laughing because she was a healthy, normal girl who had just learned that she was free.

The next day Elizabeth tried the shower nozzle.

At Easter vacation, in her final year at school, when she was eighteen, Elizabeth went to the villa in Sardinia to spend ten days. She had learned to drive, and for the first time she was free to explore the island on her own. She took long drives along the beaches and visited tiny fishing villages. She swam at the villa; under the warm Mediterranean sun, and at night lay in her bed listening to the mournful sound of the singing rocks, as the wind gently blew through them. She went to a carnival in Tempio, where the entire village dressed up in national costumes. Hidden behind the anonymity of domino masks, the girls invited the boys to dance, and everyone felt free to do things they would not dare do at any other time. A boy might *think* he knew which girl he made love to that night, but the next morning he could not be certain. It was, Elizabeth thought, like an entire village playing *The Guardsman.*

She drove to Punta Murra and watched the Sardos cook small lambs on open fires. The native islanders gave her *seada,* a goat cheese covered in a dough, with hot honey over it. She drank the delicious *selememont,* the local white wine that could be had nowhere else in the world because it was too delicate to travel.

One of Elizabeth's favorite haunts was the Red Lion Inn at Porto Cervo. It was a little pub in a basement, with ten tables for dining, and an old-fashioned bar.

Elizabeth dubbed that vacation the Time of the Boys. They were the sons of the rich, and they came in swarms, inviting Elizabeth to a constant round of swimming and riding parties. It was the first move in the mating rite.

"They're all highly eligible," Elizabeth's father assured her.

To Elizabeth they were all clods. They drank too much, talked too much and pawed her. She was sure they wanted her not for herself, because she might be an intelligent or worthwhile human being, but because she was a Roffe, heiress to the Roffe dynasty. Elizabeth had no idea that she had grown into a beauty, for it was easier to believe the truth of the past than the reflection in her mirror.

The boys wined and dined her and tried to get her into bed. They sensed that Elizabeth was a virgin, and some aberration in the male ego deluded each boy into the conviction that if he could take away Elizabeth's virginity, she would fall madly in love with him and be his slave forever. They refused to give up. No matter where they took Elizabeth, the evenings always ended up the same. "Let's go to bed." And always she politely refused them.

They did not know what to make of her. They knew she was beautiful, so it followed that she must be stupid. It never occurred to them that she was more intelligent than they. Who ever heard of a girl being both beautiful *and* intelligent?

And so Elizabeth went out with the boys to please her father, but they all bored her.

Rhys Williams came to the villa, and Elizabeth was surprised at how excited and pleased she was to see him again. He was even more attractive than she had remembered.

Rhys seemed glad to see her. "What's happened to you?" he asked.

"What do you mean?"

"Have you looked in your mirror lately?"

She blushed. "No."

He turned to Sam. "Unless the boys are all deaf, dumb and blind, I have a feeling Liz isn't going to be with us much longer."

Us! Elizabeth enjoyed hearing him say that. She hung around the two men as much as she dared, serving them drinks, running errands for them, enjoying just looking at Rhys. Sometimes Elizabeth would sit in the background, listening as they discussed business affairs, and she was fascinated. They spoke of mergers and of new factories, and products that had succeeded and others that had failed, and why. They talked about their competitors, and planned strategies and counter-strategies. To Elizabeth it was all heady stuff.

One day when Sam was up in the tower room, working, Rhys invited Elizabeth to lunch. She took him to the Red Lion and watched him shoot darts with the men at the bar. Elizabeth marveled at how much at home Rhys was. He seemed to fit in anywhere. She had heard a Spanish expression that she had never understood, but she did now as she watched Rhys. *He's a man easy in his skin.*

They sat at a small corner table with a red-and-white tablecloth, and had shepherd's pie and ale, and they talked. Rhys asked her about school.

"It's really not too bad," Elizabeth confessed. "I'm learning how little I know."

Rhys smiled. "Very few people get that far. You finish in June, don't you?"

Elizabeth wondered how he had known. "Yes."

"Do you know what you want to do after that?"

It was the question she had been asking herself. "No. Not really."

"Interested in getting married?"

For one quick instant her heart missed a beat. Then she realized that it was a general question. "I haven't found anyone yet." She thought of Mlle. Harriot and the cozy dinners in front of the fireplace and the snow falling, and she laughed aloud.

"Secret?" Rhys asked.

"Secret." She wished she could share it with him, but she did not know him well enough. The truth was, Elizabeth realized, that she did not know Rhys at all. He was a charming, handsome stranger who had once taken pity on her and flown her to Paris for a birthday dinner. She knew that he was brilliant in business and that her father depended on him. But she knew nothing about his personal life, or what he was really like. Watching him, Elizabeth had the feeling that he was a many-layered man, that the emotions he showed were to conceal the emotions he felt, and Elizabeth wondered if anyone really knew him.

It was Rhys Williams who was responsible for Elizabeth's losing her virginity.

The idea of going to bed with a man had become more and more appealing to Elizabeth. Part of it was the strong physical urge that sometimes caught her unaware and gripped her in waves of frustration, an urgent physical ache that would not leave. But there was also a strong curiosity, the need to know what *it* was like. She could not go to bed with just anyone, of course. He had to be someone special, someone she could cherish, someone who would cherish her.

On a Saturday night Elizabeth's father gave a gala at the villa.

"Put on your most beautiful dress," Rhys told Elizabeth. "I want to show you off to everyone."

Thrilled, Elizabeth had taken it for granted that she would be Rhys's date. When Rhys arrived, he had with him a beautiful blond Italian princess. Elizabeth felt so outraged and betrayed that at midnight she left the party and went to bed with a bearded drunken Russian painter named Vassilov.

The entire, brief affair was a disaster. Elizabeth was so nervous and Vassilov was so drunk that it seemed to Elizabeth that there was no beginning, middle or end. The foreplay consisted of Vassilov pulling down his pants and flopping onto the bed. At that point Elizabeth was tempted to flee but she was determined to punish Rhys for his perfidy. She got undressed and crawled into bed. A moment later, with no warning, Vassilov was entering her. It was a strange sensation. It was not unpleasant, but neither did the earth shake. She felt Vassilov's body give a quick shudder, and a moment later he was snoring. Elizabeth lay there filled with self-disgust. It was hard to believe that all the songs and books and poems were about *this*. She thought of Rhys, and she wanted to weep. Quietly, Elizabeth put on her clothes and went home. When the painter telephoned her the next morning, Elizabeth had the housekeeper tell him that she was not in. The following day Elizabeth returned to school.

She flew back in the company jet with her father and Rhys. The plane, which had been built to carry a hundred passengers, had been converted into a luxury ship. It had two large, beautifully decorated bedrooms in the rear, with full bathrooms, a comfortable office, a sitting room amidship, with paintings, and an elaborately equipped galley up front. Elizabeth thought of it as her father's magic carpet.

The two men talked business most of the time. When Rhys was free, he and Elizabeth played a game of chess. She played him to a draw, and when Rhys said, "I'm impressed," Elizabeth blushed with pleasure.

The last few months of school went by swiftly. It was time to begin thinking about her future. Elizabeth thought of Rhys's question, *Do you know what you want to do with your life?* She was not sure yet. But because of old Samuel, Elizabeth had become fascinated by the family business, and knew that she would like to become a part of it. She was not sure what she could do. Perhaps she could start by helping her father. She remembered all the tales of the wonderful hostess her mother had become, how invaluable she had been to Sam. She would try to take her mother's place.

It would be a start.

The Swedish Ambassador's free hand was squeezing Elizabeth's bottom, and she tried to ignore it as they danced around the room, her lips smiling, her eyes expertly scanning the elegantly dressed guests, the orchestra, the liveried servants, the buffet heaped with a variety of exotic dishes and fine wines, and she thought to herself with satisfaction, It's a good party.

They were in the ballroom of the Long Island estate. There were two hundred guests, all of them important to Roffe and Sons. Elizabeth became aware that the Ambassador was pressing his body closer to hers, trying to arouse her. He flicked his tongue in her ear and whispered, "You're a beautiful dancer."

"So are you," Elizabeth said with a smile, and she made a sudden misstep and came down hard on his toe with the sharp heel of her shoe. He gave a cry of pain and Elizabeth exclaimed contritely, "I'm so sorry, Ambassador. Let me get you a drink."

She left him and threaded her way toward the bar, making her way easily through the guests, her eyes moving carefully around the room, checking to see that everything was perfect.

Perfection—that was what her father demanded. Elizabeth had been the hostess for a hundred of Sam's parties now, but she had never learned to relax. Each party was an event, an opening night, with dozens of things that could go wrong. Yet she had never known such happiness. Her girlhood dream of being close to her father, of his wanting her, needing her, had come true. She had learned to adjust to the fact that his needs were impersonal, that her value to him was based on how much she could contribute to the company. That was Sam Roffe's only criterion for judging people. Elizabeth had been able to fill the gap that had existed since her mother's death. She had become her father's hostess. But because Elizabeth was a highly intelligent girl, she had become much more than that. She attended business conferences with Sam, in airplanes and in foreign hotel suites and factories and at embassies and palaces. She watched her father wield his power, deploying the billions of dollars at his command to buy and sell, tear down and build. Roffe and Sons was a vast cornucopia, and Elizabeth watched her father bestow its largesse on its friends, and withhold its bounty from its enemies. It was a fascinating world, filled with interesting people, and Sam Roffe was the master of all.

As Elizabeth looked around the ballroom now, she saw Sam standing at the bar, chatting with Rhys, a prime minister and a senator from California. Her father saw Elizabeth and waved her over. As Elizabeth moved toward him, she thought of the time, three years earlier, when it had all begun.

Elizabeth had flown home the day of her graduation. She was eighteen. Home, at the moment, had been the apartment at Beekman Place in Manhattan. Rhys had been there with her father. She had somehow known that he would be. She carried pictures of him in the secret places of her thoughts, and whenever she was lonely or depressed or discouraged, she would take them out and warm herself with her memories. In the beginning it had seemed hopeless. A fifteen-year-old schoolgirl and a man of twenty-five. Those ten years might as well have been a hundred. But through some wonderful mathematical alchemy, at eighteen the difference in years was less important. It was as though she were growing older faster than Rhys, trying to catch up to him.

Both men rose as she walked into the library, where they were talking business. Her father said casually, "Elizabeth. Just get in?"

"Yes."

"Ah. So school's finished."

"Yes."

"That's fine."

And that was the extent of her welcome home. Rhys was walking toward her, smiling. He seemed genuinely pleased to see her.

"You look wonderful, Liz. How was the graduation? Sam wanted to be there but he couldn't get away."

He was saying all the things her father should have been saying.

Elizabeth was angry with herself for being hurt. It was not that her father did not love her, she told herself, it was just that he was dedicated to a world in which she had no part. He would have taken a son into his world; a daughter was alien to him. She did not fit into the Corporate Plan.

"I'm interrupting." She moved toward the door.

"Wait a minute," Rhys said. He turned to Sam. "Liz has come home just in time. She can help with the party Saturday night."

Sam turned to Elizabeth, studying her objectively, as though newly assessing her. She resembled her mother. She had the same beauty, the same natural elegance. A flicker of interest came into Sam's eyes. It had not occurred to him before that his daughter might be a potential asset to Roffe and Sons. "Do you have a formal dress?"

Elizabeth looked at him in surprise. "I—"

"It doesn't matter. Go buy one. Do you know how to give a party?"

Elizabeth swallowed and said, "Certainly." Wasn't that one of the advantages of going to a Swiss finishing school? They taught you all the social graces. "Of course I know how to give a party."

"Good. I've invited a group from Saudi Arabia. There'll be about—" He turned to Rhys.

Rhys smiled at Elizabeth and said, "Forty. Give or take a few."

"Leave everything to me," Elizabeth said confidently.

The dinner was a complete fiasco.

Elizabeth had told the chef to prepare crab cocktails for the first course, followed by individual cassoulets, served with vintage wines. Unfortunately the cassoulet had pork in it, and the Arabs touched neither shellfish nor pork. Nor did they drink alcoholic beverages. The guests stared at the food, eating nothing. Elizabeth sat at the head of the long table, across the room from her father, frozen with embarrassment, dying inside.

It was Rhys Williams who saved the evening. He disappeared into the study for a few moments and spoke into the telephone. Then he came back into the dining room and entertained the guests with amusing stories, while the staff began to clear the table.

In what seemed no time at all, a fleet of catering trucks drove up, and as if by magic a variety of dishes began appearing. Couscous and lamb *en brochette* and rice and platters of roast chicken and fish, followed by sweetmeats and cheese and fresh fruits. Everyone enjoyed the food except Elizabeth. She was so upset that she could not swallow a bite. Each time she looked up at Rhys, he was watching her, a conspiratorial look in his eyes. Elizabeth could not have said why, but she was mortified that Rhys should not only witness her shame but save her from it. When the evening finally ended, and the last of the guests had reluctantly departed in the early hours of the morning, Elizabeth and Sam and Rhys were in the drawing room. Rhys was pouring a brandy.

Elizabeth took a deep breath and turned to her father, "I'm sorry about the dinner. If it hadn't been for Rhys—"

"I'm sure you'll do better next time," Sam said flatly.

Sam was right. From that time on, when Elizabeth gave a party, whether it was for four people or for four hundred, she researched the guests, found out their likes and dislikes, what they ate and drank, and what type of entertainment they enjoyed. She kept a catalog with file cards on each person. The guests were flattered to find that their favorite brand of wine or whiskey or cigars had been stocked for them, and that Elizabeth was able to discuss their work knowledgeably.

Rhys attended most of the parties, and he was always with the most beautiful girl there. Elizabeth hated them all. She tried to copy them. If Rhys brought a girl who wore her hair pinned up in the back, Elizabeth did her hair the same way. She tried to dress the way Rhys's girls dressed, to act the way they acted. But none of it seemed to make any impression on Rhys. He did not even seem to notice. Frustrated, Elizabeth decided that she might as well be herself.

On the morning of her twenty-first birthday, when Elizabeth came down to breakfast, Sam said, "Order some theater tickets for tonight. Supper afterward at 'Twenty-one.'"

Elizabeth thought, He remembered, and she was inordinately pleased.

Then her father added, "There'll be twelve of us. We'll be going over the new Bolivian contracts."

She said nothing about her birthday. She received telegrams

from a few former schoolmates, but that was it. Until six o'clock that evening, when an enormous bouquet of flowers arrived for her. Elizabeth was sure it was from her father. But the card read: "What a lovely day for a lovely lady." It was signed "Rhys."

Her father left the house at seven o'clock that evening on his way to the theater. He noticed the flowers and said absently, "Got a beau, huh?"

Elizabeth was tempted to say, "They're a birthday present," but what would have ben the point? If you had to remind someone you loved that it was your birthday, then it was futile.

She watched her father leave, and wondered what she would do with her evening. Twenty-one had always seemed such an important milestone. It signified growing up, having freedom, becoming a woman. Well, here was the magic day, and she felt no different from the way she had felt last year, or the year before. Why couldn't he have remembered? Would he have remembered if she were his son?

The butler appeared to ask her about dinner. Elizabeth was not hungry. She felt lonely and deserted. She knew she was feeling sorry for herself, but it was more than this uncelebrated birthday she was regretting. It was all the lonely birthdays of the past, the pain of growing up alone, without a mother or a father or anyone to give a damn.

At ten o'clock that night she dressed in a robe, sitting in the living room in the dark, in front of the fireplace, when a voice said, "Happy birthday."

The lights came on and Rhys Williams stood there. He walked over to her and said reprovingly, "This is no way to celebrate. How many times does a girl have a twenty-first birthday?"

"I—I thought you were supposed to be with my father tonight," Elizabeth said, flustered.

"I was. He mentioned that you were staying home alone tonight. Get dressed. We're going to dinner."

Elizabeth shook her head. She refused to accept his pity. "Thank you, Rhys. I—I'm really not hungry."

"I am, and I hate eating alone. I'm giving you five minutes to get into some clothes, or I'm taking you out like that."

They ate at a diner in Long Island, and they had hamburgers and chili and french-fried onions and root beer, and they talked, and Elizabeth thought it was better than the dinner she had had at Maxim's. All of Rhys's attention was focused on her, and she could understand why he was so damned attractive to women. It was not just his looks. It was the fact that he truly liked women, that he enjoyed being with them. He made Elizabeth feel like someone special, that he wanted to be with her more than with anyone else in the world. No wonder, Elizabeth thought, everyone fell in love with him.

Rhys told her a little about his boyhood in Wales, and he made it sound wonderful and adventurous and gay. "I ran away from home," he said, "because there was a hunger in me to see everything and do everything. I wanted to be everyone I saw. *I* wasn't enough for me. Can you understand that?"

Oh, how well she understood it!

"I worked at the parks and the beaches and one summer I had a job taking tourists down the Rhosili in coracles, and—"

"Wait a minute," Elizabeth interrupted. "What's a Rhosili and what's a—a coracle?"

"The Rhosili is a turbulent, swift-flowing river, full of dangerous rapids and currents. Coracles are ancient canoes, made of wooden lathes and waterproof animal skins, that go back to pre-Roman days. You've never seen Wales, have you?" She shook her head: "Ah, you would love it." She knew she would. "There's a waterfall at the Vale of Neath that's one of the beautiful sights of this world. And the lovely places to see: Aber-Eiddi and Caerbwdi and Porthclais and Kilgetty and Llangwm," and the words rolled off his tongue like the lilt of music. "It's a wild, untamed country, full of magical surprises."

"And yet you left Wales."

Rhys smiled at her and said, "It was the hunger in me. I wanted to own the world."

What he did not tell her was that the hunger was still there.

Over the next three years Elizabeth became indispensable to her father. Her job was to make his life comfortable, so that he could concentrate on the thing that was all-important to him: the Business. The details of running his life were left entirely to Elizabeth. She hired and fired servants, opened and closed the various houses as her father's needs required, and entertained for him.

More than that, she became his eyes and ears. After a business meeting Sam would ask Elizabeth her impression of a man, or explain to her why he had acted in a particular fashion. She watched him make decisions that affected the lives of thousands of people and involved hundreds of millions of dollars. She heard heads of state plead with Sam Roffe to open a factory, or beg him not to close one down.

After one of those meetings Elizabeth said, "It's unbelievable. It's—it's as though you're running a country."

Her father laughed and replied, "Roffe and Sons has a larger income than three quarters of the countries in the world."

In her travels with her father Elizabeth became reacquainted with the other members of the Roffe family, her cousins and their husbands or wives.

As a young girl Elizabeth had seen them during holidays when they had come to one of her father's houses, or when she had gone to visit them during brief school vacations.

Simonetta and Ivo Palazzi, in Rome, had always been the most fun to be with. They were open and friendly, and Ivo had always made Elizabeth feel like a woman. He was in charge of the Italian division of Roffe and Sons, and he had done very well. People enjoyed dealing with Ivo. Elizabeth remembered what a classmate had said when she had met him. "You know what I like about your cousin? He has warmth and charmth."

That was Ivo, warmth and charmth.

Then there was Hélène Roffe-Martel, and her husband, Charles, in Paris. Elizabeth had never really understood Hélène, or felt at ease with her. She had always been nice to Elizabeth, but there was a cool reserve that Elizabeth had never been able to break through. Charles was head of the French branch of Roffe and Sons. He was competent, though from what Elizabeth had overheard her father say, he lacked drive. He could follow orders, but he had no initiative. Sam had never replaced him, because the French branch ran very profitably. Elizabeth suspected that Hélène Roffe-Martel had a great deal to do with its success.

Elizabeth liked her German cousin Anna Roffe Gassner, and her husband, Walther. Elizabeth remembered hearing family gossip that Anna Roffe had married beneath her. Walther Gassner was reputed to be a black sheep, a fortune hunter, who had married an unattractive woman years older than himself, for her money. Elizabeth did not think her cousin was unattractive. She had always found Anna to be a shy, sensitive person, withdrawn, and a little frightened by life. Elizabeth had liked Walther on sight. He had the classic good looks of a movie star, but he seemed to be neither arrogant nor phony. He appeared to be genuinely in love with Anna, and Elizabeth did not believe any of the terrible stories she had heard about him.

Of all her cousins, Alec Nichols was Elizabeth's favorite. His mother had been a Roffe, and she had married Sir George Nichols, the third baronet. It was Alec to whom Elizabeth had always turned when she had a problem. Somehow, perhaps because of Alec's sensitivity and gentleness, he had seemed to the young child to be her peer, and she realized now what a great compliment that was to Alec. He had always treated her as an equal, ready to offer whatever aid and advice he could. Elizabeth remembered that once, in a moment of black despair, she had decided to run away from home. She had packed a suitcase and then, on a sudden impulse, had telephoned Alec in London to say good-bye. He had been in the middle of a conference, but he had come to the phone and talked to Elizabeth for more than an hour. When he had finished, Elizabeth had decided to forgive her father and give him another chance. That was Sir Alec Nichols. His wife, Vivian, was something else. Where Alec was generous and thoughtful, Vivian was selfish and thoughtless. She was the most self-centered woman Elizabeth had ever known.

Years ago, when Elizabeth was spending a weekend in their country home in Gloucestershire, she went on a picnic by herself. It had begun to rain, and she had returned to the house early. She had gone in the back door, and as she had started down the hallway, she had heard voices from the study, raised in a quarrel.

"I'm damned tired of playing nursemaid," Vivian was saying. "You can take your precious little cousin and amuse her yourself tonight. I'm going up to London. I have an engagement."

"Surely you can cancel it, Viv. The child is only going to be with us another day, and she—"

"Sorry, Alec. I feel like a good fuck, and I'm getting one tonight."

"For God's sake, Vivian!"

"Oh, shove it up your ass! Don't try to live my life for me."

At that moment, before Elizabeth could move, Vivian had stormed out of the study. She had taken one quick look at Elizabeth's stricken face, and said cheerily, "Back so soon, pet?" And strode upstairs.

Alec had come to the doorway. He had said gently, "Come in, Elizabeth."

Reluctantly she had walked into the study. Alec's face was aflame with embarrassment. Elizabeth had wanted desperately to comfort him, but she did not know how. Alec had walked over to a large refectory table, picked up a pipe, filled it with tobacco and lit it. It had seemed to Elizabeth that he took forever.

"You must understand Vivian."

Elizabeth had replied, "Alec, it's none of my business. I—"

"But in a sense it is. We're all family. I don't want you to think harshly of her."

Elizabeth could not believe it. After the incredible scene she had just heard, Alec was defending his wife.

"Sometimes in a marriage," Alec had continued, "a husband and a wife have different needs." He had paused awkwardly, searching for the right phrase. "I don't want you to blame Vivian because I—I can't fulfill some of those needs. That's not her fault, you see."

Elizabeth had not been able to stop herself. "Does—does she go out with other men often?"

"I'm rather afraid she does."

Elizabeth had been horrified. "Why don't you leave her?"

He had given her his gentle smile. "I can't leave her, dear child. You see, I love her."

The next day Elizabeth had returned to school. From that time on, she had felt closer to Alec than to any of the others.

Of late, Elizabeth had become concerned about her father. He seemed preoccupied and worried about something, but Elizabeth had no idea what it was. When she asked him about it, he replied, "Just a little problem I have to clear up. I'll tell you about it later."

He had become secretive, and Elizabeth no longer had access to his private papers. When he had said to her, "I'm leaving tomorrow for Chamonix to do a little mountain climbing," Elizabeth had been pleased. She knew he needed a rest. He had lost weight and had become pale and drawn-looking.

"I'll make the reservations for you," Elizabeth had said.

"Don't bother. They're already made."

That, too, was unlike him. He had left for Chamonix the next morning. That was the last time she had seen him. The last time she would ever see him . . .

Elizabeth lay there in her darkened bedroom, remembering the past. There was an unreality about her father's death, perhaps because he had been so alive.

He was the last to bear the name of Roffe. Except for her. What would happen to the company now? Her father had held the controlling interest. She wondered to whom he had left the stock.

Elizabeth learned the answer late the next afternoon. Sam's lawyer had appeared at the house. "I brought a copy of your father's will with me. I hate to intrude on your grief at a time like this, but I thought it best that you know at once. You are your father's sole beneficiary. That means that the controlling shares of Roffe and Sons are in your hands."

Elizabeth could not believe it. Surely he did not expect *her* to run the company. "Why?" she asked. "Why me?"

The attorney hesitated, then said, "May I be frank, Miss Roffe? Your father was a comparatively young man. I'm sure he didn't expect to die for many years. In time, I'm confident he would have made another will, designating someone to take over the company. He probably had not made up his mind yet." He strugged. "All that is academic, however. The point is that the control now rests in your hands. You will have to decide what you want to do with it, who you want to give it to." He studied her for a moment, then continued, "There has never before been a woman on the board of directors of Roffe and Sons, but—well, for the moment you're taking your father's place. There's a board meeting in Zurich this Friday. Can you be there?"

Sam would have expected it of her.

And so would old Samuel.

"I'll be there," Elizabeth said.

Book Two

In the bedroom of a small rented apartment in Rua dos Bombeiros, one of the winding, dangerous back alleys of Alto Estoril, a motion-picture scene was being filmed. There were four people in the room. A cameraman, and on a bed the two actors in the scene, the man in his thirties and a young blond girl with a stunning figure. She wore nothing except a vivid red ribbon tied around her neck. The man was large, with a wrestler's shoulders and a barrel-shaped, incongruously hairless chest. His phallus, even in detumescence, was huge. The fourth person in the room was a spectator, seated in the background, wearing a black broad-brimmed hat and dark glasses.

The cameraman turned to the spectator, questioningly, and the spectator nodded. The cameraman pressed a switch and the camera began to whir. He said to the actors, "All right. Action."

The man knelt over the girl and she took his penis in her mouth until it began to grow hard. The girl took it out and said, "Jesus, that's big!"

"Shove it in her," the cameraman ordered.

The man slid down over the girl and put his penis between her legs.

"Take it easy, honey." She had a high, querulous voice.

"Look as though you're enjoying it."

"How can I? It's the size of a fucking watermelon."

The spectator was leaning forward, watching every move as the man entered her. The girl said, "Oh, my God, that feels wonderful. Just take it slow, baby."

The spectator was breathing harder now, staring at the scene on the bed. This girl was the third, and she was even prettier than the others.

She was writhing from side to side now, making little moaning noises. "Oh, yes," she gasped. "Don't stop!" She grasped the man's hips and began pulling them toward her. The man began to pump harder and faster, in a frantic, pounding motion. Her movements began to quicken, and her nails dug into the man's naked back. "Oh, yes," she moaned. "Yes, yes, yes! I'm coming!"

The cameraman looked toward the spectator, and the spectator nodded, eyes glistening behind the dark glasses.

"Now!" the cameraman called to the man on the bed.

The girl, caught in her own furious frenzy, did not even hear him. As her face filled with a wild ecstasy, and her body began to shudder, the man's huge hands closed around her throat and began to squeeze, closing off the air so that she could not breathe. She stared up at him, bewildered, and then her eyes filled with a sudden, terrified comprehension.

The spectator thought: *This is the moment. Now! Jesus God! Look at her eyes!* They were dilated with terror. She fought to tear away the iron bands around her throat, but it was useless. She was still coming, and the deliciousness of her orgasm and the frantic shudder of her death throes were blending into one.

The spectator's body was soaked with perspiration. The excitement was unbearable. In the middle of life's most exquisite pleasure the girl was dying, her eyes staring into the eyes of death. It was so beautiful.

Suddenly it was over. The spectator sat there, exhausted, shaken with spasms of pleasure, lungs filled with long, deep breaths. The girl had been punished.

The spectator felt like God.

Zurich.
Friday, September 11.
Noon.

The World Headquarters of Roffe and Sons occupied sixty acres along the Sprettenbach on the western outskirts of Zurich. The administration building was a twelve-story modern glass structure, towering over a nest of research buildings, manufacturing plants, experimental laboratories, planning divisions, and railroad spurs. It was the brain center of the far-flung Roffe and Sons empire.

The reception lobby was starkly modern, decorated in green and white, with Danish furniture. A receptionist sat behind a glass desk, and those who were admitted by her into the recesses of the building had to be accompanied by a guide. To the right rear of the lobby was a bank of elevators, with one private express elevator for the use of the company president.

On this morning the private elevator had been used by the members of the board of directors. They had arrived within the past few hours from various parts of the world by plane, train, helicopter and limousine. They were gathered now in the enormous, high-ceilinged, oak-paneled boardroom; Sir Alec Nichols, Walther Gassner, Ivo Palazzi and Charles Martel. The only nonmember of the board in the room was Rhys Williams.

Refreshments and drinks had been laid out on a sideboard, but no one in the room was interested. They were tense, nervous, each preoccupied with his own thoughts.

Kate Erling, an efficient Swiss woman in her late forties, came

139

into the room. "Miss Roffe's car has arrived."

Her eye swept around the room to make sure that everything was in order: pens, note pads, a silver carafe of water at each place, cigars and cigarettes, ashtrays, matches. Kate Erling had been Sam Roffe's personal secretary for fifteen years. The fact that he was dead was no reason for her to lower his standards, or hers. She nodded, satisfied, and withdrew.

Downstairs, in front of the administration building, Elizabeth Roffe was stepping out of a limousine. She wore a black tailored suit with a white blouse. She had on no makeup. She looked much younger than her twenty-four years, pale and vulnerable.

The press was waiting for her. As she started into the building, she found herself surrounded by television and radio and newspaper reporters, with cameras and microphones.

"I'm from *L'Europeo*, Miss Roffe. Could we have a statement? Who's going to take over the company now that your father—?"

"Look this way, please, Miss Roffe. Can you give our readers a big smile?"

"Associated Press, Miss Roffe. What about your father's will?"

"New York *Daily News*. Wasn't your father an expert mountain climber? Did they find out how—?"

"*Wall Street Journal*. Can you tell us something about the company's financial—?"

"I'm from the London *Times*. We're planning to do an article on the Roffe—"

Elizabeth was fighting her way into the lobby, escorted by three security guards, pushing through the sea of reporters.

"One more picture, Miss Roffe—"

And Elizabeth was in the elevator, the door closing. She took a deep breath and shuddered. Sam was dead. Why couldn't they leave her alone?

A few moments later, Elizabeth walked into the boardroom. Alec Nichols was the first to greet her. He put his arms around her shyly and said, "I'm so sorry, Elizabeth. It was such a shock to all of us. Vivian and I tried to telephone you but—"

"I know. Thank you, Alec. Thank you for your note."

Ivo Palazzi came up and gave her a kiss on each cheek. "*Cara*, what is there to say? Are you all right?"

"Yes, fine. Thank you, Ivo." She turned. "Hello, Charles."

"Elizabeth, Hélène and I were devastated. If there is anything at all—"

"Thank you."

Walther Gassner walked over to Elizabeth and said awkwardly, "Anna and I wish to express our great sorrow at what has happened to your father."

Elizabeth nodded, her head high. "Thank you, Walther."

She did not want to be here, surrounded by all the reminders of her father. She wanted to flee, to be alone.

Rhys Williams was standing off to one side, watching Elizabeth's face, and he was thinking, If they don't stop, she's going to break down. He deliberately moved through the group, held out his hand and said, "Hello, Liz."

"Hello, Rhys." She had last seen him when he had come to the house to bring her the news of Sam's death. It seemed like years ago. Seconds ago. It had been one week.

Rhys was aware of the effort it was costing Elizabeth to keep her composure. He said, "Now that everyone's here, why don't we begin?" He smiled reassuringly. "This won't take long."

She gave him a grateful smile. The men took their accustomed places at the large rectangular oak table. Rhys led Elizabeth to the head of the table and pulled out a chair for her. My father's chair, Elizabeth thought. Sam sat here, chairing these meetings.

Charles was saying, "Since we do not have a—" He caught himself and turned to Alec. "Why don't you take over?"

Alec glanced around, and the others murmured approval. "Very well."

Alec pressed a button on the table in front of him, and Kate Erling returned, carrying a notebook. She closed the door behind her and pulled up a straight chair, her notebook and pen poised.

Alec said, "I think that under the circumstances we can dispense with the formalities. All of us have suffered a terrible loss. But"—he looked apologetically at Elizabeth—"the essential thing now is that Roffe and Sons show a strong public face."

"D'accord. We have been taking enough of a hammering in the press lately," Charles growled.

Elizabeth looked over at him and asked, "Why?"

Rhys explained, "The company is facing a lot of unusual problems just now, Liz. We're involved in heavy lawsuits, we're under government investigation, and some of the banks are pressing us. The point is that none of it is good for our image. The public buys pharmaceutical products because they trust the company that makes them. If we lose that trust, we lose our customers."

Ivo said reassuringly, "We have no problems that can't be solved. The important thing is to reorganize the company immediately."

"How?" Elizabeth asked.

Walther replied, "By selling our stock to the public."

Charles added, "In that way we can take care of all our bank loans, and have enough money left—" He let the sentence trail off.

Elizabeth looked at Alec. "Do you agree with that?"

"I think we're all in agreement, Elizabeth."

She leaned back in her chair, thoughtful. Rhys picked up some papers, rose and carried them to Elizabeth. "I've had all the necessary documents prepared. All you have to do is sign."

Elizabeth glanced at the papers lying before her. "If I sign these, what happens?"

Charles spoke up. "We have a dozen international brokerage firms ready to form a consortium to underwrite the stock issue. They will guarantee the sale at a price we mutually agree upon. In an offering as large as this one, there will be several institutional purchases, as well as private ones."

"You mean like banks and insurance companies?" Elizabeth asked.

Charles nodded. "Exactly."

"And they'll put their people on the board of directors?"

"That's usual . . ."

Elizabeth said, "So, in effect, they would control Roffe and Sons."

"We would still remain on the board of directors," Ivo interposed quickly.

Elizabeth turned to Charles. "You said a consortium of stockbrokers is ready to move ahead."

Charles nodded. "Yes."

"Then why haven't they?"

He looked at her, puzzled. "I don't understand."

"If everyone is in agreement that the best thing for the company is to let it get out of the family and into the hands of outsiders, why hasn't it been done before?"

There was an awkward silence. Ivo said, "It has to be by mutual consent, *cara. Everyone* on the board must agree."

"Who didn't agree?" Elizabeth asked.

The silence was longer this time.

Finally Rhys spoke up. "Sam."

And Elizabeth suddenly realized what had disturbed her from the moment she had walked into this room. They had all expressed their condolences and their shock and grief over her father's death, and yet at the same time there had been an atmosphere of charged excitement in the room, a feeling of—strangely, the word that came into her mind was *victory*. They had had the papers all drawn up for her, everything ready. *All you have to do is sign.* But if what they wanted was right, then why had her father objected to it? She asked the question aloud.

"Sam had his own ideas," Walther explained. "Your father could be very stubborn."

Like old Samuel, Elizabeth thought. Never let a friendly fox into your hen house. One day he's going to get hungry. And Sam had not wanted to sell. He must have had good reason.

Ivo was saying, "Believe me, *cara*, it is much better to leave all this to us. You don't understand these things."

Elizabeth said quietly, "I would like to."

"Why bother yourself with this?" Walther objected. "When your stock is sold, you will have an enormous amount of money, more than you'll ever be able to spend. You can go off anywhere you like and enjoy it."

What Walther said made sense. Why *should* she get involved? All she had to do was sign the papers in front of her, and leave.

Charles said impatiently, "Elizabeth, we're simply wasting time. You have no choice."

It was at that instant that Elizabeth knew she did have a choice. Just as her father had had a choice. She could walk away and let them do as they pleased with the company, or she could stay and find out why they were all so eager to sell the stock, why they were pressuring her. For she could feel the pressure. It was so strong it was almost physical. Everyone in that room was *willing* her to sign the papers.

She glanced over at Rhys, wondering what he was thinking. His expression was noncommittal. Elizabeth looked at Kate Erling.

She had been Sam's secretary for a long time. Elizabeth wished she could have had a chance to speak to her alone. They were all looking at Elizabeth, waiting for her to agree.

"I'm not going to sign," she said. "Not now."

There was a moment of stunned silence. Then Walther said, "I don't understand, Elizabeth." His face was ashen. "Of course you must! Everything is arranged."

Charles said angrily, "Walther's right. You must sign."

They were all speaking at once, in a confused and angry storm of words that beat at Elizabeth.

"*Why* won't you sign?" Ivo demanded.

She could not say: *Because my father would not sign. Because you're rushing me.* She had a feeling, an instinct that something was wrong, and she was determined to find out what it was. So now she merely said, "I'd like a little more time to think about it."

The men looked at one another.

"How much time, *cara?*" Ivo asked.

"I don't know yet. I'd like to get a better understanding of what's involved here."

Walther exploded. "Damn it, we can't—"

Rhys cut in firmly, "I think Elizabeth is right."

The others turned to look at him. Rhys went on, "She should have a chance to get a clear picture of the problems the company is facing, and then make up her own mind."

They were all digesting what Rhys had said.

"I agree with that," Alec said.

Charles said bitterly, "Gentlemen, it doesn't make any difference whether we agree with it or not. Elizabeth is in control."

Ivo looked at Elizabeth. "*Cara*—we need a decision quickly."

"You'll have it," Elizabeth promised.

They were all watching her, each busy with his own thoughts.

One of them was thinking, Oh, God. *She's going to have to die, too.*

E lizabeth was awed.

    She had been here in her father's Zurich headquarters often, but always as a visitor. The power belonged to him. And now it belonged to her. She looked around the huge office and felt like an imposter. The room had been magnificently decorated by Ernst Hohl. At one end stood a Roentgen cabinet with a Millet landscape over it. There was a fireplace, and in front of it a chamois leather couch, a large coffee table and four easy chairs. Around the walls were Renoirs, Chagalls, Klees and two early Courbets. The desk was a solid block of black mahogany. Next to it, on a large console table, was a communications complex—a battery of telephones with direct lines to company headquarters around the world. There were two red phones with scramblers, an intricate intercom system, a ticker tape machine, and other equipment. Hanging behind the desk was a portrait of old Samuel Roffe.

A private door led to a large dressing room, with cedar closets and lined drawers. Someone had removed Sam's clothing, and Elizabeth was grateful. She walked through a tiled bathroom that included a marble bathtub and a stall shower. There were fresh Turkish towels hanging on warming racks. The medicine chest was empty. All the daily paraphernalia of her father's life had been taken away. Kate Erling, probably. Elizabeth idly wondered whether Kate had been in love with Sam.

The executive suite included a large sauna, a fully equipped gymnasium, a barbershop, and a dining room that could seat a hundred people. When foreign guests were being entertained, a little flag representing their country was placed in the floral center-piece on the table.

In addition, there was Sam's private dining room, tastefully decorated, with muraled walls.

Kate Erling had explained to Elizabeth, "There are two chefs on duty during the day, and one at night. If you are having more than twelve guests for luncheon or dinner, they need two hours' notice."

Now Elizabeth sat at the desk, piled high with papers, memoranda, and statistics and reports, and she did not know where to begin. She thought of her father sitting here, in this chair, behind this desk, and she was suddenly filled with a sense of unbearable loss. Sam had been so able, so brilliant. How she needed him now!

Elizabeth had managed to see Alec for a few moments before he returned to London.

"Take your time," he had advised her. "Don't let anyone pressure you."

So he had sensed her feelings.

"Alec, do you think I should vote to let the company go public?"

He had smiled at her and said awkwardly, "I'm afraid I do, old girl, but then I've got my own ax to grind, haven't I? Our shares are no good to any of us until we can sell them. That's up to you now."

Elizabeth was remembering that conversation as she sat alone in the huge office. The temptation to telephone Alec was overpowering. All she had to say was, "I've changed my mind." And get out. She did not belong here. She felt so inadequate.

She looked at the set of intercom buttons on the console. Opposite one of them was the name RHYS WILLIAMS. Elizabeth debated a moment, then flicked down the switch.

Rhys was seated across from her, watching her. Elizabeth knew exactly what he must be thinking, what they were all thinking. That she had no business being there.

"That was quite a bomb you dropped at the meeting this morning," Rhys said.

"I'm sorry if I upset everyone."

He grinned. " 'Upset' is hardly the word. You put everyone in a state of shock. It was all supposed to have been cut-and-dried. The publicity releases were ready to send out." He studied her a moment. "What made you decide not to sign, Liz?"

How could she explain that it was nothing more than a feeling, an intuition? He would laugh at her. And yet Sam had refused to let Roffe and Sons go public. She had to find out why.

As though reading her thoughts, Rhys said, "Your great-great grandfather set this up as a family business, to keep away outsiders. But it was a small company then. Things have changed. We're running one of the biggest drugstores in the world. Whoever sits in your father's chair has to make all the final decisions. It's one hell of a responsibility."

She looked at him and wondered whether this was Rhys's way of telling her to get out. "Will you help me?"

"You know I will."

She felt a rush of relief and she realized how much she had been counting on him.

"The first thing we'd better do," Rhys said, "is take you on a tour of the plant here. Do you know about the physical structure of this company?"

"Not much."

That was not true. Elizabeth had been in enough meetings with Sam over the past few years to have picked up a good deal of knowledge about the workings of Roffe and Sons. But she wanted to hear it from Rhys's point of view.

"We manufacture much more than drugs, Liz. We make chemicals and perfumes and vitamins and hair sprays and pesticides. We produce cosmetics and bio-electronic instruments. We have a food division, and a division of animal nitrates." Elizabeth was aware of all that, but she let Rhys go on. "We publish magazines for distribution to doctors. We make adhesives, and building protection agents and plastic explosives."

Elizabeth could sense that he was becoming caught up by what he was saying, she could hear the undertone of pride in his voice, and she was oddly reminded of her father.

"Roffe and Sons owns factories and holding companies in over a hundred countries. Every one of them reports to this office." He paused, as though to make sure that she understood the point. "Old Samuel went into business with a horse and a test tube. It's grown to sixty factories around the world, ten research centers and a network of thousands of salesmen and detail men and women." They were the ones, Elizabeth knew, who called on the doctors and hospitals. "Last year, in the United States alone, they spent over fourteen billion dollars on drugs—and we have a healthy share of that market."

And yet Roffe and Sons was in trouble with the banks. Something was wrong.

Rhys took Elizabeth on a tour of the company's headquarters' factory. In actuality, the Zurich division was a dozen factories, with seventy-five buildings on the sixty acres of ground. It was a world in microcosm, completely self-sustaining. They visited the manufacturing plants, the research departments, the toxicology laboratories, the storage plants. Rhys brought Elizabeth to a sound stage, where they made motion pictures for research and for their world-wide advertising and products divisions. "We use more film here," Rhys told Elizabeth, "than the major Hollywood studios."

They went through the molecular biology department, and the liquid center, where fifty giant stainless steel, glass-lined tanks hung suspended from the ceiling, filled with liquids ready to be bottled. They saw the tablet-compression rooms, where powders were formed into tablets, sized, stamped with ROFFE AND SONS, packaged and labeled, without anyone ever touching them. Some of the drugs were ethical products, available only on prescription, others were proprietary items, sold over the counter.

Set apart from the other buildings were several small buildings. These were for the scientists: the analytical chemists, biochemists, organic chemists, parasitologists, pathologists.

"More than three hundred scientists work here," Rhys told Elizabeth. "Most of them are Ph.D.'s. Would you like to see our hundred-million-dollar room?"

Elizabeth nodded, intrigued.

It was in an isolated brick building, guarded by a uniformed policeman with a gun. Rhys showed his security pass, and he and Elizabeth were permitted to enter a long corridor with a steel door at the end of it. The guard used two keys to open the door, and Elizabeth and Rhys entered. The room contained no windows. It was lined from floor to ceiling with shelves filled with every variety of bottles, jars and tubes.

"Why do they call this the hundred-million-dollar room?" Elizabeth asked.

"Because that's what it cost to furnish it. See all those compounds on the shelves? None of them have names, only numbers. They're the ones that didn't make it. They're the failures."

"But a hundred million—"

"For every new drug that works, there are about a thousand that end up in this room. Some drugs are worked on for as long as ten years, and then abandoned. A single drug can cost five or ten million dollars in research before we find out that it's no good, or that someone else has beaten us to it. We don't throw any of these things away because now and then one of our bright young men will back into a discovery that can make something in this room valuable."

The amounts of money involved were awesome.

"Come on," Rhys said. "I'll show you the Loss Room."

It was in another building, this one unguarded, containing, like the other rooms, only shelves filled with bottles and jars.

"We lose a fortune here too," Rhys said. "But we plan it that way."

"I don't understand."

Rhys walked over to a shelf and picked up a bottle. It was labeled "Botulism." "Do you know how many cases of botulism there were in the United States last year? Twenty-five. But it costs us millions of dollars to keep this drug in stock." He picked up another bottle at random. "This is an antidote for rabies. This room is full of drugs that are cures for rare diseases—snakebites, poisonous plants. We furnish them free to the armed forces and to hospitals, as a public service."

"I like that," Elizabeth said. Old Samuel would have liked it too, she thought.

Rhys took Elizabeth to the capsule rooms, where empty bottles were carried in on a giant conveyor belt. By the time they had crossed the room, the bottles had been sterilized, filled with capsules, labeled, topped with cotton, and sealed. All done by automation.

There was a glassblowing factory, an architectural center to plan new buildings, a real estate division to acquire the land for them. In one building there were scores of writers turning out pamphlets in fifty languages, and printing presses to print them.

Some of the departments reminded Elizabeth of George Orwell's *1984*. The Sterile Rooms were bathed in eerie ultraviolet lights. Adjoining rooms were painted in different colors—white, green or blue—and the workers wore uniforms to match. Each time they entered or left the room, they had to go through a special sterilizing chamber. Blue workers were locked in for the entire day. Before they could eat or rest or go to the toilet, they had to undress, enter a neutral green zone, put on other clothes, and reverse the process when they returned.

"I think you'll find this interesting," Rhys said.

They were walking down the gray corridor of a research building. They reached a door marked "RESTRICTED—DO NOT ENTER." Rhys pushed the door open, and he and Elizabeth walked through. They went through a second door and Elizabeth found herself in a dimly lit room filled with hundreds of cages containing animals. The room was hot and humid, and she felt as if she had suddenly been transported to a jungle. As her eyes grew accustomed to the half-light, she saw that the cages were filled with monkeys and hamsters and cats and white mice. Many of the animals had obscene-looking growths protruding from various parts of their bodies. Some had their heads shaven, and were crowned with electrodes that had been implanted in their brains. Some of the animals were screaming and gibbering, racing around in their cages, while others were comatose and lethargic. The noise and the stench were unbearable. It was like some kind of hell. Elizabeth walked up to a cage that contained a single white kitten. Its brain was exposed, enclosed in a clear plastic covering through which protruded half a dozen wires.

"What—what's going on here?" Elizabeth asked.

A tall, bearded young man making notes in front of a cage explained. "We're testing a new tranquilizer."

"I hope it works," Elizabeth said weakly. "I think I could use it." And she walked out of the room before she could become sick.

Rhys was at her side in the corridor. "Are you all right?"

She took a deep breath. "I—I'm fine. Is all that really necessary?"

Rhys looked at her and replied. "Those experiments save a lot of lives. More than one third of the people born since nineteen fifty are alive only because of modern drugs. Think about that."

Elizabeth thought about it.

It took six full days to tour the key buildings, and when Elizabeth had finished, she was exhausted, her head spinning with the vastness of it. And she realized she was seeing just one Roffe plant. There were dozens of others scattered around the world.

The facts and figures were stunning. "It takes between five and ten years to market a new drug, and out of every two thousand compounds tested, we'll average only three products. . . ."

And ". . . Roffe and Sons has three hundred people working here in quality control alone."

And ". . . Worldwide, Roffe and Sons is responsible for over half a million employees. . . ."

And ". . . our gross income last year was . . ."

Elizabeth listened, trying to digest the incredible figures that Rhys was throwing at her. She had known that the company was large, but "large" was such an anonymous word. Having it actually translated into terms of people and money was staggering.

That night as Elizabeth lay in bed, recalling all the things she had seen and heard, she was filled with an overpowering feeling of inadequacy.

IVO: *Believe me, cara, it is much better to leave all this to us. You don't understand these things.*

ALEC: *I think you should sell but I have an ax to grind.*

WALTHER: *Why bother yourself with this? You can go off anywhere you like and enjoy your money.*

They were right, all of them, Elizabeth thought. I'm going to get out and let them do what they like with the company. I do not belong in this position.

The moment she made the decision, she felt a deep sense of relief. She fell asleep almost immediately.

The following day, Friday, was the beginning of a holiday weekend. When Elizabeth arrived at the office, she sent for Rhys to announce her decision.

"Mr. Williams had to fly to Nairobi last night," Kate Erling informed her. "He said to tell you he would be back on Tuesday. Can anyone else help you?"

Elizabeth hesitated. "Put in a call to Sir Alec, please."

"Yes, Miss Roffe." Kate added, a note of hesitation in her voice, "A package for you was delivered this morning by the police department. It contains the personal belongings your father had with him at Chamonix."

The mention of Sam brought back that sharp sense of loss, of grief.

"The police apologized because they could not give it to your messenger. It was already on its way to you."

Elizabeth frowned. "My messenger?"

"The man you sent to Chamonix to pick it up."

"I didn't send anyone to Chamonix." It was obviously some bureaucratic mix-up. "Where is it?"

"I put it in your closet."

There was a Vuitton suitcase, containing Sam's clothes, and a locked attaché case with a key taped to it. Probably company reports. She would let Rhys handle them. Then she remembered that he was away. Well, she decided, she would go away for the weekend too. She looked at the attaché case and thought, Perhaps there's something personal belonging to Sam. I'd better look at it first.

Kate Erling buzzed. "I'm sorry, Miss Roffe. Sir Alec's out of the office."

"Leave a message for him to call me, please. I'll be at the villa in Sardinia. Leave the same message for Mr. Palazzi, Mr. Gassner and Mr. Martel."

She would tell them all that she was leaving, that they could sell the stock, do as they pleased with the company.

She was looking forward to the long weekend. The villa was a retreat, a soothing cocoon, where she could be alone to think about herself and her future. Events had been flung at her so rapidly that she had had no chance to put things into any kind of perspective. Sam's accident—Elizabeth's mind tripped over the word "death"; inheriting the controlling stock of Roffe and Sons; the urgent pressure from the family to let the company go public. And the company itself. The awesome heartbeat of a behemoth whose power spanned the world. It was too much to cope with all at once.

When she flew to Sardinia late that afternoon, Elizabeth had the attaché case with her.

She took a taxi from the airport. There was no one at the villa because it had been closed, and Elizabeth had not told anyone she was coming. She let herself in and walked slowly through the large familiar rooms and it was as if she had never been away. She had not realized how much she had missed this place. It seemed to Elizabeth that the few happy memories of her childhood had been here. It felt strange to be alone in this labyrinth where there had always been half a dozen servants bustling around, cooking, cleaning, polishing. Now there was only herself. And the echoes of the past.

She left Sam's attaché case in the downstairs hallway and carried her suitcase upstairs. With the habit of long years, she started to head for her bedroom in the center of the hallway, then stopped. Her father's room was at the far end. Elizabeth turned and walked toward it. She opened the door slowly, because while her mind understood the reality, some deep, atavistic instinct made her half expect to see Sam there, to hear the sound of his voice.

The room was empty, of course, and nothing had changed since Elizabeth had last seen it. It contained a large double bed, a beautiful highboy, a dressing table, two comfortable overstuffed chairs, and a couch in front of the fireplace. Elizabeth set down her suitcase and walked over to the window. The iron shutters had been closed against the late September sun, and the draperies were drawn. She opened them wide and let the fresh mountain air flow in, soft and cool with the promise of fall. She would sleep in this room.

Elizabeth returned downstairs and went into the library. She sat down in one of the comfortable leather chairs, rubbing her hands along the sides. This was where Rhys always sat when he had a conference with her father.

She thought about Rhys and wished that he were here with her. She remembered the night he had brought her back to school after the dinner in Paris, and how she had gone back to her room and had written "Mrs. Rhys Williams" over and over. On an impulse Elizabeth walked over to the desk, picked up a pen and slowly wrote "Mrs. Rhys Williams." She looked at it and smiled. "I wonder," she mocked herself aloud, "how many other idiots are doing the same thing right now?"

She turned her thoughts away from Rhys, but still he was at the back of her mind, pleasantly comforting. She got up and wandered around the house. She explored the large, old-fashioned kitchen, with its wood-burning stove, and two ovens.

She walked over to the refrigerator and opened it. It was empty. She should have anticipated that, with the house shut down. Because the refrigerator was empty, she became suddenly hungry. She searched the cupboards. There were two small cans of tuna fish, a half-filled jar of Nescafé, and an unopened package of crackers. If she was going to be here for a long weekend, Elizabeth decided, she had better do some planning. Rather than drive into town for every meal, she would shop at one of the little markets in Cala di Volpe and stock enough food for several days. A utility Jeep was always kept in the carport and she wondered if it was still there. She went to the back of the kitchen and through the door that led to the carport, and there was the Jeep. Elizabeth walked back into the kitchen, where, on a board behind the cupboard, were hooks with labeled keys on them. She found the key to the Jeep and returned to the carport. Would there be gasoline in it? She turned the key and pressed the starter. Almost immediately the motor sparked into life. So *that* problem was eliminated. In the morning she would drive into town and pick up whatever groceries she needed.

She went back into the house. As she walked across the tiled floor of the reception hall, she could hear the echo of her footsteps, and it was a hollow, lonely sound. She wished that Alec would call, and even as she was thinking it the telephone rang, startling her.

She walked to it and picked it up. "Hello."

"Elizabeth. It's Alec here."

Elizabeth laughed aloud.

"What's so funny?"

"You wouldn't believe me if I told you. Where are you?"

"Down in Gloucester." And Elizabeth felt a sudden, urgent impulse to see him, to tell him her decision about the company. But not over the telephone. "Would you do me a favor, Alec?"

"You know I will."

"Could you fly down here for the weekend? I'd like to discuss something with you."

There was only the slightest hesitation, and then Alec said, "Of course."

Not a word about what engagements he would have to break, how inconvenient it might be. Just "Of course." That was Alec.

Elizabeth forced herself to say, "And bring Vivian."

"I'm afraid she won't be able to come. She's—ah—rather involved in London. I can arrive tomorrow morning. Will that do?"

"Perfect. Let me know what time, and I'll pick you up at the airport."

"It will be simpler if I just take a taxi."

"All right. Thank you, Alec. Very much."

When Elizabeth replaced the receiver, she was feeling infinitely better.

She knew she had made the right decision. She was in this position only because Sam had died before he had had the time to name his successor.

Elizabeth wondered who the next president of Roffe and Sons would be. The board could decide that for themselves. She thought about it from Sam's point of view, and the name that sprang instantly to mind was Rhys Williams. The others were competent in their own areas, but Rhys was the only one who had a working knowledge of the company's complete global operation. He was brilliant and effective. The problem, of course, was that Rhys was not eligible to be president. Because he was not a Roffe, or married to a Roffe, he could not even sit on the board.

Elizabeth walked into the hallway and saw her father's attaché case. She hesitated. There was hardly any point in her going through it now. She could give it to Alec when he arrived in the morning. Still, if there *was* something personal in it . . . She carried it into the library, set it on the desk, untaped the key and opened the little locks on each side. In the center of the case lay a large manila envelope. Elizabeth opened it and removed a sheaf of typewritten papers lying loosely in a cardboard cover labeled:

MR. SAM ROFFE
CONFIDENTIAL
NO COPIES.

It was obviously a report of some kind, but without anyone's name on it so that Elizabeth could not know who had drawn it. She started to skim through the report, then slowed down, then stopped. She could not believe what she was reading. She carried the papers over to an armchair, kicked off her shoes, curled her legs up underneath her and turned to page one again.

This time she read every word, and she was filled with horror.

It was an astonishing document, a confidential report of an investigation into a series of events that had occurred over the past year.

In Chile a chemical plant owned by Roffe and Sons had exploded, sending tons of poisonous materials spouting over a ten-square-mile area. A dozen people had been killed, hundreds more had been taken to hospitals. All the livestock had died, the vegetation was poisoned. The entire region had had to be evacuated. The lawsuits filed against Roffe and Sons had run into hundreds of millions of dollars. But the shocking thing was that the explosion had been deliberate. The report read: "The Chilean government's investigation into the accident was cursory. The official attitude seems to be: the Company is rich, the people are poor, let the Company pay. There is no question in the minds of our investigating staff but that it was an act of sabotage, by a person or persons unknown, using plastic explosives. Because of the antagonistic official attitude here, it will be impossible to prove."

Elizabeth remembered the incident only too well. Newspapers and magazines had been full of horror stories complete with photographs of the victims, and the world's press had attacked Roffe and Sons, accusing it of being careless and indifferent to human suffering. It had damaged the image of the company badly.

The next section of the report dealt with major research projects that Roffe and Sons' scientists had been working on for a number of years. There were four projects listed, each of them of inestimable potential value. Combined, they had cost more than fifty million dollars to develop. In each case a rival pharmaceutical firm had applied for a patent to one of the products, just ahead of Roffe and Sons, using the identical formula. The report continued: "One isolated incident might have been put down as coincidence. In a field where dozens of companies are working in related areas, it is inevitable that several companies might be working on the same type of product. But four such incidents in a period of a few months force us to the conclusion that someone in the employ of Roffe and Sons gave or sold the research material to the competitive firms. Because of the secret nature of the experiments, and the fact that they were conducted in widely separated laboratories under conditions of maximum security, our investigation indicates that the person, or persons, behind this would need to have access to top security clearances. We therefore conclude that whoever is responsible is someone in the highest executive echelon of Roffe and Sons."

There was more.

A large batch of toxic drugs had been mislabeled and shipped. Before they could be recalled there were several deaths, and more bad publicity for the company. No one could learn where the wrong labels had come from.

A deadly toxin had disappeared from a heavily guarded laboratory. Within an hour an unidentified person had leaked the story to the newspapers and started a scare-hunt.

The afternoon shadows had long since lengthened into evening, and the night air had turned chilly. Elizabeth remained totally absorbed in the document she held in her hands. When the study became dark, she switched on a lamp and continued to read, the horror piled on horror.

Not even the dry, terse tone of the report could conceal the drama in it. One thing was clear. Someone was methodically attempting to damage or destroy Roffe and Sons.

Someone in the highest echelon of the company. On the last page was a marginal note in her father's neat, precise handwriting. "Additional pressure on me to let the company go public? Trap the bastard."

She remembered now how worried Sam had been, and his sudden secrecy. He had not known whom to trust.

Elizabeth looked at the front page of the report again. "No COPIES."

Elizabeth was sure the report had been done by an outside investigative agency. So in all probability no one had been aware of this report but Sam. And now herself. The guilty person had no idea he was under suspicion. Had Sam known who he was? Had Sam confronted him before his accident? Elizabeth had no way of knowing. All she knew was that there was a traitor.

Someone in the highest echelon of the company.

No one else would have the opportunity or the ability to carry out so much destruction on so many different levels. Was that why Sam had refused to let the company go public? Was he trying to find the guilty person first? Once the company was sold, it would be impossible to conduct a secret investigation, with every move being reported to a group of strangers.

Elizabeth thought about the board meeting, and how they had urged her to sell. All of them.

Elizabeth suddenly felt very alone in the house. The loud ringing of the telephone made her jump. She walked over to it and picked it up. "Hello?"

"Liz? It's Rhys. I just received your message."

She was glad to hear his voice, but she suddenly remembered why she had called him. To tell him that she was going to sign the papers, let the company be sold. In a few short hours everything had completely changed. Elizabeth glanced out into the hallway, at the portrait of old Samuel. He had founded this company and had fought for it. Elizabeth's father had built it up, helped turn it into a giant, had lived for it, dedicated himself to it.

"Rhys," Elizabeth said, "I'd like to have a board meeting Tuesday. Two o'clock. Would you please arrange for everyone to be there?"

"Tuesday at two o'clock," Rhys agreed. "Anything else?"

She hesitated. "No. That's all. Thank you."

Elizabeth slowly replaced the receiver. She was going to fight them.

She was high on a mountain with her father, climbing at his side. *Don't look down*, Sam kept saying, and Elizabeth disobeyed, and there was nothing below but thousands of feet of empty space. There was a loud rumble of thunder, and a bolt of lightning came hurtling toward them. It hit Sam's rope and set it on fire, and Sam started falling through space. Elizabeth watched her father's body tumble end over end, and she began to scream, but her screams were drowned out by the roar of the thunder.

Elizabeth awakened suddenly, her nightgown drenched with perspiration, her heart pounding wildly. There was a loud clap of thunder, and she looked toward the window and saw that it was pouring outside. The wind was driving the rain into the bedroom through the open French doors. Quickly, Elizabeth got out of bed, crossed over to the doors and pushed them tightly shut. She looked out at the storm clouds that filled the sky, and at the lightning flashes across the horizon, but she was not seeing them.

She was thinking about her dream.

In the morning the storm had passed over the island, leaving only a light drizzle. Elizabeth hoped that the weather would not delay Alec's arrival. After reading the report she desperately needed someone to talk to. In the meantime she decided it would be a good idea to put it away in a secure place. There was a safe up in the tower room. She would keep it there. Elizabeth bathed, put on a pair of old slacks and a sweater, and went down into the library to get the report.

It was gone.

The room looked as though a hurricane had swept through it. The storm had blown open the French doors during the night, and the wind and the rain had wreaked havoc, scattering everything before it. A few loose pages of the report lay on the wet rug, but the rest of the pages had obviously been carried away by the wind.

Elizabeth stepped to the French windows and looked out. She could see no papers on the lawn, but the wind could easily have blown them over the cliff. That must have been what happened.

No COPIES. She must find out the name of the investigator Sam had hired. Perhaps Kate Erling would know. But Elizabeth could not be sure now that Sam had trusted Kate. This had become like a terrible game, where no one could trust anybody. She would have to move very carefully.

Elizabeth suddenly remembered that there was no food in the house. She could shop at Cala di Volpe and be back before Alec arrived. She went to the hall closet and got her raincoat and a scarf for her hair. Later, when the rain let up, she would search the grounds for the missing papers. She went into the kitchen and took the key to the Jeep from the key rack. She walked out the back door that led to the carport.

Elizabeth started the engine and carefully backed the Jeep out of the carport. She turned it around and headed out the private driveway, braking to slow down because of the wet surface. At the bottom of the driveway she turned right, onto the narrow mountain road that led to the little village of Cala di Volpe below. There was no traffic on the road at this hour, but there seldom was, for few houses had been built up this high. Elizabeth glanced down to her left and saw that the sea below had become dark and angry, swollen with the night storm.

She drove slowly, for this part of the road became treacherous. It was narrow, with two lanes that had been cut into the side of the mountain, along a sheer precipice. On the inside lane was the solid rock of the mountain, and on the outside, a drop of hundreds of feet to the sea below. Elizabeth kept as close as she could to the inside lane, braking to fight the momentum of the steep mountain gradient.

The car was approaching a sharp curve. Automatically, Elizabeth put her foot on the brakes to slow the Jeep down.

The brakes were dead.

It took a long moment to register. Elizabeth pressed again, harder, pushing down on the pedal with all her strength, and her heart began to pound as the Jeep kept gathering speed. It took the curve and was moving faster now, racing down the steep mountain road, gaining momentum with each second. She pressed down on the brakes again. They were useless.

Another curve lay ahead. Elizabeth was afraid to take her eyes off the road to look at the speedometer, but out of the corner of her eye she could see the needle racing upward and she was filled with an icy terror. She reached the curve and skidded around it, much too fast. The back wheels slid toward the edge of the precipice, then the tires found their traction and the Jeep plunged forward again, hurtling down the steep road ahead. There was nothing to stop it now, no barriers, no controls, only the swift roller-coaster ride down, and the deadly, beckoning curves ahead.

Elizabeth's mind raced frantically, seeking some escape. She thought of jumping. She risked a quick look at the speedometer. She was going seventy miles an hour now, and building up speed every moment, trapped between the solid mountain wall on one side and the deadly drop into space on the other. She was going to die. And in an instant revelation, Elizabeth knew that she was being murdered, and that her father had been murdered. Sam had read the report, and he had been killed. As she was going to be killed. And she had no idea who her murderer was, who hated them enough to do this terrible thing. Somehow she could have borne it better if it had been a stranger. But it was someone she knew, someone who knew her. Faces flashed through her mind. Alec . . . Ivo . . . Walther . . . Charles . . . It had to be one of them. *Someone in the highest echelon of the company.*

Her death would be listed as an accident, as Sam's had been. Elizabeth was crying now, silently, her tears mixing with the fine mist of rain that was falling, but she was not even aware of it. The Jeep was beginning to skid out of control on the wet surface, and Elizabeth fought to keep the wheels on the road. She knew it was only a matter of seconds before she hurtled over the cliff, into oblivion. Her body became rigid, and her hands were numb from gripping the steering wheel. There was nothing in the universe now but herself, careering down the mountain road, with the roaring wind tugging at her, saying *Come join me,* tearing at the car, trying to push it over the brink of the cliff. The Jeep started into another skid, and Elizabeth fought desperately to straighten it out, remembering what she had been taught. *Steer into the skid, always into the skid,* and the rear wheels straightened out and the car continued racing downhill. Elizabeth stole another quick glance at the speedometer . . . eighty miles an hour. She was catapulting toward a steep hairpin curve ahead, and she knew she was not going to make this one.

Something in her mind seemed to freeze, and it was as if there was a thin veil between her and reality. She heard her father's voice saying, *What are you doing down here alone in the dark?* and he was picking her up and carrying her to bed and she was on stage dancing and turning and turning and turning and she could not stop, and Mme. Netturova was screaming at her (or was it the wind?) and Rhys was there, saying, *How many times does a girl have her twenty-first birthday?* And Elizabeth thought, I'll never see Rhys again, and she screamed his name and the veil disappeared, but the nightmare was still there. The sharp curve was looming closer now, the car speeding toward it like a bullet. She would go over the cliff. *Let it happen quickly,* she prayed silently.

At that moment, to the right, just before the hairpin curve, Elizabeth caught a glimpse of a small firebreak trail that had been cut through the rock, going up the mountainside. She had to make a decision in a split second. She had no idea where the trail led. All she knew was that it went *upward,* that it might slow her momentum, give her a chance. And she took it. At the last instant, as the Jeep reached the trail, Elizabeth swung the wheel hard to the right. The rear wheels started to skid, but the front wheels were on the gravel road and the momentum gave them enough traction to hold. The Jeep was now hurtling upward, and Elizabeth was fighting the wheel, trying to keep the car on the narrow trail. There was a thin line of trees and their branches were slashing at her as she raced by them, tearing at her face and her hands. She looked ahead, and to her horror, she could see the Tyrrhenian Sea below. The path had merely led to the other side of the cliff. There was no safety here at all.

She was getting closer and closer to the brink now, moving too fast to jump from the Jeep. The edge of the cliff was just ahead of her, the sea hundreds of feet below. As the Jeep hurtled toward the edge, it went into a wild skid, and the last thing Elizabeth remembered was a tree looming up in front of her and then an explosion that seemed to fill the universe.

After that the world became still and white and peaceful and silent.

S he opened her eyes and she was in a hospital bed and the first thing she saw was Alec Nichols.

"There's nothing in the house for you to eat," she whispered, and started to cry.

Alec's eyes filled with pain, and he put his arms around her and held her close. "Elizabeth!"

And she mumbled, "It's all right, Alec. Everything is fine."

And it was. Every inch of her body felt bruised and beaten, but she was alive, and she could not believe it. She remembered the terror of that drive down the mountain, and her body went cold.

"How long have I been here?" Her voice was weak and hoarse.

"They brought you in two days ago. You've been unconscious since then. The doctor says it was a miracle. According to everybody who saw the scene of the accident, you should be dead. A service crew came across you and rushed you in here. You have a concussion and a hell of a lot of bruises, but, thank the Lord, there's nothing broken." He looked at her, puzzled, and said, "What were you doing up there on that firebreak road?"

Elizabeth told him. She could see the horror on his face as he lived through the terrible ride with her. He kept repeating, "Oh, my God," over and over. When Elizabeth had finished, Alec was pale. "What a stupid, terrible accident!"

"It wasn't an accident, Alec."

He looked at her, puzzled. "I don't understand."

How could he? He had not read the report. Elizabeth said, "Someone tampered with the brakes."

He shook his head incredulously. "Why would anyone do that?"

"Because—" She could not tell him. Not yet. She trusted Alec more than she trusted anyone else, but she was not ready to talk. Not until she felt stronger, not until she had had time to think.

"I don't know," she said evasively. "I'm just sure someone did."

She watched him and she could read the changing expressions on his face. They went from disbelief to puzzlement to anger.

"Well, we're certainly going to find out." His voice was grim.

He picked up the telephone, and a few minutes later he was talking to the Chief of Police in Olbia. "This is Alec Nichols," he said. "I—Yes, she's fine, thank you. . . . Thank you. I'll tell her. I'm calling about the Jeep she was driving. Could you tell me where it is? . . . Would you keep it there, please? And I'd like you to get hold of a good mechanic. I'll be there in half an hour." He replaced the receiver. "It's in the police garage. I'm going over."

"I'm coming with you."

He looked at her in surprise. "The doctor said you must stay in bed for at least another day or two. You can't—"

"I'm coming with you," she insisted stubbornly.

Forty-five minutes later Elizabeth checked her bruised and swollen body out of the hospital over a doctor's protests, and was on her way to the police garage with Alec Nichols.

Luigi Ferraro, the Chief of Police of Olbia, was a swarthy, middle-aged Sardo, with a large stomach and bandy legs. Next to him was Detective Bruno Campagna, who towered over his chief. Campagna was a muscularly built man in his fifties, with an air of solid competence. He stood next to Elizabeth and Alec, watching a mechanic examine the underside of a Jeep that was raised on a hydraulic hoist. The left front fender and radiator had been smashed, and they were streaked with the sap of the trees they had crashed into. Elizabeth had felt faint at her first sight of the car, and she had had to lean on Alec for support. He looked at her with concern. "Are you sure you're up to this?"

"I feel fine," Elizabeth lied. She felt weak and terribly tired. But she had to see for herself.

The mechanic wiped his hands on a greasy cloth and walked

over to the group. "They don't build them like that no more," he said.

Thank God, Elizabeth thought.

"Any other car woulda been in bits and pieces."

"What about the brakes?" Alec asked.

"The brakes? They're in perfect condition."

Elizabeth felt a sudden sense of unreality engulfing her. "What—what do you mean?"

"They're workin' fine. The accident didn't hurt them at all. That's what I meant when I said that they don't build—"

"That's impossible," Elizabeth interrupted. "The brakes weren't working on that Jeep."

"Miss Roffe believes that someone tampered with them," Chief Ferraro explained.

The mechanic shook his head. "No, sir." He walked back to the Jeep and pointed to the underside. "There's only two ways you can *fregare*—" He turned to Elizabeth. "Excuse me, signorina—screw up the brakes on a Jeep. You can either cut the brake links or you can loosen this nut"—he indicated a piece of metal on the underside—"and let the brake fluid run out. You can see for yourself that this link is solid, and I checked the brake drum. It's full."

Chief Ferraro said to Elizabeth soothingly, "I can understand how in your condition it could—"

"Just a moment," Alec interrupted. He turned to the mechanic. "Isn't it possible that those links were cut and then replaced or that someone drained the brake fluid and then filled it again?"

The mechanic shook his head stubbornly. "Mister, those links ain't been touched." He took his rag again and carefully wiped off the oil around the nut that held the brake fluid. "See this nut? If anyone had loosened it, there'd be fresh wrench marks on it. I'll guarantee that no one's touched it in the last six months. There's not a thing wrong with these brakes. I'll show you."

He walked over to the wall and pulled a switch. There was a whirring sound and the hydraulic lift began to lower the Jeep to the floor. They watched as the mechanic got in it, started the engine and backed the Jeep up. When it was touching the back wall, he put the Jeep in first gear and pressed down on the accelerator. The car raced toward Detective Campagna. Elizabeth opened her mouth to scream, and at that instant the Jeep jerked to a stop an inch away from him. The mechanic ignored the look the detective gave him and said, "See? These brakes are perfect."

They were all looking at Elizabeth now, and she knew what they were thinking. But that did not change the terror of that ride down the mountain. She could feel her foot pressing on the brakes, and nothing happening. Yet the police mechanic had proved that they worked. Unless he was in on it. And that meant the Chief of Police probably knew too. I'm becoming paranoiac, Elizabeth thought.

Alec said helplessly, "Elizabeth——"

"When I drove that Jeep, those brakes were not working."

Alec studied her for a moment, then said to the mechanic, "Let's suppose that someone *did* arrange it so that the brakes on this Jeep wouldn't work. How else could it have been done?"

Detective Campagna spoke up. "They could have wet the brake lining."

Elizabeth could feel an excitement stirring in her. "What would happen if they did that?"

Detective Campagna said, "When the brake lining pressed against the drum, it would have no traction."

The mechanic nodded. "He's right. The only thing is—" He turned to Elizabeth. "Were your brakes working when you started driving?"

Elizabeth remembered using the brakes to back out of the carport, and braking again later when she came to the first curves. "Yes," she said, "they were working."

"There's your answer," the mechanic said triumphantly. "Your brakes got wet in the rain."

"Hold on," Alec objected. "Why couldn't someone have wet them *before* she started?"

"Because," the mechanic said patiently, "if anyone had wet them *before* she started, she wouldn'ta had no brakes at all."

The Chief of Police turned to Elizabeth. "Rain can be dangerous, Miss Roffe. Particularly on these narrow mountain roads. This sort of thing happens all too often."

Alec was watching Elizabeth, not knowing what to do next. She felt like a fool. It *had* been an accident after all. She wanted to get out of here. She looked at the Chief of Police. "I—I'm sorry to have put you to all this trouble."

"*Please.* It is a pleasure. I mean—I am distressed about the circumstances, but it is always a pleasure to be of service. Detective Campagna will drive you back to your villa."

Alec said to her. "If you don't mind my saying so, old girl, you look ghastly. Now, I want you to hop into your bed and stay there for a few days. I'll order some groceries by telephone."

"If I stay in bed, who's going to cook?"

"I am," Alec declared.

That evening he prepared dinner and served it to Elizabeth in bed.

"I'm afraid I'm not a very good cook," he said cheerfully, as he set a tray down in front of Elizabeth.

It was the understatement of the year, Elizabeth thought. Alec was a terrible cook. Every dish was either burned, underdone or oversalted. But she managed to eat, partly because she was starving, and partly because she did not want to hurt Alec's feelings. He sat with her, making cheerful small talk. Not a word about what a fool she had made of herself at the police garage. She loved him for it.

The two of them spent the next few days at the villa, with Elizabeth remaining in bed, and Alec fussing over her, cooking all the meals, reading to her. During that time it seemed to Elizabeth that the telephone never stopped ringing. Ivo and Simonetta called every day to see how she was, and Hélène and Charles, and Walther. Even Vivian called. They all offered to come and stay with her.

"I'm really all right," she told them. "There's no reason for you to come. I'll be returning to Zurich in a few days."

Rhys Williams called. Elizabeth had not realized how much she had missed him until she heard the sound of his voice.

"I hear you decided to give Hélène some competition," he said. But she could hear the concern in his voice.

"Wrong. I only race on mountains, downhill." It was incredible to her that she could joke about it now.

Rhys said, "I'm glad you're all right, Liz."

His tone, as much as his words, warmed her. She wondered if he was with another woman now, and who she was. It would be someone beautiful, of course.

Damn her.

"Did you know you made the headlines?" Rhys asked.

"No."

" 'Heiress narrowly escapes death in car accident. Only a few weeks after her father, the well-known—' You can write the rest of the story yourself."

They spoke on the phone for half an hour, and when Elizabeth hung up she was feeling much better. Rhys seemed so genuinely interested in her, and concerned. She wondered whether he made every woman he knew feel that way about him. It was part of his charm. She remembered how they had celebrated her birthdays together. *Mrs. Rhys Williams.*

Alec walked into the bedroom. He said, "You look like the Cheshire cat."

"Do I?"

Rhys had always been able to make her feel that way. Perhaps, she thought, I should tell Rhys about the confidential report.

Alec had arranged for one of the company planes to fly them back to Zurich.

"I hate to take you back so soon," he said apologetically, "but there are some rather urgent decisions that have to be made."

The flight to Zurich was uneventful. There were reporters at the airport. Elizabeth made a brief statement about her accident, and then Alec had her safely inside the limousine and they were on their way to the company headquarters.

She was in the conference room with all the members of the board, and Rhys, present. The meeting had been going on for the past three hours, and the air was stale with cigar and cigarette smoke. Elizabeth was still shaken from her experience, and she had a pounding headache—*Nothing to be concerned about, Miss Roffe. When the concussion wears off, the headaches will go away.*

She looked around the room, at the tense, angry faces. "I've decided not to sell," Elizabeth had told them. They thought she was being arbitrary and stubborn. If they only knew how close she had come to giving in. But now it was impossible. Someone in this room was an enemy. If she quit now, it would be his victory.

They had all tried to convince her, each in his own fashion.

Alec said reasonably, "Roffe and Sons needs an experienced president, Elizabeth. Particularly now. For your own sake, as well as everyone else's, I would like to see you walk away from this."

Ivo used his charm. "You're a beautiful young girl, *carissima*. The whole world is yours. Why do you want to become a slave to something as dull as business when you could be out, having a wonderful time, traveling—"

"I've traveled," Elizabeth said.

Charles used Gallic logic. "You happen to hold the controlling stock, through a tragic accident, but it makes no sense for you to try to run the company. We have serious problems. You will only make them worse."

Walther spoke bluntly. "The company is in enough trouble. You have no idea how much trouble. If you do not sell now, it will be too late."

Elizabeth felt as though she were under siege. She listened to them all, studying them, evaluating what they were telling her. Each of them based his argument on the good of the company— yet one of them was working to destroy it.

One thing was clear. They all wanted her to get out, to let them sell their stock, and bring in outsiders to take over Roffe and Sons. Elizabeth knew that the moment she did that, her chances of finding out who was behind this were finished. As long as she stayed here, on the inside, there was the possibility that she could learn who was sabotaging the company. She would stay only as long as she had to. She had not spent the last three years with Sam without learning something about the business. With the help of the experienced staff he had built up, she would continue to carry out her father's policies. The insistence from all the board members that she get out now only made her more stubbornly determined to remain.

She decided it was time to end the meeting.

"I've made my decision," Elizabeth said. "I don't plan to run this company alone. I'm aware of how much I have to learn. I know I can count on all of you to help me. We'll deal with the problems one by one."

She sat at the head of the table, still pale from her accident, looking small and defenseless.

Ivo threw up his hands helplessly. "Can't anyone talk logic into her?"

Rhys turned to Elizabeth and smiled. "I think everyone's going to have to go along with whatever the lady wants to do."

"Thank you, Rhys." Elizabeth looked at the others. "There's one thing more. Since I'm taking my father's place, I think it would be best to make it official."

Charles stared at her. "You mean—you want to become president?"

"In effect," Alec reminded him dryly, "Elizabeth is already president. She's merely showing us the courtesy of letting us handle the situation gracefully."

Charles hesitated, then said, "All right. I move that Elizabeth Roffe be nominated president of Roffe and Sons."

"I second the motion." Walther.

The motion was carried.

It was such a bad time for presidents, he thought sadly. *So many were being assassinated.*

No one was more aware than Elizabeth of the enormous responsibility she had assumed. As long as she was running the company, the jobs of thousands of people depended upon her. She needed help, but she had no idea whom she could trust. Alec and Rhys and Ivo were the ones she most wanted to confide in, but she was not ready yet. It was too soon. She sent for Kate Erling.

"Yes, Miss Roffe?"

Elizabeth hesitated, wondering how to begin. Kate Erling had worked for Elizabeth's father for many years. She would have a sense of the undercurrents that flowed beneath the deceptively calm surface. She would know about the inner workings of the company, about Sam Roffe's feelings, his plans. Kate Erling would make a strong ally.

Elizabeth said, "My father was having some kind of confidential report drawn up for him, Kate. Do you know anything about it?"

Kate Erling frowned in concentration, then shook her head. "He never discussed it with me, Miss Roffe."

Elizabeth tried another approach. "If my father had wanted a confidential investigation, to whom would he have gone?"

This time the answer was unhesitating. "Our security division."

The last place Sam would have gone. "Thank you," Elizabeth said.

There was no one she could talk to.

There was a current financial report on her desk. Elizabeth read it with growing dismay, and then sent for the company comptroller. His name was Wilton Kraus. He was younger than Elizabeth had expected. Bright, eager, an air of faint superiority. The Wharton School, she decided, or perhaps Harvard.

Elizabeth began without preamble. "How can a company like Roffe and Sons be in financial difficulty?"

Kraus looked at her and shrugged. He was obviously not used to reporting to a woman. He said condescendingly, "Well, putting it in words of one syllable—"

"Let's begin with the fact," Elizabeth said curtly, "that up until two years ago Roffe and Sons had always done its own capital financing."

She watched his expression change, trying to adjust. "Well— yes, ma'am."

"Then why are we so heavily indebted to banks now?"

He swallowed and said, "A few years ago, we went through a period of unusually heavy expansion. Your father and the other members of the board felt that it would be wise to raise that money by borrowing from banks on short-term loans. We have current net commitments to various banks for six hundred and fifty million dollars. Some of those loans are now due."

"Overdue," Elizabeth corrected him.

"Yes, ma'am. Overdue."

"We're paying the prime rate, plus one percent, plus penalty interest. Why haven't we paid off the overdue loans and reduced the principal on the others?"

He was beyond surprise now. "Because of—er—certain unfortunate recent occurrences, the company's cash-flow position is considerably less than we had anticipated. Under ordinary circumstances we would go to the banks and ask for extensions. However, with our current problems, the various litigation settlements, the write-offs in our experimental laboratory, and . . ." His voice trailed off.

Elizabeth sat there, studying him, wondering whose side he was on. She looked down at the balance sheets again, trying to pinpoint where things had gone wrong. The statement showed a sharp decline over the past three quarters, largely because of the heavy lawsuit payoffs listed under the column "Extraordinary Expenses (Nonrecurring)." In her mind's eye she saw the explosion in Chile, the cloud of poisonous chemicals spouting into the air. She could hear the screams of the victims. A dozen people dead. Hundreds more taken to hospitals. And in the end all the human pain and misery had been reduced to money, to Extraordinary Expenses (Nonrecurring).

She looked up at Wilton Kraus. "According to your report, Mr. Kraus, our problems are of a temporary nature. We are Roffe and Sons. We're still a first-class risk for any bank in the world."

It was his turn to study her. His supercilious air was gone, but he was wary now.

"You must realize, Miss Roffe," he began cautiously, "that a drug firm's reputation is as important as its products."

Who had said that to her before? Her father? Alec? She remembered. Rhys.

"Go on."

"Our problems are becoming too well-known. The business world is a jungle. If your competitors suspect that you've been wounded, they move in for the kill." He hesitated, then added, "They're moving in for the kill."

"In other words," Elizabeth replied, "our competitors bank with our bankers, too."

He gave her a brief congratulatory smile. "Exactly. The banks have a limited amount of funds to loan out. If they're convinced that A is a better risk than B—"

"And *do* they think that?"

He ran his fingers through his hair, nervously. "Since your father's death I've had several calls from Herr Julius Badrutt. He heads up the banking consortium we're dealing with."

"What did Herr Badrutt want?" She knew what was coming.

"He wanted to know who was going to be the new president of Roffe and Sons."

"Do you know who the new president is?" Elizabeth asked.

"No ma'am."

"I am." She watched him try to conceal his surprise. "What do you think will happen when Herr Badrutt learns the news?"

"He'll pull the plugs on us," Wilton Kraus blurted out.

"I'll talk to him," Elizabeth said. She leaned back in her chair and smiled. "Would you care for some coffee?"

"Why that's—that's very kind of you. Yes, thank you."

Elizabeth watched him relax. He had sensed that she had been testing him, and he felt that he had passed the test.

"I'd like your advice," Elizabeth said. "If you were in my position, Mr. Kraus, what would you do?"

That faintly patronizing air was back. "Well," he said confidently, "that's very simple. Roffe and Sons has enormous assets. If we sold off a substantial block of stock to the public, we could easily raise more than enough money to satisfy all our bank loans."

She knew now whose side he was on.

The wind was blowing from the sea, and the early-morning air was chill and damp. In the Reeperbahn section of Hamburg the streets were crowded with visitors eager to experience the forbidden pleasures of the city of sin. The Reeperbahn catered to all tastes impartially. Drinks, drugs, girls or boys—they were all available at a price.

The garishly lighted hostess bars were on the main street, while the Grosse Freiheit featured the lewd strip shows. The Herbertstrasse, one block away, was for pedestrians only, and both sides of the street were lined with prostitutes sitting in the windows of their flats, displaying their wares through flimsy soiled nightgowns that concealed nothing. The Reeperbahn was a vast market, a human butcher shop, where you could select any piece of meat you could afford to pay for. For the straitlaced there was simple sex, missionary style; for those who enjoyed a bit of variety there was cunnilingus and analingus and sodomy. On the Reeperbahn you could buy a twelve-year-old boy or girl, or get into bed with a mother and daughter. If your tastes ran that way, you could watch a woman being serviced by a Great Dane, or get yourself whipped until you achieved orgasm. You could hire a toothless crone to perform fellatio on you in a busy alley or buy yourself an orgy in an elaborately mirrored bedroom with as many girls or boys as your libido required. The Reeperbahn prided itself on having something for everyone. Younger whores in short skirts and tight-fitting blouses cruised the pavements, propositioning men, women and couples impartially.

The cameraman walked down the street slowly, the target for a dozen girls and brightly rouged boys. He ignored them all until he came to a girl who looked to be no more than eighteen. She had blond hair. She was leaning against a wall, talking to a girl friend. She turned as the man approached, and smiled. "Would you like a party, *liebchen?* My friend and I will show you a good time."

The man studied the girl and said, "Just you."

The other girl shrugged and moved off.

"What's your name?"

"Hildy."

"Would you like to be in the movies, Hildy?" the cameraman asked.

The young girl studied him with cold eyes. *"Herrgott!* You're not going to give me that old Hollywood *Scheiss?"*

He smiled reassuringly. "No, no. This is a genuine offer. It's a porno film. I make them for a friend of mine."

"It will cost you five hundred marks. In advance."

"Gut."

She regretted instantly that she had not asked for more. Well, she would find some way to get a bonus out of him. "What do I have to do?" Hildy asked.

Hildy was nervous.

She lay sprawled out naked on the bed in the small, shabbily furnished apartment, watching the three people in the room, and thinking. There's something wrong here. Her instincts had been sharpened on the streets of Berlin and Munich and Hamburg. She had learned to rely on them. There was something about these people she did not trust. She would have liked to have walked out before it started, but they had already paid her five hundred marks, and promised her another five hundred if she did a good job. She would do a good job. She was a professional and she took pride in her work. She turned to the naked man in bed beside her. He was strong and well built; his body was hairless. What bothered Hildy was his face. He was too old for this sort of film. But it was the spectator who sat quietly at the back of the room who disturbed Hildy the most. The spectator wore a long coat, a large hat and dark glasses. Hildy could not even tell if it was a man or a woman. The vibrations were bad. Hildy fingered the red ribbon tied around her neck, wondering why they had asked her to wear it. The cameraman said, "All right. We're ready now. Action."

The camera began whirring. Hildy had been told what to do. The man was lying on his back. Hildy went to work.

She started with a trip around the world, skillfully using her tongue and lips on the man's ears and neck, moving down across his chest and stomach and belly, lightly flicking her tongue in quick butterfly strokes against his groin and penis, then each leg, down to his toes, slowly licking each toe, watching his erection begin. She rolled him over on his stomach, and her tongue began to work its way back up his body, moving slowly, expertly, finding all the erotic crevices and sensitive areas and exploring them. The man was fully aroused now, rock-hard.

"Get inside her," the cameraman said. The man rolled her over and was on top of her, forcing her thighs apart, his penis swollen to an enormous tumescence, and as he entered her, Hildy forgot her earlier fears. It felt wonderful.

"Shove it in me, *liebchen!*" she cried.

The man was deep, deep inside her, rocking back and forth, and Hildy started to move with him, her hips writhing in quickening spasms. In the back of the room the spectator was leaning forward, watching every movement. The girl on the bed closed her eyes.

She was spoiling it!

"Her eyes!" the spectator shouted.

The director called out, "*Öffne die Augen!*"

Startled, Hildy opened her eyes. She watched the man on top of her. He was good. It was the kind of sex she liked. Hard and thrusting. He was moving faster now, and she began to respond to him. Usually she did not have orgasms, except with her girl friend. With customers she always faked it, and they never knew the difference. But the cameraman had warned her that if she did not have an orgasm, she would not be paid the bonus. And so now she relaxed and let herself think about all the beautiful things she was going to buy with the money, and she felt herself beginning to climax.

"*Schneller!*" she cried. "*Schneller!*"

Her body began to shudder. *"Ah, jetzt!"* she screamed. *"Es kommt! Es kommt!"*

The spectator nodded, and the cameraman cried, "Now!"

The man's hands moved up toward the girl's neck. His enormous fingers closed over the windpipe and squeezed. She looked up into his eyes and saw what was there, and she was filled with terror. She tried to scream, but she was unable to breathe. She fought desperately to fight free, her body jerking in great, orgiastic spasms, but he had her pinned down. There was no escape.

The spectator sat there drinking it in, feasting on it, looking into the dying girl's eyes, watching her being punished.

The girl's body shuddered once, and then was still.

When Elizabeth arrived at her office, a sealed envelope marked "CONFIDENTIAL," with her name on it, was lying on her desk. She opened it. In it was a report from the chemical laboratory. It was signed "Emil Joeppli." It was full of technical terms, and Elizabeth read it through without understanding it. Then she read it again. And again. Each time more slowly. When finally she had grasped its significance, she said to Kate, "I'll be back in an hour." And she went to find Emil Joeppli.

He was a tall man about thirty-five, with a thin, freckled face, and a scalp that was bald except for a tonsure of bright red hair. He fidgeted uncomfortably, as though unused to having visitors in his little laboratory.

"I read your report," Elizabeth told him. "There's a great deal in it that I don't understand. I wonder if you would mind explaining it to me."

Instantly, Joeppli's nervousness vanished. He leaned forward in his chair, sure and confident, and began to speak rapidly. "I've been experimenting with a method of inhibiting rapid differentiation of the collagens, by using mucopolysaccharides and enzyme blocking techniques. Collagen, of course, is the fundamental protein basis of all connective tissue."

"Of course," Elizabeth said.

She did not even try to understand the technical part of what Joeppli was saying. What Elizabeth did understand was that the project he was working on could retard the aging process. It was a breathtaking concept.

She sat there, silent, listening, thinking about what this could mean in terms of revolutionizing the lives of men and women all over the world. According to Joeppli, there was no reason why everyone should not live to be a hundred, or a hundred and fifty, or even two hundred years old.

"It would not even be necessary to have injections," Joeppli told Elizabeth. "With this formula the ingredients could be taken orally in a pill or a capsule."

The possibilities were staggering. It would mean nothing less than a social revolution. And billions of dollars for Roffe and Sons. They would manufacture it themselves, and license it out to other companies as well. There was no one over fifty years of age who would not take a pill that would keep him or her young. It was difficult for Elizabeth to conceal her excitement.

"How far along are you on this project?"

"As I wrote in my report, I've been doing tests with animals for the last four years. All the recent results have been positive. It's just about ready for testing on human beings." She liked his enthusiasm.

"Who else knows about this?" Elizabeth asked.

"Your father knew. It's a Red Folder project. Top security. That means that I report only to the president of the company and to one member of the board."

Elizabeth suddenly felt chilled. "Which member?"

"Mr. Walther Gassner."

Elizabeth was silent for a moment. "From this time on," she said, "I want you to report directly to me. And only to me."

Joeppli looked at her in surprise. "Yes, Miss Roffe."

"How soon could we have this on the market?"

"If everything goes well, eighteen to twenty-four months from now."

"Fine. If you need anything—money, extra help, equipment—let me know. I want you to move as quickly as possible."

"Yes, ma'am."

Elizabeth rose, and instantly Emil Joeppli jumped to his feet.

"It's a pleasure meeting you." He smiled, and added shyly, "I liked your father."

"Thank you," Elizabeth said. Sam had known about this project. Was that another reason he refused to sell the company?

"At the door Emil Joeppli turned to Elizabeth.

"It's going to work on people!"

"Yes," Elizabeth said. "Of course it will."

It had to.

"How is a Red Folder project handled?"

Kate Erling asked, "From the beginning?"

"From the beginning."

"Well. As you know, we have several hundred new products in various experimental stages. They—"

"Who authorizes them?"

"Up to a certain amount of money, the heads of the different departments involved," Kate Erling said.

"What amount of money?"

"Fifty thousand dollars."

"And after that?"

"There must be board approval. Of course, a project does not come into the Red Folder category until it has passed its initial tests."

"You mean until it looks like it has a chance of being successful?" Elizabeth asked.

"That's right."

"How is it protected?"

"If it's an important project, all the work is transferred to one of our high-security laboratories. All the papers are removed from the general files and put into a Red Folder file. Only three people have access to that. The scientist in charge of the project, the president of the company, and one member of the board."

"Who decides who that member will be?" Elizabeth asked.

"Your father selected Walther Gassner."

The moment the words were out of her mouth, Kate realized her mistake.

The two women looked at each other, and Elizabeth said, "Thank you, Kate. That will be all."

Elizabeth had made no mention of Joeppli's project. Yet Kate had known what Elizabeth was talking about. There were two possibilities. Either Sam had trusted her and told her about Joeppli's project, or she had learned about it on her own. For someone else.

This was too important to allow anything to go wrong. She would check on the security herself. And she had to speak to Walther Gassner. She reached for the telephone, then stopped. There was a better way.

Late that afternoon Elizabeth was on a commercial airliner to Berlin.

Walther Gassner was nervous.

They were seated at a corner booth in the upstairs dining room of the Papillon on the Kurfürstendamm. Whenever Elizabeth had visited Berlin in the past, Walther had always insisted that Elizabeth have dinner at his home, with Anna and him. This time there had been no mention of that. He had suggested instead that they meet at this restaurant. And he had come without Anna.

Walther Gassner still had the clear-cut, boyish, moviestar handsomeness, but the surface gloss had begun to crack. There were lines of tension in his face, and his hands never stopped moving. He seemed to be under some extraordinary tension. When Elizabeth asked about Anna, Walther was vague. "Anna's not feeling well. She couldn't come."

"Is it anything serious?"

"No, no. She'll be fine. She's at home, resting."

"I'll call her and—"

"Better not to disturb her."

It was a puzzling conversation, totally unlike Walther, whom Elizabeth had always found so open and outgoing.

She brought up the subject of Emil Joeppli. "We need what he's working on very badly," Elizabeth said.

Walther nodded. "It's going to be big."

"I've asked him not to report to you anymore," Elizabeth told him.

Walther's hands suddenly went very still. It was like a shout. He looked at Elizabeth and asked, "Why did you do that?"

"It has nothing to do with you, Walther. I would have done exactly the same thing with any other board member working with him. I simply want to handle this my own way."

He nodded. "I see." But his hands remained motionless on the table. "You have a right, of course." He forced a smile and she could see what it was costing him. "Elizabeth," he said, "Anna has a lot of stock in the company. She can't sell it unless you vote yes. It's—it's very important. I—"

"I'm sorry, Walther, I can't let the stock be sold now."

His hands suddenly began to move again.

Herr Julius Badrutt was a thin, brittle man who resembled a praying mantis in a black suit. He was like a stick figure drawn by a child, with angular arms and legs, and a dry, unfinished face sketched on top of his body. He was seated stiffly at the conference table of the Roffe and Sons boardroom, facing Elizabeth. There were five other bankers with him. They all wore black suits with waistcoats, white shirts and dark ties. They appeared, Elizabeth thought, not so much *dressed* as in uniform. Looking around at the cold, impassive eyes at the table, Elizabeth was filled with a sense of misgiving. Before the meeting had begun, Kate had brought in a tray of coffee and delicious, freshly baked pastries. The men had all declined. Just as they had declined Elizabeth's invitation to come to lunch. She decided it was a bad sign. They were there to get the money that was owed them.

Elizabeth said, "First of all, I wish to thank all of you for coming here today."

There were polite, meaningless murmurs in response.

She took a deep breath. "I asked you here to discuss an extension on the loans owed to you by Roffe and Sons."

Julius Badrutt shook his head in tiny, jerky movements. "I am sorry, Miss Roffe. We have already informed—"

"I haven't finished," Elizabeth said. She glanced around the room. "If I were you, gentlemen, I would refuse."

They stared at her, then looked at one another in confusion.

Elizabeth continued, "If you were concerned about the loans when my father was running this company—and he was a brilliant

185

businessman—why would you extend them for a woman who is inexperienced in business?"

Julius Badrutt said dryly, "I think you have answered your own question, Miss Roffe. We have no intention of—"

Elizabeth said, "I haven't finished."

They were eyeing her more warily now. She looked at each of them in turn, making sure she had their full attention. They were Swiss bankers, admired, respected and envied by their lesser colleagues in other parts of the financial world. They were leaning forward now, listening carefully, their attitude of impatience and boredom replaced by curiosity.

"You have all known Roffe and Sons for a long time," Elizabeth went on. "I am sure most of you knew my father and, if you did, you must have respected him."

There were nods of agreement from some of the men.

"I imagine," Elizabeth continued, "that you gentlemen must have choked over your morning coffee when you learned that I was taking his place here."

One of the bankers smiled, then laughed aloud, and said, "You are quite right, Miss Roffe. I do not mean to be ungallant, but I think I am speaking for the rest of my colleagues when I say that—what were your words?—we choked over our morning coffee."

Elizabeth smiled ingenuously. "I don't blame you. I'm sure I would have reacted in exactly the same way."

Another banker spoke up. "I am curious, Miss Roffe. Since we are all in agreement about the outcome of this meeting"—he spread his hands expressively—"why are we here?"

"You're here," Elizabeth said, "because in this room are some of the greatest bankers in the world. I can't believe that you became so successful by looking at everything only in terms of dollars and cents. If that were true, then any of your bookkeepers could run your business for you. I am sure that there is much more to banking than that."

"Of course there is," another banker murmured, "but we're businessmen, Miss Roffe, and—"

"And Roffe and Sons is a business. It's a great business. I didn't know how great until I sat behind my father's desk. I had no idea how many lives this company has saved in countries all over the world. Or of the enormous contributions we've made to medicine. Or how many thousands of people depend on this company for their livelihood. If—"

Julius Badrutt interrupted. "That is all very commendable, but we seem to be getting off the point. I understand that it has been suggested to you that if you release the company stock, there will be more than sufficient monies to satisfy our loans."

His first mistake, Elizabeth thought. *I understand that it has been suggested to you.*

The suggestion had been made in the privacy of a board of directors' meeting, where everything was confidential. Someone at that meeting had talked. Someone who was trying to put pressure on her. She intended to find out who, but that would have to come later.

"I want to ask you a question," Elizabeth said. "If your loans are repaid, would it matter to you where the money came from?"

Julius Badrutt studied her, his mind circling the question, looking for a trap. Finally he said, "No. Not as long as we receive the money due us."

Elizabeth leaned forward and said earnestly, "So it doesn't matter whether you're paid from the sale of company stock to outsiders, or from our own financial resources. All of you know that Roffe and Sons isn't going out of business. Not today. Not tomorrow. Not ever. All I'm asking is the courtesy of a little extra time."

Julius Badrutt smacked his dry lips and said, "Believe me, Miss Roffe, we are most sympathetic. We understand the terrible emotional stress you have gone through, but we cannot—"

"Three months," Elizabeth said. "Ninety days. With your getting additional penalty interest, of course."

There was a silence around the table. But it was a negative silence. Elizabeth could see their cold, hostile faces. She decided on one last desperate gamble.

"I—I don't know whether it's proper for me to reveal this," she said with deliberate hesitation, "and I must ask you to keep it confidential." She looked around and saw that she had their interest again. "Roffe and Sons is on the verge of a breakthrough that's going to revolutionize the entire pharmaceutical industry." She paused to heighten the suspense. "This company is about to reveal a new product that our projections show will *far outsell every drug available on the market today.*"

She could feel the change in the atmosphere.

It was Julius Badrutt who rose to the bait first. "What—er—type of—?"

Elizabeth shook her head. "I'm sorry, Herr Badrutt. Perhaps I've already said too much. I can only tell you that it will be the biggest innovation in the history of this business. It will require a tremendous expansion of our facilities. We'll have to double them, perhaps triple them. Of course, we'll be looking for new financing on a large scale."

The bankers were glancing at one another, exchanging silent signals. The silence was broken by Herr Badrutt. "If we *were* to give you a ninety-day extension, we would naturally expect to act as the prime bankers for Roffe and Sons in all future transactions."

"Naturally."

Another exchange of meaningful looks. It's like a form of jungle drums, Elizabeth thought.

"In the meantime," Herr Badrutt said, "we would have your assurance that at the end of ninety days all your outstanding notes will be met in full?"

"Yes."

Herr Badrutt sat there, staring into space. He looked at Elizabeth, then looked around at the others, and received their silent signals. "For my part, I am willing to agree. I do not think a delay—with penalty interest—will do any harm."

One of the other bankers nodded. "If you think we should go along, Julius . . ."

And it was done. Elizabeth leaned back in her chair, trying to conceal the feeling of relief flooding through her. She had gained ninety days.

She would need every minute of that time.

I t was like being in the eye of a hurricane.

Everything flowed across Elizabeth's desk from the hundreds of departments at headquarters, from the factories in Zaire, the laboratories in Greenland, the offices in Australia and Thailand, from the four corners of the earth. There were reports on new products, sales, statistical projections, advertising campaigns, experimental programs.

There were decisions to be made on building new factories, selling old ones, acquiring companies, hiring and firing executives. Elizabeth had expert advice on every phase of the business, but all final decisions had to be made by her. As they had once been made by Sam. She was grateful now for the three years she had worked with her father. She knew much more about the company than she had realized, and much less. Its very scope was awesome. Elizabeth had once thought of it as a kingdom, but it was a *series* of kingdoms, run by viceroys, with the president's office as the throne room. Each of her cousins had charge of his own domain, but in addition they supervised other overseas territories, so that they were all traveling constantly.

Elizabeth soon learned that she had a special problem. She was a woman in a man's world, and she discovered that it made a difference. She had never really believed that men subscribed to the myth of the inferiority of women, but she quickly learned better. No one ever put it into words or acted overtly, but Elizabeth was faced with it every day. It was an attitude born of ancient prejudices and it was inescapable. The men did not like taking orders from a woman. They resented the idea of a woman questioning their judgments, trying to improve on their ideas. The fact that Elizabeth was young and attractive made it worse. They tried to make her feel that she should be at home, in a bed or kitchen, and that she should leave serious business matters to the men.

Elizabeth scheduled meetings with different department heads every day. Not all were hostile. Some were predatory. A beautiful girl sitting behind the president's desk was a challenge to the male ego. Their minds were easy to read: If I can fuck her, I can control her.

Like the grown-up version of the boys in Sardinia.

The men went after the wrong part of Elizabeth. They should have gone after her mind, because in the end that was where she controlled them. They underestimated her intelligence, and that was their mistake.

They miscalculated her capacity to assume authority, and that was another error.

And they misjudged her strength, and that was their greatest mistake. She was a Roffe, with the bloodline of old Samuel and her father in her, and she had their determination and spirit.

While the men around her were trying to use Elizabeth, she used them. She tapped the knowledge and the experience and the insights that they had accumulated, and she made them her own. She let the men talk, and she listened. She asked questions, and she remembered the answers.

She learned.

Every night Elizabeth took home two heavy briefcases filled with reports to be studied. Sometimes she worked until four in the morning. One evening a newspaper photographer snapped a picture of Elizabeth walking out of the building with a secretary carrying her two briefcases. The photograph appeared in the newspapers the next day. The caption read: "Working Heiress."

Elizabeth had become an international celebrity overnight. The story of a beautiful young girl inheriting a multibillion-dollar corporation and then taking command was irresistible. The press jumped at it. Elizabeth was lovely, intelligent, and down-to-earth, a combination they rarely came across in celebrities. She made herself available to them whenever possible, trying to build up the damaged image of the company, and they appreciated it. When she didn't know the answer to a reporter's question, she was not afraid to pick up a telephone and ask someone. Her cousins flew into Zurich once a week for meetings and Elizabeth spent as much time with them as possible. She saw them together, and one at a time. She talked to them and studied them, searching for a clue as to which one of them had allowed innocent people to die in an explosion, had sold secrets to competitors, and which one of them was trying to destroy Roffe and Sons. One of her cousins.

Ivo Palazzi, with his irresistible warmth and charmth.

Alec Nichols, a correct and proper gentleman, and gentle man, always helpful when Elizabeth needed him.

Charles Martel, a dominated, frightened man. And frightened men could be dangerous when cornered.

Walther Gassner. The All-German boy. Beautiful-looking and friendly on the outside. What was he like on the inside? He had married Anna, an heiress, thirteen years his senior. Had he married for love or money?

When Elizabeth was with them, she watched, and listened, and probed. She mentioned the explosion in Chile and studied their reactions, and she talked about the patents that Roffe had lost to other companies, and she discussed the impending government suits.

She learned nothing. Whoever it was, he was too clever to give himself away. He would have to be trapped. Elizabeth recalled Sam's marginal note on the report. *Trap the bastard*. She would have to find a way.

Elizabeth found herself becoming more and more fascinated by the inside operation of the pharmaceutical business.

Bad news was deliberately spread. If there was a report that a patient had died from a competitor's medication, within half an hour a dozen men were placing telephone calls all around the world. "By the way, did you happen to hear about . . . ?"

Yet on the surface all the companies appeared to be on the best of terms. The heads of some of the large firms held regular informal get-togethers, and Elizabeth was invited to one. She was the only woman present. They talked about their mutual problems.

The president of one of the large companies, a pompous, mid-

dle-aged roué, who had been following Elizabeth around all evening, said, "Government restrictions get more unreasonable every
Goddamned day. If some genius invented aspirin tomorrow, the
government would never okay it." He gave Elizabeth a superior
smile. "And do you have any idea, little lady, how long we've had
aspirin?"

Little lady replied, "Since four hundred B.C., when Hippocrates
discovered salicin in the bark of the willow tree."

He stared at her a moment, and the smile died. "Right." He
walked away.

The company heads all agreed that one of their biggest problems was the me-too firms, the copycat houses that stole the formu-
las of successful products, changed the names and rushed them
onto the market. It was costing the reputable drug firms hundreds
of millions of dollars a year.

In Italy it was not even necessary to steal it.

"Italy is one of the countries that has no patent regulations
protecting new drugs," one of the executives told Elizabeth. "For
a bribe of a few hundred thousand lire, anyone can buy the formu-
las and pirate them under another name. We spend millions of
dollars on research—they walk off with the profits."

"Is it just Italy?" Elizabeth asked.

"Italy and Spain are the worst. France and West Germany
aren't bad. England and the United States are clean."

Elizabeth looked around at all these indignant, moral men and
wondered if any of them was involved in the thefts of the patents
of Roffe and Sons.

It seemed to Elizabeth that she spent most of her time in
airplanes. She kept her passport in the top drawer of her desk. At
least once a week there was a frantic call from Cairo or Guatemala
or Tokyo, and within a few hours Elizabeth would find herself in
a plane with half a dozen members of her staff, to cope with some
emergency.

She met factory managers and their families in large cities like
Bombay, and at remote outposts like Puerto Vallarta, and gradually Roffe and Sons began to take on a new perspective. It was no
longer an impersonal mass of reports and statistics. A report
headed "Guatemala" now meant Emil Nunoz and his fat, happy

wife and their twelve children; "Copenhagen" was Nils Bjorn and the crippled mother with whom he lived; "Rio de Janeiro" was an evening spent with Alessandro Duval and his exquisite mistress.

Elizabeth kept in regular touch with Emil Joeppli. She always telephoned him on her private line, calling him at his little flat in Aussersihl in the evenings.

She was cautious even over the telephone.

"How are things going?"

"A little slower than I hoped, Miss Roffe."

"Do you need anything?"

"No. Just time. I ran into a little problem but I think it's solved now."

"Good. Call me if you need anything—anything at all."

"I will. Thank you, Miss Roffe."

Elizabeth hung up. She had an urge to push him, to tell him to hurry, for she knew that her time with the banks was running out. She desperately needed what Emil Joeppli was working on, but pressing him was not the answer, and so she kept her impatience to herself. Elizabeth knew that the experiments could not possibly be completed by the time the bank notes were due. But she had a plan. She intended to let Julius Badrutt into the secret, take him into the laboratory and let him see for himself what was happening. The banks would give them all the time they needed.

Elizabeth found herself working with Rhys Williams more and more closely, sometimes late into the night. They often worked alone, just the two of them, having dinner in her private dining room at the office, or at the elegant apartment she had taken. It was a modern condominium in Zurichberg, overlooking the Lake of Zurich, and it was large and airy and bright. Elizabeth was more aware than ever of the strong animal magnetism of Rhys, but if he felt an attraction for her, he was careful not to show it. He was always polite and friendly. *Avuncular* was the word that came into Elizabeth's mind, and somehow it had a pejorative sound. She wanted to lean on him, confide in him, and yet she knew she had to be careful. More than once she had found herself on the verge of telling Rhys about the efforts to sabotage the company, but something held her back. She was not ready to discuss it with anyone yet. Not until she knew more.

Elizabeth was gaining more confidence in herself. At a sales meeting they were discussing a new hair conditioner that was selling badly. Elizabeth had tried it, and she knew that it was superior to similar products on the market.

"We're getting heavy returns from drugstores," one of the sales executives complained. "It's just not catching on. We need more advertising."

"We're already over our advertising budget," Rhys objected. "We'll have to find a different approach."

Elizabeth said, "Take it out of the drugstores."

They all looked at her. "What?"

"It's too available." She turned to Rhys. "I think we should continue the advertising campaign, but sell it only at beauty salons. Make it exclusive, hard to get. That's the image it should have."

Rhys thought for a moment, then nodded and said, "I like it. Let's try it."

It became a big seller overnight.

Afterward, Rhys had complimented her. "You're not just another pretty face," he had said, grinning.

So he *was* beginning to notice!

Alec Nichols was alone in the club sauna when the door opened and a man walked into the steam-filled room, wearing a towel around his waist. He sat down on the wooden bench, next to Alec. "Hot as a witch's tit in here, ain't it, Sir Alec?"

Alec turned. It was Jon Swinton. "How did you get in here?"

Swinton winked. "I said you was expectin' me. He looked into Alec's eyes and asked, "You *was* expectin' me, wasn't you, Sir Alec?"

"No," Alec replied. "I told you I need more time."

"You also told us your little cousin was going to sell the stock, and you'd give us our money."

"She—she changed her mind."

"Ah, then you'd better change it back for her, hadn't you?"

"I'm trying. It's a question of—"

"It's a question of how much more horseshit we're going to take from you." Jon Swinton was moving closer, forcing Alec to slide along the bench. "We don't want to get rough with you 'cause it's nice to have a good friend like you in Parliament. You know what I mean? But there's a limit." He was leaning against Alec now, and Alec slid farther away from him. "We did you a favor. Now it's time to pay us back. You're gonna get hold of a shipment of drugs for us."

"No! That's impossible," Alec said. "I can't. There's no way—"

Alec suddenly found that he had been crowded to the end of the bench, next to the large metal container filled with hot rocks. "Be careful," Alec said. "I—"

Swinton grabbed hold of Alec's arm and twisted it, forcing it toward the bed of rocks. Alec could feel the hair on his arm begin to singe.

"No!"

The next instant his arm was pressed down onto the rocks, and he screamed with pain and fell to the floor in agony. Swinton was standing over him.

"You find a way. We'll be in touch."

Anna Roffe Gassner did not know how much longer she would be able to stand it.

She had become a prisoner in her own home. Except for the cleaning woman who came in for a few hours once a week, Anna and the children were alone, completely at Walther's mercy. He no longer bothered to conceal his hatred. Anna had been in the children's room as they listened together to one of their favorite records.

> *"Welch ein Singen, Musizieren,*
> *Pfeifen, Zwitschken, Tiriliern . . ."*

Walther had stormed in. "I'm sick of that!" he had yelled.

And he had smashed the record, while the children cowered in terror.

Anna had tried to placate him. "I—I'm sorry, Walther. I—I didn't know you were home. Can I do something for you?"

He had walked up to her, his eyes blazing, and he said, "We're going to get rid of the children, Anna."

In front of them!

He put his hands on her shoulders. "What happens in this house must be our secret." *Our secret. Our secret. Our secret.*

She could feel the words reverberating in her head, and his arms started to crush her until she could not breathe. She fainted.

When Anna woke up, she was lying in her bed. The shades were drawn. She looked at the bedside clock. Six P.M. The house was quiet. Too quiet. Her first thought was of the children, and terror swept through her. She rose from the bed on shaky legs, and stumbled over to the door. It was locked from the outside. She pressed her ear hard against the panel, listening. There should have been the sounds of the children. They should have come up to see her.

If they had been able to. If they were still alive.

Her legs were trembling so hard that she could barely walk to the telephone. She breathed a silent prayer, then picked it up. She heard the familiar dial tone. She hesitated, dreading the thought of what Walther would do to her if he caught her again. Without giving herself a chance to think, Anna began to dial 110. Her hands shook so badly that she dialed a wrong number. And another. She began to sob. There was so little time left. Fighting her growing hysteria, she tried again, willing her fingers to move slowly. She heard a ringing, then miraculously a man's voice said, *"Hier ist de Notruf der Polizei."*

Anna could not find her voice.

"Hier ist der Notruf der Polizei. Kann ich Ihnen helfen?"

"Ja!" It was a high-pitched sob. *"Ja, bitte! Ich bin in grosser Gefahr. Bitte schicken sie jeman-den—"*

Walther loomed in front of her, ripping the telephone out of her hand and hurling her against the bed. He slammed down the receiver, breathing hard, tore the cord out of the wall, and turned to Anna.

"The children," she whispered. "What have you done with the children?"

Walther did not answer.

The Central Division of the Berlin Kriminal Polizei was located at 2832 Keithstrasse in a district of ordinary-looking apartment houses and office buildings. The emergency number of the *Delikt am Mensch* department was equipped with an automatic hold system, so that a caller was unable to disconnect until the line had been electronically released by the switchboard. In this way every number calling in could be traced, no matter how brief the conversation. It was a sophisticated piece of equipment of which the department was proud.

Within five minutes of Anna Gassner's telephone call, Detective Paul Lange walked into the office of his chief, Major Wageman, carrying a cassette player.

"I would like you to listen to this." Detective Lange pressed a button. A metallic male voice said, *"Hier ist der Notruf der Polizei. Kann ich Ihnen helfen?"*

Then a woman's voice, filled with terror. *"Ja! Ja, bitte! Ich bin in grosser Gefahr. Bitte schicken sie jemanden—"*

There was the sound of a thud, a click, and the line went dead. Major Wageman looked up at Detective Lange. "You've traced the call?"

"We know whose residence it came from," Detective Lange replied carefully.

"Then what's the problem?" Major Wageman demanded impatiently. "Have Central send a car to investigate."

"I wanted your authority first." Detective Lange placed a slip of paper on the desk in front of the major.

"Scheiss!" Major Wageman stared at him. "Are you sure?"

"Yes, Major."

Major Wageman looked down at the slip of paper again. The telephone was listed in the name of Gassner, Walther. Head of the German division of Roffe and Sons, one of the industrial giants of Germany.

There was no need to discuss the implications. Only an idiot could miss them. One wrong move and they would both be walking the streets, looking for a job. Major Wageman thought for a moment and then said, "All right. Check it out. I want you to go there yourself. And walk on fucking eggs. Do you understand?"

"I understand, Major."

The Gassner estate was in Wannsee, an exclusive suburb in southwest Berlin. Detective Lange took the longer Hohenzollerndamm instead of the speedier autobahn, because the traffic was lighter. He went through the Clayalle, past the CIA building, hidden behind half a mile of barbed-wire fences. He passed the

American Army Headquarters and turned right on what was once known as Road One, the longest road in Germany, running from East Prussia to the Belgian border. On his right was the Brücke der Einheit, the Bridge of Unity, where the spy Abel had been exchanged for the American U-2 pilot Gary Powers. Detective Lange turned the car off the highway into the wooded hills of Wannsee.

The houses were beautiful, impressive. On Sundays, Detective Lange sometimes took his wife out here, just to look at the outside of the houses and the grounds.

He found the address he was looking for and turned into the long driveway leading to the Gassner estate. The estate represented something more than money: it represented power. The Roffe dynasty was big enough to make governments fall. Major Wageman had been right: he would be very careful.

Detective Lange drove to the front door of the three-story stone house, got out of the car, took off his hat and pressed the doorbell. He waited. There was the heavy hanging silence of a house that has been deserted. He knew that was impossible. He rang again. Nothing but that still, oppressive silence. He was debating whether to go around to the back when the door unexpectedly opened. A woman stood in the doorway. She was middle-aged, plain-looking, wearing a wrinkled dressing gown. Detective Lange took her for the housekeeper. He pulled out his identification. "I'd like to see Mrs. Walther Gassner. Please tell her Detective Lange."

"I am Mrs. Gassner," the woman said.

Detective Lange tried to conceal his surprise. She was totally unlike his image of the lady of this house.

"I—we received a telephone call at police headquarters a short time ago," he began.

She watched him, her face blank, disinterested. Detective Lange felt that he was handling this badly, but he did not know why. He had a feeling that he was missing something important.

"Did you make that call, Mrs. Gassner?" he asked.

"Yes," she answered. "It was a mistake."

There was a dead, remote quality to her voice that was disturbing. He remembered the shrill, hysterical voice on the tape recorder half an hour earlier.

"Just for our records, may I ask what kind of mistake?"

Her hesitation was barely perceptible. "There was—I thought that a piece of my jewelry was missing. I found it."

The emergency number was for murder, rape, mayhem. *Walk on fucking eggs.*

"I see." Detective Lange hesitated, wanting to get inside the house, wanting to find out what she was covering up. But there was nothing more he could say or do. "Thank you, Mrs. Gassner. I'm sorry to have troubled you."

He stood there, frustrated, and watched the door close in his face. He slowly got into his car and drove off.

Behind the door Anna turned.

Walther nodded and said softly, "You did very well, Anna. Now we're going back upstairs."

He turned toward the stairway, and Anna pulled out a pair of shears that had been concealed in the folds of her dressing gown and plunged them into his back.

Rome.
Sunday, November 4.
Noon.

It was a perfect day, Ivo Palazzi thought, for visiting the Villa d'Este with Simonetta and their three beautiful daughters. As Ivo strolled through the fabled Tivoli Gardens arm in arm with his wife, watching the girls race ahead from fountain to splashing fountain, he idly wondered whether Pirro Ligorio, who had built the park for his patrons, the D'Este family, had ever dreamed how much joy he would one day give to millions of sightseers. The Villa d'Este was a short distance northeast of Rome, nestled high in the Sabine Hills. Ivo had been there often, but it always gave him a feeling of special pleasure to stand at the very top level and look down on the dozens of sparkling fountains below, each one cunningly designed, each one different from the others.

In the past Ivo had taken Donatella and his three sons here. How they had adored it! The thought of them made Ivo sad. He had not seen or talked to Donatella since that horrifying afternoon at the apartment. He still remembered vividly the terrible scratches she had inflicted on him. He knew what remorse she must be going through, and how she must be longing for him. Well, it would do her good to suffer for a while, as he had suffered. In his mind he could hear Donatella's voice, and she was saying, "Come along. This way, boys."

It was so clear it seemed almost real. He could hear her say, "Faster, Francesco!" And Ivo turned and Donatella was in back of him, with their three boys, moving determinedly toward him and Simonetta and the three girls. Ivo's first thought was that Donatella had happened to be here at the Tivoli Gardens by coincidence, but the instant he saw the expression on her face, he knew better. The *putana* was trying to bring his two families together, trying to destroy him! Ivo rose to the occasion like a madman.

He shouted to Simonetta, "There's something I must show you. Quickly, everybody."

And he swept his family down the long winding stone steps toward a lower level, pushing tourists aside, casting frantic glances over his shoulder. Above, Donatella and the boys were moving toward the steps. Ivo knew that if the boys saw him, everything was lost. All it needed was for one of them to shout "Papa!" and he might as well drown himself in the fountains. He hurried Simonetta and the girls along, not giving them a chance to pause, not daring to let them stop for an instant.

"Where are we rushing to?" Simonetta gasped. "What's the hurry?"

"It's a surprise," Ivo said gaily. "You'll see."

He risked another quick glance back. Donatella and the three boys were out of sight for the moment. Ahead was a labyrinth, with one set of stairs leading up and another leading down. Ivo chose the stairs going up.

"Come along," he called to the girls. "Whoever gets to the top first gets a prize!"

"Ivo! I'm exhausted!" Simonetta complained. "Can't we rest a minute?"

He looked at her in shock. *"Rest?* That would spoil the surprise. Hurry!"

He took Simonetta's arm and dragged her up the steep steps, his three daughters racing ahead of them. Ivo found himself gasping for breath. It would serve them all right, he thought bitterly, if I have a heart attack and die right here. Goddamn women! You can't trust any of them. How could she do this to me? She adores me. I'll kill the bitch for this.

He could visualize himself strangling Donatella in her bed. She was wearing nothing by a flimsy negligée. He ripped it off and began to mount her, while she screamed for mercy. Ivo could feel himself getting an erection.

"Can we stop now?" Simonetta begged.

"No! We're almost there!"

They had reached the upper level again. Ivo took a hasty look around. Donatella and the boys were nowhere in sight.

"Where are you taking us?" Simonetta demanded.

"You'll see," Ivo said hysterically. "Follow me!" He shoved them toward the exit.

Isabella, the oldest girl, said, "Are we leaving, Papa? We just got here!"

"We're going to a better place," Ivo panted. He glanced back. Coming into sight, climbing the stairs, were Donatella and the boys.

"Faster, girls!"

A moment later Ivo and one of his families were outside the gates of the Villa d'Este, racing toward their car on the large square.

"I've never seen you like this," Simonetta gasped.

"I've never been like this," Ivo said truthfully. He had the motor going before the car doors were closed, and he raced out of the parking lot like the devil was pursuing him.

"Ivo!"

He patted Simonetta's hand. "I want everybody to relax now. As a special treat I'm—I'm taking you to lunch at the Hassler."

They sat at a picture window overlooking the Spanish Steps, with Saint Peter's looming gloriously in the distance.

Simonetta and the children had a marvelous time. The food was delicious. Ivo could have been eating cardboard. His hands were trembling so badly that he could hardly hold his knife and fork. I can't stand much more of this, he thought. I'm not going to let her ruin my life.

For he had no doubt now that that was exactly what Donatello intended to do. *Il giuoco è stato fatto.* The game was up. Unless he could find a way to give Donatella the money she was demanding.

He had to get it. It did not matter how.

The instant Charles Martel arrived home he knew he was in trouble. Hélène was waiting for him, and with her was Pierre Richaud, the jeweler who had made the replicas of her stolen jewelry. Charles stood in the doorway, in shock.

"Come in, Charles," Hélène said. There was an undercurrent in her voice that terrified him. "I believe that you and M. Richard know each other."

Charles stared, knowing that whatever he said would hang him. The jeweler was studying the floor in embarrassment, obviously ill at ease.

"Sit down, Charles." It was a command. Charles sat down.

Hélène said, "What you're facing, *mon cher mari*, is a criminal charge of grand theft. You have been stealing my jewelry and replacing the pieces with clumsy imitation paste, made by M. Richaud."

To his horror Charles found himself wetting his pants, a thing he had not done since he was a small boy. He blushed. He wished desperately that he could leave the room for a moment to clean himself. No, he wanted to flee and never return.

Hélène knew everything. It did not matter how she had found him out. There would be no escape and no mercy. It was terrifying enough that Hélène had discovered he had been stealing from her. Wait until she learned his motive! Wait until she found out that he had been planning to use the money to run away from her! Hell was going to have a new meaning. No one knew Hélène as Charles did. She was *une sauvage,* capable of anything. She would destroy him, without a moment's thought, turn him into a *clochard,* one of those sad bums who sleep on the streets of Paris in rags. His life had suddenly turned into an *emmerdement,* a shower of shit.

"Did you really think you could get away with anything so stupid!" Hélène was asking.

Charles remained miserably silent. He could feel his pants getting wetter, but he did not dare look down.

"I have persuaded M. Richaud to give me all the facts."

Persuaded. Charles dreaded to think how.

"I have photostatic copies of the receipts for the money you stole from me. I can put you in prison for the next twenty years." She paused, and added, "If I choose to."

Her words only served to increase Charles's panic. Experience had taught him that a generous Hélène was a dangerous Hélène. Charles was afraid to meet her glance. He wondered what it was she would demand from him. Something monstrous.

Hélène turned to Pierre Richaud. "You will say nothing of this to anyone until I have made up my mind what I wish to do."

"Of course, Mme. Roffe-Martel, of course, of course." The man was babbling. He looked hopefully toward the door. "May I—?"

Hélène nodded, and Pierre Richaud scurried out.

Hélène watched him go, then swung around to study her husband. She could smell his fear. And something else. Urine. She smiled. Charles had pissed himself out of fear. She had taught him well. Hélène was pleased with Charles. It was a very satisfying marriage. She had broken Charles, then made him her creature. The innovations he had brought to Roffe and Sons were brilliant, for they had all come from Hélène. She ruled a small part of Roffe and Sons through her husband, but now it was not enough. She was a Roffe. She was wealthy in her own right; her earlier marriages had made her even wealthier. But it was not money she was interested in. It was the control of the company. She had planned to use her stock to acquire more stock, to buy up the interest of the others. She had already discussed it with them. They were willing to go along with her, to form a minority group. First, Sam had stood in the way of her plan, and now Elizabeth. But Hélène had no intention of allowing Elizabeth or anyone else to keep her from getting what she wanted. Charles was going to get it for her. If anything went wrong, he would be her scapegoat.

Now, of course, he must be punished for his *petite révolte*. She watched his face and said, "No one steals from me, Charles. No one. You're finished. Unless I decide to save you."

He sat there, silent, wishing her dead, terrified of her. She walked over to where he sat, her thighs brushing against his face.

She said, "Would you like me to save you, Charles?"

"Yes," he said hoarsely. She was stepping out of her skirt, her eyes vicious, and he thought, *Oh, my God! Not now!*

"Then listen to me. Roffe and Sons is my company. I want the controlling interest."

He looked up at her miserably and said, "You know Elizabeth won't sell."

Hélène slipped out of her blouse and pants. She stood there, animal naked, her body lean and magnificent, her nipples hard. "Then you must do something about her. Or spend the next twenty years of your life in prison. Don't worry. I'll tell you what you will do. But first, come here, Charles."

The following morning, at ten o'clock, Elizabeth's private phone rang. It was Emil Joeppli. She had given him the number so that no one would be aware of their conversations. "I wonder if I could see you," he said. He sounded excited.

"I'll be there in fifteen minutes."

Kate Erling looked up in surprise as Elizabeth came out of her office wearing a coat. "You have an appointment at—"

"Cancel everything for the next hour," Elizabeth said, and walked out.

In the Development Building an armed guard examined Elizabeth's pass. "Last door to the left, Miss Roffe."

Elizabeth found Joeppli alone in his laboratory. He greeted her with enthusiasm.

"I finished the final tests last night. It works. The enzymes completely inhibit the aging process. Look."

He led her to a cage holding four young rabbits, alert and filled with restless vitality. Next to it was another cage containing four more rabbits, quieter, more mature.

"This is the five hundredth generation to receive the enzyme," Joeppli said.

Elizabeth stood in front of the cage. "They look healthy."

Joeppli smiled. *"That's* part of the control group." He pointed to the cage on the left. *"Those* are the senior citizens."

Elizabeth stared at the energetic rabbits, frisking around in the cage like newborn bunnies, and she could not believe it.

"They'll outlive the others by at least three to one," Joeppli told her.

When you applied that ratio to human beings, the implications were staggering. She could barely contain her excitement.

"When—when will you be ready to start testing it on people?"

"I'm getting my final notes together. After that, another three or four weeks at the most."

"Emil, don't discuss this with anyone," Elizabeth warned.

Emil Joeppli nodded. "I won't, Miss Roffe. I'm working alone. I'm being very careful."

The entire afternoon had been taken up with a board meeting, and it had gone well. Walther had not appeared. Charles had again brought up the subject of selling the stock, but Elizabeth had firmly vetoed it. After that, Ivo had been his charming self, as had Alec. Charles seemed unusually tense. Elizabeth wished she knew why.

She invited them all to stay in Zurich and have dinner with her. As casually as possible, Elizabeth brought up the problems that had been mentioned in the report, watching for a reaction of some kind, but she could detect no sign of nervousness or guilt. And everyone who could have been involved, except for Walther, was seated at that table.

Rhys had not attended the meeting or the dinner. "I have some urgent business to take care of," he had said, and Elizabeth had wondered if it was a girl. Elizabeth was aware that whenever Rhys stayed late at night to work with her, he had had to cancel a date. Once, when he had been unable to reach the girl in time, she had appeared at the office. She was a stunning redhead, with a figure that made Elizabeth feel like a boy. The girl had been furious at being stood up, and she had not bothered to hide her displeasure. Rhys had escorted her to the elevator and returned.

"Sorry about that," he had said.

Elizabeth could not help herself. "She's charming," she said sweetly. "What does she do?"

"She's a brain surgeon," Rhys had replied earnestly, and Elizabeth had laughed. The following day Elizabeth had learned that the girl *was* a brain surgeon.

There were others, and Elizabeth found herself resenting all of them. She wished that she understood Rhys better. She knew the gregarious and public Rhys Williams; she wanted to meet the private Rhys Williams, the self he kept hidden. More than once, Elizabeth had thought, *Rhys should be running this company instead of taking orders from me. I wonder how he really feels about it?*

That evening after dinner, when the members of the board had dispersed to catch trains and planes back to their homes, Rhys walked into Elizabeth's office where she was working with Kate. "Thought I ought to give you a hand," Rhys said lightly.

No explanation of where he had been. *Why should there be?* Elizabeth thought. *He doesn't have to account to me.*

They all set to work and the time flew. Elizabeth watched Rhys now, bent over some papers, rapidly scanning them, his eyes quick and alert. He had found several flaws in some important contracts, that the attorneys had missed. Now Rhys straightened up, stretched and glanced at his watch.

"Oops! It's after midnight. I'm afraid I have an appointment. I'll come in early tomorrow and finish checking these agreements."

Elizabeth wondered if his appointment was with the brain surgeon or with one of his other— She stopped herself. What Rhys Williams did with his private life was his own business.

"I'm sorry," Elizabeth said. "I didn't realize it was so late. You run along. Kate and I will finish reading these papers."

Rhys nodded. "See you in the morning. Good night, Kate."

"Good night, Mr. Williams."

Elizabeth watched Rhys leave, then forced her mind back to the contracts. But a moment later her thoughts were on Rhys again. She had been eager to tell him about the progress that Emil Joeppli was making on the new drug, to share it with him, yet she had held back. *Soon,* she told herself.

By one o'clock in the morning, they were finished.

Kate Erling said, "Will there be anything else, Miss Roffe?"

"No, I think that's all. Thank you, Kate. Come in late tomorrow."

Elizabeth stood up, and realized how stiff her body felt from sitting so long.

"Thank you. I'll have everything typed up for you tomorrow afternoon."

"That will be fine."

Elizabeth got her coat and purse, waited for Kate, and they walked to the door. They went out into the corridor together and headed toward the private express elevator that stood there, door open, waiting. The two of them stepped inside the elevator. As Elizabeth reached for the lobby button, they heard the sudden ringing of the telephone from the office.

"I'll answer it, Miss Roffe," Kate Erling said. "You go on ahead." She stepped out of the car.

Downstairs the night guard on duty in the lobby looked up at the elevator control board as a red light at the top of the board flashed on and began descending. It was the signal light for the private elevator. That meant Miss Roffe was on her way down. Her chauffeur was sitting in a chair in a corner, drowsing over a newspaper.

"The boss is coming," the guard said.

The chauffeur stretched, and started lazily to his feet.

An alarm bell suddenly shattered the peace of the lobby. The guard's eyes flashed to the control board. The red light was moving in a quick plunging pattern, gathering speed, marking the descent of the elevator.

It was out of control.

"Oh, Jesus!" the guard mumbled.

He hurried to the board, jerked open a panel and pulled the emergency switch to activate the safety brake. The red light continued its downward plunge. The chauffeur had hurried over to the control panel. He saw the look on the guard's face.

"What's going—?"

"Get away!" the guard yelled. "It's going to crash!"

They ran from the bank of elevators toward the farthest wall. The lobby was beginning to vibrate with the speed of the runaway car inside the shaft, and the guard thought, *Don't let her be in it,* and as the plunging elevator shot past the lobby, he heard the terrified screams from inside.

An instant later, there was a loud roar, and the building shuddered as thought it had been hit by an earthquake.

C hief Inspector Otto Schmied of the Zurich Kriminal Polizei was seated at his desk, eyes closed, taking deep yoga breaths, trying to calm himself, trying to control the fury that filled him.

In police procedure there were rules that were so basic, so obvious, that no one had thought it even necessary to put them in the police manual. They were simply taken for granted, like eating, or sleeping, or breathing. For example, when an accident-related fatality occurred, the first thing the investigating detective did—the *very* first thing a detective did, the simple, obvious, you-don't-have-to-draw-it-on-a-fucking-blackboard thing he did—was to visit the scene of the accident. Nothing could be more elementary than that. Yet staring up at Chief Inspector Otto Schmied from his desk was a report from Detective Max Hornung that violated every element of police procedure. I should have expected it, the inspector told himself bitterly. Why am I even surprised?

Detective Hornung was Inspector Schmied's albatross, his bête noire, his—Inspector Schmied was an ardent admirer of Melville—his Moby Dick. The inspector took another deep breath and slowly exhaled. Then, only slightly less agitated, he picked up Detective Hornung's report and read it again from the beginning.

I began an immediate investigation. By 1:35 A.M. I obtained the name of the superintendent of the Roffe and Sons administration building and from him got the name of the chief architect of the building.

Wednesday, November 7

TIME:	1:15 A.M.
SUBJECT:	Report from central switchboard of accident at Roffe and Sons administration building at Eichenbahn factory
TYPE OF ACCIDENT:	Unknown
CAUSE OF ACCIDENT:	Unknown
NUMBER OF INJURED OR DECEASED:	Unknown
TIME:	1:27 A.M.
SUBJECT:	Second message from central switchboard re accident at Roffe and Sons
TYPE OF ACCIDENT:	Elevator crash
CAUSE OF ACCIDENT:	Unknown
NUMBER OF INJURED OR DECEASED:	One female, deceased

2:30 A.M. I located the chief architect. He was celebrating his birthday at La Puce. He gave me the name of the company that had installed the elevators in the building, Rudolf Schatz, A. G.

At 3:15 A.M. I telephoned Mr. Rudolf Schatz at his home and requested him to immediately locate the plans for the elevators. I also requested the master budget sheets along with preliminary estimates, final estimates and final costs; I also requested a complete inventory of all mechanical and electrical materials used.

At this point Inspector Schmied could feel a familiar twitch starting in his right cheek. He took several deep breaths and read on.

6:15 A.M. The requested documents were delivered to me here at police headquarters by Mr. Schatz's wife. After an

213

examination of the preliminary budget and final costs I was satisfied that:

a) no inferior materials were substituted in building the elevators;

b) because of the reputation of the builders, inferior workmanship could be ruled out as a cause of the crash;

c) the safety measures built into the elevators were adequate;

d) my conclusion therefore was that the cause of the crash was not an accident. [Signed] *Max Hornung, CID*

N.B. Since my phone calls took place during the course of the night and early morning, it is possible that you may receive one or two complaints from some of the people I might have awakened.

Inspector Schmied savagely slammed the report down on his desk. "It is possible!" "Might have awakened!" The chief inspector had been under attack the entire morning by half of the officials of the Swiss government. What did he think he was running—a gestapo? How dare he awaken the president of a respectable building corporation and order him to deliver documents in the middle of the night? How dare he impugn the integrity of a reputable firm like Rudolf Schatz? And on and on and on.

But the thing that was so stunning—that was so incredible—was that Detective Max Hornung had not even *appeared* at the scene of the accident until *fourteen hours* after it was reported! By the time he arrived the victim had been removed, identified and autopsied. Half a dozen other detectives had examined the scene of the accident, had questioned witnesses and had filed their reports.

When Chief Inspector Schmied finished rereading Detective Max Hornung's report, he summoned him to his office.

The very sight of Detective Max Hornung was anathema to the chief inspector. Max Hornung was a dumpy, wistful-looking man, egg-bald, with a face that had been put together by an absent-minded prankster. His head was too large, his ears were too small, and his mouth was a raisin stuck in the middle of a pudding face. Detective Max Hornung was six inches too short to meet the rigid standards of the Zurich Kriminal Polizei, fifteen pounds too light, and hopelessly nearsighted. To top it all off, he was arrogant. All the men on the force felt unanimously about Detective Hornung: they hated him.

"Why don't you fire him?" the chief inspector's wife had asked, and he had almost struck her.

The reason that Max Hornung was on the Zurich detective force was that he had single-handedly contributed more to the Swiss national income than all the chocolate and watch factories combined. Max Hornung was an accountant, a mathematical genius with an encyclopedic knowledge of fiscal matters, an instinct for the chicanery of man, and a patience that would have made Job weep with envy. Max had been a clerk in the Betrug Abteilung, the department set up to investigate financial frauds, irregularities in stock sales and banking transactions, and the ebb and flow of currency in and out of Switzerland. It was Max Hornung who had brought the smuggling of illegal money into Switzerland to a standstill, who had ferreted out billions of dollars' worth of ingenious but illicit financial schemes, and who had put half a dozen of the world's most respected business leaders in prison. No matter how cunningly assets were concealed, mingled, remingled, sent to the Seychelles to be laundered, transferred and retransferred through a complex series of dummy corporations, in the end Max Hornung would ferret out the truth. In short, he had made himself the terror of the Swiss financial community.

Above all things that they held sacred and dear, the Swiss valued their privacy. With Max Hornung on the loose, there was no privacy.

Max's salary as a financial watchdog was meager. He had been offered bribes of a million francs in numbered bank accounts, a chalet at Cortina d'Ampezzo, a yacht, and in half a dozen instances beautiful, nubile women. In each case the bribe had been rejected and the authorities promptly notified. Max Hornung cared nothing for money. He could have become a millionaire simply by applying his financial skills to the stock market, but the idea never even occurred to him. Max Hornung was interested in but one thing: catching those who strayed from the path of financial probity. Ah, yes, there was one other wish that consumed Max Hornung, and in the end it proved to be a blessing to the business community.

For reasons which no one could fathom, Max Hornung wanted to be a police detective. He envisioned himself as a kind of Sherlock Holmes or Maigret, patiently following a labyrinth of clues, relentlessly stalking the criminal to his lair. When one of Switzerland's leading financiers accidentally learned of Max Hornung's ambitions to be a sleuth, he immediately got together with a few powerful friends, and within forty-eight hours Max Hornung was offered a job on the Zurich police force as a detective. Max could not believe his good fortune. He accepted with alacrity, and the entire business community breathed a collective sigh of relief and resumed its arcane activities.

Chief Inspector Schmied had not even been consulted about the matter. He had received a telephone call from the most powerful political leader in Switzerland, had been given his instructions, and there the matter had ended. Or, to be more accurate, there it had begun. For the chief inspector, it was the beginning of a Gethsemane that showed no sign of ending. He had honestly tried to get over his resentment at having a detective—an inexperienced and unqualified one at that—forced upon him. He assumed that there had to be some strong political motivation for such an unheard-of move. Very well, he was determined to cooperate, confident that he could handle the situation easily. His confidence was shaken the moment Max Hornung reported to him. The detective's appearance was ridiculous enough. But what stunned Inspector Schmied as he looked at this lump of humanity was the man's attitude of superiority. He exuded an air that said: Max Hornung is here—now you can all relax and stop worrying.

Inspector Schmied's thoughts of any easy cooperation vanished. Instead he devised another approach. He tried to sweep Max Hornung under the rug, as it were, by transferring him from department to department, assigning him unimportant jobs. Max worked in the Kriminal-Tech Abteilung, the fingerprint-and-identification division, and the Fahn-dungsabteilung, the division for stolen property and missing persons. But always Max Hornung kept returning, like a bad centime.

There was a rule that every detective had to work as *Brandtour Offizier*, on the night emergency desk, one week out of every twelve. Without fail, each time Max was on duty, something important would occur, and while Inspector Schmied's other detectives ran around trying to track down clues, Max would solve the case. It was infuriating.

He knew absolutely nothing about police procedure, criminology, forensics, ballistics, or criminal psychology—all the things that the other detectives were experienced in—and yet he kept solving cases that baffled everyone else. Chief Inspector Schmied came to the conclusion that Max Hornung was the luckiest man who ever lived.

In reality, luck had nothing to do with it. Detective Max Hornung solved criminal cases in exactly the same way that accountant Max Hornung had exposed a hundred ingenious schemes to defraud banks and the government. Max Hornung had a single-track mind, and it was a very narrow-gauge track at that. All he needed was one loose thread, one tiny piece that did not fit into the rest of the fabric, and once he had that he would begin to unravel it, until somebody's brilliant, foolproof scheme fell apart at the seams.

The fact that Max had a photographic memory drove his colleagues crazy. Max could instantly recall anything he had ever heard, read or seen.

Another mark against him, if indeed one was needed, was that his expense accounts were an embarrassment to the entire detective squadron. The first time he had turned in an expense sheet, the *Oberleutnant* had summoned him to his office and said genially, "You've obviously made a mistake in your figures here, Max."

The equivalent of informing Capablanca that he had sacrificed his queen through stupidity.

Max blinked. "A mistake in my figures?"

"Yes. Several, in fact." The *Oberleutnant* pointed to the paper in front of him. "Transportation across town, eighty centimes. Return, eighty centimes." He looked up and said, "The maximum taxi fare would be thirty-four francs each way."

"Yes, sir. That's why I used the bus."

The *Oberleutnant* stared at him. "A *bus?*"

None of the detectives was required to ride buses while on a case. It was unheard of. The only reply he could think of was "Well, it's—it's not necessary. I mean—we naturally don't encourage spendthrifts in this department, Hornung, but we do have a decent expense budget. Another thing. You were out in the field on this case for three days. You forgot to include meals."

"No, Herr Oberleutnant. I only take coffee in the morning and I prepare my own lunches and carry a lunch pail. My dinners are listed there."

And so they were. Three dinners, total: sixteen francs. He must have eaten at the Salvation Army kitchen.

The *Oberleutnant* said coldly, "Detective Hornung, this department existed for a hundred years before you joined it, and it will exist for a hundred years after you leave it. There are certain traditions that we observe here." He shoved the expense account back to Max. "You must think about your colleagues, you know. Now take this, revise it, and return it."

"Yes, Herr Oberleutnant. I—I'm sorry if I did it incorrectly."

A generous wave of the hand. "Quite all right. After all, you're new here."

Thirty minutes later Detective Max Hornung turned in his revised account. He had decreased his expenses by another 3 percent.

Now, on this day in November, Chief Inspector Schmied was holding Detective Max Hornung's report in his hand while the author of the report stood before him. Detective Hornung was wearing a bright-blue suit, brown shoes and white socks. In spite of his resolves, and the calming yoga breathing exercises, Inspector Schmied found himself yelling. "You were in charge here when that report came in. It was *your* job to investigate the accident and you arrived on the scene *fourteen hours later!* The whole fucking New Zealand police force could have been flown here and been back home in that time."

"Oh, no, sir. The flying time from New Zealand to Zurich by jet is—"

"Oh, shut up!"

Chief Inspector Schmied ran his hands through his thick, rapidly graying hair, trying to think what to say to this man. You could not insult him, you could not reason with him. He was an idiot, shot with luck.

Chief Inspector Schmied barked, "I will not tolerate incompetence in my department, Hornung. When the other detectives came on duty and saw the report, they immediately went to the scene to inspect the accident. They called an ambulance, had the body taken to the morgue, identified it—" He knew he was talking too fast again, and he forced himself to calm down. "In short, Hornung, they did everything a good detective is supposed to do. While you were sitting in your office waking up half of the most important men in Switzerland, in the middle of the night."

"I thought—"

"Don't! I've been on the phone apologizing the whole damned morning because of you."

"I had to find out—"

"Oh, get out of here Hornung!"

"Yes, sir. Is it all right if I attend the funeral? It's this morning."

"Yes! Go!"

"Thank you, sir. I—"

"Just go!"

It was thirty minutes before Chief Inspector Schmied was breathing normally again.

32

The funeral parlor at Sihlfeld was crowded. It was an ornate, old-fashioned building of stone and marble, with preparation rooms and a crematorium. Inside the large chapel two dozen executives and employees of Roffe and Sons occupied the front row of seats. Toward the rear were the friends, the community representatives and the press. Detective Hornung was seated in the last row, thinking that death was illogical. Man reached his prime and then, when he had the most to give, the most to live for, he died. It was inefficient.

The casket was mahogany and covered with flowers. More waste, Detective Hornung thought. The casket had been ordered sealed. Max could understand why. The minister was speaking in a doomsday voice, ". . . death in the midst of life, born in sin, ashes to ashes." Max Hornung paid little attention. He was studying those in the chapel.

"The Lord giveth, and the Lord taketh away," and people were beginning to stand and head for the exit. The services were over.

Max stood near the door, and as a man and a woman approached him, he stepped in front of the woman and said, "Miss Elizabeth Roffe? I wonder if I might have a word with you?"

Detective Max Hornung was seated with Elizabeth Roffe and Rhys Williams in a booth at a *Konditorei* across from the funeral parlor. Through the window they could see the coffin being loaded into a gray hearse. Elizabeth looked away. Her eyes were haunted.

"What's this all about?" Rhys demanded. "Miss Roffe has already given her statement to the police."

Detective Max Hornung said, "Mr. Williams, isn't it? There are just a few little details I want to check out."

"Can't they wait? Miss Roffe has been through a very trying—"

Elizabeth put her hand on Rhys's. "It's all right. If I can be of any help—" She turned to Max. "What would you like to know, Detective Hornung?"

Max stared at Elizabeth, and for the first time in his life he was at a loss for words. Women were as foreign to Max as creatures from an alien planet. They were illogical and unpredictable, subject to emotional reactions rather than rational ones. They did not compute. Max had few sexual stirrings, for he was mind-oriented, but he could appreciate the precise logic of sex. It was the mechanical construction of moving parts fitting together into a coordinated, functioning whole that excited him. That, for Max, was the poetry of loving. The sheer dynamics of it. Max felt that the poets had all missed the point. Emotions were imprecise and untidy, a waste of energy that could not move the smallest grain of sand one inch, while logic could move the world. What was puzzling Max now was that he felt comfortable with Elizabeth. It made him uneasy. No woman had ever affected him that way before. She did not seem to think he was an ugly, ridiculous little man, the way other women did. He forced himself to look away from her eyes so that he could concentrate.

"Were you in the habit of working late at night, Miss Roffe?"

"Very often," Elizabeth said. "Yes."

"How late?"

"It varied. Sometimes until ten. Sometimes until midnight, or after."

"So it was a kind of pattern? That is, people around you would have known about it?"

She was studying him, puzzled. "I suppose so."

"On the night the elevator crashed, you and Mr. Williams and Kate Erling were all working late?"

"Yes."

"But you didn't leave together?"

Rhys said, "I left early. I had an engagement."

Max regarded him a moment, then turned back to Elizabeth. "How long after Mr. Williams left did you leave?"

"I think it was about an hour."

"Did you and Kate Erling leave together?"

"Yes. We got our coats and went out into the hall." Elizabeth's voice faltered. "The—the elevator was there, waiting for us."

The special express elevator.

"What happened then?"

"We both got in. The telephone in the office rang. Kate—Miss Erling—said, 'I'll get it,' and she started to get out. But I was expecting an overseas call I had placed earlier, so I told her I would answer it." Elizabeth stopped, her eyes suddenly brimming with tears. "I got out of the elevator. She asked if she should wait, and I said, 'No, go ahead.' She pressed the lobby button. I started back to the office, and as I was opening the door, I heard—I heard the screaming, then—" She was unable to go on.

Rhys turned to Max Hornung, his face clouded with anger. "That's enough. Will you tell us what this is all about?"

It was about murder, Max thought. Someone had tried to kill Elizabeth Roffe. Max sat there concentrating, recalling everything he had learned in the past forty-eight hours about Roffe and Sons. It was a deeply plagued company, forced to pay astronomical damages in lawsuits, swamped by bad publicity, losing customers, owing enormous sums of money to banks that had grown impatient. A company ripe for a change. Its president, Sam Roffe, who had held the controlling vote, had died. An expert mountain climber who had been killed in a climbing accident. The controlling stock had gone to his daughter, Elizabeth, who had almost died in a Jeep accident in Sardinia, and had narrowly missed being killed in an elevator that had passed a recent inspection. Someone was playing deadly games.

Detective Max Hornung should have been a happy man. He had found a loose thread. But now he had met Elizabeth Roffe, and she was no longer simply a name, an equation in a mathematical puzzle. There was something very special about her. Max felt an urge to shield her, to protect her.

Rhys said, "I asked what this—"

Max looked at him and said vaguely, "Er—police procedure, Mr. Williams. Just routine." He rose. "Excuse me."

He had some urgent work to do.

33

C hief Inspector Schmied had had a full morning. There had
been a political demonstration in front of Iberia Air Lines,
three men detained for questioning. A fire of suspicious
origin at a paper factory in Brunau. It was being investigated. A
girl had been raped in Platzspitz Park. A smash-and-grab job at
Guebelin and another at Grima, next to the Baur-au-Lac. And if
that weren't enough, Detective Max Hornung was back, filled with
some kind of nonsensical theory. Chief Inspector Schmied found
himself starting to hyperventilate again.

"The elevator cable drum was cracked," Max was saying.
"When it collapsed, all the safety controls went out. Someone—"

"I saw the reports, Hornung. Normal wear and tear."

"No, Chief Inspector. I examined the specifications for the
cable drum. It should have lasted another five or six years."

Chief Inspector Schmied felt the tic in his cheek. "What are you
trying to say?"

"Someone tampered with the elevator."

Not, I think someone tampered with the elevator, or, In my
opinion someone tampered with the elevator. Oh, no! Someone
tampered with the elevator.

"Why would they do that?"

"That's what I would like to find out."

"You want to go back to Roffe and Sons?"

Detective Max Hornung looked at Inspector Schmied in genuine surprise. "No, sir. I want to go to Chamonix."

The town of Chamonix lies forty miles southeast of Geneva, 3,400 feet above sea level in the French department of Haute-Savoie, between the Mont Blanc massif and the Aiguille Rouge range, with one of the most breathtaking vistas in the world.

Detective Max Hornung was completely unaware of the scenery as he debouched from the train at the Chamonix station, carrying a battered cardboard suitcase. He waved a taxi away and headed on foot for the local police station, a small building situated on the main square in the center of town. Max entered, feeling instantly at home, reveling in the warm camaraderie that he shared with the fraternity of policemen all over the world. He was one of *them*.

The French sergeant behind the desk looked up and asked, *"On vous pourrait aider?"*

"Oui." Max beamed. And he started to talk. Max approached all foreign languages in the same fashion: he slashed his way through the impenetrable thicket of irregular verbs and tenses and participles, using his tongue like a machete. As he spoke, the expression on the desk sergeant's face changed from puzzlement to disbelief. It had taken the French people hundreds of years to develop their tongues and soft palates and larynxes to form the glorious music that was the French language. And now this man standing before him was somehow managing to turn it into a series of horrible, incomprehensible noises.

The desk sergeant could bear no more. He interrupted. "What—what are you trying to *say?*"

Max replied, "What do you mean? I'm speaking French."

The desk sergeant leaned forward and asked with unabashed curiosity, "Are you speaking it *now?*"

The fool doesn't even speak his own language, Max thought. He pulled out his warrant card and handed it to the sergeant. The sergeant read it through twice, looked up to study Max, and then read it again. It was impossible to believe that the man standing before him was a detective.

Reluctantly he handed the identification back to Max. "What can I do for you?"

"I'm investigating a climbing accident that happened here two months ago. The victim's name was Sam Roffe."

The sergeant nodded. "Yes, I remember."

"I would like to talk to someone who can give me some information about what happened."

224

"That would be the mountain-rescue organization. It is called the Société Chamoniarde de Secours en Montagne. You will find it in Place du Mont Blanc. The telephone number is five-three-one-six-eight-nine. Or they might have some information at the clinic. That's in Rue du Valais. The telephone number there is five-three-zero-one-eight-two. Here. I'll write all this down for you." He reached for a pen.

"That won't be necessary," Max said. "Société Chamoniarde de Secours en Montagne, Place du Mont Blanc, five-three-one-six-eight-nine. Or the clinic in Rue du Valais, five-three-zero-one-eight-two."

The sergeant was still staring, long after Max had disappeared through the door.

The Société Chamoniarde de Secours was in the charge of a dark, athletic-looking young man seated behind a battered pine desk. He looked up as Max walked in, and his instant thought was that he hoped this odd-looking visitor did not plan to climb a mountain.

"Can I help you?"

"Detective Max Hornung." He showed his warrant card.

"What can I do for you, Detective Hornung?"

"I am investigating the death of a man named Sam Roffe," Max said.

The man behind the desk sighed. "Ah, yes. I liked Mr. Roffe very much. It was an unfortunate accident."

"Did you see it happen?"

A shake of the head. "No. I took my rescue team up as soon as we received their distress signal, but there was nothing we could do. Mr. Roffe's body had fallen into a crevasse. It will never be found."

"How did it happen?"

"There were four climbers in the party. The guide and Mr. Roffe were last. As I understand it, they were traversing an icy moraine. Mr. Roffe slipped and fell."

"Wasn't he wearing a harness?"

"Of course. His rope broke."

"Does a thing like that happen often?"

"Only once." He smiled at his little joke, then saw the detective's look and added quickly, "Experienced climbers always

225

check their equipment thoroughly, but accidents still happen."

Max stood there a moment, thinking. "I'd like to speak to the guide."

"Mr. Roffe's regular guide didn't make the climb that day."

Max blinked, "Oh? Why not?"

"As I recall, he was ill. Another guide took his place."

"Do you have his name?"

"If you'll wait a minute, I can look it up for you."

The man disappeared into an inner office. In a few minutes he returned with a slip of paper in his hand. "The guide's name was Hans Bergmann."

"Where can I find him?"

"He's not a local." He consulted the piece of paper. "He comes from a village called Lesgets. It's about sixty kilometers from here."

Before Max left Chamonix, he stopped at the desk of the Kleine Scheidegg hotel and talked to the room clerk. "Were you on duty when Mr. Roffe was staying here?"

"Yes," the clerk said. "The accident was a terrible thing, terrible."

"Mr. Roffe was alone here?"

The clerk shook his head. "No. He had a friend with him."

Max stared. "A friend?"

"Yes. Mr. Roffe made the reservation for both of them."

"Could you give me the name of his friend?"

"Certainly," the clerk said. He pulled out a large ledger from beneath the desk and began to turn back the pages. He stopped, ran his fingers down a page and said, "Ah, here we are . . ."

It took almost three hours for Max to drive to Lesgets in a Volkswagen, the cheapest rental car he could find, and he almost passed through it. It was not even a village. The place consisted of a few shops, a small Alpine lodge, and a general store with a single gas pump in front of it.

Max parked in front of the lodge and walked in.

There were half a dozen men seated in front of an open fireplace, talking. The conversation trailed off as Max entered.

"Excuse me," he said, "I'm looking for Herr Hans Bergmann."

"Who?"

"Hans Bergmann. The guide. He comes from this village."

An elderly man with a face that was a weather map of his years spat into the fireplace and said. "Somebody's been kidding you, mister. I was born in Lesgets. I never heard of any Hans Bergmann."

I t was the first day that Elizabeth had gone to the office since the death of Kate Erling a week earlier. Elizabeth entered the downstairs lobby with trepidation, responding mechanically to the greetings of the doorman and guards. At the far end of the lobby she saw workmen replacing the smashed elevator car. She thought about Kate Erling, and Elizabeth could visualize the terror she must have felt as she plunged twelve interminable stories to her death. She knew that she could never ride in that elevator again.

When she walked into her office, her mail had already been opened by Henriette, the second secretary, and neatly placed on her desk. Elizabeth went through it quickly, initialing some memos, writing questions on others, or marking them for various department heads. At the bottom of the pile was a large sealed envelope marked "Elizabeth Roffe—Personal." Elizabeth took a letter opener and slit the envelope across the top. She reached in and took out an 8-by-10 photograph. It was a close-up of a mongoloid child, its bulging eyes staring out of its encephalic head. Attached to the picture was a note printed in crayon: "THIS IS MY BEAUTIFUL SON JOHN. YOUR DRUGS DID THIS TO HIM. I AM GOING TO KILL YOU."

Elizabeth dropped the note and the picture, and found that her hands were trembling. Henriette walked in with a handful of papers.

"These are ready to be signed, Miss—" She saw the look on Elizabeth's face. "Is something wrong?"

Elizabeth said, "Please—ask Mr. Williams to come in here."

Her eyes went back to the picture on her desk.

Roffe and Sons could not be responsible for anything so dreadful.

"It was our fault," Rhys said. "A shipment of drugs was mislabeled. We managed to recall most of it, but—" He raised his hands expressively.

"How long ago did this happen?"

"Almost four years ago."

"How many people were affected?"

"About a hundred." He saw the expression on her face and added quickly. "They received compensation. They weren't all like this, Liz. Look, we're damned careful here. We take every safety precaution we can devise, but people are human. Mistakes are sometimes made."

Elizabeth sat staring at the picture of the child. "It's horrible."

"They shouldn't have shown you the letter." Rhys ran his fingers through his thick black hair and said, "This is a hell of a time to bring it up, but we have a few other problems more important than this."

She wondered what could be more important. "Yes?"

"The FDA just gave a decision against us on our aerosol sprays. There's going to be a complete ban on aerosols within two years."

"How will that affect us?"

"It's going to hurt us badly. It means we'll have to close down half a dozen factories around the world and lose one of our most profitable divisions."

Elizabeth thought about Emil Joeppli and the culture he was working on, but she said nothing. "What else?"

"Have you seen the morning papers?"

"No."

"A government minister's wife in Belgium, Mme. van den Logh, took some Benexan."

"That's one of our drugs?"

"Yes. It's an antihistamine. It's contraindicated for anyone with essential hypertension. Our label carries a clear warning. She ignored it."

Elizabeth felt her body beginning to tense. "What happened to her?"

Rhys said, "She's in a coma. She may not live. The newspaper stories mention that it's our product. Cancellations on orders are pouring in from all over the world. The FDA notified us that it's starting an investigation, but that will take at least a year. Until they finish, we can keep selling the drug."

Elizabeth said, "I want it taken off the market."

"There's no reason to do that. It's a damned effective drug for—"

"Have any other people been hurt by it?"

"Hundreds of thousands of people have been helped by it." Rhys tone was cool. "It's one of our most effective—"

"You haven't answered my question."

"A few isolated cases, I suppose, yes. But—"

"I want it taken off the market. Now."

He sat there, fighting his anger, then he said, "Right. Would you like to know what that will cost the company?"

"No," Elizabeth said.

Rhys nodded. "So far you've only heard the good news. The bad news is that the bankers want a meeting with you. Now. They're calling in their loans."

Elizabeth sat in her office alone, thinking about the mongoloid child, and about the woman who lay in a coma because of a drug that Roffe and Sons had sold her. Elizabeth was well aware that these kinds of tragedies involved other pharmaceutical firms as well as Roffe and Sons. There were almost daily stories in the newspapers about similar cases, but they had not touched her as this had. She felt responsible. She was determined to have a talk with the department heads who were in charge of safety measures to see if they could not be improved.

This is my beautiful son John.

Mme. van den Logh is in a coma. She may not live.

The bankers want a meeting with you. Now. They've decided to call in their loans.

She felt choked, as though everything was beginning to close in on her at once. For the first time Elizabeth wondered if she was going to be able to cope. The burdens were too heavy, and they were piling up too fast. She swung around in her chair, to look up at the portrait of old Samuel hanging on the wall. He looked so competent, so sure. But she knew about his doubts and uncertainties, and his black despairs. Yet he had come through. She would survive somehow, too. She was a Roffe.

She noticed that the portrait was askew. Probably as a result of the elevator crash. Elizabeth got up to straighten it. As she tilted the picture, the hook holding it gave way, and the painting crashed to the floor. Elizabeth did not even look at it. She was staring at the place where the painting had hung. Taped to the wall was a tiny microphone.

It was 4 A.M., and Emil Joeppli was working late again. It had become a habit of his recently. Even though Elizabeth Roffe had not given him a specific deadline, Joeppli knew how important this project was to the company and he was pushing to get it finished as quickly as possible. He had heard disturbing rumors about Roffe and Sons lately. He wanted to do everything he could to help the company. It had been good to him. It gave him a handsome salary and complete freedom. He had liked Sam Roffe, and he liked his daughter too. Elizabeth Roffe would never know, but these late hours were Joeppli's gift to her. He was hunched over his small desk, checking out the results of his last experiment. They were even better than he had anticipated. He sat there, deep in concentration, unaware of the fetid smell of the caged animals in the laboratory or the cloying humidity of the room or the lateness of the hour. The door opened, and the guard on the graveyard shift, Sepp Nolan, walked in. Nolan hated this shift. There was something eerie about the deserted experimental laboratories at night. The smell of the caged animals made him ill. Nolan wondered whether all the animals they had killed here had souls and came back to haunt these corridors. I ought to put in for spook pay, he thought. Everyone in the building had long since gone home. Except for this fucking mad scientist with his cages full of rabbits and cats and hamsters.

"How long you gonna be, Doc?" Nolan asked.

Joeppli looked up, aware of Nolan for the first time. "What?"

"If you're gonna be here awhile, I can bring you back a sandwich or something. I'm gonna run over to the commissary for a quick bite."

Joeppli said, "Just coffee, please." He turned back to his charts.

231

Nolan said, "I'll lock the outside door behind me when I leave the building. Be right back."

Joeppli did not even hear him.

Ten minutes later the door to the laboratory opened, and a voice said, "You're working late, Emil."

Joeppli looked up, startled. When he saw who it was, he got to his feet, flustered, and said, "Yes, sir." He felt flattered that this man had dropped in to see him.

"The Fountain of Youth project, top secret, eh?"

Emil hesitated. Miss Roffe had said no one was supposed to know about it. But, of course, that did not include his visitor. It was this man who had brought him into the company. So Emil Joeppli smiled and said, "Yes, sir. Top secret."

"Good. Let's keep it that way. How is it going?"

"Wonderfully, sir."

The visitor wandered over to one of the rabbit cages. Emil Joeppli followed him. "Is there anything I can explain to you?"

The man smiled. "No. I'm pretty familiar with it, Emil." As the visitor started to turn away, he brushed against an empty feeding dish on the ledge and it fell to the floor. "Sorry."

"Don't worry about it, sir. I'll get it." Emil Joeppli reached down to pick it up and the back of his head seemed to explode in a shower of red, and the last thing he saw was the floor racing up to meet him.

The insistent ringing of the telephone awakened Elizabeth. She sat up in bed, heavy with sleep, and looked at the digital clock on the little table. Five A.M. She fumbled the telephone off the hook. A frantic voice said, "Miss Roffe? This is the security guard at the plant. There's been an explosion at one of the laboratories. It was completely destroyed."

Instantly she was wide-awake. "Was anybody hurt?"

"Yes, ma'am. One of the scientists was burned to death."

He did not have to tell Elizabeth the name.

35

Detective Max Hornung was thinking. The detective bureau was filled with the noise of typewriters clattering, voices raised in argument, telephones ringing, but Hornung saw and heard nothing of these things. He had the single-minded concentration of a computer. He was thinking about the charter of Roffe and Sons, as old Samuel had set it up, keeping control within the family. Ingenious, Max thought. And dangerous. It reminded him of the tontine, the Italian insurance plan devised by the banker Lorenzo Tonti in 1695. Every member of the tontine put in an equal amount of money, and as each member died, the survivors inherited his share. It provided a powerful motive to eliminate the other members. Like Roffe and Sons. It was too much of a temptation to let people inherit stock worth millions, and then tell them they could not sell it unless everyone agreed.

Max had learned that Sam Roffe had not agreed. He was dead. Elizabeth Roffe had not agreed. She had narrowly escaped death twice. Too many accidents. Detective Max Hornung did not believe in accidents. He went to see Chief Inspector Schmied.

The chief inspector listened to Max Hornung's report on Sam Roffe's climbing accident and growled, "So there's been a mix-up about the name of a guide. That hardly constitutes a case for murder, Hornung. Not in *my* department, it doesn't."

The little detective said patiently, "I think there's more to it. Roffe and Sons is having big internal problems. Perhaps someone thought that getting rid of Sam Roffe would solve them."

Chief Inspector Schmied sat back and eyed Detective Hornung.

He was certain that there was nothing to his theories. But the idea of having Detective Max Hornung out of sight for a while filled Chief Inspector Schmied with a deep pleasure. His absence would be a boost to the morale of the entire department. And there was something else to consider: The people Max Hornung wanted to investigate. No less than the powerful Roffe family. Ordinarily, Schmied would have ordered Max Hornung to keep a million miles away from them. If Detective Hornung irritated them—and how could he not!—they had enough power to have him thrown off the force. And no one could blame Chief Inspector Schmied. Hadn't the little detective been forced on him? And so he said to Max Hornung, "The case is yours. Take your time."

"Thank you," Max said happily.

As Max was walking through the corridor toward his office, he ran into the coroner, "Hornung! Can I borrow your memory for a minute?"

Max blinked. "I beg your pardon?"

"The river patrol has just fished a girl out of the river. Will you take a look at her?"

Max swallowed and said, "If you wish."

This was not a part of the job that Max enjoyed, but he felt that it was his duty.

She lay in the impersonal metal drawer in the chill of the morgue. She had blond hair and was in her late teens or early twenties. Her body was bloated from the water, and naked, except for a red ribbon knotted around her neck.

"There are signs of sexual intercourse just before death. She was strangled and then dumped into the river," the coroner said. "There's no water in her lungs. We can't get any fingerprints on her. Ever seen her before?"

Detective Max Hornung looked down at the girl's face and said, "No."

He left to catch his bus to the airport.

When Detective Max Hornung landed at the Costa Smeralda airport in Sardinia, he rented the cheapest car available, a Fiat 500, and drove into Olbia. Unlike the rest of Sardinia, Olbia was an industrial city, and the outskirts were an ugly sprawl of mills and factories, a city dump and a giant graveyard of once-beautiful automobiles, now useless old hulks, good only for scrap. Every city in the world had its automobile junkyards, Max thought. Monuments to civilization.

Max reached the center of town and drove up in front of a building with a sign that read: "QUESTURA DI SASSARI COMMIS-SARIATO DI POLIZIA OLBIA." The moment Max entered, he felt that familiar sense of identity, of belonging. He showed his warrant card to the desk sergeant, and a few minutes later he was ushered into the office of the Chief of Police, Luigi Ferraro. Ferraro rose to his feet, a welcoming smile on his face. It died as he saw his visitor. There was something about Max that did not spell "detective."

"Could I see your identification?" Chief Ferraro asked politely.

"Certainly," Max said. He pulled out his warrant card and Chief Ferraro examined both sides of it carefully, then returned it. His immediate conclusion was that Switzerland must be very hard up for detectives. He took a seat behind his desk and said, "What can I do for you?"

Max started to explain, in fluent Italian. The problem was that it took Chief Ferraro some moments to figure out what language Max was speaking. When he realized what it was supposed to be, he held up a horrified hand and said, "*Basta!* Do you speak English?"

"Of course," Max replied.

"Then I beg of you! Let us speak in English."

When Max was through talking, Chief Ferraro said, "You are mistaken, signore. I can tell you that you are wasting your time. My mechanics have already examined the Jeep. Everyone is agreed that it was an accident."

Max nodded, unperturbed. *"I haven't looked at it."*

Chief Ferraro said, "Very well. It is in a public garage now, up for sale. I will have one of my men take you there. Would you like to see the scene of the accident?"

Max blinked and said, "What for?"

Detective Bruno Campagna was elected as Max's escort. "We've already checked it out. It was an accident," Campagna said.

"No," Max replied.

The Jeep was in a corner of the garage, its front still dented and splashed with dried green sap.

"I haven't had time to work on it yet," the mechanic explained.

Max walked around the Jeep, examining it. "How were the brakes tampered with?" he asked.

The mechanic said, *"Gesù!* You, too?" A note of irritation crept into his voice. "I been a mechanic for twenty-five years, signore. I examined this Jeep myself. The last time anyone touched these brakes was when this car left the factory."

"Someone tampered with them," Max said.

"How?" The mechanic was spluttering.

"I don't know yet, but I will," Max assured him confidently. He took a last look at the Jeep, then turned and walked out of the garage.

Chief of Police Luigi Ferraro looked at Detective Bruno Campagna and demanded, "What did you *do* with him?"

"I didn't do anything. I took him to the garage, he made an ass of himself with the mechanic, then he said he wanted to go for a stroll by himself."

"Incredible!"

Max was standing on the shore, staring out at the emerald Tyrrhenian waters, seeing nothing. He was concentrating, his mind busily putting pieces together. It was like working a giant jigsaw puzzle. Everything always went neatly into place when you knew where it fitted. The Jeep was a small but important part of the puzzle. Its brakes had been examined by expert mechanics. Max had no reason to doubt either their honesty or competence. He therefore accepted the fact that the brakes of the Jeep had not been tampered with. Because Elizabeth had been driving the Jeep and someone wanted her dead, he also accepted the fact that they *had* been tampered with. There was no way it could have been done. Yet someone had done it. Max was up against someone clever. It made things more interesting.

Max stepped out onto the sandy beach, sat down on a large rock, closed his eyes and began to concentrate again, focusing on the pieces, shifting, dissecting, rearranging the bits of the puzzle.

Twenty minutes later the last piece clicked into place. Max's eyes flew open and he thought admiringly, Bravo! I must meet the man who thought of this.

After that, Detective Max Hornung had two stops to make, the first just outside Olbia and the second in the mountains. He caught the late afternoon plane back to Zurich.

Economy class.

T he head of the security forces of Roffe and Sons said to
Elizabeth, "It all happened too fast, Miss Roffe. There was
nothing we could do. By the time the fire-fighting equipment got into action, the whole laboratory was gone."

They had found the remains of Emil Joeppli's charred body.
There was no way of knowing whether his formula had been
removed from the laboratory before the explosion.

Elizabeth asked, "The Development Building was under
twenty-four-hour guard, was it not?"

"Yes, ma'am. We—"

"How long have you been in charge of our security department?"

"Five years. I—"

"You're fired."

He started to say something in protest, then changed his mind.
"Yes, ma'am."

"How many men are there on your staff?"

"Sixty-five."

Sixty-five! And they could not save Emil Joeppli. "I'm giving
them twenty-four hours' notice," Elizabeth said. "I want them all
out of here."

He looked at her a moment. "Miss Roffe, do you think you're
being fair?"

She thought of Emil Joeppli, and the priceless formula that had
been stolen, and of the bug that had been planted in her office that
she had ground under the heel of her shoe.

"Get out," Elizabeth said.

She filled every minute that morning, trying to wipe out the vision of the charred body of Emil Joeppli and his laboratory full of burned animals. She tried not to think about what the loss of that formula was going to cost the company. There was a chance a rival company might patent it and there was nothing Elizabeth could do about it. It *was* a jungle. When your competitors thought you were weak, they moved in for the kill. But this wasn't a competitor doing this. This was a friend. A deadly friend.

Elizabeth arranged for a professional security force to take over immediately. She would feel safer with strangers around her.

She phoned the Hôpital Internationale in Brussels to check on the condition of Mme van den Logh, the wife of the Belgian minister. They reported that she was still in a coma. They did not know whether she would live.

Elizabeth was thinking about Emil Joeppli and the mongoloid child and the minister's wife when Rhys walked in. He looked at her face and said gently, "As bad as that?"

She nodded, miserable.

Rhys walked over to her and studied her. She looked tired, drained. He wondered how much more she could stand. He took her hands in his and asked gently, "Is there anything I can do to help?"

Everything, Elizabeth thought. She needed Rhys desperately. She needed his strength and his help and his love. Their eyes met and she was ready to go into his arms, to tell him everything that had happened, that was happening.

Rhys said, "There's nothing new on Mme. van den Logh?"

And the moment had passed.

"No," Elizabeth said.

He asked, "Have you had any calls yet on the *Wall Street Journal* story?"

"What story?"

"You haven't seen it?"

"No."

Rhys sent to his office for a copy. The article enumerated all the recent troubles of Roffe and Sons, but the major theme of the story was that the company needed someone experienced to run it. Elizabeth put the newspaper down. "How much damage will this do?"

Rhys shrugged. "The damage has already been done. They're

239

just reporting it. We're beginning to lose a lot of our markets. We—"

The intercom buzzed. Elizabeth pressed the switch. "Yes?"

"Herr Julius Badrutt is on line two, Miss Roffe. He says it's urgent."

Elizabeth looked up at Rhys. She had been postponing the meeting with the bankers. "Put him on." She picked up the phone. "Good morning, Herr Badrutt."

"Good morning." Over the phone, his voice sounded dry and brittle. "Are you free this afternoon?"

"Well, I'm—"

"Fine. Will four o'clock be satisfactory?"

Elizabeth hesitated. "Yes. Four o'clock."

There was a dry, rustling sound over the phone and Elizabeth realized that Herr Badrutt was clearing his throat. "I was sorry to hear about Mr. Joeppli," he said.

Joeppli's name had not been mentioned in the newspaper accounts of the explosion.

She hung up slowly, and found that Rhys was watching her.

"The sharks smell blood," Rhys said.

The afternoon was filled with phone calls. Alec telephoned. "Elizabeth, did you see the story in the newspaper this morning?"

"Yes," Elizabeth said. *"The Wall Street Journal* was exaggerating."

There was a pause, and then Alec said, "I'm not talking about *The Wall Street Journal.* The *Financial Times* has a headline story on Roffe and Sons. It's not good. My phones haven't stopped ringing. We're getting heavy cancellations. What are we going to do?"

"I'll get back to you, Alec," Elizabeth promised.

Ivo called. *"Carissima,* I think you'd better prepare yourself for a shock."

I'm prepared, Elizabeth thought wryly. "What is it?"

Ivo said, "An Italian minister was arrested a few hours ago for accepting bribes."

Elizabeth had a sudden feeling of what was coming. "Go on."

There was a note of apology in Ivo's voice. "It wasn't our fault," Ivo said. "He got greedy and he was careless. They caught him at the airport, trying to smuggle money out of Italy. They've traced the money to us."

Even though Elizabeth was prepared for it, she still felt a shock of disbelief. "Why were we bribing him?"

Ivo said matter-of-factly, "So that we could do business in Italy. It's a way of life here. Our crime was not in bribing the minister, *cara*—it was in getting caught."

She sat back in her chair, her head beginning to pound.

"What happens now?"

"I would suggest that we meet with the company attorneys as quickly as possible," Ivo said. "Don't worry. Only the poor go to jail in Italy."

Charles called from Paris, his voice frantic with worry. The French press was full of Roffe & Sons. Charles urged Elizabeth to sell the company while it still had a reputation.

"Our customers are losing faith," Charles said. "Without that, there is no company."

Elizabeth thought about the phone calls, the bankers, her cousins, the press. Too much was happening too quickly. Someone was making it happen. She *had* to find out who.

The name was still in Elizabeth's private telephone book. Maria Martinelli. It brought back long-ago memories of the tall, leggy Italian girl who had been a classmate of Elizabeth's in Switzerland. They had corresponded from time to time. Maria had become a model and she had written to Elizabeth that she was engaged to marry an Italian newspaper publisher in Milan. It took Elizabeth fifteen minutes to reach Maria. When the social amenities had been disposed of, Elizabeth said into the phone, "Are you still engaged to that newspaper publisher?"

"Of course. The minute Tony gets his divorce, we're going to be married."

"I want you to do me a favor, Maria."

"Name it."

Less than one hour later Maria Martinelli called back. "I got that information you wanted. The banker who was caught trying to smuggle money out of Italy was set up. Tony says a man tipped off the border police."

"Was he able to find out the name of the man?"
"Ivo Palazzi."

Detective Max Hornung had made an interesting discovery. He had learned that not only was the explosion at the Roffe and Sons laboratory set deliberately, but that it had been caused by an explosive called Rylar X, made exclusively for the military, and not available to anyone else. What intrigued Max was that Rylar X was manufactured at one of the factories of Roffe and Sons. It took Max only one telephone call to learn which one.

The factory outside Paris.

At exactly 4 P.M. Herr Julius Badrutt lowered his angular figure into a chair and said without preamble, "As much as we would like to accommodate you, Miss Roffe, I am afraid our responsibility toward our stockholders must take precedence."

It was the kind of statement, Elizabeth thought, that bankers made to widows and orphans before they foreclosed their mortgages. But this time she was ready for Herr Badrutt.

". . . My board of directors has therefore instructed me to inform you that our bank is calling in the notes on Roffe and Sons immediately."

"I was told I had ninety days," Elizabeth said.

"Unfortunately, we feel that the circumstances have changed for the worse. I should also inform you that the other banks you are dealing with have reached the same decision."

With the banks refusing to help her, there would be no way to keep the company private.

"I'm sorry to bring you such bad news, Miss Roffe, but I felt that I should tell you personally."

"You know, of course, that Roffe and Sons is still a very strong and healthy company."

Herr Julius Badrutt nodded his head, once. "Of course. It's a great company."

"Yet you won't give us more time."

Herr Badrutt looked at her for a moment, then said, "The bank thinks your problems are manageable, Miss Roffe. But . . ." He hesitated.

"But you don't think there's anyone to manage them?"

"I'm afraid that is correct." He started to rise.

"What if someone else were president of Roffe and Sons?" Elizabeth asked.

He shook his head. "We have discussed that possibility. We don't feel that any of the present members of the board have the overall ability to cope with—"

She said, "I was thinking of Rhys Williams."

38

Constable Thomas Hiller of the Thames Marine Police Division was in terrible shape. He was sleepy, hungry, horny and wet; and he could not decide which was the greatest of his miseries.

He was sleepy because his fiancée, Flo, had kept him awake all night, fighting; he was hungry because by the time she was through screaming at him, he was late for duty, and he had had no time to pick up a bite; he was horny because she had refused to let him touch her; and he was wet because the thirty-foot police boat on which he was traveling had been built for service, not comfort, and a rising wind was driving the rain into the small wheelhouse where he stood. On days like this there was bloody little to see and even bloody less to do. The Thames Division covered fifty-four miles of river from Dartford Creek to Staines Bridge, and ordinarily Constable Hiller enjoyed patrol duty. But not when he was in this shape. Damn all women! He thought about Flo in bed, naked as a pouter pigeon, her large tits waving up and down as she yelled at him. He glanced at his watch. Another half hour and this miserable tour would be finished. The boat had turned and was headed back toward Waterloo Pier. His only problem now was deciding what to do first: sleep, eat, or jump in the kip with Flo. Maybe all three at once, he thought. He rubbed his eyes to force the sleep out of them, and turned to look at the muddy, swollen river pimpled by the rain.

It seemed to loom out of nowhere. It looked like a large white fish floating belly up, and Constable Hiller's first thought was: If we haul it aboard, we're going to stink of it. It was about ten yards to starboard and the boat was moving away from it. If he opened his mouth, the bloody fish was going to delay his getting off duty. They would have to stop and grapple it, and either pull it over the side or tow it in. Whichever they did would delay his getting to Flo. Well, he didn't *have* to report it. What if he had not seen it? What if—? They were moving farther away.

Constable Hiller called out, "Sergeant, there's a floating fish twenty degrees off starboard. Looks like a big shark."

The hundred-horsepower diesel engine suddenly changed rhythm, and the boat began to slow. Sergeant Gaskins stepped to his side. "Where is it?" he asked.

The dim shape was gone now, buried in the rain. "It was over there."

Sergeant Gaskins hesitated. He too was anxious to get home. His impulse was to ignore the damned fish.

"Was it big enough to menace navigation?" he asked.

Constable Hiller fought with himself and lost. "Yes," he said.

And so the patrol boat turned and slowly headed toward where the object had last been seen. It materialized again unexpectedly, almost under the bow, and they both stood there, staring down at it. It was the body of a young, blond girl.

She was naked, except for a red ribbon tied around her swollen neck.

At the moment when Constable Hiller and Sergeant Gaskins were fishing the body of the murdered girl out of the Thames, ten miles on the other side of London, Detective Max Hornung was entering the gray-and-white marble lobby of New Scotland Yard. Just walking through the storied portals gave him a sense of pride. They were all part of the same great fraternity. He enjoyed the fact that the Yard's cable address was HAND-CUFFS. Max was very fond of the English. His only problem concerned their ability to communicate with him. The English spoke their native language so strangely.

The policeman behind the reception desk asked, "Can I help you, sir?"

Max turned. "I have an appointment with Inspector Davidson."

"Name, sir?"

Max said, slowly and distinctly, "Inspector Davidson."

The guard looked at him with interest. "Your name is Inspector Davidson?"

"My name is *not* Inspector Davidson. My name is Max Hornung."

The policeman behind the desk said apologetically, "Excuse me, sir, but do you speak any English?"

Five minutes later Max was seated in the office of Inspector Davidson, a large, middle-aged man with a florid face and uneven yellow teeth. Typically British-looking, Max thought happily.

"Over the phone you said you were interested in information on Sir Alec Nichols as a possible suspect in a murder case."

"He's one of half a dozen."

Inspector Davidson stared at him. "His wanted toes are frozen?"

Max sighed. He repeated what he had just said, slowly and carefully.

"Ah." The inspector thought for a moment. "Tell you what I'll do. I'll turn you over to C-Four Criminal Records Department. If they have nothing on him, we'll try C-Eleven and C-Thirteen— Criminal Intelligence."

Sir Alec Nichols' name was not listed in any of the files. But Max knew where he could get the information he wanted.

Earlier that morning Max had phoned a number of executives who worked in the City, the financial center of London.

Their reactions were identical. When Max announced his name, they were filled with trepidation, for everyone doing business in the City had *something* to hide, and Max Hornung's reputation as a financial avenging angel was international. The moment that Max informed them that he was seeking information about someone else, they fell over themselves to cooperate with him.

Max spent two days visiting banks and finance companies, credit rating organizations and vital statistics offices. He was not interested in talking to the people at those places: he was interested in talking to their computers.

Max was a genius with computers. He would sit before the console board and play the machines like a virtuoso. It did not matter what language the computer had been taught, for Max spoke all of them. He talked to digital computers and low-level and high-level language computers. He was at ease with FORTRAN and FORTRAN IV, the giant IBM 370's and the PDP 10's and 11's and ALGOL 68.

He was at home with COBOL, programmed for business, and BASIC, used by the police, and the high speed APL, which conversed solely in charts and graphs. Max talked to LISP and APT, and PL-1. He held conversations in the binary code, and questioned the arithmetic units and the CPV units, and the high-speed printer answered his questions at the rate of eleven hundred lines a minute. The giant computers had spent their lives sucking up information like insatiable pumps, storing it, analyzing it, remembering it, and now they were spewing it out in Max's ear, whispering their secrets to him in their secluded air-conditioned crypts.

Nothing was sacred, nothing was safe. Privacy in today's civilization was a delusion, a myth. Every citizen was exposed, his deepest secrets laid bare, waiting to be read. People were on record if they had a Social Security number, an insurance policy, a driver's license or a bank account. They were listed if they had paid taxes or drawn unemployment insurance or welfare funds. Their names were stored in computers if they were covered by a medical plan, had made mortgage payments on a home, owned an automobile or bicycle or had a savings or checking account. The computers knew their names if they had been in a hospital, or in the military service, had a fishing or hunting license, had applied for a passport, or telephone, or electricity, or if they had been married or divorced or born.

If one knew where to look, and if one was patient, all the facts were available.

Max Hornung and the computers had a wonderful rapport. They did not laugh at Max's accent, or the way he looked, or acted or dressed. To the computers Max was a giant. They respected his intelligence, admired him, loved him. They happily gave up their secrets to him, sharing their delicious gossip about the fools that mortals made of themselves. It was like old friends chatting.

"Let's talk about Sir Alec Nichols," Max said.

The computers began. They gave Max a mathematical sketch of Sir Alec, drawn in digits and binary codes and charts. In two hours Max had a composite picture of the man, a financial identi-kit.

Copies of bank receipts and canceled checks and bills were all laid out before him. The first puzzling item that caught Max's eye was a series of checks for large amounts, all made out to "Bearer," cashed by Sir Alec Nichols. Where had the money gone? Max looked to see if it had been reported as a business or personal expense, or as a tax deduction. Negative. He went back over the lists of expenditures again: a check to White's Club, a meatmarket bill, unpaid . . . an evening gown from John Bates . . . the Guinea . . . a dentist's bill, unpaid . . . Annabelle's . . . one challis robe from Saint Laurent in Paris . . . a bill from the White Elephant, unpaid . . . a rates bill . . . John Wyndham, the hairdresser, unpaid . . . four dresses from Yves Saint Laurent, Rive Gauche . . . household salaries . . .

Max asked a question of the computer at the Vehicle Licensing Center.

Affirmative. Sir Alec owns a Bentley and a Morris.

Something was missing. There was no mechanic's bill.

Max had the computers search their memories. In seven years no such bill existed.

Did we forget something? the computers asked.

No, Max replied, *you didn't forget.*

Sir Alec did not use a mechanic. He repaired his own cars. A man with that mechanical ability would have no trouble causing an elevator, or a Jeep, to crash. Max Hornung pored over the arcane figures that his friends set before him, with the eagerness of an Egyptologist translating a set of newly discovered hieroglyphics. He found further mysteries. Sir Alec was spending a great deal more than his income.

Another loose thread.

Max's friends in the City had connections in many quarters. Within two days Max learned that Sir Alec had been borrowing money from Tod Michaels, the owner of a club in Soho.

Max turned to the police computers and asked questions. They listened, and they replied. *Yes, we have Tod Michaels for you. Has been charged with several crimes, but never convicted. Suspected of being involved in blackmail, dope, prostitution and loan-sharking.*

Max went down to Soho and asked more questions. He found out that Sir Alec Nichols did not gamble. But his wife did.

When Max was finished, there was no doubt in his mind that Sir Alec Nichols was being blackmailed. He had unpaid bills, he needed money fast. He had stock that would be worth millions, if he could sell it. Sam Roffe had stood in his way, and now Elizabeth Roffe.

Sir Alec Nichols had a motive for murder.

Max checked out Rhys Williams. The machines tried, but the information proved too sketchy.

The computers informed Max that Rhys Williams was male, born in Wales, thirty-four years of age, unmarried. An executive of Roffe and Sons. Salary eighty thousand dollars a year, plus bonuses. A London savings account with a balance of twenty-five thousand pounds, a checking account with an average balance of eight hundred pounds. A safety-deposit box in Zurich, contents unknown. All major charge accounts and credit cards. Many of the items purchased with them were for women. Rhys Williams had no criminal record. He had been employed at Roffe and Sons for nine years.

Not enough, Max thought. Not nearly enough. It was as though Rhys Williams was hiding behind the computers. Max remembered how protective the man had been when Max had questioned Elizabeth, after Kate Erling's funeral. Whom had he been protecting Elizabeth Roffe? Or himself?

At six o'clock that evening Max booked himself on an Alitalia economy flight to Rome.

I vo Palazzi had spent almost ten years carefully and skillfully building an intricate double life that not even his closest associates had penetrated.

It took Max Hornung and his computer friends in Rome less than twenty-four hours. Max held discussions with the computer at the Anagrafe Building, where vital statistics and city-administration data were kept, and he visited the computers at SID, and went to call on the bank computers. They all welcomed Max.

Tell me about Ivo Palazzi, Max said.

Happily, they replied.

The conversations began.

A grocery bill from Amici . . . a beauty salon bill from Sergio in the Via Condoitti . . . one blue suit from Angelo . . . flowers from Carducci . . . two evening dresses from Irene Galitzine . . . shoes from Gucci . . . a Pucci purse . . . utility bills . . .

Max kept reading the print-outs, examining, analyzing, smelling. Something smelled wrong. There were tuition fees for six children.

Have you made an error? Max asked.

Sorry. What type of error?

The computers at Anagrafe told me that Ivo Palazzi is registered as the father of three children. Do you verify six tuition fees?

We do.

You show Ivo Palazzi's address as being in Olgiata?

That is correct.

But he is paying for an apartment in Via Montemignaio?
Yes.
Are there two Ivo Palazzis?
No. One man. Two families. Three daughters by his wife.
Three sons by Donatella Spolini.

Before Max was through, he knew the tastes of Ivo's mistress, her age, the name of her hairdresser, and the names of Ivo's illegitimate children. He knew that Simonetta was a blonde, and Donatella a brunette. He knew what size dresses and bras and shoes each wore and how much they cost.

Among the expenses several interesting items caught Max's eye. The amounts were small, but they stood out like beacons. There was a receipted check for a lathe, a plane and a saw. Ivo Palazzi liked to work with his hands. Max thought about the fact that an architect would probably know something about elevators.

Ivo Palazzi applied for a large bank loan recently, the computers informed Max.

Did he receive it?

No. The bank asked him to have his wife cosign. He withdrew the request.

Thank you.

Max took a bus to the Polizia Scientifica center at EUR, where the giant computer was kept in a large round room.

Does Ivo Palazzi have a criminal record? Max asked.

Affirmative. Ivo Palazzi was convicted on an assault-and-battery charge at age twenty-three. His victim went to the hospital. Palazzi went to jail for two months.

Anything else?

Ivo Palazzi keeps a mistress at Via Montemignaio.

Thank you. I know.

There are several police reports of complaints from neighbors.

What sort of complaints?

Disturbing the peace. Fighting, yelling. One night she smashed all the dishes. Is that important?

Very, Max said. *Thank you.*

So Ivo Palazzi had a temper. And Donatella Spolini had a temper. Had something happened between her and Ivo? Was she threatening to expose him? Was that why he had suddenly gone to the bank for a large loan? How far would a man like Ivo Palazzi go to protect his marriage, his family, his way of life?

There was one final item that caught the little detective's attention. A large payment had been made to Ivo Palazzi by the financial section of the Italian security police. It was a reward, a percentage of the money found on the banker whom Ivo had turned in. If Ivo Palazzi was that desperate for money, what else would he do for it?

Max bade farewell to his computers and caught a noon flight to Paris on Air France.

41

The taxi fare from Charles de Gaulle Airport to the Notre Dame area is seventy francs, not including a tip. The fare by city bus Number 351, to the same area, is seven and a half francs, no tip required. Detective Max Hornung took the bus. He checked into the inexpensive Hôtel Meublé and began making phone calls. /

He talked to the people who held in their hands the secrets of the citizens of France. The French were normally more suspicious than even the Swiss, but they were eager to cooperate with Max Hornung. There were two reasons. The first was that Max Hornung was a virtuoso in his field, greatly admired, and it was an honor to cooperate with such a man. The second was that they were terrified of him. There were no secrets from Max. The odd-looking little man with the funny accent stripped everyone naked. "Certainly," they told Max. "You're welcome to use our computers. Everything to be kept confidential, of course."

"Of course."

Max dropped in at the Inspecteurs des Finances, the Crédit Lyonnais, and the Assurance Nationale and chatted with the tax computers. He visited the computers at the *gendarmerie* at Rosny-sous-Bois and the ones at the Préfecture of Police at Île de la Cité.

They started off with the light, easy gossip of old friends. *Who are Charles and Hélène Roffe-Martel?* Max asked.

Charles and Hélène Roffe-Martel, residence Rue François Premier 5, Vésinet, married May 24, 1970, at the Mairie in Neuilly, children none, Hélène three times divorced, maiden name Roffe, bank account at the Crédit Lyonnais in Avenue Montaigne in name of Hélène Roffe-Martel, average balance in excess of twenty thousand francs.

Expenditures?

With pleasure. A bill from Librairie Marceau for books . . . a dental bill for root-canal work for Charles Martel . . . hospital bills for Charles Martel . . . doctor's bill for examination of Charles Martel.

Do you have result of diagnosis?

Can you wait? I will have to speak to another computer.

Yes, please. Max waited.

The machine containing the doctor's report began to speak. *I have the diagnosis.*

Go ahead.

A nervous condition.

Anything else?

Severe bruises and contusions on thighs and buttocks.

Any explanation?

None given.

Go on, please.

A bill for a pair of men's shoes from Pinet . . . one hat from Rose Valois . . . foie gras from Fauchon . . . Carita beauty salon . . . Maxim's dinner party for eight . . . flat silver from Christofle . . . a man's robe from Sulka . . . Max stopped the computer. Something was bothering him. Something about the bills. He realized what it was. Every purchase had been signed by Mme. Roffe-Martel. The bill for men's clothes, the restaurant bills—all the accounts were in her name. Interesting.

And then the first loose thread.

A company named Belle Paix had purchased a land tax stamp. One of the owners of Belle Paix was named Charles Dessain. Charles Dessain's Social Security number was the same as Charles Martel's. Concealment.

Tell me about Belle Paix, Max said.

Belle Paix is owned by René Duchamps and Charles Dessain, also known as Charles Martel.

What does Belle Paix do?

It owns a vineyard.

How much is the company capitalized at?

Four million francs.

Where did Charles Martel get his share of the money?
From Chez ma Tante.
The house of your aunt?
Sorry. A French slang expression. The proper name is Crédit Municipal.
Is the vineyard profitable?
No. It failed.

Max needed more. He kept talking to his friends, probing, cajoling, demanding. It was the insurance computer that confided to Max that there was a warning on file of a possible insurance fraud. Max felt something delicious stir within him.

Tell me about it, he said.

And they talked, like two women gossiping back and forth over the Monday wash.

When Max was through he went to see a jeweler named Pierre Richaud.

In thirty minutes Max knew to a franc how much of Hélène Roffe-Martel's jewelry had been duplicated. It came to just over two million francs, the amount Charles Martel had invested in the vineyard. So Charles Dessain-Martel had been desperate enough to steal his wife's jewelry.

What other acts of desperation had he committed?

There was one other entry that interested Max. It might be of little significance, but Max methodically filed it away in his mind. It was a bill for the purchase of one pair of mountain-climbing boots. It gave Max pause, because mountain climbing did not fit in with his image of Charles Martel-Dessain, a man who was so dominated by his wife that he was allowed no charge accounts of his own, had no bank account in his name, and was forced to steal in order to make an investment.

No, Max could not visualize Charles Martel challenging a mountain. Max went back to his computers.

The bill you showed me yesterday from Timwear Sports Shop. I would like to see an itemized statement, please.
Certainly.

It flashed on the screen before him. There was the bill for the boots. Size 36A. A woman's size. It was Hélène Roffe-Martel who was the mountain climber.

Sam Roffe had been killed on a mountain.

42

Rue Armengaud was a quiet Paris street lined with one- and two-story private residences, each with its sloping guttered roof. Towering above its neighbors was Number 26, an eight-story modern structure of glass, steel and stone, the headquarters of Interpol, the clearinghouse for information in international criminal activities.

Detective Max Hornung was talking to a computer in the huge, air-conditioned basement room when one of the staff members walked in and said, "They're running a snuff film upstairs. Want to see it?"

Max looked up and said, "I don't know. What is a snuff film?"

"Come take a look."

Two dozen men and women were seated in the large screening room on the third floor of the building. There were members of the Interpol staff, police inspectors from the Sûreté, plainclothes detectives and a scattering of uniformed policemen.

Standing at the front of the room next to a blank screen, René Almedin, an assistant to the secretary of Interpol, was speaking. Max entered and found a seat in the back row.

René Almedin was saying, ". . . for the last several years we have been hearing increasing rumors of snuff films, pornographic films in which at the end of the sexual act the victim is murdered on camera. There has never been proof that such films actually existed. The reason, of course, is obvious. These films would not have been made for the public. They would have been made to be shown privately to wealthy individuals who got their pleasure in twisted, sadistic ways." René Almedin carefully removed his glasses. "As I have said, everything has been rumor and speculation. That has now changed, however. In a moment you are going to see footage from an actual snuff film." There was an expectant stir from the audience. "Two days ago, a male pedestrian carrying an attaché case was struck down in a hit-and-run accident in Passy. The man died on the way to the hospital. He is still unidentified. The Sûreté found this reel of film in his attaché case and turned it over to the laboratory, where it was developed." He gave a signal and the lights began to dim. The film began.

The blond girl could not have been more than eighteen. There was something unreal about watching that young face and budding woman's body performing fellatio, analingus and a variety of other sexual acts with the large hairless man in bed with her. The camera moved in to a close-up to show his enormous penis driving into her body, then pulled back to show her face. Max Hornung had never seen her face before. But he had seen something else that was familiar. His eyes were fixed on the ribbon that the girl was wearing around her neck. It triggered a memory. A red ribbon. Where? Slowly, the girl on the screen began to build to a peak, and as she started to climax, the man's fingers went around her throat and began to squeeze. The look on the girl's face changed from ecstasy to horror. She fought wildly to escape, but his hands pressed tighter, until at the final moment of orgasm the girl died. The camera moved in for a close-up of her face. The film ended. The lights suddenly came on in the room. Max remembered.

The girl who had been fished out of the river in Zurich.

At Interpol headquarters in Paris, replies from urgent inquiry cables were beginning to arrive from all over Europe. Six similar murders had taken place—in Zurich, London, Rome, Portugal, Hamburg and Paris.

René Almedin said to Max, "The descriptions match exactly. The victims were all blond, female, young; they were strangled during sexual intercourse and their bodies were nude except for a red ribbon around their necks. We're dealing with a mass murderer. Someone who has a passport, and is either affluent enough to travel extensively on his own or is on an expense account."

A man in plain clothes walked into the office and said, "We ran into some good luck. The raw stock of the film is manufactured by a small outfit in Brussels. This particular batch had a color-balance problem, which makes it easy for them to identify. We're getting a list of the customers they sold it to."

Max said, "I would like to see that list when you have it."

"Of course," René Almedin said. He studied the little detective. Max Hornung looked like no detective he had ever seen. And yet it was Max Hornung who had tied the snuff murders together.

"We owe you a debt of gratitude," Almedin said.

Max Hornung looked at him and blinked. "What for?" he asked.

Alec Nichols had not wanted to attend the banquet, but he had not wished Elizabeth to go alone. They were both scheduled to speak. The banquet was in Glasgow, a city Alec hated. A car was outside the hotel, waiting to take them to the airport as soon as they could decently make their excuses. He had already given his speech but his mind had been elsewhere. He was tense and nervous, and his stomach was upset. Some fool had had the bad judgment to serve haggis. Alec had barely tasted it. Elizabeth was seated next to him. "Are you all right, Alec?"

"Fine." He patted her hand reassuringly.

The speeches were almost finished when a waiter came up to Alec and whispered, "Excuse me, sir. There's a trunk call for you. You can take it in the office."

Alec followed the waiter out of the large dining room into the small office behind the reception desk. He picked up the telephone. "Hello?"

Swinton's voice said, "This is your last warning!" The line went dead.

T he last city on Detective Max Hornung's agenda was Berlin.
His friends the computers were waiting for him. Max
spoke to the exclusive Nixdorf computer, to which one had
access only with a specially punched card. He talked to the great
computers at Allianz and Schuffa and to the ones at the Bundesk-
rimalamt at Wiesbaden, the collection point for all criminal activity in Germany.

What can we do for you? they asked.

Tell me about Walther Gassner.

And they told him. When they were through telling Max Hornung their secrets, Walther Gassner's life was spread out before
Max in beautiful mathematical symbols. Max could see the man as
clearly as if he were looking at a photograph of him. He knew his
taste in clothes, wines, food, hotels. A handsome young ski instructor who had lived off women and had married an heiress
much older than himself.

There was one item that Max found curious: a canceled check
made out to a Dr. Heissen, for two hundred marks. On the check
was written "For consultation." What kind of consultation? The
check had been cashed at the Dresdner Bank in Dusseldorf. Fifteen minutes later Max was speaking to the branch manager of the
bank. Yes, of course the branch manager knew Dr. Heissen. He
was a valued client of the bank.

What kind of doctor was he?

A psychiatrist.

When Max had hung up, he sat back, his eyes closed, thinking.

A loose thread. He picked up the telephone and placed a call to Dr. Heissen in Dusseldorf.

An officious receptionist told Max that the doctor could not be disturbed. When Max insisted, Dr. Heissen got on the telephone and rudely informed Max that he never revealed any information about his patients, and that he would certainly not dream of discussing such matters over the telephone. He hung up on the detective.

Max went back to the computers. *Tell me about Dr. Heissen*, he said.

Three hours later Max was speaking to Dr. Heissen on the telephone again.

"I told you before," the doctor snapped, "that if you want any information about any of my patients, you will have to come to my office with a court order."

"It is inconvenient for me to come to Dusseldorf just now," the detective explained.

"That's your problem. Anything else? I'm a busy man."

"I know you are. I have in front of me your income tax reports for the past five years."

"So?"

Max said, "Doctor, I don't want to make trouble for you. But you are illegally concealing twenty-five percent of your income. If you prefer, I can just forward your files to the German income tax authorities and tell them where to look. They could start with your safe-deposit box in Munich, or your numbered bank account in Basel."

There was a long silence, and then the doctor's voice asked, "Who did you say you were?"

"Detective Max Hornung of the Swiss Kriminal Polizei."

There was another pause. The doctor said politely, "And what is it exactly you wish to know?"

Max told him.

Once Dr. Heissen began talking, there was no stopping him. Yes, of course he remembered Walther Gassner. The man had barged in without an appointment and had insisted on seeing him. He had refused to give his name. He had used the pretext that he wanted to discuss the problems of a friend.

"Of course, that alerted me instantly," Dr. Heissen confided to

Max. "It is a classic syndrome of people unwilling or afraid to face their problems."

"What *was* the problem?" Max asked.

"He said his friend was schizophrenic and homicidal, and would probably kill someone unless he could be stopped. He asked if there was some kind of treatment that could help. He said he could not bear to have his friend locked away in an insane asylum."

"What did you tell him?"

"I told him that first, of course, I would have to examine his *friend*, that some types of mental illness could be helped with modern drugs and other psychiatric and therapeutic treatments, and that other types were incurable. I also mentioned that in a case such as he described, treatment might be necessary for an extended period of time."

"What happened then?" Max asked.

"Nothing. That was really all. I never saw the man again. I would like to have helped him. He was very distraught. His coming to me was obviously a cry for help. It is similar to a killer who writes on the wall of his victim's apartment, 'Stop me before I kill again!' "

There was one thing still puzzling Max. "Doctor, you said he wouldn't give you his name, and yet he gave you a check and signed it."

Dr. Heissen explained, "He had forgotten to bring any money with him. He was very upset about that. In the end he had to write the check. That's how I happened to learn his name. Is there anything else you need to know, sir?"

"No."

Something was disturbing Max, a loose thread dangling tantalizingly out of reach. It would come to him—meanwhile, he had finished with the computers. The rest was up to him now.

When Max returned to Zurich the following morning, he found a teletype on his desk from Interpol. It contained a list of customers who had purchased the batch of raw stock used to make the snuff murder film.

There were eight names on the list.

Among them was Roffe and Sons.

★

Chief Inspector Schmied was listening to Detective Max Hornung make his report. There was no doubt about it. The lucky little detective had stumbled onto another big case.

"It's one of five people," Max was saying. "They all have a motive and they had the opportunity. They were all in Zurich for a board meeting the day the elevator crashed. Any one of them could have been in Sardinia at the time of the Jeep accident."

Chief Inspector Schmied frowned. "You said there were five suspects. Aside from Elizabeth Roffe, there are only four members of the board. Who's your other suspect?"

Max blinked and said patiently, "The man who was in Chamonix with Sam Roffe, when he was murdered. Rhys Williams."

*M*rs. *Rhys Williams.*
Elizabeth could not believe it. The whole thing had an air of unreality. It was something out of a blissful girl-hood dream. Elizabeth remembered how she had written in her exercise book, over and over, *Mrs. Rhys Williams, Mrs. Rhys Williams.* She glanced down now at the wedding ring on her finger.

Rhys said, "What are you grinning about?" He was seated in an easy chair across from her in the luxurious Boeing 707-320. They were thirty-five thousand feet somewhere above the Atlantic ocean, dining on Iranian caviar and drinking chilled Don Perignon, and it was such a cliché of *La Dolce Vita* that Elizabeth had to laugh aloud.

Rhys smiled. "Something I said?"

Elizabeth shook her head. She looked at him and marveled at how attractive he was. Her husband. "I'm just happy."

He would never know how happy. How could she tell him how much this marriage meant to her? He would not understand, because to Rhys it was not a marriage, it was a business proposition. But she loved Rhys. It seemed to Elizabeth that she had always loved him. She wanted to spend the rest of her life with him, have his children, belong to him, have him belong to her. Elizabeth looked over at Rhys again and thought wryly, But first I have to solve one small problem. I have to find a way to make him fall in love with me.

★

Elizabeth had proposed to Rhys the day of her meeting with Julius Badrutt. After the banker had left, Elizabeth had carefully brushed her hair, walked into Rhy's office, taken a deep breath and said, "Rhys—would you marry me?"

She had seen the look of surprise on his face, and before he could speak, she had gone hurriedly on, trying to sound efficient and cool. "It would be a purely business arrangement. The banks are willing to extend our loans if you take over as president of Roffe and Sons. The only way you can do that"—to Elizabeth's horror her voice had cracked—"is to marry a member of the family, and I—I seem to be the only one available."

She felt her face flush. She could not look at him.

"It wouldn't be a real marriage, of course," Elizabeth had said, "in the sense that—I mean—you'd be free to—to come and go as you pleased."

He had watched her, not helping her. Elizabeth wished he would say something. Anything.

"Rhys—"

"Sorry. You took me by surprise." He had smiled. "It isn't every day a man gets proposed to by a beautiful girl."

He was smiling, trying to get out of this without hurting her feelings. *I'm sorry, Elizabeth, but—*

"You have a deal," Rhys said.

And Elizabeth had suddenly felt as though a heavy burden had been lifted from her. She had not realized until that moment how important this had been. She had bought time now to learn who the enemy was. Together she and Rhys could stop all the terrible things that had been happening. There was one thing she had to make clear to him.

"You will be president of the company," she had said, "but the voting control of the stock will remain in my hands."

Rhys had frowned. "If I'm running the company—"

"You will be," Elizabeth had assured him.

"But the controlling stock—"

"Stays in my name. I want to make sure that it can't be sold."

"I see."

She could sense his disapproval. She had wanted to tell him that she had reached a decision. She had decided that the company should go public, that the members of the board should be able to sell their shares. With Rhys as president, Elizabeth would no longer have any fears about strangers coming in and taking over. Rhys would be strong enough to handle them. But Elizabeth could not let that happen until she found out who was trying to destroy the company. She had wanted desperately to tell Rhys all these things, but she knew that now was not the time, and so all she said was "Other than that, you'll have complete control."

Rhys had stood there, silently studying her for what seemed a long time. When he spoke, he said, "When would you like to get married?"

"As soon as possible."

Except for Anna and Walther, who was home, ill, they all came to Zurich for the wedding. Alec and Vivian, Hélène and Charles, Simonetta and Ivo. They seemed delighted for Elizabeth, and their pleasure made her feel like a fraud. She had not made a marriage, she had made a business deal.

Alec hugged her and said, "You know I wish you everything wonderful."

"I know, Alec. Thank you."

Ivo waxed ecstatic. *"Carissima, tanti auguri e figli maschi.* 'To find riches is a beggar's dream, but to find love is the dream of kings.' "

Elizabeth smiled. "Who said that?"

"I did," Ivo declared. "I hope Rhys appreciates what a lucky man he is."

"I keep telling him," she said lightly.

Hélène took Elizabeth aside. "You are full of surprises, *ma chère.* I had no idea that you and Rhys were interested in each other."

"It happened suddenly."

Hélène studied her with cool, calculating eyes. "Yes. I'm sure it did." And she walked away.

After the ceremony there was a wedding reception at the Baur-au-Lac. On the surface it was gay and festive, but Elizabeth felt the undercurrents. There was something evil in the room, a malediction, but she could not tell from whom it was coming. All she knew was that someone in the room hated her. She could feel it, deep down inside her, yet when she looked around, all she saw were

267

smiles and friendly faces. Charles raising his glass in a toast to her . . . Elizabeth had received a report on the laboratory explosion. *The explosive was manufactured by your factory outside Paris.*

Ivo, a happy grin on his face . . . *The banker who was caught trying to smuggle money out of Italy was set up. A man tipped off the border police. Ivo Palazzi.*

Alec? Walther? Which? Elizabeth wondered.

The following morning a board meeting was held, and Rhys Williams was unanimously elected president and chief operating officer of Roffe and Sons. Charles raised the question that was on everyone's mind. "Now that you are running the company, are we going to be allowed to sell our stock?"

Elizabeth could feel the sudden tension in the room.

"The controlling stock is still in Elizabeth's hands," Rhys informed them. "It's her decision."

Every head turned toward Elizabeth.

"We're not selling," she announced.

When Elizabeth and Rhys were alone, he said, "How would you like to honeymoon in Rio?"

Elizabeth looked at him, and her heart soared. He added matter-of-factly, "Our manager there is threatening to quit. We can't afford to lose him. I was planning to fly there tomorrow to straighten things out. It would look a bit strange if I went without my bride."

Elizabeth nodded and said, "Yes, of course." You're a fool, she told herself. This was your idea. It's an arrangement, not a marriage. You have no right to expect anything from Rhys. And still, a small voice, deep inside her, said, Who knows what can happen? . . .

When they got off the plane at the Galeão airport, the air was surprisingly warm, and Elizabeth realized that in Rio it was summer. A Mercedes 600 was waiting for them. The chauffeur was a thin, dark-skinned man in his late twenties. When they got into the car, Rhys asked the driver, "Where's Luis?"

"Luis is sick, Mr. Williams. I'll be driving you and Mrs. Williams."

"Tell Luis I hope he'll be better soon."

The driver studied them in the rearview mirror and said, "I will."

Half an hour later they were driving along the esplanade, over the colorful tiles of the broad avenue along the Copacabana Beach. They pulled up in front of the modern Princessa Sugarloaf Hotel and a moment later, their luggage was being attended to. They were ushered into an enormous suite with four bedrooms, a beautiful living room, a kitchen, and a huge terrace overlooking the bay. The suite had been stocked with flowers in silver vases, champagne, whiskey, and boxes of chocolates. The manager himself had escorted them to their suite.

"If there is anything at all we can do for you—anything—I am personally at your service twenty-four hours a day." And he bowed himself out.

"They're certainly friendly," Elizabeth said.

Rhys laughed and replied, "They should be. You own this hotel."

Elizabeth felt herself color. "Oh. I—I didn't know."

"Hungry?"

"I—No, thank you," Elizabeth replied.

"Some wine?"

"Yes, thank you."

In her own ears her voice sounded stilted and unnatural. She was not certain how she was supposed to behave, or what to expect from Rhys. He had suddenly become a stranger, and she felt terribly conscious of the fact that they were alone in the honeymoon suite of a hotel, that it was getting late, and that it would soon be time for bed.

She watched Rhys as he deftly opened a bottle of champagne. He did everything so smoothly, with the easy assurance of a man who knows exactly what he wants and how to get it. What did he want?

Rhys carried a glass of champagne to Elizabeth and raised his own glass in a toast. "To beginnings," he said.

"To beginnings," Elizabeth echoed. *And happy endings*, she added silently.

They drank.

We should smash our glasses into a fireplace. Elizabeth thought, to celebrate. She gulped down the rest of her champagne.

They were in Rio on their honeymoon, and she wanted Rhys. Not just for now, but forever.

The phone rang. Rhys picked it up and spoke into it briefly. When he finished he hung up and said to Elizabeth, "It's late. Why don't you get ready for bed?"

It seemed to Elizabeth that the word "bed" hung heavily in the air.

"Right," she said weakly. She turned and went into the bedroom where the bellboys had put their luggage. There was a large double bed in the center of the room. A maid had unpacked their suitcases and prepared the bed. On one side was a sheer silk nightgown of Elizabeth's, and on the other side a pair of men's blue pajamas. She hesitated a moment, then began to undress. When she was naked, she walked into the large mirrored dressing room and carefully removed her makeup. She wrapped a Turkish towel around her head, went into the bathroom and showered, slowly lathering her body and feeling the warm soapy water running between her breasts and down her belly and thighs, like warm wet fingers.

All the time she was trying not to think about Rhys, and she could think of nothing else. She thought of his arms around her and his body on hers. Had she married Rhys to help save the company, or was she using the company as an excuse because she wanted him? She no longer knew. Her desire had turned into one burning, all-consuming need. It was as though the fifteen-year-old child had been waiting for him all these years without being aware of it, and the need had turned into a hunger. She stepped out of the shower, dried herself with a soft warmed towel, put on the sheer silk nightgown, let her hair fall loose and free and climbed into bed. She lay there waiting, thinking about what was going to happen, wondering what he would be like, and she found that her heart was beginning to pound faster. She heard a sound and looked up. Rhys was standing in the doorway. He was fully dressed.

"I'll be going out now," he said.

Elizabeth sat up. "Where—where are you going?"

"It's a business problem I have to take care of." And he was gone.

Elizabeth lay awake all that night, tossing and turning, filled with conflicting emotions, telling herself how grateful she was that

Rhys had kept to their agreement, feeling like a fool for what she had been anticipating, furious with him for rejecting her.

It was dawn when Elizabeth heard Rhys return. His footsteps moved toward the bedroom, and Elizabeth closed her eyes, pretending to be asleep. She could hear Rhys's breathing as he came over to the bed. He stood there, watching her for a long time. Then he turned and walked into the other room.

A few minutes later Elizabeth was asleep.

In the late morning they had breakfast on the terrace. Rhys was pleasant and chatty, telling her what the city was like at Carnival time. But he volunteered no information about where he had spent the night, and Elizabeth did not ask. One waiter took their order for breakfast. Elizabeth noticed that it was a different waiter who served it. She thought no more about it, nor about the maids who were constantly in and out of the suite.

Elizabeth and Rhys were at the Roffe and Sons factory on the outskirts of Rio, seated in the office of the plant manager, Señor Tumas, a middle-aged, frog-faced man who perspired copiously.

He was addressing Rhys. "You must understand how it is. Roffe and Sons is dearer to me than my own life. It is my family. When I leave here, it will be like leaving home. A part of my heart will be torn out. More than anything in the world, I want to stay here." He stopped to wipe his brow. "But I have a better offer from another company, and I have my wife and children and mother-in-law to think of. You understand?"

Rhys was leaning back in his chair, his legs casually stretched out before him. "Of course, Roberto. I know how much this company means to you. You have spent many years here. Still, a man has to think of his family."

"Thank you," Roberto said gratefully. "I knew I could count on you, Rhys."

"What about your contract with us?"

Tumas shrugged. "A piece of paper. We will tear it up, no? What good is a contract if a man is unhappy in his heart?"

Rhys nodded. "That's why we flew down here, Roberto—to make you happy in your heart."

Tumas sighed. "Ah, if only it were not too late. But I have already agreed to go to work for this other company."

271

"Do they know you're going to prison?" Rhys asked conversationally.

Tumas gasped at him. "Prison?"

Rhys said, "The United States government has ordered every company doing business overseas to turn in a list of all foreign bribes they've paid over the past ten years. Unfortunately, you're heavily involved in that, Roberto. You've broken a few laws here. We had planned to protect you—as a faithful member of the family—but if you're not with us, there's no longer any reason to, is there?"

All the color had drained from Roberto's face. "But—but it was for the company that I did it," he protested. "I was only following orders."

Rhys nodded sympathetically. "Of course. You can explain that to the government at your trial." He rose to his feet and said to Elizabeth, "We'd better be starting back."

"Wait a minute," Roberto yelled. "You can't walk out and leave me like this."

Rhys said, "I think you're confused. *You're* the one who's leaving."

Tumas was mopping his brow again, his lips twitching uncontrollably. He walked over to the window and looked out. A heavy silence hung over the room. Finally, without turning, he said, "If I stay with the company—will I be protected?"

"All the way," Rhys assured him.

They were in the Mercedes, the thin dark chauffeur at the wheel, driving back to the city. "You blackmailed him," Elizabeth declared.

Rhys nodded. "We couldn't afford to lose him. He was going over to a competitor. He knows too much about our business. He would have sold us out."

Elizabeth looked at Rhys and thought, I have so much to learn about him.

That evening they went to Mirander for dinner, and Rhys was charming and amusing and impersonal. Elizabeth felt as though he were hiding behind a facade of words, putting up a verbal smoke screen to conceal his feelings. When they finished dinner, it was after midnight. Elizabeth wanted to be alone with Rhys. She had hoped they would return to the hotel. Instead he said, "I'm going to show you some of the night life in Rio."

They made the rounds of nightclubs, and everyone seemed to know Rhys. Wherever they went, he was the center of attention, charming everyone. They were invited to join couples at other tables, and groups of people joined them at their table. Elizabeth and Rhys were never alone for a moment. It seemed to Elizabeth that it was intentional, that Rhys was deliberately putting a wall of people between them. They had been friends before, and now they were—what? Elizabeth only knew that there was some unseen barrier between them. What was he afraid of and why?

At the fourth nightclub, where they had joined a table with half a dozen of Rhys's friends, Elizabeth decided she had had enough. She broke into the conversation between Rhys and a lovely-looking Spanish girl. "I haven't had a chance to dance with my husband. I'm sure you'll excuse us."

Rhys looked at her in quick surprise, then rose to his feet. "I'm afraid I've been neglecting my bride," he said lightly to the others. He took Elizabeth's arm and led her out to the dance floor. She was holding herself stiffly, and he looked at her face and said, "You're angry."

He was right, but it was an anger directed at herself. She had made the rules, and was upset now because Rhys would not break them. But it was more than that, of course. It was not knowing how Rhys felt. Was he sticking to their agreement because of a sense of honor, or because he was simply not interested in her? She had to know.

Rhys said, "Sorry about all these people, Liz, but they're in the business, and in one way or another they can be helpful to us."

So he was aware of her feelings. She could feel his arms around her, his body against hers. She thought, It feels right. Everything about Rhys was right for her. They belonged together. She knew it. But did he know how much she wanted him? Elizabeth's pride would not let her tell him. And yet he must feel something. She closed her eyes and pressed closer to him. Time had stopped and there was nothing but the two of them and the soft music and the magic of this moment. She could have gone on dancing forever in Rhys's arms. She relaxed and gave herself up to him completely and she began to feel his male hardness pressing against her thighs. She opened her eyes and looked up at him and there was something in his eyes she had never seen there before, an urgency, a wanting, that was a reflection of her own.

When he spoke, his voice was hoarse. He said, "Let's go back to the hotel."

And she could not speak.

When he helped her on with her wrap, his fingers burned her skin. They sat apart in the back of the limousine, afraid to touch. Elizabeth felt as if she were on fire. It seemed to her that it took an eternity for them to reach their suite. She did not think she could wait another moment. As the door closed, they came together in a wonderful wild hunger that swept through both of them. She was in his arms and there was a ferocity in him that she had never known. He picked her up and carried her into the bedroom. They could not get their clothes off quickly enough. We're like eager children, Elizabeth thought, and she wondered why it had taken Rhys all this time. But it did not matter now. Nothing mattered except their nakedness and the wonderful feel of his body against hers. They were in bed, exploring each other, and Elizabeth gently pulled away from his embrace and started kissing him, her tongue moving down his lean, taut body, embracing him with her lips, feeling his velvet hardness inside her mouth. His hands were on her hips, turning her on her side, and his mouth was running down between her thighs, parting them to his tongue and thrusting into the sweetness there, and when neither of them could bear it an instant longer, he moved on top of her and slowly slid inside her, thrusting deep and making gently circling motions and she began to move to his rhythm, their rhythm, the rhythm of the universe, and everything began to move faster and faster, spinning out of control, until there was a vast ecstatic explosion and the earth became still and peaceful again.

They lay there, holding each other close, and Elizabeth thought joyfully, *Mrs. Rhys Williams.*

46

"Excuse me, Mrs. Williams," Henriette's voice said on the intercom, "there's a Detective Hornung here to see you. He says it's urgent."

Elizabeth turned to look up at Rhys, puzzled. They had just returned from Rio to Zurich the evening before, and they had only been in the office a few minutes. Rhys shrugged. "Tell her to send the man in. Let's find out what's so important."

A few moments later the three of them were seated in Elizabeth's office. "What did you want to see me about?" Elizabeth asked.

Max Hornung had no small talk. He said, "Someone is trying to murder you." As he watched the color drain from Elizabeth's face, Max was genuinely distressed, wondering if there might have been a more tactful way he could have phrased it.

Rhys Williams said, "What the hell are you talking about?"

Max continued to address himself to Elizabeth. "There have already been two attempts on your life. There will probably be more."

Elizabeth stammered, "I—you must be mistaken."

"No, ma'am. That elevator crash was meant to kill you."

She stared at him in silence, her dark eyes filled with bewilderment, and some other emotion buried deeper, that Max could not define. "So was the Jeep."

Elizabeth found her voice again. "You're wrong. That was an accident. There was nothing the matter with the Jeep. The police in Sardinia examined it."

"No."

"I saw them," Elizabeth insisted.

"No, ma'am. You saw them examine *a* Jeep. It wasn't yours." They were both staring at him now.

Max went on, "Your Jeep was never in that garage. I found it in an auto junkyard at Olbia. The bolt that sealed the master cylinder had been loosened, and the brake fluid had run out. That's why you had no brakes. The left front fender was still bashed in and there were green markings on it from the sap of the trees you ran into. The lab checked it out. It matches."

The nightmare was back. Elizabeth felt it sweep through her, as though the floodgates of her hidden fears had suddenly opened, and she was filled again with the terror of that ride down the mountains.

Rhys was saying, "I don't understand. How could anyone—?"

Max turned to look at Rhys. "All Jeeps look alike, That's what they were counting on. When she crashed instead of going off the mountain, they had to improvise. They couldn't let anyone examine that Jeep because it had to look like an accident. They had expected it to be at the bottom of the sea. They probably would have finished her off there, but a maintenance crew came along, found her and took her to the hospital. They got hold of another Jeep, smashed it up a little and made the switch before the police came."

Rhys said, "You keep saying 'they.' "

"Whoever was behind it had help."

"Who—who would want to kill me?" Elizabeth asked.

"The same person who killed your father."

She had a sudden feeling of unreality, as if none of this was happening. It was all a nightmare that would go away.

"Your father was murdered," Max went on. "He was set up with a phony guide who killed him. Your father didn't go to Chamonix alone. There was someone with him."

When Elizabeth spoke, her voice was a hollow whisper. "Who?"

Max looked at Rhys and said, "Your husband."

The words echoed in her ears. They seemed to come from far away, fading in and out, and she wondered if she was losing her mind.

"Liz," Rhys said, "I wasn't there with Sam when he was killed."

"You were in Chamonix with him, Mr. Williams," Max insisted.

"That's true." Rhys was talking to Elizabeth now. "I left before Sam went on his climb."

She turned to look at him. "Why didn't you tell me?"

He hesitated a moment, then seemed to make a decision. "It's something I couldn't discuss with anyone. For the past year someone has been sabotaging Roffe and Sons. It was done very cleverly, so that it seemed to be a series of accidents. But I began to see a pattern. I went to Sam with it, and we decided to hire an outside agency to investigate."

Elizabeth knew then what was coming, and she was simultaneously filled with a deep sense of relief and a feeling of guilt. Rhys had known about the report all along. She should have trusted him enough to tell him about it, instead of keeping her fears to herself.

Rhys turned to Max Hornung, "Sam Roffe got a report that confirmed my suspicions. He asked me to go up to Chamonix to discuss it with him. I went. We decided to keep it just between the two of us until we could find out who was responsible for what was happening." When he continued, there was a note of bitterness in his voice. "Obviously, it wasn't kept quiet enough. Sam was killed because someone knew we were getting on to him. The report is missing."

"I had it," Elizabeth said. Rhys looked at her in surprise. "It was with Sam's personal effects." She said to Max, "The report indicates that it was someone on the board of Roffe and Sons, but they all have stock in the company. Why would they want to destroy it?"

Max explained, "They're not trying to destroy it, Mrs. Williams. They're trying to cause enough trouble to make the banks nervous enough to start calling in their loans. They wanted to force your father to sell the stock and go public. Whoever is behind this hasn't gotten what he wanted yet. Your life is still in danger."

"Then you've got to give her police protection," Rhys demanded.

Max blinked and said tonelessly, "I wouldn't worry about that, Mr. Williams. She hasn't been out of our sight since she married you."

The pain was unbearable and he had lived with it for four weeks.

The doctor had left some pills for him, but Walther Gassner was afraid to take them. He had to stay constantly alert to see that Anna did not try to kill him again, or to escape.

"You should get right to a hospital," the doctor had told him. "You've lost a good deal of blood—"

"No!" That was the last thing Walther wanted. Stab wounds were reported to the police. Walther had sent for the company doctor because he knew he would not report it. Walther could not afford to have the police snooping around. Not now. The doctor had silently stitched up the gaping wound, his eyes filled with curiosity. When he had finished, he had asked, "Would you like me to send a nurse to the house, Mr. Gassner?"

"No. My—my wife will take care of me."

That had been a month ago. Walther had telephoned his secretary and told her that he had had an accident and would be staying home.

He thought about that terrible moment when Anna had tried to kill him with the shears. He had turned just in time to catch the blade in his shoulder instead of through the heart. He had almost fainted from the pain and shock, but he had retained consciousness long enough to drag Anna to her bedroom and lock her in. And all the while she was screaming, "What have you done with

278

the children? What have you done with the children? . . ."

Since then Walther had kept her in the bedroom. He prepared all her meals. He would take a tray up to Anna's room, unlock the door and enter. She would be huddled in a corner, cringing from him, and she would whisper, "What have you done with the children?"

Sometimes he would open the bedroom door and find her with her ear pressed against the wall, listening for the sounds of their son and daughter. The house was silent now, except for the two of them. Walther knew there was very little time left. His thoughts were interrupted by a faint noise. He listened. And then he heard it again. *Someone was moving around in the hallway upstairs. There was not supposed to be anyone in the house. He had locked all the doors himself.*

Upstairs, Frau Mendler was dusting. She was a dayworker, and this was only her second time in this house. She did not like it. When she had worked here on Wednesday the week before, Herr Gassner had followed her around as though expecting her to steal something. When she had tried to go upstairs to clean, he had angrily stopped her, given her her wages and sent her away. There was something about his manner that frightened her.

Today he was nowhere in sight, *Gott sei Dank*. Frau Mendler had let herself in with the key she had taken the week before, and she had gone upstairs. The house was unnaturally silent, and she decided that no one was at home. She had cleaned one bedroom and had found some loose change lying around, and a gold pillbox. She started down the hallway toward the next bedroom and tried to open the door. It was locked. Strange. She wondered if they kept something valuable inside. She turned the handle again, and a woman's voice from behind the door whispered, "Who is it?"

Frau Mendler jerked her hand away from the knob, startled.

"Who is it? Who's out there?"

"Frau Mendler, the cleaning lady. Do you want me to do your bedroom?"

"You can't. I'm locked in." The voice was louder now, filled with hysteria. "Help me! Please! Call the police. Tell them my husband has killed our children. He's going to kill me. Hurry! Get away from here before he—"

A hand spun Frau Mendler around and she found herself staring up into the face of Herr Gassner. He looked as pale as death.

"What are you sneaking around here for?" he demanded. He was holding her arm, hurting it.

"I—I'm not sneaking," she said. "Today is my day to clean. The agency—"

"I told the agency I didn't want anyone here. I—" He stopped. Had he telephoned the agency? He had meant to, but he was in such pain that he could no longer remember. Frau Mendler looked into his eyes and she was terrified by what she saw there.

"They never told me," she said.

He stood still, listening for sounds from behind the locked door. Silence.

He turned to Frau Mendler. "Get out of here. Don't come back."

She could not leave the house fast enough. He had not paid her, but she had the gold pillbox and the coins she had found on the dresser. She felt sorry for the poor woman behind the door. She wished she could help her, but she could not afford to get involved. She had a police record.

In Zurich, Detective Max Hornung was reading a teletype from Interpol headquarters in Paris.

INVOICE NUMBER ON SNUFF FILM RAW STOCK USED FOR ROFFE AND SONS GENERAL EXECUTIVE ACCOUNT. PURCHASING AGENT NO LONGER WITH COMPANY. TRYING TO TRACE, WILL KEEP YOU IN-FORMED. END MESSAGE.

In Paris the police were fishing a nude body out of the Seine. She was a blonde in her late teens. She wore a red ribbon around her neck.

In Zurich, Elizabeth Williams had been placed under twenty-four-hour police protection.

48

The white light flashed, signaling a call on Rhys's private line. Fewer than half a dozen people had the number. He picked up the telephone. "Hello."

"Good morning, darling." There was no mistaking the husky, distinctive voice.

"You shouldn't be calling me."

She laughed. "You never used to worry about things like that. Don't tell me that Elizabeth has tamed you already."

"What do you want?" Rhys asked.

"I want to see you this afternoon."

"That's impossible."

"Don't make me cross, Rhys. Shall I come to Zurich or—?"

"No. I can't see you here." He hesitated. I'll come there."

"That's better. Our usual place, *chéri.*"

And Hélène Roffe-Martel hung up.

Rhys replaced the receiver slowly and sat thinking. As far as he was concerned, he had had a brief physical affair with an exciting woman, and it had been finished for some time. But Hélène was not a woman who let go easily. She was bored with Charles, and she wanted Rhys. "You and I would make a perfect team," she had said, and Hélène Roffe-Martel could be very determined. And very dangerous. Rhys decided the trip to Paris was necessary. He had to make her understand once and for all that there could be nothing further between them.

A few moments later he walked into Elizabeth's office, and her eyes brightened. She put her arms around him and whispered,

"I've been thinking about you. Let's go home and play hooky this afternoon."

He grinned. "You're becoming a sex maniac."

She held him closer. "I know. Isn't it lovely?"

"I'm afraid I have to fly to Paris this afternoon, Liz."

She tried to conceal her disappointment. "Shall I come with you?"

"No point. It's just a minor business problem. I'll be back tonight. We'll have a late supper."

When Rhys walked into the familiar small hotel on the Left Bank, Hélène was already there, seated in the dining room, waiting for him. Rhys had never known her to be late. She was organized and efficient, extraordinarily beautiful, intelligent, a wonderful lover; and yet something was missing. Hélène was a woman without compassion. There was a ruthlessness about her, a killer's instinct. Rhys had seen others hurt by it. He had no intention of becoming one of her victims. He sat down at the table.

She said, "You're looking well, darling. Marriage agrees with you. Is Elizabeth taking good care of you in bed?"

He smiled to take the sting out of his words. "That's none of your business."

Hélène leaned forward and took one of his hands, "Ah, but it is, *chéri*. It is *our* business."

She began stroking his hand, and he thought of her in bed. A tiger, wild, skilled and insatiable. He withdrew his hand.

Hélène's eyes chilled. She said, "Tell me, Rhys. How does it feel to be president of Roffe and Sons?"

He had almost forgotten how ambitious she was, how greedy. He remembered the long conversations they had once had. She was obsessed by the idea of taking control of the company. *You and I, Rhys. If Sam were out of the way, we could run it.*

Even in the midst of their lovemaking: *It's my company, darling. Samuel Roffe's blood is in me. It's mine. I want it. Fuck me, Rhys.*

Power was Hélène's aphrodisiac. And danger. "What did you want to see me about?" Rhys asked.

"I think it's time you and I made some plans."

"I don't know what you're talking about."

She said maliciously, "I know you too well, darling. You're as ambitious as I am. Why did you serve as Sam's shadow all those years when you had dozens of offers to run other companies? Because you knew that one day you would be running Roffe and Sons."

"I stayed because I liked Sam."

She grinned. "Of course, *chéri*. And now you've married his charming little daughter." She took a thin black cigar from her purse and lit it with a platinum lighter. "Charles tells me that Elizabeth has arranged to keep control of the stock and that she refuses to sell."

"That's right, Hélène."

"It's occurred to you, of course, that if she had an accident, you would inherit her estate."

Rhys stared at her for a long time.

49

I n his home in Olgiata, Ivo Palazzi was casually looking out the window of his living room when he saw a terrifying sight. Coming up the driveway were Donatella and their three sons. Simonetta was upstairs, taking a nap. Ivo hurried out the front door and went to meet his second family. He was filled with such rage that he could have killed. He had been so wonderful to this woman, so kind, so loving, and now she was deliberately trying to destroy his career, his marriage, his life. He watched Donatella get out of the Lancia Flavia he had so generously given her. Ivo thought she had never looked more beautiful. The boys climbed out of the car, and were hugging and kissing him. Oh, how Ivo loved them. Oh, how he hoped that Simonetta would not wake up from her nap!

"I came to see your wife," Donatella said stiffly. She turned to the boys "Come on, boys."

"No!" Ivo commanded.

"How are you going to stop me? If I don't see her today, I'll see her tomorrow."

Ivo was cornered. There was no way out. Yet he knew that he could not let her or anyone else ruin everything he had worked so hard for. Ivo thought of himself as a decent man, and he hated what he must do. Not just for himself, but for Simonetta and Donatella and all his children.

"You will have your money," Ivo promised. "Give me five days."

Donatella looked into his eyes. "Five days," she said.

In London, Sir Alec Nichols was taking part in a floor debate in the House of Commons. He had been chosen to make a major policy speech dealing with the crucial subject of the labor strikes that were crippling the British economy. But it was difficult for him to concentrate. He was thinking about the series of telephone calls he had received over the past few weeks. They had managed to find him wherever he was, at his club, at his barber, restaurants, business meetings. And each time Alec had hung up on them. He knew that what they were asking was only the beginning. Once they controlled him, they would find a way to take over his stock, they would own a piece of a gigantic pharmaceutical company that manufactured drugs of every description. He could not let that happen. They had begun telephoning him four and five times a day until his nerves were stretched to the breaking point. What worried Alec now was that on this day he had *not* heard from them. He had expected a call at breakfast, and then again when he had lunched at White's. But there were no calls and somehow he could not shake off the feeling that the silence was more ominous than the threats. He tried to push these thoughts away now as he addressed the House.

"No man has been a stauncher friend of labor than I. Our labor force is what makes our country great. Workers feed our mills, turn the wheels in our factories. They are the true elite of this country, the backbone that makes England stand tall and strong among nations." He paused. "However, there comes a time in the fortunes of every nation when certain sacrifices must be made . . ."

He spoke by rote. He was wondering whether he had frightened them off by calling their bluff. After all, they were just small-time hoodlums. He was Sir Alec Nichols, Baronet, M.P. What could they do to him? In all probability he would not hear from them again. From now on they would leave him in peace. Sir Alec finished his speech amid vociferous applause from the back benches.

He was on his way out when an attendant came up to him and said, "I have a message for you, Sir Alec."

Alec turned. "Yes?"

"You're to go home as quickly as possible. There has been an accident."

★

They were carrying Vivian into the ambulance when Alec arrived at the house. The doctor was at her side. Alec slammed the car against the curb and was out running before it had stopped. He took one look at Vivian's white unconscious face and turned to the doctor. "What happened?"

The doctor said helplessly, "I don't know, Sir Alec. I received an anonymous call that there had been an accident. When I got here, I found Lady Nichols on the floor of her bedroom. Her—her kneecaps had been hammered to the floor with spikes."

Alec closed his eyes, fighting off the spasm of nausea that gripped him. He could feel the bile rising in his throat.

"We'll do everything we can, of course, but I think you had better be prepared. It's unlikely that she'll ever walk again."

Alec felt as though he could not breathe. He started toward the ambulance.

"She's under heavy sedation," the doctor said. "I don't think she'll recognize you."

Alec did not even hear him. He climbed into the ambulance and sat in a jump seat, staring down at his wife, oblivious to the back doors being closed, the sound of the siren, and the ambulance beginning to move. He took Vivian's cold hands in his. Her eyes opened. "Alec." Her voice was a slurred whisper.

Alec's eyes filled with tears. "Oh, my darling, my darling . . ."

"Two men . . . wore masks . . . they held me down . . . broke my legs. . . . I'll never be able to dance again . . . I'm going to be a cripple, Alec. . . . Will you still want me?"

He buried his head in her shoulder and wept. They were tears of despair and agony, and yet there was something else, something he hardly dared admit to himself. He felt a sense of relief. If Vivian were crippled, he would be able to take care of her, she could never leave him for anyone else.

But Alec knew that this was not over. They were not finished with him. This was only their warning. The only way he would ever get rid of them was to give them what they wanted.

Quickly.

Zurich.
Thursday, December 4.

It was exactly noon when the call came through the switchboard at the Kriminal Polizei headquarters in Zurich. It was routed through to Chief Inspector Schmied's office, and when the chief inspector had finished talking, he went to find Detective Max Hornung.

"It's all over," he told Max. "The Roffe case has been solved. They've found the killer. Get out to the airport. You've just got time to catch your plane."

Max blinked at him. "Where am I going?"

"To Berlin."

Chief Inspector Schmied telephoned Elizabeth Williams. "I am calling to bring you some good news," he said. "You will no longer need a bodyguard. The murderer has been caught."

Elizabeth found herself gripping the telephone. At long last she was going to learn the name of her faceless enemy. "Who is it?" she asked.

"Walther Gassner."

They were speeding along the autobahn, heading for Wannsee. Max was in the back seat, next to Major Wageman, and two detectives sat in front. They had met Max at Tempelhof Airport, and Major Wageman had briefed Max on the situation as they

287

drove. "The house is surrounded, but we have to be careful how we move in. He's holding his wife hostage."

Max asked, "How did you get on to Walther Gassner?"

"Through you. That's why I thought you would like to be here."

Max was puzzled. "Through me?"

"You told me about the psychiatrist he visited. On a hunch, I sent out Gassner's description to other psychiatrists and found out that he had gone to half a dozen of them, looking for help. Each time he used a different name, then ran away. He knew how ill he was. His wife had phoned us for help a couple of months ago, but when one of our men went out to investigate, she sent him away." They were turning off the autobahn now, only a few minutes from the house. "This morning we received a call from a cleaning woman, a Frau Mendler. She told us she was working at the Gassner house on Monday and that she talked to Mrs. Gassner through the locked door of her bedroom. Mrs. Gassner told her that her husband had killed their two children and was going to kill her."

Max blinked. "This happened on *Monday?* And the woman didn't call you until this morning?"

"Frau Mendler has a long police record. She was afraid to come to us. Last night she told her boyfriend what had happened, and this morning they decided to call us."

They had reached the Wannsee. The car pulled up a block away from the entrance to the Gassner estate, behind an unmarked sedan. A man got out of the sedan and hurried toward Major Wageman and Max. "He's still inside the house, Major. I have men all around the grounds."

"Do you know if the woman is still alive?"

The man hesitated. "No, sir. All the blinds are drawn."

"All right. Let's make it fast and quiet. Get everyone in place. Five minutes."

The man hurried off. Major Wageman reached into the car and pulled out a small walkie-talkie. He began rapidly to issue orders. Max was not listening. He was thinking of something that Major Wageman had said to him a few minutes ago. Something that made no sense. But there was no time to ask him about it now. Men were starting to move toward the house, using trees and shrubs as cover. Major Wageman turned to Max. "Coming, Hornung?"

It seemed to Max that there was an army of men infiltrating the garden. Some of them were supplied with telescopic rifles and armored vests; others carried snubnosed tear gas rifles. The operation was carried out with mathematical precision. At a signal from Captain Wageman, tear gas grenades were simultaneously hurled through the downstairs and upstairs windows of the house and at the same instant the front and rear doors were smashed in by men wearing gas masks. Behind them came more detectives with drawn guns.

When Max and Major Wageman ran through the open front door, the hallway was filled with acrid smoke, but it was rapidly being dispersed by the open windows and doors. Two detectives were bringing Walther Gassner into the hallway in handcuffs. He was wearing a robe and pajamas and he was unshaven and his face looked gaunt and his eyes swollen.

Max stared at him, seeing him for the first time in person. Somehow he seemed unreal to Max. It was the *other* Walther Gassner who was real, the man in the computer, whose life had been spelled out in digits. Which was the shadow and which was the substance?

Major Wageman said, "You're under arrest, Herr Gassner. Where is your wife?"

Walther Gassner said hoarsely, "She's not here. She's gone! I—"

Upstairs there was the sound of a door being forced open, and a moment later a detective called down, "I've found her. She was locked in her room."

The detective appeared on the staircase, supporting a trembling Anna Gassner. Her hair was stringy and her face was streaked and blotchy, and she was sobbing.

"Oh, thank God," she said. "Thank God you've come!"

Gently the detective led her downstairs toward the group standing in the enormous reception hall. When Anna Gassner looked up and saw her husband, she began to scream.

"It's all right, Frau Gassner," Major Wageman said soothingly. "He can't harm you anymore."

"My children," she cried. "He killed my children!"

Max was watching Walther Gassner's face. He was staring at his wife with an expression of utter hopelessness. He looked broken and lifeless.

"Anna," he whispered. "Oh, Anna."

Major Wageman said, "You have the right to remain silent or to ask for a lawyer. For your own sake I hope you will cooperate with us."

Walther was not listening. "Why did you have to call them, Anna?" he pleaded. "Why? Weren't we happy together?"

"The children are dead," Anna Gassner shrieked. "They're dead."

Major Wageman looked at Walther Gassner and asked, "Is that true?"

Walther nodded, and his eyes looked old and defeated. "Yes . . . They're dead."

"Murderer! Murderer!" his wife was shrieking.

Major Wageman said, "We would like you to show us the bodies. Will you do that?"

Walther Gassner was crying now, the tears rolling down his cheeks. He could not speak.

Major Wageman said, "Where are they?"

It was Max who answered. "The children are buried in Saint Paul's graveyard."

Everyone in the room turned to stare at him. "They died at birth five years ago." Max explained.

"Murderer!" Anna Gassner screamed at her husband.

And they turned and saw the madness blazing out of her eyes.

The cold winter night had fallen, snuffing out the brief twilight. It had begun to snow, a soft, windblown powder that dusted the city. In the administration building of Roffe and Sons, the lights of the deserted offices glowed against the darkness like pale yellow moons.

In her office Elizabeth was alone, working late, waiting for Rhys to return from Geneva, where he had gone for a meeting. She wished that he would hurry. Everyone had long since left the building. Elizabeth felt restless, unable to concentrate. She could not get Walther and Anna out of her mind. She remembered Walther as she had first met him, boyish and handsome and madly in love with Anna. Or pretending to be. It was so hard to believe that Walther was responsible for all those terrible acts. Elizabeth's heart went out to Anna. Elizabeth had tried several times to telephone her, but there had been no answer. She would fly to Berlin, to give her whatever comfort she could. The telephone rang, startling her. She picked it up. It was Alec on the other end of the line, and Elizabeth was pleased to hear his voice.

"You've heard about Walther?" Alec asked.

"Yes. It's horrible. I can't believe it."

"Don't, Elizabeth."

She thought she had misunderstood him. "What?"

"Don't believe it. Walther's not guilty."

"The police said—"

"They've made a mistake. Walther was the first person Sam and I checked out. We cleared him. He's not the one we were looking for."

Elizabeth stared at the phone, filled with a sense of confusion. *He's not the one we were looking for.* She said, "I—I don't understand what you're saying."

Alec replied hesitantly, "It's awkward doing this over a telephone, Elizabeth, but I haven't had an opportunity to speak to you alone."

"Speak to me about what?" Elizabeth asked.

"For the past year," Alec said, "someone has been sabotaging the company. There was an explosion in one of our South American factories, patents have been stolen, dangerous drugs have been mislabeled. There isn't time to go into it all now. I went to Sam and suggested that we engage an outside investigating agency to try to find out who was behind it. We agreed not to discuss it with anyone else."

It was as though the earth had suddenly stopped and time was frozen. A dizzying feeling of *déjà vu* swept through Elizabeth. Alec's words were coming through the telephone, but it was Rhys's voice she was hearing. Rhys saying, *Someone has been sabotaging Roffe and Sons. It was done very cleverly, so that it seemed to be a series of accidents. But I began to see a pattern. I went to Sam with it and we decided to hire an outside agency to investigate.*

Alec's voice was going on. "They finished their report and Sam took it with him to Chamonix. We discussed it over the telephone."

Elizabeth could hear Rhys's voice saying, *Sam asked me to come up to Chamonix to discuss it with him. . . . We decided to keep it just between the two of us until we could find out who was responsible for what was happening.*

Elizabeth was suddenly finding it hard to breathe. When she spoke, she tried to make her voice sound normal. "Alec, who—who else knew about the report beside you and Sam?"

"No one. That was the whole point. According to Sam, the report showed that whoever was guilty had to be someone high up in the company."

The highest echelon. And Rhys had not mentioned being in Chamonix until the detective had brought it up.

She asked slowly, the words dragged out of her, "Could Sam have told Rhys about it?"

"No. Why?"

There was only one way Rhys could have known what was in the report. He had stolen it. There was only one reason he could have gone to Chamonix. To kill Sam. Elizabeth did not hear the rest of what Alec was saying. The roaring in her ears drowned out his words. She dropped the receiver, her head spinning, fighting off the horror that was starting to engulf her. Her mind was a series of chaotic, jumbled images. At the time she had had the Jeep accident, she had left a message for Rhys that she would be in Sardinia. The night of the elevator crash, Rhys had not been at the board meeting, but he had appeared later when she and Kate were alone. *Thought I ought to give you a hand.* And soon afterward he had left the building. *Or had he?* Her body was trembling now. It had to be some terrible mistake. Not Rhys. *No!* It was a scream in her mind.

Elizabeth rose from the desk and on unsteady legs walked through the connecting door to Rhys's office. The room was dark. She turned on the lights and stood looking around uncertainly, not sure what she expected to find. She was not searching for evidence of Rhys's guilt, she was looking for evidence of his innocence. It was unbearable to think that the man she loved, the man who had held her in his arms and made love to her, could be a cold-blooded murderer.

There was an engagement book on Rhys's desk. Elizabeth opened it, turning the pages back to September, to the holiday weekend of the Jeep accident. Nairobi was marked on his calendar. She would need to check his passport to see if he had gone there. She started to look through Rhys's desk for the passport, feeling guilty, knowing that somehow there had to be an innocent explanation.

The bottom drawer of Rhys's desk was locked. Elizabeth hesitated. She knew she had no right to break into it. Somehow it was a violation of faith, the crossing of a forbidden boundary, from which there could be no return. Rhys would know that she had done this and she would have to tell him why. And yet Elizabeth had to know. She picked up a letter opener from the desk and broke the lock, splintering the wood.

In the drawer were stacks of notes and memoranda. She lifted them out. There was an envelope addressed to Rhys Williams in a woman's handwriting. It was postmarked a few days earlier, from Paris. Elizabeth hesitated a moment, then opened it. The letter was from Hélène. It began, *"Chéri,* I tried to reach you by phone. It is urgent that we meet again soon to make our plans. . . ." Elizabeth did not finish reading the letter.

She was staring at the stolen report in the drawer.

> MR. SAM ROFFE
> CONFIDENTIAL
> NO COPIES

She felt the room begin to spin and she clutched the edge of the desk for support. She stood there forever, eyes closed, waiting for the dizziness to pass. Her killer had a face now. It was the face of her husband.

The silence was broken by the insistent ringing of a distant telephone. It took Elizabeth a long time to realize where the sound was coming from. Slowly she walked back to her office. She picked up the telephone.

It was the attendant in the lobby, his voice cheerful. "Just checkin' that you're still there, Mrs. Williams. Mr. Williams is on his way up to you."

To stage another accident.

Her life was all that stood between Rhys and the control of Roffe and Sons. She could not face him, could not pretend that nothing was wrong. The moment he saw her, he would know. She had to escape. In a blind panic, Elizabeth grabbed her purse and coat and started out of the office. She stopped. She had forgotten something. Her passport! She had to get far away from Rhys, someplace where he could not find her. She hurried back to her desk, found the passport and ran out into the corridor, her heart pounding as though it would burst. The indicator on the private elevator was swinging upward.

Eight . . . nine . . . ten . . .

Elizabeth began racing down the stairs, running for her life.

There was a ferryboat that ran between Civitavecchia and Sardinia, carrying passengers and automobiles. Elizabeth drove aboard in a rental car, lost among a dozen other cars. Airports kept records, but the huge boat was anonymous. Elizabeth was one of a hundred passengers crossing over to the island of Sardinia for a holiday. She was sure she could not have been followed, and yet she was filled with an unreasoning fear. Rhys had gone too far to let anything stop him now. She was the only one who could expose him. He would have to get rid of her.

When Elizabeth had fled from the building, she had had no idea where she was going. She knew only that she must get out of Zurich and hide somewhere, that she would not be safe until Rhys was caught. *Sardinia.* It was the first place she thought of. She had rented a small car and had stopped at a phone booth along the auto route to Italy and had tried to call Alec. He was out. She left a message for him to call her in Sardinia. Unable to reach Detective Max Hornung, she left the same message for him.

She would be at the villa in Sardinia. But this time she would not be alone. The police would be there to protect her.

When the ferryboat landed in Olbia, Elizabeth found that it would not be necessary to go to the police. They were waiting for her in the person of Bruno Campagna, the detective she had met with Chief of Police Ferraro. It had been Campagna who had taken her to look at the Jeep following the accident. The detective hurried over to Elizabeth's car and said, "We were beginning to get very worried about you, Mrs. Williams."

Elizabeth looked at him, surprised.

"We received a call from the Swiss police," Campagna explained, "asking us to keep an eye out for you. We've been covering all the boats and airports."

Elizabeth was filled with a feeling of gratitude. Max Hornung! He had gotten her message. Detective Campagna looked at her tired, drawn face. "Would you like me to drive?"

"Please," Elizabeth said gratefully.

She slid over to the passenger seat, and the tall detective got behind the wheel. "Where would you rather wait—the police station or your villa?"

"The villa, if someone could stay with me. I'd—I'd rather not be there alone."

Campagna nodded reassuringly. "Don't worry. We have orders to keep you well guarded. I'll stay there with you tonight, and we'll have a radio car stationed at the driveway leading to your place. No one will be able to get near you."

His confidence was enough to let Elizabeth relax. Detective Campagna drove swiftly and expertly, winding through the little streets of Olbia, heading up the mountain road that led to the Costa Smeralda. Every place they passed reminded her of Rhys.

Elizabeth asked, "Has there been any—any news of my husband?"

Detective Campagna gave her a quick, compassionate glance, then turned his eyes back to the road. "He's on the run, but he won't get far. They expect to have him in custody by morning."

Elizabeth knew that she should feel a sense of relief, and instead the words brought a terrible, aching pain. It was Rhys they were talking about, Rhys who was being hunted like some animal. He had placed her in this terrible nightmare, and now he was caught up in his own nightmare, fighting for his life, as he had made her fight for hers. And how she had trusted him! How she had believed in his kindness and his gentleness and his love! She shuddered. Detective Campagna asked her, "Are you cold?"

"No. I'm fine." She felt feverish. A warm wind seemed to be whistling through the car, setting her nerves on edge. At first she thought it was her imagination until Detective Campagna said, "I'm afraid we're in for a scirocco. It's going to be a busy night."

Elizabeth understood what he meant. The scirocco could drive people and animals crazy. The wind blew in from the Sahara, hot and dry and grainy with sand, with a macabre keening sound that had an eerie, unbalancing effect on the nerves. The crime rate always went up during a scirocco, and the judges treated criminals leniently.

An hour later, out of the dark, the villa loomed ahead of them. Detective Campagna turned into the driveway, drove into the empty carport and turned off the engine. He walked around to the side of the car and opened Elizabeth's door. "I'd like you to stay right behind me, Mrs. Williams," he said. "Just in case."

"All right," Elizabeth replied.

They moved toward the front door of the darkened villa. Detective Campagna said, "I'm sure he's not here but we won't take any chances. May I have your key?"

Elizabeth handed him the key. He gently edged her to one side of the door, inserted the key and opened the door, his other hand hovering near his gun. He reached inside and flicked on the light switch, and the hallway was suddenly flooded with brilliant light.

"I'd like you to show me the house," Detective Campagna said. "Make sure we cover every room. Okay?"

"Yes."

They started walking through the house, and everywhere they went the huge detective turned the lights on. He looked in all the closets and corners and checked to make sure the windows and doors were locked. There was no one else in the house. When they returned to the living room downstairs, Detective Campagna said, "If you don't mind, I'd like to call headquarters."

"Of course," Elizabeth said. She led him into the study.

He picked up the telephone and dialed. A moment later he said, "Detective Campagna. We're at the villa. I'll camp here for the night. You can send a cruiser up to park at the foot of the driveway." He listened a moment then said into the phone, "She's fine. Just a little tired. I'll check in later." He replaced the receiver.

Elizabeth sank into a chair. She was feeling tense and nervous, but she knew that it was going to be worse tomorrow. Much worse. She would be safe but Rhys would be either dead or in prison. Somehow, in spite of everything he had done, she could not bear the thought of that.

Detective Campagna was studying her, a look of concern on his face. "I could use a cup of coffee," he said. "How about you?"

She nodded. "I'll make some." She started to rise.

"You stay where you are, Mrs. Williams. My wife says I make the best coffee in the world."

Elizabeth managed a smile. "Thank you." She sank back gratefully. She had not realized how emotionally drained she felt. For the first time now, Elizabeth admitted to herself that even during the telephone conversation with Alec she had felt that there might be some mistake, some explanation, that Rhys must be innocent. Even while she was fleeing, she had held on to the thought that he could not have done all those terrible things, that he could not have killed her father and then made love to her and tried to kill her. It would take a monster to do those things. And so she had kept that tiny ember of hope flickering in her. It had died when Detective Campagna had said, *He's on the run, but he won't get far. They expect to have him in custody by morning.*

She could not bear to think about it anymore, but she could think of nothing else. How long had Rhys been planning to take over the company? Probably from the moment he had met that impressionable fifteen-year-old girl, alone and lonely in a Swiss boarding school. That was when he must have first decided how he was going to outwit Sam—through his daughter. How easy it had been for him. The dinner at Maxim's and the long friendly talks during the years, and the charm—oh, the incredible charm! He had been patient. He had waited until she had become a woman, and the greatest irony of all was that Rhys did not even have to woo her. She had wooed *him*. How he must have laughed at her. He and Hélène Elizabeth wondered whether they were in it together, and she wondered where Rhys was now, and whether the police would kill him when they caught him. She began to weep uncontrollably.

"Mrs. Williams . . ." Detective Campagna was standing over her, holding out a cup of coffee.

"Drink this," he said. "You'll feel better."

"I—I'm sorry," Elizabeth apologized. "I don't usually carry on this way."

He said to her gently, "I think you're doing *molto bene.*"

Elizabeth took a sip of the hot coffee. He had put something in it. She looked up at him, and he grinned. "I decided a shot of Scotch wouldn't do you any harm."

He sat down across from her in a companionable silence. She was grateful for his company. She could never have stayed here alone. Not until she knew what had happened to Rhys, not until she knew whether he was dead or alive. She finished her coffee.

Detective Campagna looked at his watch. "The patrol car should be here any minute. There'll be two men in it on guard duty all night. I'll stay downstairs. I suggest you go up to bed now and try to get some sleep."

Elizabeth shivered. "I couldn't sleep." But even as she said it, her body was filled with an enormous lassitude. The long drive and the tremendous strain she had been under for so long were finally taking their toll.

"Maybe I'll just lie down for a bit," she said. She found it difficult to get the words out.

Elizabeth lay in her bed, fighting against sleep. Somehow it did not seem fair that she should be asleep while Rhys was being hunted. She visualized him being shot down on some cold dark street and she shuddered. She tried to keep her eyes open, but they were heavy weights, and the instant they closed she began to feel herself sinking down, down, into a soft cushion of nothingness.

Sometime later she was awakened by the screams.

Elizabeth sat up in bed, her heart beating wildly, not knowing what it was that had awakened her. Then she heard it again. An eerie, high-pitched scream that seemed to come from right outside her window, the sound of someone in the agony of death. Elizabeth arose and stumbled over to the window and looked out into the night. It was a landscape by Daumier, lit by a chill winter moon. The trees were black and stark, their branches whipped by a wild wind. In the distance, far below, the sea was a boiling caldron.

The scream came again. And again. And Elizabeth realized what it was. The singing rocks. The sirocco had risen in intensity and was blowing through them, making that terrible keening sound, over and over. And it became Rhys's voice she was hearing, crying out for her, begging her to help him. She could not stand it. She covered her ears with her hands, but the sound would not go away.

Elizabeth started toward the bedroom door, and she was surprised at how weak she was. Her mind was hazy with exhaustion. She walked out into the hallway and started down the stairs. She felt dazed, as though she had been drugged. She tried to call out to Detective Campagna, but her voice was a hoarse croak. She kept descending the long flight of stairs, fighting to keep her balance. She called aloud, "Detective Campagna."

There was no answer. Elizabeth stumbled into the living room. He was not there. She moved from room to room, holding on to furniture to keep from falling down.

Detective Campagna was not in the house.

She was alone.

Elizabeth stood in the hallway, her mind confused, trying to force herself to think. The detective had stepped outside to talk to the policemen in the patrol car. Of course that was it. She walked to the front door and opened it and looked outside.

No one was there. Only the black night and the screaming wind. With a growing feeling of fear, Elizabeth turned and made her way back to the study. She would call the police station and find out what had happened. She picked up the telephone, and the line was dead.

It was at that instant that all the lights went out.

54

In London, at Westminster Hospital, Vivian Nichols regained consciousness as she was being wheeled out of the operating room, down the long bleak corridor. The operation had taken eight hours. In spite of everything the skilled surgeons had been able to do, she would never walk again. She woke in agonizing pain, whispering Alec's name over and over. She needed him, she needed to have him at her side, to have him promise that he would still love her.

The hospital staff was unable to locate Alec.

In Zurich, in the communications room of the Kriminal Polizei, an Interpol message was received from Australia. The former film purchasing agent for Roffe and Sons had been located in Sydney. He had died of a heart attack three days earlier. His ashes were being shipped home. Interpol had been unable to obtain any information regarding the purchase of the film. They were awaiting further instructions.

In Berlin, Walther Gassner was seated in the discreet waiting room of an exclusive private sanatorium in a pleasant suburb outside the city. He had been there, motionless for almost ten hours. From time to time a nurse or an attendant would stop by to speak to him and offer him something to eat or drink. Walther paid no attention to them. He was waiting for his Anna.

It would be a long wait.

In Olgiata, Simonetta Palazzi was listening to a woman's voice on the telephone. "My name is Donatella Spolini," the voice said. "We've never met, Mrs. Palazzi, but we have a great deal in common. I suggest we meet for luncheon at the Bolognese in the Piazza del Popolo. Shall we say one o'clock tomorrow?"

Simonetta had a conflicting appointment at the beauty parlor the next day, but she adored mysteries. "I'll be there," she said. "How will I know you?"

"I'll have my three sons with me."

In her villa in Le Vésinet, Hélène Roffe-Martel was reading a note she had found waiting for her on the mantelpiece in the drawing room. It was from Charles. He had left her, run away. "You will never see me again," the note said. "Don't try to find me." Hélène tore the note into small pieces. She would see him again. She would find him.

In Rome, Max Hornung was at Leonardo da Vinci Airport. For the past two hours he had been trying to get a message through to Sardinia, but because of the storm all communications were down. Max went back to the flight operations office to talk to the airport manager again. "You've *got* to get me on a plane to Sardinia," Max said. "Believe me, it's a matter of life and death."

The airport manager said, "I believe you, signore, but there is nothing I can do about it. Sardinia is shut up tight. The airports are closed. Even the boats have stopped running. Nothing is going in or out of that island until the scirocco is over."

"When will that be?" Max asked.

The airport manager turned to study the large weather map on the wall. "It looks like it's good for at least another twelve hours."

Elizabeth Williams would not be alive in twelve hours.

T he dark was hostile, filled with invisible enemies waiting to
strike at her. And Elizabeth realized now that she was completely at their mercy. Detective Campagna had brought her
here to be murdered. He was Rhys's man. Elizabeth remembered
Max Hornung explaining about switching the Jeeps. *Whoever did
it had help. Someone who knew the island.* How convincing
Detective Campagna had been. *We've been covering all the boats
and airports.* Because Rhys had known she would come here to
hide. *Where would you like to wait—at the police station or your
villa?* Detective Campagna had had no intention of letting her go
to the police. It had not been headquarters he had phoned. It had
been Rhys. *We're at the villa.*

Elizabeth knew she had to flee, but she no longer had the
strength. She was fighting to keep her eyes open, and her arms and
legs felt heavy. She suddenly realized why. He had drugged her
coffee. Elizabeth turned and made her way into the dark kitchen.
She opened a cabinet and fumbled around until she found what
she wanted. She took down a bottle of vinegar and splashed some
into a glass with water and forced herself to drink it. Immediately
she began to retch into the sink. In a few minutes she felt a little
better, but she was still weak. Her brain refused to function. It was
as if all the circuits inside her had already closed down, were
preparing for the darkness of death.

"No," she told herself fiercely. "You're not going to die like
that. You're going to fight. They're going to have to kill you."
She raised her voice and said, "Rhys, come and kill me," but her

voice was barely a whisper. She turned and headed for the hallway, feeling her way by instinct. She stopped under the portrait of old Samuel, while outside the moaning, alien wind tore against the house, screaming at her, taunting her, warning her. She stood there in the blackness, alone, facing a choice of terrors. She could go outside, into the unknown, and try to escape from Rhys, or she could stay here and try to fight him. But how?

Her mind was trying to tell her something but she was still dazed by the drug. She could not concentrate. Something about an accident.

She remembered then and said aloud. "He has to make it look like an accident."

You must stop him, Elizabeth. Had Samuel spoken? Or was it in her mind?

"I can't. It's too late." Her eyes were closing, and her face was pressed against the coolness of the portrait. It would be so wonderful to go to sleep. But there was something she had to do. She tried to remember what it was, but it kept slipping away.

Don't let it look like an accident. Make it look like murder. Then the company will never belong to him.

Elizabeth knew what she had to do. She walked into the study. She stood there a moment, then reached for a table lamp and hurled it against a mirror. She could hear them both smash. She lifted a small chair and pounded it against the wall until the chair began to splinter. She moved over to the bookcase and began ripping pages out of the books, scattering them around the room. She tore the useless telephone cord out of the wall. Let Rhys explain this to the police, she thought. Do not go gentle into that good night. Well, she would not go gentle. They would have to take her by force.

A sudden gale swept through the room, swirling the papers through the air, then died away. It took Elizabeth a moment to realize what had happened.

She was no longer alone in the house.

At Leonardo da Vinci Airport, near the *merci* area where freight was handled, Detective Max Hornung was watching a helicopter land. By the time the pilot had his door open Max was at his side. "Can you fly me to Sardinia?" he asked.

The pilot stared at him. "What's going on? I just flew somebody there. There's a bad storm blowing."

"Will you take me?"

"It'll cost you triple."

Max did not even hesitate. He climbed into the helicopter. As they took off, Max turned to the pilot and asked, "Who was the passenger you took to Sardinia?"

"His name was Williams."

The dark was Elizabeth's ally now, concealing her from her killer. It was too late to get away. she had to try to find a place to hide somewhere in the house. She went upstairs, putting distance between herself and Rhys. At the top of the stairs she hesitated, then turned toward Sam's bedroom. Something leaped at her out of the dark, and she started to scream, but it was only the shadow of a wind-whipped tree through the window. Her heart was pounding so hard that she was sure that Rhys would be able to hear it downstairs.

Delay him, her mind said. *But how?* Her head felt heavy. Everything was fuzzy. Think! she told herself. What would old Samuel have done? She walked to the bedroom at the end of the hall, took the key from the inside and locked the door from the outside. Then she locked the other doors and they were the doors of the gates of the ghetto in Krakow, and Elizabeth was not sure why she was doing it, and then she remembered that she had killed Aram and that they must not catch her. She saw the beam of a flashlight below, starting to move up the stairs, and her heart leaped. Rhys was coming for her. Elizabeth began to climb the tower stairs, and halfway up, her knees began to buckle. She slid to the floor and crawled the rest of the way on her hands and knees. She reached the top of the stairs and dragged herself upright. She opened the door to the tower room and went in. *The door,* Samuel said. *Lock the door.*

Elizabeth locked the door, but she knew that that would not keep Rhys out. At least, she thought, he will have to break it down. More violence to explain. Her death was going to look like murder. She pushed furniture against the door, moving slowly, as though the darkness were a heavy sea dragging her down. She pushed a table against the door, then an armchair and another table, working like an automaton, fighting for time, building her pitiable fortress against death. From the floor below she heard a crash and a moment later another and then a third. Rhys was breaking down the bedroom doors, looking for her. Signs of an attack, a trail for the police to follow. She had tricked him, as he had tricked her. Yet something was vaguely bothering her. If Rhys had to make her death look like an accident, why was he breaking down doors? She moved to the French doors and looked outside, listening to the mad wind singing a dirge to her. Beyond the balcony there was a sheer drop to the sea below. There was no escape from this room. This was where Rhys would have to come to get her. Elizabeth felt around for a weapon, but there was nothing that could help her.

She waited in the dark for her killer.

What was Rhys waiting for? Why didn't he break the door down and get it over with? *Break the door down.* Something was wrong. Even if he took her body away from here and disposed of it somewhere else, Rhys would still not be able to explain the violence of the house, the smashed mirror, the broken doors. Elizabeth tried to put herself into Rhys's mind, to figure out what plan he could have that would explain all those things without the police suspecting him of her death. There was only one way.

And even as Elizabeth thought of it, she could smell the smoke.

56

From the helicopter Max could see the coast of Sardinia, thickly blanketed by a cloud of swirling red dust. The pilot shouted above the kin of the rotor blades, "It's gotten worse. I don't know if I can land."

"You've got to!" Max yelled. "Head for Porto Cervo."

The pilot turned to look at Max. "That's at the top of a fucking mountain."

"I know," Max said. "Can you do it?"

"Our chances are about seventy-thirty."

"Which way?"

"Against."

The smoke was seeping in under the door, coming up from below through the floorboards, and a new sound had been added to the shrieking of the wind. The roar of flames. Elizabeth knew now, she had the answer, but it was too late to save her life. She was trapped here. Of course it did not matter whether doors and mirrors and furniture had been smashed, because in a few minutes nothing would be left of this house or of her. Everything would be ruined by the fire, as the laboratory and Emil Joeppli had been destroyed, and Rhys would have an alibi in some other place, so that he could not be blamed. He had beaten her. He had beaten them all.

The smoke was beginning to billow into the room now—yellow, acrid fumes that made Elizabeth choke. She could see the edges of flame start to lick at the cracks of the door, and she began to feel the heat.

It was her anger that gave Elizabeth the strength to move.

Through the blinding haze of smoke she felt her way toward the French doors. She pushed them open and stepped onto the balcony. The instant the doors opened, the flames from the hallway leaped into the room, licking at the walls. Elizabeth stood on the balcony, gratefully gulping in deep breaths of fresh air as the wind tore at her clothes. She looked down. The balcony protruded from the side of the building, a tiny island hanging over an abyss. There was no hope, no escape.

Unless . . . Elizabeth looked up at the sloping slate roof above her head. If there was some way for her to reach the roof and get to the other side of the house that was not burning yet, she might get away. She stretched her arms as high as she could, but the eave of the roof was beyond her reach. The flames were beginning to move closer now, enveloping the room. There was one slender chance. Elizabeth took it. She forced herself to go back into the blazing, smoke-filled room, choking from the acrid fumes. She grabbed the chair behind her father's desk and dragged it onto the balcony. Fighting to keep her balance, she positioned the chair and stood on top of it. Her fingers could reach the roof now, but they could not find a grip. She fumbled blindly, vainly, searching to get a purchase.

Inside, the flames had reached the curtains and were dancing all around the room, attacking the books and the carpet and the furniture, moving toward the balcony. Elizabeth's fingers suddenly found a grip on a protruding slate. Her arms were leaden; she was not sure she could hold on. She started to pull herself up, and the chair began to slip away from her. With her last remaining strength she pulled herself up and held on. She was climbing the walls of the ghetto now, fighting for her life. She kept pulling and straining and suddenly she found herself lying on the sloping roof, gasping for breath. She forced herself to move, inching her way upward, pressing her body hard against the steep pitch of the roof, aware that one slip would hurtle her into the black abyss below. She reached the peak of the roof and paused to catch her breath and take her bearings. The balcony she had just escaped from was blazing. There could be no turning back.

Looking down on the far side of the house, Elizabeth could see the balcony of one of the guest bedrooms. There were no flames there yet. But Elizabeth did not know whether she would be able to reach it. The roof slanted sharply downward, the slates were loose, the wind was pulling madly at her. If she slipped, there would be nothing to stop her fall. She stayed where she was, frozen, afraid to try it. And then, like a sudden miracle, a figure appeared on the guest balcony, and it was Alec, and he was looking up and calling out calmly, "You can make it, old girl. Nice and easy."

And Elizabeth's heart soared within her.

"Take it slow," Alec counseled. "One step at a time. It's a piece of cake."

And Elizabeth began to let herself move toward him, carefully, sliding down inch by inch, not letting go of one slate until she had found a firm grip on another. It seemed to take forever. And all the while she heard Alec's encouraging voice, urging her on. She was almost there now, sliding toward the balcony. A slate loosened, and she started to fall.

"Hold on!" Alec called.

Elizabeth found another hold, grabbing it fiercely. She had reached the edge of the roof now, with nothing below her but endless space. She would have to drop down onto the balcony where Alec stood waiting. If she missed . . .

Alec was looking up at her, his face filled with quiet confidence. "Don't look down," he said. "Close your eyes, and let yourself go. I'll catch you."

She tried. She took a deep breath, and then another She knew she had to let go and yet she could not bring herself to do it. Her fingers were frozen to the tiles.

"Now!" Alec called, and Elizabeth let herself drop and she was falling into space, and suddenly she was caught in Alec's arms as he pulled her to safety. She closed her eyes in relief.

"Well done," Alec said.

And she felt the muzzle of the gun against her head.

T he helicopter pilot was flying as low as he dared over the island, skimming the treetops, trying to avoid the punishing winds. Even at that altitude the air was filled with turbulence. In the distance ahead the pilot saw the mountain peak of Porto Cervo. Max saw it at the same moment. "There it is!" Max shouted. "I can see the villa." And then he saw something else that made his heart jump. "It's on fire!"

On the balcony Elizabeth heard the sound of the approaching helicopter over the wind, and she looked up. Alec paid no attention. He was watching Elizabeth, his eyes filled with pain. "It was for Vivian. I had to do it for Vivian. You see that, don't you? They have to find you in the fire."

Elizabeth was not listening. She could only think, *It wasn't Rhys. It wasn't Rhys.* All the time it had been Alec. Alec had killed her father and had tried to kill her. He had stolen the report and then tried to frame Rhys with it. He had terrified her into running away from Rhys because Alec had known that she would come here.

The helicopter had disappeared from sight now, beyond some nearby trees.

Alec said, "Close your eyes, Elizabeth."

She said fiercely, "No!"

And Rhys's voice suddenly called, "Drop the gun, Alec!"

They both looked down, and on the lawn below, in the light of the flickering flames, they saw Rhys and Chief of Police Luigi Ferraro and half a dozen detectives, armed with rifles.

311

"It's finished, Alec," Rhys shouted. "Let her go."

One of the detectives with a telescopic rifle said, "I can't shoot at him unless she moves out of the way."

Move, Rhys prayed. *Move!*

From behind the trees across the lawn Max Hornung came hurrying up to Rhys. He stopped as he saw the tableau above. Rhys said, "I got your message. I was too late."

They were both staring up at the two figures on the balcony, puppets, backlit by the rising flames coming from the far side of the villa. The wind was whipping the house into a gigantic torch, lighting the surrounding mountains, turning the night into an inferno, a blazing Valhalla.

Elizabeth turned and looked into Alec's face, and it was a mask of death, his eyes unseeing. He moved away from her toward the balcony door.

On the ground the detective said, "I've got him," and raised his rifle. He fired once. Alec staggered, then disappeared through the door into the house.

One moment there were two figures on the balcony, and then only one.

Elizabeth screamed, "Rhys!"

But he was already racing toward her.

Everything after that happened in a quick, confused kaleidoscope of motion. Rhys was picking her up and carrying her down to safety and she clung tightly to him and could not hold him close enough.

She was lying on the grass, with her eyes closed, and Rhys was holding her in his arms, saying, "I love you, Liz. I love you, my darling."

She listened to his voice washing over her, caressing her. She could not speak. She looked into his eyes and saw all the love and anguish, and there was so much she wanted to tell him. She was filled with guilt for all of her terrible suspicions. She would spend the rest of her life making it up to him.

She was too weary to think about it now, too weary to think about any of it. It was as though it had all happened to someone else in some other place, at some other time.

The only important thing was that she and Rhys were together. She felt his strong arms holding her close, forever, and it was enough.

58

It was like stepping into a blazing corner of hell. The smoke was getting thicker, filling the room with dancing chimeras that kept vanishing. The fire leaped down at Alec, fondling his hair, and the crackle of the flames became Vivian's voice calling to him in an irresistible siren song.

In a sudden flare of brightness, he saw her. She was stretched out on the bed, her beautiful body naked except for the scarlet ribbon tied around her neck, the same red ribbon she had worn the first time he had made love to her. She called his name again, her voice filled with longing. And this time she wanted *him,* not the others. He moved closer, and she whispered, "You're the only one I ever loved."

And Alec believed it. He had had to punish her because of the things she had done. But he had been clever—he had made those others pay for her sins. The terrible things he had done had been for her. As he moved toward her, Vivian whispered again, "You're the only one I ever loved, Alec," and he knew that it was true.

She was holding out her beckoning arms to him, and he sank down beside her. He embraced her, and they became one. He was inside her, and he *was* her. And this time he was able to satisfy her. And he felt such pleasure that it became an exquisite pain beyond bearing. He could feel the heat from her body consuming him, and even as he watched in wonder, the ribbon around Vivian's neck turned into a vivid tongue of flame caressing him, licking at him. In the next instant, a blazing beam from the ceiling crashed on top of him in a fiery pyre.

Alec died as the others had. In ecstasy.

A
STRANGER
IN THE
MIRROR

NOTE TO THE READER

The art of making others laugh is surely a wondrous gift from the gods. I affectionately dedicate this book to the comedians, the men and women who have that gift and share it with us. And to one of them in particular: my daughter's godfather, Groucho.

This is a work of fiction. Except for the names of theatrical personalities, all characters are imaginary.

If you would seek to find yourself
Look not in a mirror
For there is but a shadow there,
A stranger . . .
   —SILENIUS, *Odes to Truth*

PROLOGUE

On a Saturday morning in November in 1969, a series of bizarre and inexplicable events occurred aboard the fifty-five-thousand-ton luxury liner *S.S. Bretagne* as it was preparing to sail from the Port of New York to Le Havre.

Claude Dessard, chief purser of the *Bretagne*, a capable and meticulous man, ran, as he was fond of saying, a "tight ship." In the fifteen years Dessard had served aboard the *Bretagne*, he had never encountered a situation he had not been able to deal with efficiently and discreetly. Considering that the *S.S. Bretagne* was a French ship, this was high tribute, indeed. However, on this particular day it was as though a thousand devils were conspiring against him. It was of small consolation to his sensitive Gallic pride that the intensive investigations conducted afterward by the American and French branches of Interpol and the steamship line's own security forces failed to turn up a single plausible explanation for the extraordinary happenings of that day.

Because of the fame of the persons involved, the story was told in headlines all over the world, but the mystery remained unsolved.

As for Claude Dessard, he retired from the Cie. Trans-atlantique and opened a bistro in Nice, where he never tired of reliving with his patrons that strange, unforgettable November day.

It had begun, Dessard recalled, with the delivery of flowers from the President of the United States.

One hour before sailing time, an official black limousine bearing government license plates had driven up to Pier 92 on the lower Hudson River. A man wearing a charcoal-gray suit had disembarked from the car, carrying a bouquet of thirty-six Sterling Silver roses. He had made his way to the foot of the gangplank and exchanged a few words with Alain Safford, the *Bretagne*'s officer on duty. The flowers were ceremoniously transferred to Janin, a junior deck officer, who delivered them and then sought out Claude Dessard.

"I thought you might wish to know," Janin reported. "Roses from the President to Mme. Temple."

Jill Temple. In the last year, her photograph had appeared on the front pages of daily newspapers and on magazine covers from New York to Bangkok and Paris to Leningrad. Claude Dessard recalled reading that she had been number one in a recent poll of the world's most admired women, and that a large number of newborn girls were being christened Jill. The United States of America had always had its heroines. Now, Jill Temple had become one. Her courage and the fantastic battle she had won and then so ironically lost had captured the imagination of the world. It was a great love story, but it was much more than that: it contained all the elements of classic Greek drama and tragedy.

Claude Dessard was not fond of Americans, but in this case he was delighted to make an exception. He had tremendous admiration for Mme. Temple. She was—and this was the highest accolade Dessard could tender—*galante*. He resolved to see to it that her voyage on his ship would be a memorable one.

The chief purser turned his thoughts away from Jill Temple and concentrated on a final check of the passenger list. There was the usual collection of what the Americans referred to as V.I.P.'s, an acronym Dessard detested, particularly since Americans had such barbaric ideas about what made a person important. He noted that the wife of a wealthy industrialist was traveling alone. Dessard smiled knowingly and scanned the passenger list for the name of Matt Ellis, a black football star. When he found it, he nodded to himself, satisfied. Dessard was also interested to note that in adjoining cabins were a prominent senator and Carlina Rocca, a South American stripper, whose names had been linked in recent news stories. His eye moved down the list.

David Kenyon. Money. An enormous amount of it. He had

sailed on the *Bretagne* before. Dessard remembered David Kenyon as a good-looking, deeply tanned man with a lean, athletic body. A quiet, impressive man. Dessard put a C.T., for captain's table, after David Kenyon's name.

Clifton Lawrence. A last-minute booking. A small frown appeared on the chief purser's face. Ah, here was a delicate problem. What did one do with Monsieur Lawrence? At one time the question would not even have been raised, for he would automatically have been seated at the captain's table, where he would have regaled everyone with amusing anecdotes. Clifton Lawrence was a theatrical agent who in his day had represented many of the major stars in the entertainment business. But, alas, M. Lawrence's day was over. Where once the agent had always insisted on the luxurious Princess Suite, on this voyage he had booked a single room on a lower deck. First class, of course, but still . . . Claude Dessard decided he would reserve his decision until he had gone through the other names.

There was minor royalty aboard, a famous opera singer and a Nobel-Prize-declining Russian novelist.

A knock at the door interrupted Dessard's concentration. Antoine, one of the porters, entered.

"Yes—what?" Claude Dessard asked.

Antoine regarded him with rheumy eyes. "Did you order the theater locked?"

Dessard frowned. "What are you talking about?"

"I assumed it was you. Who else would do it? A few minutes ago I checked to see that everything was in order. The doors were locked. It sounded like someone was inside the theater, running a movie."

"We never run films in port," Dessard said firmly. "And at no time are those doors locked. I'll look into it."

Ordinarily, Claude Dessard would have investigated the report immediately, but now he was harassed by dozens of urgent last-minute details that had to be attended to before the twelve o'clock sailing. His supply of American dollars did not tally, one of the best suites had been booked twice by mistake, and the wedding gift ordered by Captain Montaigne had been delivered to the wrong ship. The captain was going to be furious. Dessard stopped to listen to the familiar sound of the ship's four powerful turbines starting. He felt the movement of the *S.S. Bretagne* as she slipped away from the pier and began backing her way into the channel. Then Dessard once again became engrossed in his problems.

Half an hour later, Léon, the chief veranda-deck steward, came in. Dessard looked up, impatiently. "Yes, Léon?"

"I'm sorry to bother you, but I thought you should know . . ."

"Hm?" Dessard was only half-listening, his mind on the delicate task of completing the seating arrangements for the captain's table for each night of the voyage. The captain was not a man gifted with social graces, and having dinner with his passengers every night was an ordeal for him. It was Dessard's task to see that the group was *agréable*.

"It's about Mme. Temple . . ." Léon began.

Dessard instantly laid down his pencil and looked up, his small black eyes alert. "Yes?"

"I passed her cabin a few minutes ago, and I heard loud voices and a scream. It was difficult to hear clearly through the door, but it sounded as though she was saying, 'You've killed me, you've killed me.' I thought it best not to interfere, so I came to tell you."

Dessard nodded. "You did well. I shall check to make certain that she is all right."

Dessard watched the deck steward leave. It was unthinkable that anyone would harm a woman like Mme. Temple. It was an outrage to Dessard's Gallic sense of chivalry. He put on his uniform cap, stole a quick look in the wall mirror and started for the door. The telephone rang. The chief purser hesitated, then picked it up. "Dessard."

"Claude—" It was the third mate's voice. "For Christ's sake, send someone down to the theater with a mop, would you? There's blood all over the place."

Dessard felt a sudden sinking sensation in the pit of his stomach. "Right away," Dessard promised. He hung up, arranged for a porter, then dialed the ship's physician.

"André? Claude." He tried to make his voice casual. "I was just wondering whether anyone has been in for medical treatment. . . . No, no. I wasn't thinking of seasick pills. This person would be bleeding, perhaps badly. . . . I see. Thank you." Dessard hung up, filled with a growing sense of unease. He left his office and headed for Jill Temple's suite. He was halfway there when the next singular event occurred. As Dessard reached the boat deck, he felt the rhythm of the ship's motion change. He glanced out at the ocean and saw that they had arrived at the Ambrose Lightship, where they would drop their pilot tug and the liner would head for the open sea. But instead, the *Bretagne* was slowing to a stop. Something out of the ordinary was happening.

Dessard hurried to the railing and looked over the side. In the sea below, the pilot tug had been snugged against the cargo hatch of the *Bretagne*, and two sailors were transferring luggage from the liner to the tug. As Dessard watched, a passenger stepped from the ship's hatch onto the small boat. Dessard could only catch a glimpse of the person's back, but he was sure that he must have been mistaken in his identification. It was simply not possible. In fact, the incident of a passenger leaving the ship in this fashion was so extraordinary that the chief purser felt a small *frisson* of alarm. He turned and hurriedly made his way to Jill Temple's suite. There was no response to his knock. He knocked again, this time a little more loudly. "Madame Temple . . . This is Claude Dessard, the chief purser. I was wondering if I might be of any service."

There was no answer. By now, Dessard's internal warning system was screaming. His instincts told him that there was something terribly wrong, and he had a premonition that it centered, somehow, around this woman. A series of wild, outrageous thoughts danced through his brain. She had been murdered or kidnapped or—He tried the handle of the door. It was unlocked. Slowly, Dessard pushed the door open. Jill Temple was standing at the far end of the cabin, looking out the porthole, her back to him. Dessard opened his mouth to speak, but something in the frozen rigidity of her figure stopped him. He stood there awkwardly for a moment, debating whether to quietly withdraw, when suddenly the cabin was filled with an unearthly, keening sound, like an animal in pain. Helpless before such a deep private agony, Dessard withdrew, carefully closing the door behind him.

Dessard stood outside the cabin a moment, listening to the wordless cries from within. Then, deeply shaken, he turned and headed for the ship's theater on the main deck. A porter was mopping up a trail of blood in front of the theater.

Mon Dieu, Dessard thought. *What next?* He tried the door to the theater. It was unlocked. Dessard entered the large, modern auditorium that could seat six hundred passengers. The auditorium was empty. On an impulse, he went to the projection booth. The door was locked. Only two people had keys to this door, he and the projectionist. Dessard opened it with his key and went inside. Everything seemed normal. He walked over to the two Century 35-mm. projectors in the room and put his hands on them.

One of them was warm.

In the crew's quarters on D deck, Dessard found the projectionist, who assured him that he knew nothing about the theater being used.

On the way back to his office, Dessard took a shortcut through the kitchen. The chef stopped him, in a fury. "Look at this," he commanded Dessard. "Just look what some idiot has done!"

On a marble pastry table was a beautiful six-tiered wedding cake, with delicate, spun-sugar figures of a bride and groom on top.

Someone had crushed in the head of the bride.

"It was at that moment," Dessard would tell the spellbound patrons at his bistro, "that I knew something terrible was about to happen."

Book One

I n 1919, Detroit, Michigan, was the single most successful
industrial city in the world. World War I had ended, and
Detroit had played a significant part in the Allies' victory,
supplying them with tanks and trucks and aeroplanes. Now, with
the threat of the Hun over, the automobile plants once again
turned their energies to retooling for motorcars. Soon four thousand automobiles a day were being manufactured, assembled and
shipped. Skilled and unskilled labor came from all parts of the
world to seek jobs in the automotive industry. Italians, Irish,
Germans—they came in a flood tide.

Among the new arrivals were Paul Templarhaus and his bride,
Frieda. Paul had been a butcher's apprentice in Munich. With
the dowry he received when he married Frieda, he emigrated to
New York and opened a butcher shop, which quickly showed a
deficit. He then moved to St. Louis, Boston and, finally, Detroit,
failing spectacularly in each city. In an era when business was
booming and an increasing affluence meant a growing demand
for meat, Paul Templarhaus managed to lose money everywhere
he opened a shop. He was a good butcher but a hopelessly incompetent businessman. In truth he was more interested in writing poetry than in making money. He would spend hours
dreaming up rhymes and poetic images. He would set them
down on paper and mail them off to newspapers and magazines,
but they never bought any of his masterpieces. To Paul, money
was unimportant. He extended credit to everyone, and the word
quickly spread: if you had no money and wanted the finest of
meats, go to Paul Templarhaus.

Paul's wife, Frieda, was a plain-looking girl who had had no experience with men before Paul had come along and proposed to her—or, rather, as was proper—to her father. Frieda had pleaded with her father to accept Paul's suit, but the old man had needed no urging, for he had been desperately afraid he was going to be stuck with Frieda the rest of his life. He had even increased the dowry so that Frieda and her husband would be able to leave Germany and go to the New World.

Frieda had fallen shyly in love with her husband at first sight. She had never seen a poet before. Paul was thin and intellectual-looking, with pale myopic eyes and receding hair, and it was months before Frieda could believe that this handsome young man truly belonged to her. She had no illusions about her own looks. Her figure was lumpy, the shape of an oversized, uncooked potato kugel. Her best feature was her vivid blue eyes, the color of gentians, but the rest of her face seemed to belong to other people. Her nose was her grandfather's, large and bulbous, her forehead was an uncle's, high and sloping, and her chin was her father's, square and grim. Somewhere inside Frieda was a beautiful young girl, trapped with a face and body that God had given her as some kind of cosmic joke. But people could see only the formidable exterior. Except for Paul. Her Paul. It was just as well that Frieda never knew that her attraction lay in her dowry, which Paul saw as an escape from the bloody sides of beef and hog brains. Paul's dream had been to go into business for himself and make enough money so that he could devote himself to his beloved poetry.

Frieda and Paul went to an inn outside Salzburg for their honeymoon, a beautiful old castle on a lovely lake, surrounded by meadows and woods. Frieda had gone over the honeymoon-night scene a hundred times in her mind. Paul would lock the door and take her into his arms and murmur sweet endearments as he began to undress her. His lips would find hers and then slowly move down her naked body, the way they did it in all the little green books she had secretly read. His organ would be hard and erect and proud, like a German banner, and Paul would carry her to the bed (perhaps it would be safer if he *walked* her to it) and tenderly lay her down. *Mein Gott, Frieda,* he would say. *I love your body. You are not like those skinny little girls. You have the body of a woman.*

The actuality came as a shock. It was true that when they reached their room, Paul locked the door. After that, the reality was a stranger to the dream. As Frieda watched, Paul quickly stripped off his shirt, revealing a high, thin, hairless chest. Then he pulled down his pants. Between his legs lay a limp, tiny penis, hidden by a foreskin. It did not resemble in any way the exciting pictures Frieda had seen. Paul stretched out on the bed, waiting for her, Frieda realized that he expected her to undress herself. Slowly, she began to take off her clothes. *Well, size is not everything*, Frieda thought. *Paul will be a wonderful lover.* Moments later, the trembling bride joined her groom on the marital bed. While she was waiting for him to say something romantic, Paul rolled over on top of her, made a few thrusts inside her, and rolled off again. For the stunned bride, it was finished before it began. As for Paul, his few previous sexual experience had been with the whores of Munich, and he was reaching for his wallet when he remembered that he no longer had to pay for it. From now on it was free. Long after Paul had fallen asleep, Frieda lay in bed, trying not to think about her disappointment. *Sex is not everything*, she told herself. *My Paul will make a wonderful husband.*

As it turned out, she was wrong again.

It was shortly after the honeymoon that Frieda began to see Paul in a more realistic light. Frieda had been reared in the German tradition of a *Hausfrau*, and so she obeyed her husband without question, but she was far from stupid. Paul had no interest in life except his poems, and Frieda began to realize that they were very bad. She could not help but observe that Paul left a great deal to be desired in almost every area she could think of. Where Paul was indecisive, Frieda was firm, where Paul was stupid about business, Frieda was clever. In the beginning, she had sat by, silently suffering, while the head of the family threw away her handsome dowry by his softhearted idiocies. By the time they moved to Detroit, Frieda could stand it no longer. She marched into her husband's butcher shop one day and took over the cash register. The first thing she did was to put up a sign: NO CREDIT. Her husband was appalled, but that was only the beginning. Frieda raised the prices of meat and began advertising, showering the neighborhood with pamphlets, and the business expanded over-night. From that moment on, it was Frieda who made all the important decisions, and Paul who followed them. Frieda's disappointment had turned her into a tyrant. She found that she had a talent for running things and people, and she was inflexible. It was Frieda who decided how their money was to be invested, where they would live, where they would vacation, and when it was time to have a baby.

She announced her decision to Paul one evening and put him to work on the project until the poor man almost suffered a nervous breakdown. He was afraid too much sex would undermine his health, but Frieda was a woman of great determination. "Put it in me," she would command.

"How *can* I?" Paul protested. "It is not interested."

Frieda would take his shriveled little penis and pull back the foreskin, and when nothing happened, she would take it in her mouth—"*Mein Gott!* Frieda! What are you *doing?*"—until it got hard in spite of him, and she would insert it between her legs until Paul's sperm was inside her.

Three months after they began, Frieda told her husband that he could take a rest. She was pregnant. Paul wanted a girl and Frieda wanted a boy, so it was no surprise to any of their friends that the baby was a boy.

The baby, at Frieda's insistence, was delivered at home by a midwife. Everything went smoothly up to and throughout the actual delivery. It was then that those who were gathered around the bed got a shock. The newborn infant was normal in every way, except for its penis. The baby's organ was enormous, dangling like a swollen, outsized appendage between the baby's innocent thighs.

His father's not built like that, Frieda thought with fierce pride.

She named him Tobias, after an alderman who lived in their precinct. Paul told Frieda that he would take over the training of the boy. After all, it was the father's place to bring up his son.

Frieda listened and smiled, and seldom let Paul go near the child. It was Frieda who brought the boy up. She ruled him with a Teutonic fist, and she did not bother with the velvet glove. At five, Toby was a thin, spindly-legged child, with a wistful face and the bright, gentian-blue eyes of his mother. Toby adored his mother and hungered for her approval. He wanted her to pick him up and hold him on her big, soft lap so that he could press his head deep into her bosom. But Frieda had no time for such things. She was busy making a living for her family. She loved little Toby, and she was determined that he would not grow up to be a weakling like his father. Frieda demanded perfection in everything Toby did. When he began school, she would supervise his homework, and if he was puzzled by some assignment, his mother would admonish him, "Come on, boy—roll up your sleeves!" And she would stand over him until he had solved the problem. The sterner Frieda was with Toby, the more he loved her. He trembled at the thought of displeasing her. Her punishment was swift and her praise was slow, but she felt that it was for Toby's own good. From the first moment her son had been placed in her arms, Frieda had known that one day he was going to become a famous and important man. She did not know how or when, but she knew it would happen. It was as though God had whispered it into her ear. Before her son was even old enough to understand what she was saying, Frieda would tell him of his greatness to come, and she never stopped telling him. And so, young Toby grew up knowing that he was going to be famous, but having no idea how or why. He only knew that his mother was never wrong.

Some of Toby's happiest moments occurred when he sat in the enormous kitchen doing his homework while his mother stood at the large old-fashioned stove and cooked. She would make heavenly smelling, thick black bean soup with whole frankfurters floating in it, and platters of succulent bratwurst, and potato pancakes with fluffy edges of brown lace. Or she would stand at the large chopping block in the middle of the kitchen, kneading dough with her thick, strong hands, then sprinkling a light snowflake of flour over it, magically transforming the dough into a mouth-watering *Pflaumenkuchen* or *Apfelkuchen*. Toby would go to her and throw his arms around her large body, his face reaching only up to her waist. The exciting musky female smell of her would become a part of all the exciting kitchen smells, and an unbidden sexuality would stir within him. At those moments Toby would gladly have died for her. For the rest of his life, the smell of fresh apples cooking in butter brought back an instant, vivid image of his mother.

One afternoon, when Toby was twelve years old, Mrs. Durkin,

the neighborhood gossip, came to visit them. Mrs. Durkin was a bony-faced woman with black, darting eyes and a tongue that was never still. When she departed, Toby did an imitation of her that had his mother roaring with laughter. It seemed to Toby that it was the first time he had ever heard her laugh. From that moment on, Toby looked for ways to entertain her. He would do devastating imitations of customers who came into the butcher shop and of teachers and schoolmates, and his mother would go into gales of laughter.

Toby had finally discovered a way to win his mother's approval.

He tried out for a school play, *No Account David,* and was given the lead. On the opening night, his mother sat in the front row and applauded her son's success. It was at that moment that Frieda knew how God's promise was going to come true.

It was the early 1930's, the beginning of the Depression, and movie theaters all over the country were trying every conceivable stratagem to fill their empty seats. They gave away dishes and radios, and had keno nights and bingo nights, the hired organists to accompany the bouncing ball while the audience sang along.

And they held amateur contests. Frieda would carefully check the theatrical section of the newspaper to see where contests were taking place. Then she would take Toby there and sit in the audience while he did his imitations of Al Jolson and James Cagney and Eddie Cantor and yell out, *"Mein Himmel!* What a talented boy!" Toby nearly always won first prize.

He had grown taller, but he was still thin, an earnest child with guileless, bright blue eyes set in the face of a cherub. One looked at him and instantly thought: *innocence.* When people saw Toby they wanted to put their arms around him and hug him and protect him from Life. They loved him and on stage they applauded him. For the first time Toby understood what he was destined to be; he was going to be a star, for his mother first, and God second.

Toby's libido began to stir when he was fifteen. He would masturbate in the bathroom, the one place he was assured of privacy, but that was not enough. He decided he needed a girl.

One evening, Clara Connors, the married sister of a classmate, drove Toby home from an errand he was doing for his mother.

Clara was a pretty blonde with large breasts, and as Toby sat next to her, he began to get an erection. Nervously, he inched his hand across to her lap and began to fumble under her skirt, ready to withdraw instantly if she screamed. Clara was more amused than angry, but when Toby pulled out his penis and she saw the size of it, she invited him to her house the following afternoon and initiated Toby into the joys of sexual intercourse. It was a fantastic experience. Instead of a soapy hand, Toby had found a soft, warm receptacle that throbbed and grabbed at his penis. Clara's moans and screams made him grow hard again and again, so that he had orgasm after orgasm without ever leaving the warm, wet nest. The size of his penis had always been a source of secret shame to Toby. Now it had suddenly become his glory. Clara could not keep this phenomenon to herself, and soon Toby found himself servicing half a dozen married women in the neighborhood.

During the next two years, Toby managed to deflower nearly half the girls in his class. Some of Toby's classmates were football heroes, or better looking than he, or rich—but where they failed, Toby succeeded. He was the funniest, cutest thing the girls had ever seen, and it was impossible to say no to that innocent face and those wistful blue eyes.

In Toby's senior year in high school, when he was eighteen, he was summoned to the principal's office. In the room were Toby's mother, grim-faced, a sobbing sixteen-year-old Catholic girl named Eileen Henegan and her father, a uniformed police sergeant. The moment Toby entered the room, he knew he was in deep trouble.

"I'll come right to the point, Toby," the principal said. "Eileen is pregnant. She says you're the father of her child. Have you had a physical relationship with her?"

Toby's mouth suddenly went dry. All he could think of was how much Eileen had enjoyed it, how she had moaned and begged for more. And now this.

"Answer him, you little son of a bitch!" Eileen's father bellowed. "Did you touch my daughter?"

Toby sneaked a look at his mother. That she was here to witness his shame upset him more than anything else. He had let her down, disgraced her. She would be repelled by his behavior. Toby resolved that if he ever got out of this, if God would only help him this once and perform some kind of miracle, he would never touch another girl as long as he lived. He would go straight to a doctor and have himself castrated, so that he would never even think about sex again, and . . .

"Toby . . ." His mother was speaking, her voice stern and cold. "Did you go to bed with this girl?"

Toby swallowed, took a deep breath and mumbled, "Yes, Mother."

"Then you will marry her." There was finality in her tone. She looked at the sobbing, puffy-eyed girl. "Is that what you want?"

"Y-yes," Eileen cried. "I love Toby." She turned to Toby. "They *made* me tell. I didn't want to give them your name."

Her father, the police sergeant, announced to the room at large, "My daughter's only sixteen. It's statutory rape. He could be sent to jail for the rest of his miserable life. But if he's going to marry her . . ."

They all turned to look at Toby. He swallowed again and said, "Yes, sir. I—I'm sorry it happened."

During the silent ride home with his mother, Toby sat at her side, miserable, knowing how much he had hurt her. Now he would have to find a job to support Eileen and the child. He would probably have to go to work in the butcher shop and forget his dreams, all his plans for the future. When they reached the house, his mother said to him, "Come upstairs."

Toby followed her to his room, steeling himself for a lecture. As he watched, she took out a suitcase and began packing his clothes. Toby stared at her, puzzled. "What are you doing, Mama?"

"Me? I'm not doing anything. *You* are. You're going away from here."

She stopped and turned to face him. "Did you think I was going to let you throw your life away on that nothing of a girl? So you took her to bed and she's going to have a baby. That proves two things—that *you're* human, and *she's* stupid! Oh, no—no one traps my son into marriage. God meant you to be a big man, Toby. You'll go to New York, and when you're a famous star, you'll send for me."

He blinked back tears and flew into her arms, and she cradled him in her enormous bosom. Toby suddenly felt lost and frightened at the thought of leaving her. And yet, there was an excitement within him, the exhilaration of embarking on a new life. He was going to be in Show Business. He was going to be a star; he was going to be famous.

His mother had said so.

In 1939, New York City was a mecca for the theater. The Depression was over. President Franklin Roosevelt had promised that there was nothing to fear but fear itself, that America would be the most prosperous nation on earth, and so it was. Everyone had money to spend. There were thirty shows playing on Broadway, and all of them seemed to be hits.

Toby arrived in New York with a hundred dollars his mother had given him. Toby knew he was going to be rich and famous. He would send for his mother and they would live in a beautiful penthouse and she would come to the theater every night to watch the audience applaud him. In the meantime, he had to find a job. He went to the stage doors of all the Broadway theaters and told them about the amateur contests he had won and how talented he was. They threw him out. During the weeks that Toby hunted for a job, he sneaked into theaters and nightclubs and watched the top performers work, particularly the comedians. He saw Ben Blue and Joe E. Lewis and Frank Fay. Toby knew that one day he would be better than all of them.

His money running out, he took a job as a dishwasher. He telephoned his mother every Sunday morning, when the rates were cheaper. She told Toby about the furor caused by his running away.

"You should see them," his mother said. "The policeman comes over here in his squad car every night. The way he carries on, you would think we were all gangsters. He keeps asking where you are."

"What do you tell him?" Toby asked anxiously.

"The truth. That you slunk away like a thief in the night, and that if I ever got my hands on you I would personally wring your neck."

Toby laughed aloud.

During the summer, Toby managed to get a job as an assistant to a magician, a beady-eyed, untalented mountebank who performed under the name of the Great Merlin. They played a series of second-rate hotels in the Catskills, and Toby's primary job was to haul the heavy paraphernalia in and out of Merlin's station wagon, and to guard the props, which consisted of six white rabbits, three canaries and two hamsters. Because of Merlin's fears that the props would "get eaten," Toby was forced to live with them in rooms the size of broom closets, and it seemed to Toby that the whole summer consisted of one overpowering stench. He was in a state of physical exhaustion from carrying the heavy cabinets with trick sides and bottoms and running after props that were constantly escaping. He was lonely and disappointed. He sat staring at the dingy, little rooms, wondering what he was doing here and how this was going to get him started in show business. He practiced his imitations in front of the mirror, and his audience consisted of Merlin's smelly little animals.

One Sunday as the summer was drawing to a close, Toby made his weekly telephone call home. This time it was his father who answered.

"It's Toby, Pop. How are you?"

There was a silence.

"Hello! Are you there?"

"I'm here, Toby." Something in his father's voice chilled Toby.

"Where's Mom?"

"They took her to the hospital last night."

Toby clutched the receiver so hard that it almost broke in his fist. "What happened to her?"

"The doctor said it was a heart attack."

No! Not his mother! "She's going to be all right," Toby demanded. "Isn't she?" He was screaming into the mouthpiece. "Tell me she's going to be all right, goddam you!"

From a million miles away he could hear his father crying. "She—she died a few hours ago."

The words washed over Toby like white-hot lava, burning him, scalding him, until his body felt as though it were on fire. His father was lying. She *couldn't* be dead. They had a pact. Toby was going to be famous and his mother was going to be at his side. There was a beautiful penthouse waiting for her, and a limousine and chauffeur and furs and diamonds. . . . He was sobbing so hard he could not breathe. He heard the distant voice saying, "Toby! Toby!"

"I'm on my way home. When is the funeral?"

"Tomorrow," his father said. "But you mustn't come here. They'll be expecting you, Toby. Eileen is going to have her baby soon. Her father wants to kill you. They'll be looking for you at the funeral."

So he could not even say goodbye to the only person in the world he loved. Toby lay in his bed all that day, remembering. The images of his mother were so vivid and alive. She was in the kitchen, cooking, telling him what an important man he was going to be, and at the theater, sitting in the front row and calling out, *"Mein Himmel!* What a talented boy!"

And laughing at his imitations and jokes. And packing his suitcase. *When you're a famous star, you'll send for me.* He lay there, numbed with grief, thinking, *I'll never forget this day. Not as long as I live. August the fourteenth, 1939. This is the most important day of my life.*

He was right. Not because of the death of his mother but because of an event that was taking place in Odessa, Texas, fifteen hundred miles away.

The hospital was an anonymous four-story building, the color of charity. Inside was a rabbit warren of cubicles designed to diagnose sickness, alleviate it, cure it or sometimes bury it. It was a medical supermarket, and there was something there for everyone.

It was four A.M., the hour of quiet death or fitful sleep. A time for the hospital staff to have a respite before girding for the battles of another day.

The obstetrical team in Operating Room 4 was in trouble. What had started out as a routine delivery had suddenly turned into an emergency. Up until the actual delivery of the baby of Mrs. Karl

Czinski, everything had been normal. Mrs. Czinski was a healthy woman in her prime, with wide peasant hips that were an obstetrician's dream. Accelerated contractions had begun, and things were moving along according to schedule.

"Breech delivery," Dr. Wilson, the obstetrician, announced. The words caused no alarm. Although only three percent of births are breech deliveries—the lower part of the infant emerging first— they are usually handled with ease. There are three types of breech deliveries: spontaneous, where no help is required; assisted, where the obstetrician lends nature a hand; and a complete "breakup," where the baby is wedged in the mother's womb.

Dr. Wilson noted with satisfaction that this was going to be a spontaneous delivery, the simplest kind. He watched the baby's feet emerge, followed by two small legs. There was another contraction from the mother, and the baby's thighs appeared.

"We're almost there," Dr. Wilson said encouragingly. "Bear down once more."

Mrs. Czinski did. Nothing happened.

He frowned. "Try again. Harder."

Nothing.

Dr. Wilson placed his hands on the baby's legs and tugged, very gently. There was no movement. He squeezed his hand past the baby, through the narrow passage into the uterus, and began to explore. Beads of perspiration appeared on his forehead. The maternity nurse moved close to him and mopped his brow.

"We've got a problem," Dr. Wilson said, in a low voice.

Mrs. Czinski heard. "What's wrong?" she asked.

"Everything's fine." Dr. Wilson reached in farther, gently trying to push the infant downward. It would not budge. He could feel the umbilical cord compressed between the baby's body and the maternal pelvis, cutting off the baby's air supply.

"Fetoscope!"

The maternity nurse reached for the instrument and applied it to the mother's belly, listening for the baby's heartbeat. "It's down to thirty," she reported. "And there's marked arrhythmia."

Dr. Wilson's fingers were inside the mother's body, like remote antennae of his brain, probing, searching.

"I'm losing the fetal heartbeat—" There was alarm in the maternity nurse's voice. "It's negative!"

They had a dying baby inside the womb. There was still a slim chance that the baby could be revived if they could get it out in time. They had a maximum of four minutes to deliver it, clear its lungs and get its tiny heart beating again. After four minutes, brain damage would be massive and irreversible.

"Clock it," Dr. Wilson ordered.

Everyone in the room instinctively glanced up as the electric clock on the wall clocked to the twelve o'clock position, and the large red second hand began making its first sweep.

The delivery team went to work. An emergency respiratory tank was wheeled to the table while Dr. Wilson tried to dislodge the infant from the pelvic floor. He began the Bracht maneuver, trying to shift the infant around, twisting its shoulders so that it could clear the vaginal opening. It was useless.

A student nurse, participating in her first delivery, felt suddenly ill. She hurried out of the room.

Outside the door of the operating room stood Karl Czinski, nervously kneading his hat in his large, calloused hands. This was the happiest day of his life. He was a carpenter, a simple man who believed in early marriage and large families. This child would be their first, and it was all he could do to contain his excitement. He loved his wife very much, and he knew that without her he would be lost. He was thinking about his wife as the student nurse came rushing out of the delivery room, and he called to her, "How is she?"

The distraught young nurse, her mind preoccupied with the baby, cried, "She's dead, she's dead!" and hurried away to be sick.

Mr. Czinski's face went white. He clutched his chest and began gasping for air. By the time they got him to the emergency ward, he was beyond help.

Inside the delivery room, Dr. Wilson was working frantically, racing the clock. He could reach inside and touch the umbilical cord and feel the pressure against it, but there was no way to release it. Every impulse in him screamed for him to pull the half-delivered baby out by force, but he had seen what happened to babies that had been delivered that way. Mrs. Czinski was moaning now, half delirious.

"Bear down, Mrs. Czinski. Harder! Come on!"

It was no use, Dr. Wilson glanced up at the clock. Two precious minutes were gone, without any blood circulating through the baby's brain. Dr. Wilson faced another problem: what was he going to do if the baby were saved *after* the four minutes had elapsed? Let it live and become a vegetable? Or let it have a merciful, quick death? He put the thought out of his mind and began to move faster. Closing his eyes, working by touch, all his concentration focused on what was happening inside the woman's body. He tried the Mauriceau-Smellie-Veit maneuver, a complicated series of moves designed to loosen and free the baby's body. And suddenly there was a shift. He felt it begin to move. "Piper forceps!"

The maternity nurse swifty handed him the special forceps and Dr. Wilson reached in and placed them around the baby's head. A moment later the head emerged.

The baby was delivered.

This was always the instant of glory, the miracle of a newly created life, red-faced and bawling, complaining of the indignity of being forced out of that quiet, dark womb into the light and the cold.

But not this baby. This baby was blue-white and still. It was a female.

The clock. A minute and a half left. Every move was swiftly mechanical now, the result of long years of practice. Gauzed fingers cleared the back of the infant's pharynx so air could get into the larnegeal opening. Dr. Wilson placed the baby flat on its back. The maternity nurse handed him a small-size laryngoscope connecting with an electric suction apparatus. He set it in place and nodded, and the nurse clicked a switch. The rhythmic sucking sound of the machine began.

Dr. Wilson looked up at the clock.

Twenty seconds left to go. Heartbeat negative.

Fifteen . . . fourteen . . . Heartbeat negative.

The moment of decision was at hand. It might already be too late to prevent brain damage. No one could ever be really sure about these things. He had seen hospital wards filled with pathetic creatures with the bodies of adults and the minds of children, or worse.

Ten seconds. And no pulse, not even a thread to give him hope.

Five seconds. He made his decision then, and hoped that God would understand and forgive him. He was going to pull the plug, say that the baby could not be saved. No one would question his action. He felt the baby's skin once more. It was cold and clammy.

Three seconds.

He looked down at the infant and he wanted to weep. It was such a pity. She was a pretty baby. She would have grown up to be a beautiful woman. He wondered what her life would have been like. Would she have gotten married and had children? Or perhaps become an artist or a teacher or a business executive? Would she have been rich or poor? Happy or unhappy?

One second. Negative heartbeat.

Zero.

He reached his hand toward the switch, and at that instant the baby's heart began to beat. It was a tentative, irregular spasm, and then another and then it steadied down to a strong, regular beat. There was a spontaneous cheer in the room and cries of congratulation. Dr. Wilson was not listening.

He was staring up at the clock on the wall.

Her mother named her Josephine, after her grandmother in Krakow. A middle name would have been pretentious for the daughter of a Polish seamstress in Odessa, Texas.

For reasons that Mrs. Czinski did not understand, Dr. Wilson insisted that Josephine be brought back to the hospital for an examination every six weeks. The conclusions each time were the same: she *seemed* normal.

Only time would tell.

On Labor Day, the summer season in the Catskills was over and the Great Merlin was out of a job, and along with him, Toby. Toby was free to go. But where? He was homeless, jobless and penniless. Toby's decision was made for him when a guest offered him twenty-five dollars to drive her and her three children from the Catskills to Chicago.

Toby left without saying good-bye to the Great Merlin or his smelly props.

Chicago, in 1939, was a prosperous, wide-open city. It was a city with a price, and those who knew their way around could buy anything from women to dope to politicians. There were hundreds of nightclubs that catered to every taste. Toby made the rounds of all of them, from the big, brassy Chez Paree to the little bars on Rush Street. The answer was always the same. No one wanted to hire a young punk as a comic. The sands were running out for Toby. It was time he started to fulfill his mother's dream.

He was almost nineteen years old.

One of the clubs Toby hung around was the Knee High, where the entertainment consisted of a tired three-piece combo, a broken-down, middle-aged drunken comic and two strippers, Meri and Jeri, who were billed as the Perry Sisters and were, improbably enough, really sisters. They were in their twenties, and attractive in a cheap, blowsy way. Jeri came up to the bar one evening and sat next to Toby. He smiled and said politely, "I like your act."

Jeri turned to look at him and saw a naive, baby-faced kid, too young and too poorly dressed to be a mark. She nodded indifferently and started to turn away, when Toby stood up, Jeri stared at the telltale bulge in his pants, then turned to look up at the innocent young face again. "Jesus Christ," she said. "Is that all you?"

He smiled. "There's only one way to find out."

At three o'clock that morning, Toby was in bed with both of the Perry Sisters.

Everything had been meticulously planned. One hour before showtime, Jeri had taken the club comic, a compulsive gambler, to an apartment on Diversey Avenue where a crap game was in progress. When he saw the action, he licked his lips and said, "We can only stay a minute."

Thirty minutes later, when Jeri slipped away, the comic was rolling the dice, screaming like a maniac. "An eighter from Decatur, you son of a bitch!" lost in some fantasy world where success and stardom and riches all hung on each roll of the dice.

At the Knee High, Toby sat at the bar, neat and tidy, waiting.

When showtime came and the comic had not appeared, the owner of the club began to rage and curse. "That bastard's through this time, you hear? I won't have him near my club again."

"I don't blame you," Meri said. "But you're in luck. There's a new comic sitting at the bar. He just got in from New York."

"What? Where?" The owner took one look at Toby. "For chrissakes, where's his nanny? He's a baby!"

"He's great!" Jeri said. And she meant it.

"Try him," Meri added. "What can you lose?"

"My fuckin' customers!" But he shrugged and walked over to where Toby was sitting. "So you're a comic, huh?"

"Yeah," Toby said casually. "I just finished doing a gig in the Catskills."

The owner studied him a moment. "How old are you?"

"Twenty-two," Toby lied.

"Horseshit. All right. Get out there. And if you lay an egg, you won't *live* to see twenty-two."

And there it was. Toby Temple's dream had finally come true. He was standing in the spotlight while the band played a fanfare for him, and the audience, *his* audience, sat there waiting to discover him, to adore him. He felt a surge of affection so strong that the feeling brought a lump to his throat. It was as though he and the audience were one, bound together by some wonderful, magical cord. For an instant he thought of his mother and hoped that wherever she was, she could see him now. The fanfare stopped. Toby went into his routine.

"Good evening, you lucky people. My name is Toby Temple. I guess you all know *your* names."

Silence.

He went on. "Did you hear about the new head of the Mafia in Chicago? He's a queer. From now on, the Kiss of Death includes dinner and dancing."

There was no laughter. They were staring at him, cold and hostile, and Toby began to feel the sharp claws of fear tearing at his stomach. His body was suddenly soaked in perspiration. That wonderful bond with the audience had vanished.

He kept going. "I just played an engagement in a theater up in Maine. The theater was so far back in the woods that the manager was a bear."

Silence. They hated him.

"Nobody told me this was a deaf-mute convention. I feel like the social director on the *Titanic*. Being here is like walking up the gangplank and there's no ship."

They began to boo. Two minutes after Toby had begun, the owner frantically signaled to the musicians, who started to play loudly, drowning out Toby's voice. He stood there, a big smile on his face, his eyes stinging with tears.

He wanted to scream at them.

It was the screams that awakened Mrs. Czinski. They were high-pitched and feral, eerie in the stillness of the night, and it was not until she sat up in bed that she realized it was the baby screaming. She hurried into the other room where she had fixed up a nursery. Josephine was rolling from side to side, her face blue from convulsions. At the hospital, an intern gave the baby an intravenous sedative, and she fell into a peaceful sleep. Dr. Wilson, who had delivered Josephine, gave her a thorough examination. He could find nothing wrong with her. But he was uneasy. He could not forget the clock on the wall.

4

Vaudeville had flourished in America from 1881 until its final
demise when the Palace Theatre closed its doors in 1932.
Vaudeville had been the training ground for all the aspiring
young comics, the battlefield where they sharpened their wits
against hostile, jeering audiences. However, the comics who won
out went on to fame and fortune. Eddie Cantor and W. C. Fields,
Jolson and Benny, Abbott and Costello, and Jessel and Burns and
the Marx Brothers, and dozens more. Vaudeville was a haven, a
steady paycheck, but with vaudeville dead, comics had to turn to
other fields. The big names were booked for radio shows and
personal appearances, and they also played the important nightclubs around the country. For the struggling young comics like
Toby, however, it was another story. They played nightclubs, too,
but it was a different world. It was called the Toilet Circuit, and
the name was a euphemism. It consisted of dirty saloons all over
the country where the great unwashed public gathered to guzzle
beer and belch at the strippers and destroy the comics for sport.
The dressing rooms were stinking toilets, smelling of stale food
and spilled drinks and urine and cheap perfume and, overlaying
it all, the rancid odor of fear: flop sweat. The toilets were so filthy
that the female performers squatted over the dressing room sinks
to urinate. Payment varied from an indigestible meal to five, ten
or sometimes as much as fifteen dollars a night, depending on the
audience reaction.

Toby Temple played them all, and they became his school. The
names of the towns were different, but the places were all the same,

and the smells were the same, and the hostile audiences were the same. If they did not like a performer, they threw beer bottles at him and heckled him throughout his performance and whistled him off. It was a tough school, but it was a good one, because it taught Toby all the tricks of survival. He learned to deal with drunken tourists and sober hoodlums, and never to confuse the two. He learned how to spot a potential heckler and quiet him by asking him for a sip of his drink or borrowing his napkin to mop his brow.

Toby talked himself into jobs at places with names like Lake Kiamesha and Shawanga Lodge and the Avon. He played Wildwood, New Jersey, and the B'nai B'rith and the Sons of Italy and Moose halls.

And he kept learning.

Toby's act consisted of parodies of popular songs, imitations of Gable and Grant and Bogart and Cagney, and material stolen from the big-name comics who could afford expensive writers. All the struggling comics stole their material, and they bragged about it. "I'm doing Jerry Lester"—meaning they were using his material—"and I'm twice as good as he is." "I'm doing Milton Berle." "You should see my Red Skelton."

Because material was the key, they stole only from the best.

Toby would try anything. He would fix the indifferent, hard-faced audience with his wistful blue eyes and say, "Did you ever see an Eskimo pee?" He would put his two hands in front of his fly, and ice cubes would dribble out.

He would put on a turban and wrap himself in a sheet. "Abdul, the snake charmer," he would intone. He would play a flute, and out of a wicker basket a cobra began to appear, moving rhythmically to the music as Toby pulled wires. The snake's body was a douche bag, and its head was the nozzle. There was always someone in the audience who thought it was funny.

He did the standards and the stockies and the platters, where you laid the jokes in their laps.

He had dozens of *shticks*. He had to be ready to switch from one *bit* to another, before the beer bottles started flying.

And no matter where he played, there was always the sound of a flushing toilet during his act.

★

Toby traveled across the country by bus. When he arrived at a new town he would check into the cheapest hotel or boardinghouse and size up the nightclubs and bars and horse parlors. He stuffed cardboard in the soles of his shoes and whitened his shirt collars with chalk to save on laundry. The towns were all dreary, and the food was always bad; but it was the loneliness that ate into him. He had no one. There was not a single person in the vast universe who cared whether he lived or died. He wrote to his father from time to time, but it was out of a sense of duty rather than love. Toby desperately needed someone to talk to, someone who would understand him, share his dreams with him.

He watched the successful entertainers leave the big clubs with their entourages and their beautiful, classy girls and drive off in shiny limousines, and Toby envied them. *Someday . . .*

The worst moments were when he flopped, when he was booed in the middle of his act, thrown out before he had a chance to get started. At those times Toby hated the people in the audience; he wanted to kill them. It wasn't only that he had failed, it was that he had failed at the bottom. He could go down no further; he was *there*. He hid in his hotel room and cried and begged God to leave him alone, to take away his desire to stand in front of an audience and entertain them. *God*, he prayed, *let me want to be a shoe salesman or a butcher. Anything but this.* His mother had been wrong. God had not singled him out. He was never going to be famous. Tomorrow, he would find some other line of work. He would apply for a nine-to-five job in an office and live like a normal human being.

And the next night Toby would be on stage again, doing his imitations, telling jokes, trying to win over the people before they turned on him and attacked.

He would smile at them innocently and say, "This man was in love with his duck, and he took it to a movie with him one night. The cashier said, 'You can't bring that duck in here,' so the man went around the corner and stuffed the duck down the front of his trousers, bought a ticket and went inside. The duck started getting restless, so the man opened his fly and let the duck's head out. Well, next to the man was a lady and her husband. She turned to her husband and said, 'Ralph, the man next to me has his penis out.' So Ralph said, 'Is he bothering you?' 'No,' she said. 'Okay. Then forget it and enjoy the movie.' A few minutes later the wife nudged her husband again. 'Ralph—his penis—' And her husband said, 'I told you to ignore it.' And she said, 'I can't—it's eating my popcorn!' ' "

He made one-night appearances at the Three Six Five in San Francisco, Rudy's Rail in New York and Kin Wa Low's in Toledo. He played plumbers conventions and bar mitzvahs and bowling banquets.

And he learned.

He did four and five shows a day at small theaters named the Gem and the Odeon and the Empire and the Star.

And he learned.

And, finally, one of the things that Toby Temple learned was that he could spend the rest of his life playing the Toilet Circuit, unknown and undiscovered. But an event occurred that made the whole matter academic.

On a cold Sunday afternoon in early December in 1941, Toby was playing a five-a-day act at the Dewey Theatre on Fourteenth Street in New York. There were eight acts on the bill, and part of Toby's job was to introduce them. The first show went well. During the second show, when Toby introduced the Flying Kanazawas, a family of Japanese acrobats, the audience began to hiss them. Toby retreated backstage. "What the hell's the matter with them out there?" he asked.

"Jesus, haven't you heard? The Japs attacked Pearl Harbor a few hours ago," the stage manager told him.

"So what?" Toby asked. "Look at those guys—they're great."

The next show, when it was the turn of the Japanese troupe, Toby went out on stage and aaid, "Ladies and gentlemen, it's a great privilege to present to you, fresh from their triumph in Manila—the Flying Filipinos!" The moment the audience saw the Japanese troupe, they began to hiss. During the rest of the day Toby turned them into the Happy Hawaiians, the Mad Mongolians and, finally, the Eskimo Flyers. But he was unable to save them. Nor, as it turned out, himself. When he telephoned his father that evening, Toby learned that there was a letter waiting for him at home. It began, "Greetings," and was signed by the President. Six weeks later, Toby was sworn into the United States Army. The day he was inducted, his head was pounding so hard that he was barely able to take the oath.

★

The headaches came often, and when they happened, little Josephine felt as though two giant hands were squeezing her temples. She tried not to cry, because it upset her mother. Mrs. Czinski had discovered religion. She had always secretly felt that in some way she and her baby were responsible for the death of her husband. She had wandered into a revival meeting one afternoon, and the minister had thundered, "You are all soaked in sin and wickedness. The God that holds you over the pit of Hell like a loathsome insect over a fire abhors you. You hang by a slender thread, every damned one of you, and flames of His wrath will consume you unless you repent!" Mrs. Czinski instantly felt better, for she knew that she was hearing the word of the Lord.

"It's a punishment from God because we killed your father," her mother would tell Josephine, and while she was too young to understand what the words meant, she knew that she had done something bad, and she wished she knew what it was, so that she could tell her mother that she was sorry.

I n the beginning, Toby Temple's war was a nightmare.
     In the army, he was a nobody, a serial number in a uniform
     like millions of others, faceless, nameless, anonymous.

He was sent to basic training camp in Georgia and then shipped
out to England, where his outfit was assigned to a camp in Sussex.
Toby told the sergeant he wanted to see the commanding general.
He got as far as a captain. The captain's name was Sam Winters.
He was a dark-complexioned, intelligent-looking man in his early
thirties. "What's your problem, soldier?"

"It's like this, Captain," Toby began. "I'm an entertainer. I'm
in show business. That's what I did in civilian life."

Captain Winters smiled at his earnestness. "What exactly do
you do?" he asked.

"A little of everything," Toby replied. "I do imitations and
parodies and . . ." He saw the look in the captain's eyes and ended
lamely. "Things like that."

"Where have you worked?"

Toby started to speak, then stopped. It was hopeless. The captain would only be impressed by places like New York and Hollywood. "No place you would have heard of," Toby replied. He
knew now that he was wasting his time.

Captain Winters said, "It's not up to me, but I'll see what I can
do."

"Sure," Toby said. "Thanks a lot, Captain." He gave a salute
and exited.

Captain Sam Winters sat at his desk, thinking about Toby long after the boy had gone. Sam Winters had enlisted because he felt that this was a war that had to be fought and had to be won. At the same time he hated it for what it was doing to young kids like Toby Temple. But if Temple really had talent, it would come through sooner or later, for talent was like a frail flower growing under solid rock. In the end, nothing could stop it from bursting through and blooming. Sam Winters had given up a good job as a motion-picture producer in Hollywood to go into the army. He had produced several successful pictures for Pan-Pacific Studios and had seen dozens of young hopefuls like Toby Temple come and go. The least they deserved was a chance. Later that afternoon he spoke to Colonel Beech about Toby. "I think we should let Special Services audition him," Captain Winters said. "I have a feeling he might be good. God knows the boys are going to need all the entertainment they can get."

Colonel Beech stared up at Captain Winters and said coolly, "Right, Captain. Send me a memo on it." He watched as Captain Winters walked out the door. Colonel Beech was a professional soldier, a West Point man. The Colonel despised all civilians, and to him, Captain Winters was a civilian. Putting on a uniform and captain's bars did not make a man a soldier. When Colonel Beech received Captain Winter's memo on Toby Temple, he glanced at it, then savagely scribbled across it, "REQUEST DENIED," and initialed it.

He felt better.

What Toby missed most was the lack of an audience. He needed to work on his sense of timing, his skills. He would tell jokes and do imitations and routines at every opportunity. It did not matter whether his audience was two GIs doing guard duty with him in a lonely field, a busload of soldiers on their way into town or a dishwasher on KP. Toby had to make them laugh, win their applause.

Captain Sam Winters watched one day as Toby went through one of his routines in the recreation hall. Afterward, he went up to Toby and said, "I'm sorry your transfer didn't work out, Temple. I think you have talent. When the war's over, if you get to Hollywood, look me up." He grinned and added, "Assuming I still have a job out there."

The following week Toby's battallion was sent into combat.

In later years, when Toby recalled the war, what he remembered were not the battles. At Saint-Lô he had been a smash doing a mouth-sync act to a Bing Crosby record. At Aachen he had sneaked into the hospital and told jokes to the wounded for two hours before the nurses threw him out. He remembered with satisfaction that one GI had laughed so hard all his stitches had broken open. Metz was where he had bombed out, but Toby felt that that was only because the audience was jittery about the Nazi planes flying overhead.

The fighting that Toby did was incidental. He was cited for bravery in the capture of a German command post. Toby had really no idea what was going on. He had been playing John Wayne, and had gotten so carried away that it was all over before he had time to be frightened.

To Toby, it was the entertaining that was important. In Cherbourg he visited a whorehouse with a couple of friends, and while they were upstairs, Toby stayed in the parlor doing a routine for the madame and two of her girls. When he had finished, the madame sent him upstairs, on the house.

That was Toby's war. All in all, it was not a bad war, and time went by very quickly. When the war ended, it was 1945 and Toby was almost twenty-five years old. In appearance he had not aged one day. He had the same sweet face and beguiling blue eyes, and that hapless air of innocence about him.

Everyone was talking about going home. There was a bride waiting in Kansas City, a mother and father in Bayonne, a business in St. Louis. There was nothing waiting for Toby. Except Fame.

He decided to go to Hollywood. It was time that God made good on His promise.

"Do you know God? Have you seen the face of Jesus? I have seen Him, brothers and sisters, and I have heard His voice, but he speaks only to those who kneel before Him and confess their sins. God abhors the unrepentant. The bow of God's wrath is bent and the flaming arrow of His righteous anger is pointed at your wicked hearts, and at any moment He will let go and the arrow of His retribution shall smite your hearts! Look up to Him now, before it is too late!"

Josephine looked up toward the top of the tent, terrified, expecting to see a flaming arrow shooting at her. She clutched her mother's hand, but her mother was unaware of it. Her face was flushed and her eyes were bright with fervor.

"Praise Jesus!" the congregation roared.

The revival meetings were held in a huge tent, on the outskirts of Odessa, and Mrs. Czinski took Josephine to all of them. The preacher's pulpit was a wooden platform raised six feet above the ground. Immediately in front of the platform was the glory pen, where sinners were brought to repent and experience conversion. Beyond the pen were rows and rows of hard wooden benches, packed with chanting, fanatic seekers of salvation, awed by the threats of Hell and Damnation. It was terrifying for a six-year-old child. The evangelists were Fundamentalists, Holy Rollers and Pentecostalists and Methodists and Adventists, and they all breathed Hell-fire and Damnation.

"Get on your knees, O ye sinners, and tremble before the might of Jehovah! For your wicked ways have broken the heart of Jesus Christ, and for that ye shall bear the punishment of His Father's wrath! Look around at the faces of the young children here, conceived in lust and filled with sin."

And little Josephine would burn with shame, feeling everyone staring at her. When the bad headaches came, Josephine knew that they were a punishment from God. She prayed every night that they would go away, so she would know that God had forgiven her. She wished she knew what she had done that was so bad.

"And I'll sing Hallelujah, and you'll sing Hallelujah, and we'll all sing Hallelujah when we arrive at Home."

"Liquor is the blood of the Devil, and tobacco is his breath, and fornication is his pleasure. Are you guilty of trafficking with Satan? Then you shall burn eternally in Hell, damned forever, because Lucifer is coming to get you!"

And Josephine would tremble and look around wildly, fiercely clutching the wooden bench so that the Devil could not take her.

They sang, "I want to get to Heaven, my long-sought rest." But little Josephine misunderstood and sang, "I want to get to Heaven with my long short dress."

*After the thundering sermons would come the Miracles. Jose-
phine would watch in frightened fascination as a procession of
crippled men and women limped and crawled and rode in wheel-
chairs to the glory pen, where the preacher laid hands on them
and willed the powers of Heaven to heal them. They would throw
away their canes and their crutches, and some of them would
babble hysterically in strange tongues, and Josephine would
cower in terror.*

*The revival meetings always ended with the plate being
passed. "Jesus is watching you—and He hates a miser." And
then it would be over. But the fear would stay with Josephine for
a long time.*

In 1946, the town of Odessa, Texas, had a dark brown taste.
Long ago, when the Indians had lived there, it had been the taste
of desert sand. Now it was the taste of oil.

There were two kinds of people in Odessa: Oil People and the
Others. The Oil People did not look *down* on the Others—they
simply felt sorry for them, for surely God meant everyone to have
private planes and Cadillacs and swimming pools and to give
champagne parties for a hundred people. That was why He had put
oil in Texas.

Josephine Czinski did not know that she was one of the Others.
At six, Josephine Czinski was a beautiful child, with shiny black
hair and deep brown eyes and a lovely oval face.

Josephine's mother was a skilled seamstress who worked for the
wealthy people in town, and she would take Josephine along as she
fitted the Oil Ladies and turned bolts of fairy cloth into stunning
evening gowns. The Oil People liked Josephine because she was a
polite, friendly child, and they liked themselves for liking her.
They felt it was democratic of them to allow a poor kid from the
other side of town to associate with their children. Josephine was
Polish, but she did not *look* Polish, and while she could never be
a member of the Club, they were happy to give her visitors'
privileges. Josephine was allowed to play with the Oil Children and
share their bicycles and ponies and hundred-dollar dolls, so that
she came to live a dual life. There was her life at home in the tiny
clapboard cottage with battered furniture and outdoor plumbing
and doors that sagged on their hinges. Then there was Josephine's

life in beautiful colonial mansions on large country estates. If Josephine stayed overnight at Cissy Topping's or Lindy Ferguson's, she was given a large bedroom all to herself, with breakfast served by maids and butlers. Josephine loved to get up in the middle of the night when everyone was asleep and go down and stare at the beautiful things in the house, the lovely paintings and heavy monogrammed silver and antiques burnished by time and history. She would study them and caress them and tell herself that one day she would have such things, one day she would live in a grand house and be surrounded by beauty.

But in both of Josephine's worlds, she felt lonely. She was afraid to talk to her mother about her headaches and her fear of God because her mother had become a brooding fanatic, obsessed with God's punishment, welcoming it. Josephine did not want to discuss her fears with the Oil Children because they expected her to be bright and gay, as they were. And so, Josephine was forced to keep her terrors to herself.

On Josephine's seventh birthday, Brubaker's Department Store announced a photographic contest for the Most Beautiful Child in Odessa. The entry picture had to be taken in the photograph department of the store. The prize was a gold cup inscribed with the name of the winner. The cup was placed in the department-store window, and Josephine walked by the window every day to stare at it. She wanted it more than she had ever wanted anything in her life. Josephine's mother would not let her enter the contest— "Vanity is the devil's mirror," she said—but one of the Oil Women who liked Josephine paid for her picture. From that moment on, Josephine knew that the gold cup was hers. She could visualize it sitting on her dresser. She would polish it carefully every day. When Josephine found out that she was in the finals, she was too excited to go to school. She stayed in bed all day with an upset stomach, her happiness too much for her to bear. This would be the first time that she had owned anything beautiful.

The following day Josephine learned that the contest had been won by Tina Hudson, one of the Oil Children. Tina was not nearly as beautiful as Josephine, but Tina's father happened to be on the board of directors of the chain that owned Brubaker's Department Store.

When Josephine heard the news, she developed a headache that made her want to scream with pain. She was afraid for God to know how much that beautiful gold cup meant to her, but He must have known because her headaches continued. At night she would cry into her pillow, so that her mother could not hear her.

A few days after the contest ended, Josephine was invited to Tina's home for a weekend. The gold cup was sitting in Tina's room on a mantle. Josephine stared at it for a long time.

When Josephine returned home, the cup was hidden in her overnight case. It was still there when Tina's mother came by for it and took it back.

Josephine's mother gave her a hard whipping with a switch made from a long, green twig. But Josephine was not angry with her mother.

The few minutes Josephine had held the beautiful gold cup in her hands had been worth all the pain.

Hollywood, California, in 1946, was the film capital of the world, a magnet for the talented, the greedy, the beautiful, the hopeful and the weird. It was the land of palm trees and Rita Hayworth and the Holy Temple of the Universal Spirit and Santa Anita. It was the agent who was going to make you an overnight star; it was a con game, a whorehouse, an orange grove, a shrine. It was a magical kaleidoscope, and each person who looked into it saw his own vision.

To Toby Temple, Hollywood was where he was meant to come. He arrived in town with an army duffel bag and three hundred dollars in cash, moving into a cheap boardinghouse on Cahuenga Boulevard. He had to get into action fast, before he went broke. Toby knew all about Hollywood. It was a town where you had to put up a front. Toby went into a haberdashery on Vine Street, ordered a new wardrobe, and with twenty dollars remaining in his pocket, strolled into the Hollywood Brown Derby, where all the stars dined. The walls were covered with caricatures of the most famous actors in Hollywood. Toby could feel the pulse of show business here, sense the power in the room. He saw the hostess walking toward him. She was a pretty redhead in her twenties and she had a sensational figure.

She smiled at Toby and said, "Can I help you?"

Toby could not resist it. He reached out with his two hands and grabbed her ripe melon breasts. A look of shock came over her face. As she opened her mouth to cry out, Toby fixed his eyes in a glazed stare and said apologetically, "Excuse me, miss—I'm not a sighted person."

"Oh! I'm sorry!" She was contrite for what she had been thinking, and sympathetic. She conducted Toby to a table, holding his
arm and helping him sit down, and arranged for his order. When
she came back to his table a few minutes later and caught him
studying the pictures on the wall, Toby beamed up at her and said,
"It's a miracle! I can see again!"

He was so innocent and so funny that she could not help laughing. She laughed all through dinner with Toby, and at his jokes in
bed that night.

Toby took odd jobs around Hollywood because they brought
him to the fringes of show business. He parked cars at Ciro's, and
as the celebrities drove up, Toby would open the car door with a
bright smile and an apt quip. They paid no attention. He was just
a parking boy, and they did not even know he was alive. Toby
watched the beautiful girls as they got out of the cars in their
expensive, tight-fitting dresses, and he thought to himself, *If you
only knew what a big star I'm going to be, you'd drop all those
creeps.*

Toby made the rounds of agents, but he quickly learned that he
was wasting his time. The agents were all star-fuckers. You could
not look for *them*. They had to be looking for *you*. The name that
Toby heard most often was Clifton Lawrence. He handled only the
biggest talent and he made the most incredible deals. *One day*,
Toby thought, *Clifton Lawrence is going to be my agent.*

Toby subscribed to the two bibles of show business: *Daily
Variety* and the *Hollywood Reporter*. It made him feel like an
insider. *Forever Amber* had been bought by Twentieth Century-
Fox, and Otto Preminger was going to direct. Ava Gardner had
been signed to star in *Whistle Stop* with George Raft and Jorja
Curtright, and *Life with Father* had been bought by Warner
Brothers. Then Toby saw an item that made his pulse start pound-
ing. "Producer Sam Winters has been named Vice-President in
Charge of Production at Pan-Pacific Studios."

W hen Sam Winters returned from the war his job at Pan-
Pacific Studios was waiting for him. Six months later,
there was a shakeup. The head of the studio was fired, and
Sam was asked to take over until a new production head could be
found. Sam did such a good job that the search was abandoned,
and he was officially made Vice-President in Charge of Production. It was a nerve-racking, ulcer-making job, but Sam loved it
more than he loved anything in the world.

Hollywood was a three-ring circus filled with wild, insane characters, a minefield with a parade of idiots dancing across it. Most
actors, directors and producers were self-centered megalomaniacs,
ungrateful, vicious and destructive. But as far as Sam was concerned, if they had talent, nothing else mattered. Talent was the
magic key.

Sam's office door opened and Lucille Elkins, his secretary, came
in with the freshly opened mail. Lucille was a permanent fixture,
one of the competent professionals who stayed on forever and
watched her bosses come and go.

"Clifton Lawrence is here to see you," Lucille said.

"Tell him to come in."

Sam liked Lawrence. He had style. Fred Allen had said, "All the
sincerity in Hollywood could be hidden in a gnat's navel and
there'd still be room for four caraway seeds and an agent's heart."

Cliff Lawrence was more sincere than most agents. He was a
Hollywood legend, and his client list ran the gamut of who's who
in the entertainment field. He had a one-man office and was con-

stantly on the move, servicing clients in London, Switzerland, Rome and New York. He was on intimate terms with all the important Hollywood executives and played in a weekly gin game that included the production heads of three studios. Twice a year, Lawrence chartered a yacht, gathered half a dozen beautiful "models" and invited top studio executives for a week's "fishing trip." Clifton Lawrence kept a fully stocked beachhouse at Malibu that was available to his friends anytime they wanted to use it. It was a symbiotic relationship that Clifton had with Hollywood, and it was profitable for everyone.

Sam watched as the door opened and Lawrence bounced in, elegant in a beautifully tailored suit. He walked up to Sam, extended a perfectly manicured hand and said, "Just wanted to say a quick hello. How's everything, dear boy?"

"Let me put it this way," Sam said. "If days were ships, today would be the *Titanic.*"

Clifton Lawrence made a commiserating noise.

"What did you think of the preview last night?" Sam asked.

"Trim the first twenty minutes and shoot a new ending, and you've got yourself a big hit."

"Bull's-eye." Sam smiled. "That's exactly what we're doing. Any clients to sell me today?"

Lawrence grinned. "Sorry. They're all working."

And it was true. Clifton Lawrence's select stable of top stars, with a sprinkling of directors and producers, were always in demand.

"See you for dinner Friday, Sam," Clifton said. *"Ciao."* He turned and walked out the door.

Lucille's voice came over the intercom. "Dallas Burke is here."

"Send him in."

"And Mel Foss would like to see you. He said it's urgent."

Mel Foss was head of the television division of Pan-Pacific Studios.

Sam glanced at his desk calendar. "Tell him to make it breakfast tomorrow morning. Eight o'clock. The Polo Lounge."

In the outer office, the telephone rang and Lucille picked it up. "Mr. Winter's office."

An unfamiliar voice said, "Hello there. Is the great man in?"

"Who's calling, please?"

"Tell him it's an old buddy of his—Toby Temple. We were in the army together. He said to look him up if I ever got to Hollywood, and here I am."

"He's in a meeting, Mr. Temple. Could I have him call you back?"

"Sure." He gave her his telephone number, and Lucille threw it into the wastebasket. This was not the first time someone had tried the old-army-buddy routine on her.

Dallas Burke was one of the motion-picture industry's pioneer directors. Burke's films were shown at every college that had a course in movie making. Half a dozen of his earlier pictures were considered classics, and none of his work was less than brilliant and innovative. Burke was in his late seventies now, and his once massive frame had shrunk so that his clothes seemed to flap around him.

"It's good to see you again, Dallas," Sam said as the old man walked into the office.

"Nice to see you, kid." He indicated the man with him. "You know my agent."

"Certainly. How are you, Peter?"

They all found seats.

"I hear you have a story to tell me," Sam said to Dallas Burke.

"This one's a beauty." There was a quavering excitement in the old man's voice.

"I'm dying to hear it, Dallas," Sam said. "Shoot."

Dallas Burke leaned forward and began talking. "What's everybody in the world most interested in, kid? Love—right? And this idea's about the most holy kind of love there is—the love of a mother for her child." His voice grew stronger as he became immersed in his story. "We open in Long Island with a nineteen-year-old girl working as a secretary for a wealthy family. Old money. Gives us a chance for a slick background—know what I mean? High-society stuff. The man she works for is married to a tight-assed blueblood. He likes the secretary, and she likes him, even though he's older."

Only half-listening, Sam wondered whether the story was going to be *Back Street* or *Imitation of Life*. Not that it mattered, because whichever it was, Sam was going to buy it. It had been almost twenty years since anyone had given Dallas Burke a picture to direct. Sam could not blame the industry. Burke's last three pictures had been expensive, old-fashioned and box-office disasters. Dallas Burke was finished forever as a picture maker. But he was a human being and he was still alive, and somehow he had to be taken care of, because he had not saved a cent. He had been offered a room in the Motion Picture Relief Home, but he had indignantly turned it down. "I don't want your fucking charity!" he had shouted. "You're talking to the man who directed Doug Fairbanks and Jack Barrymore and Milton Sills and Bill Farnum. I'm a giant, you pygmy sons of bitches!"

And he was. He was a legend; but even legends had to eat.

When Sam had become a producer, he had telephoned an agent he knew and told him to bring in Dallas Burke with a story idea. Since then, Sam had bought unusable stories from Dallas Burke every year for enough money for the old man to live on, and while Sam had been away in the army, he had seen to it that the arrangement continued.

". . . so you see," Dallas Burke was saying, "the baby grows up without knowing her mother. But the mother keeps track of *her*. At the end, when the daughter marries this rich doctor, we have a big wedding. And do you know what the twist is, Sam? Listen to this—it's great. They won't let the mother in! She has to sneak in to the back of the church to watch her own kid getting married. There won't be a dry eye in the audience. . . . Well, that's it. What do you think?"

Sam had guessed wrong. *Stella Dallas*. He glanced at the agent, who averted his eyes and studied the tips of his expensive shoes in embarrassment.

"It's great," Sam said. "It's exactly the kind of picture the studio's looking for." Sam turned to the agent. "Call Business Affairs and work out a deal with them, Peter. I'll tell them to expect your call."

The agent nodded.

"Tell them they're gonna have to pay a stiff price for this one, or I'll take it to Warner Brothers," Dallas Burke said. "I'm giving you first crack at it because we're friends."

"I appreciate that," Sam said.

He watched as the two men left the office. Strictly speaking,

Sam knew he had no right to spend the company's money on a sentimental gesture like this. But the motion-picture industry owed something to men like Dallas Burke, for without him and his kind, there would have been no industry.

At eight o'clock the following morning, Sam Winters drove up under the portico of the Beverly Hills Hotel. A few minutes later, he was threading his way across the Polo Lounge, nodding to friends, acquaintances and competitors. More deals were made in this room over breakfast, lunch and cocktails than were consummated in all the offices of all the studios combined. Mel Foss looked up as Sam approached.

"Morning, Sam."

The two men shook hands and Sam slid into the booth across from Foss. Eight months ago Sam had hired Foss to run the television division of Pan-Pacific Studios. Television was the new baby in the entertainment world, and it was growing with incredible rapidity. All the studios that had once looked down on television were now involved in it.

The waitress came to take their orders, and when she had left, Sam said, "What's the good news, Mel?"

Mel Foss shook his head. "There is no good news," he said. "We're in trouble."

Sam waited, saying nothing.

"We're not going to get a pickup on 'The Raiders.' "

Sam looked at him in surprise. "The ratings are great. Why would the network want to cancel it? It's tough enough to get a hit show."

"It's not the show," Foss said. "It's Jack Nolan." Jack Nolan was the star of "The Raiders," and he had been an instant success, both critically and with the public.

"What's the matter with him?" Sam asked. He hated Mel Foss's habit of forcing him to draw information from him.

"Have you read this week's issue of *Peek* Magazine?"

"I don't read it any week. It's a garbage pail." He suddenly realized what Foss was driving at. "They nailed Nolan!"

"In black and white," Foss replied. "The dumb son of a bitch put on his prettiest lace dress and went out to a party. Someone took pictures."

"How bad is it?"

"Couldn't be worse. I got a dozen calls from the network yesterday. The sponsors and the network want out. No one wants to be associated with a screaming fag."

"Transvestite," Sam said. He had been counting heavily on presenting a strong television report at the board meeting in New York next month. The news from Foss would put an end to that. Losing "The Raiders" would be a blow.

Unless he could do something.

When Sam returned to his office, Lucille waved a sheaf of messages at him. "The emergencies are on top," she said. "They need you—"

"Later. Get me William Hunt at IBC."

Two minutes later, Sam was talking to the head of the International Broadcasting Company. Sam had known Hunt casually for a number of years, and liked him. Hunt had started as a bright young corporate lawyer and had worked his way to the top of the network ladder. They seldom had any business dealings because Sam was not directly involved with television. He wished now that he had taken the time to cultivate Hunt. When Hunt came on the line, Sam forced himself to sound relaxed and casual. "Morning, Bill."

"This is a pleasant surprise," Hunt said. "It's been a long time, Sam."

"Much too long. That's the trouble with this business, Bill. You never have time for the people you like."

"Too true."

Sam made his voice sound offhand. "By the way, did you happen to see that silly article in *Peek?*"

"You know I did," Hunt said quietly. "That's why we're canceling the show, Sam." The words had a finality to them.

"Bill." Sam said, "what would you say if I told you that Jack Nolan was framed?"

There was a laugh from the other end of the line. "I'd say you should think about becoming a writer."

"I'm serious," Sam said, earnestly. "I *know* Jack Nolan. He's as straight as we are. That photograph was taken at a costume party. It was his girlfriend's birthday, and he put the dress on as a gag." Sam could feel his palms sweating.

"I can't—"

"I'll tell you how much confidence I have in Jack," Sam said into the phone. "I've just set him for the lead in *Laredo*, our big Western feature for next year."

There was a pause. "Are you serious, Sam?"

"You're damn right I am. It's a three-million-dollar picture. If Jack Nolan turned out to be a fag, he'd be laughed off the screen. The exhibitors wouldn't touch it. Would I take that kind of gamble if I didn't know what I was talking about?"

"Well . . ." There was hesitation in Bill Hunt's voice.

"Come on, Bill, you're not going to let a lousy gossip sheet like *Peek* destroy a good man's career. You *like* the show, don't you?"

"Very much. It's a damned good show. But the sponsors—"

"It's your network. You've got more sponsors than you have air time. We've given you a hit show. Let's not fool around with a success."

"Well . . ."

"Has Mell Foss talked to you yet about the studio's plans for 'The Raiders' for next season?"

"No . . ."

"I guess he was planning to surprise you," Sam said. "Wait until you hear what he has in mind! Guest stars, big-name Western writers, shooting on location—the works! If 'The Raiders' doesn't skyrocket to number one, I'm in the wrong business."

There was a brief hesitation. Then Bill Hunt said, "Have Mel phone me. Maybe we all got a little panicked here."

"He'll call you," Sam promised.

"And, Sam—you understand my position. I wasn't trying to hurt anybody."

"Of course you weren't," Sam said, generously. "I know you too well to think that, Bill. That's why I felt I owed it to you to let you hear the truth."

"I appreciate that."

"What about lunch next week?"

"Love it. I'll call you Monday."

They exchanged good-byes and hung up. Sam sat there, drained. Jack Nolan was as queer as an Indian dime. Someone should have taken him away in a net long ago. And Sam's whole future depended on maniacs like that. Running a studio was like walking a high wire over Niagara Falls in a blizzard. *Anyone's crazy to do this job,* Sam thought. He picked up his private phone and dialed. A few moments later, he was talking to Mel Foss.

" 'The Raiders' stays on the air," Sam said.

"What?" There was stunned disbelief in Foss's voice.

"That's right. I want you to have a fast talk with Jack Nolan. Tell him if he ever steps out of line again, I'll personally run him out of this town and back to Fire Island! I mean it. If he gets the urge to suck something, tell him to try a banana!"

Sam slammed the phone down. He leaned back in his chair, thinking. He had forgotten to tell Foss about the format changes he had ad-libbed to Bill Hunt. He would have to find a writer who could come up with a Western script called *Laredo*.

The door burst open and Lucille stood there, her face white. "Can you get right down to Stage Ten? Someone set it on fire."

Toby Temple had tried to reach Sam Winters half a dozen times, but he was never able to get past his bitch of a secretary, and he finally gave up. Toby made the rounds of the nightclubs and studios without success. During the next year, he took jobs to support himself. He sold real estate and insurance and haberdashery, and in between he played in bars and obscure nightclubs. But he was not able to get past the studio gates.

"You're going about it the wrong way," a friend of his told him. "Make *them* come to *you*."

"How do I do that?" Toby asked, cynically.

"Get into Actors West."

"An *acting* school?"

"It's more than that. They put on plays, and every studio in town covers them."

Actors West had the smell of professionalism. Toby could sense it the moment he walked in the door. On the wall were photographs of graduates of the school. Toby recognized many of them as successful actors.

The blond receptionist behind the desk said, "May I help you?"

"Yes. I'm Toby Temple. I'd like to enroll."

"Have you had acting experience?" she asked.

"Well, no," Toby said. "But, I—"

She shook her head. "I'm sorry, Mrs. Tanner won't interview anyone without professional experience."

Toby stared at her a moment. "Are you kidding me?"

"No. That's our rule. She never—"

"I'm not talking about that," Toby said. "I mean—you really don't know who I am?"

The blonde looked at him and said, "No."

Toby let his breath out softly. "Jesus," he said. "Leland Hayward was right. If you work in England, Hollywood doesn't even know you're alive." He smiled and said apologetically, "I was joking. I figured you'd know me."

The receptionist was confused now, not knowing what to believe. "You *have* worked professionally?"

Toby laughed. "I'll say I have."

The blonde picked up a form. "What parts have you played, and where?"

"Nothing here," Toby said quickly. "I've been in England for the last two years, working in rep."

The blonde nodded. "I see. Well, let me talk to Mrs. Tanner."

The blonde disappeared into the inner office, returning a few minutes later. "Mrs. Tanner will see you. Good luck."

Toby winked at the receptionist, took a deep breath and walked into Mrs. Tanner's office.

Alice Tanner was a dark-haired woman, with an attractive, aristocratic face. She appeared to be in her middle thirties, about ten years older than Toby. She was seated behind her desk, but what Toby could see of her figure was sensational. *This place is going to be just fine*, Toby decided.

Toby smiled winningly and said, "I'm Toby Temple."

Alice Tanner rose from behind the desk and walked toward him. Her left leg was encased in a heavy metal brace and she limped with the practiced, rolling walk of someone who has lived with it for a long time.

Polio, Toby decided. He did not know whether to comment on it.

"So you want to enroll in our classes."

"Very much," Toby said.

"May I ask why?"

He made his voice sincere. "Because everywhere I go, Mrs. Tanner, people talk about your school and the wonderful plays you put on here. I'll bet you have no idea of the reputation this place has."

She studied him a moment. "I do have an idea. That's why I have to be careful to keep out phonies."

Toby felt his face begin to redden, but he smiled boyishly and said, "I'll bet. A lot of them, must try to crash in here."

"Quite a few," Mrs. Tanner agreed. She glanced at the card she held in her hand. "Toby Temple."

"You probably haven't heard the name," he explained, "because for the last couple of years, I've been——"

"Playing repertory in England."

He nodded. "Right."

Alice Tanner looked at him and said quietly, "Mr. Temple, Americans are not permitted to play in English repertory. British Actors Equity doesn't allow it."

Toby felt a sudden sinking sensation in the pit of his stomach.

"You might have checked first and saved us both this embarrassment. I'm sorry, but we only enroll professional talent here." She started back toward her desk. The interview was over.

"Hold it!" His voice was like a whiplash.

She turned in astonishment. At that instant, Toby had no idea what he was going to say or do. He only knew that his whole future was hanging in the balance. The woman standing in front of him was the stepping-stone to everything he wanted, everything he had worked and sweated for, and he was not going to let her stop him.

"You don't judge talents by rules, lady! Okay—so I haven't acted. And why? Because people like you won't give me a chance. You see what I mean?" It was W. C. Field's voice.

Alice Tanner opened her mouth to interrupt him, but Toby never gave her the opportunity. He was Jimmy Cagney telling her to give the poor kid a break, and James Stewart agreeing with him, and Clark Gable saying he was dying to work with the kid and Cary Grant adding that he thought the boy was brilliant. A host of Hollywood stars was in that room, and they were all saying funny things, things that Toby Temple had never thought of before. The words, the jokes poured out of him in a frenzy of desperation. He was a man drowning in the darkness of his own oblivion, clinging to a life raft of words, and the words were all that were keeping him afloat. He was soaked in perspiration, running around the room, imitating the movement of each character who was talking. He was

372

manic, totally outside of himself, forgetting where he was and what he was here for until he heard Alice Tanner saying, "Stop it! Stop it!"

Tears of laughter were streaming down her face.

"Stop it!" she repeated, gasping for breath.

And slowly, Toby came down to earth. Mrs. Tanner had taken out a handkerchief and was wiping her eyes.

"You—you're insane," she said. "Do you know that?"

Toby stared at her, a feeling of elation slowly filling him, lifting, exalting him. "You liked it, huh?"

Alice Tanner shook her head and took a deep breath to control her laughter and said, "Not—not very much."

Toby looked at her, filled with rage. She had been laughing *at* him, not with him. He had been making a fool of himself.

"Then what were you laughing at?" Toby demanded.

She smiled and said quietly. "You. That was the most frenetic performance I've ever seen. Somewhere, hidden beneath all those movie stars, is a young man with a lot of talent. You don't have to imitate other people. You're naturally funny."

Toby felt his anger begin to seep away.

"I think one day you could be really good if you're willing to work hard at it. Are you?"

He gave her a slow, beatific grin and said, "Let's roll up our sleeves and go to work."

Josephine worked very hard Saturday morning, helping her mother clean the house. At noon, Cissy and some other friends picked her up to take her on a picnic.

Mrs. Czinski watched Josephine being driven off in the long limousine filled with the children of the Oil People. She thought, one day something bad is going to happen to Josephine. I shouldn't let her be with those people. They're the Devil's children. And she wondered if there was a devil in Josephine. She would talk to the Reverend Damian. He would know what to do.

A ctors West was divided into two sections: the Showcase group, which consisted of the more experienced actors, and the Workshop group. It was the Showcase actors who staged plays that were covered by the studio talent scouts. Toby had been put with the Workshop actors. Alice Tanner had told him that it might be six months to a year before he would be ready for a Showcase play.

Toby found the classes interesting, but the magic ingredient was missing: the audience, the applauders, the laughers, the people who would adore him.

In the weeks since Toby had begun classes, he had seen very little of the head of the school. Occasionally, Alice Tanner would drop into the Workshop to watch improvisations and give a word of encouragement, or Toby would run into her on his way to class. But he had hoped for something more intimate. He found himself thinking about Alice Tanner a great deal. She was what Toby thought of as a classy dame, and that appealed to him; he felt it was what he deserved. The idea of her crippled leg had bothered him at first, but it had slowly begun to take on a sexual fascination.

Toby talked to her again about putting him in a Showcase play where the critics and talent scouts could see him.

"You're not ready yet," Alice Tanner told him.

She was standing in his way, keeping him from his success. I *have to do something about that*, Toby decided.

A Showcase play was being staged, and on the opening night Toby was seated in a middle row next to a student named Karen, a fat little character actress from his class. Toby had played scenes with Karen, and he knew two things about her: she never wore underclothes and she had bad breath. She had done everything but send up smoke signals to let Toby know that she wanted to go to bed with him, but he had pretended not to understand. *Jesus,* he thought, *fucking her would be like being sucked into a tub of hot lard.*

As they sat there waiting for the curtain to go up, Karen excitedly pointed out the critics from the Los Angeles *Times* and *Herald-Express,* and the talent scouts from Twentieth Century-Fox, MGM and Warner Brothers. It enraged Toby. They were here to see the actors up on the stage, while *he* sat in the audience like a dummy. He had an almost uncontrollable impulse to stand up and do one of his routines, dazzle them, show them what *real* talent looked like.

The audience enjoyed the play, but Toby was obsessed with the talent scouts, who sat within touching distance, the men who held his future in their hands. Well, if Actors West was the lure to bring them to him, Toby would use it; but he had no intention of waiting six months, or even six weeks.

The following morning, Toby went to Alice Tanner's office.

"How did you like the play?" she asked.

"It was wonderful," Toby said. "Those actors are really great." He gave a self-deprecating smile. "I see what you mean when you say I'm not ready yet."

"They've had more experience than you, that's all, but you have a unique personality. You're going to make it. Just be patient."

He sighed. "I don't know. Maybe I'd be better off forgetting the whole thing and selling insurance or something."

She looked at him in quick surprise. "You mustn't," she said.

Toby shook his head. "After seeing those pros last night, I—I don't think I have it."

"Of course you have, Toby. I won't let you talk like that."

In her voice was the note he had been waiting to hear. It was not a teacher talking to a pupil now, it was a woman talking to a man, encouraging him, caring about him. Toby felt a small thrill of satisfaction.

He shrugged helplessly. "I don't know, anymore. I'm all alone in this town. I have no one to talk to."

"You can always talk to me, Toby. I'd like to be your friend."

He could hear the sexual huskiness come into her voice. Toby's blue eyes held all the wonder in the world as he gazed at her. As she watched him, he walked over and locked the office door. He returned to her, fell on his knees, buried his head in her lap and, as her fingers touched his hair, he slowly lifted her skirt, exposing the poor thigh encased in the cruel steel brace. Gently removing the brace, he tenderly kissed the red marks left by the steel bars. Slowly, he unfastened her garter belt, all the time telling Alice of his love and his need for her, and kissed his way down to the moist lips exposed before him. He carried her to the deep leather couch and made love to her.

That evening, Toby moved in with Alice Tanner.

In bed that night, Toby found that Alice Tanner was a pitiful lonely woman, desperate for someone to talk to, someone to love. She had been born in Boston. Her father was a wealthy manufacturer who had given her a large allowance and paid no further attention to her. Alice had loved the theater and had studied to be an actress, but in college she had contracted polio and that had put an end to her dream. She told Toby how it had affected her life. The boy she was engaged to had jilted her when he learned the news. Alice had left home and married a psychiatrist, who committed suicide six months later. It was as though all her emotions had been bottled up inside her. Now they poured out in a violent eruption that left her feeling drained and peaceful and marvelously content.

Toby made love to Alice until she almost fainted with ecstasy, filling her with his huge penis and making slow circles with his hips until he seemed to be touching every part of her body. She moaned, "Oh, darling, I love you so much. Oh, God, how I love this!"

But when it came to school, Toby found that he had no influence with Alice. He talked to her about putting him in the next Showcase play, introducing him to casting directors, speaking to important studio people about him, but she was firm. "You'll hurt yourself if you push too fast, darling. Rule one: the first impression you make is the most important. If they don't like you the first time, they'll never go back to see you a second time. You've got to be ready."

The instant the words were out, she became The Enemy. She was against him. Toby swallowed his fury and forced himself to smile at her. "Sure. It's just that I'm impatient. I want to make it for you as much as for me."

"Do you? Oh, Toby, I love you so much!"

"I love you, too, Alice." And he smiled into her adoring eyes. He knew he had to circumvent this bitch who was standing in the way of what he wanted. He hated her and he punished her.

When they went to bed, he made her do things she had never done before, things he had never asked a whore to do, using her mouth and her fingers and her tongue. He pushed her further and further, forcing her into a series of humiliations. And each time he got her to do something more degrading, he would praise her, the way one praises a dog for learning a new trick, and she would be happy because she had pleased him. And the more he degraded her, the more degraded he felt. He was punishing himself, and he had not the faintest idea why.

Toby had a plan in mind, and his chance to put it into action came sooner than he had anticipated. Alice Tanner announced that the Workshop class was going to put on a private show for the advanced classes and their guests on the following Friday. Each student could choose his own project. Toby prepared a monologue and rehearsed it over and over.

On the morning of the show, Toby waited until class was over and walked up to Karen, the fat actress who had sat next to him during the play. "Would you do me a favor?" he asked casually.

"Sure, Toby." Her voice was surprised and eager.

Toby stepped back to get away from her breath. "I'm pulling a gag on an old friend of mine. I want you to telephone Clifton Lawrence's secretary and tell her you're Sam Goldwyn's secretary, and that Mr. Goldwyn would like Mr. Lawrence to come to the show tonight to see a brilliant new comic. There'll be a ticket waiting at the box office."

Karen stared at him. "Jesus, old lady Tanner would have my head. You know she never allows outsiders at the Workshop shows."

"Believe me, it'll be all right." He took her arm and squeezed it. "You busy this afternoon?"

She swallowed, her breath coming a little faster. "No—not if you'd like to do something."

"I'd like to do something."

Three hours later, an ecstatic Karen made the phone call.

The auditorium was filled with actors from the various classes and their guests, but the only person Toby had eyes for was the man who sat in an aisle seat in the third row. Toby had been in a panic, fearful that his ruse would not work. Surely a man as clever as Clifton Lawrence would see through the trick. But he had not. He was here.

A boy and girl were on stage now, doing a scene from *The Sea Gull*. Toby hoped they would not drive Clifton Lawrence out of the theater. Finally, the scene was finished, and the actors took their bows and left the stage.

It was Toby's turn. Alice suddenly appeared at his side in the wings, whispering, "Good luck, darling," unaware that his luck was sitting in the audience.

"Thanks, Alice." Toby breathed a silent prayer, straightened his shoulders, bounced out on stage and smiled boyishly at the audience. "Hello, there. I'm Toby Temple. Hey, did you ever stop to think about names, and how our parents choose them? It's crazy. I asked my mother why she named me Toby. She said she took one look at my mug, and that was it."

His look was what got the laugh. Toby appeared so innocent and wistful, standing up there on that stage, that they loved him. The jokes he told were terrible, but somehow that did not matter. He was so vulnerable that they wanted to protect him, and they did it with their applause and their laughter. It was like a gift of love that flowed into Toby, filling him with an almost unbearable exhilaration. He was Edward G. Robinson and Jimmy Cagney, and Cagney was saying, "You dirty rat! Who do you think you're giving orders to?"

And Robinson's, "To you, you punk. I'm Little Caesar. I'm the boss. You're nuthin'. Do you know what that means?"

"Yeah, you dirty rat. You're the boss of nuthin'."

A roar. The audience adored Toby.

Bogart was there, snarling, "I'd spit in your eye, punk, if my lip wasn't stuck over my teeth."

And the audience was enchanted.

Toby gave them his Peter Lorre. "I saw this little girl in her room, playing with it, and I got excited. I don't know what came over me. I couldn't help myself. I crept into her room, and I pulled the rope tighter and tighter, and I broke her yo-yo."

A big laugh. He was rolling.

He switched over to Laurel and Hardy, and a movement in the audience caught his eye and he glanced up. Clifton Lawrence was walking out of the theater.

The rest of the evening was a blur to Toby.

When the show was over, Alice Tanner came up to Toby. "You were wonderful, darling! I . . ."

He could not bear to look at her, to have anyone look at him. He wanted to be alone with his misery, to try to cope with the pain that was tearing him apart. His world had collapsed around him. He had had his chance, and he had failed. Clifton Lawrence had walked out on him, had not even waited for him to finish. Clifton Lawrence was a man who knew talent, a professional who handled the best. If Lawrence did not think Toby had anything . . . He felt sick to his stomach.

"I'm going for a walk," he said to Alice.

He walked down Vine Street and Gower, past Columbia Pictures and RKO and Paramount. All the gates were locked. He walked along Hollywood Boulevard and looked up at the huge mocking sign on the hill that said, "HOLLYWOODLAND." There was no Hollywoodland. It was a state of mind, a phony dream that lured thousands of otherwise normal people into the insanity of trying to become a star. The word *Hollywood* had become a lodestone for miracles, a trap that seduced people with wonderful promises, siren songs of dreams fulfilled, and then destroyed them.

Toby walked the streets all night long, wondering what he was going to do with his life. His faith in himself had been shattered and he felt rootless and adrift. He had never imagined himself doing anything other than entertaining people, and if he could not do that, all that was left for him were dull, monotonous jobs where he would be caged up for the rest of his life. Mr. Anonymous. No one would ever know who he was. He thought of the long, dreary years, the bitter loneliness of the thousand nameless towns, of the people who had applauded him and laughed at him and loved him. Toby wept. He wept for the past and for the future.

He wept because he was dead.

It was dawn when Toby returned to the white stucco bungalow he shared with Alice. He walked into the bedroom and looked down at her sleeping figure. He had thought that she would be the open sesame to the magic kingdom. Not for him. He would leave. He had no idea where he would go. He was almost twenty-seven years old and he had no future.

He lay down on the couch, exhausted. He closed his eyes, listening to the sounds of the city stirring into life. The morning sounds of cities are the same, and he thought of Detroit. His mother. She was standing in the kitchen cooking apple tarts for him. He could smell her wonderful musky female odor mingled with the smell of apples cooking in butter, and she was saying, *God wants you to be famous.*

He was standing alone on an enormous stage, blinded by floodlights, trying to remember his lines. He tried to speak but he had lost his voice. He grew panicky. There was a great rumbling noise from the audience, and through the blinding lights Toby could see the spectators leaving their seats and running toward the stage to attack him, to kill him. Their love had turned to hate. They were surrounding him, grabbing him, chanting, "Toby! Toby! Toby!"

Toby suddenly jerked awake, his mouth dry with fright. Alice Tanner was leaning over him, shaking him.

"Toby! Telephone. It's Clifton Lawrence."

Clifton Lawrence's office was in a small, elegant building on Beverly Drive, just south of Wilshire. French Impressionist paintings hung from the carved *boiserie,* and before the dark green marble fireplace a sofa and some antique chairs were grouped around an exquisite tea table. Toby had never seen anything like it.

A shapely, redheaded secretary was pouring tea. "How do you like your tea, Mr. Temple?"

Mr. Temple! "One sugar, please."

"There you are." A little smile and she was gone.

Toby did not know that the tea was a special blend imported

from Fortnum and Mason, nor that it was steeping in Irish Baleek, but he knew it tasted wonderful. In fact, everything about this office was wonderful, especially the dapper little man who sat in an armchair studying him. Clifton Lawrence was smaller than Toby had expected, but he radiated a sense of authority and power.

"I can't tell you how much I appreciate your seeing me," Toby said. "I'm sorry I had to trick you into—"

Clifton Lawrence threw his head back and laughed. "Trick me? I had lunch with Goldwyn yesterday. I went to watch you last night because I wanted to see if your talent matched your nerve. It did."

"But you walked out—" Toby exclaimed.

"Dear boy, you don't have to eat the entire jar of caviar to know it's good, right? I knew what you had in sixty seconds."

Toby felt that sense of euphoria building up in him again. After the black despair of the night before, to be lifted to the heights like this, to have his life handed back to him—

"I have a hunch about you, Temple," Clifton Lawrence said. "I think it would be exciting to take someone young and build his career. I've decided to take you on as a client."

The feeling of joy was exploding inside Toby. He wanted to stand up and scream aloud. *Clifton Lawrence was going to be his agent!*

". . . handle you on one condition," Clifton Lawrence was saying, "That you do exactly as I tell you. I don't stand for temperament. You step out of line just once, and we're finished. Do you understand?"

Toby nodded quickly. "Yes, sir. I understand."

"The first thing you have to do is face the truth." He smiled at Toby and said, "Your act is terrible. Definitely bottom drawer."

It was as though Toby had been kicked in the stomach. Clifton Lawrence had brought him here to punish him for that stupid phone call; he was not going to handle him. He . . .

But the little agent continued. "Last night was amateur night, and that's what you are—an amateur." Clifton Lawrence rose from his chair and began to pace. "I'm going to tell you what you have, and I'm going to tell you what you need to become a star."

Toby sat there.

"Let's start with your material," Clifton said. "You could put butter and salt on it and peddle it in theater lobbies."

"Yes, sir. Well, some of it might be a little corny, but—"

"Next. You have no style."

Toby felt his hands begin to clench. "The audience seemed to—"

"Next. You don't know how to move. You're a lox."

Toby said nothing.

The little agent walked over to him, looked down and said softly, reading Toby's mind, "If you're so bad, what are you doing here? You're here because you've got something that money can't buy. When you stand up on that stage, the audience wants to eat you up. They love you. Do you have any idea how much that could be worth?"

Toby took a deep breath and sat back. "Tell me."

"More than you could ever dream. With the right material and the proper kind of handling, you can be a star."

Toby sat there, basking in the warm glow of Clifton Lawrence's words, and it was as though everything Toby had done all his life had led to this moment, as though he were *already* a star, and it had all happened. Just as his mother had promised him.

"The key to an entertainer's success is personality," Clifton Lawrence was saying. "You can't buy it and you can't fake it. You have to be born with it. You're one of the lucky ones, dear boy." He glanced at the gold Piaget watch on his wrist. "I've set up a meeting for you with O'Hanlon and Rainger at two o'clock. They're the best comedy writers in the business. They work for all the top comics."

Toby said nervously, "I'm afraid I haven't much mon—"

Clifton Lawrence dismissed it with a wave of his hand. "Not to worry, dear boy. You'll pay me back later."

Long after Toby Temple had left, Clifton Lawrence sat there thinking about him, smiling to himself at that wide-eyed innocent face and those trusting, guileless blue eyes. It had been many years since Clifton had represented an unknown. All his clients were important stars, and every studio fought for their services. The excitement had long since gone. The early days had been more fun, more stimulating. It would be a challenge to take this raw, young kid and develop him, build him into a hot property. Clifton had a feeling that he was really going to enjoy this experience. He liked the boy. He liked him very much, indeed.

The meeting took place at the Twentieth Century-Fox studio on Pico Boulevard in West Los Angeles, where O'Hanlon and Rainger had their offices. Toby had expected something lavish, on the order of Clifton Lawrence's suite, but the writers' quarters were drab and dingy, located in a small wooden bungalow on the lot.

An untidy, middle-aged secretary in a cardigan ushered Toby into the inner office. The walls were a dirty apple-green, and the only adornment was a battered dart board and a "PLAN AHEAD" sign with the last three letters squeezed together. A broken venetian blind partially filtered out the sun's rays that fell across a dirty brown carpet worn down to the canvas. There were two scarred desks, back to back, each littered with papers and pencils and half-empty cartons of cold coffee.

"Hi, Toby. Excuse the mess. It's the maid's day off," O'Hanlon greeted him. "I'm O'Hanlon." He indicated his partner. "This is —er—?"

"Rainger."

"Ah, yes. This is Rainger."

O'Hanlon was large and rotund and wore horn-rimmed glasses. Rainger was small and frail. Both men were in their early thirties and had been a successful writing team for ten years. In all the time that Toby was to work with them, he always referred to them as "the boys."

Toby said, "I understand you fellas are going to write some jokes for me."

O'Hanlon and Rainger exchanged a look. Rainger said, "Cliff Lawrence thinks you might be America's new sex symbol. Let's see what you can do. Have you got an act?"

"Sure," Toby replied. He remembered what Clifton had said about it. Suddenly, he felt diffident.

The two writers sat down on the couch and crossed their arms. "Entertain us," O'Hanlon said.

Toby looked at them. "Just like that?"

"What would you like?" Rainger asked. "An introduction from a sixty-piece orchestra?" He turned to O'Hanlon "Get the music department on the phone."

You prick, thought Toby. *You're on my shit list, both of you.*

He knew what they were trying to do. They were trying to make him look bad so that they could go back to Clifton Lawrence and say, *We can't help him. He's a stiff.* Well, he was not going to let them get away with it. He put on a smile he did not feel, and went into his Abbott and Costello routine. "Hey Lou, ain't you ashamed of yourself? You're turnin' into a bum. Why don't you go out and get yourself a job?"

"I got a job."

"What kind of job?"

"Lookin' for work."

"You call that a job?"

"Certainly. It keeps me busy all day, I got regular hours, and I'm home in time for dinner every night."

The two of them were studying Toby now, weighing him, analyzing him, and in the middle of his routine they began talking, as though Toby were not in the room.

"He doesn't know how to stand."

"He uses his hands like he's chopping wood. Maybe we could write a woodchopper act for him."

"He pushes too hard."

"Jesus, with that material—wouldn't you?"

Toby was getting more upset by the moment. He did not have to stay here and be insulted by these two maniacs. Their material was probably lousy anyway.

Finally, he could stand it no longer. He stopped, his voice trembling with rage. "I don't need you bastards! Thanks for the hospitality." He started for the door.

Rainger stood up in genuine amazement. "Hey! What's the matter with you?"

Toby turned on him in fury. "What the fuck do you *think* is the matter? You—you—" He was so frustrated, he was on the verge of tears.

Rainger turned to look at O'Hanlon in bewilderment. "We must have hurt his feelings."

"Golly."

Toby took a deep breath. "Look, you two. I don't care if you don't like me, but—"

"We *love* you!" O'Hanlon exclaimed.

"We think you're darling!" Rainger chimed in.

Toby looked from one to the other in complete bafflement. "What? You acted like—"

"You know your trouble, Toby? You're insecure. Relax. Sure, you've got a lot to learn, but on the other hand, if you were Bob Hope, you wouldn't be here."

O'Hanlon added, "And do you know why? Because Bob's up in Carmel today."

"Playing golf. Do you play golf?" Rainger asked.

"No."

The two writers looked at each other in dismay. "There go all the golf jokes. Shit!"

O'Hanlon picked up the telephone. "Bring in some coffee, will you, Zsa Zsa?" He put down the phone and turned to Toby. "Do you know how many would-be comics there are in this quaint little business we're in?"

Toby shook his head.

"I can tell you exactly. Three billion seven hundred and twenty-eight million, as of six o'clock last night. And that's not including Milton Berle's brother. When there's a full moon, they all crawl out of the woodwork. There are only half a dozen really top comics. The others will never make it. Comedy is the most serious business in the world. It's goddamned hard work being funny, whether you're a comic or a comedian."

"What's the difference?"

"A big one. A comic opens funny doors. A comedian opens doors funny."

Rainger asked, "Did you ever stop to think what makes one comedian a smash and another a failure?"

"Material," Toby said, wanting to flatter them.

"Buffalo shit. The last new joke was invented by Aristophanes. Jokes are basically all the same. George Burns can tell six jokes that the guy on the bill ahead of him just told, and Burns will get bigger laughs. Do you know why? Personality." *It was what Clifton Lawrence had told him.* "Without it, you're nothing, nobody. You start with a personality and you turn it into a charac-ter. Take Hope. If he came out and did a Jack Benny monologue, he'd bomb. Why? Because he's built up a character. That's what the audiences expect from him. When Hope walks out, they want to hear those rapid-fire jokes. He's a likeable smart-ass, the big city fellow who gets his lumps. Jack Benny—just the opposite. He wouldn't know what to do with a Bob Hope monologue, but he can take a two-minute pause and make an audience scream. Each of the Marx Brothers has his own character. Fred Allen is unique. That brings us to you. Do you know your problem, Toby? You're a little of everybody. You're imitating all the big boys. Well, that's great if you want to play Elks smokers for the rest of your life. But if you want to move up into the big time, you've got to create a character of your own. When you're out on that stage, before you even open your mouth, the audience has to know that it's Toby Temple up there. Do you read me?"

"Yes."

O'Hanlon took over. "Do you know what you've got, Toby? A lovable face. If I weren't already engaged to Clark Gable, I'd be crazy about you. There's a naive sweetness about you. If you package it right, it could be worth a fucking fortune."

"To say nothing of a fortune in fucking," Rainger chimed in.

"You can get away with things that the other boys can't. It's like a choirboy saying four-letter words—it's cute because you don't believe he really understands what he's saying. When you walked in here, you asked if we were the fellows who were going to write your jokes. The answer is no. This isn't a joke shop. What we are going to do is show you what you've got and how to use it. We're going to tailor a character for you. Well—what do you say?"

Toby looked from one to the other, grinned happily and said, "Let's roll up our sleeves and go to work."

Every day after that, Toby had lunch with O'Hanlon and Rainger at the studio. The Twentieth Century-Fox commissary was an enormous room filled with wall-to-wall stars. On any given day, Toby could see Tyrone Power and Loretta Young and Betty Grable and Don Ameche and Alice Faye and Richard Widmark and Victor Mature and the Ritz Brothers, and dozens of others. Some were seated at tables in the large room, and others ate in the smaller executive dining room which adjoined the main commissary. Toby loved watching them all. In a short time, he would be one of *them*, people would be asking for *his* autograph. He was on his way, and he was going to be bigger than any of them.

★

Alice Tanner was thrilled by what was happening to Toby. "I know you're going to make it, darling. I'm so proud of you."

Toby smiled at her and said nothing.

Toby and O'Hanlon and Rainger had long discussions about the new character Toby was to be.

"He should think he's a sophisticated man of the world," O'Hanlon said, "But every time he comes to bat, he lays an egg."

"What's his job?" asked Rainger. "Mixing metaphors?"

"This character should live with his mother. He's in love with a girl, but he's afraid to leave home to marry her. He's been engaged to her for five years."

"Ten is a funnier number."

"Right! Make it ten years. His mother shouldn't happen to a dog. Every time Toby wants to get married, his mother develops a new disease. *Time* Magazine calls *her* every week to find out what's happening in medicine."

Toby sat there listening, fascinated by the fast flow of dialogue. He had never worked with real professionals before, and he enjoyed it. Particularly since he was the center of attention. It took O'Hanlon and Rainger three weeks to write an act for Toby. When they finally showed it to him, he was thrilled. It was *good*. He made a few suggestions, they added and threw out some lines, and Toby Temple was ready. Clifton Lawrence sent for him.

"You're opening Saturday night at the Bowling Ball."

Toby stared at him. He had had expectations of being booked into Ciro's or the Trocadero. "What's—what's the Bowling Ball?"

"A little club on south Western Avenue."

Toby's face fell. "I never heard of it."

"And they never heard of you. That's the point, dear boy. If you should bomb there, no one will ever know it."

Except Clifton Lawrence.

The Bowling Ball was a dump. There was no other word to describe it. It was a duplicate of ten thousand other sleazy little bars scattered throughout the country, a watering hole for losers. Toby had played there a thousand times, in a thousand cities. The patrons were mostly middle-aged males, blue-collar workers indulging in their ritual get-together with their buddies, ogling the tired waitresses in their tight skirts and low-cut blouses, exchanging dirty jokes over a shot of cheap whiskey or a glass of beer. The floor show took place in a small cleared area at the far end of the room, where three bored musicians played. A homosexual singer opened the show, followed by an acrobatic dancer in a leotard, and then a stripper who worked with a somnolent cobra.

Toby sat at a table in the back of the room with Clifton Lawrence and O'Hanlon and Rainger, watching the other acts, listening to the audience, trying to gauge its mood.

"Beer drinkers," Toby said contemptuously.

Clifton started to retort, then looked at Toby's face and checked himself. Toby was scared. Clifton knew that Toby had played places like this before, but this time was different. This was the test.

Clifton said gently, "If you can put the beer drinkers in your pocket, the champagne crowd will be a pushover. These people work hard all day, Toby. When they go out at night, they want their nickel's worth. If you can make *them* laugh, you can make anyone laugh."

At that moment, Toby heard the bored MC announce his name.

"Give 'em hell, tiger!" O'Hanlon said.

Toby was on.

He stood on the stage, on guard and tense, appraising the audience like a wary animal sniffing for danger in a forest.

An audience was a beast with a hundred heads, each one different; and he had to make the beast laugh. He took a deep breath. *Love me*, he prayed.

He went into his act.

And no one was listening to him. No one was laughing. Toby could feel the flop sweat begin to pop out on his forehead. The act was not working. He kept his smile pasted on and went on talking over the loud noise and conversation. He could not get their attention. They wanted the naked broads back. They had been exposed on too many Saturday nights to too many talentless, unfunny comedians. Toby kept talking, in the face of their indifference. He went on because there was nothing else he could do. He looked out and saw Clifton Lawrence and the boys, watching him with worried expressions.

Toby continued. There was no audience in the room, just people, talking to one another, discussing their problems and their lives. For all they cared, Toby Temple could have been a million miles away. Or dead. His throat was dry now with fear, and it was becoming hard to get the words out. From the corner of his eye, Toby saw the manager start toward the bandstand. He was going to begin the music, pull the plug on him. It was all over. Toby's palms were wet and his bowels had turned to water. He could feel hot urine trickle down his leg. He was so nervous that he was beginning to mix up his words. He did not dare look at Clifton Lawrence or the writers. He was too filled with shame. The manager was at the bandstand, talking to the musicians. They glanced over at Toby and nodded. Toby went on, talking desperately, wanting it to be over, wanting to run away somewhere and hide.

A middle-aged woman seated at a table directly in front of Toby giggled at one of his jokes. Her companions stopped to listen. Toby kept talking, in a frenzy. The others at the table were listening now, laughing. And then the next table.

And the next. And, slowly, the talking began to die down. They were *listening* to him. The laughs were starting to come, long and regular, and they were getting bigger, and building. And building. The people in the room had become an audience. And he had them. *He fucking had them!* It no longer mattered that he was in a cheap saloon filled with beer-drinking slobs. What mattered was their laughter, and their love. It came out at Toby in waves. First he had them laughing, then he had them screaming. They had never heard anything like him, not in this crummy place, not anywhere. They applauded and they cheered and before they were through, they damned near tore the place apart. They were witnessing the birth of a phenomenon. Of course, they could not know that. But Clifton Lawrence and O'Hanlon and Rainger knew it. And Toby Temple knew it.

God had finally come through.

Reverend Damian shoved the blazing torch into Josephine's face and screamed, "O God Almighty, burn away the evil in this sinful child," and the congregation roared "Amen!" And Josephine could feel the flame licking at her face and the Reverend Damian yelled out, "Help this sinner exorcise the Devil, O God.

We will pray him out, we will burn him out, we will drown him out," and hands grabbed Josephine, and her face was suddenly plunged into a wooden tub of cold water, and she was held under while voices chanted into the night air, beseeching the Almighty One for His help, and Josephine struggled to get loose, fighting for breath, and when they finally pulled her out, half-conscious, the Reverend Damian declared. *"We thank you, sweet Jesus, for your mercy. She is saved! She is saved!"* And there was great rejoicing, and everyone was raised in spirit. Except Josephine, whose headaches became worse.

10

"I've gotten you a booking in Las Vegas," Clifton Lawrence told Toby. "I've arranged for Dick Landry to work on your act. He's the best nightclub director in the business."

"Fantastic! Which hotel? The Flamingo? The Thunderbird?"

"The Oasis."

"The Oasis?" Toby looked at Cliff to see if he was joking. "I never—"

"I know." Cliff smiled. "You never heard of it. Fair enough. They never heard of you. They're really not booking you—they're booking me. They're taking my word that you're good."

"Don't worry," Toby promised. "I will be."

Toby broke the news to Alice Tanner about his Las Vegas booking just before he was to leave. "I know you're going to be a big star," she said. "It's your time. They'll adore you, darling." She hugged him and said, "When do we leave, and what do I wear to the opening night of a young comic genius?"

Toby shook his head ruefully. "I wish I could take you, Alice. The trouble is I'll be working night and day thinking up a lot of new material."

She tried to conceal her disappointment. "I understand." She held him tighter. "How long will you be gone?"

"I don't know yet. You see, it's kind of an open booking."

She felt a small stab of worry, but she knew that she was being silly. "Call me the moment you can," she said.

Toby kissed her and danced out the door.

It was as though Las Vegas, Nevada, had been created for the sole pleasure of Toby Temple. He felt it the moment he saw the town. It had a marvelous kinetic energy that he responded to, a pulsating power that matched the power burning inside him. Toby flew in with O'Hanlon and Rainger, and when they arrived at the airport, a limousine from the Oasis Hotel was waiting for them. It was Toby's first taste of the wonderful world that was soon to be his. He enjoyed leaning back in the huge black car and having the chauffeur ask, "Did you have a nice flight, Mr. Temple?"

It was always the little people who could smell a success even before it happened, Toby thought.

"It was the usual bore," Toby said carelessly. He caught the smile that O'Hanlon and Rainger exchanged, and he grinned back at them. He felt very close to them. They were all a team, the best goddamned team in show business.

The Oasis was off the glamorous Strip, far removed from the more famous hotels. As the limousine approached the hotel, Toby saw that it was not as large or as fancy as the Flamingo or the Thunderbird, but it had something better, much better. It had a giant marquee in front that read:

OPENING SEPT. 4TH
LILI WALLACE
TOBY TEMPLE

Toby's name was in dazzling letters that seemed a hundred feet high. No sight was as beautiful as this in the whole goddamn world.

"Look at that!" he said in awe.

O'Hanlon glanced at the sign and said, "Yeah! How about that? *Lili Wallace!*" And he laughed. "Don't worry, Toby. After the opening you'll be on top of her."

The manager of the Oasis, a middle-aged, sallow-faced man named Parker, greeted Toby and personally escorted him to his suite, fawning all the way. "I can't tell you how pleased we are to have you with us, Mr. Temple. If there's anything at all you need—anything—just give me a call."

The welcome, Toby realized, was for Clifton Lawrence. This was the first time the fabulous agent had deigned to book one of his clients into this hotel. The manager of the Oasis hoped that now the hotel would get some of Lawrence's really big stars.

The suite was enormous. It consisted of three bedrooms, a large living room, a kitchen, a bar and a terrace. On a table in the living room were bottles of assorted liquors, flowers and a large bowl of fresh fruit and cheeses, compliments of the management.

"I hope this will be satisfactory, Mr. Temple," Parker said.

Toby looked around and thought of all the dreary little cock-roach-ridden fleabag hotel rooms he had lived in. "Yeah. It's okay."

"Mr. Landry checked in an hour ago. I've arranged to clear the Mirage Room for your rehearsal at three o'clock."

"Thanks."

"Remember, if there's *anything* at all you need—" And the manager bowed himself out.

Toby stood there, savoring his surroundings. He was going to live in places like this for the rest of his life. He would have it all— the broads, the money, the applause. Mostly the applause. People sitting out there laughing and cheering and loving him. *That* was his food and drink. He did not need anything else.

Dick Landry was in his late twenties, a slight, thin man with an alopecian head and long, graceful legs. He had started out as a gypsy on Broadway and had graduated from the chorus to lead dancer to choreographer to director. Landry had taste and a sense of what an audience wanted. He could not make a bad act good, but he could make it *look* good, and if he was given a good act, he could make it sensational. Until ten days ago, Landry had never heard of Toby Temple, and the only reason Landry had cut into his frantic schedule to come to Las Vegas and stage Temple's act was because Clifton Lawrence had asked him to. It was Clifton who had given Landry his start.

Fifteen minutes after Dick Landry met Toby Temple, Landry knew he was working with a talent. Listening to Toby's mono-logue, Landry found himself laughing aloud—something he rarely did. It was not the jokes so much as Toby's wistful way of deliver-ing them. He was so pathetically sincere that it broke your heart. He was an adorable Chicken Little, terrified that the sky was about to fall on his head. You wanted to run up there and hug him and assure him that everything would be all right.

When Toby finished, it was all that Landry could do to keep from applauding. He went up to the stage where Toby stood. "You're good," he said enthusiastically. "Really good."

Toby said, pleased, "Thanks. Cliff says you can show me how to be great."

Landry said, "I'm going to try. The first thing is for you to learn to diversify your talents. As long as you can only stand up there and tell jokes, you'll never be more than a standup comic. Let me hear you sing."

Toby grinned. "Rent a canary. I can't sing."

"Try it."

Toby tried. Landry was pleased. "Your voice isn't much," he told Toby, "but you have an ear. With the right songs, you can fake it so that they'll think you're Sinatra. We'll arrange to have some song writers do some special material for you. I don't want you singing the same songs that everyone else is doing. Let's see you move."

Toby moved.

Landry studied him carefully. "Fair, fair. You'll never be a dancer, but I'm going to make you look like one."

"Why?" Toby asked. "Song-and-dance men are a dime a dozen."

"So are comics," Landry retorted. "I'm going to turn you into an entertainer."

Toby grinned and said, "Let's roll up our sleeves and get to work."

They went to work. O'Hanlon and Rainger were at every rehearsal, adding lines, creating new routines, watching Landry drive Toby. It was a grueling schedule. Toby rehearsed until every muscle in his body ached, but he burned off five pounds and became trim and hard. He took a singing lesson every day and vocalized until he was singing in his sleep. He worked on new comedy routines with the boys, then stopped to learn new songs that had been written for him, and it was time to rehearse again.

Almost every day, Toby found a message in his box that Alice Tanner had telephoned. He remembered how she had tried to hold him back. *You're not ready yet.* Well, he was ready now, and he had done it in *spite* of her. To hell with her. He threw the messages away. Finally, they stopped. But the rehearsals went on.

Suddenly it was opening night.

There is a mystique about the birth of a new star. It is as though some telepathic message is instantaneously transmitted to the four corners of the world of show business. Through some magic alchemy, the news spreads to London and Paris, to New York and Sydney; wherever there is theater, the word is carried.

Five minutes after Toby Temple walked onto the stage of the Oasis Hotel, the word was out that there was a new star on the horizon.

Clifton Lawrence flew in for Toby's opening and stayed for the supper show. Toby was flattered. Clifton was neglecting his other clients for him. When Toby finished the show, the two of them went to the hotel's all-night coffee shop.

"Did you see all the celebrities out there?" Toby asked. "When they came back to my dressing room, I damn near died."

Clifton smiled at Toby's enthusiasm. It was such a pleasant change from all his other, jaded clients. Toby was a pussycat. A sweet, blue-eyed pussycat.

"They know talent when they see it," Clifton said. "So does the Oasis. They want to make a new deal with you. They want to raise you from six-fifty to a thousand a week."

Toby dropped his spoon. "A thousand a week? That's fantastic, Cliff!"

"And I've had a couple of feelers from the Thunderbird and the El Rancho Hotel."

"Already?" Toby asked, elated.

"Don't wet your pants. It's just to play the lounge." He smiled. "It's the old story, Toby. To *me* you're a headliner, and to *you* you're a headliner—but to a *headliner* are you a headliner?" He stood up. "I have to catch a plane to New York. I'm flying to London tomorrow."

"London? When will you be back?"

"In a few weeks." Clifton leaned forward and said, "Listen to me, dear boy. You have two more weeks here. Treat it like a school. Every night you're up on that stage, I want you to figure out how you can be better. I've persuaded O'Halon and Rainger not to leave. They're willing to work with you day and night. Use them. Landry will come back weekends to see how everything is going.''

"Right," Toby said. "Thanks, Cliff."

"Oh, I almost forgot," Clifton Lawrence said casually. He pulled a small package from his pocket and handed it to Toby.

Inside was a pair of beautiful diamond cufflinks. They were in the shape of a star.

Whenever Toby had some free time, he relaxed around the large swimming pool at the back of the hotel. There were twenty-five girls in the show and there were always a dozen or so from the chorus line in bathing suits, sunning themselves. They appeared in the hot noon air like late-blooming flowers, one more beautiful than the next. Toby had never had trouble getting girls, but what happened to him now was a totally new experience. The showgirls had never heard of Toby Temple before, but his name was up in lights on the marquee. That was enough. He was a *Star*, and they fought each other for the privilege of going to bed with him.

The next two weeks were marvelous for Toby. He would wake up around noon, have breakfast in the dining room where he was kept busy signing autographs and then rehearse for an hour or two. Afterward, he would pick one or two of the long-legged beauties around the pool and they would go up to his suite for an afternoon romp in bed.

And Toby learned something new. Because of the skimpy costumes the girls wore, they had to get rid of their pubic hair. But they waxed it in such a way that only a curly strip of hair was left in the center of the mound, making the opening more available.

"It's like an aphrodisiac," one of the girls confided to Toby. "A few hours in a pair of tight pants and a girl becomes a raving nymphomaniac."

Toby did not bother to learn any of their names. They were all "baby" or "honey," and they became a marvelous, sensuous blur of thighs and lips and eager bodies.

During the final week of Toby's engagement at the Oasis, he had a visitor. Toby had finished the first show and was in his dressing room, creaming off his makeup, when the dining room captain opened the door and said in hushed tones, "Mr. Al Caruso would like you to join his table."

Al Caruso was one of the big names in Las Vegas. He owned one hotel outright, and it was rumored that he had points in two or three others. It was also rumored that he had mob connections, but that was no concern of Toby's. What was important was that if Al Caruso liked him, Toby could get bookings in Las Vegas for the rest of his life. He hurriedly finished dressing and went into the dining room to meet Caruso.

Al Caruso was a short man in his fifties with gray hair, twinkling, soft brown eyes and a little paunch. He reminded Toby of a miniature Santa Claus. As Toby came up to the table, Caruso rose, held out his hand, smiled warmly and said, "Al Caruso. Just wanted to tell you what I think of you, Toby. Pull up a chair."

There were two other men at Caruso's table, dressed in dark suits. They were both burly, sipped Coca-Colas and did not say a word during the entire meeting. Toby never learned their names. Toby usually had his dinner after the first show. He was ravenous now, but Caruso had obviously just finished eating, and Toby did not want to appear to be more interested in food than in his meeting with the great man.

"I'm impressed with you, kid," Caruso said. "Real impressed." And he beamed at Toby with those mischievous brown eyes.

"Thanks, Mr. Caruso," Toby said happily. "That means a lot to me."

"Call me Al."

"Yes, sir—Al."

"You got a future, Toby. I've seen 'em come and I've seen 'em go. But the ones with talent last a long time. You got talent."

Toby could feel a pleasant warmth suffusing his body. He fleetingly debated whether to tell Al Caruso to discuss business with Clifton Lawrence; but Toby decided it might be better if he made the deal himself. *If Caruso is this excited about me,* Toby thought, *I can make a better deal than Cliff.* Toby decided he would let Al Caruso make the first offer and then he would do some hard bargaining.

"I almost wet my pants," Caruso was telling him. "That monkey routine of yours is the funniest thing I ever heard."

"Coming from you, that's a real compliment," Toby said with sincerity.

The little Santa Claus eyes were filled with tears of laughter. He took out a white silk handkerchief and wiped them away. He turned to his two escorts. "Did I say he's a funny man?"

The two men nodded.

Al Caruso turned back to Toby. "Tell you why I came to see you, Toby."

This was the magical moment, his entrance into the big time. Clifton Lawrence was off in Europe somewhere, making deals for has-been clients when he should have been here making *this* deal. Well, Lawrence would have a real surprise in store for him when he returned.

Toby leaned forward and said, smiling engagingly, "I'm listening, Al."

"Millie loves you."

Toby blinked, sure that he had missed something. The old man was watching him, his eyes twinkling.

"I—I'm sorry," Toby said, in confusion. "What did you say?"

Al Caruso smiled warmly. "Millie loves you. She told me."

Millie? Could that be Caruso's wife? His daughter? Toby started to speak, but Al Caruso interrupted.

"She's a great kid. I been keepin' her for three, four years." He turned to the other two men. "Four years?"

They nodded.

Al Caruso turned back to Toby. "I love that girl, Toby. I'm really crazy about her."

Toby could feel the blood beginning to drain from his face. "Mr. Caruso—"

Al Caruso said, "Millie and me got a deal. I don't cheat on her except with my wife, and she don't cheat on me unless she tells me." He beamed at Toby, and this time Toby saw something beyond the cherubic smile that turned his blood to ice.

"Mr. Caruso—"

"You know somethin', Toby? You're the first guy she ever cheated on me with." He turned to the two men at the table. "Is that the honest truth?"

They nodded.

When Toby spoke, his voice was trembling. "I—I swear to God

I didn't know Millie was your girlfriend. If I had even *dreamed* it, I wouldn't have touched her. I wouldn't have come within a mile of her, Mr. Caruso—"

The Santa Claus beamed at him. "Al. Call me Al."

"Al." It came out as a croak. Toby could feel the perspiration running down under his arms. "Look, Al," he said. "I'll—I'll never see her again. *Ever.* Believe me, I—"

Caruso was staring at him. "Hey! I don't think you were listening to me."

Toby swallowed. "Yes. Yes, I was. I heard every word you said. And you don't have to worry about—"

"I said the kid loves you. If she wants you, then I want her to have you. I want her to be happy. Understand?"

"I—" Toby's brain was spinning. For a crazy moment he had actually thought that the man sitting across from him was looking for revenge. Instead Al Caruso was offering him his girlfriend. Toby almost laughed aloud with relief. "Jesus, Al," Toby said. "Sure. Whatever you want."

"Whatever Millie wants."

"Yeah. Whatever Millie wants."

"I knew you were a nice man," Al Caruso said. He turned to the two men at the table. "Did I say Toby Temple was a nice man?"

They nodded and silently sipped their Cokes.

Al Caruso rose, and the two men with him were instantly on their feet, one positioned on either side of him. "I'm gonna give the wedding myself," Al Caruso said. "We'll take over the big banquet room at the Morocco. You don't have to worry about nothin'. I'll take care of everything."

The words came at Toby as though filtered, from a far distance. His mind registered what Al Caruso was saying, but it made no sense to him.

"Wait a minute," Toby protested. "I can't—"

Caruso put a powerful hand on Toby's shoulder. "You're a lucky man," Caruso said. "I mean, if Millie hadn't convinced me that you two really love each other, if I thought you were just laying her like she was some two-dollar hoor, this whole thing coulda had a different ending. You get my meaning?"

Toby found himself involuntarily looking up at the two men in black, and they both nodded.

"You finish up here Saturday night," Al Caruso said. "We'll make the wedding Sunday."

Toby's throat had gone dry again. "I—the thing is, Al, I'm afraid I have some bookings. I—"

"They'll wait," the cherubic face beamed. "I'm gonna pick out Millie's wedding dress myself. Night, Toby."

Toby stood there, staring in the direction of the three figures long after they had disappeared.

He did not have the faintest notion who Millie was.

By the next morning, Toby's fears had evaporated. The unexpectedness of what had happened had thrown him off guard. But this was not the era of Al Capone. No one could force him to marry anyone he did not want to marry. Al Caruso was not some cheap, strongarm hoodlum; he was a respectable hotel owner. The more Toby thought about the situation, the funnier it became. He kept embellishing it in his mind, building up the laughs. He had not really let Caruso scare him, of course, but he would tell it as though he had been terrified. *I go up to this table, and there's Caruso sitting with these six gorillas, see? They've all got big bulges where they're carrying guns.* Oh, yes, it would make a great story. He might even get a hilarious routine out of it.

For the rest of the week Toby stayed away from the swimming pool and the casino and avoided all the girls. He was not afraid of Al Caruso, but why take unnecessary chances? Toby had planned to leave Las Vegas by plane Sunday noon. Instead, he arranged for a rental car to be delivered to the back of the hotel parking lot Saturday night. The car would be waiting for him there. He packed his bags before he went downstairs to do his last show, so that he would be ready to leave for Los Angeles the moment he finished. He would stay away from Las Vegas for a while. If Al Caruso was really serious, Clifton Lawrence could straighten things out.

Toby's closing performance was sensational. He got a standing ovation, the first one he had ever received. He stood on the stage, feeling the waves of love coming from the audience, bathing him in a warm, soft glow. He did one encore, begged off and hurried upstairs. This had been the greatest three weeks of his life. In that short period of time, he had gone from a nobody who slept with waitresses and cripples to a Star who had laid Al Caruso's mistress.

Beautiful girls were begging him to take them to bed, audiences admired him and the big hotels wanted him. He had it made, and he knew that this was only the beginning. He took out the key to his door. As he opened it, a familiar voice called out, "Come on in, kid."

Slowly, Toby entered the room. Al Caruso and his two friends were inside. A quick shiver of apprehension went down Toby's back. But it was all right. Caruso was beaming and saying, "You were great tonight, Toby, really great."

Toby began to relax. "It was a good audience."

Caruso's brown eyes twinkled and he said, "You *made* them a good audience, Toby. I told you—you got talent."

"Thanks, Al." He wished they would all leave, so he could be on his way.

"You work hard," Al Caruso said. He turned to his two lieutenants. "Did I say I never seen nobody work so hard?"

The two men nodded.

Caruso turned back to Toby. "Hey—Millie was kinda upset you didn't call her. I told her it was because you was workin' so hard."

"That's right," Toby said quickly. "I'm glad you understand, Al."

Al smiled benignly. "Sure. But you know what I don't understand? You didn't call to find out what time the wedding is."

"I was going to call in the morning."

Al Caruso laughed and said chidingly, "From L.A.?"

Toby felt a small pang of anxiety. "What are you talking about, Al?"

Caruso regarded him reproachfully. "You got your suitcases all packed in there." He pinched Toby's cheek playfully. "I told you I'd kill anyone who hurt Millie."

"Wait a minute! Honest to God, I wasn't—"

"You're a good kid, but you're stupid, Toby. I guess that's part of bein' a genius, huh?"

Toby stared at the chubby, beaming countenance, not knowing what to say.

"You gotta believe me," Al Caruso said warmly, "I'm your friend. I wanna make sure nothin' bad happens to you. For Millie's sake. But if you won't listen to me, what can I do? You know how you get a mule to pay attention?"

Toby shook his head dumbly.

"First, you hit it over the head with a two-by-four."

Toby felt fear rising in his throat.

"Which is your good arm?" Caruso asked.

"My—my right one," Toby mumbled.

Caruso nodded genially and turned to the two men. "Break it," he said.

From out of nowhere, a tire iron appeared in the hands of one of the men. The two of them began closing in on Toby. The river of fear became a sudden flood that made his whole body shake.

"For Christ's sake," Toby heard himself say, inanely. "You can't do this."

One of the men hit him hard in the stomach. In the next second, Toby felt excruciating pain as the tire iron slammed against his right arm, shattering bones. He fell to the floor, writhing in an unbearable agony. He tried to scream, but he could not catch his breath. Through tear-filled eyes, he looked up and saw Al Caruso standing over him, smiling.

"Have I got your attention?" Caruso asked softly.

Toby nodded, in torment.

"Good," Caruso said. He turned to one of the men. "Open up his pants."

The man leaned down and unzipped Toby's fly. He took the tire iron and flicked out Toby's penis.

Caruso stood there a moment, looking down at it. "You're a lucky man, Toby. You're really hung."

Toby was filled with a dread such as he had never known. "Oh, God . . . please . . . don't . . . don't do it to me," he croaked.

"I wouldn't hurt you," Caruso told him. "As long as you're good to Millie, you're my friend. If she ever tells me you did anything to hurt her—anything—you understand me?" He nudged Toby's broken arm with the toe of his shoe and Toby screamed aloud. "I'm glad we understand each other," Caruso beamed. "The wedding is at one o'clock."

Caruso's voice was fading in and out as Toby felt himself slipping into unconsciousness. But he knew he had to hang on. "I c-can't," he whimpered. "My arm . . ."

"Don't worry about that," Al Caruso said. "There's a doc on his way up to take care of you. He's gonna set your arm and give you some stuff so you won't feel no pain. The boys will be here tomorrow to pick you up. You be ready, huh?"

Toby lay there in a nightmare of agony, staring up at Santa Claus's smiling face, unable to believe that any of this was really happening. He saw Caruso's foot moving toward his arm again.

"So—sure," Toby moaned. "I'll be ready . . ."

And he lost consciousness.

11

The wedding, a gala event, was held in the ballroom of the Morocco Hotel. It seemed that half of Las Vegas was there. There were entertainers and owners from all the other hotels and showgirls and, in the center of it all, Al Caruso and a couple dozen of his friends, quiet, conservatively dressed men, most of whom did not drink. There were lavish arrangements of flowers everywhere, strolling musicians, a gargantuan buffet and two fountains that flowed champagne. Al Caruso had taken care of everything.

Everyone sympathized with the groom, whose arm was in a cast as a result of an accidental fall down some stairs. But they all commented on what a marvelous-looking couple the bride and groom made and what a wonderful wedding it was.

Toby had been in such a daze from the opiates that the doctor had given him that he had walked through the ceremony almost oblivious of what was going on. Then, as the drugs began to wear off and the pain began to take hold again, the anger and hate flooded back into him. He wanted to scream out to everyone in the room the unspeakable humiliation that had been forced upon him.

Toby turned to look at his bride across the room. He remembered Millie now. She was a pretty girl in her twenties, with honey-blond hair and a good figure. Toby recalled that she had laughed louder than the others at his stories and had followed him around. Something else came back to him, too. She was one of the few who had refused to go to bed with him, which had only served to whet Toby's appetite. It was *all* coming back to him now.

"I'm crazy about you," he had said. "Don't you like me?"

"Of course I do," she had replied. "But I have a boyfriend."

Why hadn't he listened to her! Instead, he had coaxed her up to his room for a drink and then had started telling her funny stories. Millie was laughing so hard that she hardly noticed what Toby was doing until he had her undressed and in bed.

"Please, Toby," she had begged. "Don't. My boyfriend will be angry."

"Forget about him. I'll take care of the jerk later," Toby had said. "I'm going to take care of *you*, now."

They had had a wild night of lovemaking. In the morning, when Toby had awakened, Millie was lying beside him, crying. In a benevolent mood, Toby had taken her in his arms and said, "Hey, baby, what's the matter? Didn't you enjoy it?"

"You know I did. But—"

"Come on, stop that," Toby had said. "I love you."

She had propped herself up on her elbows, looked into his eyes and said, "Do you really, Toby? I mean *really?*"

"Damned right I do." All she needed was what he would give her right now. It proved to be a real cheerer-upper.

She had watched him return from the shower, toweling his still wet hair and humming snatches of his theme song. Happy, she had smiled and said, "I think I loved you from the first moment I saw you, Toby."

"Hey, that's wonderful. Let's order breakfast."

And that had been the end of that. . . . Until now. Because of a stupid broad he had fucked only one night, his whole life was turned topsy-turvy.

Now, Toby stood there, watching Millie coming toward him in her long, white wedding gown, smiling at him, and he cursed himself and he cursed his cock and he cursed the day he was born.

In the limousine, the man in the front seat chuckled and said admiringly, "I sure gotta hand it to you, boss. The poor bastard never knew what hit him."

Caruso smiled benignly. It had worked out well. Ever since his wife, who had the temper of a virago, had found out about his affair with Millie, Caruso had known that he would have to find a way to get rid of the blond showgirl.

"Remind me to see that he treats Millie good," Caruso said softly.

Toby and Millie moved into a small home in Benedict Canyon. In the beginning, Toby spent hours scheming about ways to get out of his marriage. He would make Millie so miserable that she would ask for a divorce. Or he would frame her with another guy and then demand a divorce. Or he would simply leave her and defy Caruso to do something about it. But he changed his mind after a talk with Dick Landry, the director.

They were having lunch at the Bel Air Hotel a few weeks after the wedding, and Landry asked, "How well do you really know Al Caruso?"

Toby looked at him. "Why?"

"Don't get mixed up with him, Toby. He's a killer. I'll tell you something I know for a fact. Caruso's kid brother married a nineteen-year-old girl fresh out of a convent. A year later, the kid caught his wife in bed with some guy. He told Al about it."

Toby was listening, his eyes fastened on Landry. "What happened."

"Caruso's goons took a meat cleaver and cut off the guy's prick. They soaked it in gasoline and set it on fire while the guy watched. Then they left him to bleed to death."

Toby remembered Caruso saying, *Open up his pants*, and the hard hands fumbling at his zipper, and Toby broke out in a cold sweat. He felt suddenly sick to his stomach. He knew now with an awful certainty that there was no escape.

Josephine found an escape when she was ten. It was a door to another world where she could hide from her mother's punishments and the constant threat of Hell-fire and Damnation. It was a world filled with magic and beauty. She would sit in the darkened movie house hour after hour and watch the glamorous people on the screen. They all lived in beautiful houses and wore lovely clothes, and they were all so happy. And Josephine thought, I will go to Hollywood one day and live like that. She hoped that her mother would understand.

Her mother believed that movies were the thoughts of the Devil, so Josephine had to sneak away to the theater, using money she earned by baby-sitting. The picture that was playing today was a love story, and Josephine leaned forward in joyous anticipation as it began. The credits came on first. They read, "Produced by Sam Winters."

T here were days when Sam Winters felt as though he were running a lunatic asylum instead of a motion-picture studio, and that all the inmates were out to get him. This was one of those days, for the crises were piled a foot high. There had been another fire at the studio the night before—the fourth; the sponsor of "My Man Friday" had been insulted by the star of the series and wanted to cancel the show; Bert Firestone, the studio's boy-genius director, had shut down production in the middle of a five-million-dollar picture; and Tessie Brand had walked out on a picture that was scheduled to start shooting in a few days.

The fire marshal and the studio comptroller were in Sam's office.

"How bad was last night's fire?" Sam asked.

The comptroller said, "The sets are a total loss, Mr. Winters. We're going to have to rebuild Stage Fifteen completely. Sixteen is fixable, but it will take us three months."

"We haven't got three months," Sam snapped. "Get on the phone and rent some space at Goldwyn. Use this weekend to start building new sets. Get everybody moving."

He turned to the fire marshal, a man named Reilly, who reminded Sam of George Bancroft, the actor.

"Somebody sure as hell don't like you, Mr. Winters," Reilly said. "each fire has been a clear case of arson. Have you checked on grunts?"

Grunts were disgruntled employees who had been recently fired or who felt they had a grievance against their employer.

"We've gone through all the personnel files twice," Sam replied. "We haven't come up with a thing."

"Whoever is setting these babies knows exactly what he's doing. He's using a timing device attached to a homemade incendiary. He could be an electrician or a mechanic."

"Thanks," Sam said. "I'll pass that on."

"Roger Tapp is calling from Tahiti."

"Put him on," Sam said. Tapp was the producer of "My Man Friday," the television series being shot in Tahiti, starring Tony Fletcher.

"What's the problem?" Sam asked.

"You won't fucking believe this, Sam. Philip Heller, the chairman of the board of the company that's sponsoring the show, is visiting here with his family. They walked on the set yesterday afternoon, and Tony Fletcher was in the middle of a scene. He turned to them and insulted them."

"What did he say?"

"He told them to *get off his island.*"

"Jesus Christ!"

"That's who he thinks he is. Heller's so mad he wants to cancel the series."

"Get over to Heller and apologize. Do it right now. Tell him Tony Fletcher's having a nervous breakdown. Send Mrs. Heller flowers, take them to dinner. I'll talk to Tony Fletcher myself."

The conversation lasted thirty minutes. It began with Sam saying, "Hear this, you stupid cocksucker . . ." and ended with, "I love you, too, baby. I'll fly over there to see you as soon as I can get away. And for God's sake, Tony, don't lay Mrs. Heller!"

The next problem was Bert Firestone, the boy-genius director who was breaking Pan-Pacific Studios. Firestone's picture, *There's Always Tomorrow,* had been shooting for a hundred and ten days, and was more than a million dollars over budget. Now Bert Firestone had shut the production down, which meant that, besides the stars, there were a hundred and fifty extras sitting around on their asses doing nothing. Bert Firestone. A thirty-year-old whiz kid who came from directing prize-winning television shows at a Chicago station to directing movies in Hollywood. Firestone's first three motion pictures had been mild successes, but his fourth one had been a box-office smash. On the basis of that money-maker, he had become a hot property. Sam remembered his first meeting with him. Firestone looked a not-yet-ready-to-shave fifteen. He was a pale, shy man with black horn-rimmed glasses that concealed tiny, myopic pink eyes. Sam had felt sorry for the kid. Firestone had not known anyone in Hollywood, so Sam had gone out of his way to have him to dinner and to see that he was invited to parties. When they had first discussed *There's Always Tomorrow*, Firestone was very respectful. He told Sam that he was eager to learn. He hung on every word that Sam said. He could not have agreed more with Sam. If he were signed for this picture, he told Sam, he would certainly lean heavily on Mr. Winters's expertise.

That was *before* Firestone signed the contract. *After* he signed it, he made Adolf Hitler look like Albert Schweitzer. The little apple-cheeked kid turned into a killer overnight. He cut off all communication. He completely ignored Sam's casting suggestions, insisted on totally rewriting a fine script that Sam had approved, and he changed most of the shooting locales that had already been agreed upon. Sam had wanted to throw him off the picture, but the New York office had told Sam to be patient. Rudolph Hergershorn, the president of the company, was hypnotized by the enormous grosses on Firestone's last movie. So Sam had been forced to sit tight and do nothing. It seemed to him that Firestone's arrogance grew day by day. He would sit quietly through a production meeting, and when all the experienced department heads had finished speaking, Firestone would begin chopping down everyone. Sam gritted his teeth and bore it. In no time at all, Firestone acquired the nickname of Emperor, and when his coworkers were not calling him that, they referred to him as Kid Prick from Chicago. Somebody said about him, "He's a hermaphrodite. He could probably fuck himself and give birth to a two-headed monster."

Now, in the middle of shooting, Firestone had closed down the company.

Sam went over to see Devlin Kelly, the head of the art department. "Give it to me fast," Sam said.

"Right. Kid Prick ordered—"

"Cut that out. It's *Mr.* Firestone."

"Sorry. *Mr. Firestone* asked me to build a castle set for him. He drew the sketches himself. You okayed them."

"They were good. What happened?"

"What happened was that we built him exactly what the little—what he wanted, and when he took a look at it yesterday, he decided he didn't want it anymore. A half-million bucks down the—"

"I'll talk to him," Sam said.

Bert Firestone was outside, in back of Stage Twenty-Three, playing basketball with the crew. They had rigged up a court and had painted in boundary lines and put up two baskets.

Sam stood there, watching a moment. The game was costing the studio two thousand dollars an hour. "Bert!"

Firestone turned, saw Sam, smiled and waved. The ball came to him, he dribbled it, feinted, and sank a basket. Then he strolled over to Sam. "How are things?" As though nothing were wrong.

As Sam looked at the boyish, smiling young face, it occurred to him that Bert Firestone was a psycho. Talented, maybe even a genius, but a certifiable lunatic. And five million dollars of the company's money was in his hands.

"I hear there's a problem with the new set," Sam said. "Let's straighten it out."

Bert Firestone smiled lazily and said, "There's nothing to straighten out, Sam. The set won't work."

Sam exploded. "What the hell are you talking about? We gave you exactly what you ordered. You did the sketches yourself. Now you tell me what's wrong with it!"

Firestone looked at him and blinked. "Why, there's nothing wrong with it. It's just that I've changed my mind. I don't want a castle. I've decided that's not the right ambience. Do you know what I mean? This is Ellen and Mike's farewell scene. I'd like to have Ellen come to visit Mike on the deck of his ship as he's getting ready to sail."

Sam stared at him. "We don't have a ship set, Bert."

Bert Firestone stretched his arms and smiled lazily and said, "Build one for me, Sam."

★

"Sure, I'm pissed off, too," Rudolph Hergershorn said, over the long-distance line, "but you *can't* replace him, Sam. We're in too deep now. We have no stars in the picture. *Bert Firestone's* our star."

"Do you know how far over the budget he's—"

"I know. And like Goldwyn said, 'I'll never use the son of a bitch again, until I need him.' We need him to finish this picture."

"It's a mistake," Sam argued. "He shouldn't be allowed to get away with this."

"Sam—do you like the stuff Firestone has shot so far?"

Sam had to be honest. "It's great."

"Build him his ship."

The set was ready in ten days, and Bert Firestone put the *There's Always Tomorrow* company back into production. It turned out to be the top grosser of the year.

The next problem was Tessie Brand.

Tessie was the hottest singer in show business. It had been a coup when Sam Winters had managed to sign her to a three-picture deal at Pan-Pacific Studios. While the other studios were negotiating with Tessie's agents, Sam had quietly flown to New York, seen Tessie's show and taken her out to supper afterward. The supper had lasted until seven o'clock the following morning.

Tessie Brand was one of the ugliest girls Sam had ever seen, and probably the most talented. It was the talent that won out. The daughter of a Brooklyn tailor, Tessie had never had a singing lesson in her life. But when she walked onto a stage and began belting out a song in a voice that rocked the rafters, audiences went wild. Tessie had been an understudy in a flop Broadway musical that had lasted only six weeks. On closing night, the ingenue made the mistake of phoning in sick and staying home. Tessie Brand made her debut that evening, singing her heart out to the sprinkling of people in the audience. Among them happened to be Paul Varrick, a Broadway producer. He starred Tessie in his next musical. She turned the show, which was fair, into a smash. The critics ran out of superlatives trying to describe the incredible, ugly Tessie and her amazing voice. She recorded her first single record. Overnight it became number one. She did an album, and it sold two million copies in the first month. She was Queen Midas, for everything she touched turned to gold. Broadway producers and record companies were making their fortunes with Tessie Brand, and Hollywood wanted in on the action. Their enthusiasm dimmed when they got a look at Tessie's face, but her box-office figures gave her an irresistible beauty.

After spending five minutes with her, Sam knew how he was going to handle her.

"What makes me nervous," Tessie confessed to Sam the first night they met, "is how I'm gonna look on that great big screen. I'm ugly enough *life-sized*, right? All the studios tell me they can make me look beautiful, but I think that's a load of horseshit."

"It *is* a load of horseshit," Sam said. Tessie looked at him in surprise. "Don't let anyone try to change you, Tessie. They'll ruin you."

"Yeah?"

"When MGM signed Danny Thomas, Louie Mayer wanted him to get a nose job. Instead, Danny quit the studio. He knew that what he had to sell was *himself*. That's what *you* have to sell— Tessie Brand, not some plastic stranger up there."

"You're the first one who's leveled with me," Tessie said. "You're a real *Mensch*. You married?"

"No," Sam said.

"Do you fool around?"

Sam laughed. "Never with singers—I have no ear."

"You wouldn't need an ear." Tessie smiled. "I like you."

"Do you like me well enough to make some movies with me?"

She looked at him and said, "Yeah."

"Wonderful. I'll work out the deal with your agent."

She stroked Sam's hand and said, "Are you sure you don't fool around?"

Tessie Brand's first two pictures went through the box-office roof. She received an Academy nomination for the first one and was awarded the golden Oscar for the second. Audiences all over the world lined up at motion-picture theaters to see Tessie and to hear that incredible voice. She had everything. She was funny, she could sing and she could act. Her ugliness turned out to be an asset, because audiences identified with it. Tessie Brand became a surrogate for all the unattractive, the unloved, the unwanted.

Tessie married the leading man in her first picture, divorced him after the retakes and married the leading man in her next picture. Sam had heard rumors that this marriage too was sinking, but Hollywood was a hotbed of gossip. He paid no attention, for he felt that it was none of his business.

As it turned out, he was mistaken.

Sam was talking on the phone to Barry Herman, Tessie's agent. "What's the problem, Barry?"

"Tessie's new picture. She's not happy, Sam."

Sam felt his temper rising. "Hold it! Tessie's approved the producer, the director and the shooting script. We've got the sets built and we're ready to roll. There's no way she can walk away now. I'll—"

"She doesn't want to walk away."

Sam was taken aback. "What the hell *does* she want?"

"She wants a new producer on the picture."

Sam yelled into the phone. "She *what?*"

"Ralph Dastin doesn't understand her."

"Dastin's one of the best producers in the business. She's lucky to have him."

"I couldn't agree with you more, Sam. But the chemistry's wrong. She won't make the picture unless he's out."

"She's got a contract, Barry."

"I know that, sweetheart. And, believe me, Tessie has every intention of honoring it. As long as she's physically able. It's just that she gets nervous when she's unhappy and she can't seem to remember her lines."

"I'll call you back," Sam said savagely. He slammed down the phone.

The goddamned bitch! There was no reason to fire Dastin from the picture. He had probably refused to go to bed with her, or something equally ridiculous. He said to Lucille, "Ask Ralph Dastin to come up here."

Ralph Dastin was an amiable man in his fifties. He had started as a writer and had eventually become a producer. His movies had taste and charm.

"Ralph," Sam began, "I don't know how to—"

Dastin held up his hand. "You don't have to say it, Sam. I was on my way up here to tell you I'm quitting."

"What the hell's going on?" Sam demanded.

Dastin shrugged. "Our star's got an itch. She wants someone else to scratch it."

"You mean she has your replacement already picked out?"

"Jesus, where have you been—on Mars? Don't you read the gossip columns?"

"Not if I can help it. Who is he?"

"It's not a he."

Sam sat down, slowly. *"What?"*

"It's the costume designer on Tessie's picture. Her name is Barbara Carter—like the little liver pills."

"Are you sure about this?" Sam asked.

"You're the only one in the entire Western Hemisphere who doesn't know it."

Sam shook his head. "I always thought Tessie was straight."

"Sam, life's a cafeteria. Tessie's a hungry girl."

"Well, I'm not about to put a goddamned female costume designer in charge of a four-million-dollar picture."

Dastin grinned. "You just said the wrong thing."

"What does *that* mean?"

"It means that part of Tessie's pitch is that women aren't given a fair chance in this business. Your little star has become very feminist-minded."

"I won't do it," Sam said.

"Suit yourself. But I'll give you some free advice. It's the only way you're ever going to get this picture made."

Sam telephoned Barry Herman. "Tell Tessie that Ralph Dastin walked off the picture," Sam said.

"She'll be pleased to hear that."

Sam gritted his teeth, then asked, "Did she have anyone else in mind to produce the picture?"

"As a matter of fact, she did," Herman said smoothly. "Tessie has discovered a very talented young girl who she feels is ready for a challenge like this. Under the guidance of someone as brilliant as you, Sam—"

"Cut out the commercial," Sam said. "Is that the bottom line?"

"I'm afraid it is, Sam. I'm sorry."

★

Barbara Carter had a pretty face and a good figure and, as far as Sam could tell, was completely feminine. He watched her as she took a seat on the leather couch in his office and daintily crossed her long, shapely legs. When she spoke, her voice sounded a trifle husky, but that may have been because Sam was looking for some kind of sign. She studied him with soft gray eyes and said, "I seem to be in a terrible spot, Mr. Winters. I had no intention of putting anyone out of work. And yet"—she raised her hands helplessly— "Miss Brand says she simply won't make the picture unless I produce it. What do you think I should do?"

For an instant, Sam was tempted to tell her. Instead, he said, "Have you had any experience with show business—besides being a costume designer?"

"I've ushered, and I've seen lots of movies."

Terrific! "What makes Miss Brand think you can produce a motion picture?"

It was as though Sam had touched a hidden spring. Barbara Carter was suddenly full of animation. "Tessie and I have talked a lot about this picture." No more *"Miss Brand,"* Sam noticed. "I feel there are a lot of things wrong with the script, and when I pointed them out to her, she agreed with me."

"Do you think you know more about writing a script than an Academy Award-winning writer who's done half a dozen successful pictures and Broadway plays?"

"Oh, no, Mr. Winters! I just think I know more about *women.*" The gray eyes were harder now, the tone a little tougher. "Don't you think it's ridiculous for men to always be writing women's parts? Only *we* really know how we feel. Doesn't that make sense to you?"

Sam was tired of the game. He knew he was going to hire her, and he hated himself for it, but he was running a studio, and his job was to see that pictures got made. If Tessie Brand wanted her pet squirrel to produce this picture, Sam would start ordering nuts. A Tessie Brand picture could easily mean a profit of from twenty to thirty million dollars. Besides, Barbara Carter couldn't do anything to really hurt the picture. Not now. It was too close to shooting for any major changes to be made.

"You've convinced me," Sam said, with irony. "You've got the job. Congratulations."

The following morning, the *Hollywood Reporter* and *Variety* announced on their front pages that Barbara Carter was producing the new Tessie Brand movie. As Sam started to throw the papers in his wastebasket, a small item at the bottom of the page caught his eye: "TOBY TEMPLE SIGNED FOR LOUNGE AT TAHOE HOTEL."

Toby Temple. Sam remembered the eager young comic in uniform, and the memory brought a smile to Sam's face. Sam made a mental note to see his act if Temple ever played in town.

He wondered why Toby Temple had never gotten in touch with him.

I n a strange way, it was Millie who was responsible for Toby Temple's rise to stardom. Before their marriage, he had been just another up-and-coming comic, one of dozens. Since the wedding, a new ingredient had been added: hatred. Toby had been forced into a marriage with a girl he despised, and there was such rage in him that he could have killed her with his bare hands.

Although Toby did not realize it, Millie was a wonderful, devoted wife. She adored him and did everything she could to please him. She decorated the house in Benedict Canyon, and did it beautifully. But the more Millie tried to please Toby, the more he loathed her. He was always meticulously polite to her, careful never to do or say anything that might upset her enough to call Al Caruso. As long as he lived, Toby would not forget the awful agony of that tire iron smashing into his arm, or the look on Al Caruso's face when he said, "If you ever hurt Millie . . ."

Because Toby could not take out his aggressions on his wife, he turned his fury on his audiences. Anyone who rattled a dish' or rose to go to the washroom or dared talk while Toby was on stage was the instant object of a savage tirade. Toby did it with such wide-eyed, naive charm that the audiences adored it, and when Toby ripped apart some hapless victim, people laughed until they cried. The combination of his innocent, guileless face and his wicked, funny tongue made him irresistible. He could say the most outrageous things and get away with them. It became a mark of distinction to be singled out for a tongue lashing by Toby Temple.

It never even occurred to his victims that Toby meant every word he said. Where before Toby had been just another promising young comedian, now he became the talk of the entertainment circuit.

When Clifton Lawrence returned from Europe, he was amazed to learn that Toby had married a showgirl. It had seemed out of character, but when he asked Toby about it, Toby looked him in the eye and said, "What's there to tell, Cliff? I met Millie, fell in love with her and that was that."

Somehow, it had not rung true. And there was something else that puzzled the agent. One day in his office, Clifton told Toby, "You're really getting hot. I've booked you into the Thunderbird for a four-week gig. Two thousand a week."

"What about that tour?"

"Forget it. Las Vegas pays ten times as much, and everybody will see your act."

"Cancel Vegas. Get me the tour."

Clifton looked at him in surprise. "But Las Vegas is—"

"Get me the tour." There was a note in Toby's voice that Clifton Lawrence had never heard before. It was not arrogance or temperament; it was something beyond that, a deep, controlled rage.

What made it frightening was that it emanated from a face that had grown more genial and boyish than ever.

From that time on, Toby was on the road constantly. It was his only escape from his prison. He played night clubs and theaters and auditoriums, and when those bookings ran out, he badgered Clifton Lawrence to book him into colleges. Anywhere, to get away from Millie.

The opportunities to go to bed with eager, attractive women were limitless. It was the same in every town. They waited in Toby's dressing room before and after the show and waylaid him in his hotel lobby.

Toby went to bed with none of them. He thought of the man's penis being hacked off and set on fire and Al Caruso saying to Toby, *You're really hung. . . . I wouldn't hurt you. You're my friend. As long as you're good to Millie . . .*

And Toby turned all the women away.

"I'm in love with my wife," he would say shyly. And they

believed him and admired him for it, and the word spread, as Toby meant it to spread: Toby Temple did not fool around; he was a real family man.

But the lovely, nubile young girls kept coming after him, and the more Toby refused, the more they wanted him. And Toby was so hungry for a woman that he was in constant physical pain. His groin ached so much that sometimes it was difficult for him to work. He started to masturbate again. Each time he did, he thought of all the beautiful girls waiting to go to bed with him, and he cursed and raged against fate.

Because Toby could not have it, sex was on his mind all the time. Whenever he returned home after a tour, Millie was waiting for him, eager and loving and ready. And the moment Toby saw her, all his sexual desire drained away. She was the enemy, and Toby despised her for what she was doing to him. He forced himself to go to bed with her, but it was Al Caruso he was satisfying. Whenever Toby took Millie, it was with a savage brutality that forced gasps of pain from her. He pretended that he thought they were sounds of pleasure, and he pounded into her harder and harder, until finally he came in an explosion of fury that poured his venomous semen into her. He was not making love.

He was making hate.

In June, 1950, the North Koreans moved across the 38th Parallel and attacked the South Koreans, and President Truman ordered United States troops in. No matter what the rest of the world thought about it, to Toby the Korean War was the best thing that ever happened.

In early December, there was an announcement in *Daily Variety* that Bob Hope was getting ready to make a Christmas tour to entertain the troops in Seoul. Thirty seconds after he read it, Toby was on the telephone, talking to Clifton Lawrence.

"You've got to get me on it, Cliff."

"What for? You're almost thirty years old. Believe me, dear boy, those tours are no fun. I—"

"I don't give a damn whether they're fun or not," Toby shouted into the phone. "Those soldiers are out there risking their lives. The least I can do is give them a few laughs."

It was a side of Toby Temple that Clifton had not seen before. He was touched and pleased.

"Okay. If you feel that strongly about it, I'll see what I can do," Clifton promised.

An hour later he called Toby back. "I talked to Bob. He'd be happy to have you. But if you should change your mind—"

"No chance," Toby said, hanging up.

Clifton Lawrence sat there a long time, thinking about Toby. He was very proud of him. Toby was a wonderful human being, and Clifton Lawrence was delighted to be his agent, delighted to be the man helping to shape his growing career.

Toby played Taegu and Pusan and Chonju, and he found solace in the laughter of the soldiers. Millie faded into the background of his mind.

Then Christmas was over. Instead of returning home, Toby went to Guam. The boys there loved him. He went to Tokyo and entertained the wounded in the army hospital. But finally, it was time to return home.

In April, when Toby came back from a ten-week tour in the Midwest, Millie was waiting at the airport for him. Her first words were, "Darling—I'm going to have a baby!"

He stared at her, stunned. She mistook his expression for happiness.

"Isn't it wonderful?" she exclaimed. "Now, when you're away, I'll have the baby to keep me company. I hope it's a boy so that you can take him to baseball games and . . ."

Toby did not hear the rest of the stupidities she was mouthing. It was as though her words were being filtered from far away. Somewhere in the back of his mind, Toby had believed that someday, somehow, there would be an escape for him. They had been married two years, and it seemed like an eternity. Now this. Millie would *never* let him go.

Never.

The baby was due around Christmastime. Toby had made arrangements to go to Guam with a troupe of entertainers, but he had no idea whether Al Caruso would approve of his being away while Millie was having the baby. There was only one way to find out. Toby called Las Vegas.

Caruso's cheerful, familiar voice came on the line immediately and said, "Hi, kid. Good to hear your voice."

"It's good to hear yours, Al."

"I hear you're gonna be a father. You must be real excited."

"Excited isn't the word for it," Toby said truthfully. He let his voice take on a note of careful concern. "That's the reason I'm calling you, Al. The baby's going to be born around Christmas, and—" He had to be very careful. "I don't know what to do. I want to be here with Millie when the kid's born, but they asked me to go back to Korea and Guam to entertain the troops."

There was a long pause. "That's a tough spot."

"I don't want to let our boys down, but I don't want to let Millie down, either."

"Yeah." There was another pause. Then, "I'll tell you what I think, kid. We're all good Americans, right? Those kids are out there fighting for us, right?"

Toby felt his body suddenly relax. "Sure. But I hate to—"

"Millie'll be okay," Caruso said. "Women have been havin' babies a hell of a long time. You go to Korea."

Six weeks later, on Christmas Eve, as Toby walked off a stage to thunderous applause at the army post in Pusan, he was handed a cable, informing him that Millie had died while giving birth to a stillborn son.

Toby was free.

August 14, 1952, was Josephine Czinski's thirteenth birthday. She was invited to a party by Mary Lou Kenyon, who had been born on the same day. Josephine's mother had forbidden her to go. "Those are wicked people," Mrs. Czinski admonished her. "You'll be better off stayin' home and studyin' your Bible."

But Josephine had no intention of remaining at home. Her friends were *not* wicked. She wished that there was some way she could make her mother understand. As soon as her mother left, Josephine took five dollars that she had earned by baby-sitting and went downtown, where she bought a lovely white bathing suit. Then she headed for Mary Lou's house. She had a feeling it was going to be a wonderful day.

Mary Lou Kenyon lived in the most beautiful of all the Oil People mansions. Her home was filled with antiques and priceless tapestries and beautiful paintings. On the grounds were guest cottages, stables, a tennis court, a private landing strip and two swimming pools, an enormous one for the Kenyons and their guests and a smaller one in back for the staff.

Mary Lou had an older brother, David, of whom Josephine had caught glimpses from time to time. He was the most handsome boy Josephine had ever seen. He seemed about ten feet tall with broad, football shoulders and teasing gray eyes. He was an All-America halfback and had been given a Rhodes scholarship. Mary Lou had also had an older sister, Beth, who had died when Josephine was a little girl.

Now, at the party, Josephine kept looking around hopefully for David, but she did not see him anywhere. In the past, he had stopped to speak to her several times, but each time Josephine had reddened and stood there, tongue-tied.

The party was a big success. There were fourteen boys and girls. They had eaten an enormous lunch of barbecue beef, chicken, chili and potato salad and lemonade, served on the terrace by uniformed butlers and maids. Then Mary Lou and Josephine opened their presents, while everyone stood around and commented on them.

Mary Lou said, "Let's all go for a swim."

Everyone made a dash for the dressing rooms at their side of the pool. As Josephine changed into her new bathing suit, she thought that she had never been so happy. It had been a perfect day, spent with her friends. She was one of them, sharing the beauty that surrounded them everywhere. There was nothing evil about it. She wished she could stop time and freeze this day so that it would never end.

Josephine stepped out into the bright sunlight. As she walked toward the pool, she became aware that the others were watching her, the girls with open envy, the boys with sly, covert looks. In the past few months Josephine's body had matured dramatically. Her breasts were firm and full, straining against her bathing suit, and her hips hinted at the lush, rounded curves of a woman. Josephine dived into the pool, joining the others.

"Let's play Marco Polo," someone called out.

Josephine loved the game. She enjoyed moving around in the warm water with her eyes tightly closed. She would call out, "Marco!" and the others would have to reply, "Polo!" Josephine would dive after the sound of their voices before they got away, until she tagged someone, and then that person became "it."

They began the game. Cissy Topping was "it." She went after the boy she liked, Bob Jackson, but could not get him, so she tagged Josephine. Josephine closed her eyes tightly and listened for the telltale sound of splashes.

"Marco!" she called out.

There was a chorus of "Polo!" Josephine made a dive for the nearest voice. She felt around in the water. There was no one there.

"Marco!" she called.

Again, a chorus of "Polo!" She made a blind grab but reached only thin air. It did not matter to Josephine that they were faster than she; she wanted this game to go on forever, as she wanted this day to last until eternity.

She stood still, straining to hear a splash, a giggle, a whisper. She moved around in the pool, eyes closed, hands outstretched, and reached the steps. She took a step up to quiet the sound of her own movements.

"Marco!" she called out.

And there was no answer. She stood there, still.

"Marco!"

Silence. It was as though she were in a warm, wet, deserted world, alone. They were playing a trick on her. They had decided that no one would answer her. Josephine smiled and opened her eyes.

She was alone on the pool steps. Something made her look down. The bottom of her white bathing suit was stained with red, and there was a thin trickle of blood coming from between her thighs. The children were all standing on the sides of the pool, staring at her. Josephine looked up at them, stricken. "I—" She stopped, not knowing what to say. She quickly moved down the steps into the water, to cover her shame.

"We don't do that in the swimming pool," Mary Lou said.

"Polacks do," someone giggled.

"Hey, let's go take a shower."

"Yeah. I feel icky."

"Who wants to swim in *that?*"

Josephine closed her eyes again and heard them all moving toward the poolhouse, leaving her. She stayed there, keeping her eyes squeezed closed, pressing her legs together to try to stop the shameful flow. She had never had her period before. It had been totally unexpected. They would all come back in a moment and tell her that they had only been teasing, that they were still her friends, that the happiness would never stop. They would return and explain that it was all a game. Perhaps they were back already, ready to play. Eyes tightly shut, she whispered, "Marco," and the echo died on the afternoon air. She had no idea how long she stood there in the water with her eyes closed.

We don't do that in the swimming pool.

425

Polacks do.

Her head had begun pounding violently. She felt nauseous, and her stomach was suddenly cramping. But Josephine knew that she must keep standing there with her eyes tightly shut. Just until they returned and told her it was a joke.

She heard footsteps and a rustling sound above her and she suddenly knew that everything was all right. They had come back. She opened her eyes and looked up.

David, Mary Lou's older brother, was standing at the side of the pool, a terrycloth robe in his hands.

"I apologize for all of them," he said, his voice tight. He held out the robe. "Here. Come out and put this on."

But Josephine closed her eyes and stayed there, rigid. She wanted to die as quickly as possible.

15

It was one of Sam Winters's good days. The rushes on the Tessie Brand picture were wonderful. Part of the reason, of course, was that Tessie was breaking her neck to vindicate her behavior. But whatever the reason, Barbara Carter was going to emerge as the hottest new producer of the year. It was going to be a terrific year for costume designers.

The television shows produced by Pan-Pacific were doing well, and "My Man Friday" was the biggest of them all. The network was talking to Sam about a new five-year contract for the series.

Sam was preparing to leave for lunch when Lucille hurried in and said, "They just caught someone setting a fire in the prop department. They're bringing him over here now."

The man sat in a chair facing Sam in silence, two studio guards standing behind him. His eyes were bright with malice. Sam had still not gotten over his shock. "Why?" he asked. "For God's sake —why?"

"Because I didn't want your fucking charity," Dallas Burke said. "I hate you and this studio and the whole rotten business. I *built* this business, you son of a bitch. I paid for half the studios in this lousy town. Everybody got rich off me. Why didn't you give me a picture to direct instead of trying to pay me off by pretending to buy a bunch of fucking stolen fairy tales? You would have bought the phone book from me, Sam. I didn't want any favors from you—I wanted a job. You're making me die a failure, you prick, and I'll never forgive you for that."

Long after they had taken Dallas Burke away, Sam sat there thinking about him, remembering the great things Dallas had done, the wonderful movies he had made. In any other business, he would have been a hero, the chairman of the board or would have been retired with a nice, fat pension and glory.

But this was the wonderful world of show business.

I n the early 1950's, Toby Temple's success was growing. He
played the top nightclubs—the Chez Paree in Chicago, the
Latin Casino in Philadelphia, the Copacabana in New York.
He played benefits and children's hospitals and charity affairs—he
would play for anybody, anywhere, at any time. The audience was
his lifeblood. He needed the applause and the love. He was totally
absorbed in show business. Major events were occuring around the
world, but to Toby they were merely grist for his act.

In 1951, when General MacArthur was fired and said, "Old
soldiers don't die—they just fade away," Toby said, "Jesus—we
must use the same laundry."

In 1952, when the hydrogen bomb was dropped, Toby's response was, "That's nothing. You should have caught my opening
in Atlanta."

When Nixon made his "Checkers" speech, Toby said, "I'd vote
for him in a minute. Not Nixon—Checkers."

Ike was President and Stalin died and young America was
wearing Davy Crockett hats and there was a bus boycott in
Montgomery.

And everything was material for Toby's act.

When he delivered his zingers with that wide-eyed look of
baffled innocence, the audiences screamed.

Toby's whole life consisted of punch lines. ". . . so he said, 'Wait
a minute; I'll get my hat and go with you . . .' " and ". . . to tell
the truth, it looked so good I ate it myself!" and ". . . it's a
candystore, but they'll call me. . . ." and ". . . I would have

been a Shamus . . ." and ". . . now I've got you and there's no ship . . ." and "Just my luck. I get the part that eats. . . ." and on and on, with the audiences laughing until they cried. His audiences loved him, and he fed on their love and battened on it and climbed ever higher.

But there was a deep, wild restlessness in Toby. He was always looking for something more. He could never enjoy himself because he was afraid he might be missing a better party somewhere, or playing to a better audience, or kissing a prettier girl. He changed girls as frequently as he changed his shirts. After the experience with Millie, he was afraid to become deeply involved with anyone. He remembered when he had played the Toilet Circuit and envied the comics with the big limousines and the beautiful women. He had made it, and he was as lonely now as he had been then. Who was it who had said, "When you get there, there is no there. . . ."

He was dedicated to becoming Number One and he knew he would make it. His one regret was that his mother would not be there to watch her prediction come true.

The only reminder left of her was his father.

The nursing home in Detroit was an ugly brick building from another century. Its walls held the sweet stench of old age and sickness and death.

Toby Temple's father had suffered a stroke and was almost a vegetable now, a man with listless, apathetic eyes and a mind that cared for nothing except Toby's visits. Toby stood in the dingy green-carpeted hall of the home that now held his father. The nurses and inmates crowded adoringly around him.

"I saw you on the Harold Hobson show last week, Toby. I thought you were just marvelous. How do you think of all those clever things to say?"

"My writers think of them," Toby said, and they laughed at his modesty.

A male nurse was coming down the corridor, wheeling Toby's father. He was freshly shaved and had his hair slicked down. He had let them dress him in a suit in honor of his son's visit.

"Hey, it's Beau Brummel!" Toby called, and everyone turned to look at Mr. Temple with envy, wishing that they had a wonderful, famous son like Toby to come and visit them.

Toby walked over to his father, leaned down and gave him a hug. "Who you trying to kid?" Toby asked. He pointed to the male nurse. "*You* should be wheeling *him* around, Pop."

Everyone laughed, filing the quip away in their minds so that they could tell their friends what they had heard Toby Temple say. *I was with Toby Temple the other day and he said . . . I was standing as close as I am to you, and I heard him . . .*

He stood around entertaining them, insulting them gently, and they loved it. He kidded them about their sex lives and their health and their children, and for a little while they were able to laugh at their own problems. Finally, Toby said ruefully, "I hate to leave you, you're the best-looking audience I've had in years"—*They would remember that, too*— "but I have to spend a little time alone with Pop. He promised to give me some new jokes."

They smiled and laughed and adored him.

Toby was alone in the small visitors room with his father. Even this room had the smell of death, and yet, *That was what this place was all about, wasn't it,* Toby thought. *Death?* It was filled with used-up mothers and fathers who were in the way. They had been taken out of the small back bedrooms at home, out of the dining rooms and parlors where they were becoming an embarrassment whenever there were guests, and had been sent to this nursing home by their children, nieces and nephews. *Believe me, it's for your own good, Father, Mother, Uncle George, Aunt Bess. You'll be with a lot of very nice people your own age. You'll have company all the time. You know what I mean?* What they really meant was, *I'm sending you there to die with all the other useless old people. I'm sick of your drooling at the table and telling the same stories over and over and pestering the children and wetting your bed.* The Eskimos were more honest about it. They sent their old people out onto the ice and abandoned them there.

"I'm sure glad you came today," Toby's father said. His speech was slow. "I wanted to talk to you. I got some good news. Old Art Riley next door died yesterday."

Toby stared at him. "*That's* good news?"

"It means I can move into his room," his father explained. "It's a single."

And that was what old age was all about: Survival, hanging on to the few creature comforts that still remained. Toby had seen people here who would have been better off dead, but they clung to life, fiercely. *Happy birthday, Mr. Dorset. How do you feel about being ninety-five years old today? . . . When I think of the alternative, I feel great.*

At last, it was time for Toby to leave.

"I'll be back to see you as soon as I can," Toby promised. He gave his father some cash and handed out lavish tips to all the nurses and attendants. "You take good care of him, huh? I need the old man for my act."

And Toby was gone. The moment he walked out the door, he had forgotten them all. He was thinking about his performance that evening.

For weeks they would talk about nothing but his visit.

At seventeen, Josephine Czinski was the most beautiful girl in Odessa, Texas. She had a golden, tanned complexion and her long black hair showed a hint of auburn in the sunlight, and her deep brown eyes held flecks of gold. She had a stunning figure, with a full, rounded bosom, a narrow waist that tapered to gently swelling hips, and long, shapely legs.

Josephine did not socialize with the Oil People anymore. She went out with the Others now. After school she worked as a waitress at the Golden Derrick, a popular drive-in. Mary Lou and Cissy Topping and their friends came there with their dates. Josephine always greeted them politely; but everything had changed.

Josephine was filled with a restlessness, a yearning for something she had never known. It was nameless, but it was there. She wanted to leave this ugly town, but she did not know where she wanted to go or what she wanted to do. Thinking about it too long made her headaches begin.

She went out with a dozen different boys and men. Her mother's favorite was Warren Hoffman.

"Warren'd make you a fine husband. He's a regular church-goer, he earns good money as a plumber and he's half out of his head about you."

"He's twenty-five years old and he's fat."

Her mother studied Josephine. "Poor Polack girls don't find no knights in shinin' armor. Not in Texas and not noplace else. Stop foolin' yourself."

Josephine would permit Warren Hoffman to take her to the

movies once a week. He would hold her hand in his big, sweaty, calloused palms and keep squeezing it throughout the picture. Josephine hardly noticed. She was too engrossed in what was happening on the screen. What was up there was an extension of the world of beautiful people and things that she had grown up with, only it was even bigger and even more exciting. In some dim recess of her mind, Josephine felt that Hollywood could give her everything she wanted: the beauty, the fun, the laughter and happiness. Aside from marrying a rich man, she knew there was no other way she would ever be able to have that kind of life. And the rich boys were all taken, by the rich girls.

Except for one.

David Kenyon. Josephine thought of him often. She had stolen a snapshot of him from Mary Lou's house long ago. She kept it hidden in her closet and took it out to look at whenever she was unhappy. It brought back the memory of David standing by the side of the pool saying, *I apologize for all of them,* and the feeling of hurt had gradually disappeared and been replaced by his gentle warmth. She had seen David only once after that terrible day at his swimming pool when he had brought her a robe. He had been in a car with his family, and Josephine later heard that he had been driven to the train depot. He was on his way to Oxford, England. That had been four years ago, in 1952. David had returned home for summer vacations and at Christmas, but their paths had never crossed. Josephine often heard the other girls discussing him. In addition to the estate David had inherited from his father, his grandmother had left him a trust fund of five million dollars. He was a real catch. *But not for the Polish daughter of a seamstress.*

Josephine did not know that David Kenyon had returned from Europe. It was a late Saturday evening in July, and Josephine was working at the Golden Derrick. It seemed to her that half the population of Odessa had come to the drive-in to defeat the hot spell with gallons of lemonade and ice cream and sodas. It had been so busy that Josephine had been unable to take a break. A ring of autos constantly circled the neon-lighted drive-in like metallic animals lined up at some surrealistic water hole. Josephine delivered a car tray with what seemed to her to be her millionth order of cheeseburgers and Cokes, pulled out a menu and walked over to a white sports car that had just driven up.

"Good evening," Josephine said cheerfully. "Would you like to look at a menu?"

"Hello, stranger."

At the sound of David Kenyon's voice, Josephine's heart suddenly began to pound. He looked exactly as she remembered him, only he seemed even more handsome. There was a maturity now, a sureness, that being abroad had given him. Cissy Topping was seated next to him, looking cool and beautiful in an expensive silk skirt and blouse.

Cissy said, "Hi, Josie. You shouldn't be working on a hot night like this, honey."

As though it was something Josephine had chosen to do instead of going to an air-conditioned theater or riding around in a sports car with David Kenyon.

Josephine said evenly, "It keeps me off the streets," and she saw that David Kenyon was smiling at her. She knew that he understood.

Long after they had gone, Josephine thought about David. She went over every word—*Hello, stranger . . . I'll have a pig in a blanket and a root beer—make that coffee. Cold drinks are bad on a hot night. . . . How do you like working here? . . . I'm ready for the check. . . . Keep the change. . . . It was nice seeing you again, Josephine*—looking for hidden meanings, nuances that she might have missed. Of course, he could not have said anything with Cissy seated beside him, but the truth was that he really had nothing to say to Josephine. She was surprised that he had even remembered her name.

She was standing in front of the sink in the little kitchen of the drive-in, lost in her thoughts, when Paco, the young Mexican cook, came up behind her and said, *¿Que pasa*, Josita? You have that look een your eye."

She liked Paco. He was in his late twenties, a slim, dark-eyed man with a ready grin and a flip joke when pressure built up and everyone was tense.

"Who ees he?"

Josephine smiled. "Nobody, Paco."

"Bueno. Because there are seex hungry cars goin' crazy out there. *Vamos!*"

He telephoned the next morning, and Josephine knew who it was before she lifted the receiver. She had not been able to get him out of her mind all night. It was as though this call was the extension of her dream.

His first words were, "You're a cliché. While I was away, you've grown up and become a beauty," and she could have died of happiness.

He took her out to dinner that evening. Josephine had been prepared for some out-of-the-way little restaurant where David would not be likely to run into any of his friends. Instead they went to his club, where everyone stopped by their table to say hello. David was not only unashamed to be seen with Josephine, he seemed proud of her. And she loved him for it and for a hundred other reasons. The look of him, his gentleness and understanding, the sheer joy of being with him. She had never known that anyone as wonderful as David Kenyon could exist.

Each day, after Josephine finished work, they were together. Josephine had had to fight men off from the time she was fourteen, for there was a sexuality about her that was a challenge. Men were always pawing and grabbing at her, trying to squeeze her breasts or shove their hands up her skirt, thinking that that was the way to excite her, not knowing how much it repelled her.

David Kenyon was different. He would occasionally put his arm around her or touch her casually, and Josephine's whole body would respond. She had never felt this way about anyone before. On the days when she did not see David, she could think of nothing else.

She faced the fact that she was in love with him. As the weeks went by, and they spent more and more time together, Josephine realized that the miracle had happened. David was in love with her.

He discussed his problems with her, and his difficulties with his family. "Mother wants me to take over the businesses," David told her, "but I'm not sure that's how I want to spend the rest of my life."

The Kenyon interests included, besides oil wells and refineries, one of the largest cattle ranches in the Southwest, a chain of hotels, some banks and a large insurance company.

"Can't you just tell her no, David?"

David sighed. "You don't know my mother."

Josephine had met David's mother. She was a tiny woman (it seemed impossible that David had come out of that stick figure) who had borne three children. She had been very ill during and after each pregnancy and had had a heart attack following the third delivery. Over the years she repeatedly described her suffering to her children, who grew up with the belief that their mother had deliberately risked death in order to give each of them life. It gave her a powerful hold on her family, which she wielded unsparingly.

"I want to live my own life," David told Josephine, "but I can't do anything to hurt Mother. The truth is—Doc Young doesn't think she's going to be with us much longer."

One evening, Josephine told David about her dreams of going to Hollywood and becoming a star. He looked at her and said, quietly, "I won't let you go." She could feel her heart beating wildly. Each time they were together, the feeling of intimacy between them grew stronger. Josephine's background did not mean a damn to David. He did not have an ounce of snobbery in him. It made the incident at the drive-in one night that much more shocking.

It was closing time, and David was parked in his car, waiting for her. Josephine was in the small kitchen with Paco, hurriedly putting away the last of the trays.

"Heavy date, huh?" Paco said.

Josephine smiled. "How did you know?"

"Because you look like Chreestmas. Your pretty face ees all lit up. You tell heem for me he's one lucky hombre!"

Josephine smiled and said, "I will." On an impulse, she leaned over and gave Paco a kiss on the cheek. An instant later, she heard the roar of a car engine and then the scream of rubber. She turned in time to see David's white convertible smash the fender of another car and race away from the drive-in. She stood there, unbelievingly, watching the tail lights disappear into the night.

At three o'clock in the morning, as Josephine lay tossing in bed, she heard a car pull up outside her bedroom. She hurried to the window and looked out. David was sitting behind the wheel. He was very drunk. Quickly, Josephine put on a robe over her nightgown and went outside.

"Get in," David commanded. Josephine opened the car door and slid in beside him. There was a long, heavy silence. When David finally spoke, his voice was thick, but it was more than the whiskey he had drunk. There was a rage in him, a savage fury that propelled the words out of him like small explosions. "I don't own you," David said. "You're free to do exactly as you please. But as long as you go out with me, I expect you not to kiss any god-damned Mexicans. Y'understand?"

She looked at him, helplessly, then said, "When I kissed Paco, it was because—he said something that made me happy. He's my friend."

David took a deep breath, trying to control the emotions that were churning inside him. "I'm going to tell you something I've never told to a living soul."

Josephine sat there waiting, wondering what was coming next.

"I have an older sister," David said. "Beth. I—I adore her."

Josephine had a vague recollection of Beth, a blond, fair-skinned beauty, whom Josephine used to see when she went over to play with Mary Lou. Josephine had been eight when Beth passed away. David must have been about fifteen. "I remember when Beth died," Josephine said.

David's next words were a shock. "Beth is alive."

She stared at him. "But, I—everyone thought—"

"She's in an insane asylum." He turned to face her, his voice dead. "She was raped by one of our Mexican gardeners. Beth's bedroom was across the hall from mine. I heard her screams and I raced into her room. He had ripped off her nightgown and he was on top of her and—" His voice broke with the memory. "I struggled with him until my mother ran in and called the police. They finally arrived and took the man to jail. He committed suicide in his cell that night. But Beth had lost her mind. She'll never leave that place. Never. I can't tell you how much I love her, Josie. I miss her so damned much. Ever since that night, I—I—I can't—stand—"

She placed a hand over his and said, "I'm so sorry, David. I understand. I'm glad you told me."

In some strange way, the incident served to bring them even closer together. They discussed things they had never talked about before. David smiled when Josephine told him about her mother's religious fanaticism. "I had an uncle like that once," he said. "He went off to some monastery in Tibet."

"I'm going to be twenty-four next month," David told Josephine one day. "It's an old family tradition that the Kenyon men marry by the time they're twenty-four," and her heart leaped within her.

The following evening, David had tickets for a play at the Globe Theatre. When he came to pick Josephine up, he said, "Let's forget the play. We're going to talk about our future."

The moment Josephine heard the words, she knew that everything she had prayed for was coming true. She could read it in David's eyes. They were filled with love and wanting.

She said, "Let's drive out to Dewey Lake."

She wanted it to be the most romantic proposal ever made, so that one day it would become a tale that she would tell her children, over and over. She wanted to remember every moment of this night.

Dewey Lake was a small body of water about forty miles outside of Odessa. The night was beautiful and star-spangled, with a soft, waxing gibbous moon. The stars danced on the water, and the air was filled with the mysterious sounds of a secret world, a microcosm of the universe, where millions of tiny unseen creatures made love and preyed and were preyed upon and died.

Josephine and David sat in the car, silent, listening to the sounds of the night. Josephine watched him, sitting behind the wheel of the car, his handsome face intense and serious. She had never loved him as much as she loved him at that moment. She wanted to do something wonderful for him, to give him something to let him know how much she cared for him. And suddenly she knew what she was going to do.

"Let's go for a swim, David," she said.

"We didn't bring bathing suits."

"It doesn't matter."

He turned to look at her and started to speak, but Josephine was out of the car, running down to the shore of the lake. As she started to undress she could hear him moving behind her. She plunged into the warm water. A moment later David was beside her.

"Josie . . ."

She turned toward him, then into him, her body hurting with wanting, hungry for him. They embraced in the water and she could feel the male hardness of him pressed against her, and he said, "We can't, Josie." His voice was choked with his desire for her. She reached down for him and said, "Yes. Oh, yes, David."

They were back on the shore and he was on top of her and inside her and one with her and they were both a part of the stars and the earth and the velvet night.

They lay together a long time, holding each other. It was not until much later, when David had dropped her off at home, that Josephine remembered that he had not proposed to her. But it no longer mattered. What they had shared together was more binding than any marriage ceremony. He would propose tomorrow.

Josephine slept until noon the next day. She woke up with a smile on her face. The smile was still there when her mother came into the bedroom carrying a lovely old wedding dress. "Go down to Brubaker's and get me twelve yards of tulle right away. Mrs. Topping just brought me her wedding dress. I have to make it over for Cissy by Saturday. She and David Kenyon are getting married."

David Kenyon had gone to see his mother as soon as he drove Josephine home. She was in bed, a tiny, frail woman who had once been very beautiful.

His mother opened her eyes when David walked into her dimly lit bedroom. She smiled when she saw who it was. "Hello, son. You're up late."

"I was out with Josephine, Mother."

She said nothing, just watching him with her intelligent gray eyes.

"I'm going to marry her," David said.

She shook her head slowly. "I can't let you make a mistake like that, David."

"You don't really know Josephine. She's—"

"I'm sure she's a lovely girl. But she's not suitable to be a Kenyon wife. Cissy Topping would make you happy. And if you married her, it would make me happy."

He took her frail hand in his and said, "I love you very much, Mother, but I'm capable of making my own decisions."

"Are you really?" she asked softly. "Do you always do the right thing?"

He stared at her and she said, "Can you always be trusted to act properly, David? Not to lose your head? Not to do terrible—"

He snatched his hand away.

"Do you always know what you're doing, son?" Her voice was even softer now.

"Mother, for God's sake!"

"You've done enough to this family already, David. Don't burden me any further. I don't think I could bear it."

His face was white. "You know I didn't—I couldn't help—"

"You're too old to send away again. You're a man now. I want you to act like one."

His voice was anguished. "I—I love her—"

She was seized with a spasm, and David summoned the doctor. Later, he and the doctor had a talk.

"I'm afraid your mother hasn't much longer, David."

And so the decision was made for him.

He went to see Cissy Topping.

"I'm in love with someone else," David said. "My mother always thought that you and I—"

"So did I, darling."

"I know it's a terrible thing to ask, but—would you be willing to marry me until—until my mother dies, and then give me a divorce?"

Cissy looked at him and said softly, "If that's what you want, David."

He felt as though an unbearable weight had been lifted from his shoulders. "Thank you, Cissy, I can't tell you how much—"

She smiled and said, "What are old friends for?"

The moment David left, Cissy Topping telephoned David's mother. All she said was, "It's all arranged."

The one thing David Kenyon had not anticipated was that Josephine would hear about the forthcoming marriage before he could explain everything to her. When David arrived at Josephine's home, he was met at the door by Mrs. Czinski.

"I'd like to see Josephine," he said.

She glared at him with eyes filled with malicious triumph. "The Lord Jesus shall overcome and smite down His enemies, and the wicked shall be damned forever."

David said patiently, "I want to talk to Josephine."

"She's gone," Mrs. Czinski said. "She's gone away!"

The dusty Greyhound Odessa-El Paso-San Bernardino-Los Angeles bus pulled into the Hollywood depot on Vine Street at seven A.M., and somewhere during the fifteen-hundred-mile, two-day journey, Josephine Czinski had become Jill Castle. Outwardly, she looked like the same person. It was inside that she had changed. Something in her was gone. The laughter had died.

The moment she had heard the news, Josephine knew that she must escape. She began to mindlessly throw her clothes into a suitcase. She had no idea where she was going or what she would do when she got there. She only knew that she had to get away from this place at once.

It was when she was walking out of her bedroom and saw the photographs of the movie stars on her wall that she suddenly knew where she was going. Two hours later, she was on the bus for Hollywood. Odessa and everyone in it receded in her mind, fading faster and faster as the bus swept her toward her new destiny. She tried to make herself forget her raging headache. Perhaps she should have seen a doctor about the terrible pains in her head. But now she no longer cared. That was part of her past, and she was sure they would go away. From now on life was going to be wonderful. Josephine Czinski was dead.

Long live Jill Castle.

Book Two

19

Toby Temple became a superstar because of the unlikely juxtaposition of a paternity suit, a ruptured appendix and the President of the United States.

The Washington Press Club was giving its annual dinner, and the guest of honor was the President. It was a prestigious affair attended by the Vice-President, senators, Cabinet members, Chief Justices and anyone else who could buy, borrow or steal a ticket. Because the event was always given international press coverage, the job of master of ceremonies had become a highly prized plum. This year, one of America's top comedians had been chosen to emcee the show. One week after he had accepted, he was named defendant in a paternity suit involving a fifteen-year-old girl. On the advice of his attorney, the comedian immediately left the country for an indefinite vacation. The dinner committee turned to their number two choice, a popular motion-picture and television star. He arrived in Washington the night before the dinner. The following afternoon, on the day of the banquet, his agent telephoned to announce that the actor was in the hospital, undergoing emergency surgery for a burst appendix.

There were only six hours left before the dinner. The committee frantically went through a list of possible replacements. The important names were busy doing a movie or a television show, or were too far away to get to Washington in time. One by one, the candidates were eliminated and finally, near the bottom of the list, the name of Toby Temple appeared. A committee member shook his head. "Temple's a nightclub comic. He's too wild. We wouldn't dare turn him loose on the President."

"He'd be all right if we could get him to tone down his material."

The chairman of the committee looked around and said, "I'll tell you what's great about him, fellows. He's in New York City and he can be here in an hour. The goddamned dinner is tonight!"

That was how the committee selected Toby Temple.

As Toby looked around the crowded banquet hall, he thought to himself that if a bomb were dropped here tonight, the federal government of the United States would be leaderless.

The President was seated in the center of the speakers' table on the dais. Half a dozen Secret Service men stood behind him. In the last-minute rush of putting everything together, no one had remembered to introduce Toby to the President, but Toby did not mind. *The President will remember me*, Toby thought. He recalled his meeting with Downey, the chairman of the dinner committee. Downey had said, "We love your humor, Toby. You're very funny when you attack people. However—" He had paused to clear his throat. "This is—er—a sensitive group here tonight. Don't get me wrong. It's not that they can't take a little joke on themselves, but everything said in this room tonight is going to be reported by the news media all over the world. Naturally, none of us wants anything said that would hold the President of the United States or members of Congress up to ridicule. In other words, we want you to be funny, but we don't want you to get anyone mad."

"Trust me." Toby had smiled.

The dinner plates were being cleared and Downey was standing in front of the microphone. "Mr. President, honored guests, it's my pleasure to introduce to you our master of ceremonies, one of our brightest young comedians, Mr. Toby Temple!"

There was polite applause as Toby rose to his feet and walked over to the microphone. He looked out at the audience, then turned to the President of the United States.

The President was a simple, homespun man. He did not believe in what he called top-hat diplomacy. "People to people," he had said in a nationwide speech, "that's what we need. We've got to quit depending on computers and start trusting our instincts again. When I sit down with the heads of foreign powers, I like to negotiate by the seat of my pants." It had become a popular phrase.

Now Toby looked at the President of the United States and said, his voice choked with pride, "Mr. President, I cannot tell you what a thrill it is for me to be up here on the same podium with the man who has the whole world wired to his ass."

There was a shocked hush for a long moment, then the President grinned, guffawed, and the audience suddenly exploded with laughter and applause. From that moment on, Toby could do no wrong. He attacked the senators in the room, the Supreme Court, the press. They adored it. They screamed and howled, because they knew Toby did not really mean a word of what he said. It was excruciatingly funny to hear these insults coming from that boyish, innocent face. There were foreign ministers there that night. Toby addressed them in a double-talk version of their own languages that sounded so real that they were nodding in agreement. He was an idiot-savant, reeling off patter that praised them, berated them, and the meaning of his wild gibberish was so clear that every person in the room understood what Toby was saying.

He received a standing ovation. The President walked over to Toby and said, "That was brilliant, absolutely brilliant. We're giving a little supper at the White House Monday night, Toby, and I'd be delighted . . ."

The following day, all the newspapers wrote about Toby Temple's triumph. His remarks were quoted everywhere. He was asked to entertain at the White House. There, he was an even bigger sensation. Important offers began pouring in from all over the world. Toby played the Palladium in London, he gave a command performance for the Queen, he was asked to conduct symphony orchestras for charity and to serve on the National Arts Committee. He played golf with the President frequently and was invited to dinner at the White House again and again. Toby met legislators and governors and the heads of America's largest corporations. He insulted them all, and the more he attacked them, the more charmed they were. They adored having Toby around, turning his acerbic wit loose on their guests. Toby's friendship became a symbol of prestige among the Brahmins.

The offers that were coming in were phenomenal. Clifton Lawrence was as excited about them as Toby, and Clifton's excitement had nothing to do with business or money. Toby Temple had been the most wonderful thing that had happened to him in years, for he felt as though Toby were his son. He had spent more time on Toby's career than on any of his other clients, but it had been worth it. Toby had worked hard, had perfected his talent until it shone like a diamond. And he was appreciative and generous, something that was rare in this business.

"Every top hotel in Vegas is after you," Clifton Lawrence told Toby. "Money is no object. They want you, period. I have scripts on my desk from Fox, Universal, Pan-Pacific—all starring parts. You can do a tour of Europe, any guest shot you want, or you can have your own television show on any of the networks. That would still give you time to do Vegas and a picture a year."

"How much could I make with my own television show, Cliff?"

"I think I can push them up to ten thousand a week for an hour variety show. They'll have to give us a firm two years, maybe three. If they want you badly enough, they'll go for it."

Toby leaned back on the couch, exulting. Ten thousand a show, say forty shows a year. In three years, that would come to over one million dollars for telling the world what he thought of it! He looked over at Clifton. The little agent was trying to play it cool, but Toby could see that he was eager. He wanted Toby to make the television deal. Why not? Clifton could pick up a hundred-and-twenty-thousand-dollar commission for Toby's talent and sweat. Did Clifton really deserve that kind of money? He had never had to work his ass off in filthy little clubs or have drunken audiences throw empty beer bottles at him or go to greedy quacks in nameless villages to have a clap treated because the only girls available were the raddled whores around the Toilet Circuit. What did Clifton Lawrence know of the cockroach-ridden rooms and the greasy food and the endless procession of all-night bus rides going from one hell-hole to another? He could never understand. One critic had called Toby an overnight success, and Toby had laughed aloud. Now, sitting in Clifton Lawrence's office, he said, "I want my own television show."

Six weeks later, the deal was signed with Consolidated Broadcasting.

"The network wants a studio to do the deficit financing," Clifton Lawrence told Toby. "I like the idea because I can parlay it into a picture deal."

"Which studio?"

"Pan-Pacific."

Toby frowned. "Sam Winters?"

"That's right. For my money, he's the best studio head in the business. Besides, he owns a property I want for you, *The Kid Goes West*."

Toby said, "I was in the army with Winters. Okay. But he owes me one. Shaft the bastard!"

Clifton Lawrence and Sam Winters were in the steam room in the gymnasium at Pan-Pacific Studios, breathing in the eucalyptus scent of the heated air.

"This is the life," the little agent sighed. "Who needs money?"

Sam grinned. "Why don't you talk like that when we're negotiating, Cliff?"

"I don't want to spoil you, dear boy."

"I hear that you made a deal with Toby Temple at Consolidated Broadcasting."

"Yeah. Biggest deal they've ever made."

"Where are you going to get the deficit financing for the show?"

"Why, Sam?"

"We could be interested. I might even throw in a picture deal. I just bought a comedy called *The Kid Goes West*. It hasn't been announced yet. I think Toby'd be perfect for it."

Clifton Lawrence frowned and said, "Shit! I wish I'd known about this earlier, Sam. I've already made a deal at MGM."

"Have you closed yet?"

"Well, practically. I gave them my word . . ."

Twenty minutes later, Clifton Lawrence had negotiated a lucrative arrangement for Toby Temple in which Pan-Pacific Studios would produce "The Toby Temple Show" and star him in *The Kid Goes West*.

The negotiations could have gone on longer, but the steam room had become unbearably hot.

One of the stipulations in Toby Temple's contract was that he did not have to come to rehearsals. Toby's stand-in would work with the guest stars in the sketches and dance routines, and Toby would appear for the final rehearsal and taping. In this way, Toby could keep his part fresh and exciting.

On the afternoon of the show's premiere, in September, 1956, Toby walked into the theater on Vine Street where the show would be taped and sat watching the run-through. When it was over, Toby took his stand-in's place. Suddenly the theater was filled with electricity. The show came to life and crackled and sparkled. And when it was taped that evening and went on the air, forty million people watched it. It was as though television had been made for Toby Temple. In closeup, he was even more adorable, and everyone wanted him in his living room. The show was an instant success. It jumped to number one in the Nielsen Ratings, and there it firmly remained. Toby Temple was no longer a star.

He had become a superstar.

Hollywood was more exciting than Jill Castle had ever dreamed. She went on sightseeing tours and saw the outside of the stars' homes. And she knew that one day she would have a beautiful home in Bel-Air or Beverly Hills. Meanwhile, Jill lived in an old rooming-house, an ugly two-story wooden structure that had been converted into an even uglier twelve-bedroom house with tiny bedrooms. Her room was inexpensive, which meant that she could stretch out the two hundred dollars she had saved up. The house was located on Bronson, a few minutes from Hollywood and Vine streets, the heart of Hollywood, and was convenient to the motion-picture studios.

There was another feature about the house that attracted Jill. There were a dozen roomers, and all of them were either trying to get into pictures, were working in pictures as extras or bit players or had retired from the Business. The old-timers floated around the house in yellowed robes and curlers, frayed suits and scuffed shoes that would no longer take a shine. The roomers looked used up, rather than old. There was a common living room with battered and sprung furniture where they all gathered in the evening to exchange gossip. Everyone gave Jill advice, most of it contradictory.

"The way to get into pictures, honey, is you find yourself an AD who likes you." This from a sour-faced lady who had recently been fired from a television series.

"What's an AD?" Jill asked.

"An assistant director." In a tone that pitied Jill's ignorance. "He's the one who hires the supes."

Jill was too embarrassed to ask what the "supes" were.

"If you want *my* advice, you'll find yourself a horny casting director. An AD can only use you on *his* picture. A casting director can put you into *everything*." This from a toothless woman who must have been in her eighties.

"Yeah? Most of them are fags." A balding character actor.

"What's the difference? I mean, if it gets one launched?" An intense, bespectacled young man who burned to be a writer.

"What about starting out as an extra?" Jill asked. "Central Casting—"

"Forget it. Central Casting's books are closed. They won't even register you unless you're a specialty."

"I'm—I'm sorry. What's a specialty?"

"It's like if you're an amputee. That pays thirty-three fifty-eight instead of the regular twenty-one fifty. Or if you own dinner clothes or can ride a horse, you make twenty-eight thirty-three. If you know how to deal cards or handle the stick at a crap table, that's twenty-eight thirty-three. If you can play football or baseball, that pays thirty-three fifty-eight—same as an amputee. If you ride a camel or an elephant, it's fifty-five ninety-four. Take my advice, forget about being an extra. Go for a bit part."

"I'm not sure what the difference is," Jill confessed.

"A bit player's got at least one line to say. Extras ain't allowed to talk, except the omnies."

"The what?"

"The omnies—the ones who make background noises."

"First thing you gotta do is get yourself an agent."

"How do I find one?"

"They're listed in the *Screen Actor*. That's the magazine the Screen Actors Guild puts out. I got a copy in my room. I'll get it."

They all looked through the list of agents with Jill, and finally narrowed it down to a dozen of the smaller ones. The consensus of opinion was that Jill would not have a chance at a large agency.

Armed with the list, Jill began to make the rounds. The first six agents would not even talk to her. She ran into the seventh as he was leaving his office.

"Excuse me," Jill said. "I'm looking for an agent."

He eyed her a moment and said, "Let's see your portfolio."

She stared at him blankly. "My what?"

"You must have just gotten off the bus. You can't operate in this town without a book. Get some pictures taken. Different poses. Glamour stuff. Tits and ass."

Jill found a photographer in Culver City near the David Selznick Studios, who did her portfolio for thirty-five dollars. She picked up the pictures a week later and was very pleased with them. She looked beautiful. All of her moods had been captured by the camera. She was pensive . . . angry . . . loving . . . sexy. The photographer had bound the pictures together in a book with looseleaf cellophane pages.

"At the front here," he explained, "you put your acting credits."

Credits. That was the next step.

By the end of the next two weeks, Jill had seen, or tried to see, every agent on her list. None of them was remotely interested. One of them told her, "You were in here yesterday, honey."

She shook her head. "No, I wasn't."

"Well, she looked exactly like you. That's the problem. You all look like Elizabeth Taylor or Lana Turner or Ava Gardner. If you were in any other town trying to get a job in any other business, everybody would grab you. You're beautiful, you're sexy-looking, and you've got a great figure. But in Hollywood, looks are a drug on the market. Beautiful girls come here from all over the world. They starred in their high school play or they won a beauty contest or their boyfriend told them they ought to be in pictures—and whammo! They flock here by the thousands, and they're all the same girl. Believe me, honey, you were in here yesterday."

The boarders helped Jill make a new list of agents. Their offices were smaller and the locations were in the cheap-rent district, but the results were the same.

"Come back when you've got some acting experience, kid. You're a looker, and for all I know you could be the greatest thing since Garbo, but I can't waste my time finding out. You go get yourself a screen credit and I'll be your agent."

"How can I get a screen credit if no one will give me a job?"

He nodded. "Yeah. That's the problem. Lots of luck."

★

There was only one agency left on Jill's list, recommended by a girl she had sat next to at the Mayflower Coffee Shop on Hollywood Boulevard. The Dunning Agency was located in a small bungalow off La Cienega in a residential area. Jill had telephoned for an appointment, and a woman had told her to come in at six o'clock.

Jill found herself in a small office that had once been someone's living room. There was an old scarred desk littered with papers, a fake-leather couch mended with white surgical tape and three rattan chairs scattered around the room. A tall, heavyset woman with a pock-marked face came out of another room and said, "Hello. Can I help you?"

"I'm Jill Castle. I have an appointment to see Mr. Dunning."

"*Miss* Dunning," the woman said. "That's me."

"Oh," said Jill, in surprise. "I'm sorry, I thought—"

The woman's laugh was warm and friendly. "It doesn't matter."

But it does matter, Jill thought, filled with a sudden excitement. Why hadn't it occurred to her before? A *woman* agent! Someone who had gone through all the traumas, someone who would understand what it was like for a young girl just starting out. She would be more sympathetic than any man could ever be.

"I see you brought your portfolio," Miss Dunning was saying. "May I look at it?"

"Certainly," Jill said. She handed it over.

The woman sat down, opened the portfolio and began to turn the pages, nodding approval. "The camera likes you."

Jill did not know what to say. "Thank you."

The agent studied the pictures of Jill in a bathing suit. "You've got a good figure. That's important. Where you from?"

"Texas," Jill said. "Odessa."

"How long have you been in Hollywood, Jill?"

"About two months."

"How many agents have you been to?"

For an instant, Jill was tempted to lie, but there was nothing but compassion and understanding in the woman's eyes. "About thirty, I guess."

The agent laughed. "So you finally got down to Rose Dunning. Well, you could have done worse. I'm not MCA or William Morris, but I keep my people working."

"I haven't had any acting experience."

The woman nodded, unsurprised. "If you had, you'd be at MCA or William Morris. I'm a kind of breaking-in station. I get the kids with talent started, and then the big agencies snatch them away from me."

For the first time in weeks, Jill began to feel a sense of hope. "Do—do you think you'd be interested in handling me?" she asked.

The woman smiled. "I have clients working who aren't half as pretty as you. I think I can put you to work. That's the only way you'll ever get experience, right?"

Jill felt a glow of gratitude.

"The trouble with this damned town is that they won't give kids like you a chance. All the studios scream that they're desperate for new talent, and then they put up a big wall and won't let anybody in. Well, we'll fool 'em. I know of three things you might be right for. A daytime soap, a bit in the Toby Temple picture and a part in the new Tessie Brand movie."

Jill's head was spinning. "But would they—"

"If *I* recommend you, they'll take you. I don't send clients who aren't good. They're just bit parts, you understand, but it will be a start."

"I can't tell you how grateful I'd be," Jill said.

"I think I've got the soap-opera script here." Rose Dunning lumbered to her feet, pushing herself out of her chair, and walked into the next room, beckoning Jill to follow her.

The room was a bedroom with a double bed in a corner under a window and a metal filing cabinet in the opposite corner. Rose Dunning waddled over to the filing cabinet, opened a drawer, took out a script and brought it over to Jill.

"Here we are. The casting director is a good friend of mine, and if you come through on this, he'll keep you busy."

"I'll come through," Jill promised fervently.

The agent smiled and said, "Course, I can't send over a pig in a poke. Would you mind reading for me?"

"No. Certainly not."

The agent opened the script and sat down on the bed. "Let's read this scene."

Jill sat on the bed next to her and looked at the script.

"Your character is Natalie. She's a rich girl who's married to a weakling. She decides to divorce him, and he won't let her. You make your entrance *here*."

Jill quickly scanned the scene. She wished she had had a chance to study the script overnight or even for an hour. She was desperately anxious to make a good impression.

"Ready?"

"I—I think so," Jill said. She closed her eyes and tried to think like the character. A rich woman. Like the mothers of the friends that she had grown up with, people who took it for granted that they could have anything they wanted in life, believing that other people were there for their convenience. The Cissy Toppings of the world. She opened her eyes, looked down at the script and began to read. "I want to talk to you, Peter."

"Can't it wait?" That was Rose Dunning, cueing her.

"I'm afraid it's waited too long already. I'm catching a plane for Reno this afternoon."

"Just like that?"

"No. I've been trying to catch that plane for five years, Peter. This time I'm going to make it."

Jill felt Rose Dunning's hand patting her thigh. "That's very good," the agent said, approvingly. "Keep reading." She let her hand rest on Jill's leg.

"Your problem is that you haven't grown up yet. You're still playing games. Well, from now on, you're going to have to play by yourself."

Rose Dunning's hand was stroking her thigh. It was disconcerting. "Fine. Go on," she said.

"I—I don't want you to try to get in touch with me ever again. Is that *quite* clear?"

The hand was stroking Jill faster, moving toward her groin. Jill lowered the script and looked at Rose Dunning. The woman's face was flushed and her eyes had a glazed look in them.

"Keep reading," she said huskily.

"I—I can't," Jill said. "If you—"

The woman's hand began to move faster. "This is to get you in the mood, darling. It's a sexual fight, you see. I want to feel the sex in you." Her hand was pressing harder now, moving between Jill's legs.

"No!" Jill got to her feet, trembling.

Saliva was dribbling out of the corner of the woman's mouth. "Be good to me and I'll be good to you." Her voice was pleading. "Come here, baby." She held out her arms and made a grab for her, and Jill ran out of the office.

In the street outside, she vomited. Even when the wracking spasms were over and her stomach had quieted down, she felt no better. Her headache had started again.

It was not fair. The headaches didn't belong to her. They belonged to Josephine Czinski.

During the next fifteen months, Jill Castle became a full-fledged member of the Survivors, the tribe of people on the fringes of show business who spent years and sometimes a whole lifetime trying to break into the Business, working at other jobs temporarily. The fact that the temporary jobs sometimes lasted ten or fifteen years did not discourage them.

As ancient tribes once sat around long-ago campfires and recounted sagas of brave deeds, so the Survivors sat around Schwab's Drugstore, telling and retelling heroic tales of show business, nursing cups of cold coffee while they exchanged the latest bits of inside gossip. They were outside the Business, and yet, in some mysterious fashion, they were at the very pulse and heartbeat of it. They could tell you what star was going to be replaced, what producer had been caught sleeping with his director, what network head was about to be kicked upstairs. They knew these things before anyone else did, through their own special kind of jungle drums. For the Business *was* a jungle. They had no illusions about that. Their illusions lay in another direction. They thought they could find a way to get through the studio gates, scale the studio walls. They were artists, they were the Chosen. Hollywood was their Jericho and Joshua would blow his golden trumpet and the mighty gates would fall before them and their enemies would be smitten, and lo, Sam Winters's magic wand would be waved and they would be wearing silken robes and be Movie Stars and adored ever after by their grateful public, Amen. The coffee at Schwab's was heady sacramental wine, and they were the Disciples of the future, huddling together for comfort, warming one another with their dreams, on the very brink of *making it.* They had met an assistant director who told them a producer who said a casting director who promised and any second now, and the reality would be in their grasp.

In the meantime, they worked in supermarkets and garages and beauty parlors and car washes. They lived with each other and married each other and divorced each other, and they never noticed how time was betraying them. They were unaware of the new lines and the graying temples, and the fact that it took half an hour longer in the morning to put on makeup. They had become shopworn without having been used, aged without mellowing, too old for a career with a plastics company, too old to have babies, too old for those younger parts once so coveted.

They were now character actors. But they still dreamed.

The younger and prettier girls were picking up what they called mattress money.

"Why break your ass over some nine-to-five job when all you have to do is lay on your back a few minutes and pick up an easy twenty bucks? Just till your agent calls."

Jill was not interested. Her only interest in life was her career. A poor Polish girl could never marry a David Kenyon. She knew that now. But Jill Castle, the movie star, could have anybody and anything she wanted. Unless she could achieve that, she would change back into Josephine Czinski again.

She would never let that happen.

Jill's first acting job came through Harriet Marcus, one of the Survivors who had a third cousin whose ex-brother-in-law was a second assistant director on a television medical series shooting at Universal Studios. He agreed to give Jill a chance. The part consisted of one line, for which Jill was to receive fifty-seven dollars, minus deductions for Social Security, withholding taxes and the Motion Picture Relief Home. Jill was to play the part of a nurse. The script called for her to be in a hospital room at a patient's bedside, taking his pulse when the doctor entered.

DOCTOR: "How is he, Nurse?"

NURSE: "Not very good, I'm afraid, Doctor."

That was it.

Jill was given a single, mimeographed page from the script on a Monday afternoon and told to report for makeup at six A.M. the following morning. She went over the scene a hundred times. She wished the studio had given her the entire script. How did they expect her to figure out what the character was like from *one page?* Jill tried to analyze what kind of a woman the nurse might be. Was she married? Single? She could be secretly in love with the doctor. Or maybe they had had an affair and it was over. How did she feel about the patient? Did she hate the thought of his death? Or would it be a blessing?

"Not very good, I'm afraid, Doctor." She tried to put concern in her voice.

She tried again. "Not very good. I'm *afraid*, Doctor." Alarmed. He was going to die.

"*Not* very good, I'm afraid, Doctor." Accusing. It was the doctor's fault. If he had not been away with his mistress . . .

Jill stayed up the entire night working on the part, too keyed-up to sleep, but in the morning, when she reported to the studio, she felt exhilarated and alive. It was still dark when she arrived at the guard's gate off Lankershim Boulevard, in a car borrowed from her friend Harriet. Jill gave the guard her name, and he checked it against a roster and waved her on.

"Stage Seven," he said. "Two blocks down, turn right."

Her name was on the roster. Universal Studios was expecting *her*. It was like a wonderful dream. As Jill drove toward the sound stage, she decided she would discuss the part with the director, let him know that she was capable of giving him any interpretation he wanted. Jill pulled into the large parking lot and went onto Stage Seven.

The sound stage was crowded with people busily moving lights, carrying electrical equipment, setting up the camera, giving orders in a foreign language she did not understand. "Hit the inky dink and give me a brute. . . . I need a scrim here. . . . Kill the baby. . . ."

Jill stood there watching, savoring the sights and smells and sounds of show business. This was her world, her future. She would find a way to impress the director, show him that she was someone special. He would get to know her as a person, not as just another actress.

The second assistant director herded Jill and a dozen other actors over to Wardrobe, where Jill was handed a nurse's uniform and sent back to the sound stage, where she was made up with all the other bit players in a corner of the sound stage. Just as they were finished with her, the assistant director called her name. Jill hurried on to the hospital-room set where the director stood near the camera, talking to the star of the series. The star's name was Rod Hanson, and he played a surgeon full of compassion and wisdom. As Jill approached them, Rod Hanson was saying, "I have a German shepherd that can fart better dialogue than this shit. Why can't the writers give me some character, for Christ's sake?"

"Rod, we've been on the air five years. Don't improve a hit. The public loves you the way you are."

The cameraman walked up to the director. "All lit, chief."

"Thanks, Hal," the director said. He turned to Rod Hanson. "Can we make this, baby? We'll finish the discussion later."

"One of these days, I'm going to wipe my ass with this studio," Hanson snapped. He strode away.

Jill turned to the director, who was now alone. This was her opportunity to discuss the interpretation of the character, to show him that she understood his problems and was there to help make the scene great. She gave him a warm, friendly smile. "I'm Jill Castle," she said. "I'm playing the nurse. I think she can really be very interesting and I have some ideas about—"

He nodded absently and said, "Over by the bed," and walked away to speak to the cameraman.

Jill stood looking after him, stunned. The second assistant director, Harriet's third cousin's ex-brother-in-law, hurried up to Jill and said in a low voice, "For Chrissakes, didn't you hear him? Over by the bed!"

"I wanted to ask him—"

"Don't blow it!" he whispered fiercely. "Get out there!"

Jill walked over to the patient's bed.

"All right. Let's have it quiet, everybody." The assistant director looked at the director. "Do you want a rehearsal, chief?"

"For this? Let's go for a take."

"Give us a bell. Settle down, everybody. Nice and quiet. We're rolling. Speed."

Unbelievingly, Jill listened to the sound of the bell. She looked frantically toward the director, wanting to ask him how he would like her to interpret the scene, what her relationship was to the dying man, what she was—

A voice called, "Action!"

They were all looking at Jill expectantly. She wondered whether she dare ask them to stop the cameras for just a second, so she could discuss the scene and—

The director yelled, "Jesus Christ! Nurse! This isn't a morgue—it's a hospital. Feel his goddamned pulse before he dies of old age!"

Jill looked anxiously into the circle of bright lights around her. She took a deep breath, lifted the patient's hand and took his pulse. If they would not help her, she would have to interpret the scene in her own way. The patient was the father of the doctor. The two of them had quarreled. The father had been in an accident and the doctor had just been notified. Jill looked up and saw Rod Hanson approaching. He walked up to her and said, "How is he, Nurse?"

Jill looked into the doctor's eyes and read the concern there. She wanted to tell him the truth, that his father was dying, that it was too late for them to make up their quarrel. Yet she had to break it to him in such a way that it would not destroy him and—

The director was yelling, "Cut! Cut! Cut! Goddamn it, the idiot's got *one* line, and she can't even remember it. Where did you find her—in the Yellow Pages?"

Jill turned toward the voice shouting from the darkness, aflame with embarrassment. "I—I know my line," she said shakily. "I was just trying to—"

"Well, if you know it, for Chrissakes, would you *mind saying it?* You could drive a train through that pause. When he *asks* you the fucking question, *answer it.* Okay?"

"I was just wondering if I should—"

"Let's go again, right away. Give us a bell."

"We're on a bell. Hold it down. We're rolling."

"Speed."

"Action."

Jill's legs were trembling. It was as though she was the only one here who cared about the scene. All she had wanted to do was create something beautiful. The hot lights were making her dizzy, and she could feel the perspiration running down her arms ruining the crisp, starched uniform.

"Action! Nurse!"

Jill stood over the patient and put her hand on his pulse. If she did the scene wrong again, they would never give her another chance. She thought of Harriet and of her friends at the rooming-house and of what they would say.

The doctor entered and walked up to her. "How is he, Nurse?"

She would no longer be one of them. She would be a laughing-stock. Hollywood was a small town. Word got around fast.

"Not very good, I'm afraid, Doctor."

No other studio would touch her. It would be her last job. It would be the end of everything, her whole world.

The doctor said, "I want this man put in intensive care immediately."

"Good!" the director called. "Cut and print."

Jill was hardly aware of the people rushing past her, starting to dismantle the set to make room for the next one. She had done her first scene—and she had been thinking about something else. She could not believe it was over. She wondered whether she should find the director and thank him for the opportunity, but he was at the other end of the stage talking to a group of people. The second assistant director came up to her and squeezed her arm and said, "You did okay, kid. Only next time, learn your lines."

There was film on her; she had her first credit.
From now on, Jill thought, *I'll be working all the time.*

Jill's next acting job was thirteen months later, when she did a bit part at MGM. In the meantime, she held a series of civilian jobs. She became the local Avon lady, she worked behind a soda fountain and—briefly—she drove a taxi.

With her money running low, Jill decided to share an apartment with Harriet Marcus. It was a two-bedroom apartment and Harriet kept her bedroom working overtime. Harriet worked at a down-town department store as a model. She was an attractive girl with short dark hair, black eyes, a model's boyish figure and a sense of humor.

"When you come from Hoboken," she told Jill, "you'd *better* have a sense of humor."

In the beginning, Jill had been a bit daunted by Harriet's cool self-sufficiency, but she soon learned that underneath that sophis-ticated facade, Harriet was a warm, frightened child. She was in love constantly. The first time Jill met her, Harriet said, "I want you to meet Ralph. We're getting married next month."

A week later, Ralph had left for parts unknown, taking with him Harriet's car.

A few days after Ralph had departed, Harriet met Tony. He was in import-export and Harriet was head-over-heels in love with him.

"He's very important," Harriet confided to Jill. But someone obviously did not think so, because a month later, Tony was found floating in the Los Angeles River with an apple stuffed in his mouth.

Alex was Harriet's next love.

"He's the best-looking thing you've ever seen," Harriet confided to Jill.

Alex *was* handsome. He dressed in expensive clothes, drove a flashy convertible and spent a lot of time at the racetracks. The romance lasted until Harriet started running out of money. It angered Jill that Harriet had so little sense about men.

"I can't help it," Harriet confessed. "I'm attracted to guys who are in trouble. I think it's my mother instinct." She grinned and added, "My mother was an idiot."

Jill watched a procession of Harriet's fiancés come and go. There was Nick and Bobby and John and Raymond, until finally Jill could no longer keep track of them.

A few months after they had moved in together, Harriet announced that she was pregnant.

"I think it's Leonard," she quipped, "but you know—they all look alike in the dark."

"Where is Leonard?"

"He's either in Omaha or Okinawa. I always was lousy at geography."

"What are you going to do?"

"I'm going to have my baby."

Because of her slight figure, Harriet's pregnancy became obvious in a matter of weeks and she had to give up her modeling job. Jill found a job in a supermarket so that she could support the two of them.

One afternoon when Jill returned home from work, she found a note from Harriet. It read: "I've always wanted my baby to be born in Hoboken. Have gone back home to my folks. I'll bet there's a wonderful guy there, waiting for me. Thanks for everything." It was signed: "Harriet, The Nun."

The apartment had suddenly become a lonely place.

It was a heady time for Toby Temple. He was forty-two years old and owned the world. He joked with kings and golfed with Presidents, but his millions of beer-drinking fans did not mind because they knew Toby was one of *them,* their champion who milked all the sacred cows, ridiculed the high and the mighty, shattered the shibboleths of the Establishment. They loved Toby, just as they knew that Toby loved them.

He spoke about his mother in all his interviews, and each time she became more saintlike. It was the only way Toby could share his success with her.

Toby acquired a beautiful estate in Bel-Air. The house was Tudor, with eight bedrooms and an enormous staircase and hand-carved paneling from England. It had a movie theater, a game room, a wine cellar, and on the grounds were a large swimming pool, a housekeeper's cottage and two guest cottages. He bought a lavish home in Palm Springs, a string of race-horses and a trio of stooges. Toby called them all "Mac" and they adored him. They ran errands, chauffeured him, got him girls at any hour of the day or night, took trips with him, gave him massages. Whatever the master desired, the three Macs were always there to give him. They were the jesters to the Nation's Jester. Toby had four secretaries, two just to handle the enormous flow of fan mail. His private secretary was a pretty twenty-one-year-old honey-blonde named Sherry. Her body had been designed by a sex maniac, and Toby insisted that she wear short skirts with nothing under them. It saved them both a lot of time.

★

The premiere of Toby Temple's first movie had gone remarkably well. Sam Winters and Clifton Lawrence were at the theater. Afterward they all went to Chasen's to discuss the picture.

Toby had enjoyed his first meeting with Sam after the deal had been made. "It would have been cheaper if you had returned my phone calls," Toby said, and he told Sam of how he had tried to reach him.

"My tough luck," Sam said, ruefully.

Now, as they sat in Chasen's, Sam turned to Clifton Lawrence. "If you don't take an arm and a leg, I'd like to make a new three-picture deal for Toby."

"Just an arm. I'll give you a call in the morning," the agent said to Sam. He looked at his watch. "I have to run along."

"Where you going?" Toby asked.

"I'm meeting another client. I *do* have other clients, dear boy."

Toby looked at him oddly, then said, "Sure."

The reviews the next morning were raves. Every critic predicted that Toby Temple was going to be as big a star in movies as he was in television.

Toby read all the reviews, then got Clifton Lawrence on the phone.

"Congratulations, dear boy," the agent said. "Did you see the *Reporter* and *Variety?* Those reviews were love letters."

"Yeah. It's a green-cheese world, and I'm a big fat rat. Can I have any more fun than that?"

"I told you you'd own the world one day, Toby, and now you do. It's all yours." There was a deep satisfaction in the agent's voice.

"Cliff, I'd like to talk to you. Can you come over?"

"Certainly. I'll be free at five o'clock and—"

"I meant now."

There was a brief hesitation, then Clifton said, "I have appointments until—"

"Oh, if you're too busy, forget it." And Toby hung up.

One minute later, Clifton Lawrence's secretary called and said, "Mr. Lawrence is on his way over to see you, Mr. Temple."

★

Clifton Lawrence was seated on Toby's couch. "For God's sake, Toby, you know I'm never too busy for you. I had no idea you would want to see me today, or I wouldn't have made other appointments."

Toby sat there staring at him, letting him sweat it out. Clifton cleared his throat and said, "Come on! You're my favorite client. Didn't you know that?"

And it was true, Clifton thought. *I made him. He's my creation. I'm enjoying his success as much as he is.*

Toby smiled. "Am I really, Cliff?" He could see the tension easing out of the dapper little agent's body. "I was beginning to wonder."

"What do you mean?"

"You've got so many clients that sometimes I think you don't pay enough attention to me."

"That's not true. I spend more time—"

"I'd like you to handle just me, Cliff."

Clifton smiled. "You're joking."

"No. I'm serious." He watched the smile leave Clifton's face. "I think I'm important enough to have my own agent—and when I say my own agent, I don't mean someone who's too busy for me because he has a dozen other people to take care of. It's like a group fuck, Cliff. Somebody always gets left with a hard-on."

Clifton studied him a moment, then said, "Fix us a drink." While Toby went over to the bar, Clifton sat there, thinking. He knew what the real problem was, and it was not Toby's ego, or his sense of importance.

It had to do with Toby's loneliness. Toby was the loneliest man Clifton had ever known. Clifton had watched Toby buy women by the dozens and try to buy friends with lavish gifts. No one could ever pick up a check when Toby was around. Clifton once heard a musician say to Toby, "You don't have to *buy* love, Toby. Everybody loves you, anyway." Toby winked and said, "Why take a chance?"

The musician never worked on Toby's show again.

Toby wanted *all* of everybody. He had a need, and the more he acquired the bigger his need grew.

Clifton had heard that Toby went to bed with as many as half a dozen girls at a time, trying to appease the hunger in him. But of course, it did not work. What Toby needed was *one* girl, and he had not found her. So he went on playing the numbers game.

He had a desperate need to have people around him all the time.

Loneliness. The only time it was not there was when Toby was in front of an audience, when he could hear the applause and feel the love. *It was all really very simple,* Clifton thought. When Toby was not on stage, he carried his audience with him. He was always surrounded by musicians and stooges and writers and showgirls and down-and-out comics, and everyone else he could gather into his orbit.

And now he wanted Clifton Lawrence. *All* of him.

Clifton handled a dozen clients, but their total income was not a great deal more than Toby's income from night clubs, television and motion pictures, for the deals Clifton had been able to make for Toby were phenomenal. Nevertheless, Clifton did not make his decision on the basis of money. He made it because he loved Toby Temple, and Toby needed him. Just as *he* needed Toby. Clifton remembered how flat his life had been before Toby came into it. There had been no new challenges for years. He had been coasting on old successes. And he thought now of the electric excitement around Toby, the fun and the laughter and the deep camaraderie the two of them shared.

When Toby came back to Clifton and handed him his drink, Clifton raised his glass in a toast and said, "To the two of us, dear boy."

It was the season of successes and fun and parties, and Toby was always "on." People expected him to be funny. An actor could hide behind the words of Shakespeare or Shaw or Molière, and a singer could count on the help of Gershwin or Rodgers and Hart or Cole Porter. But a comedian was naked. His only weapon was his wit.

Toby Temple's ad libs quickly became famous around Hollywood. At a party for the elderly founder of a studio, someone asked Toby, "Is he really ninety-one years old?"

Toby replied, "Yep. When he reaches one hundred, they're going to split him two-for-one."

At dinner one evening, a famous physician who took care of many of the stars told a long and labored joke to a group of comedians.

"Doc," Toby pleaded, "don't amuse us—save us!"

One day the studio was using lions in a movie, and as Toby saw them being trucked by, he yelled, "Christians—ten minutes!"

Toby's practical jokes became legend. A Catholic friend of his went to the hospital for a minor operation. While he was recuperating, a beautiful young nun stopped by his bed. She stroked his forehead. "You feel nice and cool. Such soft skin."

"Thank you, Sister."

She leaned over him and began straightening his pillows, her breasts brushing against his face. In spite of himself, the poor man began to get an erection. As the Sister started to straighten the blankets, her hand brushed against him. He was in an agony of mortification.

"Good Lord," the nun said. "What have we here?" And she pulled the covers back, revealing his rock-hard penis.

"I—I'm terribly sorry, Sister," he stammered. "I—"

"Don't be sorry. It's a great cock," the nun said, and began to go down on him.

It was six months before he learned that it was Toby who had sent the hooker in to him.

As Toby was stepping out of an elevator one day, he turned to a pompous network executive and said, "By the way, Will, how did you ever come out on that morals charge?" The elevator door closed and the executive was left with a half a dozen people eyeing him warily.

When it came time to negotiate a new contract, Toby arranged for a trained panther to be delivered to him at the studio. Toby opened Sam Winters's office door while Sam was in the middle of a meeting.

"My agent wants to talk to you," Toby said. He shoved the panther inside the office and closed the door.

When Toby told the story later, he said, "Three of the guys in that office almost had heart attacks. It took them a month to get the smell of panther piss out of that room."

Toby had a staff of ten writers working for him, headed by O'Hanlon and Rainger. Toby complained constantly about the material his writers gave him. Once Toby made a whore a member of the writing team. When Toby learned that his writers were spending most of their time in the bedroom, he had to fire her.

Another time, Toby brought an organ grinder and his monkey to a story conference. It was humiliating and demeaning, but O'Hanlon and Rainger and the other writers took it because Toby turned their material into pure gold. He was the best in the business.

Toby's generosity was profligate. He gave his employees and his friends gold watches and cigarette lighters and complete wardrobes and trips to Europe. He carried an enormous amount of money with him and paid for everything in cash, including two Rolls-Royces. He was a soft touch. Every Friday a dozen hangers-on in the business would line up for a handout. Once Toby said to one of the regulars, "Hey, what are you doing here today? I just read in *Variety* that you got a job in a picture." The man looked at Toby and said, "Hell, don't I get two weeks' notice?"

There were myriad stories about Toby, and nearly all of them were true. One day, during a story conference, a writer walked in late, an unforgivable sin. "I'm sorry I'm late," he apologized. "My kid was run over by a car this morning."

Toby looked at him and said, "Did you bring the jokes?"

Everyone in the room was shocked. After the meeting, one of the writers said to O'Hanlon, "That's the coldest son of a bitch in the world. If you were on fire, he'd sell you water."

Toby flew in a top brain surgeon to operate on the injured boy and paid all the hospital bills. He said to the father, "If you ever mention this to anyone, you're out on your ass."

Work was the only thing that made Toby forget his loneliness, the only thing that brought him real joy. If a show went well, Toby was the most amusing companion in the world, but if the show went badly, he was a demon, attacking every target within reach of his savage wit.

He was possessive. Once, during a story conference, he took Rainger's head between his two hands and announced to the room, "This is mine. It belongs to me."

At the same time he grew to hate writers, because he needed them and he did not want to need anyone. So he treated them with contempt. On pay day, Toby made airplanes of the writers' paychecks and sailed them through the air. Writers would be fired for the smallest infraction. One day a writer walked in with a tan and

Toby immediately had him discharged. "Why did you do that?" O'Hanlon asked. "He's one of our best writers."

"If he was working," Toby said, "he wouldn't have had time for a tan."

A new writer brought in a joke about mothers and was let go.

If a guest on his show got big laughs, Toby would exclaim, "You're great! I want you on this show every week." He would look over at the producer and say, "You hear me?" and the producer would know that the actor was never to appear on the show again.

Toby was a mass of contradictions. He was jealous of the success of other comics, yet the following happened. One day as Toby was leaving his rehearsal stage, he passed the dressing room of an old-time comedy star, Vinnie Turkel, whose career had long since gone downhill. Vinnie had been hired to do his first dramatic part, in a live television play. He hoped that it would mean a comeback for him. Now, as Toby looked into the dressing room, he saw Vinnie on the couch, drunk. The director of the show came by and said to Toby, "Let him be, Toby. He's finished."

"What happened?"

"Well, you know Vinnie's trademark has always been his high, quavery voice. We started rehearsing and every time Vinnie opened his mouth and tried to be serious, everyone began to laugh. It destroyed the old guy."

"He was counting on this part, wasn't he?" Toby asked.

The director shrugged. "Every actor counts on every part."

Toby took Vinnie Turkel home with him and stayed with the old comedy star, sobering him up. "This is the best role you've ever had in your life. Are you gonna blow it?"

Vinnie shook his head, miserable. "I've already blown it, Toby. I can't cut it."

"Who says you can't?" Toby demanded. "You can play that part better than anyone in the world."

The old man shook his head. "They laughed at me."

"Sure they did. And do you know why? Because you've made them laugh all your life. They *expected* you to be funny. But if you keep going, you'll win them over. You'll kill them."

He spent the rest of the afternoon restoring Vinnie Turkel's confidence. That evening, Toby telephoned the director at home.

"Turkel's all right now," Toby said. "You have nothing to worry about."

"I know I haven't," the director retorted. "I've replaced him."

"*Un*-replace him," Toby said. "You've got to give him a shot."

"I can't take the chance, Toby. He'll get drunk again and—"

"Tell you what I'll do," Toby offered. "Keep him in. If you still don't want him after dress rehearsal, I'll take over his part and do it for nothing."

There was a pause, and the director said, "Hey! Are you serious?"

"You bet your ass."

"It's a deal," the director said quickly. "Tell Vinnie to be at rehearsal at nine o'clock tomorrow morning."

When the show went on the air, it was the hit of the season. And it was Vinnie Turkel whose performance the critics singled out. He won every prize that television had to offer and a new career opened up for him as a dramatic actor. When he sent Toby an expensive gift to show his appreciation, Toby returned it with a note. "I didn't do it, *you* did." That was Toby Temple.

A few months later, Toby signed Vinnie Turkel to do a sketch in his show. Vinnie stepped on one of Toby's laugh lines and from that moment on, Toby gave him wrong cues, killed his jokes and humiliated him in front of forty million people.

That was Toby Temple, too.

Someone asked O'Hanlon what Toby Temple was really like, and O'Hanlon replied, "Do you remember the picture where Charlie Chaplin meets the millionaire? When the millionaire is drunk, he's Chaplin's buddy. When he's sober, he throws him out on his ass. That's Toby Temple, only without the liquor."

Once during a meeting with the heads of a network, one of the junior executives hardly said a word. Later, Toby said to Clifton Lawrence, "I don't think he liked me."

"Who?"

"The kid at the meeting."

"What do you care? He's a thirty-second Assistant Nobody."

"He didn't say a word to me," Toby brooded. "He really doesn't like me."

Toby was so upset that Clifton Lawrence had to track down the young executive. He called the bewildered man in the middle of the night and said, "Do you have anything against Toby Temple?"

"*Me?* I think he's the funniest man in the whole world!"

"Then would you do me a favor, dear boy? Call him and tell him so."

"*What?*"

"Call Toby and tell him you like him."

"Well, sure. I'll call him first thing tomorrow."

"Call him now."

"It's three o'clock in the morning!"

"It doesn't matter. He's waiting for you."

When the executive called Toby, the phone was answered immediately. He heard Toby's voice say, "Hi."

The young executive swallowed and said, "I—I just wanted to tell you that I think you're great."

"Thanks, pal," Toby said, and hung up.

The size of Toby's entourage grew. Sometimes he would awaken in the middle of the night and telephone friends to come over for a gin game, or he would awaken O'Hanlon and Rainger and summon them to a story conference. He would often sit up all night running movies at home, with the three Macs and Clifton Lawrence and half a dozen starlets and hangers-on.

And the more people there were around him, the lonelier Toby became.

I t was November, 1963, and the autumn sunshine had given
way to a thin, unwarming light from the sky. The early mornings were foggy and chilling now, and the first rains of winter
had begun.

Jill Castle still stopped in at Schwab's every morning, but it
seemed to her that the conversations were always the same. The
Survivors talked about who had lost a part and why. They gloated
over each disastrous review that came out and deprecated the good
ones. It was the threnody of losers, and Jill began to wonder if she
were becoming like the rest of them. She was still sure that she was
going to be Somebody, but as she looked around at the same
familiar faces, she realized they all felt the same way about themselves. Was it possible they were all out of touch with reality, all
of them gambling on a dream that was never going to happen? She
could not bear the thought of it.

Jill had become the mother confessor to the group. They came
to her with problems, and she listened and tried to help; with
advice, a few dollars or a place to sleep for a week or two. She
seldom dated because she was absorbed in her career and she had
not met anyone who interested her.

Whenever Jill was able to put a little money aside, she sent it to
her mother with long, glowing letters about how well she was
doing. In the beginning, Jill's mother had written back urging Jill
to repent and become a bride of God. But as Jill made occasional
movies and sent more money home, her mother began to take a

certain reluctant pride in her daughter's career. She was no longer against Jill's being an actress but she pressed Jill to get parts in religious pictures. "I'm sure Mr. DeMille would give you a role if you explained your religious background to him," she wrote.

Odessa was a small town. Jill's mother still worked for the Oil People, and she knew that her mother would talk about her, that sooner or later David Kenyon would hear of her success. And so, in her letters, Jill made up stories about all the stars she worked with, always careful to use their first names. She learned the bit players' trick of having the set photographer snap her picture as she stood next to the star. The photographer would give her two prints and Jill would mail one to her mother and keep the other. She made her letters sound as though she was just one step short of stardom.

It is the custom in Southern California, where it never snows, that three weeks before Christmas a Santa Claus Parade marches down Hollywood Boulevard and that each night after that until Christmas Eve a Santa Claus float makes the journey. The citizens of Hollywood are as conscientious about the celebration of the Christ child as are their neighbors in northern climes. They are not to be held responsible if "Glory Be to God on High" and "Silent Night" and "Rudolph the Red-Nosed Reindeer" pour out of home and car radios in a community that is sweltering in a temperature of eighty-five or ninety degrees. They long for an old-fashioned white Christmas as ardently as other red-blooded patriotic Americans, but because they know that God is not going to supply it, they have learned to create their own. They festoon the streets with Christmas lights and plastic Christmas trees and papier-mâché cutouts of Santa Claus and his sled and his reindeer. Stars and character actors vie for the privilege of riding in the Santa Claus Parade; not because they are concerned about bringing holiday cheer to the thousands of children and adults who line the path of the parade, but because the parade is televised and their faces will be seen coast to coast.

Jill Castle stood on a corner, alone, watching the long parade of floats go by, the stars on top waving to their loving fans below. The Grand Marshal of the parade this year was Toby Temple. The adoring crowds cheered wildly as his float passed by. Jill caught a quick glimpse of Toby's beaming, ingenuous face and then he was gone.

There was music from the Hollywood High School Band, followed by a Masonic Temple float, and a marine corps band. There were equestrians in cowboy outfits and a Salvation Army band, followed by Shriners. There were singing groups carrying flags and streamers, a Knott's Berry Farm float with animals and birds made of flowers; fire engines, clowns and jazz bands. It might not have been the spirit of Christmas, but it was pure Hollywood spectacle.

Jill had worked with some of the character actors on the floats. One of them waved to her and called down, "Hiya, Jill! How ya doin'?"

Several people in the crowd turned to look enviously at her, and it gave her a delightful feeling of self-importance that people knew she was in the Business. A deep, rich voice beside her said, "Excuse me—are you an actress?"

Jill turned. The speaker was a tall, blond, good-looking boy in his middle twenties. His face was tanned and his teeth were white and even. He wore a pair of old jeans and a blue tweed jacket with leather-patch elbows.

"Yes."

"Me, too. An *actor*, I mean." He grinned and added, "Struggling."

Jill pointed to herself and said, "Struggling."

He laughed. "Can I buy you a cup of coffee?"

His name was Alan Preston and he came from Salt Lake City where his father was an elder in the Mormon Church. "I grew up with too much religion and not enough fun," he confided to Jill.

It's almost prophetic, Jill thought. *We have exactly the same kind of background.*

"I'm a good actor," Alan said ruefully, "but this is sure a rough town. Back home, everybody wants to help you. Here, it seems like everybody's out to *get* you."

They talked until the coffee shop closed, and by that time they were old friends. When Alan asked, "Do you want to come back to my place?" Jill hesitated only a moment. "All right."

Alan Preston lived in a boardinghouse off Highland Avenue, two blocks from the Hollywood Bowl. He had a small room at the back of the house.

"They ought to call this place The Dregs," he told Jill. "You should see the weirdos who live here. They all think they're going to make it big in show business."

Like us, Jill thought.

The furniture in Alan's room consisted of a bed, a bureau, a chair and a small rickety table. "I'm just waiting until I move into my palace," Alan explained.

Jill laughed. "Same with me."

Alan started to take her in his arms, and she stiffened. "Please don't."

He looked at her a moment and said gently, "Okay," and Jill was suddenly embarrassed. What was she doing here in this man's room, anyway? She knew the answer to that. She was desperately lonely. She was hungry for someone to talk to, hungry for the feel of a man's arms around her, holding her and reassuring her and telling her that everything was going to be wonderful. It had been so long. She thought of David Kenyon, but that was another life, another world. She wanted him so much that it was an ache. A little later, when Alan Preston put his arms around Jill again, she closed her eyes and it became David kissing her and undressing her and making love to her.

Jill spent the night with Alan, and a few days later he moved into her small apartment.

Alan Preston was the most uncomplicated man Jill had ever met. He was easygoing and relaxed, taking each day as it came, totally unconcerned with tomorrow. When Jill would discuss his way of life with him, he would say, "Hey, remember *Appointment in Samarra?* If it's going to happen, it'll happen. Fate will find *you*. You don't have to go looking for it."

Alan would stay in bed long after Jill had gone out looking for work. When she returned home, she would find him in an easy chair, reading or drinking beer with his friends. He brought no money into the house.

"You're a dope," one of Jill's girlfriends told her. "He's using your bed, eating your food, drinking your liquor. Get rid of him."

But Jill didn't.

For the first time, Jill understood Harriet, understood all her friends who clung desperately to men they did not love, men they hated.

It was the fear of being alone.

Jill was out of a job. Christmas was only a few days away and she was down to her last few dollars, yet she *had* to send her mother a Christmas present. It was Alan who solved the problem. He had left early one morning without saying where he was going. When he returned, he said to Jill, "We've got a job."

"What kind of job?"

"Acting, of course. We're actors, aren't we?"

Jill looked at him, filled with sudden hope. "Are you serious?"

"Of course I am. I ran into a friend of mine who's a director. He's got a picture starting tomorrow. There's parts for both of us. A hundred bucks apiece, for one day's work."

"That's wonderful!" Jill exclaimed. "A hundred dollars!" With that she could buy her mother some lovely English wool for a winter coat and have enough left over to buy a good leather purse.

"It's just a little indie. They're shooting it in back of someone's garage."

Jill said, "What can we lose? It's a part."

The garage was on the south side of Los Angeles, in an area that in one generation had gone from exclusivity to middle-class gentility to seed.

They were greeted at the door by a short, swarthy man who took Alan's hand and said, "You made it, buddy. Great."

He turned to Jill and whistled appreciatively. "You told it like it is, pal. She's an eyeful."

Alan said, "Jill, this is Peter Terraglio. Jill Castle."

"How do you do!" Jill said.

"Pete's the director," Alan explained.

"Director, producer, chief bottle washer. I do a little of everything. Come on in." He led them through the empty garage into a passageway that had at one time been servants' quarters. There were two bedrooms off the corridor. The door to one was open. As they approached it, they could hear the sound of voices. Jill reached the doorway, looked inside and stopped in shocked disbelief. In the middle of the room four naked people were lying on a bed; a black man, a Mexican man, and two girls, one white and one black. A cameraman was lighting the set while one of the girls practiced fellatio on the Mexican. The girl paused for a moment, out of breath, and said, "Come on, you cock. Get hard."

Jill felt faint. She wheeled around in the doorway to start back down the passageway, and she felt her legs start to give way. Alan had his arm around her, supporting her.

"Are you all right?"

She could not answer him. Her head was suddenly splitting, and her stomach was filled with knives.

"Wait here," Alan ordered.

He was back in a minute with a bottle of red pills and a pint of vodka. He took out two of the pills and handed them to Jill. "These will make you feel better."

Jill put the pills in her mouth, her head pounding.

"Wash it down with this," Alan told her.

She did as he said.

"Here." Alan handed her another pill. She swallowed it with vodka. "You need to lie down a minute."

He led Jill into the empty bedroom, and she lay down on the bed, moving very slowly. The pills were beginning to work. She started to feel better. The bitter bile had stopped coming up into her mouth.

Fifteen minutes later, her headache was fading away. Alan handed her another pill. Without even thinking about it, Jill swallowed it. She took another drink of vodka. It was such a blessing to have the pain disappear. Alan was behaving peculiarly, moving all around the bed. "Sit still," she said.

"I am sitting still."

Jill thought that was funny and began to laugh. She laughed until the tears streamed down her face. "What—what were those pills?"

"For your headache, honey."

Terraglio peered into the room and said, "How we doin'? Everybody happy?"

"Every—everybody's happy," Jill mumbled.

Terraglio looked at Alan and nodded. "Five minutes," Terraglio said. He hurried off.

Alan was leaning over Jill, stroking her breast and her thighs, lifting her skirt and working his fingers between her legs. It felt marvelously exciting, and Jill suddenly wanted him inside her.

"Look, baby," Alan said, "I wouldn't ask you to do anything bad. You'd just make love to *me*. It's what we do anyway, only this time we get paid for it. Two hundred bucks. And it's all yours."

She shook her head, but it seemed to take forever to move it from side to side. "I couldn't do that," she said, fuzzily.

"Why not?"

She had to concentrate to remember. "Because I'm—I'm gonna be a star. Can't do porno films."

"Would you like me to fuck you?"

"Oh, yes! I want you, David."

Alan started to say something, then grinned. "Sure, baby. I want you, too. Come on." He took Jill's hand and lifted her off the bed. Jill felt as though she were flying.

They were in the hallway, then moving into the other bedroom.

"Okay," Terraglio said as he saw them. "Keep the same setup. We've got some fresh blood coming in."

"Do you want me to change the sheets?" one of the crew asked.

"What the fuck do you think we are, MGM?"

Jill was clinging to Alan. "David, there are people here."

"They'll leave," Alan assured her. "Here." He took out another pill and gave it to Jill. He put the bottle of vodka to her lips, and she swallowed the pill. From that point on, everything happened in a haze. David was undressing her and saying comforting things. Then she was on the bed with him. He moved his naked body closer to her. A bright light came on, blinding her.

"Put this in your mouth," he said, and it was David talking.

"Oh, yes." She stroked it lovingly and started to put it in her mouth and someone in the room said something that Jill could not hear, and David moved away so that Jill was forced to turn her face into the light and squint in the glare. She felt herself being pushed down on her back and then David was inside her making love to her, and at the same time she had his penis in her mouth. She loved him so much. The lights bothered her and the talking in the background. She wanted to tell David to stop them, but she was in an ecstasy of delirium, having orgasm after orgasm until she thought that her body would tear itself apart. David loved *her*, not Cissy, and he had come back to her and they were married. They were having such a wonderful honeymoon.

"David . . ." she said. She opened her eyes and the Mexican was on top of her, moving his tongue down her body. She tried to ask him where David was, but she could not get the words out. She closed her eyes while the man did delicious things to her body. When Jill opened her eyes again, the man had somehow turned into a girl with long red hair and large bosoms trailing across Jill's belly. Then the woman started doing something with her tongue and Jill closed her eyes and fell into unconsciousness.

The two men stood looking down at the figure on the bed.

"She gonna be all right?" Terraglio asked.

"Sure," Alan said.

"You really come up with 'em," Terraglio said admiringly. "She's terrific. Best looker yet."

"My pleasure." He held out his hand.

Terraglio pulled a thick wad of bills out of his pocket and peeled off two of them. "Here y'are. Wanna drop by for a little Christmas dinner? Stella'd love to see you."

"Can't," Alan said. "I'm spending Christmas with the wife and kids. I'm catching the next plane out to Florida."

"We're gonna have a hell of a picture here." Terraglio nodded toward the unconscious girl. "What kind of billing should we give her?"

Alan grinned. "Why don't you use her real name? It's Josephine Czinski. When the picture plays in Odessa, it'll give all her friends a real kick."

They had lied. Time was not a friend that healed all wounds; it was the enemy that ravaged and murdered youth. The seasons came and went and each season brought a new crop of Product to Hollywood. The competition hitchhiked and came on motorcycles and trains and planes. They were all eighteen years old, as Jill had once been. They were long-legged and lithe, with fresh, eager young faces and bright smiles that did not need caps. And with each new crop that came in, Jill was one year older. One day she looked in the mirror and it was 1964 and she had become twenty-five years old.

At first, the experience of making the pornographic film had terrified her. She had lived in dread that some casting director would learn about it and blackball her. But as the weeks went by and then months, Jill gradually forgot her fears. But she had changed. Each succeeding year had left its mark upon her, a patina of hardness, like the annual rings on a tree. She began to hate all the people who would not give her a chance to act, the people who made promises they never kept.

She had embarked on an endless series of monotonous, thankless jobs. She was a secretary and a receptionist and a short-order cook and a baby-sitter and a model and a waitress and a telephone operator and a salesgirl. Just until she got The Call.

But The Call never came. And Jill's bitterness grew. She did occasional walk-ons and one-liners, but they never led to anything. She looked in the mirror and received Time's message: *Hurry*. Seeing her reflection was like looking back into layers of the past.

There were still traces of the fresh young girl who had come to Hollywood seven endless years ago. But the fresh young girl had small wrinkles near the edges of her eyes and deeper lines that ran from the corners of her nose down to her chin, warning signals of time fleeting and success ungrasped, the souvenirs of all the countless, dreary little defeats. *Hurry, Jill, hurry!*

And so it was that when Fred Kapper, an eighteen-year-old assistant director at Fox, told Jill he had a good part for her if she would go to bed with him, she decided it was time to say yes.

She met Fred Kapper at the studio during his lunch hour.

"I only got half an hour," he said. "Lemme think where we can have some privacy." He stood there a moment, frowning in deep thought, then brightened. "The dubbing room. Come on."

The dubbing room was a small soundproof projection chamber where all the sound tracks were combined on one reel.

Fred Kapper looked around the bare room and said, "Shit! They used to have a little couch here." He glanced at his watch. "We'll have to make do. Get your clothes off sweetheart. The dubbing crew'll be back in twenty minutes."

Jill stared at him a moment, feeling like a whore, and she loathed him. But she did not let it show. She had tried it her way and had failed. Now she was going to do it *their* way. She took off her dress and pants. Kapper did not bother undressing. He merely opened his zipper and took out his tumescent penis. He looked at Jill and grinned. "That's a beautiful ass. Bend over."

Jill looked around for something to lean against. In front of her was the laugh machine, a console on wheels, filled with laugh-track loops controlled by buttons on the outside.

"Come on, bend over."

Jill hesitated a moment, then leaned forward, propping herself up by her hands, Kapper moved in back of her and Jill felt his fingers spreading her cheeks. An instant later she felt the tip of his penis pressing against her anus. "Wait!" Jill said. "Not there! I— I can't—"

"Scream for me, baby!" and he plunged his organ inside her, ripping her with a terrible pain. With each scream, he thrust deeper and harder. She tried frantically to get away, but he was grabbing her hips, shoving himself in and out, holding her fast. She was off balance now. As she reached out to get leverage, her fingers touched the buttons of the laugh machine, and instantly the room was filled with maniacal laughter. As Jill squirmed in a burning agony, her hands pounded the machine, and a woman tittered and a small crowd guffawed and a girl giggled and a hundred voices cackled and chuckled and roared at some obscene, secret joke. The echoes bounced hysterically around the walls as Jill cried out with pain.

Suddenly she felt a series of quick shudders and a moment later the alien piece of flesh inside her was withdrawn, and slowly the laughter in the room died away. Jill stayed still, her eyes shut, fighting the pain. When finally she was able to straighten up and turn around, Fred Kapper was zipping up his fly.

"You were sensational, sweetheart. That screaming really turns me on."

And Jill wondered what kind of an animal he would be when he was nineteen.

He saw that she was bleeding. "Get yourself cleaned up and come over to Stage Twelve. You start working this afternoon."

After that first experience, the rest was easy. Jill began to work regularly at all the studios: Warner Brothers, Paramount, MGM, Universal, Columbia, Fox. Everywhere, in fact, except at Disney, where sex did not exist.

The role that Jill created in bed was a fantasy, and she acted it out with skill, preparing herself as though she were playing a part. She read books on Oriental erotica and bought philters and stimulants from a sex shop on Santa Monica Boulevard. She had a lotion that an airline stewardess brought her from the Orient, with the faintest touch of wintergreen in it. She learned to massage her lovers slowly and sensuously. "Lie there and think about what I'm doing to your body," she whispered. She rubbed the lotion across the man's chest and down his stomach toward his groin, making gentle, circling motions. "Close your eyes and enjoy it."

Her fingers were as light as butterfly wings, moving down his body, caressing him. When he began to have an erection, Jill would take his growing penis in her hand and softly stroke it, moving her tongue down between his legs until he was squirming with pleasure, then continuing down slowly, all the way to his toes. Then Jill would turn him over, and it all began again. When a man's organ was limp, she put the head of it just inside the lips of her vagina, and slowly drew him inside her, feeling it grow hard and stiff. She taught the men the waterfall, and how to peak and stop just before an orgasm and then build again and peak again, so that when they finally came, it was an ecstatic explosion. They had their pleasure and got dressed and left. No one ever stayed long enough to give her the loveliest five minutes in sex, the quiet holding afterward, the peaceful oasis of a lover's arms.

Providing Jill with acting parts was a small price to pay for the pleasure she gave the casting men, the assistant directors, the directors and the producers. She became known around town as a "red-hot piece of ass," and everyone was eager for his share. And Jill gave it. Each time she did, there was that much less self-respect and love in her, and that much more hatred and bitterness.

She did not know how, or when, but she knew that one day this town would pay for what it had done to her.

During the next few years, Jill appeared in dozens of movies and television shows and commercials. She was the secretary who said, "Good morning, Mr. Stevens," and the baby-sitter who said, "Don't worry now, you two have a good evening. I'll put the children to bed," and the elevator operator who announced, "Sixth floor next," and the girl in the ski outfit who confided, "All my girlfriends use Dainties." But nothing ever *happened*. She was a nameless face in the crowd. She was in the Business, and yet she was not, and she could not bear the thought of spending the rest of her life like this.

In 1966 Jill's mother died and Jill drove to Odessa for the funeral. It was late afternoon and there were fewer than a dozen people at the service, none of them the women her mother had worked for all those years. Some of the churchgoers were there, the doomsaying revivalists. Jill remembered how terrified she had been at those meetings. But her mother had found some sort of solace in them, the exorcising of whatever demons had tormented her.

A familiar voice said quietly, "Hello, Josephine." She turned and he was standing at her side and she looked into his eyes and it was as though they had never been apart, as though they still belonged to each other. The years had stamped a maturity on his face, added a sprinkling of gray to his sideburns. But he had not changed, he was still David, her David. Yet they were strangers.

He was saying, "I'm very sorry about your mother."

And she heard herself replying, "Thank you, David."

As though they were reciting lines from a play.

"I have to talk to you. Can you meet me tonight?" There was an urgent pleading in his voice.

She thought of the last time they had been together and of the hunger in him then and the promise and the dreams. She said, "All right, David."

"The lake? Do you have a car?"

She nodded.

"I'll meet you there in an hour."

Cissy was standing in front of a mirror, naked, getting ready to dress for a dinner party when David arrived home. He walked into her bedroom and stood there watching her. He could judge his wife with complete dispassion, for he felt no emotion whatsoever toward her. She was beautiful. Cissy had taken care of her body, keeping it in shape with diet and exercise. It was her primary asset and David had reason to believe that she was liberal in sharing it with others, her golf coach, her ski teacher, her flight instructor. But David could not blame her. It had been a long time since he had gone to bed with Cissy.

In the beginning, he had really believed that she would give him a divorce when Mama Kenyon died. But David's mother was still alive and flourishing. David had no way of knowing whether he had been tricked or whether a miracle had taken place. A year after their marriage, David had said to Cissy, "I think it's time we talked about that divorce."

Cissy had said, "What divorce?" And when she saw the astonished look on his face she laughed. "I *like* being Mrs. David Kenyon, darling. Did you really think I was going to give you up for that little Polish whore?"

He had slapped her.

The following day he had gone to see his attorney. When David was finished talking, the attorney said, "I can get you the divorce. But if Cissy is set on hanging on to you, David, it's going to be bloody expensive."

488

"Get it."

When Cissy had been served the divorce papers, she had locked herself in David's bathroom and had swallowed an overdose of sleeping pills. It had taken David and two servants to smash the heavy door. Cissy had hovered on the brink of death for two days. David had visited her in the private hospital where she had been taken.

"I'm sorry, David," she had said. "I don't want to live without you. It's as simple as that."

The following morning, he had dropped the divorce suit.

That had been almost ten years ago, and David's marriage had become an uneasy truce. He had completely taken over the Kenyon empire and he devoted all of his energies to running it. He found physical solace in the strings of girls he kept in the various cities around the world to which his business carried him. But he had never forgotten Josephine.

David had no idea how she felt about him. He wanted to know, and yet he was afraid to find out. She had every reason to hate him. When he had heard the news about Josephine's mother, David had gone to the funeral parlor just to look at Josephine. The moment he saw her, he knew that nothing had changed. Not for him. The years had been swept away in an instant, and he was as much in love with her as ever.

I have to talk to you. . . . meet me tonight. . . .

All right, David. . . .

The lake.

Cissy turned around as she saw David watching her in the pier glass. "You'd better hurry and change, David. We'll be late."

"I'm going to meet Josephine. If she'll have me, I'm going to marry her. I think it's time this farce ended, don't you?"

She stood there, staring at David, her naked image reflected in the mirror.

"Let me get dressed," she said.

David nodded and left the room. He walked into the large drawing room, pacing up and down, preparing for the confrontation. Surely after all these years, Cissy would not want to hang onto a marriage that was a hollow shell. He would give her anything she—

He heard the sound of Cissy's car starting and then the scream of tires as it careened down the driveway. David raced to the front door and looked out. Cissy's Maserati was racing toward the highway. Quickly, David got into his car, started the engine and gunned down the driveway after Cissy.

As he reached the highway, her car was just disappearing in the distance. He stepped down hard on the accelerator. The Maserati was a faster car than David's Rolls. He pressed down harder on the gas pedal: 70 . . . 80 . . . 90. Her car was no longer in sight.

100 . . . 110 . . . still no sign of her.

He reached the top of a small rise, and there he saw the car, like a distant toy, careening around a curve. The torque was pulling the car to one side, the tires fighting to hold their traction on the road. The Maserati swayed back and forth, yawing across the highway. Then it leveled off and made it past the curve. And suddenly the car hit the shoulder of the road and shot into the air like a catapult and rolled over and over across the fields.

David pulled Cissy's unconscious body out of the car moments before the ruptured gas tank exploded.

It was six o'clock the next morning before the chief surgeon came out of the operating room and said to David, "She's going to live."

Jill arrived at the lake just before sunset. She drove to the edge of the water. Turning off the motor, she gave herself up to the sounds of the wind and the air. *I don't know when I've ever been so happy*, she thought. And then she corrected herself. *Yes, I do. Here. With David.* And she remembered how his body had felt on hers and she grew faint with wanting. Whatever had spoiled their happiness was over. She had felt it the moment she had seen David. He was still in love with her. She knew it.

She watched the blood-red sun slowly drown in the distant water, and darkness fell. She wished that David would hurry.

An hour passed, then two, and the air became chilled. She sat in the car, still and quiet. She watched the huge dead-white moon float into the sky. She listened to the night sounds all around her and she said to herself, *David is coming.*

Jill sat there all night and, in the morning, when the sun began to stain the horizon, she started the car and drove home to Hollywood.

J ill sat in front of her dressing table and studied her face in the mirror. She saw a barely perceptible wrinkle at the corner of her eye and frowned. *It's unfair,* she thought. *A man can completely let himself go. He can have gray hair, a pot-belly and a face like a road map, and no one thinks anything of it. But let a woman get one tiny wrinkle . . .* She began to apply her makeup. Bob Schiffer, Hollywood's top makeup artist had taught her some of his techniques. Jill put on a pan-stick base instead of the powder base that she had once used. Powder dried the skin, while the pan stick kept it moist. Next, she concentrated on her eyes, the makeup under the lower lids three or four shades lighter than her other makeup, so that the shadows were softened. She rubbed in a small amount of eye shadow to give her eyes more color, then carefully applied false eyelashes over her own lashes, tilting them at the outer edges at a forty-five-degree angle. She brushed some Duo adhesive on her own outer lashes and joined them with the false lashes, making the eyes look larger. To give the lashes a fuller look, she drew fine dots on her lower eyelid beneath her own lashes. After that, Jill applied her lipstick, then powdered her lips before applying a second coat of lipstick. She applied a blusher to her cheeks and dusted her face with powder, avoiding the areas around her eyes where the powder would accentuate the faint wrinkles.

Jill sat back in her chair and studied the effect in the mirror. She looked beautiful. Someday, she would have to resort to the tape trick, but thank God that was still years away. Jill knew of older actresses who used the trick. They fastened tiny pieces of Scotch tape to their skin just below the hairline. Attached to these tapes were threads which they tied around their heads and concealed beneath their hair. The result was to pull the slackened skin of their faces taut, giving the effect of a face lift without the expense and pain of surgery. A variation was also used to disguise their sagging breasts. A piece of tape attached to the breast on one end and to the firmer flesh higher on the chest on the other provided a simple temporary solution to the problem. Jill's breasts were still firm.

She finished combing her soft, black hair, took one final look in the mirror, glanced at her watch and realized that she would have to hurry.

She had an interview for "The Toby Temple Show."

Eddie Berrigan, the casting director for Toby's show, was a married man. He had made arrangements to use a friend's apartment three afternoons a week. One of the afternoons was reserved for Berrigan's mistress and the other two afternoons were reserved for what he called "old talent" and "new talent."

Jill Castle was new talent. Several buddies had told Eddie that Jill gave a fantastic "trip around the world" and wonderful head. Eddie had been eager to try her. Now, a part in a sketch had come up that was right for her. All the character had to do was look sexy, say a few lines and exit.

Jill read for Eddie and he was satisfied. She was no Kate Hepburn, but the role didn't call for one. "You're in," he said.

"Thank you, Eddie."

"Here's your script. Rehearsal starts tomorrow morning, ten o'clock sharp. Be on time, and know your lines."

"Of course." She waited.

"Er—how about meeting me this afternoon for a cup of coffee?"
Jill nodded.

"A friend of mine has an apartment at ninety-five thirteen Argyle. The Allerton."

"I know where it is," Jill said.

"Apartment Six D. Three o'clock."

Rehearsals went smoothly. It was going to be a good show. That week's talent included a spectacular dance team from Argentina, a popular rock and roll group, a magician who made everything in sight disappear and a top vocalist. The only one missing was Toby Temple. Jill asked Eddie Berrigan about Toby's absence. "Is he sick?"

Eddie snorted. "He's sick like a fox. The peasants rehearse while old Toby has himself a ball. He'll show up Saturday to tape the show, and then split."

Toby Temple appeared on Saturday morning, breezing into the studio like a king. From a corner of the stage, Jill watched him make his entrance, followed by his three stooges, Clifton Lawrence and a couple of old-time comics. The spectacle filled Jill with contempt. She knew all about Toby Temple. He was an egomaniac who, according to rumor, bragged that he had been to bed with every pretty actress in Hollywood. No one ever said no to him. Oh, yes, Jill knew about the Great Toby Temple.

The director, a short, nervous man named Harry Durkin, introduced the cast to Toby. Toby had worked with most of them. Hollywood was a small village, and the faces soon became familiar. Toby had not met Jill Castle before. She looked beautiful in a beige linen dress, cool and elegant.

"What are you doing, honey?" Toby asked.

"I'm in the astronaut sketch, Mr. Temple."

He gave her a warm smile and said, "My friends call me Toby."

The cast started to work. The rehearsal went unusually well, and Durkin quickly realized why. Toby was showing off for Jill. He had laid every other girl in the show, and Jill was a new challenge.

The sketch that Toby did with Jill was the high point of the show. Toby gave Jill a couple of additional lines and a funny piece of business. When rehearsal was over, Toby said to her, "How about a little drink in my dressing room?"

"Thank you, I don't drink." Jill smiled and walked away. She had a date with a casting director and that was more important than Toby Temple. *He* was a one-shot. A casting director meant steady employment.

When they taped the show that evening it was an enormous success, one of the best shows Toby had ever done.

"Another smash," Clifton told Toby. "That astronaut sketch was top drawer."

Toby grinned. "Yeah. I like that little chick in it. She's got something."

"She's pretty," Clifton said. Every week there was a different girl. They all had something, and they all went to bed with Toby and became yesterday's conversation piece.

"Fix it for her to have supper with us, Cliff."

It was not a request. It was a command. A few years ago, Clifton would have told Toby to do it himself. But these days, when Toby asked you to do something, you did it. He was a king and this was his kingdom, and those who did not want to be exiled stayed in his favor.

"Of course, Toby," Clifton said. "I'll arrange it."

Clifton walked down the hall to the dressing room where the girl dancers and female members of the cast changed. He rapped once on the door and walked in. There were a dozen girls in the room in various stages of undress. They paid no attention to him except to call out greetings. Jill had removed her makeup and was getting into her street clothes. Clifton walked up to her. "You were very good," he said.

Jill glanced at him in the mirror without interest. "Thanks." At one time she would have been excited to be this close to Clifton Lawrence. He could have opened every door in Hollywood for her. Now everyone knew that he was simply Toby Temple's stooge.

"I have good news for you. Mr. Temple wants you to join him for supper."

Jill lightly tousled her hair with her fingertips and said, "Tell him I'm tired. I'm going to bed." And she walked out.

Supper that evening was a misery. Toby, Clifton Lawrence and Durkin, the director, were in La Rue's at a front booth. Durkin had suggested inviting a couple of the showgirls, but Toby had furiously rejected the idea.

The table captain was saying, "Are you ready to order, Mr. Temple?"

Toby pointed to Clifton and said, "Yeah. Give the idiot here an order of tongue."

Clifton joined the laughter of the others at the table, pretending that Toby was simply being amusing.

Toby snapped, "I asked you to do a simple thing like inviting a girl to dinner. Who told you to scare her off?"

"She was tired," Clifton explained. "She said—"

"*No* broad is too tired to have dinner with me. You must have said something that pissed her off." Toby had raised his voice. The people at the next booth had turned to stare. Toby gave them his boyish smile and said, "This is a farewell dinner, folks." He pointed at Clifton. "He's donated his brain to the zoo."

There was laughter from the other table. Clifton forced a grin, but under the table his hands were clenched.

"Do you want to know how dumb he is?" Toby asked the people at the adjoining booth. "In Poland, they tell jokes about *him.*"

The laughter increased. Clifton wanted to get up and walk out, but he did not dare. Durkin sat there embarrassed, too wise to say anything. Toby now had the attention of several nearby booths. He raised his voice again, giving them his charming smile. "Cliff Lawrence here gets his stupidity honestly. When he was born, his parents had a big fight over him. His mother claimed it wasn't her baby."

Mercifully, the evening finally came to an end. But tomorrow Clifton Lawrence stories were going to be told all over town.

Clifton Lawrence lay in his bed that night, unable to sleep. He asked himself why he allowed Toby to humiliate him. The answer was simple: money. The income from Toby Temple brought him over a quarter of a million dollars a year. Clifton lived expensively and generously, and he had not saved a cent. With his other clients gone, he needed Toby. That was the problem. Toby knew it, and baiting Clifton had become a blood sport. Clifton had to get away before it was too late.

But he was aware that it was already too late.

He had been trapped into this situation because of his affection for Toby: he had really loved him. He had watched Toby destroy others—women who had fallen in love with him, comics who had tried to compete with him, critics who had panned him. But those were *others.* Clifton had never believed that Toby would turn on him. He and Toby were too close, Clifton had done too much for him.

He dreaded to think about what the future held.

Ordinarily, Toby would not have given Jill Castle more than a second glance. But Toby was not used to being denied anything he wanted. Jill's refusal only acted as a goad. He invited her to dinner again. When she declined, Toby shrugged it off as some kind of stupid game she was playing and decided to forget about her. The irony was that if it had been a game, Jill would never have been able to deceive Toby, because Toby understood women too well. No, he sensed that Jill really did *not* want to go out with him, and the thought galled him. He was unable to get her out of his mind.

Casually, Toby mentioned to Eddie Berrigan that it might be a good idea to use Jill Castle on the show again. Eddie telephoned her. She told him she was busy doing a bit role in a Western. When Eddie reported back to Toby, the comedian was furious.

"Tell her to cancel whatever she's doing," he snapped. "We'll pay her more. For Christ's sake, this is the number one show on the air. What's the matter with that dizzy broad?"

Eddie called Jill again and told her how Toby felt. "He really wants you back on the show, Jill. Can you make it?"

"I'm sorry," Jill said. "I'm doing a part at Universal. I can't get out of it."

Nor would she try. An actress did not get ahead in Hollywood by walking out on a studio. Toby Temple meant nothing to Jill except a day's work. The following evening, the Great Man himself telephoned her. His voice on the telephone was warm and charming.

"Jill? This is your little old co-star, Toby."

"Hello, Mr. Temple."

"Hey, come on! What's with the 'mister' bit?" There was no response. "Do you like baseball?" Toby asked. "I've got box seats for—"

"No, I don't."

"Neither do I." He laughed. "I was testing you. Listen, how about having dinner with me Saturday night? I stole my chef from Maxim's in Paris. He—"

"I'm sorry. I have a date, Mr. Temple." There was not even a flicker of interest in her voice.

Toby felt himself gripping the receiver more tightly. "When *are* you free?"

"I'm a hard-working girl. I don't go out much. But thank you for asking me."

And the line went dead. The bitch had hung up on him—a fucking bit player had hung up on Toby Temple! There was not a woman Toby had met who would not give a year of her life to spend one night with him—and this stupid cunt had turned him down! He was in a violent rage, and he took it out on everyone around him. Nothing was right. The script stank, the director was an idiot, the music was terrible and the actors were lousy. He summoned Eddie Berrigan, the casting director, to his dressing room.

"What do you know about Jill Castle?" Toby demanded.

"Nothing," Eddie said instantly. He was not a fool. Like everyone else on the show, he knew exactly what was going on. Whichever way it turned out, he had no intention of getting caught in the middle.

"Does she sleep around?"

"No, sir," Eddie said firmly. "If she did, I'd know about it."

"I want you to check her out," Toby ordered. "Find out if she's got a boyfriend, where she goes, what she does—you know what I want."

"*Yes*, sir," Eddie said earnestly.

At three o'clock the next morning, Eddie was awakened by the telephone at his bedside.

"What did you find out?" a voice asked.

Eddie sat up in bed, trying to blink himself awake. "Who the hell—" He suddenly realized who was at the other end of the telephone. "I checked," Eddie said hastily. "She's got a clean bill of health."

"I didn't ask you for her fucking medical certificate," Toby snapped. "Is she laying anybody?"

"No, sir. Nobody. I talked to my buddies around town. They all like Jill and they use her because she's a fine actress." He was talking faster now, anxious to convince the man at the other end of the phone. If Toby Temple ever learned that Jill had slept with Eddie—had chosen *him* over Toby Temple!—Eddie would never work in this town again. He *had* talked to his casting-director friends, and they were all in the same position he was. No one wanted to make an enemy of Toby Temple, so they had agreed on a conspiracy of silence. "She doesn't play around with *anybody*."

Toby's voice softened, "I see. I guess she's just some kind of crazy kid, huh?"

"I guess she is," said Eddie, relieved.

"Hey! I hope I didn't wake you up?"

"No, no, that's all right, Mr. Temple."

But Eddie lay awake a long time, contemplating what could happen to him if the truth ever came out.

For this was Toby Temple's town.

Toby and Clifton Lawrence were having lunch at the Hillcrest Country Club. Hillcrest had been created because few of the top country clubs in Los Angeles admitted Jews. This policy was so rigidly observed that Groucho Marx's ten-year-old child, Melinda, had been ordered out of the swimming pool of a club where a Gentile friend had taken her. When Groucho heard what had happened, he telephoned the manager of the club and said, "Listen—my daughter's only *half*-Jewish. Would you let her go into the pool up to her waist?"

As a result of incidents like this, some affluent Jews who enjoyed golf, tennis, gin rummy and baiting anti-Semites got together and formed their own club, selling shares exclusively to Jewish members. Hillcrest was built in a beautiful park a few miles from the heart of Beverly Hills, and it quickly became famous for having the best buffet and the most stimulating conversation in town. The Gentiles clamored to be admitted. In a gesture toward tolerance, the board ruled that a few non-Jews would be allowed to join the club.

Toby always sat at the comedians' table, where the Hollywood wits gathered to exchange jokes and top one another. But today Toby had other things on his mind. He took Clifton to a corner table. "I need your advice, Cliff," Toby said.

The little agent glanced up at him in surprise. It had been a long time since Toby had asked for his advice. "Certainly, dear boy."

"It's this girl," Toby began, and Clifton was instantly ahead of him. Half the town knew the story by now. It was the biggest joke in Hollywood. One of the columnists had even run it as a blind item. Toby had read it and commented, "I wonder who the schmuck is?" The great lover was hooked on a girl on the town who had turned him down. There was only one way to handle this situation.

"Jill Castle," Toby was saying, "remember her? The kid who was on the show?"

"Ah, yes, a very attractive girl. What's the problem?"

"I'll be goddamned if I know," Toby admitted. "It's like she's got something against me. Every time I ask her for a date, I get a turn-down. It makes me feel like some kind of shit-kicker from Iowa."

Clifton took a chance. "Why don't you stop asking her?"

"That's the crazy part, pal. I can't. Between you and me and my cock, I've never wanted a broad so much in my life. It's getting so I can't think about anything else." He smiled self-consciously and said, "I told you it was crazy. You've been around the track a few times, Cliff. What do I do?"

For one reckless moment, Clifton was tempted to tell Toby the truth. But he couldn't tell him that his dream girl was sleeping around town with every assistant casting director who could give her a day's work. Not if he wanted to keep Toby as a client. "I have an idea," Clifton suggested. "Is she serious about her acting?"

"Yes. She's ambitious."

"All right. Then, give her an invitation she *has* to accept."

"What do you mean?"

"Have a party at your house."

"I just told you, she won't—"

"Let me finish. Invite studio heads, producers, directors—people who could do her some good. If she's really interested in being an actress, she'll be dying to meet them."

Toby dialed her number. "Hello, Jill."

"Who is this?" she asked.

Everyone in the country recognized his voice, and she was asking who it was!

"Toby. Toby Temple."

"Oh." It was a sound that could have meant anything.

"Listen, Jill, I'm giving a little dinner party at my home next Wednesday night and I"—he heard her start to refuse and hurried on—"I'm having Sam Winters, head of Pan-Pacific, and a few other studio heads there, and some producers and directors. I thought it might be good for you to meet them. Are you free?"

There was the briefest of pauses, and Jill Castle said, "Wednesday night. Yes, I'm free. Thank you, Toby."

And neither of them knew that it was an appointment in Samarra.

On the terrace, an orchestra played, while liveried waiters passed trays of hors d'oeuvres and glasses of champagne.

When Jill arrived, forty-five minutes late, Toby nervously hurried to the door to greet her. She was wearing a simple white silk dress, and her black hair fell softly against her shoulders. She looked ravishing. Toby could not take his eyes off her. Jill was aware that she looked beautiful. She had washed and styled her hair very carefully and had taken a long time with her makeup.

"There are a lot of people here I want you to meet." Toby took Jill's hand and led her across the large reception hall into the formal drawing room. Jill stopped at the entrance, staring at the guests. Almost every face in the room was familiar to her. She had seen them on the cover of *Time* and *Life* and *Newsweek* and *Paris Match* and *OGGI* or on the screen. This was the *real* Hollywood. These were the picture makers. Jill had imagined this moment a thousand times, being with these people, talking with them. Now that the reality was here, it was difficult for her to realize that it was actually happening.

Toby was handing her a glass of champagne. He took her arm and led her to a man surrounded by a group of people. "Sam, I want you to meet Jill Castle."

Sam turned. "Hello, Jill Castle," he said pleasantly.

"Jill, this is Sam Winters, chief Indian of Pan-Pacific Studios."

"I know who Mr. Winters is," Jill said.

"Jill's an actress, Sam, a damned clever actress. You could use her. Give your joint a little class."

"I'll keep that in mind," Sam said politely.

Toby took Jill's hand, holding it firmly. "Come on, honey," he said. "I want everybody to meet you."

Before the evening was over, Jill had met three studio heads, half a dozen important producers, three directors, a few writers, several newspaper and television columnists and a dozen stars. At dinner, Jill sat at Toby's right. She listened to the various conversations, savoring the feeling of being on the Inside for the first time.

". . . the trouble with these epics is that if one of them flops, it can wipe out the whole studio. Fox is hanging on by its teeth, waiting to see what *Cleopatra* does."

". . . have you seen the new Billy Wilder picture yet? Sensational!"

"Yeah? I liked him better when he was working with Brackett. Brackett has class."

"Billy has talent."

". . . so, I sent Peck a mystery script last week, and he's crazy about it. He said he'd give me a definite answer in a day or two."

". . . I received this invitation to meet the new guru, Krishi Pramananada. Well, my dear, it turned out I'd already met him; I attended his bar mitzvah."

". . . the problem with budgeting a picture at two is that by the time you have an answer print, the cost of inflation plus the goddamned unions has pushed it up to three or four."

Millions, Jill thought excitedly. *Three or four millions.* She remembered the endless penny-ante conversations at Schwab's where the hangers-on, the Survivors, avidly fed each other crumbs of information about what the studios were doing. Well, the people at this table tonight were the *real* survivors, the ones who made everything in Hollywood happen.

These were the people who had kept the gates shut against her, who had refused to give her a chance. Any person at this table could have helped her, could have changed her life, but none of them had had five minutes to spare for Jill Castle. She looked over at a producer who was riding high with a big new musical picture. He had refused to give Jill even an interview.

At the far end of the table, a famous comedy director was in animated conversation with the star of his latest film. He had refused to see Jill.

Sam Winters was talking to the head of another studio. Jill had sent a telegram to Winters, asking him to watch her performance on a television show. He had never bothered answering.

They would pay for their slights and insults, they and everybody else in this town who had treated her so shabbily. Right now, she meant nothing to the people here, but she would. Oh, yes. One day she would.

The food was superb, but Jill was too preoccupied to notice what she ate. When dinner was over, Toby rose and said, "Hey! We better hurry before they start the picture without us." Holding Jill's arm, he led the way to the large projection room where they were to watch a movie.

The room was arranged so that sixty people could comfortably view the picture in couches and easy chairs. An open cabinet filled with candy bars stood at one side of the entrance. A popcorn machine stood on the other side.

Toby had seated himself next to Jill. She was aware that all through the screening his eyes were on her rather than on the movie. When the picture ended and the lights went up, coffee and cake were served. Half an hour later, the party began to dissolve. Most of the guests had early studio calls.

Toby was standing at the front door saying good night to Sam Winters when Jill walked up, wearing her coat. "Where are you going?" Toby demanded. "I'm gonna take you home."

"I have my car," Jill answered, sweetly. "Thank you for a lovely evening, Toby." And she left.

Toby stood there in disbelief, watching her drive away. He had made exciting plans for the rest of the evening. He was going to take Jill upstairs to the bedroom and—he had even picked out the tapes he was going to play! *Any woman here tonight would have been grateful to jump into my bed,* Toby thought. They were stars, too, not some dumb bit player. Jill Castle was just too damned stupid to know what she was turning down. It was over as far as Toby was concerned. He had learned his lesson.

He was never going to talk to Jill again.

Toby telephoned Jill at nine o'clock the next morning, and he was answered by a tape-recorded message. "Hello, this is Jill Castle. I'm sorry I'm not at home now. If you'll leave your name and telephone number, I'll call back when I return. Please wait until you hear the signal. Thank you." There was a sharp beep.

Toby stood there clutching the telephone in his hand, then slammed down the receiver without leaving a message. He was damned if he was going to carry on a conversation with a mechanical voice. A moment later, he redialed the number. He listened to the recording again and spoke. "You've got the cutest voice-over in town. You should package it. I don't usually call back girls who eat and run, but in your case, I've decided to make an exception. What are you doing for dinner to—?" The phone went dead. He had talked too long for the goddamned tape. He froze, not knowing what to do, feeling like a fool. It infuriated him to have to call back again, but he dialed the number for the third time and said,

"As I was saying before the rabbi cut me off, how about dinner tonight? I'll wait for your call." He left his number and hung up.

Toby waited restlessly all day and did not hear from her. By seven o'clock, he thought, *To hell with you. That was your last chance, baby.* And this time it was final. He took out his private phone book and began to thumb through it. There was no one in it who interested him.

I t was the most tremendous role in Jill's life.

She had no idea why Toby wanted her so much when he could have any girl in Hollywood, nor did the reason matter. The fact was that he did. For days Jill had been able to think of nothing but the dinner party and how everyone there—all those important people—had catered to Toby. They would do anything for him. Somehow, Jill had to find a way to make Toby do anything for *her*. She knew she had to be very clever. Toby's reputation was that once he took a girl to bed, he lost interest in her. It was the pursuit he enjoyed, the challenge. Jill spent a great deal of time thinking about Toby and about how she was going to handle him.

Toby telephoned her every day and she let a week go by before she agreed to have dinner with him again. He was in such a euphoric state that everyone in the cast and crew commented on it.

"If there were such an animal," Toby told Clifton, "I'd say I was in love. Every time I think about Jill, I get an erection." He grinned and added, "And when I get an erection, pal, it's like putting up a billboard on Hollywood Boulevard."

The night of their first date, Toby picked Jill up at her apartment and said, "We have a table at Chasen's." He was sure it would be a treat for her.

"Oh?" There was a note of disappointment in Jill's voice.

He blinked. "Is there someplace else you'd rather go?" It was

Saturday night, but Toby knew he could get a table anywhere: Perino's, the Ambassador, the Derby. "Name it."

Jill hesitated, then said, "You'll laugh."

"No, I won't."

"Tommy's."

Toby was getting a poolside massage from one of the Macs, while Clifton Lawrence looked on. "You wouldn't believe it," Toby marveled. "We stood in line at that hamburger joint for twenty minutes. Do you know where the hell Tommy's is? Downtown Los Angeles. The only people who go to downtown Los Angeles are wetbacks. She's crazy. I'm ready to blow a hundred bucks on her with French champagne and the whole bit, and the evening costs me two dollars and forty cents. I wanted to take her to Pip's afterward. Do you know what we did instead? We walked along the beach at Santa Monica. I got sand in my Guccis. No one walks along the beach at night. You get mugged by scuba divers." He shook his head in admiration. "Jill Castle. Do you believe her?"

"No," Clifton said dryly.

"She wouldn't come back to my place for a little nightcap, so I figured I'd get in the kip at *her* place, right?"

"Right."

"Wrong. She doesn't even let me in the door. I get a kiss on my cheek and I'm on my way home, alone. Now what the hell kind of night out on the town is that for Charlie-superstar?"

"Are you gonna see her again?"

"Are you demented? You bet your sweet ass I am!"

After that, Toby and Jill were together almost every night. When Jill would tell Toby she could not see him because she was busy or had an early morning call, Toby would be in despair. He telephoned Jill a dozen times a day.

He took her to the most glamorous restaurants and the most exclusive private clubs in town. In return, Jill took him to the old boardwalk in Santa Monica and the Trancas Inn and the little French family restaurant called Taix and to Papa DeCarlos and all the other out-of-the-way places a struggling actress with no money learns about. Toby did not care where he went, as long as Jill was with him.

She was the first person he had ever known who made his feeling of loneliness vanish.

Toby was almost afraid to go to bed with Jill now, for fear the magic might disappear. And yet he wanted her more than he had ever desired any woman in his life. Once, at the end of an evening, when Jill was giving him a light good night kiss, Toby reached between her legs and said, "God, Jill, I'll go crazy if I can't have you." She pulled back and said coldly, "If that's all you want, you can buy it anywhere in town for twenty dollars." She slammed the door in his face. Afterward, she leaned against the door, trembling, afraid that she had gone too far. She lay awake all night, worrying.

The next day Toby sent her a diamond bracelet, and Jill knew that everything was all right. She returned the bracelet with a carefully thought-out note. "Thank you, anyway. You make me feel very beautiful."

"It cost me three grand," Toby told Clifton proudly, "and she sends it back!" He shook his head incredulously. "What do you think of a girl like that?"

Clifton could have told him exactly what he thought, but all he said was, "She's certainly unusual, dear boy."

"Unusual!" Toby exclaimed. "Every broad in this town is on the make for everything they can get their hot little hands on. Jill is the first girl I've ever met who doesn't give a damn about material things. Do you blame me for being crazy about her?"

"No," Clifton said. But he was beginning to get worried. He knew all about Jill, and he wondered if he should not have spoken up sooner.

"I wouldn't object if you wanted to take Jill on as a client," Toby said to Clifton. "I'll bet she could be a big star."

Clifton parried it deftly but firmly. "No, thanks, Toby. One superstar on my hands is enough." He laughed.

That night Toby repeated the remark to Jill.

After his unsuccessful attempt with Jill, Toby was careful not to broach the subject of their going to bed together. Toby was actually proud of Jill for refusing him. All the other girls he had gone with had been doormats. But not Jill. When Toby did something Jill thought was out of line, she told him so. One night Toby tongue-lashed a man who was pestering him for an autograph.

Later, Jill said, "It's funny when you're sarcastic on stage, Toby, but you hurt that man's feelings."

Toby had gone back to the man and apologized.

Jill told Toby that she thought his drinking so much was not good for him. He cut down on his consumption. She made a casually critical remark about his clothes, and he changed tailors. Toby allowed Jill to say things that he would not have tolerated from anyone else in the world. No one had ever dared boss him around or criticize him.

Except, of course, his mother.

Jill refused to accept money or expensive gifts from Toby, but he knew that she could not have much money, and her courageous behavior made Toby even more proud of her. One evening at Jill's apartment, while Toby was waiting for her to finish dressing before dinner, he noticed a stack of bills in the living room. Toby slipped them into his pocket and the next day ordered Clifton to pay them. Toby felt as though he had scored a victory. But he wanted to do something big for Jill, something important.

And he suddenly knew what it was going to be.

"Sam—I'm going to do you a great big favor!"

Beware of stars bearing gifts, Sam Winters thought wryly.

"You've been going crazy looking for a girl for Keller's picture, right?" Toby asked. "Well, I got her for you."

"Anyone I know?" Sam inquired.

"You met her at my house. Jill Castle."

Sam remembered Jill. Beautiful face and figure, black hair. Far too old to play the teen-ager in the Keller movie. But if Toby Temple wanted her to test for the part, Sam was going to oblige. "Have her come in to see me this afternoon," he said.

Sam saw to it that Jill Castle's test was carefully handled. She was given one of the studio's top cameramen, and Keller himself directed the test.

Sam looked at the rushes the following day. As he had guessed, Jill was too mature for the part of the young girl. Aside from that, she was not bad. What she lacked was charisma, the magic that leaped out from the screen.

He telephoned Toby Temple. "I looked at Jill's test this morning, Toby. She photographs well, and she can read lines, but she's not a leading lady. She could earn a good living playing minor roles, but if she has her heart set on becoming a star, I think she's in the wrong business."

Toby picked up Jill that evening to take her to a dinner being given for a celebrated English director who had just arrived in Hollywood. Jill had been looking forward to it.

She opened the door for Toby and the moment he entered she knew that something was wrong. "You heard some news about my test," she said.

He nodded reluctantly. "I talked to Sam Winters." He told her what Sam had said, trying to soften the blow.

Jill stood there listening, not saying a word. She had been so *sure*. The part had felt so *right*. Out of nowhere came the memory of the gold cup in the department-store window. The little girl had ached with the wanting and the loss; Jill felt the same feelings of despair now.

Toby was saying, "Look, honey, don't worry about it. Winters doesn't know what he's talking about."

But he *did* know! She was not going to make it. All the agony and the pain and the hope had been for nothing. It was as though her mother had been right and a vengeful God was punishing Jill for she knew not what. She could hear the preacher screaming, *See that little girl? She will burn in Hell for her sins if she does not give her soul up to God and repent.* She had come to this town with love and dreams, and the town had degraded her.

She was overcome with an unbearable feeling of sadness and she was not even aware that she was sobbing until she felt Toby's arm around her.

"Sh! It's all right," he said, and his gentleness made her cry all the harder.

She stood there while he held her in his arms and she told him about her father dying when she was born, and about the gold cup and the Holy Rollers and the headaches and the nights filled with terror while she waited for God to strike her dead. She told him about the endless, dreary jobs she had taken in order to become an actress and the series of failures. Some deep-rooted instinct kept her from mentioning the men in her life. Although she had started out playing a game with Toby, she was now beyond pretense. It was in this moment of her naked vulnerability that she reached him. She touched a chord deep within him that no one else had ever struck.

He took out his pocket handkerchief and dried her tears. "Hey, if you think *you* had it tough," he said, "listen to *this*. My old man was a butcher and . . ."

They talked until three o'clock in the morning. It was the first time in his life Toby had talked to a girl as a human being. He understood her. How could he not; she was *him*.

Neither of them ever knew who made the first move. What had started as a gentle, understanding comforting slowly became a sensual, animal wanting. They were kissing hungrily, and he was holding her tightly. She could feel his maleness pressing against her. She needed him and he was taking off her clothes, and she was helping him and then he was naked in the dark beside her, and there was an urgency in both of them. They went to the floor. Toby entered her and Jill moaned once at the enormous size of him, and Toby started to withdraw. She pulled him closer to her, holding him fiercely. He began to make love to her then, filling her, completing her, making her body whole. It was gentle and loving and it kept building and became frantic and demanding and suddenly it was beyond that. It was an ecstasy, an unbearable rapture, a mindless animal coupling, and Jill was screaming, "Love me, Toby! Love me, love me!" His pounding body was on her, in her, was part of her, and they were one.

They made love all night and talked and laughed, and it was as though they had belonged together always.

If Toby had thought he cared for Jill before, he was insane about her now. They lay in bed, and he held her in his arms protectively, and he thought wonderingly, *This is what love is.* He turned to gaze at her. She looked warm and disheveled and breathtakingly beautiful, and he had never loved anyone so much. He said, "I want to marry you."

It was the most natural thing in the world.

She hugged him tightly and said, "Oh, yes, Toby." She loved him and she was going to marry him.

And it was not until hours later that Jill remembered why all this had started in the first place. She had wanted Toby's power. She had wanted to pay back all the people who had used her, hurt her, degraded her. She had wanted vengeance.

Now she was going to have it.

27

Clifton Lawrence was in trouble. In a way, he supposed, it was his own fault for letting things get this far. He was seated at Toby's bar, and Toby was saying, "I proposed to her this morning, Cliff, and she said yes. I feel like a sixteen-year-old kid."

Clifton tried not to let the shock show on his face. He had to be extremely careful about the way he handled this. He knew one thing: He could not let that little tramp marry Toby Temple. The moment the wedding announcement was made, every cocksman in Hollywood would crawl out of the woodwork, announcing that he had gotten in there first. It was a miracle that Toby had not found out about Jill before now, but it could not be kept from him forever. When he learned the truth, Toby would kill. He would lash out at everyone around him, everyone who had let this happen to him, and Clifton Lawrence would be the first to feel the brunt of Toby's rage. No, Clifton could not let this marriage take place. He was tempted to point out that Toby was twenty years older than Jill, but he checked himself. He looked over at Toby and said cautiously, "It might be a mistake to rush things. It takes a long time to really get to know a person. You might change your—"

Toby brushed it aside. "You're gonna be my best man. You think we should have the wedding here or up in Vegas?"

Clifton knew that he was wasting his breath. There was only one way to prevent this disaster from happening. He had to find a way to stop Jill.

That afternoon, the little agent telephoned Jill and asked her to come to his office. She arrived an hour late, gave him a cheek to kiss, sat down on the edge of the couch and said, "I haven't much time. I'm meeting Toby."

"This won't take long."

Clifton studied her. It was a different Jill. She bore almost no resemblance to the girl he had first met a few months ago. There was a confidence about her now, an assurance that she had not had earlier. Well, he had dealt with girls like her before.

"Jill, I'm going to lay it on the line," Clifton said. "You're bad for Toby. I want you to get out of Hollywood." He took a white envelope out of a drawer. "Here's five thousand dollars' cash. That's enough to take you anywhere you want to go."

She stared at him a moment, a surprised expression on her face, then leaned back on the couch and began to laugh.

"I'm not joking," Clifton Lawrence said. "Do you think Toby would marry you if he found out you've laid everybody in town?"

She regarded Clifton for a long moment. She wanted to tell him that *he* was responsible for everything that had happened to her. He and all the other people in power who had refused to give her a chance. They had made her pay with her body, her pride, her soul. But she knew there was no way she could ever make him understand. He was trying to bluff her. He would not dare tell Toby about her; it would be Lawrence's word against hers.

Jill rose to her feet and walked out of the office.

One hour later, Clifton received a call from Toby.

Clifton had never heard Toby sound so excited. "I don't know what you said to Jill, pal, but I have to hand it to you—she can't wait. We're on our way to Las Vegas to get married!"

The Lear jet was thirty-five miles from the Los Angeles International Airport, flying at 250 knots. David Kenyon made contact with the LAX approach control and gave them his position.

David was exhilarated. He was on his way to Jill.

Cissy had recovered from most of her injuries suffered in the automobile accident, but her face had been badly lacerated. David had sent her to the best plastic surgeon in the world, a doctor in Brazil. She had been gone for six weeks, during which time she had been sending him glowing reports about the doctor.

Twenty-four hours ago, David had received a telephone call from Cissy, saying she was not returning. She had fallen in love.

David could not believe his good fortune.

"That's—that's wonderful," he managed to stammer. "I hope you and the doctor will be happy."

"Oh, it's not the doctor," Cissy replied. "It's someone who owns a little plantation here. He looks exactly like you, David. The only difference is that he loves me."

The crackling of the radio interrupted his thoughts. "Lear Three Alpha Papa, this is Los Angeles Approach Control. You're clear for approach to Runway Twenty-five Left. There will be a United seven-oh-seven behind you. When you land, please taxi to the ramp on your right."

"Roger." David began to make his descent, and his heart started to pound. He was on his way to find Jill, to tell her he still loved her, to ask her to marry him.

He was walking through the terminal when he passed the news-stand and saw the headline: "TOBY TEMPLE WEDS ACTRESS." He read the story twice and then turned and went into the airport bar.

He stayed drunk for three days and then flew back to Texas.

It was a storybook honeymoon. Toby and Jill flew in a private jet to Las Hadas, where they were the guests of the Patinos at their fairyland resort carved out of the Mexican jungle and beach. The newlyweds were given a private villa surrounded by cacti, hibiscus and brilliantly colored bougainvillea, where exotic birds serenaded them all night. They spent ten days exploring and yachting and being partied. They ate delicious dinners at the Legazpi prepared by gourmet chefs and swam in the fresh-water pools. Jill shopped at the exquisite boutiques at the Plaza.

From Mexico they flew to Biarritz where they stayed at L'Hotel du Palais, the spectacular palace that Napoleon III built for his Empress Eugenie. The honeymooners gambled at the casinos and went to the bullfights and fished and made love all night.

From the Côte Basque they drove east to Gstaad, thirty-five hundred feet above sea level in the Bernese Oberland. They took sightseeing flights among the peaks, skimming Mont Blanc and the Matterhorn. They skied the dazzling white slopes and rode dog sleds and attended fondue parties and danced. Toby had never been so happy. He had found the woman to make his life complete. He was no longer lonely.

Toby could have continued the honeymoon forever, but Jill was eager to get home. She was not interested in any of these places, nor in any of these people. She felt like a newly crowned queen who was being kept from her country. Jill Castle was burning to return to Hollywood.

Mrs. Toby Temple had scores to settle.

Book Three

There is a smell to failure. It is a stench that clings like a miasma. Just as dogs can detect the odor of fear in a human being, so people can sense when a man is on his way down. Particularly in Hollywood.

Everyone in the Business knew that Clifton Lawrence was finished, even before he knew it. They could smell it in the air around him.

Clifton had not heard from Toby or Jill in the week since they had returned from their honeymoon. He had sent an expensive gift and had left three telephone messages, which had been ignored. Jill. Somehow she had managed to turn Toby's mind against him. Clifton knew that he had to effect a truce. He and Toby meant too much to each other to let anyone come between them.

Clifton drove out to the house on a morning when he knew Toby would be at the studio. Jill saw him coming up the driveway and opened the door for him. She looked stunningly beautiful, and he said so. She was friendly. They sat in the garden and had coffee, and she told him about the honeymoon and the places they had been. She said, "I'm sorry Toby hasn't returned your calls, Cliff. You can't believe how frantic it's been around here." She smiled apologetically, and Clifton knew then that he had been wrong about her. She was not his enemy.

"I'd like us to start fresh and be friends," he said.

"Thank you, Cliff. So would I."

Clifton felt an immeasurable sense of relief. "I want to give a dinner party for you and Toby. I'll take over the private room at the Bistro. A week from Saturday. Black tie, a hundred of your most intimate friends. How does that sound?"

"Lovely. Toby will be pleased."

Jill waited until the afternoon of the party to telephone and say, "I'm so sorry, Cliff. I'm afraid I'm not going to be able to make it tonight. I'm a little tired. Toby thinks I should stay home and rest."

Clifton managed to hide his feelings. "I'm sorry about that, Jill, but I understand. Toby will be able to come, won't he?"

He heard her sigh over the telephone. "I'm afraid not, dear boy. He won't go anywhere without me. But you have a nice party." And she hung up.

It was too late to call off the party. The bill was three thousand dollars. But it cost Clifton much more than that. He had been stood up by the guest of honor, his one and only client, and everyone there, the studios heads, the stars, the directors—all the people who mattered in Hollywood—were aware of it. Clifton tried to cover up by saying that Toby was not feeling well. It was the worst thing he could have done. When he picked up a copy of the *Herald Examiner* the next afternoon, there was a photograph of Mr. and Mrs. Toby Temple that had been taken at the Dodgers Stadium the night before.

Clifton Lawrence knew now that he was fighting for his life. If Toby dropped him, there would be no one around to pick him up. None of the big agencies would take him on, because he could bring them no clients; and he could not bear the thought of starting all over again on his own. It was too late for that. He *had* to find a way to make peace with Jill. He telephoned Jill and told her he would like to come to the house to talk to her.

"Of course," she said. "I was telling Toby last night that we haven't seen enough of you lately."

"I'll be over in fifteen minutes," Clifton said. He walked over to the liquor cabinet and poured himself a double Scotch. He had been doing too much of that lately. It was a bad habit to drink during a working day, but who was he kidding? What work? Every day he received important offers for Toby, but he could not get the great man to sit down and even discuss them with him. In the past, they had talked over everything. He remembered all the wonderful times they had had, the trips they had taken, the parties and the laughs and the girls. They had been as close as twins. Toby had needed him, had counted on him. And now . . . Clifton poured another drink and was pleased to see his hands were not trembling so much.

When Clifton arrived at the Temples' house, Jill was seated on the terrace, having coffee. She looked up and smiled as she saw him approach. *You're a salesman,* Clifton told himself. *Sell her on you.*

"It's nice to see you, Cliff. Sit down."

"Thanks, Jill." He took a seat across from her at a large wrought-iron table and studied her. She was wearing a white summer dress, and the contrast with her black hair and golden, tanned skin was stunning. She looked younger, and—the only word he could think of somehow—innocent. She was watching him with warm, friendly eyes.

"Would you like some breakfast, Cliff?"

"No, thanks. I ate hours ago."

"Toby isn't here."

"I know. I wanted to talk to you alone."

"What can I do for you?"

"Accept my apology," Clifton urged. He had never begged anyone for anything in his life, but he was begging now. "We— I got off on the wrong foot. Maybe it was my fault. It probably was. Toby's been my client and my friend for so long that I—I wanted to protect him. Can you understand that?"

Jill nodded, her brown eyes fixed on him, and said, "Of course, Cliff."

He took a deep breath. "I don't know whether he ever told you the story, but I'm the one who got Toby started. I knew he was going to be a big star the first time I saw him." He saw that he had her full attention. "I handled a lot of important clients then, Jill. I let them all go so that I could concentrate on Toby's career."

"Toby's talked to me about how much you've done for him," she said.

"Has he?" He hated the eagerness in his voice.

Jill smiled. "He told me about the day he pretended that Sam Goldwyn telephoned you and how you went to see Toby anyway. That was nice."

Clifton leaned forward and said, "I don't want anything to

happen to the relationship that Toby and I have. I need you in my corner. I'm asking you to forget everything that happened between us. I apologize for being out of line. I thought I was protecting Toby. Well, I was wrong. I think you're going to be great for him."

"I want to be. Very much."

"If Toby drops me, I—I think it would kill me. I'm not just talking about business. He and I have—he's been like a son to me. I love him." He despised himself for it, but he heard himself begging again. "Please, Jill, for God's sake . . ." He stopped, his voice choked.

She looked at him a long moment with those deep brown eyes and then held out her hand. "I don't hold grudges," Jill said. "Can you come to dinner tomorrow night?"

Clifton took a deep breath and then smiled happily and said, "Thanks." He found that his eyes were suddenly misty. "I—I won't forget this. Ever."

The following morning, when Clifton arrived at his office, there was a registered letter notifying him that his services had been terminated and that he no longer had the authority to act as Toby Temple's agent.

J ill Castle Temple was the most exciting thing to hit Hollywood
since Cinemascope. In a company town where everyone
played the game of admiring the emperor's clothes, Jill used
her tongue like a scythe. In a city where flattery was the daily
currency of conversation, Jill fearlessly spoke her mind. She had
Toby beside her and she brandished his power like a club, attacking all the important studio executives. They had never experienced anything like it before. They did not dare offend Jill,
because they did not want to offend Toby. He was Hollywood's
most bankable star, and they wanted him, needed him.

Toby was bigger than ever. His television show was still number
one in the Nielsen Ratings every week, his movies were enormous
money makers, and when Toby played Las Vegas, the casinos
doubled their profits. Toby was the hottest property in show
business. They wanted him for guest shots, record albums, personal appearances, merchandising, benefits, movies, they wanted
they wanted they wanted.

The most important people in town fell all over themselves to
please Toby. They quickly learned that the way to please Toby was
to please Jill. She began to schedule all of Toby's appointments
herself and to organize his life so that there was room in it only for
those of whom she approved. She put up an impenetrable barricade around him, and none but the rich and the famous and the
powerful were allowed to go through it. She was the keeper of the
flame. The little Polish girl from Odessa, Texas, entertained and
was entertained by governors, ambassadors, world-renowned art-

ists and the President of the United States. This town had done terrible things to her. But it would never do them again. Not as long as she had Toby Temple.

The people who were in real trouble were the ones on Jill's hate list.

She lay in bed with Toby and made sensuous love to him. When Toby was relaxed and spent, she snuggled in his arms and said, "Darling, did I ever tell you about the time I was looking for an agent and I went to this woman—what was her name?—oh, yes! Rose Dunning. She told me she had a part for me and she sat down on her bed to read with me."

Toby turned to look at her, his eyes narrowing. "What happened?"

Jill smiled. "Stupid innocent that I was, while I was reading, I felt her hand go up my thigh." Jill threw back her head and laughed. "I was frightened out of my wits. I've never run so fast in my life."

Ten days later, Rose Dunning's agency license was permanently revoked by the City Licensing Commission.

The following weekend, Toby and Jill were at their house in Palm Springs. Toby was lying on a massage table in the patio, a heavy Turkish towel under him, while Jill gave him a long, relaxing massage. Toby was on his back, cotton pads protecting his eyes against the strong rays of the sun. Jill was working on his feet, using a soft creamy lotion.

"You sure opened my eyes about Cliff," Toby said. "He was nothing but a parasite, milking me. I hear he's going around town trying to get himself a partnership deal. No one wants him. He can't get himself arrested without me."

Jill paused a moment and said, "I feel sorry for Cliff."

"That's the goddamned trouble with you, sweetheart. You think with your heart instead of your head. You've got to learn to be tougher."

Jill smiled quietly. "I can't help it. I'm the way I am." She started to work on Toby's legs, moving her hands slowly up toward his thighs with light, sensuous movements. He began to have an erection.

"Oh, Jesus," he moaned.

Her hands were moving higher now, moving toward Toby's groin, and the hardness increased. She slid her hands between his legs, underneath him, and slipped a creamy finger inside him. His enormous penis was rock hard.

"Quick, baby," he said. "Get on top of me."

They were at the marina, on the *Jill*, the large motorsailer Toby had bought for her. Toby's first television show of the new season was to tape the following day.

"This is the best vacation I've had in my whole life," Toby said. "I hate to go back to work."

"It's such a wonderful show," Jill said. "I had fun doing it. Everyone was so nice." She paused a moment, then added lightly, "*Almost* everyone."

"What do you mean?" Toby's voice was sharp. "Who wasn't nice to you?"

"No one, darling. I shouldn't have even mentioned it."

But she finally allowed Toby to worm it out of her, and the next day Eddie Berrigan, the casting director, was fired.

In the months that followed, Jill told Toby little fictions about other casting directors on her list, and one by one they disappeared. Everyone who had ever used her was going to pay. It was, she thought, like the rite of mating with the queen bee. They had all had their pleasure, and now they had to be destroyed.

She went after Sam Winters, the man who had told Toby she had no talent. She never said a word against him; on the contrary, she praised him to Toby. But she always praised other studio heads just a little bit more. . . . The other studios had properties better suited for Toby . . . directors who really understood him. Jill would add that she could not help thinking that Sam Winters did not really appreciate Toby's talent. Before long, Toby began feeling the same way. With Clifton Lawrence gone, Toby had no one to talk to, no one he could trust, except Jill. When Toby decided to make his movies at another studio, he believed that it was his own idea. But Jill made certain that Sam Winters knew the truth.

Retribution.

There were those around Toby who felt that Jill could not last, that she was simply a temporary intruder, a passing fancy. So they tolerated her or treated her with a thinly veiled contempt. It was their mistake. One by one, Jill eliminated them. She wanted no one around who had been important in Toby's life or who could influence him against her. She saw to it that Toby changed his lawyer and his public-relations firm and she hired people of her own choosing. She got rid of the three Macs and Toby's entourage of stooges. She replaced all the servants. It was *her* house now and she was the mistress of it.

A party at the Temples' had become the hottest ticket in town. Everyone who was anybody was there. Actors mingled with socialites and governors and heads of powerful corporations. The press was always there in full force, so that there was a bonus for the lucky guests. Not only did they go to the Temples' and have a wonderful time, but everyone *knew* that they had been to the Temples' and had had a wonderful time.

When the Temples were not hosts, they were guests. There was an avalanche of invitations. They were invited to premieres, charity dinners, political affairs, openings of restaurants and hotels.

Toby would have been content to stay at home alone with Jill, but she liked going out. On some evenings, they had three or four parties to attend, and she rushed Toby from one to the other.

"Jesus, you should have been a social director at Grossinger's," Toby laughed.

"I'm doing it for you, darling," Jill replied.

Toby was making a movie for MGM and had a grueling schedule. He came home late one night, exhausted, to find his evening clothes laid out for him. "We're not going out *again*, baby? We haven't been home one night the whole fucking year!"

"It's the Davises' anniversary party. They'd be terribly hurt if we didn't show up."

Toby sat down heavily on the bed. "I was looking forward to a nice hot bath and a quiet evening. Just the two of us."

But Toby went to the party. And because he always had to be "on," always had to be the center of attention, he drew on his enormous reservoir of energy until everyone was laughing and applauding and telling everyone else what a brilliantly funny man Toby Temple was. Late that night, lying in his bed, Toby was unable to sleep, his body drained, but his mind reliving the triumphs of the evening line by line, laugh by laugh. He was a very happy man. And all because of Jill.

How his mother would have adored her.

In March they received an invitation to the Cannes Film Festival.

"No way," Toby said, when Jill showed him the invitation. "The only Cannes I'm going to is the one in my bathroom. I'm tired, honey. I've been working my butt off."

Jerry Guttman, Toby's public-relations man, had told Jill that there was a good chance that Toby's movie would win the Best Picture Award and that it would help if Toby were there. He felt that it was important for Toby to go.

Lately, Toby had been complaining that he was tired all the time and was unable to sleep. At night he took sleeping pills, which left him groggy in the morning. Jill counteracted the feeling of tiredness by giving him benzedrine at breakfast so that Toby would have enough energy to get through the day. Now, the cycle of uppers and downers seemed to be taking its toll on him.

"I've already accepted the invitation," Jill told Toby, "but I'll cancel. No problem, darling."

"Let's go down to the Springs for a month and just lie around in the soap."

She looked at him. "What?"

He sat there, very still. "I meant *sun*. I don't know why it came out *soap*."

She laughed. "Because you're funny." Jill squeezed his hand. "Anyway, Palm Springs sounds wonderful. I love being alone with you."

"I don't know what's wrong with me," Toby sighed. "I just don't have the juice anymore. I guess I'm getting old."

"You'll never get old. You can wear me out."

He grinned. "Yeah? I guess my pecker will live long after I die." He rubbed the back of his head and said, "I think I'll take a little nap. To tell you the truth, I'm not feeling so hot. We don't have a date tonight, do we?"

"Nothing that I can't put off. I'll send the servants away and cook dinner for you myself tonight. Just us."

"Hey, that'll be great."

He watched her leave, and he thought, *Jesus, I'm the luckiest guy who ever lived.*

They were lying in bed late that night. Jill had given Toby a warm bath and a relaxing massage, kneading his tired muscles, soothing away his tensions.

"Ah, that feels wonderful," he murmured. "How did I ever get along without you?"

"I can't imagine." She nestled close to him. "Toby, tell me about the Cannes Film Festival. What's it like? I've never been to one."

"It's just a mob of hustlers who come from all over the world to sell their lousy movies to one another. It's the biggest con game in the world."

"You make it sound exciting," Jill said.

"Yeah? Well, I guess it is kind of exciting. The place is filled with characters." He studied her for a moment. "Do you really want to go to that stupid film festival?"

She shook her head quickly. "No. We'll go to Palm Springs."

"Hell, we can go to Palm Springs anytime."

"Really, Toby, it's not important."

He smiled. "Do you know why I'm so crazy about you? Any other woman in the world would have been pestering me to take her to the festival. You're dying to go, but do you say anything? No. You want to go to the Springs with me. Have you canceled that acceptance?"

"Not yet, but—"

"Don't. We're going to India." A puzzled look came over his face. "Did I say India? I meant—Cannes."

When their plane landed at Orly, Toby was handed a cablegram. His father had died in the nursing home. It was too late for Toby to go back for the funeral. He arranged to have a new wing added to the rest home, named after his parents.

The whole world was at Cannes.

It was Hollywood and London and Rome, all mixed together in a glorious, many-tongued cacophony of sound and fury, in Technicolor and Panavision. From all over the globe, picture makers flocked to the French Riviera, carrying cans of dreams under their arms, rolls of celluloid made in English and French and Japanese and Hungarian and Polish, that were going to make them rich and famous overnight. The *croisette* was packed with professionals and amateurs, veterans and tyros, comers, and has-beens, all competing for the prestigious prizes. Being awarded a prize at the Cannes Film Festival meant money in the bank, if the winner had no distribution deal, he could get one, and if he already had one, he could better it.

Every hotel in Cannes was filled, and the overflow had spilled up and down the coast to Antibes, Beaulieu, Saint-Tropez and Menton. The residents of the small villages gaped in awe at the famous faces that filled their streets and restaurants and bars.

Every room had been reserved for months ahead, but Toby Temple had no difficulty getting a large suite at the Carlton. Toby and Jill were feted everywhere they went. News photographers' cameras clicked incessantly, and their images were sent around the world. The Golden Couple, the King and Queen of Hollywood. The reporters interviewed Jill and asked for her opinions on everything from French wines to African politics. It was a far cry from Josephine Czinski of Odessa, Texas.

Toby's picture did not win the award, but two nights before the festival was to end, the Judges Committee announced that they were presenting a special award to Toby Temple for his contribution to the field of entertainment.

It was a black-tie affair, and the large banquet hall at the Carlton Hotel overflowed with guests. Jill was seated on the dais next to Toby. She noticed that he was not eating. "What's the matter, darling?" she asked.

Toby shook his head. "Probably had too much sun today. I feel a little woozy."

"Tomorrow I'm going to see that you rest." Jill had scheduled interviews for Toby with *Paris Match* and the London *Times* in the morning, luncheon with a group of television reporters, followed by a cocktail party. She decided she would cancel the least important.

At the conclusion of dinner, the mayor of Cannes rose to his feet and introduced Toby. "*Mesdames, messieurs, et invités dis-*

tingués c'est un grand privilège des vous présente un homme dont l'oeuvre a donné plaisir et bonheur au monde entier. J'ai l'honneur de lui présenter cette medaille spéciale, un signe de notre affection et de notre appréciation." He held up a gold medal and ribbon and bowed to Toby. "Monsieur Toby Temple!" There was an enthusiastic burst of applause from the audience, as everyone in the great banquet hall rose to his feet in a standing ovation. Toby was seated in his chair, not moving.

"Get up," Jill whispered.

Slowly, Toby rose, pale and unsteady. He stood there a moment, smiled, then started toward the microphone. Halfway there, he stumbled and fell to the floor, unconscious.

Toby Temple was flown to Paris in a French air force transport jet and rushed to the American Hospital, where he was put in the intensive-care ward. The finest specialists in France were summoned, while Jill sat in a private room at the hospital, waiting. For thirty-six hours she refused to eat or drink or take any of the phone calls that were flooding into the hospital from all over the world.

She sat alone, staring at the walls, neither seeing nor hearing the stir of activity around her. Her mind was focused on only one thing: *Toby had to get well.* Toby was her sun, and if the sun went out, the shadow would die. She could not allow that to happen.

It was five o'clock in the morning when Doctor Duclos, the chief of staff, entered the private room Jill had taken so she could be near Toby.

"Mrs. Temple—I am afraid there is no point in trying to soften the blow. Your husband has suffered a massive stroke. In all probability, he will never be able to walk or speak again."

W hen they finally allowed Jill into Toby's hospital room in Paris, she was shocked by his appearance. Overnight, Toby had become old and desiccated, as if all his vital fluids had drained out of him. He had lost partial use of both arms and legs, and though he was able to make grunting animal noises, he could not speak.

It was six weeks before the doctors would permit Toby to be moved. When Toby and Jill arrived back in California, they were mobbed at the airport by the press and television media and hundreds of well-wishers. Toby Temple's illness had caused a major sensation. There were constant phone calls from friends inquiring about Toby's health and progress. Television crews tried to get into the house to take pictures of him. There were messages from the President and senators, and thousands of letters and postcards from fans who loved Toby Temple and were praying for him.

But the invitations had stopped. No one was calling to find out how *Jill* felt, or whether she would like to attend a quiet dinner or take a drive or see a movie. Nobody in Hollywood cared a damn about *Jill*.

She had brought in Toby's personal physician, Dr. Eli Kaplan, and he had summoned two top neurologists, one from UCLA Medical Center and the other from Johns Hopkins. Their diagnosis was exactly the same as that of Dr. Duclos, in Paris.

"It's important to understand," Dr. Kaplan told Jill, "that Toby's mind is not impaired in any way. He can hear and understand everything you say, but his speech and motor functions are affected. He can't respond."

"Is—is he always going to be like this?"

Dr. Kaplan hesitated. "It's impossible to be absolutely certain, of course, but in our opinion, his nervous system has been too badly damaged for therapy to have any appreciable effect."

"But you don't know for sure."

"No . . ."

But Jill knew.

In addition to the three nurses who tended Toby round the clock, Jill arranged for a physiotherapist to come to the house every morning to work with Toby. The therapist carried Toby into the pool and held him in his arms, gently stretching the muscles and tendons, while Toby feebly tried to kick his legs and move his arms about in the warm water. There was no progress. On the fourth week, a speech therapist was brought in. She spent one hour every afternoon trying to help Toby learn to speak again, to form the sounds of words.

After two months, Jill could see no change. None at all. She sent for Dr. Kaplan.

"You've got to do something to help him," she demanded. "You can't leave him like this."

He looked at her helplessly. "I'm sorry, Jill. I tried to tell you. . . ."

Jill sat in the library, alone, long after Dr. Kaplan had gone. She could feel one of the bad headaches beginning, but there was no time to think of herself now. She went upstairs.

Toby was propped up in bed, staring at nothingness. As Jill walked up to him, Toby's deep blue eyes lit up. They followed Jill, bright and alive, as she approached his bed and looked down at him. His lips moved and some unintelligible sound came out. Tears of frustration began to fill his eyes. Jill remembered Dr. Kaplan's words, *It's important to understand that his mind is not impaired in any way.*

Jill sat down on the edge of the bed. "Toby, I want you to listen to me. You're going to get out of that bed. You're going to walk and you're going to talk." The tears were running down the sides of his cheeks now. "You're going to do it," Jill said. "You're going to do it for me."

The following morning, Jill fired the nurses, the psysiotherapist and the speech therapist. As soon as he heard the news, Dr. Eli Kaplan hurried over to see Jill.

"I agree with you about the physiotherapist, Jill—but the *nurses!* Toby has to have someone with him twenty-four hours a—"

"I'll be with him."

He shook his head. "You have no idea what you're letting yourself in for. One person can't—"

"I'll call you if I need you."

She sent him away.

The ordeal began.

Jill was going to attempt to do what the doctors had assured her could not be done. The first time she picked Toby up and put him into his wheelchair, it frightened her to feel how weightless he was. She took him downstairs in the elevator that had been installed and began to work with him in the swimming pool, as she had seen the physiotherapist do. But what happened now was different. Where the therapist had been gentle and coaxing, Jill was stern and unrelenting. When Toby tried to speak, signifying that he was tired and could not bear any more, Jill said, "You're not through. One more time. For me, Toby."

And she would force him to do it one more time.

And yet again, until he sat mutely crying with exhaustion.

In the afternoon, Jill set to work to teach Toby to speak again. "Ooh . . . ooooooooh."

"Ahaaahh . . . aaaaaaaaagh . . ."

"No! Ooooooooooh. Round your lips, Toby. Make them obey you. Oooooooh."

"Aaaaaaaaaah . . ."

"No goddamn you! You're going to speak! Now, say it— Ooooooooooooh!"

And he would try again.

Jill would feed him each night, and then lie in his bed, holding him in her arms. She drew his useless hands slowly up and down her body, across her breasts and down the soft cleft between her legs. "Feel that, Toby," she whispered. "That's all yours, darling. It belongs to you. I want you. I want you to get well so we can make love again. I want you to fuck me, Toby."

He looked at her with those alive, bright eyes and made incoherent, whimpering sounds.

"Soon, Toby, soon."

Jill was tireless. She discharged the servants because she did not want anyone around. After that, she did all the cooking herself. She ordered her groceries by phone and never left the house. In the beginning, Jill had been kept busy answering the telephones, but the calls had soon dwindled to a trickle, then ceased. Newscasters had stopped giving bulletins on Toby Temple's condition. The world knew that he was dying. It was just a question of time.

But Jill was not going to let Toby die. If he died, she would die with him.

The days blended into one long, endless round of drudgery. Jill was up at six o'clock in the morning. First, she would clean Toby. He was totally incontinent. Even though he wore a catheter and a diaper, he would befoul himself during the night and the bedclothes would sometimes have to be changed, as well as Toby's pajamas. The stench in the bedroom was almost unbearable. Jill filled a basin with warm water, took a sponge and soft cloth and cleaned the feces and urine from Toby's body. When he was clean, she dried him off and powdered him, then shaved him and combed his hair.

"There. You look beautiful, Toby. Your fans should see you now. But they'll see you soon. They'll fight to get in to see you. The President will be there—everybody will be there to see Toby Temple."

Then Jill prepared Toby's breakfast. She made oatmeal or cream of wheat or scrambled eggs, food she could spoon into his mouth. She fed him as though he were a baby, talking to him all the time, promising that he was going to get well.

"You're Toby Temple," she intoned. "Everybody loves you, everybody wants you back. Your fans out there are waiting for you, Toby. You've got to get well for them."

And another long, punishing day would begin.

She wheeled his useless, crippled body down to the pool for his exercises. After that, she massaged him and worked on his speech therapy. Then it was time for her to prepare his lunch, and after lunch it would begin all over again. Through it all, Jill kept telling Toby how wonderful he was, how much he was loved. He was Toby Temple, and the world was waiting for him to come back to it. At night she would take out one of his scrapbooks and hold it up so he could see it.

"There we are with the Queen. Do you remember how they all cheered you that night? That's the way it's going to be again. You're going to be bigger than ever, Toby, bigger than ever."

She tucked him in at night and crawled into the cot she had put next to his bed, drained. In the middle of the night, she would be awakened by the noisome stench of Toby's bowel movement in bed. She would drag herself from her cot and change Toby's diaper and clean him. By then it would be time to start fixing his breakfast and begin another day.

And another. In an endless march of days.

Each day Jill pushed Toby a little harder, a little further. Her nerves were so frayed that, if she felt Toby was not trying, she would slap him across the face. "We're going to beat them," she said fiercely. "You're going to get well."

Jill's body was exhausted from the punishing routine she was putting herself through, but when she lay down at night sleep eluded her. There were too many visions dancing through her head, like scenes from old movies. She and Toby mobbed by reporters at the Cannes Festival . . . The President at their Palm Springs home, telling Jill how beautiful she was . . . Fans crowding around Toby and her at a premiere . . . The Golden Couple . . . Toby stepping up to receive his medal and falling . . . falling . . . Finally, she would drift off to sleep.

Sometimes, Jill would awaken with a sudden, fierce headache that would not go away. She would lie there in the loneliness of the dark, fighting the pain, until the sun would come up, and it was time to drag herself to her feet.

And it would begin all over again. It was as though she and Toby were the lone survivors of some long-forgotten holocaust. Her world had shrunk to the dimensions of this house, these rooms, this man. She drove herself relentlessly from dawn until past midnight.

And she drove Toby, her Toby imprisoned in hell, in a world where there was only Jill, whom he must blindly obey.

The weeks, dreary and painful, dragged by and turned into months. Now, Toby would begin to cry when he saw Jill coming toward him, for he knew he was going to be punished. Each day Jill became more merciless. She forced Toby's flopping, useless limbs to move, until he was in unbearable agony. He made horrible gurgling pleas for her to stop, but Jill would say, "Not yet. Not until you're a man again, not until we show them all." She would go on kneading his exhausted muscles. He was a helpless, full-grown baby, a vegetable, a nothing. But when Jill looked at him, she saw him as he was going to be, and she declared, "You're going to walk!"

She would lift him to his feet and hold him up while she forced one leg after the other, so that he was moving in a grotesque parody of motion, like a drunken, disjointed marionette.

Her headaches had become more frequent. Bright lights or a loud noise or sudden movement would set them off. *I must see a doctor*, she thought. *Later, when Tony is well again.* Now there was no time or room for herself.

Only Toby.

It was as though Jill were possessed. Her clothes hung loosely on her, but she had no idea of how much weight she had lost or how she looked. Her face was thin and drawn, her eyes hollow. Her once beautiful shiny hair was lusterless and stringy. She did not know, nor would she have cared.

One day Jill found a telegram under the door asking her to phone Dr. Kaplan. No time. The routine must be kept.

The days and nights became a Kafkaesque blur of bathing Toby and exercising him and changing him and shaving him and feeding him.

And then starting all over again.

She got a walker for Toby and fastened his fingers around it and moved his legs, holding him up, trying to show him the motions, walking him back and forth across the room until she was asleep on her feet, not knowing any longer where or who she was, or what she was doing.

Then, one day, Jill knew that it had all come to an end.

She had been up with Toby half the night and had finally gone into her own bedroom, where she had fallen into a dazed slumber just before dawn. When Jill awakened, the sun was high in the sky. She had slept long past noon. Toby had not been fed or bathed or changed. He was lying in his bed, helpless, waiting for her, probably panicky. Jill started to rise and found that she could not move. She was filled with such a bottomless, bone-deep weariness that her exhausted body would no longer obey her. She lay there, helpless, knowing that she had lost, that it had all been wasted, all the days and nights of hell, the months of agony, none of it had meant anything. Her body had betrayed her, as Toby's had betrayed him. Jill had no strength left to give him anymore, and it made her want to weep. It was finished.

She heard a sound at her bedroom door and she raised her eyes. Toby was standing in the doorway, by himself, his trembling arms clutching his walker, his mouth making unintelligible slobbering noises, working to say something.

"Jiiiiiigh . . . Jiiiiiigh . . ."

He was trying to say "Jill." She began to sob uncontrollably and she could not stop.

From that day on, Toby's progress was spectacular. For the first time, *he* knew he was going to get well. He no longer objected when Jill pushed him beyond the limits of his endurance. He welcomed it. He wanted to get well for *her*. Jill had become his goddess; if he had loved her before, he worshiped her now.

And something had happened to Jill. Before, it had been her own life she was fighting for; Toby was merely the instrument she was forced to use. But somehow, that had changed. It was as though Toby had become a part of her. They were one body and one mind and one soul, obsessed with the same purpose. They had gone through a purging crucible. His life had been in her hands, and she had nurtured it and strengthened it, and saved it, and out of that had grown a kind of love. Toby belonged to her, just as she belonged to him.

Jill changed Toby's diet, so that he began to regain the weight he had lost. He spent time in the sun every day and took long walks around the grounds, using the walker, then a cane, building up his strength. When the day came that Toby could walk by himself, the two of them celebrated by having a candlelight dinner in the dining room.

Finally, Jill felt that Toby was ready to be seen. She telephoned Dr. Kaplan, and his nurse put him on the phone immediately.

"Jill! I've been terribly worried. I've tried to telephone you and there was never any answer. I sent a telegram, and when I didn't hear, I assumed you had taken Toby away somewhere. Is he—has he—"

"Come and see for yourself, Eli."

Dr. Kaplan could not conceal his astonishment. "It's unbelievable," he told Jill. "It's—it's like a miracle."

"It is a miracle," Jill said. *Only in this life you made your own miracles, because God was busy elsewhere.*

"People still call me to ask about Toby," Dr. Kaplan was saying. "Apparently they've been unable to get through to you. Sam Winters calls at least once a week. Clifton Lawrence has been calling."

Jill dismissed Clifton Lawrence. But Sam Winters! That was good. Jill had to find a way to let the world know that Toby Temple was still a superstar, that they were still the Golden Couple.

Jill telephoned Sam Winters the next morning and asked him if he would like to come and visit Toby. Sam arrived at the house an hour later. Jill opened the front door to let him in, and Sam tried to conceal his shock at her appearance. Jill looked ten years older than when he had last seen her. Her eyes were hollow brown pools and her face was etched with deep lines. She had lost so much weight that she looked almost skeletal.

"Thank you for coming, Sam. Toby will be pleased to see you."

Sam had been prepared to see Toby in bed, a shadow of the man he had once been, but he was in for a stunning surprise. Toby was lying on a pad alongside the pool and, as Sam approached, Toby rose to his feet, a little slowly, but steadily, and held out a firm hand. He appeared tanned and healthy, better than he had looked before his stroke. It was as though through some arcane alchemy, Jill's health and vitality had flowed into Toby's body, and the sick tides that had ravaged Toby had ebbed into Jill.

"Hey! It's great to see you, Sam."

Toby's speech was a little slower and more precise than before, but it was clear and strong. There was no sign of the paralysis Sam had heard about. There was still the same boyish face with the bright blue eyes. Sam gave Toby a hug and said, "Jesus, you really had us scared."

Toby grinned and said, "You don't have to call me 'Jesus' when we're alone."

Sam looked at Toby more closely and marveled. "I honestly can't get over it. Damn it, you look *younger*. The whole town was making funeral arrangements."

"Over my dead body," Toby smiled.

Sam said, "It's fantastic what the doctors today can—"

"No doctors." Toby turned to look at Jill and naked adoration shone from his eyes. "You want to know who did it? Jill. Just Jill. With her two bare hands. She threw everybody out and made me get on my feet again."

Sam glanced at Jill, puzzled. She had not seemed to him the kind of girl capable of such a selfless act. Perhaps he had misjudged her. "What are your plans?" he asked Toby. "I suppose you'll want to rest and—"

"He's going back to work," Jill said. "Toby's too talented to be sitting around doing nothing."

"I'm raring to go," Toby agreed.

"Perhaps Sam has a project for you," Jill suggested.

They were both watching him. Sam did not want to discourage Toby, but neither did he want to hold out any false hopes. It was not possible to make a picture with a star unless you got insurance on him, and no company was going to insure Toby Temple.

"There's nothing in the shop at the moment," Sam said carefully. "But I'll certainly keep an eye open."

"You're afraid to use him, aren't you?" It was as though she was reading his mind.

"Certainly not." But they both knew he was lying.

No one in Hollywood would take a chance on using Toby Temple again.

Toby and Jill were watching a young comedian on television.

"He's rotten," Toby snorted. "Damn it, I wish I could get back on the air. Maybe I oughta get an agent. Somebody who could check around town and see what's doing."

"No!" Jill's tone was firm. "We're not going to let anyone peddle you. You're not some bum looking for a job. You're Toby

Temple. We're going to make them come to you."

Toby smiled wryly and said, "They're not beating down the doors, baby."

"They will be," Jill promised. "They don't know what shape you're in. You're better now than you ever were. We just have to show them."

"Maybe I should pose in the nude for one of those magazines."

Jill was not listening. "I have an idea," she said slowly. "A one-man show."

"Huh?"

"A one-man show." There was a growing excitement in her voice. "I'm going to book you into the Huntington Hartford Theatre. Everybody in Hollywood will come. After *that*, they'll start beating down the doors!"

And everybody in Hollywood did come; producers, directors, stars, critics—all the people in show business who mattered. The theater on Vine Street had long since been sold out, and hundreds of people had been turned away. There was a cheering mob outside the lobby when Toby and Jill arrived in a chauffeur-driven limousine. He was *their* Toby Temple. He had come back to them from the dead, and they adored him more than ever.

The audience inside the theater was there partly out of respect for a man who had been famous and great, but mostly out of curiosity. They were there to pay final tribute to a dying hero, a burnt-out star.

Jill had planned the show herself. She had gone to O'Hanlon and Rainger, and they had written some brilliant material, beginning with a monologue kidding the town for burying Toby while he was still alive. Jill had approached a song-writing team that had won three Academy Awards. They had never written special material for anyone, but when Jill said, "Toby insists you're the only writers in the world who . . ."

Dick Landry, the director, flew in from London to stage the show.

Jill had assembled the finest talent she could find to back up Toby, but in the end everything would depend on the star himself. It was a one-man show, and he would be alone on that stage.

The moment finally arrived. The house lights dimmed, and the theater was filled with that expectant hush that precedes the ringing up of the curtain, the silent prayer that on this night magic would happen.

It happened.

As Toby Temple strolled out onto the stage, his gait strong and steady, that familiar impish smile lighting up that boyish face, there was a momentary silence and then a wild explosion of applause and yelling, a standing ovation that rocked the theater for a full five minutes.

Toby stood there, waiting for the pandemonium to subside, and when the theater was finally still, he said, "You call *that* a reception?" And they roared.

He was brilliant. He told stories and sang and danced, and he attacked everybody, and it was as though he had never been gone. The audience could not get enough of him. He was still a superstar, but now he was something more; he had become a living legend.

The *Variety* review the next day said, "They came to bury Toby Temple, but they stayed to praise him and cheer him. And how he deserved it! There is no one in show business who has the old master's magic. It was an evening of ovations, and no one who was fortunate enough to be there is likely ever to forget that memorable . . ."

The *Hollywood Reporter* review said, "The audience was there to see a great star come back, but Toby Temple proved he had never been away."

All the other reviews were in the same panegyric vein. From that moment on, Toby's phones rang constantly. Letters and telegrams poured in with invitations and offers.

They were beating the doors down.

Toby repeated his one-man show in Chicago and in Washington and New York; everywhere he went, he was a sensation. There was more interest in him now than there had ever been. In a wave of affectionate nostalgia, Toby's old movies were shown at art theaters and at universities. Television stations had a Toby Temple Week and ran his old variety shows.

There were Toby Temple dolls and Toby Temple games and Toby Temple puzzles and jokebooks and T-shirts. There were endorsements for coffee and cigarettes and toothpaste.

Toby did a cameo in a musical picture at Universal and was

signed to do guest appearances on all the big variety shows. The networks had writers at work, competing to develop a new Toby Temple Hour.

The sun was out once more, and it was shining on Jill.

There were parties again, and receptions and this ambassador and that senator and private screenings and . . . Everybody wanted them for everything. They were given a dinner at the White House, an honor usually reserved for heads of state. They were applauded wherever they appeared.

But now it was Jill they were applauding, as well as Toby. The magnificent story of what she had done, her feat of single-handedly nursing Toby back to health, against all odds, had stirred the imagination of the world. It was hailed by the press as the love story of the century. *Time* Magazine put them both on the cover, with a glowing tribute to Jill in the accompanying story.

A five-million-dollar deal was made for Toby to star in a new weekly television variety show, starting in September, only twelve weeks away.

"We'll go to Palm Springs so that you can rest until then," Jill said.

Toby shook his head. "You've been shut in long enough. We're going to live a little." He put his arms around her and added, "I'm not very good with words, baby, unless they're jokes. I don't know how to tell you what I feel about you. I—I just want you to know that I didn't start living until the day I met you."

And he abruptly turned away, so that Jill could not see the tears in his eyes.

Toby arranged to tour his one-man show in London, Paris and— the greatest coup of all—Moscow. Everyone was fighting to sign him. He was as big a cult figure in Europe as he was in America.

They were out on the *Jill*, on a sunny, sparkling day, headed for Catalina. There were a dozen guests aboard the boat, among them Sam Winters and O'Hanlon and Rainger, who had been selected as the head writers on Toby's new television show. They were all in the salon, playing games and talking. Jill looked around and noticed that Toby was missing. She went out on deck.

Toby was standing at the railing, staring at the sea. Jill walked up to him and said, "Are you feeling all right?"

"Just watching the water, baby."

"It's beautiful, isn't it?"

"If you're a shark." He shuddered. "That's not the way I want to die. I've always been terrified of drowning."

She put her hand in his. "What's bothering you?"

He looked at her. "I guess I don't want to die. I'm afraid of what's out there. *Here*, I'm a big man. Everybody knows Toby Temple. But out there. . . ? You know my idea of Hell? A place where there's no audience."

The Friars Club gave a Roast with Toby Temple as the guest of honor. A dozen top comics were on the dais, along with Toby and Jill, Sam Winters and the head of the network that Toby had signed with. Jill was asked to stand up and take a bow. It became a standing ovation.

They're cheering me, Jill thought. *Not Toby. Me!*

The master of ceremonies was the host of a famous nighttime television talk show. "I can't tell you how happy I am to see Toby here," he said. "Because if we weren't honoring him *here* tonight, we'd be holding this banquet at Forest Lawn."

Laughter.

"And believe me, the food's terrible there. Have you ever eaten at Forest Lawn? They serve leftovers from the Last Supper."

Laughter.

He turned to Toby. "We really are proud of you, Toby. I mean that. I understand you've been asked to donate a part of your body to science. They're going to put it in a jar at the Harvard Medical School. The only problem so far is that they haven't been able to find a jar big enough to hold it."

Roars.

When Toby got up for his rebuttal, he topped them all.

Everyone agreed that it was the best Roast the Friars had ever had.

Clifton Lawrence was in the audience that night.

He was seated at a table in the back of the room near the kitchen with the other unimportant people. He had been forced to impose on old friendships to get even this table. Ever since Toby Temple had fired him, Clifton Lawrence had worn the label of a loser. He had tried to make a partnership deal with a large agency. With no clients, however, he had nothing to offer. Then Clifton had tried the smaller agencies, but they were not interested in a middle-aged has-been; they wanted aggressive young men. In the end, Clifton had settled for a salaried job with a small new agency. His weekly salary was less than what he had once spent in one evening at Romanoff's.

He remembered his first new day at the new agency. It was owned by three aggressive young men—no, *kids*—all of them in their late twenties. Their clients were rock stars. Two of the agents were bearded, and they all wore jeans and sport shirts and tennis shoes without socks. They made Clifton feel a thousand years old. They spoke in a language he did not understand. They called him "Dad" and "Pop" and he thought of the respect he had once commanded in this town, and he wanted to weep.

The once dapper, cheerful agent had become seedy-looking and bitter. Toby Temple had been his whole life, and Clifton talked about those days compulsively. It was all he thought about. That and Jill. Clifton blamed her for everything that had happened to him. Toby could not help himself; he had been influenced by that bitch. But, oh, how Clifton hated Jill.

He was sitting in the back of the room watching the crowd applaud Jill Temple when one of the men at the table said, "Toby's sure a lucky bastard. I wish I had a piece of that. She's great in bed."

"Yeah?" someone asked, cynically. "How would *you* know?"

"She's in that porno flick at the Pussycat Theatre. Hell, I thought she was going to suck the guy's liver out of him."

Clifton's mouth was suddenly so dry that he could hardly get out the words. "Are you—are you sure it was Jill Castle?" he asked.

The stranger turned to him. "Sure, I'm sure. She used another name—Josephine something. A crazy Polack name." He stared at Clifton and said, "Hey! Didn't you used to be Clifton Lawrence?"

There is an area of Santa Monica Boulevard, bordering between Fairfax and La Cienega, that is County territory. Part of an island surrounded by the City of Los Angeles, it operates under County ordinances, which are more lenient than those of the City. In one six-block area, there are four movie houses that run only hard-core pornography, half a dozen bookshops where customers can stand in private booths and watch movies through individual viewers and a dozen massage parlors staffed with nubile young girls who are experts at giving everything except massages. The Pussycat Theatre sits in the midst of it all.

There were perhaps two dozen people in the darkened theater, all of them men except for two women who sat holding hands. Clifton looked around at the audience and wondered what drove these people to darkened caverns in the middle of a sunny day, to spend hours watching images of other people fornicating on film.

The main feature came on, and Clifton forgot everything except what was up on the screen. He leaned forward in his seat, concentrating on the face of each actress. The plot was about a young college professor who smuggled his female students into his bedroom for night classes. All of them were young, surprisingly attractive and incredibly endowed. They went through a variety of sexual exercises, oral, vaginal and anal, until the professor was as satisfied as his pupils.

But none of the girls was Jill. *She has to be there*, Clifton thought. This was the only chance he would ever have to avenge himself for what she had done to him. He would arrange for Toby to see the film. It would hurt Toby, but he would get over it. Jill would be destroyed. When Toby learned what kind of whore he had married, he would throw her out on her ass. Jill *had* to be in this film.

And suddenly, there she was—on the wide screen, in wonderful, glorious, living color. She had changed a great deal. She was thinner now, more beautiful and more sophisticated. But it was Jill. Clifton sat there, drinking in the scene, reveling in it, rejoicing and feasting his senses, filled with an electrifying sense of triumph and vengeance.

Clifton remained in his seat until the credits came on. There it was, *Josephine Czinski*. He got to his feet and made his way back to the projection booth. A man in shirt sleeves was inside the small room, reading a racing form. He glanced up as Clifton entered and said, "No one's allowed in here, buddy."

"I want to buy a print of that picture."

The man shook his head. "Not for sale." He went back to his handicapping.

"I'll give you a hundred bucks to run off a dupe. No one will ever know."

The man did not even look up.

"Two hundred bucks," Clifton said.

The projectionist turned a page.

"Three hundred."

He looked up and studied Clifton. "Cash?"

"Cash."

At ten o'clock the following morning, Clifton arrived at Toby Temple's house with a can of film under his arm. *No, not film,* he thought happily. *Dynamite. Enough to blow Jill Castle to hell.*

The door was opened by an English butler Clifton had not seen before.

"Tell Mr. Temple that Clifton Lawrence is here to see him."

"I'm sorry, sir. Mr. Temple is not here."

"I'll wait," Clifton said firmly.

The butler replied, "I'm afraid that won't be possible. Mr. and Mrs. Temple left for Europe this morning."

Europe was a succession of triumphs.

The night of Toby's opening at the Palladium in London, Oxford Circus was jammed with crowds frantically trying to get a glimpse of Toby and Jill. The entire area around Argyll Street had been cordoned off by the metropolitan police. When the mob got out of hand, mounted police were hastily summoned to assist. Precisely at the stroke of eight o'clock, the Royal Family arrived and the show began.

Toby exceeded everyone's wildest expectations. His face beaming with innocence, he brilliantly attacked the British government and its old-school-tie smugness. He explained how it had managed to become less powerful than Uganda and how it could not have happened to a more deserving country. They all roared with laughter, because they knew that Toby Temple was only joking. He did not mean a word of it. Toby loved them.

As they loved him.

The reception in Paris was even more tumultuous. Jill and Toby were guests at the President's Palace and were driven around the city in a state limousine. They could be seen on the front pages of the newspapers every day, and when they appeared at the theater, extra police had to be called out to control the crowds. At the end of Toby's performance, he and Jill were being escorted toward their waiting limousine when suddenly the mob broke through the police guard and hundreds of Frenchmen descended on them, screaming, "Toby, Toby . . . *on veut Toby!*" The surging crowd held out pens and autograph books, pressing forward to touch the great Toby Temple and his wonderful Jill. The police were unable to hold them back; the crowd swept them aside, tearing at Toby's clothes, fighting to obtain a souvenir. Toby and Jill were almost crushed by the press of bodies, but Jill felt no fear. This riot was a tribute to *her*. She had done this for these people; she had brought Toby back to them.

Their last stop was Moscow.

Moscow in June is one of the loveliest cities in the world. Graceful white *berezka* and Lipa trees with yellow flowerbeds line the wide boulevards crowded with natives and visitors strolling in the sunshine. It is the season for tourists. Except for official visitors, all tourists to Russia are handled through Intourist, the government-controlled agency which arranges transportation, hotels and guided sightseeing tours. But Toby and Jill were met at the Sheremetyevo International Airport by a large Zil limousine and driven to the Metropole Hotel, usually reserved for VIPs from satellite countries. The suite had been stocked with Stolichnaya vodka and black caviar.

General Yuri Romanovitch, a high party official, came to the hotel to bid them welcome. "We do not run many American pictures in Russia, Mr. Temple, but we have played your movies here often. The Russian people feel that genius transcends all boundaries."

Toby had been booked to appear at the Bolshoi Theatre for three performances. Opening night, Jill shared in the ovation. Because of the language barrier, Toby did most of his act in pantomime, and the audience adored him. He gave a diatribe in his pseudo-Russian, and their laughter and applause echoed through the enormous theater like a benediction of love.

During the next two days, General Romanovitch escorted Toby and Jill on a private sightseeing tour. They went to Gorky Park and rode on the giant ferris wheel, and saw the historic Saint Basil's Cathedral. They were taken to the Moscow State Circus and given a banquet at Aragvi, where they were served the golden roe caviar, the rarest of the eight caviars, *zakushki*, which literally means *small bites*, and *pashteet*, the delicate paté baked in a crust. For dessert, they ate *yoblochnaya*, the incredibly delicious apple charlotte pastry with apricot sauce.

And more sightseeing. They went to the Pushkin Art Museum

and Lenin's Mausoleum and the Detsky Mir, Moscow's enchanting children's shop.

They were taken to places of whose existence most Russians were unaware. Granovsko Street, crowded with chauffeur-driven Chaikas and Volgas. Inside, behind a simple door marked "Office of Special Passes," they were ushered into a store crammed with imported luxury foodstuffs from all over the world. This was where the "Nachalstvo," the Russian elite, were privileged to shop.

They went to a luxurious *dacha,* where foreign films were run in the private screening room for the privileged few. It was a fascinating insight into the People's State.

On the afternoon of the day Toby was to give his final performance, the Temples were getting ready to go out shopping. Toby said, "Why don't you go alone, baby? I think I'll sack out for a while."

She studied him for a moment. "Are you feeling all right?"

"Great. I'm just a little tired. You go buy out Moscow."

Jill hesitated. Toby looked pale. When this tour was over, she would see to it that Toby had a long rest before he began his new television show. "All right," she agreed. "Take a nap."

Jill was walking through the lobby toward the exit when she heard a man's voice call, "Josephine," and even as she turned, she knew who it was, and in a split second the magic happened again.

David Kenyon was moving toward her, smiling and saying, "I'm so glad to see you," and she felt as though her heart would stop. *He's the only man who has ever been able to do this to me,* Jill thought.

"Will you have a drink with me?" David asked.

"Yes," she said.

The hotel bar was large and crowded, but they found a comparatively quiet table in a corner where they could talk.

"What are you doing in Moscow?" Jill asked.

"Our government asked me to come over. We're trying to work out an oil deal."

A bored waiter strolled over to the table and took their order for drinks.

"How's Cissy?"

David looked at her a moment, then said, "We got a divorce a few years ago." He deliberately changed the subject. "I've followed everything that's been happening to you. I've been a fan of Toby Temple's since I was a kid." Somehow, it made Toby sound very old. "I'm glad he's well again. When I read about his stroke, I was concerned about you." There was a look in his eyes that Jill remembered from long ago, a wanting, a needing.

"I thought Toby was great in Hollywood and London," David was saying.

"Were you there?" Jill asked, in surprise.

"Yes." Then he added quickly, "I had some business there."

"Why didn't you come backstage?"

He hesitated. "I didn't want to intrude on you. I didn't know if you would want to see me."

Their drinks arrived in heavy, squat glasses.

"To you and Toby," David said. And there was something in the way he said it, an undercurrent of sadness, a hunger . . .

"Do you always stay at the Metropole?" Jill asked.

"No. As a matter of fact, I had a hell of a time getting—" He saw the trap too late. He smiled wryly. "I knew you'd be there. I was supposed to have left Moscow five days ago. I've been waiting, hoping to run into you."

"Why, David?"

It was a long time before he replied. When he spoke, he said, "It's all too late now, but I want to tell you anyway, because I think you have a right to know."

And he told her about his marriage to Cissy, how she had tricked him, about her attempted suicide, and about the night when he had asked Jill to meet him at the lake. It all came out in an outpouring of emotion that left Jill shaken.

"I've always been in love with you."

She sat listening, a feeling of happiness flowing through her body like a warm wine. It was like a lovely dream come true, it was everything she had wanted, wished for. Jill studied the man sitting across from her, and she remembered his strong hands on her, and his hard demanding body, and she felt a stirring within herself. But Toby had become a part of her, he was her own flesh; and David . . .

A voice at her elbow said, "Mrs. Temple! We have been looking everywhere for you!" It was General Romanovitch.

Jill looked at David. "Call me in the morning."

Toby's last performance in the Bolshoi Theatre was more exciting than anything that had been seen there before. The spectators threw flowers and cheered and stamped their feet and refused to leave. It was a fitting climax to Toby's other triumphs. A large party was scheduled for after the show, but Toby said to Jill, "I'm beat, goddess. Why don't you go? I'll return to the hotel and get some shut-eye."

Jill went to the party alone, but it was as though David were at her side every moment. She carried on conversations with her hosts and danced and acknowledged the tributes they were paying to her, but all the time her mind was reliving her meeting with David. *I married the wrong girl. Cissy and I are divorced. I've never stopped loving you.*

At two o'clock in the morning, Jill's escort dropped her at her hotel suite. She went inside and found Toby lying on the floor in the middle of the room, unconscious, his right hand stretched out toward the telephone.

Toby Temple was rushed in an ambulance to the Diplomatic Polyclinic at 3 Sverchkov Prospekt. Three top specialists were summoned in the middle of the night to examine him. Everyone was sympathetic toward Jill. The chief of the hospital escorted her to a private office, where she waited for news. *It's like a rerun,* Jill thought. *All this had happened before.* It had a vague, unreal quality.

Hours later, the door to the office opened and a short, fat Russian waddled in. He was dressed in an ill-fitting suit and looked like an unsuccessful plumber. "I am Dr. Durov," he said. "I am in charge of your husband's case."

"I want to know how he is."

"Sit down, Mrs. Temple, please."

Jill had not even been aware that she had stood up. "Tell me!"

"Your husband has suffered a stroke—technically called a cerebral venous thrombosis."

"How bad is it?"

"It is the most—what do you say?—hard-hitting, dangerous. If your husband lives—and it is too soon to tell—he will never walk or speak again. His mind is clear but he is completely paralyzed."

Before Jill left Moscow, David telephoned her.

"I can't tell you how sorry I am," he said. "I'll be standing by.

Anytime you need me, I'll be there. Remember that."

It was the only thing that helped Jill keep her sanity in the nightmare that was about to begin.

The journey home was a hellish déja vu. The hospital litter in the plane, the ambulance from the airport to the house, the sick-room.

Except that this time it was *not* the same. Jill had known it the moment they had allowed her to see Toby. His heart was beating, his vital organs functioning; in every respect he was a living organism. And yet he was not. He was a breathing pulsating corpse, a dead man in an oxygen tent, with tubes and needles running into his body like antennae, feeding him the vital fluids that were necessary to keep him alive. His face was twisted in a horrifying rictus that made him look as though he were grinning, his lips pulled up so that his gums were exposed. *I am afraid I can offer you no hope,* the Russian doctor had said.

That had been weeks ago. Now they were back home in Bel-Air. Jill had immediately called in Dr. Kaplan, and he had sent for specialists who had summoned more specialists, and the answer always came out the same: a massive stroke that had heavily damaged or destroyed the nerve centers, with very little chance of reversing the damage that had already been done.

There were nurses around the clock and a physiotherapist to work with Toby, but they were empty gestures.

The object of all this attention was grotesque. Toby's skin had turned yellow, and his hair was falling out in large tufts. His paralyzed limbs were shriveled and stringy. On his face was the hideous grin that he could not control. He was monstrous to look at, a death's head.

But his eyes were alive. And how alive! They blazed with the power and frustration of the mind trapped in that useless shell. Whenever Jill walked into his room, Toby's eyes would follow her hungrily, frantically, pleading. For what? For her to make him walk again? Talk again? To turn him into a man again?

She would stare down at him, silent, thinking: *A part of me is lying in that bed, suffering, trapped.* They were bound together. She would have given anything to have saved Toby, to have saved herself. But she knew that there was no way. Not this time.

The phones rang constantly, and it was a replay of all those other phone calls, all those other offers of sympathy.

But there was one phone call that was different. David Kenyon telephoned. "I just want you to know that whatever I can do—anything at all—I'm waiting."

Jill thought of how he looked, tall and handsome and strong, and she thought of the misshapen caricature of a man in the next room. "Thank you, David. I appreciate it. There's nothing. Not at the moment."

"We've got some fine doctors in Houston," he said. "Some of the best in the world. I could fly them down to him."

Jill could feel her throat tightening. Oh, how she wanted to ask David to come to her, to take her away from this place! But she could not. She was bound to Toby, and she knew that she could never leave him.

Not while he was alive.

Dr. Kaplan had completed his examination of Toby. Jill was waiting for him in the library. She turned to face him as he walked through the door. He said, with a clumsy attempt at humor, "Well, Jill, I have good news and I have bad news."

"Tell me the bad news first."

"I'm afraid Toby's nervous system is damaged too heavily to be rehabilitated. There's no question about it. Not this time. He'll never walk or talk again."

She stared at him a long time, and then said, "What's the good news?"

Dr. Kaplan smiled. "Toby's heart is amazingly strong. With proper care, he can live for another twenty years."

Jill looked at him, unbelievingly. *Twenty years. That* was the *good* news! She thought of herself saddled with the horrible gargoyle upstairs, trapped in a nightmare from which there was no escape. She could never divorce Toby. Not as long as he lived. Because no one would understand. She was the heroine who had saved his life. Everyone would feel betrayed, cheated, if she deserted him now. Even David Kenyon.

David telephoned every day now, and he kept talking about her wonderful loyalty and her selflessness, and they were both aware of the deep emotional current flowing between them.

The unspoken phrase was, *when Toby dies.*

T hree nurses attended Toby around the clock in shifts. They
were crisp and capable and as impersonal as machines. Jill
was grateful for their presence, for she could not bear to go
near Toby. The sight of that hideous, grinning mask repelled her.
She found excuses to stay away from his room. When she did force
herself to go to him, Jill could sense a change in him immediately.
Even the nurses could feel it. Toby lay motionless and impotent,
frozen in his spastic cage. Yet the moment Jill entered the room,
a vitality began to blaze from those bright blue eyes. Jill could read
Toby's thoughts as clearly as if he were speaking aloud. *Don't let
me die. Help me. Help me!*

Jill stood looking down at his ruined body and thought, *I can't
help you. You don't want to live like this. You want to die.*

The idea began to grow in Jill.

The newspapers were full of stories about terminally ill husbands whose wives had released them from their pain. Even some
doctors admitted that they deliberately let certain patients die.
Euthanasia, it was called. Mercy killing. But Jill knew that it could
also be called murder, even though nothing lived in Toby anymore
but those damned eyes that would not stop following her around.

In the weeks that followed, Jill never left the house. Most of the
time, she shut herself away in her bedroom. Her headaches had
returned, and she could find no relief.

Newspapers and magazines carried human-interest stories about
the paralyzed superstar and his devoted wife, who had once nursed
him back to health. All the periodicals speculated about whether

Jill would be able to repeat the miracle. But she knew that there would be no more miracles. Toby would never be well again.

Twenty years, Dr. Kaplan had said. And David was out there waiting for her. She had to find a way to escape from her prison.

It began on a dark, gloomy Sunday. It rained in the morning and continued all day, drumming against the roof and the windows of the house until Jill thought she would go mad. She was in her bedroom, reading, trying to get the vicious tattoo of the falling rain out of her mind, when the night nurse walked in. Her name was Ingrid Johnson. She was starched and Nordic.

"The burner upstairs isn't working," Ingrid announced. "I'll have to go down to the kitchen to prepare Mr. Temple's dinner. Could you stay with him for a few minutes?"

Jill could sense the disapproval in the nurse's voice. She thought it strange for a wife not to go near her husband's sickbed. "I'll look after him," Jill said.

She put down her book and went down the hall to Toby's bedroom. The moment Jill walked into the room, her nostrils were assailed by the familiar stench of sickness. In an instant, every fiber of her being was flooded with memories of those long, dreadful months when she had fought to save Toby.

Toby's head was propped up on a large pillow. As he watched Jill enter, his eyes suddenly came alive, flashing out frantic messages. *Where have you been? Why have you stayed away from me? I need you. Help me!* It was as though his eyes had a voice. Jill looked down at that loathsome, twisted body with the grinning death's mask and she felt nauseated. *You'll never get well, damn you! You've got to die! I want you to die!*

As Jill stared at Toby, she watched the expression in his eyes change. They registered shock and disbelief and then they began to fill with such hatred, such naked malevolence, that Jill involuntarily took a step away from the bed. She realized then what had happened. She had spoken her thoughts aloud.

She turned and fled from the room.

In the morning, the rain stopped. Toby's old wheelchair had been brought up from the basement. The day nurse, Frances Gordon, was wheeling Toby out in his chair to the garden to get some sun. Jill listened to the sound of the wheelchair moving down the hall toward the elevator. She waited a few minutes, then she went downstairs. She was passing the library when the phone rang. It was David, calling from Washington.

"How are you today?" He sounded warm and caring.

She had never been so glad to hear his voice. "I'm fine, David."

"I wish you were with me, darling."

"So do I. I love you so much. And I want you. I want you to hold me in your arms again. Oh, David . . ."

Some instinct made Jill turn. Toby was in the hallway, strapped in the wheelchair where the nurse had left him for a moment. His blue eyes blazed at Jill with such loathing, such malice that it was like a physical blow. His mind was speaking to her through his eyes, screaming at her, *I'm going to kill you!* Jill dropped the telephone in panic.

She ran out of the room and up the stairs, and she could feel Toby's hatred pursuing her, like some violent, evil force. She stayed in her bedroom all day, refusing food. She sat in a chair, in a trancelike state, her mind going over and over the moment at the telephone. Toby knew. He knew. She could not face him again.

Finally, night came. It was the middle of July, and the air still held the heat of the day. Jill opened her bedroom windows wide to catch whatever faint breeze there might be.

In Toby's room, Nurse Gallagher was on duty. She tiptoed in to take a look at her patient. Nurse Gallagher wished she could read his mind, then perhaps she might be able to help the poor man. She tucked the covers around Toby. "You get a good night's sleep now," she said, cheerily. "I'll be back to check on you." There was no reaction. He did not even move his eyes to look at her.

Perhaps it's just as well I can't read his mind, Nurse Gallagher thought. She took one last look at him and retired to her little sitting room to watch some latenight television. Nurse Gallagher enjoyed the talk shows. She loved to watch movie stars chat about themselves. It made them terribly *human,* just like ordinary, everyday people. She kept the sound low, so that it would not disturb her patient. But Toby Temple would not have heard it in any case. His thoughts were elsewhere.

The house was asleep, safe in the guarded fastness of the Bel-Air woods. A few faint sounds of traffic drifted up from Sunset Boulevard far below. Nurse Gallagher was watching a late late movie. She wished they would run an old Toby Temple film. It would be so exciting to watch Mr. Temple on television and know that he was here in person, just a few feet away.

At four A.M., Nurse Gallagher dozed off in the middle of a horror film.

In Toby's bedroom there was a deep silence.

In Jill's room, the only sound that could be heard was the ticking of the bedside clock. Jill lay in her bed, naked, sound asleep, one arm hugging a pillow, her body dark against the white sheets. The street noises were muffled and far away.

Jill turned restlessly in her sleep and shivered. She dreamed that she and David were in Alaska on their honeymoon. They were on a vast frozen plain and a sudden storm had come up. The wind was blowing the icy air into their faces, and it was difficult to breathe. She turned toward David, but he was gone. She was alone in the frigid Arctic, coughing, fighting to get her breath. It was the sound of someone choking that woke Jill up. She heard a horrid, gasping wheeze, a death rattle, and she opened her eyes, and the sound was coming from her own throat. She could not breathe. An icy cloak of air covered her like some obscene blanket, caressing her nude body, stroking her breasts, kissing her lips with a frigid, malodorous breath that reeked of the grave. Jill's heart was pounding wildly now, as she fought for air. Her lungs felt seared from the cold. She tried to sit up, and it was as though there was an invisible weight holding her down. She knew this had to be a dream, but at the same time she could hear that hideous rattle from her throat as she fought for breath. She was dying. But could a person die during a nightmare? Jill could feel the cold tendrils exploring her body, moving in between her legs, inside her now, filling her, and with a heart-stopping suddenness, she realized it was Toby. Somehow, by some means, it was Toby. And the quick rush of terror in Jill gave her the strength to claw her way to the foot of the bed, gasping for breath, mind and body fighting to stay alive. She reached the floor and struggled to her feet and ran for the door, feeling the cold pursuing her, surrounding her, clutching at her. Her fingers found the door knob and twisted it open. She ran out into the hallway, panting for air, filling her starved lungs with oxygen.

The hallway was warm, quiet, still. Jill stood there, swaying, her teeth chattering uncontrollably. She turned to look into her room.

It was normal and peaceful. She had had a nightmare. Jill hesitated a moment, then slowly walked back through the doorway. Her room was warm. There was nothing to be afraid of. Of *course*, Toby could not harm her.

In her sitting room, Nurse Gallagher awakened and went in to check on her patient.

Toby Temple was lying in his bed, exactly as she had left him. His eyes were staring at the ceiling, focused on something that Nurse Gallagher could not see.

After that the nightmare kept recurring regularly, like a black omen of doom, a prescience of some horror to come. Slowly, a terror began to build up in Jill. Wherever she went in the house, she could feel Toby's presence. When the nurse took him out. Jill could hear him. Toby's wheelchair had developed a high-pitched creak, and it got on Jill's nerves every time she heard it. *I must have it fixed*, she thought. She avoided going anywhere near Toby's room, but it did not matter. He was everywhere, waiting for her.

The headaches were constant now, a savage, rhythmic pounding that would not let her rest. Jill wished that the pain would stop for an hour, a minute, a second. She *had* to sleep. She went into the maid's room behind the kitchen, as far away from Toby's quarters as she could get. The room was warm and quiet. Jill lay down on the bed and closed her eyes. She was asleep almost instantly.

She was awakened by the fetid, icy air, filling the room, clutching at her, trying to entomb her. Jill leaped up and ran out the door.

The days were horrible enough, but the nights were terrifying. They followed the same pattern. Jill would go to her room and huddle in her bed, fighting to stay awake, afraid to go to sleep, knowing that Toby would come. But her exhausted body would take over and she would finally doze off.

She would be awakened by the cold. She would lie shivering in her bed, feeling the icy air creeping toward her, an evil presence enveloping her like a terrible malediction. She would get up and flee in silent terror.

It was three A.M.

Jill had fallen asleep in her chair, reading a book. She came out of her sleep gradually, slowly, and she opened her eyes in the pitch-black bedroom, knowing that something was terribly wrong. Then she realized what it was. *She had gone to sleep with all the lights on.* She felt her heart begin to race and she thought, *There's nothing to be afraid of. Nurse Gallagher must have come in and turned out the lights.*

Then she heard the sound. It was coming down the hallway, *creak . . . creak . . .* Toby's wheelchair, moving toward her bedroom door. Jill began to feel the hairs rise on the back of her neck. *It's only a tree branch against the roof, or the house settling,* she told herself. Yet she knew that it wasn't true. She had heard that sound too many times before *Creak . . . creak . . .* like the music of death coming to get her. *It can't be Toby,* she thought. *He's in his bed, helpless. I'm losing my mind.* But she could hear it coming closer and closer. It was at her door now. It had stopped, waiting. And suddenly there was the sound of a crash, and then silence.

Jill spent the rest of the night huddled in her chair in the dark, too terrified to move.

In the morning, outside her bedroom door, she found a broken vase on the floor, where it had been knocked over from a hallway table.

She was talking to Dr. Kaplan. "Do you believe that the—the mind can control the body?" Jill asked.

He looked at her, puzzled. "In what way?"

"If Toby wanted—wanted *very much* to get out of his bed, could he?"

"You mean unaided? In his present condition?" He gave her a look of incredulity. "He has absolutely no mobility at all. None whatsoever."

Jill was still not satisfied. "If—if he was really *determined* to get up—if there was something he felt he had to do . . ."

Dr. Kaplan shook his head. "Our minds give commands to the body, but if our motor impulses are blocked, if there are no muscles to carry out those commands, then nothing can happen."

She had to find out. "Do you believe that objects can be moved by the mind?"

"You mean psychokinesis? There are a lot of experiments being done, but no one has ever come up with any proof that's convinced me."

There was the broken vase outside her bedroom door.

Jill wanted to tell him about that, about the cold air that kept following her, about Toby's wheelchair at her door, but he would think she was crazy. *Was she? Was something wrong with her? Was she losing her mind?*

When Dr. Kaplan left, Jill walked over to look at herself in the mirror. She was shocked by what she saw. Her cheeks were sunken and her eyes enormous in a pale, bony face. *If I go on this way,* Jill thought, *I'll die before Toby.* She looked at her stringy, dull hair and her broken, cracked fingernails. *I must never let David see me looking like this. I have to start taking care of myself. From now on,* she told herself, *you're going to the beauty parlor once a week, and you're going to eat three meals a day and sleep eight hours.*

The following morning, Jill made an appointment at the beauty parlor. She was exhausted, and under the warm, comfortable hum of the hair drier, she dozed off, and the nightmare began. She was in bed, asleep. She could hear Toby come into her bedroom in his wheelchair . . . *creak* . . . *creak.* Slowly, he got out of the chair and rose to his feet and moved toward her, grinning, his skeletal hands reaching for her throat. Jill awoke screaming wildly, throwing the beauty shop into an uproar. She fled without even having her hair combed out.

After that experience, Jill was afraid to leave the house again. And afraid to remain in it.

Something seemed to be wrong with her head. It was no longer just the headaches. She was beginning to forget things. She would go downstairs for something and walk into the kitchen and stand there, not knowing what she had come for. Her memory began to play strange tricks on her. Once, Nurse Gordon came in to speak to her; Jill wondered what a nurse was doing there, and then she suddenly remembered. The director was waiting on the set for Jill. She tried to recall her line. *Not very well, I'm afraid, Doctor.* She must speak to the director and find out how he wanted her to read it. Nurse Gordon was holding her hand, saying, "Mrs. Temple! Mrs. Temple! Are you feeling all right?" And Jill was back in her own surroundings, again in the present, caught up in the terror of what was happening to her. She knew she could not go on like this. She had to find out whether there was something wrong with her mind or whether Toby was able to somehow move, whether he had found a way to attack her, to try to murder her.

She had to see him. She forced herself to walk down the long hall toward Toby's bedroom. She stood outside a moment, steeling herself, and then Jill entered Toby's room.

Toby was lying in his bed, and the nurse was giving him a sponge bath. She looked up, saw Jill and said, "Why, here's Mrs. Temple. We're just having a nice bath, aren't we?"

Jill turned to look at the figure on the bed.

Toby's arms and legs had shriveled into stringy appendages attached to his shrunken, twisted torso. Between his legs, like some long, indecent snake, lay his useless penis, flaccid and ugly. The yellow cast had gone from Toby's face, but the gaping idiotic grin was still there. His body was dead, but the eyes were frantically alive. Darting, seeking, weighing, planning, hating; cunning blue eyes filled with their secret plans, their deadly determination. It was Toby's mind she was seeing. *The important thing to remember is that his mind is unimpaired,* the doctor had told her. His mind could think and feel and hate. That mind had nothing to do but plan its revenge, figure out a way to destroy her. Toby wanted her dead, as she wanted him dead.

As Jill looked down at him now staring into those eyes blazing with loathing, she could hear him saying, *I'm going to kill you,* and she could feel the waves of abhorence hitting her like physical blows.

Jill stared into those eyes, and she remembered the broken vase and she knew that none of the nightmares had been illusions. He had found a way.

She knew now that it was Toby's life against hers.

When Dr. Kaplan finished his examination of Toby, he went to find Jill. "I think you should stop the therapy in the swimming pool," he said. "It's a waste of time. I was hoping we might get some slight improvement in Toby's musculature, but it's not working. I'll talk to the therapist myself."

"No!" It was a sharp cry.

Dr. Kaplan looked at her in surprise. "Jill, I know what you did for Toby last time. But this time it's hopeless. I—"

"We can't give up. Not yet." There was a desperation in her voice.

Dr. Kaplan hesitated, then shrugged. "Well, if it means that much to you, but—"

"It does."

At that moment, it was the most important thing in the world. It was going to save Jill's life.

She knew now what she had to do.

The following day was Friday. David telephoned Jill to tell her that he had to go to Madrid on business.

"I may not be able to call you over the weekend."

"I'll miss you," Jill said. "Very much."

"I'll miss you, too. Are you all right? You sound strange. Are you tired?"

Jill was fighting to keep her eyes open, to forget the terrible pain in her head. She could not remember the last time she had eaten or slept. She was so weak that it was difficult to stand. She forced energy into her voice. "I'm fine, David."

"I love you, darling. Take care of yourself."

"I'm going to, David. I love you. Please know that." *No matter what happens.*

She heard the physiotherapist's car turn into the driveway, and Jill started downstairs, her head pounding, her trembling legs barely able to support her. She opened the front door as the physiotherapist was about to ring the bell.

"Morning, Mrs. Temple," he said. He started to enter but Jill blocked his way. He looked at her in surprise.

"Dr. Kaplan has decided to discontinue Mr. Temple's therapy treatments," Jill said.

The physiotherapist frowned. It meant he had made an unnecessary trip out here. Someone should have told him earlier. Ordinarily he would have complained about the way it had been handled. But Mrs. Temple was such a great lady, with such big problems. He smiled at her and said, "It's okay, Mrs. Temple. I understand."

And he got back into his car.

Jill waited until she heard the car drive away. Then she started back up the stairs. Halfway up, a wave of dizziness hit her again, and she had to cling to the banister until it passed. She could not stop now. If she did, she would be dead.

She walked to the door of Toby's room, turned the knob and entered. Nurse Gallagher was seated in an easy chair working on needlepoint. She looked up in surprise as she saw Jill standing in the doorway. "Well!" she said. "You've come to visit us. Isn't that nice?" She turned toward the bed. "I know Mr. Temple is pleased. Aren't we, Mr. Temple?"

Toby was sitting up in bed, propped upright by pillows, his eyes carrying his message to Jill. *I'm going to kill you.*

Jill averted her eyes and walked over to Nurse Gallagher. "I've decided that I haven't been spending enough time with my husband."

"Well, now, that's exactly what I've been thinking," Nurse Gallagher chirped. "But then I could see that you've been ill yourself, and so I said to myself—"

"I'm feeling much better now," Jill interrupted. "I'd like to be alone with Mr. Temple."

Nurse Gallagher gathered up her needlepoint paraphernalia and got to her feet. "Of course," she said. "I'm sure we'll enjoy that."

She turned toward the grinning figure on the bed. "Won't we, Mr. Temple?" To Jill, she added, "I'll just go down to the kitchen and fix myself a nice cup of tea."

"No. You're off duty in half an hour. You can leave now. I'll stay here until Nurse Gordon arrives." Jill gave her a quick, reassuring smile. "Don't worry. I'll be here with him."

"I suppose I *could* get some shopping done, and—"

"Fine," Jill said. "You run along."

Jill stood there, immobile, until she heard the front door slam and Nurse Gallagher's car going down the driveway. When the sounds of the motor had died away on the summer air, Jill turned to look at Toby.

His eyes were focused on her face in an unwavering, unblinking stare. Forcing herself to move closer to the bed, she pulled back the covers and looked down at the wasted, paralyzed frame, the limp, useless legs.

The wheelchair was in a corner. Jill moved it over to the bedside and positioned the chair so that she could roll Toby onto it. She reached toward him, and stopped. It took every ounce of her willpower to touch him. The grinning, mummified face was only inches away from her, the mouth smiling idiotically and the bright blue eyes spewing venom. Jill leaned forward and forced herself to lift Toby by his arms. He was almost weightless, but in Jill's exhausted condition, she could barely manage it. As she touched his body, Jill could feel the icy air begin to envelop her. The pressure inside her head was becoming unbearable. There were bright colored spots before her eyes, and they began to dance around, faster and faster, making her dizzy. She felt herself starting to faint, but she knew that she must not allow that to happen. Not if she wanted to live. With a superhuman effort, she dragged Toby's limp body onto the wheelchair and strapped him in. She looked at her watch. She had only twenty minutes.

It took Jill five minutes to go into her bedroom and change into a bathing suit and return to Toby's room.

She released the brake on the wheelchair and began to wheel Toby down the corridor, into the elevator. She stood behind him as they rode down, so that she could not see his eyes. But she could feel them. And she could feel the damp cold of the noxious air that began to fill the elevator, smothering her, caressing her, filling her lungs with its putrescence until she began to choke. She could not breathe. She fell to her knees, gasping, fighting to stay conscious, trapped in there with him. As she started to feel herself blacking out, the elevator door opened. She crawled into the warm sunlight and lay there on the ground, breathing deeply, sucking in the fresh air, slowly getting back her energy. She turned toward the elevator. Toby was seated in the wheelchair, watching, waiting. Jill quickly pushed the chair out of the elevator. She started toward the swimming pool. It was a beautiful, cloudless day, warm and balmy, the sun sparkling on the blue, filtered water.

Jill rolled the wheelchair to the edge of the deep end of the pool and set the brake. She walked around to the front of the chair. Toby's eyes were fixed on her, watchful, puzzled. Jill reached for the strap holding Toby into the chair, and tightened it as hard as she could, pulling on it, yanking it with all that was left of her strength, feeling herself growing dizzy again with the effort. Suddenly it was done. Jill watched Toby's eyes change as he realized what was happening, and they began to fill with wild, demonic panic.

Jill released the brake, grasped the handle of the wheelchair and started to push it toward the water. Toby was trying to move his paralyzed lips, trying to scream, but no sound came out, and the effect was terrifying. She could not bear to look into his eyes. She did not want to know.

She shoved the wheelchair to the very edge of the pool.

And it stuck. It was held back by the cement lip. She pushed harder, but it would not go over. It was as though Toby were holding the chair back by sheer willpower. Jill could see him straining to rise out of the chair, fighting for his life. He was going to get loose, free himself, reach out for her throat with his bony fingers . . . She could hear his voice screaming, *I don't want to die . . . I don't want to die*, and she did not know whether it was her imagination or whether it was real, but in a rush of panic, she found a sudden strength and shoved as hard as she could against the back of the wheelchair. It lurched forward, upward into the air, and hung there, motionless, for what seemed an eternity, then rolled into the pool, hitting with a loud splash. The wheelchair seemed to float on top of the water for a long time, then slowly began to sink. The eddies of the water turned the chair around, so that the last thing Jill saw was Toby's eyes damning her to hell as the water closed over them.

She stood there forever, shivering in the warm noonday sun, letting the strength flow back into her mind and body. When she was finally able to move again, she walked down the steps of the swimming pool to wet her bathing suit.

Then she went into the house to telephone the police.

T oby Temple's death made newspaper headlines all over the world. If Toby had become a folk hero, then Jill had become a heroine. Hundreds of thousands of words were printed about them, their photographs appeared in all the media. Their great love story was told and retold, the tragic ending giving it an even greater poignancy. Letters and telegrams of condolence streamed in from heads of state, housewives, politicians, millionaires, secretaries. The world had suffered a personal loss; Toby had shared the gift of his laughter with his fans, and they would always be grateful. The air waves were filled with praise for him, and each network paid tribute to him.

There would never be another Toby Temple.

The inquest was held at the Criminal Court Building on Grand Avenue in downtown Los Angeles, in a small, compact courtroom. An inquest examiner was in charge of the hearings, guiding the panel of six jurors.

The room was packed to overflowing. When Jill arrived, the photographers and reporters and fans mobbed her. She was dressed in a simple black tailored wool suit. She wore no makeup and she had never looked more beautiful. In the few days that had lapsed since Toby's death, Jill had miraculously bloomed into her old self again. For the first time in months, she was able to sleep soundly and dreamlessly. She had a voracious appetite and her headaches had disappeared. The demon that had been draining her life away was gone.

Jill had talked to David every day. He had wanted to come to the inquest, but Jill insisted that he stay away. They would have enough time together later.

"The rest of our lives," David had told her.

There were six witnesses at the inquest. Nurse Gallagher, Nurse Gordon and Nurse Johnson testified about the general routine of their patient and his condition. Nurse Gallagher was giving her testimony.

"What time were you supposed to go off duty on the morning in question?" the inquest examiner asked.

"At ten."

"What time did you actually leave?"

Hesitation. "Nine-thirty."

"Was it your custom, Mrs. Gallagher, to leave your patient before your shift was up?"

"No, sir. That was the first time."

"Would you explain how you happened to leave early on that particular day?"

"It was Mrs. Temple's suggestion. She wanted to be alone with her husband."

"Thank you. That's all."

Nurse Gallagher stepped down from the stand. *Of course Toby Temple's death was an accident,* she thought. *It's a pity that they had to put a wonderful woman like Jill Temple through this ordeal.* Nurse Gallagher looked over at Jill and felt a quick stab of guilt. She remembered the night that she had gone into Mrs. Temple's bedroom and found her asleep in a chair. Nurse Gallagher had quietly turned out the lights and closed the door so that Mrs. Temple would not be disturbed. In the dark hallway, Nurse Gallagher had brushed against a vase on a pedestal and it had fallen and broken. She had meant to tell Mrs. Temple, but the vase had looked very expensive, and so, when Mrs. Temple had not mentioned it, Nurse Gallagher decided to say nothing about it.

The physiotherapist was on the witness stand.

"You usually gave Mr. Temple a treatment every day?"

"Yes, sir."

"Did this treatment take place in the swimming pool?"

"Yes, sir. The pool was heated to a hundred degrees, and—"

"Did you give Mr. Temple a treatment on the date in question?"

"No, sir."

"Would you tell us why?"

"She sent me away."

"By 'she,' you mean Mrs. Temple?"

"Right."

"Did she give you any reason?"

"She said Dr. Kaplan didn't want him to have no more treatments."

"And so you left without seeing Mr. Temple?"

"That's correct. Yeah."

Dr. Kaplan was on the stand.

"Mrs. Temple telephoned you after the accident, Dr. Kaplan. Did you examine the deceased as soon as you arrived at the scene?"

"Yes. The police had pulled the body out of the swimming pool. It was still strapped into the wheelchair. The police surgeon and I examined the body and determined that it was too late for any attempt at resuscitation. Both lungs were filled with water. We could detect no vital signs."

"What did you do then, Dr. Kaplan?"

"I took care of Mrs. Temple. She was in a state of acute hysteria. I was very concerned about her."

"Dr. Kaplan, did you have a previous discussion with Mrs. Temple about discontinuing therapy treatments?"

"I did. I told her I thought they were a waste of time."

"What was Mrs. Temple's reaction to that?"

Dr. Kaplan looked over at Jill Temple and said, "Her reaction was very unusual. She insisted that we keep trying." He hesitated. "Since I am under oath and since this inquest jury is interested in hearing the truth, I feel there is something I am obligated to say."

A complete hush had fallen over the room. Jill was staring at him. Dr. Kaplan turned toward the jury box.

"I would like to say, for the record, that Mrs. Temple is probably the finest and bravest woman I have ever had the honor to know." Every eye in the courtroom turned toward Jill. "The first time her husband suffered a stroke, none of us thought he had a chance of recovery. Well, she nursed him back to health single-handedly. She did for him what no doctor I know could have done. I could never begin to describe to you her devotion or dedication to her husband." He looked over to where Jill was sitting and said, "She is an inspiration to all of us."

The spectators broke out into applause.

"That will be all, Doctor," the inquest examiner said. "I would like to call Mrs. Temple to the stand."

They watched as Jill rose and slowly walked over to the witness stand to be sworn in.

"I know what an ordeal this is for you, Mrs. Temple, and I will try to get it over with as quickly as possible."

"Thank you." Her voice was low.

"When Dr. Kaplan said he wanted to discontinue the therapy treatments, why did you want to go ahead with them?"

She looked up at him and he could see the deep pain in her eyes. "Because I wanted my husband to have every chance to get well again. Toby loved life, and I wanted to bring him back to it. I—" Her voice faltered, but she went on. "I had to help him myself."

"On the day of your husband's death, the physiotherapist came to the house, and you sent him away."

"Yes."

"Yet, earlier, Mrs. Temple, you said that you wanted those treatments to continue. Can you explain your action?"

"It's very simple. I felt that our love was the only thing strong enough to heal Toby. It had healed him before . . ." She broke off, unable to continue. Then, visibly steeling herself, she continued in a harsh voice, "I had to let him know how much I loved him, how much I wanted him to get well again."

Everyone in the courtroom was leaning forward, straining to hear every word.

"Would you tell us what happened on the morning of the accident?"

There was a silence that lasted for a full minute while Jill gathered her strength, and then she spoke. "I went into Toby's room. He seemed so glad to see me. I told him that I was going to take him to the pool myself, that I was going to make him well again. I put on a bathing suit so that I could work with him in the water. When I started to lift him off the bed into his wheelchair, I—I became faint. I suppose I should have realized then that I wasn't physically strong enough to do what I was trying to do. But I couldn't stop. Not if it was going to help him. I put him in the wheelchair and talked to him all the way down to the pool. I wheeled him to the edge. . . ."

She stopped, and there was a breathless hush in the room. The only sound was the susurration of the reporters' pens as they frantically scribbled on their shorthand pads.

"I reached down to undo the straps that held Toby in the wheelchair, and I felt faint again and started to fall. I-I must have accidentally released the brake. The chair started to roll into the pool. I tried to grab it, but it—it went into the pool with—with Toby strapped into it." Her voice was choked. "I jumped into the pool after him and fought to free him, but the straps were too tight. I tried to lift the chair out of the water, but it was—it was too heavy. It . . . was . . . just . . . too . . . heavy." She closed her eyes a moment to hide her deep anguish. Then, almost in a whisper, "I tried to help Toby, and I killed him."

It took the inquest jury less than three minutes to reach a verdict: Toby Temple had died in an accident.

Clifton Lawrence sat in the back of the courtroom and listened to the verdict. He was certain that Jill had murdered Toby. But there was no way to prove it. She had gotten away with it.

The case was closed.

36

The funeral was standing room only. It was held at Forest Lawn on a sunny August morning, on the day Toby Temple was to have started his new television series. There were thousands of people milling about the lovely, rolling grounds, trying to get a look at all the celebrities who were there to pay their last respects. Television cameramen photographed the funeral services in long shots and zoomed in for closeups of the stars and producers and directors who were at the graveside. The President of the United States had sent an emissary. There were governors present, studio heads, presidents of large corporations, and representatives from every guild that Toby had belonged to: SAG and AFTRA and ASCAP and AGVA. The president of the Beverly Hills branch of the Veterans of Foreign Wars was there in full uniform. There were contingents from the local police and fire departments.

And the *little people* were there. The grips and prop men and extras and stunt men who had worked with Toby Temple. The wardrobe mistresses and the best boys and the go-fers and the gaffers and the assistant directors. And there were others, and all of them had come to pay homage to a great American. O'Hanlon and Rainger were there, remembering the skinny little kid who had walked into their office at Twentieth Century-Fox. *I understand you fellas are going to write some jokes for me. . . . He uses his hands like he's chopping wood. Maybe we could write a woodchopper act for him. . . . He pushes too hard. . . . Jesus, with that material—wouldn't you? . . . A comic opens funny doors. A comedian opens doors funny.* And Toby Temple had worked and learned and gone to the top. *He was a prick,* Rainger was thinking. *But he was our prick.*

Clifton Lawrence was there. The little agent had been to the barber and his clothes were freshly pressed, but his eyes gave him away. They were the eyes of a failure among his peers. Clifton was lost in memories, too. He was remembering that first preposterous phone call. *There's a young comic Sam Goldwyn wants you to see. . . .* and Toby's performance at the school. *You don't have to eat the entire jar of caviar to know if it's good, right? . . . I've decided to take you on as a client, Toby. . . . If you can put the beer drinkers in your pocket, the champagne crowd will be a pushover. . . . I can make you the biggest star in the business.* Everyone had wanted Toby Temple: the studios, the networks, the nightclubs. *You've got so many clients that sometimes I think you don't pay enough attention to me. . . . It's like a group fuck, Cliff. Somebody always gets left with a hard-on. . . . I need your advice, Cliff. . . . It's this girl. . . .*

Clifton Lawrence had a lot to remember.

Next to Clifton stood Alice Tanner.

She was absorbed in the memory of Toby's first audition in her office. *Somewhere, hidden under all those movie stars, is a young man with a lot of talent. . . . After seeing those pros last night, I—I don't think I have it.* And falling in love with him. *Oh, Toby, I love you so much. . . . I love you, too, Alice. . . .* Then he was gone. But she was grateful that she had once had him.

Al Caruso had come to pay tribute. He was stooped and gray and his brown Santa Claus eyes were filled with tears. He was remembering how wonderful Toby had been to Millie.

Sam Winters was there. He was thinking of all the pleasure Toby Temple had given to millions of people and he wondered how one measured that against the pain that Toby had given to a few.

Someone nudged Sam and he turned to see a pretty, dark-haired girl, about eighteen. "You don't know me, Mr. Winters"—she smiled—"but I heard you're looking for a girl for the new William Forbes movie. I'm from Ohio, and . . ."

David Kenyon was there. Jill had asked him not to come, but David had insisted. He wanted to be near her. Jill supposed that it could do no harm now. She was finished with her performance.

The play had closed and her part was over. Jill was so glad and so tired. It was as though the fiery ordeal she had gone through had burned away the hard core of bitterness within her, had cauterized all the hurts and the disappointments and the hatreds. Jill Castle had died in the holocaust and Josephine Czinski had been reborn in the ashes. She was at peace again, filled with a love for everyone and a contentment she had not known since she was a young girl. She had never been so happy. She wanted to share it with the world.

The funeral rites were ending. Someone took Jill's arm, and she allowed herself to be led to the limousine. When she reached the car, David was standing there, a look of adoration on his face. Jill smiled at him. David took her hands in his and they exchanged a few words. A press photographer snapped a picture of them.

Jill and David decided to wait five months before they got married, so that the public's sense of propriety would be satisfied. David spent a great part of that time out of the country, but they talked to each other every day. Four months after Toby's funeral, David telephoned Jill and said, "I had a brainstorm. Let's not wait any longer. I have to go to Europe next week for a conference. Let's sail to France on the *Bretagne*. The captain can marry us. We'll honeymoon in Paris and from there we'll go anywhere you like for as long as you like. What do you say?"

"Oh, yes, David, yes!"

She took a long last look around the house, thinking of all that had happened here. Remembering her first dinner party there and all the wonderful parties later and then Toby's sickness and her fight to bring him back to health. And then . . . there were too many memories.

She was glad to be leaving.

D avid's private jet plane flew Jill to New York, where a limousine was waiting to drive her to the Regency Hotel on Park Avenue. The manager himself ushered Jill to an enormous penthouse suite.

"The hotel is completely at your service, Mrs. Temple," he said. "Mr. Kenyon instructed us to see that you have everything you need."

Ten minutes after Jill checked in, David telephoned from Texas. "Comfortable?" he asked.

"It's a little crowded." Jill laughed. "It has *five bedrooms*, David. What am I going to do with them all?"

"If I were there, I'd show you," he said.

"Promises, promises," she teased. "When am I going to see you?"

"The *Bretagne* sails at noon tomorrow. I have some business to wind up here. I'll meet you aboard the ship. I've reserved the honeymoon suite. Happy, darling?"

"I've never been happier," Jill said. And it was true. Everything that had gone before, all the pain and the agony, it had all been worth it. It seemed remote and dim, now, like a half-forgotten dream.

"A car will pick you up in the morning. The driver will have your boat ticket."

"I'll be ready," Jill said.

Tomorrow.

It could have started with the photograph of Jill and David

Kenyon that had been taken at Toby's funeral and sold to a newspaper chain. It could have been a careless remark dropped by an employee of the hotel where Jill was staying or by a member of the crew of the *Bretagne*. In any case, there was no way that the wedding plans of someone as famous as Jill Temple could have been kept secret. The first item about her impending marriage appeared in an Associated Press bulletin. After that, it was a front-page story in newspapers across the country and in Europe.

The story was also carried in the *Hollywood Reporter* and *Daily Variety*.

The limousine arrived at the hotel precisely on the dot of ten o'clock. A doorman and three bellboys loaded Jill's luggage into the car. The morning traffic was light and the drive to Pier 90 took less than half an hour.

A senior ship's officer was waiting for Jill at the gangplank. "We're honored to have you aboard, Mrs. Temple," he said. "Everything's ready for you. If you would come this way, please."

He escorted Jill to the Promenade Deck and ushered her into a large, airy suite with its own private terrace. The rooms were filled with fresh flowers.

"The captain asked me to give you his compliments. He will see you at dinner this evening. He said to tell you how much he's looking forward to performing the wedding ceremony."

"Thank you," Jill said. "Do you know whether Mr. Kenyon is on board yet?"

"We just received a telephone message. He's on his way from the airport. His luggage is already here. If there is anything you need, please let me know."

"Thank you," Jill replied. "There's nothing." And it was true. There was not one single thing that she needed that she did not have. She was the happiest person in the world.

There was a knock at the cabin door and a steward entered, carrying more flowers. Jill looked at the card. They were from the President of the United States. Memories. She pushed them out of her mind and began to unpack.

He was standing at the railing on the Main Deck, studying the passengers as they came aboard. Everyone was in a festive mood, preparing for a holiday or joining loved ones aboard. A few of them smiled at him, but the man paid no attention to them. He was watching the gangplank.

At eleven-forty A.M., twenty minutes before sailing time, a chauffeur-driven Silver Shadow raced up to Pier 90 and stopped. David Kenyon jumped out of the car, looked at his watch and said to the chauffeur, "Perfect timing, Otto."

"Thank you, sir. And may I wish you and Mrs. Kenyon a very happy honeymoon."

"Thanks." David Kenyon hurried toward the gangplank, where he presented his ticket. He was escorted aboard by the ship's officer who had taken care of Jill.

"Mrs. Temple is in your cabin, Mr. Kenyon."

"Thank you."

David could visualize her in the bridal suite, waiting for him, and his heart quickened. As David started to move away, a voice called, "Mr. Kenyon . . ."

David turned. The man who had been standing near the railing walked over to him, a smile on his face. David had never seen him before. David had the millionaire's instinctive distrust of friendly strangers. Almost invariably, they wanted something.

The man held out his hand, and David shook it cautiously. "Do we know each other?" David asked.

"I'm an old friend of Jill's," the man said, and David relaxed. "My name is Lawrence. Clifton Lawrence."

"How do you do, Mr. Lawrence." He was impatient to leave.

"Jill asked me to come up and meet you," Clifton said. "She's planned a little surprise for you."

David looked at him. "What kind of surprise?"

"Come along, and I'll show you."

David hesitated a moment. "All right. Will it take long?"

Clifton Lawrence looked up at him and smiled. "I don't think so."

They took an elevator down to C deck, moving past the throngs of embarking passengers and visitors. They walked down a corridor to a large set of double doors. Clifton opened them and ushered David in. David found himself in a large, empty theater. He looked around, puzzled. "In here?"

"In here." Clifton smiled.

He turned and looked up at the projectionist in the booth and nodded. The projectionist was greedy. Clifton had had to give him two hundred dollars before he would agree to assist him. "If they ever found out, I would lose my job," he had grumbled.

"No one will ever know," Clifton had assured him. "It's just a practical joke. All you have to do is lock the doors when I come in with my friend, and start running the film. We'll be out of there in ten minutes."

In the end, the projectionist had agreed.

Now David was looking at Clifton, puzzled. "Movies?" David asked.

"Just sit down, Mr. Kenyon."

David took a seat on the aisle, his long legs stretched out. Clifton took a seat across from him. He was watching David's face as the lights went down and the bright images started to flicker on the large screen.

It felt as though someone was pounding him in the solar plexus with iron hammers. David stared up at the obscene images on the screen and his brain refused to accept what his eyes were seeing. Jill, a young Jill, the way she had looked when he had first fallen in love with her, was naked on a bed. He could see every feature clearly. He watched, mute with disbelief, as a man got astride the girl on the screen and rammed his penis into her mouth. She began sucking it lovingly, caressingly, and another girl came into the scene and spread Jill's legs apart and put her tongue deep inside her. David thought he was going to be sick. For one wild, hopeful instant, he thought that this might be trick photography, a fake, but the camera covered every movement that Jill made. Then the Mexican came into the scene and got on top of Jill, and a hazy red curtain descended in front of David's eyes. He was fifteen years old again, and it was his sister Beth he was watching up there, his sister sitting on top of the naked Mexican gardener in her bed, saying, *Oh, God, I love you, Juan. Keep fucking me. Don't stop!* and David standing in the doorway, unbelievingly, watching his beloved sister. He had been seized with a blind, overpowering rage, and had snatched up a steel letter opener from the desk and had run over to the bed and knocked his sister aside and plunged the opener into the gardener's chest, again and again, until the walls were covered with blood, and Beth was screaming, *Oh, God, no! Stop it, David! I love him. We're going to be married!* There was blood everywhere. David's mother had come running into the room and had sent David away. But he learned later that his mother had telephoned the district attorney, a close friend of the

Kenyon family. They had had a long talk in the study, and the Mexican's body had been taken to the jail. The next morning, it was announced that he had committed suicide in his cell. Three weeks later, Beth had been placed in an institution for the insane.

It all flooded back into David now, the unbearable guilt for what he had done, and he went berserk. He picked up the man sitting across from him and smashed his fist into his face, pounding at him, screaming meaningless, senseless words, attacking him for Beth and for Jill, and for his own shame. Clifton Lawrence tried to defend himself, but there was no way that he could stop the blows. A fist smashed into his nose and he felt something break. A fist cannoned into his mouth and the blood started running like a river. He stood there helplessly, waiting for the next blow to strike him. But suddenly there were no more. There was no sound in the room but his tortured, stertorous breathing and the sensuous sounds coming from the screen.

Clifton pulled out a handkerchief to try to stem the bleeding. He stumbled out of the theater, covering his nose and mouth with his handkerchief, and started toward Jill's cabin. As he passed the dining room, the swinging kitchen door opened for a moment, and he walked into the kitchen, past the bustling chefs and stewards and waiters. He found an ice-making machine and scooped up chunks of ice into a cloth and put them over his nose and mouth. He started out. In front of him was an enormous wedding cake with little spunsugar figures of the bride and groom on top. Clifton reached out and twisted off the bride's head and crushed it in his fingers.

Then he went to find Jill.

The ship was under way. Jill could feel the movement as the fifty-five-thousand-ton liner began to slide away from the pier. She wondered what was keeping David.

As Jill was finishing her unpacking, there was a knock at the cabin door. Jill hurried over to the door and called out, "David!" She opened it, her arms outstretched.

Clifton Lawrence stood there, his face battered and bloody. Jill dropped her arms and stared at him. "What are you doing here? What—what happened to you?"

"I just dropped by to say hello, Jill."

She could hardly understand him.

"And to give you a message from David."

Jill looked at him, uncomprehendingly. "From *David?*"

Clifton walked into the cabin.

He was making Jill nervous. "Where is David?"

Clifton turned to her and said, "Remember what movies used to be like in the old days? There were the good guys in the white hats and the bad guys in the black hats and in the end, you always knew the bad guys were going to get their just deserts. I grew up on those movies, Jill. I grew up believing that life was really like that, that the boys in the white hats always won."

"I don't know what you're talking about."

"It's nice to know that once in a while life works out like those old movies." He smiled at her through battered, bleeding lips and said, "David's gone. For good."

She stared at him in disbelief.

And at that moment, they both felt the motion of the ship come to a stop. Clifton walked out to the veranda and looked down over the side of the ship. "Come here."

Jill hesitated a moment, then followed him, filled with some nameless, growing dread. She peered over the railing. Far below on the water, she could see David getting on the pilot tug, leaving the *Bretagne*. She clutched the railing for support. "*Why?*" she demanded unbelievingly. "*What happened?*"

Clifton Lawrence turned to her and said, "I ran your picture for him."

And she instantly knew what he meant and she moaned, "Oh, my God. No! Please, no! You've killed me!"

"Then we're even."

"Get out!" she screamed. "Get out of here!" She flung herself at him and her nails caught his cheeks and ripped deep gashes down the side. Clifton swung and hit her hard across the face. She fell to her knees, clutching her head in agony.

Clifton stood looking at her for a long moment. This was how he wanted to remember her. "So long, Josephine Czinski," he said.

Clifton left Jill's cabin and walked up to the boat deck, keeping the lower half of his face covered with the handkerchief. He walked slowly, studying the faces of the passengers, looking for a fresh face, an unusual type. You never knew when you might stumble across some new talent. He felt ready to go back to work again.

Who could tell? Maybe he would get lucky and discover another Toby Temple.

Shortly after Clifton left, Claude Dessard walked up to Jill's cabin and knocked at the door. There was no response, but the chief purser could hear sounds inside the room. He waited a moment, then raised his voice and said, "Mrs. Temple, this is Claude Dessard, the chief purser. I was wondering if I might be of service?"

There was no answer. By now Dessard's internal warning system was screaming. His instincts told him that there was something terribly wrong, and he had a premonition that it centered, somehow, around this woman. A series of wild, outrageous thoughts danced through his brain. She had been murdered or kidnaped or—He tried the handle of the door. It was unlocked. Slowly, Dessard pushed the door open. Jill Temple was standing at the far end of the cabin, looking out the porthole, her back to him. Dessard opened his mouth to speak, but something in the frozen rigidity of the figure stopped him. He stood there awkwardly for a moment, debating whether to quietly withdraw, when suddenly the cabin was filled with an unearthly, keening sound, like an animal in pain. Helpless before such a deep private agony, Dessard withdrew, carefully closing the door behind him.

Dessard stood outside the cabin a moment, listening to the wordless cry from within, then, deeply disturbed, turned and headed for the theater on the main deck.

At dinner that evening, there were two empty seats at the captain's table. Halfway through the meal, the captain signaled to Dessard, who was hosting a party of less important passengers two tables away. Dessard excused himself and hurried over to the captain's table.

"Ah, Dessard," the captain said, genially. He lowered his voice, and his tone changed. "What happened with Mrs. Temple and Mr. Kenyon?"

Dessard looked around at the other guests and whispered, "As you know, Mr. Kenyon left with the pilot at the Ambrose Lightship. Mrs. Temple is in her cabin."

The captain swore under his breath. He was a methodical man

who did not like to have his routine interfered with. *"Merde!* All the wedding arrangements have been made," he said.

"I know, Captain." Dessard shrugged and rolled his eyes upward. "Americans," he said.

Jill sat alone in the darkened cabin, huddled in a chair, her knees pulled up to her chest, staring into nothingness. She was grieving, but it was not for David Kenyon or Toby Temple or even for herself. She was grieving for a little girl named Josephine Czinski. Jill had wanted to do so much for that little girl, and now all the wonderful magical dreams she had had for her were finished.

Jill sat there, unseeing, numbed by a defeat that was beyond comprehension. Only a few hours ago she had owned the world, she had had everything she ever wanted, and now she had nothing. She became slowly aware that her headache had returned. She had not noticed it before because of the other pain, the agonizing pain that was tearing deep into her bowels. But now she could feel the band around her forehead tightening. She pulled her knees up closer against her chest, in the fetal position, trying to shut out everything. She was so tired, so terribly tired. All she wanted to do was to sit here forever and not have to think. Then maybe the pain would stop, at least for a little while.

Jill dragged herself over to the bed and lay down and closed her eyes.

Then she felt it. A wave of cold, foul-smelling air moving toward her, surrounding her, caressing her. And she heard his voice, calling her name. *Yes,* she thought, *yes.* Slowly, almost in a trance, Jill got to her feet and walked out of her cabin, following the beckoning voice in her head.

It was two o'clock in the morning and the decks were deserted when Jill emerged from her cabin. She stared down at the sea, watching the gentle splashing of the waves against the ship as it cut through the water, listening to the voice. Jill's headache was worse now, a tight vise of agony. But the voice was telling her not to worry, telling her that everything was going to be fine. *Look down,* the voice said.

Jill looked down into the water and saw something floating there. It was a face. Toby's face, smiling at her, the drowned blue eyes looking up at her. The icy breeze began to blow, gently pushing her closer to the rail.

"I had to do it, Toby," she whispered. "You see that, don't you?"

The head in the water was nodding, bobbing, inviting her to come and join it. The wind grew colder and Jill's body began trembling. *Don't be afraid,* the voice told her. *The water is deep and warm. . . . You'll be here with me. . . . Forever. Come, Jill.*

She closed her eyes a moment, but when she opened them, the smiling face was still there, keeping pace with the ship, the mutilated limbs dangling in the water. *Come to me,* the voice said.

She leaned over to explain to Toby, so that he would leave her in peace, and the icy wind pushed against her, and suddenly she was floating in the soft velvet night air, pirouetting in space. Toby's face was coming closer, coming to meet her, and she felt the paralyzed arms go around her body, holding her. And they were together, forever and ever.

Then there was only the soft night wind and the timeless sea.

And the stars above, where it had all been written.

THE NAKED FACE

To the Women in my Life—

Jorja
Mary
and
Natalie

At ten minutes before eleven in the morning, the sky exploded into a carnival of white confetti that instantly blanketed the city. The soft snow turned the already frozen streets of Manhattan to gray slush and the icy December wind herded the Christmas shoppers toward the comfort of their apartments and homes.

On Lexington Avenue the tall, thin man in the yellow rain slicker moved along with the rushing Christmas crowd to a rhythm of his own. He was walking rapidly, but it was not with the frantic pace of the other pedestrians who were trying to escape the cold. His head was lifted and he seemed oblivious to the passersby who bumped against him. He was free after a lifetime of purgatory, and he was on his way home to tell Mary that it was finished. The past was going to bury its dead and the future was bright and golden. He was thinking how her face would glow when he told her the news. As he reached the corner of Fifty-ninth Street, the traffic light ambered its way to red and he stopped with the impatient crowd. A few feet away, a Salvation Army Santa Claus stood over a large kettle. The man reached in his pocket for some coins, an offering to the gods of fortune. At that instant someone clapped him on the back, a sudden, stinging blow that rocked his whole body. Some overhearty Christmas drunk trying to be friendly.

Or Bruce Boyd. Bruce, who had never known his own strength and had a childish habit of hurting him physically. But he had not seen Bruce in more than a year. The man started to turn his head to see who had hit him, and to his surprise, his knees began to buckle. In slow motion, watching himself from a distance, he could see his body hit the sidewalk. There was a dull pain in his back and it began to spread. It became hard to breathe. He was aware of a parade of shoes moving past his face as though animated with a life of their own. His cheek began to feel numb from the freezing sidewalk. He knew he must not lie there. He opened his mouth to ask someone to help him, and a warm, red river began to gush out and flow into the melting snow. He watched in dazed fascination as it moved across the sidewalk and ran down into the gutter. The pain was worse now, but he didn't mind it so much because he had suddenly remembered his good news. He was free. He was going to tell Mary that he was free. He closed his eyes to rest them from the blinding whiteness of the sky. The snow began to turn to icy sleet, but he no longer felt anything.

Carol Roberts heard the sounds of the reception door opening and closing and the men walking in, and before she even looked up, she could smell what they were. There were two of them. One was in his middle forties. He was a big mother, about six foot three, and all muscle. He had a massive head with deep-set steely blue eyes and a weary, humorless mouth. The second man was younger. His features were clean-cut, sensitive. His eyes were brown and alert. The two men looked completely different and yet, as far as Carol was concerned, they could have been identical twins.

They were fuzz. That was what she had smelled. As they moved toward her desk she could feel the drops of perspiration begin to trickle down her armpits through the shield of anti-perspirant. Frantically her mind darted over all the treacherous areas of vulnerability. Chick? Christ, he had kept out of trouble for over six months. Since that night in his apartment when he had asked her to marry him and had promised to quit the gang.

Sammy? He was overseas in the Air Force, and if anything had happened to her brother, they would not have sent these two mothers to break the news. No, they were here to bust her. She was carrying grass in her purse, and some loudmouthed prick had rapped about it. But why two of them? Carol tried to tell herself that they could not touch her. She was no longer some dumb black hooker from Harlem that they could push around. Not any more. She was the receptionist for one of the biggest psychoanalysts in the country. But as the two men moved toward her, Carol's panic increased. There was the feral memory of too many years of hiding in stinking, over-crowded tenement apartments while the white Law broke down doors and hauled away a father, or a sister, or a cousin.

But nothing of the turmoil in her mind showed on her face. At first glance the two detectives saw only a young and nubile, tawny-skinned woman in a smartly tailored beige dress. Her voice was cool and impersonal. "May I help you?" she asked.

Then Lt. Andrew McGreavy, the older detective, spotted the spreading perspiration stain under the armpit of her dress. He automatically filed it away as an interesting piece of information for future use. The doctor's receptionist was up-tight. McGreavy pulled out a wallet with a worn badge pinned onto the cracked imitation leather. "Lieutenant McGreavy, Nineteenth Precinct." He indicated his partner. "Detective Angeli. We're from the Homicide Division."

Homicide? A muscle in Carol's arm twitched involuntarily. *Chick! He had killed someone. He had broken his promise to her and gone back to the gang. He had pulled a robbery and had shot someone, or—was he shot? Dead? Is that what they had come to tell her?* She felt the perspiration stain begin to widen. Carol suddenly became conscious of it. McGreavy was looking at her face, but she knew that he had noticed it. She and the McGreavys of the world needed no words. They recognized each other on sight. They had known each other for hundreds of years.

"We'd like to see Dr. Judd Stevens," said the younger detective. His voice was gentle and polite, and went with his appearance. She noticed for the first time that he carried a small parcel wrapped in brown paper and held together with string.

It took an instant for his words to sink in. So it wasn't Chick. Or Sammy. Or the grass.

"I'm sorry," she said, barely hiding her relief. "Dr. Stevens is with a patient."

"This will only take a few minutes," McGreavy said. "We want to ask him some questions." He paused. "We can either do it here, or at Police Headquarters."

She looked at the two of them a moment, puzzled. What the hell could two Homicide detectives want with Dr. Stevens? Whatever the police might think, the doctor had not done anything wrong.

She knew him too well. How long had it been? Four years. It had started in night court. . . .

It was three A.M. and the overhead lights in the courtroom bathed everyone in an unhealthy pallor. The room was old and tired and uncaring, saturated with the stale smell of fear that had accumulated over the years like layers of flaked paint.

It was Carol's lousy luck that Judge Murphy was sitting on the bench again. She had been up before him only two weeks before and had gotten off with probation. First offense. Meaning it was the first time the bastards had caught her. This time she knew the judge was going to throw the book at her.

The case on the docket ahead of hers was almost over. A tall, quiet-looking man standing before the judge was saying something about his client, a fat man in handcuffs who trembled all over. She figured the quiet-looking man must be a mouthpiece. There was a look about him, an air of easy confidence, that made her feel the fat man was lucky to have him. She didn't have anyone.

The men moved away from the bench and Carol heard her name called. She stood up, pressing her knees together to keep them from trembling. The bailiff gave her a gentle push toward the bench. The court clerk handed the charge sheet to the judge.

Judge Murphy looked at Carol, then at the sheet of paper in front of him.

" 'Carol Roberts. Soliciting on the streets, vagrancy, possession of marijuana, and resisting arrest.' "

The last was a lot of shit. The policeman had shoved her and she had kicked him in the balls. After all, she was an American citizen.

"You were in here a few weeks ago, weren't you, Carol?"

She made her voice sound uncertain. "I believe I was, Your Honor."

"And I gave you probation."

"Yes, sir."

"How old are you?"

She should have known they would ask. "Sixteen. Today's my sixteenth birthday. Happy birthday to me," she said. And she burst into tears, huge sobs that wracked her body.

The tall, quiet man had been standing at a table at the side gathering up some papers and putting them in a leather attaché case. As Carol stood there sobbing, he looked up and watched her for a moment. Then he spoke to Judge Murphy.

The judge called a recess and the two men disappeared into the judge's chambers. Fifteen minutes later, the bailiff escorted Carol into the judge's chambers, where the quiet man was earnestly talking to the judge.

"You're a lucky girl, Carol," Judge Murphy said. "You're going to get another chance. The Court is remanding you to the personal custody of Dr. Stevens."

So the tall mother wasn't a mouthpiece—he was a quack. She wouldn't have cared if he was Jack the Ripper. All she wanted was to get out of that stinking courtroom before they found out it wasn't her birthday.

The doctor drove her to his apartment, making small talk that did not require any answers, giving Carol a chance to pull herself together and think things out. He stopped the car in front of a modern apartment building on Seventy-first Street overlooking the East River. The building had a doorman and an elevator operator, and from the calm way they greeted him, you would think he came home every morning at three A.M. with a sixteen-year-old black hooker.

Carol had never seen an apartment like the doctor's. The living room was done in white with two long, low couches covered in oatmeal tweed. Between the couches was an enormous square coffee table with a thick glass top. On it was a large chessboard with carved Venetian figures. Modern paintings hung on the wall. In the foyer was a closed-circuit television monitor that showed the entrance to the lobby. In one corner of the living room was a smoked glass bar with shelves of crystal glasses and decanters. Looking out the window, Carol could see tiny boats, far below, tossing their way along the East River.

"Courts always make me hungry," Judd said. "Why don't I whip up a little birthday supper?" And he took her into the kitchen where she watched him skillfully put together a Mexican omelette, French-fried potatoes, toasted English muffins, a salad, and coffee. "That's one of the advantages of being a bachelor," he said. "I can cook when I feel like it."

So he was a bachelor without any home pussy. If she played her cards right, this could turn out to be a bonanza. When she had finished devouring the meal, he had taken her into the guest bedroom. The bedroom was done in blue, dominated by a large double bed with a blue checked bedspread. There was a low Spanish dresser of dark wood with brass fittings.

"You can spend the night here," he said. "I'll rustle up a pair of pajamas for you."

As Carol looked around the tastefully decorated room she thought, *Carol, baby! You've hit the Jackpot! This mother's looking for a piece of jailbait black ass. And you're the baby who is gonna give it to him.*

She undressed and spent the next half hour in the shower. When she came out, a towel wrapped around her shining, voluptuous body, she saw that the motherfucking ofay had placed a pair of his pajamas on the bed. She laughed knowingly and left them there. She threw the towel down and strolled into the living room. He was not there. She looked through the door leading into a den. He was sitting at a large, comfortable desk with an old-fashioned desk lamp hanging over it. The den was crammed with books from floor to ceiling. She walked up behind him and kissed him on the neck. "Let's get started, baby," she whispered. "You got me so horny I can't stand it." She pressed closer to him. "What are we waitin' for, big daddy? If you don't ball me quick, I'll go out of my cotton-pickin' mind."

He regarded her for a second with thoughtful dark gray eyes. "Haven't you got enough trouble?" he asked mildly. "You can't help being born a Negro, but who told you you had to be a black dropout pot-smoking sixteen-year-old whore?"

She stared at him, baffled, wondering what she had said wrong. Maybe he had to get himself worked up and whip her first to get his kicks. Or maybe it was the Reverend Davidson bit. He was going to pray over her black ass, reform her, and then lay her. She tried again. She reached between his legs and stroked him, whispering, "Go, baby. Sock it to me."

He gently disengaged himself and sat her in an armchair. She had never been so puzzled. He didn't look like a fag, but these days you never knew. "What's your bag, baby? Tell me how you like to freak out and I'll give it to you."

"All right," he said. "Let's rap."

"You mean—*talk?*"

"That's right."

And they talked. All night long. It was the strangest night that Carol had ever spent. Dr. Stevens kept leaping from one subject to another, exploring, testing her. He asked her opinion about Vietnam, ghettos, and college riots. Every time Carol thought she had figured out what he was really after, he switched to another subject. They talked of things she had never heard of, and about subjects in which she considered herself the world's greatest living expert. Months afterward she used to lie awake, trying to recall the word, the idea, the magic phrase that had changed her. She had never been able to because she finally realized there had been no magic word. What Dr. Stevens had done was simple. He had talked to her. Really talked to her. No one had ever done that before. He had treated her like a human being, an equal, whose opinions and feelings he cared about.

Somewhere during the course of the night she suddenly became aware of her nakedness and went in and put on his pajamas. He came in and sat on the edge of the bed and they talked some more. They talked about Mao Tse-tung and hula hoops and the Pill. And having a mother and father who had never been married. Carol told him things she had never told anybody in her life. Things that had been long buried deep in her subconscious. And when she had finally fallen asleep, she had felt totally empty. It was as though she had had a major operation, and a river of poison had been drained out of her.

In the morning, after breakfast, he handed her a hundred dollars.

She hesitated, then finally said, "I lied. It's not my birthday."

"I know." He grinned. "But we won't tell the judge." His tone changed. "You can take this money and walk out of here and no one will bother you until the next time you get caught by the police." He paused. "I need a receptionist. I think you'd be marvelous at the job.

She looked at him unbelievingly. "You're putting me on. I can't take shorthand or type."

"You could if you went back to school."

Carol looked at him a moment and then said enthusiastically, "I never thought of that. That sounds groovy." She couldn't wait to get the hell out of the apartment with his hundred dollars and flash it at the boys and girls at Fishman's Drug Store in Harlem, where the gang hung out. She could buy enough kicks with this money to last a week.

When she walked into Fishman's Drug Store, it was as though she had never been away. She saw the same bitter faces and heard the same hip, defeated chatter. She was home. She kept thinking of the doctor's apartment. It wasn't the furniture that made the big difference. It was so—clean. And quiet. It was like a little island somewhere in another world. And he had offered her a passport to it. What was there to lose? She could try it for laughs, to show the doctor that he was wrong, that she couldn't make it.

To her own great surprise, Carol enrolled in night school. She left her furnished room with the rust-stained washbasin and broken toilet and the torn green window shade and the lumpy iron cot where she would turn tricks and act out plays. She was a beautiful heiress in Paris or London or Rome, and the man pumping away on top of her was a wealthy, handsome prince, dying to marry her. And as each man had his orgasm and crawled off her, her dream died. Until the next time.

She left the room and all her princes without a backward glance and moved back in with her parents. Dr. Stevens gave her an allowance while she was studying. She finished high school with top grades. The doctor was there on graduation day, his gray eyes bright with pride. Someone believed in her. She was somebody. She took a day job at Nedick's and took a secretarial course at night. The day after she finished, she went to work for Dr. Stevens and could afford her own apartment.

In the four years that had passed, Dr. Stevens had always treated her with the same grave courtesy he had shown her the first night. At first she had waited for him to make some reference to what she had been, and what she had become. But she had finally come to the realization that he had always seen her as what she was *now*. All he had done was to help her fulfill herself. Whenever she had a problem, he always found time to discuss it with her. Recently she had been meaning to tell him about what had happened with her and Chick and ask him whether she should tell Chick, but she kept putting it off. She wanted her Dr. Stevens to be proud of her. She would have done anything for him. She would have slept with him, killed for him . . .

And now here were these two mothers from the Homicide Squad wanting to see him.

McGreavy was getting impatient. "How about it, miss?" he asked.

"I have orders never to disturb him when he's with a patient," said Carol. She saw the expression that came into McGreavy's eyes. "I'll ring him." She picked up the phone and pressed the inter-com buzzer. After thirty seconds of silence, Dr. Stevens' voice came over the phone. "Yes?"

"There are two detectives here to see you, Doctor. They're from the Homicide Division."

She listened for a change in his voice . . . nervousness . . . fear. There was nothing. "They'll have to wait," he said. He went off the line.

A surge of pride flared through her. Maybe they could panic her, but they could never get her doctor to lose his cool. She looked up defiantly. "You heard him," she said.

"How long will his patient be in there?" asked Angeli, the younger man.

She glanced at the clock on the desk. "Another twenty-five minutes. It's his last patient for the day."

The two men exchanged a look.

"We'll wait," sighed McGreavy.

They took chairs. McGreavy was studying her. "You look famil-iar," he said.

She wasn't deceived. The mother was on a fishing expedition. "You know what they say," replied Carol. "We all look alike."

Exactly twenty-five minutes later, Carol heard the click of the side door that led from the doctor's private office directly to the corridor. A few moments later, the door to the doctor's office opened and Dr. Judd Stevens stepped out. He hesitated as he saw McGreavy. "We've met before," he said. He could not remember where.

McGreavy nodded impassively. "Yeah . . . Lieutenant McGreavy." He indicated Angeli. "Detective Frank Angeli."

Judd and Angeli shook hands. "Come in."

The men walked into Judd's private office and the door closed. Carol looked after them, trying to piece it together. The big detective had seemed antagonistic toward Dr. Stevens. But maybe that was just his natural charm. Carol was sure of only one thing. Her dress would have to go to the cleaner's.

Judd's office was furnished like a French country living room. There was no working desk. Instead, comfortable easy chairs and end tables with authentic antique lamps were scattered about the room. At the far end of the office a private door led out to the corridor. On the floor was an exquisitely patterned Edward Fields area rug, and in a corner was a comfortable damask-covered contour couch. McGreavy noted that there were no diplomas on the walls. But he had checked before coming here. If Dr. Stevens had wanted to, he could have covered his walls with diplomas and certificates.

"This is the first psychiatrist's office I've ever been in," Angeli said, openly impressed. "I wish my house looked like this."

"It relaxes my patients," Judd said easily. "And by the way, I'm a psychoanalyst."

"Sorry," Angeli said. "What's the difference?"

"About fifty dollars an hour," McGreavy said. "My partner doesn't get around much."

Partner. And Judd suddenly remembered. McGreavy's partner had been shot and killed and McGreavy had been wounded during the holdup of a liquor store four—or was it five?—years ago. A petty hoodlum named Amos Ziffren had been arrested for the crime. Ziffren's attorney had pleaded his client not guilty by reason of insanity. Judd had been called in as an expert for the defense and asked to examine Ziffren. He had found that he was hopelessly insane with advanced paresis. On Judd's testimony, Ziffren had escaped the death penalty and had been sent to a mental institution.

"I remember you now," Judd said. "The Ziffren case. You had three bullets in you; your partner was killed."

"And I remember you," McGreavy said. "You got the killer off."

"What can I do for you?"

"We need some information, Doctor," McGreavy said. He nodded to Angeli. Angeli began fumbling at the string on the package he carried.

"We'd like you to identify something for us," McGreavy said. His voice was careful, giving nothing away.

Angeli had the package open. He held up a yellow oilskin rain slicker. "Have you ever seen this before?"

"It looks like mine," Judd said in surprise.

"It is yours. At least your name is stenciled inside."

"Where did you find it?"

"Where do you think we found it?" The two men were no longer casual. A subtle change had taken place in their faces.

Judd studied McGreavy a moment, then picked up a pipe from a rack on a long, low table and began to fill it with tobacco from a jar. "I think you'd better tell me what this is all about," he said quietly.

"It's about this raincoat, Dr. Stevens," said McGreavy. "If it's yours, we want to know how it got out of your possession.

"There's no mystery about it. It was drizzling when I came in this morning. My raincoat was at the cleaners, so I wore the yellow slicker. I keep it for fishing trips. One of my patients hadn't brought a raincoat. It was beginning to snow pretty heavily, so I let him borrow the slicker." He stopped, suddenly worried. "What's happened to him?"

"Happened to who?" McGreavy asked.

"My patient—John Hanson."

"Check," Angeli said gently. "You hit the bull's-eye. The reason Mr. Hanson couldn't return the coat himself is that he's dead."

Judd felt a small shock go through him. "Dead?"

"Someone stuck a knife in his back," McGreavy said.

Judd stared at him incredulously. McGreavy took the coat from Angeli and turned it around so that Judd could see the large, ugly slash in the material. The back of the coat was covered with dull, henna-colored stains. A feeling of nausea swept over Judd.

"Who would want to kill him?"

"We were hoping that you could tell us, Dr. Stevens," said Angeli. "Who'd know better than his psychoanalyst?"

Judd shook his head helplessly. "When did it happen?"

McGreavy answered. "Eleven o'clock this morning. On Lexington Avenue, about a block from your office. A few dozen people must have seen him fall, but they were busy going home to get ready to celebrate the birth of Christ, so they let him lie there bleeding to death in the snow."

Judd squeezed the edge of the table, his knuckles white.

"What time was Hanson here this morning?" asked Angeli.

"Ten o'clock."

"How long do your sessions last, Doctor?"

"Fifty minutes."

"Did he leave as soon as it was over?"

"Yes. I had another patient waiting."

"Did Hanson go out through the reception office?"

"No. My patients come in through the reception office and leave by that door." He indicated the private door leading to the outside corridor. "In that way they don't meet each other."

McGreavy nodded. "So Hanson was killed within a few minutes of the time he left here. Why was he coming to see you?"

Judd hesitated. "I'm sorry. I can't discuss a doctor-patient relationship."

"Someone murdered him," McGreavy said. "You might be able to help us find his killer."

Judd's pipe had gone out. He took his time lighting it again.

"How long had he been coming to you?" This time it was Angeli. Police teamwork.

"Three years," Judd said.

"What was his problem?"

Judd hesitated. He saw John Hanson as he had looked that morning; excited, smiling, eager to enjoy his new freedom. "He was a homosexual."

"This is going to be another one of those beauties," McGreavy said bitterly.

"*Was* a homosexual," Judd said. "Hanson was cured. I told him this morning that he didn't have to see me any more. He was ready to move back in with the family. He has—had—a wife and two children."

"A fag with a family?" asked McGreavy.

"It happens often."

"Maybe one of his homo playmates didn't want to cut him loose. They got in a fight. He lost his temper and slipped a knife in his boyfriend's back."

Judd considered. "It's possible," he said thoughtfully, "but I don't believe it."

"Why not, Dr. Stevens?" asked Angeli.

"Because Hanson hadn't had any homosexual contacts in more

than a year. I think it's much more likely that someone tried to mug him. Hanson was the kind of man who would have put up a fight."

"A brave married fag," McGreavy said heavily. He took out a cigar and lit it. "There's only one thing wrong with the mugger theory. His wallet hadn't been touched. There was over a hundred dollars in it." He watched Judd's reaction.

Angeli said, "If we're looking for a nut, it might make it easier."

"Not necessarily," Judd objected. He walked over to the window. "Take a look at that crowd down there. One out of twenty is, has been, or will be in a mental hospital."

"But if a man's crazy . . . ?"

"He doesn't have to necessarily appear crazy," Judd explained. "For every obvious case of insanity there are at least ten cases undiagnosed.

McGreavy was studying Judd with open interest. "You know a lot about human nature, don't you, Doctor?"

"There's no such thing as human nature," Judd said. "Any more than there's such a thing as animal nature. Try to average out a rabbit and a tiger. Or a squirrel and an elephant."

"How long you been practicing psychoanalysis?" asked McGreavy.

"Twelve years. Why?"

McGreavy shrugged. "You're a good-looking guy. I'll bet a lot of your patients fall in love with you, huh?"

Judd's eyes chilled. "I don't understand the point of the question."

"Oh, come on, Doc. Sure you do. We're both men of the world. A fag walks in here and finds himself a handsome young doctor to tell his troubles to." His tone grew confidential. "Now do you mean to say that in three years on your couch Hanson didn't get a little hard-on for you?"

Judd looked at him without expression. "Is that your idea of being a man of the world, Lieutenant?"

McGreavy was unperturbed. "It could have happened. And I'll tell you what else could have happened. You said you told Hanson you didn't want to see him again. Maybe he didn't like that. He'd grown dependent on you in three years. The two of you had a fight."

Judd's face darkened with anger.

Angeli broke the tension. "Can you think of anyone who had reason to hate him, Doctor? Or someone *he* might have hated?"

"If there were such a person," Judd said, "I would tell you. I think I knew everything there was to know about John Hanson. He was a happy man. He didn't hate anyone and I don't know of anyone who hated him."

"Good for him. You must be one helluva doctor," McGreavy said. "We'll take his file along with us."

"No."

"We can get a court order."

"Get it. There's nothing in that file that can help you."

"Then what harm could it do if you gave it to us?" asked Angeli.

"It could hurt Hanson's wife and children. You're on the wrong track. You'll find that Hanson was killed by a stranger."

"I don't believe it," McGreavy snapped.

Angeli rewrapped the raincoat and tied the string around the bundle. "We'll get this back to you when we run some more tests on it."

"Keep it," Judd said.

McGreavy opened the private door leading to the corridor. "We'll be in touch with you, Doctor." He walked out. Angeli nodded to Judd and followed McGreavy out.

Judd was still standing there, his mind churning, when Carol walked in. "Is everything all right?" she asked hesitantly.

"Someone killed John Hanson."

"*Killed* him?"

"He was stabbed," Judd said.

"Oh my God! But why?"

"The police don't know."

"How terrible!" She saw his eyes and the pain in them. "Is there anything I can do, Doctor?"

"Would you close up the office, Carol? I'm going over to see Mrs. Hanson. I'd like to break the news to her myself."

"Don't worry. I'll take care of everything," said Carol.

"Thanks."

And Judd left.

Thirty minutes later Carol had finished putting the files away and was locking her desk when the corridor door opened. It was after six o'clock and the building was closed. Carol looked up as the man smiled and moved toward her.

Mary Hanson was a doll of a woman; small, beautiful, exquisitely made. On the outside, she was soft, Southern-helpless-feminine, and on the inside, granite bitch. Judd had met her a week after beginning her husband's therapy. She had fought hysterically against it and Judd had asked her to have a talk with him. "Why are you so opposed to your husband going through analysis?"

"I won't have my friends saying I married a crazy man," she had told Judd. "Tell him to give me a divorce; then he can do any damn thing he pleases."

Judd had explained that a divorce at that point could destroy John completely.

"There's nothing left to destroy," Mary had screamed. "If I'd known he was a fairy, do you think I would have married him? He's a woman."

"There's some woman in every man," Judd had said. "Just as there's some man in every woman. And in your husband's case, there are some difficult psychological problems to overcome. But he's trying, Mrs. Hanson. I think you owe it to him and his children to help him."

He had reasoned with her for more than three hours, and in the end she had reluctantly agreed to hold off on the divorce. In the months that followed, she had become interested and then in-volved in the battle that John was waging. Judd made it a rule never to treat married couples, but Mary had asked him to let her become a patient, and he had found it helpful. As she had begun to understand herself and where she had failed as a wife, John's progress had become dramatically rapid.

And now Judd was here to tell her that her husband had been senselessly murdered. She looked up at him, unable to believe what he had just said, sure that it was some kind of macabre joke. And then realization set in. "He's never coming back to me!" she screamed. "He's never coming back to me!" She started tearing at her clothes in anguish, like a wounded animal. The six-year-old twins walked in. And from that moment on, there was bedlam. Judd managed to calm the children down and take them to a neighbor's house. He gave Mrs. Hanson a sedative and called the family doctor. When he was sure there was nothing more he could do, he left. He got into his car and drove aimlessly, lost in thought. Hanson had fought his way through a hell, and at the moment of his victory . . . It was such a pointless death. *Could* it have been some homosexual who had attacked him? Some former lover who was frustrated because Hanson had left him? It was possible, of course, but Judd did not believe it. Lieutenant McGreavy had said that Hanson was killed a block away from the office. If the murderer had been a homosexual, full of hatred, he would have made a rendezvous with Hanson at some private place, either to try to persuade Hanson to come back to him or to pour out his recriminations before he killed him. He would not have plunged a knife into him on a crowded street and then fled.

On the corner ahead he saw a phone booth and suddenly remembered that he had promised to have dinner with Dr. Peter Hadley and his wife, Norah. They were his closest friends, but he was in no mood to see anyone. He stopped the car at the curb, went into the phone booth and dialed the Hadleys' number. Norah answered the phone. "You're late! Where are you?"

"Norah," Judd said, "I'm afraid I'm going to have to beg off tonight."

"You can't," she wailed. "I have a sexy blonde sitting here dying to meet you."

"We'll do it another night," Judd said. "I'm really not up to it. Please apologize for me."

"Doctors!" snorted Norah. "Just a minute and I'll put your chum on."

Peter got on the phone. "Anything wrong, Judd?"

Judd hesitated. "Just a hard day, Pete. I'll tell you about it tomorrow."

"You're missing some delicious Scandinavian smorgasbord. I mean *beautiful*."

"I'll meet her another time," promised Judd. He heard a hurried whisper, and then Norah got on the phone again.

"She'll be here for Christmas dinner, Judd. Will you come?"

He hesitated. "We'll talk about it later, Norah. I'm sorry about tonight." He hung up. He wished he knew some tactful way to stop Norah's matchmaking.

Judd had gotten married in his senior year in college. Elizabeth had been a social science major, warm and bright and gay, and they had both been young and very much in love and full of wonderful plans to remake the world for all the children they were going to have. And on the first Christmas of their marriage, Elizabeth and their unborn child had been killed in a head-on automobile collision. Judd had plunged himself totally into his work, and in time had become one of the outstanding psychoanalysts in the country. But he was still not able to bear being with other people celebrating Christmas Day. Somehow, even though he told himself he was wrong, that belonged to Elizabeth and their child.

He pushed open the door of the phone booth. He was aware of a girl standing outside the booth waiting to use the phone. She was young and pretty, dressed in a tight-fitting sweater and a miniskirt, with a bright-colored raincoat. He stepped out of the booth. "Sorry," he apologized.

She gave him a warm smile. "That's all right." There was a wistful look on her face. He had seen that look before. Loneliness seeking to break through the barrier that he had unconsciously set up.

If Judd knew that he had a quality that was attractive to women, it was deep in his subconscious. He had never analyzed why. It was more of a handicap than an asset to have his female patients falling in love with him. It sometimes made life very difficult.

He moved past the girl with a friendly nod. He sensed her standing there in the rain, watching as he got into his car and drove away.

He turned the car onto the East River Drive and headed for the Merritt Parkway. An hour and a half later he was on the Connecticut Turnpike. The snow in New York was dirty and slushy, but the same storm had magically transformed the Connecticut landscape into a Currier and Ives picture postcard.

He drove past Westport and Danbury, deliberately forcing his mind to concentrate on the ribbon of road that flashed beneath his wheels and the wintry wonderland that surrounded him. Each time his thoughts reached out to John Hanson, he made himself think of other things. He drove on through the darkness of the Connecticut countryside and hours later, emotionally worn out, finally turned the car around and headed for home.

Mike, the red-faced doorman who usually greeted him with a smile, was preoccupied and distant. Family difficulties, Judd supposed. Usually Judd would chat with him about Mike's teen-age son and married daughters, but Judd did not feel like talking this evening. He asked Mike to have the car sent down to the garage.

"Right, Dr. Stevens." Mike seemed about to add something, then thought better of it.

Judd walked into the building. Ben Katz, the manager, was crossing the lobby. He saw Judd, gave a nervous wave, and hurriedly disappeared into his apartment.

What's the matter with everyone tonight? thought Judd. Or is it just my nerves? He stepped into the elevator.

Eddie, the elevator operator, nodded. "Evening, Dr. Stevens."

"Good evening, Eddie."

Eddie swallowed and looked away self-consciously.

"Is anything wrong?" Judd asked.

Eddie quickly shook his head and kept his eyes averted.

My God, thought Judd. *Another candidate for my couch.* The building was suddenly full of them.

Eddie opened the elevator door and Judd got out. He started toward his apartment. He didn't hear the elevator door close, so he turned around. Eddie was staring at him. As Judd started to speak, Eddie quickly closed the elevator door. Judd went to his apartment, unlocked the door, and entered.

Every light in the apartment was on. Lieutenant McGreavy was opening a drawer in the living room. Angeli was coming out of the bedroom. Judd felt anger flare in him. "What are you doing in my apartment?"

"Waitin' for you, Dr. Stevens," McGreavy said.

Judd walked over and slammed the drawer shut, narrowly missing McGreavy's fingers. "How did you get in here?"

"We have a search warrant," said Angeli.

Judd stared at him incredulously. "A search warrant? For my apartment?"

"Suppose we ask the questions, Doctor," McGreavy said.

"You don't have to answer them," interjected Angeli, "without benefit of legal counsel. Also, you should know that anything you say can be used as evidence against you."

"Do you want to call a lawyer?" McGreavy asked.

"I don't need a lawyer. I told you that I loaned the raincoat to John Hanson this morning and I didn't see it again until you brought it to my office this afternoon. I couldn't have killed him. I was with patients all day. Miss Roberts can verify that."

McGreavy and Angeli exchanged a silent signal.

"Where did you go after you left your office this afternoon?" Angeli asked.

"To see Mrs. Hanson."

"We know that," McGreavy said. "Afterward."

Judd hesitated. "I drove around."

"Where?"

"I drove up to Connecticut."

"Where did you stop for dinner?" McGreavy asked.

"I didn't. I wasn't hungry."

"So no one saw you?"

Judd thought a moment. "I suppose not."

"Perhaps you stopped for gas somewhere," suggested Angeli.

"No," Judd said. "I didn't. What difference does it make where I went tonight? Hanson was killed this morning."

"Did you go back to your office any time after you left it this afternoon?" McGreavy's voice was casual.

"No," Judd said. "Why?"

"It was broken into."

"What? By whom?"

"We don't know," said McGreavy. "I want you to come down and take a look around. You can tell us if anything is missing."

"Of course," Judd replied. "Who reported it?"

"The night watchman," said Angeli. "Do you keep anything of value in the office, Doctor? Cash? Drugs? Anything like that?"

"Petty cash," Judd said. "No addictive drugs. There was nothing there to steal. It doesn't make any sense."

"Right," McGreavy said. "Let's go."

In the elevator Eddie gave Judd an apologetic look. Judd met his eyes and nodded that he understood.

Surely, Judd thought, the police couldn't suspect him of breaking into his own office. It was as though McGreavy was determined to pin something on him because of his dead partner. But that had been five years ago. Could McGreavy have been brooding all these years, blaming it on the doctor? Waiting for a chance to get him?

There was an unmarked police car a few feet from the entrance. They got in and rode to the office in silence.

When they reached the office building, Judd signed the lobby register. Bigelow, the guard, looked at him strangely. Or did he imagine it?

They took the elevator to the fifteenth floor and walked down the corridor to Judd's office. A uniformed policeman was standing in front of the door. He nodded to McGreavy and stepped aside. Judd reached for his key.

"The door's unlocked," Angeli said. He pushed the door open and they went in, Judd leading the way.

The reception office was in chaos. All the drawers had been pulled out of the desk and papers were strewn about the floor. Judd stared unbelievingly, feeling a shock of personal violation.

"What do you suppose they were looking for, Doctor?" asked McGreavy.

"I have no idea," Judd said. He walked to the inner door and opened it, McGreavy close behind him.

In his office two end tables had been overturned, a smashed lamp lay on the floor, and blood soaked the Fields rug.

In the far corner of the room, grotesquely spread out, was the body of Carol Roberts. She was nude. Her hands were tied behind her back with piano wire, and acid had been splashed on her face and breasts and between her thighs. The fingers of her right hand were broken. Her face was battered and swollen. A wadded handkerchief was stuffed in her mouth.

The two detectives watched Judd as he stared at the body.

"You look pale," Angeli said. "Sit down."

Judd shook his head and took several deep breaths. When he

spoke, his voice was shaking with rage. "Who—who could have done this?"

"That's what you're going to tell us, Dr. Stevens," said McGreavy.

Judd looked up at him. "No one could have wanted to do this to Carol. She never hurt anyone in her life."

"I think it's about time you started singing another tune," McGreavy said. "No one wanted to hurt Hanson, but they stuck a knife in his back. No one wanted to hurt Carol, but they poured acid all over her and tortured her to death." His voice became hard. "And you stand there and tell me no one would want to hurt them. What the hell are you—deaf, dumb, and blind? The girl worked for you for four years. You're a psychoanalyst. Are you trying to tell me you didn't know or care about her personal life?"

"Of course I cared," Judd said tightly. "She had a boyfriend she was going to marry—"

"Chick. We've talked to him."

"But he could never have done this. He's a decent boy and he loved Carol."

"When was the last time you saw Carol alive?" asked Angeli.

"I told you. When I left here to go to see Mrs. Hanson. I asked Carol to close up the office." His voice broke and he swallowed and took a deep breath.

"Were you scheduled to see any more patients today?"

"No."

"Do you think this could have been done by a maniac?" Angeli asked.

"It must have been a maniac, but—even a maniac has to have some motivation."

"That's what I think," McGreavy said.

Judd looked over to where Carol's body lay. It had the sad appearance of a disfigured rag doll, useless and discarded. "How long are you going to leave her like this?" Judd asked angrily.

"They'll take her away now," said Angeli. "The coroner and the Homicide boys have already finished."

Judd turned to McGreavy. "You left her like this for me?"

"Yeah," McGreavy said. "I'm going to ask you again. Is there anything in this office that someone could want badly enough to"—he indicated Carol—"do that?"

"No."

"What about the records of your patients?"

Judd shook his head. "Nothing."

"You're not being very cooperative, Doctor, are you?" asked McGreavy.

"Don't you think I want to see you find whoever did this?" Judd snapped. "If there was anything in my files that would help, I would tell you. I know my patients. There isn't any one among them who could have killed her. This was done by an outsider."

"How do you know it wasn't someone after your files?"

"My files weren't touched."

McGreavy looked at him with quickened interest. "How do you know that?" he asked. "You haven't even looked."

Judd walked over to the far wall. As the two men watched, he pressed the lower section of the paneling and the wall slid open, revealing racks of built-in shelves. They were filled with tapes. "I record every session with my patients," Judd said. "I keep the tapes here.

"Couldn't they have tortured Carol to try to force her to tell where those tapes were?"

"There is nothing in any of these tapes worth anything to anyone. There was some other motive for her murder."

Judd looked at Carol's scarred body again, and he was filled with helpless, blind rage. "You've got to find whoever did this!"

"I intend to," McGreavy said. He was looking at Judd.

On the windy, deserted street in front of Judd's office building, McGreavy told Angeli to drive Judd home. "I've got an errand to do," McGreavy said. He turned to Judd. "Good night, Doctor."

Judd watched the huge, lumbering figure move down the street.

"Let's go," Angeli said. "I'm freezing."

Judd slid into the front seat beside Angeli, and the car pulled away from the curb.

"I've got to go tell Carol's family," Judd said.

"We've already been over there."

Judd nodded wearily. He still wanted to see them himself, but it could wait.

There was a silence. Judd wondered what errand Lieutenant McGreavy could have at this hour of the morning.

As though reading his thoughts, Angeli said, "McGreavy's a good cop. He thought Ziffren should have gotten the electric chair for killing his partner.'

"Ziffren was insane."

Angeli shrugged. "I'll take your word for it, Doctor."

But McGreavy hadn't, Judd thought. He turned his mind to Carol and remembered her brightness and her affection and her deep pride in what she was doing, and Angeli was speaking to him and he saw that they had arrived at his apartment building.

Five minutes later Judd was in his apartment. There was no question of sleep. He fixed himself a brandy and carried it into the den. He remembered the night Carol had strolled in here, naked and beautiful, rubbing her warm, lithe body against his. He had acted cool and aloof because he had known that that was the only chance he had of helping her. But she had never known what willpower it had taken for him to keep from making love to her. Or had she? He raised his brandy glass and drained it.

The city morgue looked like all city morgues at three o'clock in the morning, except that someone had placed a wreath of mistletoe over the door. Someone, thought McGreavy, who had either an overabundance of holiday spirit or a macabre sense of humor.

McGreavy had waited impatiently in the corridor until the autopsy was completed. When the coroner waved to him, he walked into the sickly-white autopsy room. The coroner was scrubbing his hands at the large white sink. He was a small, birdlike man with a high, chirping voice and quick, nervous movements. He answered all of McGreavy's questions in a rapid, staccato manner, then fled. McGreavy remained there a few minutes, absorbed in what he had just learned. Then he walked out into the freezing night air to find a taxi. There was no sign of one. The sons of bitches were all vacationing in Bermuda. He could stand out here until his ass froze off. He spotted a police cruiser, flagged it down, showed his identification to the young rookie behind the wheel, and ordered him to drive him to the Nineteenth Precinct. It was against regulations, but what the hell. It was going to be a long night.

★

When McGreavy walked into the precinct, Angeli was waiting for him. "They just finished the autopsy on Carol Roberts," McGreavy said.

"And?"

"She was pregnant."

Angeli looked at him in surprise.

"She was three months gone. A little late to have a safe abortion, and a little early to show."

"Do you think that had anything to do with her murder?"

"That's a good question," McGreavy said. "If Carol's boyfriend knocked her up and they were going to get married anyway— what's the big deal? So they get married and have the kid a few months later. It happens every day of the week. On the other hand, if he knocked her up and he *didn't* want to marry her—that's no big deal, either. So she has the baby and no husband. That happens *twice* every day of the week."

"We talked to Chick. He wanted to marry her."

"I know," replied McGreavy. "So we have to ask ourselves where that leaves us. It leaves us with a colored girl who's pregnant. She goes to the father and tells him about it, and he murders her."

"He'd have to be insane."

"Or very foxy. I vote for foxy. Look at it this way: supposing Carol went to the father and broke the bad news and told him she wasn't going to have an abortion; she was going to have his baby. Maybe she used it to try to blackmail him into marrying her. But supposing he couldn't marry her because he was married already. Or maybe he was a white man. Let's say a well-known doctor with a fancy practice. If a thing like this ever got out, it would ruin him. Who the hell would go to a headshrinker who knocked up his colored receptionist and had to marry her?"

"Stevens is a doctor," said Angeli. "There are a dozen ways he could have killed her without arousing suspicion."

"Maybe," McGreavy said. "Maybe not. If there was any suspicion and it could be traced back to him, he'd have a hard time getting out of it. He buys poison—someone has a record of it. He buys a rope or a knife—they can be traced. But look at this cute little setup. Some maniac comes in for no reason and murders his receptionist and he's the griefstricken employer demanding that the police find the killer."

"It sounds like a pretty flimsy case."

"I'm not finished. Let's take his patient, John Hanson. Another senseless killing by this unknown maniac. I'll tell you something, Angeli. I don't believe in coincidences. And two coincidences like that in one day make me nervous. So I asked myself what connection there could be between the death of John Hanson and Carol Roberts, and suddenly it didn't seem so coincidental, after all. Suppose Carol walked into his office and broke the bad news that he was going to be a daddy. They had a big fight and she tried to blackmail him. She said he had to marry her, give her money— whatever. John Hanson was waiting in the outer office, listening. Maybe Stevens wasn't sure he had heard anything until he got on the couch. Then Hanson threatened him with exposure. Or tried to get him to sleep with him."

"That's a lot of guesswork."

"But it fits. When Hanson left, the doctor slipped out and fixed him so he couldn't talk. Then he had to come back and get rid of Carol. He made it look like some maniac did the job, then he stopped by to see Mrs. Hanson, and took a ride to Connecticut. Now his problems are solved. He's sitting pretty and the police are running their asses off searching for some unknown nut."

"I can't buy it," Angeli said. "You're trying to build a murder case without a shred of concrete evidence."

"What do you call 'concrete'?" McGreavy asked. "We've got two corpses. One of them is a pregnant lady who worked for Stevens. The other is one of his patients, murdered a block from his office. He's coming to him for treatment because he's a homosexual. When I asked to listen to his tapes, he wouldn't let me. Why? Who is Dr. Stevens protecting? I asked him if anyone could have broken into his office looking for something. Then maybe we could have cooked up a nice theory that Carol caught them and they tortured her to try to find out where this mysterious something was. But guess what? There is no mysterious something. His tapes aren't worth a tinker's damn to anybody. He had no drugs in the office. No money. So we're looking for some goddam maniac. Right? Except that I won't buy it. I think we're looking for Dr. Judd Stevens."

"I think you're out to nail him," said Angeli quietly.

McGreavy's face flushed with anger. "Because he's as guilty as hell."

"Are you going to arrest him?"

"I'm going to give Dr. Stevens some rope," McGreavy said. "And while he's hanging himself, I'm going to be digging into every little skeleton in his closet. When I nail him, he's going to stay nailed." McGreavy turned and walked out.

Angeli looked after him thoughtfully. If he did nothing, there was a good chance that McGreavy would try to railroad Dr. Stevens. He could not let that happen. He made a mental note to speak to Captain Bertelli in the morning.

The morning newspapers headlined the sensational torture murder of Carol Roberts. Judd was tempted to have his telephone exchange call his patients and cancel his appointments for the day. He had not gone to bed, and his eyes felt heavy and gritty. But when he reviewed the list of patients, he decided that two of them would be desperate if he canceled; three of them would be badly upset; the others could be handled. He decided it was better to continue with his normal routine, partly for his patients' sake, and partly because it was good therapy for him to try to keep his mind off what had happened.

Judd arrived at his office early, but already the corridor was crowded with newspaper and television reporters and photographers. He refused to let them in or to make a statement, and finally managed to get rid of them. He opened the door to his inner office slowly, filled with trepidation. But the blood-stained rug had been removed and everything else had been put back in place. The office looked normal. Except that Carol would never walk in here again, smiling and full of life.

Judd heard the outer door open. His first patient had arrived.

Harrison Burke was a distinguished-looking silver-haired man who looked like the proto-type of a big business executive, which he was: a vice-president of the International Steel Corporation. When Judd had first seen Burke, he had wondered whether the executive had created his stereotyped image, or whether the image had created the executive. Some day he would write a book on face values; a doctor's bedside manner, a lawyer's flamboyance in a courtroom, an actress' face and figure—these were the universal currencies of acceptance: the surface image rather than the basic values.

Burke lay down on the couch, and Judd turned his attention to him. Burke had been sent to Judd by Dr. Peter Hadley two months ago. It had taken Judd ten minutes to ascertain that Harrison Burke was a paranoiac with tendencies toward homicide. The morning headlines had been full of a murder that had taken place in this office the night before, but Burke never mentioned it. That was typical of his condition. He was totally immersed in himself.

"You didn't believe me before," Burke said, "but now I've got proof that they're after me."

"I thought we had decided to keep an open mind about that, Harrison," Judd replied carefully. "Remember yesterday we agreed that the imagination could play—"

"It isn't my imagination," shouted Burke. He sat up, his fists clenched. "They're trying to kill me!"

"Why don't you lie down and try to relax?" Judd suggested soothingly.

Burke got to his feet. "Is that all you've got to say? You don't even want to hear my proof!" His eyes narrowed. "How do I know you're not one of them?"

"You know I'm not one of them," Judd said. "I'm your friend. I'm trying to help you." He felt a stab of disappointment. The progress he had thought they were making over the past month had completely eroded away. He was looking now at the same terrified paranoiac who had first walked into his office two months ago.

Burke had started with International Steel as a mail boy. In twenty-five years his distinguished good looks and his affable personality had taken him almost to the top of the corporate ladder. He had been next in line for the presidency. Then, four years ago, his wife and three children had perished in a fire at their summer home in Southampton. Burke had been in the Bahamas with his mistress. He had taken the tragedy harder than anyone realized. Reared as a devout Catholic, he was unable to shake off his burden of guilt. He began to brood, and he saw less of his friends. He stayed home evenings, reliving the agonies of his wife and children burning to death while, in another part of his mind, he lay in bed with his mistress. It was like a motion picture that he ran over and over in his mind. He blamed himself completely for the death of his family. If only he had been there, he could have saved them. The thought became an obsession. He was a monster. He knew it and God knew it. Surely others could see it! They must hate him as he hated himself. People smiled at him and pretended sympathy, but all the while they were waiting for him to expose himself, waiting to trap him. But he was too cunning for them. He stopped going to the executive dining room and began to have lunch in the privacy of his office. He avoided everyone as much as possible.

Two years ago, when the company had needed a new president, they had passed over Harrison Burke and had hired an outsider. A year later the post of executive vice-president had opened up, and a man was given the job over Burke's head. Now he had all the proof he needed that there was a conspiracy against him. He began to spy on the people around him. At night he hid tape recorders in the offices of other executives. Six months ago he had been caught. It was only because of his long seniority and position that he was not fired.

Trying to help him and relieve some of the pressure on him, the president of the company began to cut down on Burke's responsibilities. Instead of helping, it convinced Burke more than ever that *they* were out to get him. *They* were afraid of him because he was smarter than they were. If he became president, *they* would all lose their jobs because *they* were stupid fools. He began to make more and more mistakes. When these errors were called to his attention, he indignantly denied having made them. Someone was deliberately changing his reports, altering the figures and statistics, trying to discredit him. Soon he realized that it was not only the people in the company who were after him. There were spies outside. He was constantly followed in the streets. They tapped his telephone line, read his mail. He was afraid to eat, lest they poison his food. His weight began to drop alarmingly. The worried president of the company arranged an appointment for him with Dr. Peter Hadley and insisted that Burke keep it. After spending half an hour with him, Dr. Hadley had phoned Judd. Judd's appointment book was full, but when Peter had told him how urgent it was, Judd reluctantly agreed to take him on.

Now Harrison Burke lay supine on the damask-covered contour couch, his fists clenched tightly at his sides.

"Tell me about your proof."

"They broke into my house last night. They came to kill me. But I was too clever for them. I sleep in my den now and I have extra locks on all the doors so they can't get to me."

"Did you report the break-in to the police?" Judd asked.

"Of course not! The police are in it with them. They have orders to shoot me. But they wouldn't dare do it while there are people around, so I stay in crowds."

"I'm glad you gave me this information," Judd said.

"What are you going to do with it?" Burke asked eagerly.

"I'm listening very carefully to everything you say," Judd said. He indicated the tape recorder. "I've got it all down on tape so if they do kill you, we'll have a record of the conspiracy."

Burke's face lit up. "By God, that's good! Tape! That'll really fix them!"

"Why don't you lie down again?" Judd suggested.

Burke nodded and slid onto the couch. He closed his eyes. "I'm tired. I haven't slept in months. I don't dare close my eyes. You don't know what it's like, having everybody after you.

Don't I? He thought of McGreavy.

"Didn't your houseboy hear anyone break in?" Judd asked.

"Didn't I tell you?" Burke replied. "I fired him two weeks ago."

Judd quickly went over in his mind his recent sessions with Harrison Burke. Only three days ago Burke had described a fight he had had that day with his houseboy. So his sense of time had become disoriented. "I don't believe you mentioned it," Judd said casually. "Are you sure it was two weeks ago that you let him go?"

"I don't make mistakes," snapped Burke. "How the hell do you think I got to be vice-president of one of the biggest corporations in the world? Because I've got a brilliant mind, Doctor, and don't forget it."

"Why did you fire him?"

"He tried to poison me."

"How?"

"With a plate of ham and eggs. Loaded with arsenic."

"Did you taste it?" Judd asked.

"Of course not," Burke snorted.

"How did you know it was poisoned?"

"I could smell the poison."

"What did you say to him?"

A look of satisfaction came over Burke's face. "I didn't say anything. I beat the shit out of him."

A feeling of frustration swept over Judd. Given time, he was sure he could have helped Harrison Burke. But time had run out. There was always the danger in psychoanalysis that under the venting of free-flow association, the thin veneer of the id could blow wide open, letting escape all the primitive passions and emotions that huddled together in the mind like terrified wild beasts in the night. The free verbalizing was the first step in treatment. In Burke's case, it had boomeranged. These sessions had released all the latent hostilities that had been locked in his mind. Burke had seemed to improve with each session, agreeing with Judd that there was no conspiracy, that he was only over-worked and emotionally exhausted. Judd had felt that he was guiding Burke to a point where they could begin deep analysis and start to attack the root of the problem. But Burke had been cunningly lying all along. He had been testing Judd, leading him on to try to trap him and find out whether he was one of them. Harrison Burke was a walking time bomb that could explode at any second. There was no next of kin to notify. Should Judd call the president of the company and tell him what he felt? If he did, it would instantly destroy Burke's future. He would have to be put away in an institution. Was he right in his diagnosis that Burke was a potentially homicidal paranoiac? He would like to get an-other opinion before he called, but Burke would never consent. Judd knew he would have to make the decision alone.

"Harrison, I want you to make me a promise," Judd said.

"What kind of promise?" Burke asked warily.

"If they are trying to trick you, then they want you to do something violent so they can have you locked up . . . But you're too smart for that. No matter how they provoke you, I want you to promise me that you won't do anything to them. That way, they can't touch you."

Burke's eyes lit up. "By God, you're right," he said. "So that's their plan! Well, we're too clever for them, aren't we?"

Outside, Judd heard the sound of the reception room door open and close. He looked at his watch. His next patient was here.

Judd quietly snapped off the tape recorder. "I think that's enough for today," he said.

"You got all this down on the tape recorder?" Burke asked eagerly.

"Every word," Judd said. "No one's going to hurt you." He hesitated. "I don't think you should go to the office today. Why don't you go home and get some rest?"

"I can't," Burke whispered, his voice filled with despair. "If I'm not in my office, they'll take my name off the door and put someone else's name on it." He leaned toward Judd. "Be careful. If they know you're my friend, they'll try to get you, too." Burke walked over to the door leading to the corridor. He opened it a crack and peered up and down the corridor. Then he swiftly sidled out.

Judd looked after him, his mind filled with the pain of what he would have to do to Harrison Burke's life. Perhaps if Burke had come to him six months earlier . . . And then a sudden thought sent a chill through him. Was Harrison Burke *already* a murderer? Was it possible that he had been involved in the deaths of John Hanson and Carol Roberts? Both Burke and Hanson were patients. And they could have easily met. Several times in the past few months Burke's appointments had followed Hanson's. And Burke had been late more than once. He could have run into Hanson in the corridor. And seeing him several times could easily have triggered his paranoia, made him feel that Hanson was following him, threatening him. As for Carol, Burke had seen her every time he came to the office. Had his sick mind conceived some menace from her that could only be removed by her death? How long had Burke really been mentally ill? His wife and three children had died in an accidental fire. Accidental? Somehow, he had to find out.

He went to the door leading to the reception office and opened it. "Come in," he said.

Anne Blake rose gracefully to her feet and moved toward him, a warm smile lighting her face. Judd felt again the same heart-turning feeling that had hit him when he had first seen her. It was the first time that he had felt any deep emotional response toward any woman since Elizabeth.

In no way did they look alike. Elizabeth had been blond and small and blue-eyed. Anne Blake had black hair and unbelievable violet eyes framed by long, dark lashes. She was tall, with a lovely, full-curved figure. She had an air of lively intelligence and a classic, patrician beauty that would have made her seem inaccessible, except for the warmth in her eyes. Her voice was low and soft, with a faint, husky quality.

Anne was in her middle twenties. She was, without question, the most beautiful woman Judd had ever seen. But it was something beyond her beauty that caught at Judd. There was an almost palpable force that pulled him to her, some unexplainable reaction that made him feel as though he had known her forever. Feelings that he had thought long since dead had suddenly surfaced again, surprising him by their intensity.

She had appeared in Judd's office three weeks earlier, without an appointment. Carol had explained that his schedule was full and he could not possibly take on any new patient. But Anne had quietly asked if she could wait. She had sat in the outer office for two hours, and Carol had finally taken pity on her and brought her in to Judd.

He had felt such an instant powerful emotional reaction to Anne that he had no idea what she said during the first few minutes. He remembered he had asked her to sit down and she had told him her name, Anne Blake. She was a housewife. Judd had asked her what her problem was. She had hesitated and said that she was not certain. She was not even sure she had a problem. A doctor friend of hers had mentioned that Judd was one of the most brilliant analysts in the country, but when Judd had asked her who the doctor was, Anne had demurred. For all Judd knew, she could have gotten his name out of the telephone directory.

He had tried to explain to her how impossible his schedule was, that he simply was unable to take on any new patients. He offered to recommend half a dozen good analysts. But Anne had quietly insisted that she wanted him to treat her. In the end Judd had agreed. Outwardly, except for the fact that she appeared to be under some stress, she seemed perfectly normal, and he was certain that her problem would be a relatively simple one, easily solved. He broke his rule about not taking any patient without another doctor's recommendation, and he gave up his lunch hour in order to treat Anne. She had appeared twice a week for the past three weeks, and Judd knew very little more about her than he had known when she first came in. He knew something more about himself. He was in love—for the first time since Elizabeth.

At their first session, Judd had asked her if she loved her husband, and hated himself for wanting to hear her say that she did not. But she had said, "Yes. He's a kind man, and very strong."

"Do you think he represents a father figure?" Judd had asked.

Anne had turned her incredible violet eyes on him. "No. I wasn't looking for a father figure. I had a very happy home life as a child."

"Where were you born?"

"In Revere, a small town near Boston."

"Are both your parents still alive?"

"Father is alive. Mother died of a stroke when I was twelve."

"Did your father and mother have a good relationship?"

"Yes. They were very much in love."

It shows in you, thought Judd happily. With all the sickness and aberration and misery that he had seen, having Anne here was like a breath of April freshness.

"Any brothers or sisters?"

"No. I was an only child. A spoiled brat." She smiled up at him. It was an open, friendly smile without guile or affectation.

She told him that she had lived abroad with her father, who was serving in the State Department, and when he had remarried and moved to California, she had gone to work at the UN as an interpreter. She spoke fluent French, Italian, and Spanish. She had met her future husband in the Bahamas when she was on vacation. He owned a construction firm. Anne had not been attracted to him at first, but he had been a persistent and persuasive suitor. Two months after they met, Anne had married him. She had now been married for six months. They lived on an estate in New Jersey.

And that was all Judd had been able to find out about her in half a dozen visits. He still had not the slightest clue as to what her problem was. She had an emotional block about discussing it. He remembered some of the questions he had asked her during their first session.

"Does your problem involve your husband, Mrs. Blake?"

No answer.

"Are you and your husband compatible, physically?"

"Yes." Embarrassed.

"Do you suspect him of having an affair with another woman?"

"No." Amused.

"Are you having an affair with another man?"

"No." Angry.

He hesitated, trying to figure out the best approach to take to break down the barrier. He decided on a buckshot technique: he would touch on every major category until he struck a nerve.

"Do you quarrel about money?"

"No. He's very generous."

"Any in-law problems?"

"He's an orphan. My father lives in California."

"Were you or your husband ever addicted to drugs?"

"No."

"Do you suspect your husband of being homosexual?"

A low, warm laugh. "No."

He pressed on, because he had to. "Have you ever had a sexual relationship with a woman?"

"No." Reproachful.

He had touched on alcoholism, frigidity, a pregnancy she was afraid to face—everything he could think of. And each time she had looked at him with her thoughtful, intelligent eyes and had merely shaken her head. Whenever he tried to pin her down, she would head him off with, "Please be patient with me. Let me do it my own way."

With anyone else, he might have given up. But he knew that he had to help her. And he had to keep seeing her.

He had let her talk about any subject she chose. She had traveled to a dozen countries with her father and had met fascinating people. She had a quick mind and an unexpected humor. He found that they liked the same books, the same music, the same playwrights. She was warm and friendly, but Judd could never detect the slightest sign that she reacted to him as anything other than a doctor. It was bitter irony. He had been subconsciously searching for someone like Anne for years, and now that she had walked into his life, his job was to help her solve whatever her problem was and send her back to her husband.

Now, as Anne walked into the office, Judd moved to the chair next to the couch and waited for her to lie down.

"Not today," she said quietly. "I just came to see if I could help."

He stared at her, speechless for a moment. His emotions had been stretched so tight in the past two days that her unexpected sympathy unnerved him. As he looked at her, he had a wild impulse to pour out everything that was happening to him. To tell her about the nightmare that was engulfing him, about McGreavy and his idiotic suspicions. But he knew he could not. He was the doctor and she was his patient. Worse than that. He was in love with her, and she was the untouchable wife of a man he did not even know.

She was standing there, watching him. He nodded, not trusting himself to speak.

"I liked Carol so much," said Anne. "Why would anyone kill her?"

"I don't know," said Judd.

"Don't the police have any idea who did it?"

Do they! Judd thought bitterly. *If she only knew.*

Anne was looking at him curiously.

"The police have some theories," Judd said.

"I know how terrible you must feel. I just wanted to come and tell you how very sorry I am. I wasn't even sure you'd be in the office today."

"I wasn't going to come in," Judd said. "But—well, here I am. As long as we're both here, why don't we talk a little about you?"

Anne hesitated. "I'm not sure that there's anything to talk about any more."

Judd felt his heart jump. *Please, God, don't let her say that I'm not going to see her any more.*

"I'm going to Europe with my husband next week."

"That's wonderful," he made himself say.

"I'm afraid I've wasted your time, Dr. Stevens, and I apologize."

"Please don't," Judd said. He found that his voice was husky. She was walking out on him. But of course she couldn't know that. He was being infantile. His mind told him this clinically while his stomach ached with the physical hurt of her going away. Forever.

She opened her purse and took out some money. She was in the habit of paying in cash after each visit, unlike his other patients, who sent him checks.

"No," said Judd quickly. "You came here as a friend. I'm—grateful."

Judd did something he had never done before with a patient. "I would like you to come back once more," he said.

She looked up at him quietly. "Why?"

Because I can't bear to let you go so soon, he thought. Because I'll never meet anyone like you again. Because I wish I had met you first. Because I love you. Aloud he said, "I thought we might—round things out. Talk a little to make sure that you really are over your problem."

She smiled mischievously. "You mean you want me to come back for my graduation?"

"Something like that," he said. "Will you do it?"

"If you want me to—of course." She rose. "I haven't given you a chance with me. But I know you're a wonderful doctor. If I should ever need help, I'd come to you."

She held out her hand and he took it. She had a warm, firm handclasp. He felt again that compelling current that ran between them and marveled that she felt nothing.

"I'll see you Friday," she said.

"Friday."

He watched her walk out the private door leading to the corridor, then sank into a chair. He had never felt so completely alone in his life. But he couldn't sit here and do nothing. There had to be an answer, and if McGreavy wasn't going to find it, *he* had to discover it before McGreavy destroyed him. On the dark side, Lieutenant McGreavy suspected him of two murders that he couldn't prove he did not commit. He might be arrested at any moment, which would mean that his professional life would be destroyed. He was in love with a married woman he would only see once more. He forced himself to turn to the bright side. He couldn't think of a single bloody thing.

The rest of the day went by as though he were under water. A few of the patients made reference to Carol's murder, but the more disturbed ones were so self-absorbed that they could think only of themselves and their problems. Judd tried to concentrate, but his thoughts kept drifting away, trying to find answers to what had happened. He would go over the tapes later to pick up what he had missed.

At seven o'clock, when Judd had ushered out the last patient, he went over to the recessed liquor cabinet and poured himself a stiff scotch. It hit him with a jolt, and he suddenly remembered that he had not had any breakfast or lunch. The thought of food made him ill. He sank into a chair and thought about the two murders. There was nothing in the case histories of any of his patients that would cause someone to commit murder. A blackmailer might have tried to steal them. But blackmailers were cowards, preying on the weaknesses of others, and if Carol had caught one breaking in and he had killed her, it would have been done quickly, with a single blow. He would not have tortured her. There had to be some other explanation.

Judd sat there a long time, his mind slowly sifting the events of the past two days. Finally he sighed and gave it up. He looked at the clock and was startled to see how late it was.

By the time he left his office, it was after nine o'clock. As he stepped out of the lobby into the street, a blast of icy wind hit him. It had started to snow again. The snow swirled through the sky, gently blurring everything so that it looked as though the city had been painted on a canvas that had not dried and the paints were running, melting down sky-scrapers and streets into watery grays and whites. A large red-and-white sign in a store window across the street on Lexington Avenue warned:

ONLY 6 SHOPPING DAYS 'TIL CHRISTMAS

Christmas. He resolutely turned his thoughts away from it and started to walk.

The street was deserted except for a lone pedestrian in the distance, hurrying home to his wife or sweetheart. Judd found himself wondering what Anne was doing. She was probably at home with her husband, discussing his day at the office, interested, caring. Or they had gone to bed, and . . . *Stop it!* he told himself.

There were no cars on the windswept street, so just before he reached the corner, Judd began to cross at an angle, heading toward the garage where he parked his car during the day. As he reached the middle of the street, he heard a noise behind him, and turned. A large black limousine without lights was coming toward him, its tires fighting for traction in the light powder of snow. It was less than ten feet away. *The drunken fool*, thought Judd. *He's in a skid and he's going to kill himself.* Judd turned and leaped back toward the curb and safety. The nose of the car swerved toward him, the car accelerating. Too late Judd realized the car was deliberately trying to run him down.

The last thing he remembered was something hard smashing against his chest, and a loud crash that sounded like thunder. The dark street suddenly lit up with bright Roman candles that seemed to explode in his head. In that split second of illumination, Judd suddenly knew the answer to everything. He knew why John Hanson and Carol Roberts had been murdered. He felt a sense of wild elation. He had to tell McGreavy. Then the light faded, and there was only the silence of the wet darkness.

From the outside, the Nineteenth Police Precinct looked like an ancient, weatherbeaten four-story school building: brown brick, plaster facade, and cornices white with the droppings of generations of pigeons. The Nineteenth Precinct was responsible for the area of Manhattan from Fifty-ninth Street to Eighty-sixth Street, from Fifth Avenue to the East River.

The call from the hospital reporting the hit-and-run accident came through the police switchboard a few minutes after ten and was transferred to the Detective Bureau. The Nineteenth Precinct was having a busy night. Because of the weather, there had been a heavy increase in rapes and muggings. The deserted streets had become a frozen wasteland where marauders preyed on the hapless stragglers who wandered into their territory.

Most of the detectives were out on squeals, and the Detective Bureau was deserted except for Detective Frank Angeli and a sergeant, who was interrogating an arson suspect.

When the phone rang, Angeli answered. It was a nurse who had a hit-and-run patient at the city hospital. The patient was asking for Lieutenant McGreavy. McGreavy had gone to the Hall of Records. When she gave Angeli the name of the patient, he told the nurse that he would be right over.

Angeli was hanging up the receiver as McGreavy walked in. Angeli quickly told him about the call. "We'd better get right over to the hospital," Angeli said.

"He'll keep. First I want to talk to the captain of the precinct where that accident occurred."

Angeli watched as McGreavy dialed the number. He wondered whether Captain Bertelli had told McGreavy about his conversation with Angeli. It had been short and to the point.

"Lieutenant McGreavy is a good cop," Angeli had said, "but I think he's influenced by what happened five years ago."

Captain Bertelli had given him a long, cold stare. "Are you accusing him of framing Dr. Stevens?"

"I'm not accusing him of anything, Captain. I just thought you should be aware of the situation."

"Okay, I'm aware of it." And the meeting was over.

McGreavy's phone conversation took three minutes while McGreavy grunted and made notes and Angeli impatiently paced back and forth. Ten minutes later the two detectives were in a squad car on the way to the hospital.

Judd's room was on the sixth floor at the end of a long, dreary corridor that had the sickly-sweet smell of all hospitals. The nurse who had phoned was escorting them to Judd's room.

"What shape is he in, Nurse?" asked McGreavy.

"The doctor will have to tell you that," she said primly. And then continued, compulsively. "It's a miracle the man wasn't killed. He has a possible concussion, some bruised ribs, and an injured left arm."

"Is he conscious?" asked Angeli.

"Yes. We're having a terrible time keeping him in bed." She turned to McGreavy. "He keeps saying he has to see you."

They walked into the room. There were six beds in the room, all occupied. The nurse indicated a bed at the far corner that was curtained off, and McGreavy and Angeli walked over to it and stepped behind the curtain.

Judd was in bed, propped up. His face was pale and there was a large adhesive plaster on his forehead. His left arm was in a sling.

McGreavy spoke. "I hear you had an accident."

"It wasn't an accident," said Judd. "Someone tried to kill me." His voice was weak and shaky.

"Who?" asked Angeli.

"I don't know, but it all fits in." He turned to McGreavy. "The killers weren't after John Hanson or Carol. They were after me."

McGreavy looked at him in surprise. "What makes you think so?"

"Hanson was killed because he was wearing my yellow slicker. They must have seen me go into my building wearing that coat. When Hanson came out of my office wearing it, they mistook him for me."

"That's possible," said Angeli.

"Sure," said McGreavy. He turned to Judd. "And when they learned that they had killed the wrong man, they came into your office and tore your clothes off and found out you were really a little colored girl, and they got so mad they beat you to death."

"Carol was killed because they found her there when they came to get me," Judd said.

McGreavy reached in his overcoat pocket and took out some notes. "I just talked to the captain of the precinct where the accident happened."

"It was no accident."

"According to the police report, you were jaywalking."

Judd stared at him. "Jaywalking?" he repeated weakly.

"You crossed in the middle of the street, Doctor."

"There were no cars so I—"

"There *was* a car," McGreavy corrected. "Only you didn't see it. It was snowing and the visibility was lousy. You stepped out of nowhere. The driver put on his brakes, went into a skid, and hit you. Then he panicked and drove away."

"That's not the way it happened and his headlights were off."

"And you think *that's* evidence that he killed Hanson and Carol Roberts?"

"Someone tried to kill me," repeated Judd insistently.

McGreavy shook his head. "It won't work, Doctor."

"What won't work?" asked Judd.

"Did you really expect me to start beating the bushes for some mythical killer while you take the heat off yourself?" His voice was suddenly hard. "Did you know your receptionist was pregnant?"

Judd closed his eyes and let his head sink back on the pillow. So that was what Carol had wanted to speak to him about. He had half-guessed. And now McGreavy would think . . . He opened his eyes. "No," he said wearily. "I didn't."

Judd's head began pounding again. The pain was returning. He swallowed to fight off the nausea that engulfed him. He wanted to ring for the nurse, but he was damned if he would give McGreavy the satisfaction.

"I went through the records at City Hall," said McGreavy. "What would you say if I told you that your cute little pregnant receptionist had been a hooker before she went to work for you?" The pounding in Judd's head was becoming steadily worse. "Were you aware of that, Dr. Stevens? You don't have to answer. I'll answer for you. You knew it because you picked her up in night court four years ago, when she was arrested on a charge of soliciting. Now isn't it a little far-out for a respectable doctor to hire a hooker as a receptionist in a high-class office?"

"No one is born a hooker," said Judd. "I was trying to help a sixteen-year-old child have a chance at life."

"And get yourself a little free black tail on the side?"

"You dirty-minded bastard!"

McGreavy smiled without mirth. "Where did you take Carol after you found her in night court?"

"To my apartment."

"And she slept there?"

"Yes."

McGreavy grinned. "You're a beauty! You picked up a good-looking young whore in night court and took her to your apartment to spend the night. What were you looking for—a chess partner? If you really didn't sleep with her, there's a damn good chance you're a homosexual. And guess who that ties you in with? Right. John Hanson. If you *did* sleep with Carol, then the chances are pretty good that you continued sleeping with her until you finally got her knocked up. And you have the gall to lie there and tell me some cock-and-bull story about a hit-and-run maniac who's going around murdering people?" McGreavy turned and strode out of the room, his face red with anger.

The pounding in Judd's head had turned to a throbbing agony. Angeli was watching him, worried. "You all right?"

"You've got to help me," Judd said. "Someone is trying to kill me." It sounded like a threnody in his ears.

"Who'd have a motive for killing you, Doctor?"

"I don't know."

"Do you have any enemies?"

"No."

"Have you been sleeping with anyone's wife or girl friend?"

Judd shook his head and instantly regretted the motion.

"Is there any money in your family—relatives who might want to get you out of the way?"

"No."

Angeli sighed. "OK. So there's no motive for anyone wanting to murder you. What about your patients? I think you'd better give us a list so we can check them out.

"I can't do that."

"All I'm asking for is their names."

"I'm sorry." It was an effort to speak. "If I were a dentist or a chiropodist I'd give it to you. But don't you see? These people have problems. Most of them serious problems. If you started questioning them, you'd not only shatter them, you'd destroy their confidence in me. I wouldn't be able to treat them any more. I can't give you that list." He lay back on the pillow, exhausted.

Angeli looked at him quietly, then asked, "What do you call a man who thinks that everyone's out to kill him?"

"A paranoiac," said Judd. He saw the look on Angeli's face. "You don't think I'm . . . ?"

"Put yourself in my place," Angeli said. "If I were in that bed right now, talking like you, and you were my doctor, what would you think?"

Judd closed his eyes against the stabs of pain in his head. He heard Angeli's voice continue. "McGreavy's waiting for me."

Judd opened his eyes. "Wait . . . Give me a chance to prove that I'm telling the truth."

"How?"

"Whoever's trying to kill me is going to try again. I want someone with me. Next time they try, he can catch them."

Angeli looked at Judd. "Dr. Stevens, if someone really wants to kill you, all the policemen in the world can't stop them. If they don't get you today, they'll get you tomorrow. If they don't get you here, they'll get you somewhere else. It doesn't matter whether you're a king or a president, or just plain John Doe. Life is a very thin thread. It only takes a second to snap it."

"There's nothing—nothing at all you can do?"

"I can give you some advice. Have new locks put on the doors of your apartment, and check the windows to make sure they're securely bolted. Don't let anyone in the apartment unless you know them. No delivery boys unless you've ordered the delivery yourself."

Judd nodded, his throat dry and aching.

"Your building has a doorman and an elevator man," continued Angeli. "Can you trust them?"

"The doorman has worked there for ten years. The elevator operator has been there eight years. I'd trust them with my life."

Angeli nodded approvingly. "Good. Ask them to keep their eyes open. If they're on the alert, it's going to be hard for anyone to sneak up to your apartment. What about the office? Are you going to hire a new receptionist?"

Judd thought of a stranger sitting at Carol's desk, in her chair. A spasm of helpless anger wracked him. "Not right away."

"You might think about hiring a man," said Angeli.

"I'll think about it."

Angeli turned to go, then stopped. "I have an idea," he said hesitantly, "but it's a longshot."

"Yes?" He hated the eagerness in his voice.

"This man who killed McGreavy's old partner . . ."

"Ziffren."

"Was he really insane?"

"Yes. They sent him to the Matteawan State Hospital for mentally ill criminals."

"Maybe he blames you for having him put away. I'll check him out. Just to make sure he hasn't escaped or been released. Give me a call in the morning."

"Thanks," Judd said gratefully.

"It's my job. If you're involved in any of this, I'm going to help McGreavy nail you." Angeli turned to go. He stopped again. "You don't have to mention to McGreavy that I'm checking on Ziffren for you."

"I won't."

The two men smiled at each other. Angeli left. Judd was alone again.

If the situation was bleak that morning it was even bleaker now. Judd knew that he would already have been arrested for murder except for one thing—McGreavy's character. McGreavy wanted vengeance and he wanted it so badly that he would make sure that every last bit of evidence was in place. *Could* the hit-and-run have been an accident? There had been snow on the street, and the limousine could have accidentally skidded into him. But then, why had the headlights been off? And where had the car come from so suddenly?

He was convinced now that an assassin had struck—and would strike again. With that thought, he fell asleep.

Early the next morning Peter and Norah Hadley came to the hospital to see Judd. They had heard about the accident on the morning news.

Peter was Judd's age, smaller than Judd and painfully thin. They had come from the same town in Nebraska and had gone through medical school together.

Norah was English. She was blond and chubby with a large, soft bosom a bit too large for her five feet three inches. She was vivacious and comfortable, and after five minutes' conversation with her, people felt they had known her forever.

"You look lousy," Peter said, studying Judd critically.

"That's what I like, Doctor. A bedside manner." Judd's headache was almost gone and the pain in his body had been reduced to a dull, aching soreness.

Norah handed him a bouquet of carnations. "We brought you some flowers, love," she said. "You poor old darling." She leaned over and kissed him on the cheek.

"How did it happen?" asked Peter.

Judd hesitated. "It was a hit-and-run accident."

"Everything hit the fan at once, didn't it? I read about poor Carol."

"It's dreadful," said Norah. "I liked her so much."

Judd felt a tightness in his throat. "So did I."

"Any chance of catching the bastard who did it?" Peter asked.

"They're working on it."

"In this morning's paper it said that a Lieutenant McGreavy is close to making an arrest. Do you know anything about it?"

"A little," Judd said dryly. "McGreavy likes to keep me up to date."

"You never know how wonderful the police are until you really need them," Norah said.

"Dr. Harris let me take a look at your X rays. Some nasty bruises—no concussion. You'll be out of here in a few days."

But Judd knew he had no time to spare.

They spent the next half hour in small talk, carefully avoiding the subject of Carol Roberts. Peter and Norah were unaware that John Hanson had been a patient of Judd's. For some reason of his own, McGreavy had kept that part of the story out of the newspapers.

When they got up to leave, Judd asked to speak to Peter alone. While Norah waited outside, Judd told Peter about Harrison Burke.

"I'm sorry," said Peter. "When I sent him to you, I knew he was in a bad way but I was hoping there was still time for you to help him. Of course you have to put him away. When are you going to do it?"

"As soon as I get out of here," Judd said. And he knew he was lying. He didn't want Harrison Burke sent away. Not just yet. He wanted to find out first whether Burke could have committed the two murders.

"If there's anything I can do for you, old buddy—call." And Peter was gone.

Judd lay there, planning his next move. Since there was no rational motive for anyone wanting to kill him, it stood to reason that the murders had been committed by someone who was mentally unbalanced, someone with an imagined grievance against him. The only two people he could think of who might fit into that category were Harrison Burke and Amos Ziffren, the man who had killed McGreavy's partner. If Burke had no alibi for the morning Hanson was killed, then Judd would ask Detective Angeli to check him out further. If Burke had an alibi, then he would concentrate on Ziffren. The feeling of depression that had enveloped him began to lift. He felt that at last he was doing something. He was suddenly desperately impatient to get out of the hospital.

He rang for the nurse and told her he wanted to see Dr. Harris. Ten minutes later Seymour Harris walked into the room. He was a little gnome of a man with bright blue eyes and tufts of black hair sticking out of his cheeks. Judd had known him a long time and had great respect for him.

"Well! Sleeping Beauty's awake. You look terrible."

Judd was getting tired of hearing it. "I feel fine," he lied. "I want to get out of here."

"When?"

"Now."

Dr. Harris looked at him reprovingly. "You just got here. Why don't you stick around a few days? I'll send you in a few nymphomaniac nurses to keep you company."

"Thanks, Seymour. I really do have to leave."

Dr. Harris sighed. "OK. You're the doctor, Doctor. Personally, I wouldn't let my cat walk around in your condition." He looked at Judd keenly. "Anything I can do to help?"

Judd shook his head.

"I'll have Miss Bedpan get your clothes."

Thirty minutes later the girl at the reception desk called a taxi for him. He was at his office at ten-fifteen.

His first patient, Teri Washburn, was waiting in the corridor. Twenty years earlier Teri had been one of the biggest stars in the Hollywood firmament. Her career had fizzled overnight, and she had married a lumberman from Oregon and dropped out of sight. Teri had been married five or six times since then and was now living in New York with her latest husband, an importer. She looked up angrily as Judd came down the corridor.

"Well . . ." she said. The speech of reproval she had rehearsed died away as she saw his face. "What happened to you?" she asked.

"You look like you got caught between two horny mix-masters."

"Just a little accident. Sorry I'm late." He unlocked the door and ushered Teri into the reception office. Carol's empty desk and chair loomed in front of him.

"I read about Carol," Teri said. There was an excited edge to her voice. "Was it a sex murder?"

"No," Judd said shortly. He opened the door to his inner office. "Give me ten minutes."

He went into the office, consulted his calendar pad, and began dialing the numbers of his patients, canceling the rest of his appointments for the day. He was able to reach all but three patients. His chest and arm hurt every time he moved, and his head was beginning to pound again. He took two Darvan from a drawer and washed them down with a glass of water. He walked over to the reception door and opened it for Teri. He steeled himself to put everything out of his mind for the next fifty minutes except the problems of his patient. Teri lay down on the couch, her skirt hiked up, and began talking.

Twenty years ago Teri Washburn had been a raving beauty, and traces of it were still there. She had the largest, softest, most innocent eyes that Judd had ever seen. The sultry mouth had a few hard lines around it, but it was still voluptuous, and her breasts were rounded and firm beneath a close-fitting Pucci print. Judd suspected that she had had a silicone injection, but he was waiting for her to mention it. The rest of her body was still good, and her legs were great.

At one time or another, most of Judd's female patients thought they were in love with him, the natural transference from patient-doctor to patient-protector-lover. But Teri's case was different. She had been trying to have an affair with Judd from the first minute she had walked into his office. She had tried to arouse him in every way she could think of—and Teri was an expert. Judd had finally warned her that unless she behaved herself, he would send her to another doctor. Since then she had behaved reasonably well with him: studying him, trying to find his Achilles heel. An eminent English physican had sent Teri to him after a nasty international scandal at Antibes. A French gossip columnist had accused Teri of spending a weekend on the yacht of a famous Greek shipping magnate to whom she was engaged, and sleeping with his three brothers while the ship's owner flew to Rome for a day on business. The story was quickly hushed up and the columnist printed a retraction and was then quietly fired. In her first session with Judd, Teri had boasted that the story was true.

"It's wild," she had said. "I need sex all the time. I can't get enough of it." She had rubbed her hands against her hips, sliding her skirt up, and looked at Judd innocently. "Do you know what I mean, honey?" she had asked.

Since that first visit, Judd had found out a great deal about Teri. She had come from a small coal-mining town in Pennsylvania.

"My father was a dumb Polack. He got his kicks getting drunk on boilermakers every Saturday night and beating the shit out of my old lady."

When she was thirteen, Teri had the body of a woman and the

face of an angel. She learned that she could earn nickels by going to the back of the coal tips with the miners. The day her father had found out, he had come into their small cabin screaming incoherently in Polish, and had thrown Teri's mother out. He had locked the door, taken off his heavy belt, and begun beating Teri. When he was through, he had raped her.

Judd had watched Teri as she lay there describing the scene, her face empty of any emotion.

"That was the last time I saw my father or mother."

"You ran away," Judd said.

Teri twisted around on the couch in surprise. "What?"

"After your father raped you—"

"Ran away?" Teri said. She threw back her head and let out a whoop of laughter. "I *liked* it. It was my bitch of a mother who threw me out!"

Now Judd switched on the tape recorder. "What would you like to talk about?" he asked.

"Fucking," she said. "Why don't we psychoanalyze you and find out why you're so straight?"

He ignored it. "Why did you think Carol's death might have something to do with a sexual attack?"

"Because everything reminds me of sex, honey." She squirmed and her skirt rode a little higher.

"Pull your skirt down, Teri."

She gave him an innocent look. "Sorry . . . You missed a great birthday party Saturday night, Doc."

"Tell me about it."

She hesitated, an unaccustomed note of concern in her voice. "You won't hate me?"

"I've told you that you don't need my approval. The only one whose approval you need is you. Right and wrong are the rules we make up ourselves so that we can play in the game with other people. Without rules, there can't be a game. But never forget— the rules are artificial."

There was a silence. Then she spoke. "It was a swinging party. My husband hired a six-piece band."

He waited.

She twisted around to look at him. "Are you sure you won't lose respect for me?"

"I want to help you. We've all done things we're ashamed of, but that does not signify that we have to continue doing them."

She studied him a moment, then lay back on the couch. "Did I ever tell you I suspected my husband, Harry, is impotent?"

"Yes." She talked of it constantly.

"He hasn't really done it to me since we've been married. He always has some goddam excuse . . . Well . . ." Her mouth twisted bitterly. "Well . . . Saturday night I fucked the band while Harry watched." She began to cry.

Judd handed her some kleenex and sat there, watching her.

No one had ever given Teri Washburn anything in her life that she had not been overcharged for. When she had first gone to Hollywood, she had landed a job as a waitress in a drive-in and used most of her wages to go to a third-rate dramatic coach. Within a week the coach had her move in with him, doing all his household chores and confining her coaching to the bedroom. A few weeks later, when she realized that he could not have gotten her an acting job even if he had wanted to, she had walked out on him and taken a job as a cashier in a Beverly Hills hotel drugstore. A movie executive had appeared on Christmas Eve to buy a last-minute gift for his wife. He had given Teri his card and told her to call him. Teri had made a screen test a week later. She was awkward and untrained, but she had three things going for her. She had a sensational face and figure, the camera loved her, and the studio executive was keeping her.

Teri Washburn appeared in bit parts in a dozen pictures the first year. She began to get fan mail. Her parts grew larger. At the end of a year her benefactor died of a heart attack, and Teri was afraid the studio would fire her. Instead, the new executive called her in and told her that he had big plans for her. She got a new contract, a raise, and a larger apartment with a mirrored bedroom. Teri's roles gradually grew to leads in B pictures, and finally, as the public showed their adoration by putting down their money at the box office to see each new Teri Washburn picture, she began to star in A pictures.

All that had been a long time ago, and Judd felt sorry for her as she lay on his couch, trying to control her sobs.

"Would you like some water?" he asked.

"N-no," she said. "I'm f-fine." She took a handkerchief out of her purse and blew her nose. "I'm sorry," she said, "for behaving like a goddam idiot." She sat up.

Judd sat there quietly, waiting for her to get control of herself.

"Why do I marry men like Harry?"

"That's an important question. Do you have any idea why?"

"How the hell should I know!" screamed Teri. "You're the psychiatrist. If I knew they were like that, you don't think I'd marry those creeps, do you?"

"What do you think?"

She stared at him, shocked. "You mean you think I *would?*" She got to her feet angrily. "Why, you dirty sonofabitch! You think I *liked* fucking the band?"

"Did you?"

In a fury she picked up a vase and flung it at him. It shattered against a table. "Does that answer you?"

"No. That vase was two hundred dollars. I'll put it on your bill."

She stared at him helplessly. "Did I really like it?" she whispered.

"You tell me."

Her voice dropped even lower. "I must be sick," she said. "Oh, God, I'm sick. Please help me, Judd. Help me!"

Judd walked over to her. "You've got to help me help you."

She nodded her head, dumbly.

"I want you to go home and think about how you feel, Teri. Not while you're doing these things, but before you do them. Think about why you want to do them. When you know that, you'll know a great deal about yourself."

She looked at him a moment, then her face relaxed. She took out her handkerchief and blew her nose again. "You're a helluva man, Charlie Brown," she said. She picked up her purse and gloves. "See you next week?"

"Yes," he said. "See you next week." He opened the door to the corridor, and Teri exited.

He knew the answer to Teri's problem, but she would have to work it through for herself. She would have to learn that she could not buy love, that it had to be given freely. And she could not accept the fact that it could be given to her freely until she learned to believe that she was worthy of receiving love. Until that time,

Teri would go on trying to buy it, using the only currency she had: her body. He knew the agony she was going through, the bottomless despair of self-loathing, and his heart went out to her. But the only way in which he could help her was to give the appearance of being impersonal and detached. He knew that to his patients he seemed remote and aloof from their problems, dispensing wisdom from some Olympian height. But that was a vital part of the facade of therapy. In reality, he cared deeply about the problems of his patients. They would have been amazed if they had known how often the unspeakable demons that tried to batter down the ramparts of their emotions appeared in Judd's own nightmares.

During the first six months of his practice as a psychiatrist, when he was undergoing the required two years of analysis necessary to become a psychoanalyst, Judd had developed blinding headaches. He was empathetically taking on the symptoms of all his patients, and it had taken him almost a year to learn to channel and control his emotional involvement.

Now, as Judd locked Teri Washburn's tape away, his mind came forcibly back to his own dilemma. He walked over to the phone and dialed information for the number of the Nineteenth Precinct.

The switchboard operator connected him with the Detective Bureau. He heard McGreavy's deep bass voice over the phone, "Lieutenant McGreavy."

"Detective Angeli, please."

"Hold on."

Judd heard the clatter of the phone as McGreavy put the receiver down. A moment later Angeli's voice came over the wire. "Detective Angeli."

"Judd Stevens. I wondered whether you'd gotten that information yet?"

There was an instant's hesitation. "I checked into it," said Angeli carefully.

"All you have to do is say 'yes' or 'no.' " Judd's heart was pounding. It was an effort for him to ask the next question. "Is Ziffren still at Matteawan?"

It seemed an eternity before Angeli answered. "Yes. He's still there."

A wave of disappointment surged through Judd. "Oh. I see."

"I'm sorry."

"Thanks," Judd said. Slowly he hung up. So that left Harrison Burke. Harrison Burke, a hopeless paranoiac who was convinced that everyone was out to kill him. Had Burke decided to strike first? John Hanson had left Judd's office at ten-fifty on Monday and had been killed a few minutes later. Judd had to find out whether Harrison Burke was in his office at that time. He looked up Burke's office number and dialed it.

"International Steel." The voice had the remote, impersonal timbre of an automaton.

"Mr. Harrison Burke, please."

"Mr. Harrison Burke . . . Thank you . . . One moment, please . . ."

Judd was gambling on Burke's secretary answering the phone. If she had stepped out for a moment and Burke answered it himself . . . "Mr. Burke's office." It was a girl's voice.

"This is Dr. Judd Stevens. I wonder if you could give me some information?"

"Oh, yes, Dr. Stevens!" There was a note of relief in her voice, mixed with apprehension. She must have known that Judd was Burke's analyst. Was she counting on him for help? What had Burke been doing to upset her?

"It's about Mr. Burke's bill.." Judd began.

"His *bill?*" She made no effort to conceal her disappointment.

Judd went on quickly. "My receptionist is—is no longer with me, and I'm trying to straighten out the books. I see that she charged Mr. Burke for a nine-thirty appointment this past Monday, and I wonder if you'd mind checking his calendar for that morning?"

"Just a moment," she said. There was disapproval in her voice now. He could read her mind. Her employer was cracking up and his analyst was only concerned about getting his money. She came back on the phone a few minutes later. "I'm afraid your receptionist made a mistake, Dr. Stevens," she said tartly. "Mr. Burke couldn't have been at your office Monday morning."

"Are you sure?" persisted Judd. "It's down in her book—nine-thirty to—"

"I don't care what's down in her book, Doctor." She was angry now, upset by his callousness. "Mr. Burke was in a staff meeting all morning on Monday. It began at eight o'clock."

"Couldn't he have slipped out for an hour?"

"No, Doctor," she said. "Mr. Burke never leaves his office during the day." There was an accusation in her voice. *Can't you see that he's ill? What are you doing to help him?*

"Shall I tell him you called?"

"That won't be necessary," Judd said. "Thank you." He wanted to add a word of reassurance, of comfort, but there was nothing he could say. He hung up.

So that was that. He had struck out. If neither Ziffren nor Harrison Burke had tried to kill him—then there could be no one else with any motive. He was back where he had started. Some person—or persons—had murdered his receptionist and one of his patients. The hit-and-run incident could have been deliberate or accidental. At the time it happened, it seemed to be deliberate. But looking at it dispassionately, Judd admitted to himself that he had been wrought up by the events of the last few days. In his highly emotional state he could easily have turned an accident into something sinister. The simple truth was that there was no one who could have any possible motive for killing him. He had an excellent relationship with all his patients, warm relationships with his friends. He had never, to his knowledge, harmed anyone. The phone rang. He recognized Anne's low, throaty voice instantly.

"Are you busy?"

"No. I can talk."

There was concern in her voice. "I read that you were hit by a car. I wanted to call you sooner, but I didn't know where to reach you."

He made his voice light. "It was nothing serious. It will teach me not to jaywalk."

"The papers said it was a hit-and-run accident."

"Yes."

"Did they find the person who did it?"

"No. It was probably some kid out for a lark." *In a black limousine without lights.*

"Are you sure?" asked Anne.

The question caught him by surprise. "What do you mean?"

"I don't really know." Her voice was uncertain. "It's just that— Carol was murdered. And now—this."

644

So she had put it together, too.

"It—it almost sounds as if there's a maniac running around loose."

"If there is," Judd assured her, "the police will catch him."

"Are you in any danger?"

His heart warmed. "Of course not." There was an awkward silence. There was so much he wanted to say, but he couldn't. He must not mistake a friendly phone call for anything more than the natural concern that a patient would have for her doctor. Anne was the type who would have called anyone who was in trouble. It meant no more than that.

"I'll still see you on Friday?" he asked.

"Yes." There was an odd note in her voice. Was she going to change her mind?

"It's a date," he said quickly. But of course it was not a date. It was a business appointment.

"Yes. Good-bye, Dr. Stevens."

"Good-bye, Mrs. Blake. Thanks for calling. Thanks very much." He hung up. And thought about Anne. And wondered if her husband had any idea what an incredibly lucky man he was.

What was her husband like? In the little Anne had said about him, Judd had formed the image of an attractive and thoughtful man. He was a sportsman, bright, was a successful businessman, donated money to the arts. He sounded like the kind of person Judd would have liked for a friend. Under different circumstances.

What could Anne's problem have been that she was afraid to discuss with her husband? Or her analyst? With a person of Anne's character, it was probably an overwhelming feeling of guilt because of an affair she had had either before she was married or after her marriage. He could not imagine her having casual affairs. Perhaps she would tell him on Friday. When he saw her for the last time.

The rest of the afternoon went by swiftly. Judd saw the few patients he had not been able to cancel. When the last one had departed, he took out the tape of Harrison Burke's last session and played it, making occasional notes as he listened.

When he had finished, he switched the tape recorder off. There was no choice. He had to call Burke's employer in the morning and inform him of Burke's condition. He glanced out the window and was surprised to see that night had fallen. It was almost eight o'clock. Now that he had finished concentrating on his work, he suddenly felt stiff and tired. His ribs were sore and his arm had begun to throb. He would go home and soak in a nice hot bath.

He put away all the tapes except Burke's, which he locked in a drawer of a side table. He would turn it over to a court-appointed psychiatrist. He put on his overcoat and was halfway out the door when the phone rang. He went to the phone and picked it up. "Dr. Stevens."

There was no answer on the other end. He heard breathing, heavy and nasal.

"Hello?"

There was no response. Judd hung up. He stood there a moment, frowning. Wrong number, he decided. He turned out the office lights, locked the doors, and moved toward the bank of elevators. All the tenants were long since gone. It was too early for the night shift of maintenance workers, and except for Bigelow, the watchman, the building was deserted.

Judd walked over to the elevator and pressed the call button. The signal indicator did not move. He pressed the button again. Nothing happened.

And at that moment all the lights in the corridor blacked out.

J udd stood in front of the elevator, the wave of darkness lapping at him like a physical force. He could feel his heart slow and then begin to beat faster. A sudden, atavistic fear flooded his body, and he reached in his pockets for a book of matches. He had left them in the office. Perhaps the lights were working on the floors below. Moving slowly and cautiously, he groped his way toward the door that led to the stairwell. He pushed the door open. The stairwell was in darkness. Carefully holding onto the railing, he started down into the blackness. In the distance below, he saw the wavering beam of a flashlight moving up the stairs. He was filled with sudden relief. Bigelow, the watchman. "Bigelow!" he yelled. "Bigelow! It's Dr. Stevens!" His voice bounced against the stone walls, echoing eerily through the stairwell. The figure holding the flashlight kept climbing silently, inexorably upward. "Who's there?" Judd demanded. The only answer was the echo of his words.

And Judd suddenly knew who was there. His assassins. There had to be at least two of them. One had cut off the power in the basement while the other blocked the stairs to prevent his escape.

The beam of the flashlight was coming closer, only two or three floors below now, climbing rapidly. Judd's body went cold with fear. His heart began to pound like a triphammer, and his legs felt weak. He turned quickly and went back up the stairs to his floor. He opened the door and stood, listening. What if someone were waiting up here in the dark corridor for him?

The sounds of the footsteps advancing up the stairs were louder now. His mouth dry, Judd turned and made his way along the inky corridor. When he reached the elevators, he began counting office doors. As he reached his office, he heard the stairwell door open. The keys slipped from his nervous fingers and dropped to the floor. He fumbled for them frantically, found them, opened the door to his reception room, and went in, double-locking the door behind him. No one could open it now without a special key.

From the corridor outside, he could hear the sound of approaching footsteps. He went into his private office and flicked the light switch. Nothing happened. There was no power at all in the building. He locked the inner door, then moved to the phone. He fumbled for the dial and dialed the operator. There were three long, steady rings, and then the operator's voice, Judd's only link to the outside world.

He spoke softly. "Operator, this is an emergency. This is Dr. Judd Stevens. I want to speak to Detective Frank Angeli at the Nineteenth Precinct. Please hurry!"

"Thank you. Your number please?"

Judd gave it to her.

"One moment, please."

He heard the sound of someone testing the corridor entrance to his private office. They could not get in that way because there was no outside knob on the door.

"Hurry, Operator!"

"One moment, please," replied the cool, unhurried voice.

There was a buzz on the line and then the police switchboard operator spoke. "Nineteenth Precinct."

Judd's heart leaped. "Detective Angeli," he said. "It's urgent!"

"Detective Angeli . . . just a moment, please."

Outside in the corridor, something was happening. He could hear the sound of muted voices. Someone had joined the first man. What were they planning?

A familiar voice came on the phone. "Detective Angeli's not here. This is his partner, Lieutenant McGreavy. Can—"

"This is Judd Stevens. I'm in my office. The lights are all out and someone's trying to break in and kill me!"

There was a heavy silence on the other end. "Look, Doctor," said McGreavy. "Why don't you come down here and we'll talk a—"

"I can't come down there," Judd almost shouted. "Someone's trying to murder me!"

There was another silence at the other end of the line. McGreavy did not believe him and was not going to help him. Outside, Judd heard a door open, and then the sound of voices in the reception office. They were in the reception office! It was impossible for them to have gotten in without a key. But he could hear them moving, coming toward the door to his private office.

McGreavy's voice was coming over the phone, but Judd did not even listen. It was too late. He replaced the receiver. It would not have mattered even if McGreavy had agreed to come. The assassins were here! *Life is a very thin thread and it only takes a second to snap it.* The fear that gripped him turned to a blind rage. He refused to be slaughtered like Hanson and Carol. He was going to put up a fight. He felt around in the dark for a possible weapon. An ashtray . . . a letter opener . . . useless. The assassins would have guns. It was a Kafka nightmare. He was being condemned for no reason by faceless executioners.

He heard them moving closer to the inner door and knew that he only had a minute or two left to live. With a strange, dispassionate calm, as though he were his own patient, he examined his final thoughts. He thought of Anne, and a sense of aching loss filled him. He thought of his patients, and of how much they needed him. Harrison Burke. With a pang he remembered that he had not yet told Burke's employer that Burke had to be committed. He would put the tapes where they could be . . . His heart lurched. Perhaps he *did* have a weapon to fight with!

He heard the doorknob turning. The door was locked, but it was flimsy. It would be simple for them to break it in. He quickly groped his way in the dark to the table where he had locked away Burke's tape. He heard a creak as pressure was applied against the reception-room door. Then he heard someone fumbling at the lock. *Why don't they just break it down?* he thought. Somewhere, far back in his mind, he felt the answer was important, but he had no time to think about it now. With trembling fingers he unlocked the drawer with the tape in it. He ripped it out of its cardboard container, then moved over to the tape player and started to thread it. It was an outside chance, but it was the only one he had.

He stood there, concentrating, trying to recall his exact conversation with Burke. The pressure on the door increased. Judd gave a quick, silent prayer. "I'm sorry about the power going out," he said aloud. "But I'm sure they'll have it fixed in a few minutes, Harrison. Why don't you lie down and relax?"

The noise at the door suddenly ceased. Judd had finished threading the tape into the player. He pressed the "on" button. Nothing happened. Of course! All the power in the building was off. He could hear them begin to work on the lock again. A feeling of desperation seized him. "That's better," he said loudly. "Just make yourself comfortable." He fumbled for the packet of matches on the table, found it, tore out a match and lit it. He held the flame close to the tape player. There was a switch marked "battery." He turned the knob, then pressed the "on" button again. At that moment, there was a sudden click as the lock on the door sprung open. His last defense was gone!

And then Burke's voice rang through the room. "Is that all you've got to say? You don't even want to hear my proof. How do I know you're not one of them?"

Judd froze, not daring to move, his heart roaring like thunder.

"You know I'm not one of them," said Judd's voice from the tape. "I'm your friend. I'm trying to help you. . . . Tell me about your proof."

"They broke into my house last night," Burke's voice said. "They came to kill me, but I was too clever for them. I sleep in my den now, and I have extra locks on all the doors so they can't get to me."

The sounds in the outer office had ceased.

Judd's voice again. "Did you report the break-in to the police?"

"Of course not! The police are in it with them. They have orders to shoot me. But they wouldn't dare do it while there are other people around, so I stay in crowds."

"I'm glad you gave me this information."

"What are you going to do with it?"

"I'm listening very carefully to everything you say," said Judd's voice. "I've got it all down"—at that moment a warning screamed in Judd's brain; the next words were—"on tape."

He made a dive for the switch and pressed it. "-in my mind," Judd said loudly. "And we'll work out the best way to handle it."

He stopped. He could not play the tape again because he had no way of telling where to pick it up. His only hope was that the men outside were convinced that Judd had a patient in the office with him. Even if they believed that, would it stop them?

"Cases like this," Judd said, raising his voice, "are really more common than you'd believe, Harrison." He gave an impatient exclamation. "I wish they'd get these lights back on. I know your chauffeur's waiting out in front for you. He'll probably wonder what's wrong and come up."

Judd stopped and listened. He could hear whispering from the other side of the door. What were they deciding? From the distant street below, he suddenly heard the insistent wail of an approaching siren. The whispering stopped. He listened for the sound of the outer door closing, but he could hear nothing. Were they still out there, waiting? The scream of the siren grew louder. It stopped in front of the building.

And suddenly all the lights went on.

8

"**D**rink?"

McGreavy shook his head moodily, studying Judd. Judd poured himself his second stiff scotch while McGreavy watched without comment. Judd's hands were still trembling. As the warmth of the whiskey floated through him, he felt himself beginning to relax.

McGreavy had arrived at the office two minutes after the lights had come on. With him was a stolid police sergeant who now sat making notes in a shorthand notebook.

McGreavy was talking. "Let's go over it once more, Dr. Stevens."

Judd took a deep breath and began again, deliberately keeping his voice calm and low. "I locked the office and went to the elevator. The corridor lights blacked out. I thought that the lights on the lower floors might be working, and I started to walk down." Judd hesitated, reliving the fear. "I saw someone coming up the stairs with a flashlight. I called out. I thought it was Bigelow, the guard. It wasn't."

"Who was it?"

"I've told you," said Judd. "I don't know. They didn't answer."

"What made you think they were coming to kill you?"

An angry retort came to Judd's lips, and he checked it. It was essential to make McGreavy believe him. "They followed me back to my office."

"You think there were two men trying to kill you?"

"At least two," Judd said. "I heard them whispering."

"You said that when you entered your reception office, you locked the outside door leading to the corridor. Is that right?"

"Yes."

"And that when you came into your inner office, you locked the door leading to the reception office."

"Yes."

McGreavy walked over to the door leading from the reception office to Judd's inner office. "Did they try to force this door?"

"No," admitted Judd. He remembered how puzzled he had been by that.

"Right," said McGreavy. "When you lock the reception-office door that opens onto the corridor, it takes a special key to open it from the outside."

Judd hesitated. He knew what McGreavy was leading up to. "Yes."

"Who had the keys to that lock?"

Judd felt his face reddening. "Carol and I."

McGreavy's voice was bland. "What about the cleaning people? How did they get in?"

"We had a special arrangement with them. Carol came in early three mornings a week and let them in. They were finished before my first patient arrived."

"That seems inconvenient. Why couldn't they get into these offices when they cleaned all the other offices?"

"Because the files I keep in here are of a highly confidential nature. I prefer the inconvenience to having strangers in here when no one is around."

McGreavy looked over at the sergeant to make sure he was getting it all down. Satisfied, he turned back to Judd. "When we walked into the reception office, the door was unlocked. Not forced—unlocked."

Judd said nothing.

McGreavy went on. "You just told us that the only ones who had a key to that lock were you and Carol. And we have Carol's key. Think again, Dr. Stevens. Who else had a key to that door?"

"No one."

"Then how do you suppose those men got in?" And Judd suddenly knew. "They made a copy of Carol's key when they killed her."

"It's possible," conceded McGreavy. A bleak smile touched his lips. "If they made a copy, we'll find paraffin traces on her key. I'll have the lab run a test."

Judd nodded. He felt as though he had scored a victory, but his feeling of satisfaction was short-lived.

"So the way you see it," McGreavy said, "two men—we'll assume for the moment there's no woman involved—had a key copied so they could get into your office and kill you. Right?"

"Right," said Judd.

"Now you said that when you went into your office, you locked the inner door. True?"

"Yes," Judd said.

McGreavy's voice was almost mild. "But we found that door unlocked, too."

"They must have had a key to it."

"Then after they got it open, why didn't they kill you?"

"I told you. They heard the voices on the tape and—"

"These two desperate killers went to all the trouble to knock out the lights, trap you up here, break into your office—and then just vanished into thin air without harming a hair of your head?" His voice was filled with contempt.

Judd felt cold anger rising in him. "What are you implying?"

"I'll spell it out for you, Doctor. I don't think anyone was here and I don't believe anyone tried to kill you."

"You don't have to take my word for it," Judd said angrily. "What about the lights? What about the night watchman, Bigelow?"

"He's in the lobby."

Judd's heart missed a beat. "Dead?"

"He wasn't when he let us in. There was a faulty wire in the main power switch. Bigelow was down in the basement trying to fix it. He got it working just as I arrived."

Judd looked at him numbly. "Oh," he said finally.

"I don't know what you're playing at, Dr. Stevens," McGreavy said, "but from now on, count me out." He moved toward the door. "And do me a favor. Don't call me again—I'll call you."

The sergeant snapped his notebook shut and followed McGreavy out.

The effects of the whiskey had evaporated. The euphoria had

gone, and he was left with a deep depression. He had no idea what his next move should be. He was on the inside of a puzzle that had no key. He felt like the boy who cried "wolf," except that the wolves were deadly, unseen phantoms, and every time McGreavy came, they seemed to vanish. Phantoms or . . . There was one other possibility. It was so horrifying that he couldn't bring himself to even acknowledge it. But he had to.

He had to face the possibility that he was a paranoiac.

A mind that was overstressed could give birth to delusions that seemed totally real. He had been working too hard. He had not had a vacation in years. It was conceivable that the deaths of Hanson and Carol could have been the catalyst that had sent his mind over some emotional precipice so that events became enormously magnified and out of joint. People suffering from paranoia lived in a land where everyday, commonplace things represented nameless terrors. Take the car accident. If it had been a deliberate attempt to kill him, surely the driver would have gotten out and made sure that the job was finished. And the two men who had come here tonight. He did not *know* that they had guns. Would a paranoiac not assume that they were there to kill him? It was more logical to believe that they were sneak thieves. When they had heard the voices in his inner office, they had fled. Surely, if they were assassins, they would have opened the unlocked door and killed him. How could he find out the truth? He knew it would be useless to appeal to the police again. There was no one to whom he could turn.

An idea began to form. It was born of desperation, but the more he examined it, the more sense it made. He picked up the telephone directory and began to rifle through the yellow pages.

At four o'clock the following afternoon Judd left his office and drove to an address on the lower West Side. It was an ancient, rundown brownstone apartment house. As he pulled up in front of the dilapidated building, Judd began to have misgivings. Perhaps he had the wrong address. Then a sign in a window of a first-floor apartment caught his eye:

NORMAN Z. MOODY
Private Investigator
SATISFACTION GUARANTEED

Judd alighted from the car. It was a raw, windy day with a forecast of late snow. He moved gingerly across the icy sidewalk and walked into the vestibule of the building.

The vestibule smelled of mingled odors of stale cooking and urine. He pressed the button marked "Norman Z. Moody—1," and a moment later a buzzer sounded. He stepped inside and found Apartment 1. A sign on the door read:

Norman Z. Moody
Private Investigator
RING BELL AND ENTER

He rang the bell and entered.

Moody was obviously not a man given to throwing his money away on luxuries. The office looked as though it had been furnished by a blind, hyperthyroid pack rat. Odds and ends crammed every spare inch of the room. In one corner stood a tattered Japanese screen. Next to it was an East Indian lamp, and in front of the lamp a scarred Danish-modern table. Newspapers and old magazines were piled everywhere.

A door to an inner room burst open and Norman Z. Moody emerged. He was about five foot five and must have weighed three hundred pounds. He rolled as he walked, reminding Judd of an animated Buddha. He had a round, jovial face with wide, guileless, pale blue eyes. He was totally bald and his head was egg-shaped. It was impossible to guess his age.

"Mr. Stevenson?" Moody greeted him.

"Dr. Stevens," Judd said.

"Sit down, sit down." Buddha with a Southern drawl.

Judd looked around for a seat. He removed a pile of old body-building and nudist magazines from a scrofulous-looking leather armchair with strips torn out of it, and gingerly sat down.

Moody was lowering his bulk into an oversized rocking chair. "Well, now! What can I do for you?"

Judd knew that he had made a mistake. Over the phone he had carefully given Moody his full name. A name that had been on the front page of every New York newspaper in the last few days. And he had managed to pick the only private detective in the whole city who had never even heard of him. He cast about for some excuse to walk out.

"Who recommended me?" Moody prodded.

Judd hesitated, not wanting to offend him. "I got your name out of the yellow pages."

Moody laughed. "I don't know what I'd do without the yellow pages," he said. "Greatest invention since corn liquor." He gave another little laugh.

Judd got to his feet. He was dealing with a total idiot. "I'm sorry to have taken up your time, Mr. Moody," he said. "I'd like to think about this some more before I . . ."

"Sure, sure. I understand," Moody said. "You'll have to pay me for the appointment, though."

"Of course," Judd said. He reached in his pocket and pulled out some bills. "How much is it?"

"Fifty dollars."

"Fifty—?" Judd swallowed angrily, peeled off some bills and thrust them in Moody's hand. Moody counted the money carefully.

"Thanks a lot," Moody said. Judd started toward the door, feeling like a fool. "Doctor . . ."

Judd turned. Moody was smiling at him benevolently, tucking the money into the pocket of his waistcoat. "As long as you're stuck for the fifty dollars," he said mildly, "you might as well sit down and tell me what your problem is. I always say that nothin' takes more weight off than gettin' things off your chest."

The irony of it, coming from this silly fat man, almost made Judd laugh. Judd's whole life was devoted to listening to people get things off their chests. He studied Moody a moment. What could he lose? Perhaps talking it out with a stranger would help. Slowly he went back to his chair and sat down.

"You look like you're carryin' the weight of the world, Doc. I always say that four shoulders are better than two."

Judd was not certain how many of Moody's aphorisms he was going to be able to stand.

Moody was watching him. "What brought you here? Women, or money? I always say if you took away women and money, you'd solve most of the world's problems right there." Moody was eyeing him, waiting for an answer.

"I—I think someone is trying to kill me."

Blue eyes blinked. "You think?"

Judd brushed the question aside. "Perhaps you could give me the name of someone who specializes in investigating that kind of thing."

"I certainly can," Moody said. "Norman Z. Moody. Best in the country."

Judd sighed in despair.

"Why don't you tell me about it, Doc?" Moody suggested. "Let's see if the two of us can't sort it out a little."

Judd had to smile in spite of himself. It sounded so much like himself. *Just lie down and say anything that comes into your mind.* Why not? He took a deep breath and, as concisely as possible, told Moody the events of the past few days. As he spoke, he forgot that Moody was there. He was really speaking to himself, putting into words the baffling things that had occurred. He carefully said nothing to Moody about his fears for his own sanity. When Judd had finished, Moody regarded him happily.

"You got yourself a dilly of a problem there. Either somebody's out to murder you, or you're afraid that you're becoming a schizophrenic paranoiac."

Judd looked up in surprise. Score one for Norman Z. Moody.

Moody went on. "You said there are two detectives on the case. Do you remember their names?"

Judd hesitated. He was reluctant to get too deeply committed to this man. All he really wanted to do was get out of there. "Frank Angeli," he answered, "and Lieutenant McGreavy."

There was an almost imperceptible change in Moody's expression.

"What reason would anyone have to kill you, Doc?"

"I have no idea. As far as I know, I haven't any enemies."

"Oh, come on. Everybody's got a few enemies layin' around. I always say enemies give a little salt to the bread of life."

Judd tried not to wince.

"Married?"

"No," Judd said.

"Are you a fairy?"

Judd sighed. "Look, I've been through all this with the police and—"

"Yeah. Only you're payin' me to help you," Moody said, unperturbed. "Owe anybody any money?"

"Just the normal monthly bills."

"What about your patients?"

"What about them?"

"Well, I always say if you're lookin' for seashells, go down to the seashore. Your patients are a lot of loonies. Right?"

"Wrong," Judd said curtly. "They're people with problems."

"Emotional problems that they can't solve themselves. Could one of them have it in for you? Oh, not for any real reason, but maybe somebody with an imaginary grievance against you."

"It's possible. Except for one thing. Most of my patients have been under my care for a year or more. In that length of time I've gotten to know them as well as one human being can know another."

"Don't they never get mad at you?" Moody asked innocently.

"Sometimes. But we're not looking for someone who's angry. We're looking for a homicidal paranoiac who has murdered at least two people and has made several attempts to murder me." He hesitated, then made himself go on. "If I have a patient like that and don't know it, then you're looking at the most incompetent psychoanalyst who ever lived."

He looked up and saw Moody studying him.

"I always say first things first," Moody said cheerfully. "The first thing we've gotta do is find out whether someone's trying to knock you off, or whether you're nuts. Right, Doc?" He broke into a broad smile, taking the offense out of his words.

"How?" Judd asked.

"Simple," Moody said. "Your problem is, you're standin' at home plate strikin' at curve balls, an' you don't know if anyone's pitchin'. First we're gonna find out if there's a ballgame goin' on; then we're gonna find out who the players are. You got a car?"

"Yes."

Judd had forgotten about walking out and finding another private detective. He sensed now behind Moody's bland, innocent face and his homespun maxims a quiet, intelligent capability.

"I think your nerves are shot," Moody said. "I want you to take a little vacation."

"When?"

"Tomorrow morning."

"That's impossible," Judd protested. "I have patients scheduled. . . ."

Moody brushed it aside. "Cancel them."

"But what good—"

"Do I tell you how to run your business?" Moody asked. "When you leave here, I want you to go straight to a travel agency. Have them get you a reservation at"—he thought a moment—"Grossinger's. That's a pretty drive up through the Catskills . . . Is there a garage in the apartment building where you live?"

"Yes."

"OK. Tell them to service your car for the trip. You don't want to have any breakdowns on the road."

"Couldn't I do this next week? Tomorrow is a full—"

"After you make your reservation, you're going back to your office and call all your patients. Tell them you've had an emergency and you'll be back in a week."

"I really can't," Judd said. "It's out of the—"

"You'd better call Angeli, too," Moody continued. "I don't want the police hunting for you while you're gone."

"Why am I doing this?" Judd asked.

"To protect your fifty dollars. That reminds me. I'm gonna need another two hundred for a retainer. Plus fifty a day and expenses.

Moody hauled his large bulk up out of the big rocker. "I want you to get a nice early start tomorrow," he said, "so you can get up there before dark. Can you leave about seven in the morning?"

"I . . . I suppose so. What will I find when I get up there?"

"With a little luck, a scorecard."

Five minutes later Judd was thoughtfully getting into his car. He had told Moody that he could not go away and leave his patients on such short notice. But he knew that he was going to. He was literally putting his life into the hands of the Falstaff of the private detective world. As he started to drive away, his eye caught Moody's sign in the window.

SATISFACTION GUARANTEED.

He'd better be right, Judd thought grimly.

The plan for the trip went smoothly. Judd stopped at a travel agency on Madison Avenue. They reserved a room for him at Grossinger's and provided him with a road map and a variety of color brochures on the Catskills. Next he telephoned his answering service and arranged for them to call his patients and cancel all his appointments until further notice. He phoned the Nineteenth Precinct and asked for Detective Angeli.

"Angeli's home sick," said an impersonal voice. "Do you want his home number?

"Yes."

A few moments later he was talking to Angeli. From the sound of Angeli's voice, he had a heavy cold.

"I've decided I need to get out of town for a few days," Judd said. "I'm leaving in the morning. I wanted to check it with you."

There was a silence while Angeli thought it over. "It might not be a bad idea. Where will you go?"

"I thought I'd drive up to Grossinger's."

"All right," Angeli said. "Don't worry. I'll clear it with McGreavy." He hesitated. "I heard what happened at your office last night."

"You mean you heard McGreavy's version," Judd said.

"Did you get a look at the men who tried to kill you?"

So Angeli, at least, believed him.

"No."

"Nothing at all that could help us find them? Color, age, height?"

"I'm sorry," Judd replied. "It was dark."

Angeli sniffed. "OK. I'll keep looking. Maybe I'll have some good news for you when you get back. Be careful, Doctor."

"I will," Judd said gratefully. And he hung up.

Next he phoned Harrison Burke's employer and briefly explained Burke's situation. There was no choice but to have him committed as soon as possible. Judd then called Peter, explained that he had to go out of town for a week, and asked him to make the necessary arrangements for Burke. Peter agreed.

The decks were clear.

The thing that disturbed Judd the most was that he would be unable to see Anne on Friday. Perhaps he would never see her again.

As he drove back toward his apartment, he thought about Norman Z. Moody. He had an idea what Moody was up to. By having Judd notify all his patients that he was going away, Moody was making sure that if one of Judd's patients was the killer—if there was a killer—a trap, using Judd as the bait, would be set for him.

Moody had instructed him to leave his forwarding address with his telephone exchange and with the doorman at the apartment building. He was making certain that everyone would know where Judd was going.

When Judd pulled up in front of the apartment house, Mike was there to greet him.

"I'm leaving on a trip in the morning, Mike," Judd informed him. "Will you make sure the garage services my car and fills the tank?"

"I'll have it taken care of, Dr. Stevens. What time will you be needing the car?"

"I'll be leaving at seven." Judd sensed Mike watching him as he walked into the apartment building.

When he entered his apartment, he locked the doors and carefully checked the windows. Everything seemed to be in order.

He took two codeine pills, got undressed, and ran a hot bath, gingerly easing his aching body into it, feeling the tensions soaking out of his back and neck. He lay in the blessedly relaxing tub, thinking. Why had Moody warned him not to let the car break down on the road? Because that was the most likely place for him to be attacked, somewhere on a lonely road in the Catskills? And what could Moody do about it if Judd were attacked? Moody had refused to tell him what his plan was—if there was a plan. The more Judd examined it, the more convinced he became that he was walking into a trap. Moody had said he was setting it up for Judd's pursuers. But no matter how many times he went over it, the answer always came out the same: the trap seemed designed to catch Judd. But why? What interest could Moody have in getting him killed? *My God*, thought Judd. *I've picked a name at random out of the yellow pages of the Manhattan Telephone Directory and I believe he wants to have me murdered! I am paranoiac!*

He felt his eyes beginning to close. The pills and the hot bath had done their work well. Wearily he pulled himself out of the tub, carefully patted his bruised body dry with a fluffy towel, and put on a pair of pajamas. He got into bed and set the electric alarm clock for six. The Catskills, he thought. It was an appropriate name. And he fell into a deep, exhausted sleep.

At six A.M., when the alarm went off, Judd was instantly awake. As though there had been no time lapse at all, his first thought was, *I don't believe in a series of coincidences and I don't believe that one of my patients is a mass murderer. Ergo, I am either a paranoiac, or am becoming one.* What he needed was to consult another psychoanalyst without delay. He would phone Dr. Robbie. He knew that it would mean the end of his professional career, but there was no help for it. If he were suffering from paranoia, they would have to commit him. Did Moody suspect that he was dealing with a mental case? Was that why he suggested a vacation? Not because he believed anyone was after Judd's life, but because he could see the signs of a nervous breakdown? Perhaps the wisest course would be to follow Moody's advice and go to the Catskills for a few days. Alone, with all the pressures removed, he could calmly try to evaluate himself, try to reason out when his mind had started to trick him, when he had begun to lose touch with reality. Then, when he returned, he would make an appointment with Dr. Robbie and put himself under his care.

It was a painful decision to make, but having made it, Judd felt better. He dressed, packed a small suitcase with enough clothes for five days, and carried it out to the elevator.

Eddie was not on duty yet, and the elevator was on self-service. Judd rode down to the basement garage. He looked around for Wilt, the attendant, but he was nowhere around. The garage was deserted.

Judd spotted his car parked in a corner against the cement wall. He walked over to it, put his suitcase in the back seat, opened the front door, and eased in behind the wheel. As he reached for the ignition key, a man loomed up at his side from nowhere. Judd's heart skipped a beat.

"You're right on schedule." It was Moody.

"I didn't know you were going to see me off," Judd said.

Moody beamed at him, his cherubic face breaking into a huge smile. "I had nothin' better to do and I couldn't sleep."

Judd was suddenly grateful for the tactful way Moody had handled the situation. No reference to the fact that Judd was a mental case, just an ingenuous suggestion that he drive up to the country and take a rest. Well, the least Judd could do was to keep up the pretense that everything was normal.

"I decided you were right. I'm going to drive up and see if I can find a scorecard to the ballgame."

"Oh, you don't have to go anywhere for that," Moody said. "That's all taken care of."

Judd looked at him blankly. "I don't understand."

"It's simple. I always say when you want to get to the bottom of anything, you gotta start diggin'."

"Mr. Moody . . ."

Moody leaned against the door of the car. "You know what I found intriguin' about your little problem, Doc? Seemed like every five minutes somebody was tryin' to kill you—maybe. Now that 'maybe' fascinated me. There was nothin' for us to bite into 'til we found out whether you were crackin' up, or whether someone was really tryin' to turn you into a corpse."

Judd looked at him. "But the Catskills . . ." he said weakly.

"Oh, you wasn't never goin' to the Catskills, Doc." He opened the door of the car. "Step out here."

Bewildered, Judd stepped out of the car.

"You see, that was just advertising. I always say if you wanta catch a shark, you've gotta bloody up the water first."

Judd was watching his face.

"I'm afraid you never would have got to the Catskills," Moody said gently. He walked around to the hood of the car, fumbled with the catch, and raised the hood. Judd walked over to his side. Taped to the distributor head were three sticks of dynamite. Two thin wires were dangling loose from the ignition.

"Booby-trapped," Moody said.

Judd looked at him, baffled. "But how did you . . ."

Moody grinned. "I told you, I'm a bad sleeper. I got here around midnight. I paid the night man to go out and have some fun, an' I just kinda waited in the shadows. The nightman'll cost another twenty dollars," he added. "I didn't want you to look cheap."

Judd felt a sudden wave of affection toward the little fat man. "Did you see who did it?"

"Nope. It was done before I got here. At six o'clock this mornin' I figured no one was gonna show up any more, so I took a look." He pointed to the dangling wires. "Your friends are real cute. They rigged a second booby trap so if you lifted the hood all the way, this wire would detonate the dynamite. The same thing would happen if you turned on your ignition. There's enough stuff here to wipe out half the garage."

Judd felt suddenly sick to his stomach. Moody looked at him sympathetically. "Cheer up," he said. "Look at the progress we've made. We know two things. First of all, we know you're not nuts. And secondly"—the smile left his face—"we know that somebody is God Almighty anxious to murder you, Dr. Stevens."

T hey were sitting in the living room of Judd's apartment, talking, Moody's enormous body spilling over the large couch. Moody had carefully put the pieces of the already defused bomb in the trunk of his own car.

"Shouldn't you have left it there so the police could have examined it?" Judd asked.

"I always say that the most confusin' thing in the world is too much information."

"But it would have proved to Lieutenant McGreavy that I've been telling the truth."

"Would it?"

Judd saw his point. As far as McGreavy was concerned, Judd could have placed it there himself. Still, it seemed odd to him that a private detective would withhold evidence from the police. He had a feeling that Moody was like an enormous iceberg. Most of the man was concealed under the surface, under that facade of gentle, small-town bumbler. But now, as he listened to Moody talking, he was filled with elation. He was not insane and the world had not suddenly become filled with wild coincidences. There was an assassin on the loose. A flesh-and-blood assassin. And for some reason he had chosen Judd as his target. *My God*, thought Judd, *how easily our egos can be destroyed*. A few minutes ago he had been ready to believe that he was paranoiac. He owed Moody an incalculable debt.

". . . You're the doctor," Moody was saying. "I'm just an old gumshoe. I always say when you want honey, go to a beehive."

Judd was beginning to understand Moody's jargon. "You want my opinion about the kind of man, or men, we're looking for."

"That's it," beamed Moody. "Are we dealin' with some homicidal maniac who broke out of a loony bin"—

Mental institution, Judd thought automatically. —"or have we got somethin' deeper goin' here?"

"Something deeper," said Judd instantly.

"What makes you think so, Doc?"

"First of all, *two* men broke into my office last night. I might swallow the theory of one lunatic, but two lunatics working together is too much."

Moody nodded approvingly. "Gotcha. Go on."

"Secondly, a deranged mind may have an obsession, but it works in a definite pattern. I don't know why John Hanson and Carol Roberts were killed, but unless I'm wrong, I'm scheduled to be the third and last victim."

"What makes you think you're the last?" asked Moody curiously.

"Because," replied Judd, "if there were going to be other murders, then the first time they failed to kill me, they would have gone on to get whoever else was on their list. But instead of that, they've been concentrating on trying to kill me."

"You know," said Moody approvingly, "you have the natural born makin's of a detective."

Judd was frowning. "There are several things that make no sense."

"Such as?"

"First, the motive," said Judd. "I don't know anyone who—"

"We'll come back to that. What else?"

"If someone really was that anxious to kill me, when the car knocked me down, all the driver had to do was to back up and run over me. I was unconscious."

"Ah. That's where Mr. Benson comes in."

Judd looked at him blankly.

"Mr. Benson is the witness to your accident," explained Moody benevolently. "I got his name from the police report and went to see him after you left my office. That'll be three-fifty for taxicabs. OK?"

Judd nodded, speechless.

"Mr. Benson—he's a furrier, by the way. Beautiful stuff. If you ever want to buy anything for your sweetheart, I can get you a discount. Anyway, Tuesday, the night of the accident, he was comin' out of an office building where his sister-in-law works. He dropped some pills off because his brother Matthew, who's a Bible salesman, had the flu an' she was goin' to take the pills home to him."

Judd controlled his impatience. If Norman Z. Moody had felt like sitting there and reciting the entire Bill of Rights, he was going to listen.

"So Mr. Benson dropped off these pills an' was comin' out of the building when he saw this limousine headin' toward you. Of course, he didn't know it was you at the time."

Judd nodded.

"The car was kinda crabbin' sideways, an' from Benson's angle, it looked like it was in a skid. When he saw it hit you, he started runnin' over to see if he could help. The limousine backed up to make another run at you. He saw Mr. Benson an' got out of there like a bat outta hell."

Judd swallowed. "So if Mr. Benson hadn't happened along . . ."

"Yeah," said Moody mildly. "You might say you an' me wouldn't have met. These boys aren't playin' games. They're out to get you, Doc."

"What about the attack in my office? Why didn't they break the door down?"

Moody was silent for a moment, thinking. "That's a puzzler. They coulda broken in an' killed you an' whoever was with you an' got away without anybody seein' them. But when they thought you weren't alone, they left. It don't fit in with the rest." He sat there worrying his lower lip. "Unless . . ." he said.

"Unless what?"

A speculative look came over Moody's face. "I wonder . . ." he breathed.

"What?"

"It'll keep for the time bein'. I got me a little idea, but it don't make sense until we find a motive."

Judd shrugged helplessly. "I don't know of anyone who has a motive for killing me."

Moody thought about this a moment. "Doc, could you have any

secret that you shared with this patient of yours, Hanson, an' Carol Roberts? Somethin' maybe only the three of you knew about?"

Judd shook his head. "The only secrets I have are professional secrets about my patients. And there's not one single thing in any of their case histories that would justify murder. None of my patients is a secret agent, or a foreign spy, or an escaped convict. They're just ordinary people—housewives, professional men, bank clerks—who have problems they can't cope with."

Moody looked at him guilelessly. "An' you're sure that you're not harboring a homicidal maniac in your little group?"

Judd's voice was firm. "Positive. Yesterday I might not have been sure. To tell you the truth, I was beginning to think that I was suffering from paranoia and that you were humoring me.

Moody smiled at him. "The thought had crossed my mind," he said. "After you phoned me for an appointment, I did some checking up on you. I called a couple of pretty good doctor friends of mine. You got quite a reputation."

So the "Mr. Stevenson" had been part of Moody's country bumpkin facade.

"If we go to the police now," Judd said, "with what we know, we can at least get them to start looking for whoever's behind all this."

Moody looked at him in mild surprise. "You think so? We don't really have much to go on yet, do we, Doc?"

It was true.

"I wouldn't be discouraged," Moody said. "I think we're makin' real progress. We've narrowed it down nicely."

A note of frustration crept into Judd's voice. "Sure. It could be anyone in the continental United States."

Moody sat there a moment, contemplating the ceiling. Finally he shook his head. "Families," he sighed.

"Families?"

"Doc—I believe you when you say you know your patients inside out. If you tell me they couldn't do anything like this, I have to go along with you. It's your beehive an' you're th' keeper of the honey." He leaned forward on the couch. "But tell me somethin'. When you take on a patient, do you interview his family?"

"No. Sometimes the family isn't even aware that the patient is undergoing psychoanalysis.

Moody leaned back, satisfied. "There you are," he said.

Judd looked at him. "You think that some member of a patient's family is trying to kill me?"

"Could be."

"They'd have no more motive than the patient. Less, probably."

Moody painfully pushed himself to his feet. "You never know, do you, Doc? Tell you what I'd like you to do. Get me a list of all the patients you've seen in the last four or five weeks. Can you do that?"

Judd hesitated. "No," he said, finally.

"That confidential patient-doctor business? I think maybe it's time to bend that a little. Your life's at stake.

"I think you're on the wrong track. What's been happening has nothing to do with my patients or their families. If there had been any insanity in their families, it would have come out in the psychoanalysis." He shook his head. "I'm sorry, Mr. Moody. I have to protect my patients."

"You said there was nothing in the files that was important."

"Nothing that's important to us." He thought of some of the material in the files. John Hanson picking up sailors in gay bars on Third Avenue. Teri Washburn making love to the boys in the band. Fourteen-year-old Evelyn Warshak, the resident prostitute in the ninth grade . . . "I'm sorry," he said again. "I can't show you the files."

Moody shrugged. "OK,' he said. "OK. Then you're gonna have to do part of my job for me."

"What do you want me to do?"

"Take out the tapes on everybody you've had on your couch for the last month. Listen real careful to each one. Only this time don't listen like a doctor—listen like a detective—look for anything the least bit offbeat."

"I do that anyway. That's my job."

"Do it again. An' keep your eyes open. I don't want to lose you 'til we solve this case." He picked up his overcoat and struggled into it, making it look like an elephant ballet. Fat men were supposed to be graceful, thought Judd, but that did not include Mr. Moody. "Do you know the most peculiar thing about this whole megillah?" queried Moody thoughtfully.

"What?"

"You put your finger on it before, when you said there were *two* men. Maybe one man might have a burning itch to knock you off—but why *two?*"

"I don't know."

Moody studied him a moment, speculatively. "By God!" he finally said.

"What is it?"

"I just might have a brainstorm. If I'm right, there could be *more* than two men out to kill you."

Judd stared at him incredulously. "You mean there's a whole group of maniacs after me? That doesn't make sense."

There was a look of growing excitement on Moody's face. "Doctor, I've got an idea who the umpire in this ballgame might be." He looked at Judd, his eyes bright. "I don't know how yet, or why—but it could be I know *who.*"

"Who?"

Moody shook his head. "You'd have me sent to a cracker factory if I told you. I always say if you're gonna shoot off your mouth, make sure it's loaded first. Let me do a little target practice. If I'm on the right track, I'll tell you."

"I hope you are," Judd said earnestly.

Moody looked at him a moment. "No, Doc. If you value your life worth a damn—pray I'm wrong."

And Moody was gone.

He took a taxi to the office.

It was Friday noon, and with only three more shopping days until Christmas, the streets were crowded with late shoppers, bundled up against the raw wind sweeping in from the Hudson River. The store windows were festive and bright, filled with lighted Christmas trees and carved figures of the Nativity. Peace on Earth. Christmas. And Elizabeth, and their unborn baby. One day soon—if he survived—he would have to make his own peace, free himself from the dead past and let go. He knew that with Anne he could have . . . He firmly stopped himself. What was the point in fantasizing about a married woman about to go away with her husband, whom she loved? The taxi pulled up in front of his office building and Judd got out, nervously looking around. But what could he look for? He had no idea what the murder weapon would be, or who would wield it.

When he reached his office, he locked the outer door, went to the paneling that concealed the tapes, and opened it. The tapes were filed chronologically, under the name of each patient. He selected the most recent ones and carried them over to the tape recorder. With all his appointments canceled for the day, he would be able to concentrate on trying to find some clue that might involve friends or families of his patients. He felt that Moody's suggestion was farfetched, but he had too much respect for him to ignore it.

As he put on the first tape, he remembered the last time he had used the machine. Was it only last night? The memory filled him again with the sharp sense of nightmare. Someone had planned to murder him here in this room, where they had murdered Carol.

He suddenly realized that he had given no thought to his patients at the free hospital clinic where he worked one morning a week. It was probably because the murders had revolved around this office rather than the hospital. Still . . . He walked over to a section of the cabinets labeled "CLINIC," looked through some of the tapes, and finally selected half a dozen. He put the first one on the tape recorder.

Rose Graham.

". . . an accident, Doctor. Nancy cries a lot. She's always been a whiny baby, so when I hit her, it's for her own good, y'know?"

"Did you ever try to find out why Nancy cries a lot?" Judd's voice asked.

" 'Cause she's spoiled. Her daddy spoiled her rotten and then run off and left us. Nancy always thought she was daddy's girl, but how much could Harry really have loved her if he run off like that?"

"You and Harry were never married, were you?"

"Well . . . Common law, I guess you'd call it. We was goin' to get married."

"How long did you live together?"

"Four years."

"How long was it after Harry left you that you broke Nancy's arm?"

" 'Bout a week, I guess. I didn't mean to break it. It's just that she wouldn't stop whining, so I finally picked up this curtain rod an' started beating on her."

"Do you think Harry loved Nancy more than he loved you?"

"No. Harry was crazy about me."

"Then why do you think he left you?"

"Because he was a man. An' y'know what men are? Animals! All of you! You should all be slaughtered like pigs!" Sobbing.

Judd switched off the tape and thought about Rose Graham. She was a psychotic misanthrope, and she had nearly beaten her six-year-old child to death on two separate occasions. But the pattern of the murders did not fit Rose Graham's psychosis.

He put on the next tape from the clinic.

Alexander Fallon.

"The police say that you attacked Mr. Champion with a knife, Mr. Fallon."

"I only did what I was told."

"Someone told you to kill Mr. Champion?"

"He told me to do it."

"He?"

"God."

"Why did God tell you to kill him?"

"Because Champion's an evil man. He's an actor. I saw him on the stage. He kissed this woman. This actress. In front of the whole audience. He kissed her and . . ."

Silence.

"Go on."

"He touched her—her titty."

"Did that upset you?"

"Of course! It upset me terribly. Don't you understand what that meant? He had carnal knowledge of her. When I came out of that theater, I felt like I had just come from Sodom and Gomorrah. They had to be punished."

"So you decided to kill him."

"I didn't decide it. God decided. I just carried out His orders."

"Does God often talk to you?"

"Only when there's His work to be done. He's chosen me as His instrument, because I'm pure. Do you know what makes me pure? Do you know what the most cleansing thing in the world is? Slaying the wicked!"

Alexander Fallon. Thirty-five, a part-time baker's assistant. He had been sent to a mental home for six months and then released. Could God have told him to destroy Hanson, a homosexual, and Carol, a former prostitute, and Judd, their benefactor? Judd decided that it was unlikely. Fallon's thought processes took place in brief, painful spasms. Whoever had planned the murders was highly organized.

He played several more of the tapes from the clinic, but none of them fit into the pattern he was searching for. No. It wasn't any patient at the clinic.

He looked over the office files again and a name caught his eye. Skeet Gibson.

He put on the tape.

" 'Mornin', Dockie. How do you like this bee-u-ti-ful day I cooked up for you?"

"You're feeling good today."

"If I was feelin' any better, they'd have me locked up. Did you catch my show last night?"

"No. I'm sorry, I wasn't able to."

"I was only a smash. Jack Gould called me 'the most lovable comedian in the world.' An' who am I to argue with a genius like Jack Gould? You shoulda heard that audience! They were applauding like it was going out of style. Do ya know what that proves?"

"That they can read 'Applause' cards?"

"You're sharp, you devil, you. That's what I like—a headshrinker with a sense of humor. The last one I had was a drag. Had a great big beard that really bugged me."

"Why?"

"Because it was a lady!"

Loud laughter.

"Gotcha that time, didn't I, old cock? Seriously, folks, one of the reasons I'm feelin' so good is because I just pledged a million dollars—count 'em: one million bucks—to help the kids in Biafra."

"No wonder you feel good."

"You bet your sweet ass. That story hit the front pages all over the world."

"Is that important?"

"What do you mean, 'Is that important?' How many guys

pledge that kind of loot? You've gotta blow your own horn, Peter Pan. I'm glad I can afford to pledge the money."

"You keep saying 'pledge.' Do you mean 'give?' "

"Pledge—give—what's the difference? You pledge a million—give a few grand—an' they kiss your ass . . . Did I tell you it's my anniversary today?"

"No. Congratulations."

"Thanks. Fifteen great years. You never met Sally. There's the sweetest broad that ever walked God's earth. I really got lucky with my marriage. You know what a pain in the keester in-laws can be? Well, Sally's got these two brothers, Ben an' Charley. I told you about them. Ben's head writer on my TV show an' Charley's my producer. They're geniuses. I've been on the air seven years now. An' we're never outta the top ten in the Nielsen's. I was smart to marry into a family like that, huh? Most women get fat an' sloppy once they've hooked their husband. But Sally, bless her, is slimmer now than the day we were married. What a dame! . . . Got a cigarette?"

"Here. I thought you quit smoking."

"I just wanted to show myself I had the old willpower, so I quit. Now I'm smoking because I want to. . . . I made a new deal with the network yesterday. I really shafted em. Is my time up yet?"

"No. Are you restless, Skeet?"

"To tell you the truth, sweetie, I'm in such great shape I don't know what the hell I'm coming in here any more for."

"No more problems?"

"Me? The world's my oyster an' I'm Diamond Jim Brady. I've gotta hand it to you. You've really helped me. You're my man. With the kind of money you make, maybe I should go into business and set up my own shingle, huh? . . . That reminds me of the great story of the guy who goes to a wigpicker, but he's so nervous he just lays on the couch and doesn't say anything. At the end of the hour, the shrink says, 'That'll be fifty dollars.' Well, that goes on for two whole years without the schmuck saying one word. Finally the little guy opens his mouth one day and says, 'Doctor—could I ask you a question?' 'Sure,' says the Doc. And the little guy says, 'Would you like a partner?' "

Loud laughter.

"You got a shot of aspirin or somethin'?"

"Certainly. Is it one of your bad headaches?"

"Nothin' I can't handle, old buddy . . . Thanks. That'll do the trick."

"What do you think brings these headaches on?"

"Just normal show-biz tension . . . We have our script reading this afternoon."

"Does that make you nervous?"

"Me? Hell, no! What have I got to be nervous about? If the jokes are lousy, I make a face, wink at the audience, an' they eat it up. No matter how bad the show is, little old Skeet comes out smelling like a rose."

"Why do you think you have these headaches every week?"

"How the fuck do I know? You're supposed to be a doctor. You tell me. I don't pay you to sit on your fat ass for an hour asking stupid questions. Jesus Christ, if an idiot like you can't cure a simple headache, they shouldn't let you be running around loose, messing up people's lives. Where'd you get your medical certificate? From a veterinarian school? I wouldn't trust my fuckin' cats with you. You're a goddam quack! The only reason I came to you in the first place was because Sally shitted me into it. It was the only way I could get her off my back. Do ya know my definition of Hell? Bein' married to an ugly, skinny nag for fifteen years. If you're lookin' for some more suckers to cheat, take on her two idiot brothers, Ben an' Charley. Ben, my head writer, doesn't know which end of the pencil has the lead in it, an' his brother's even stupider. I wish they'd all drop dead. They're out to get me. You think I like you? You stink! You're so goddam smug, sitting there looking down on everybody. You haven't got any problems, have you? Do you know why? Because you're not for real. You're out of it. All you do is sit on your fat keester all day long an' steal money from sick people. Well, I'm gonna get you, you sonofabitch. I'm gonna report you to the AMA. . . ."

Sobbing.

"I wish I didn't have to go to that goddam reading."

Silence.

"Well—keep your pecker up. See ya next week, sweetie."

Judd switched off the recorder. Skeet Gibson, America's most beloved comedian, should have been institutionalized ten years ago. His hobbies were beating up young, blond showgirls and getting into barroom brawls. Skeet was a small man, but he had started out as a prizefighter, and he knew how to hurt. One of his favorite sports was going into a gay bar, coaxing an unsuspecting homosexual into the men's room, and beating him unconscious. Skeet had been picked up by the police several times, but the incidents had always been hushed up. After all, he was America's most lovable comic. Skeet was paranoid enough to want to kill, and he was capable of killing in a fit of rage. But Judd did not think he was cold-blooded enough to carry out this kind of planned vendetta. And in that, Judd felt certain, lay the key to the solution. Whoever was trying to murder him was doing it not in the heat of any passion, but methodically and coldbloodedly. A madman.

Who was not mad.

T he phone rang. It was his answering service. They had been able to reach all his patients except Anne Blake. Judd thanked the operator and hung up.

So Anne was coming here today. He was disturbed at how unreasonably happy he was at the thought of seeing her. He must remember that she was only coming by because he had asked her to, as her doctor. He sat there thinking about Anne. How much he knew about her . . . and how little.

He put Anne's tape on the tape recorder and listened to it. It was one of her first visits.

"Comfortable, Mrs. Blake?"

"Yes, thank you."

"Relaxed?"

"Yes."

"You're clenching your fists."

"Perhaps I am a little tense."

"About what?"

A long silence.

"Tell me about your home life. You've been married six months."

"Yes."

"Go on."

"I'm married to a wonderful man. We live in a beautiful house."

"What kind of house is it?"

"Country French . . . It's a lovely old place. There's a long,

678

winding driveway leading to it. High up on the roof there's a funny old bronze rooster with its tail missing. I think some hunter shot it off a long time ago. We have about five acres, mostly wooded. I go for long walks. It's like living in the country.

"Do you like the country?"

"Very much."

"Does your husband?"

"I think so."

"A man doesn't usually buy five acres in the country unless he loves it."

"He loves me. He would have bought it for me. He's very generous."

"Let's talk about him."

Silence.

"Is he good-looking?"

"Anthony's very handsome."

Judd felt a pang of unreasonable, unprofessional jealousy.

"You're compatible physically?" It was like a tongue probing at a sore tooth.

"Yes."

He knew what she would be like in bed: exciting and feminine and giving. *Christ,* he thought, *get off the subject.*

"Do you want children?"

"Oh, yes."

"Does your husband?"

"Yes, of course."

A long silence except for the silky rustling of the tape. Then:

"Mrs. Blake, you came to me because you said you had a desperate problem. It concerns your husband, doesn't it?"

Silence.

"Well, I'm assuming it does. From what you told me earlier, you love each other, you're both faithful, you both want children, you live in a beautiful home, your husband is successful, handsome, and he spoils you. And you've only been married six months. I'm afraid it's a little like the old joke: "What's my problem, Doctor?""

There was silence again except for the impersonal whirring of the tape. Finally she spoke. "It's . . . it's difficult for me to talk about. I thought I could discuss it with a stranger, but"—he remembered vividly how she had twisted around on the couch to look up at him with those large, enigmatic eyes—"it's harder. You see"—she was speaking more rapidly now, trying to overcome the barriers that had kept her silent—"I overheard something and I—I could easily have jumped to the wrong conclusion."

"Something to do with your husband's personal life? Some woman?"

"No."

"His business?"

"Yes . . ."

"You thought he lied about something? Tried to get the better of someone in a deal?"

"Something like that."

Judd was on surer ground now. "And it upset your confidence in him. It showed you a side of him that you had never seen before."

"I—I can't discuss it. I feel disloyal to him even being here. Please don't ask me anything more today, Dr. Stevens."

And that had ended that session. Judd switched off the tape.

So Anne's husband had pulled a sharp business deal. He could have cheated on his taxes. Or forced someone into bankruptcy. Anne, naturally, would be upset. She was a sensitive woman. Her faith in her husband would be shaken.

He thought about Anne's husband as a possible suspect. He was in the construction business. Judd had never met him, but whatever business problem he was involved in could not, by any stretch of the imagination, have included John Hanson, Carol Roberts, or Judd.

What about Anne herself? Could she be a psychopath? A homicidal maniac? Judd leaned back in his chair and tried to think about her objectively.

He knew nothing about her except what she had told him. Her background could have been fictitious, she could have made it all up, but what would she have to gain? If this was some elaborate charade as a cover to murder, there had to be a motivation. The memory of her face and her voice flooded his mind, and he knew that she could have nothing to do with any of this. He would stake his life on it. The irony of the phrase made him grin.

He went over to get the tapes of Teri Washburn. Perhaps there was something there that he might have missed.

Teri had been having extra sessions lately at her own request. Was she under some new pressure that she had not yet confided to him? Because of her incessant preoccupation with sex, it was difficult to determine accurately her current progress. Still—why had she suddenly, urgently asked for more time with him?

Judd picked up one of her tapes at random and put it on.

"Let's talk about your marriages, Teri. You've been married five times."

"Six, but who's counting?"

"Were you faithful to your husbands?"

Laughter.

"You're putting me on. There isn't a man in the world who can satisfy me. It's a physical thing."

"What do you mean by 'a physical thing?' "

"I mean that's the way I'm built. I just got a hot hole and it's gotta be kept filled all the time."

"Do you believe that?"

"That it's gotta be kept filled?"

"That you're different, physically, from any other woman."

"Certainly. The studio doctor told me. It's a glandular thing or something." A pause. "He was a lousy lay."

"I've seen all your charts. Physiologically your body is normal in every respect."

"Fuck the charts, Charley. Why don't you find out for yourself?"

"Have you ever been in love, Teri?"

"I could be in love with you."

Silence.

"Get that look off your face. I can't help it. I told you. It's the way I'm built. I'm always hungry."

"I believe you. But it's not your body that's hungry. It's your emotions.

"I've never been fucked in my emotions. Do you want to give it a whirl?"

"No."

"What do you want?"

"To help you."

"Why don't you come over here and sit down next to me?"

"That will be all for today."

Judd switched off the tape. He remembered a dialogue they had had when Teri was talking about her career as a big star and he had asked her why she left Hollywood.

"I slapped some obnoxious jerk at a drunken party," she had said. "And he turned out to be Mr. Big. He had me thrown out of Hollywood on my Polack ass."

Judd had not probed any further because at that time he was more interested in her home background, and the subject had never come up again. Now he felt a small nagging doubt. He should have explored it further. He had never had any interest in Hollywood except in the way Dr. Louis Leakey or Margaret Mead might be interested in the natives of Patagonia. Who would know about Teri Washburn, the glamour star?

Norah Hadley was a movie buff. Judd had seen a collection of movie magazines at their house and had kidded Peter about them. Norah had spent the entire evening defending Hollywood. He picked up the receiver and dialed.

Norah answered the phone.

"Hello," said Judd.

"Judd!" Her voice was warm and friendly. "You called to tell me when you're coming to dinner."

"We'll do it soon."

"You'd better," she said. "I promised Ingrid. She's beautiful."

Judd was sure she was. But not in the way Anne was beautiful.

"You break another date with her and we'll be at war with Sweden."

"It won't happen again."

"Are you all over your accident?"

"Oh, yes."

"What a horrible thing that was."

There was a hesitant note in Norah's voice. "Judd . . . about Christmas Day. Peter and I would like you to share it with us. Please.

He felt the old familiar tightening in his chest. They went through this every year. Peter and Norah were his dearest friends, and they hated it that he spent every Christmas alone, walking among strangers, losing himself in alien crowds, driving his body to keep moving until he was too exhausted to think. It was as though he were celebrating some terrible black mass for the dead, letting his grief take possession of him and tear him apart, lacerating and shriving him in some ancient ritual over which he had no control. *You're dramatizing it,* he told himself wearily.

"Judd . . ."

He cleared his throat. "I'm sorry, Norah." He knew how much she cared. "Perhaps next Christmas."

She tried to keep the disappointment out of her voice. "Sure. I'll tell Pete."

"Thanks." He suddenly remembered why he had called. "Norah—do you know who Teri Washburn is?"

"*The* Teri Washburn? The star? Why do you ask?"

"I—I saw her on Madison Avenue this morning."

"In person? Honestly?" She was like an eager child. "How did she look? Old? Young? Thin? Fat?"

"She looked fine. She used to be a pretty big star, didn't she?"

"*Pretty* big? Teri Washburn was the *biggest*—and in every way, if you know what I mean.

"Whatever made a girl like that leave Hollywood?"

"She didn't exactly leave. She was booted out."

So Teri had told him the truth. Judd felt better.

"You doctors keep your heads buried in the sand, don't you? Teri Washburn was involved in one of the hottest scandals Hollywood ever had."

"Really?" said Judd. "What happened?"

"She murdered her boyfriend."

I t had started to snow again. From the street fifteen floors below, the sounds of traffic floated up, muted by the white, cottony flakes dancing in the arctic wind. In a lighted office across the street he saw the blurred face of a secretary streaming down the window.

"Norah—are you certain?"

"When it comes to Hollywood, you're talking to a walking encyclopedia, love. Teri was living with the head of Continental Studios but she was keeping an assistant director on the side. She caught him cheating on her one night and she stabbed him to death. The head of the studio pulled a lot of strings and paid off a lot of people and it was hushed up and called an accident. Part of the arrangement was that she get out of Hollywood and never come back. And she never has."

Judd stared at the phone numbly.

"Judd, are you there?"

"I'm here."

"You sound funny."

"Where did you hear all this?"

"Hear it? It was in all the newspapers and fan magazines. Everybody knew about it."

Except him. "Thanks, Norah," he said. "Say hello to Peter." He hung up.

So that was the "casual incident." Teri Washburn had murdered a man and had never mentioned it to him. And if she had murdered once . . .

Thoughtfully he picked up a pad and wrote down "Teri Washburn."

The phone rang. Judd picked it up. "Dr. Stevens . . ."

"Just checking to see if you're all right." It was Detective Angeli. His voice was still hoarse with a cold.

A feeling of gratitude filled Judd. Someone was on his side.

"Anything new?"

Judd hesitated. He could see no point to keeping quiet about the bomb.

"They tried again." Judd told Angeli about Moody and the bomb that had been planted in his car. "That should convince McGreavy," he concluded.

"Where's the bomb?" Angeli's voice was excited.

Judd hesitated. "It's been dismantled."

"It's been *what?*" Angeli asked incredulously. "Who did that?"

"Moody. He didn't think it mattered."

"*Didn't* matter! What does he think the Police Department is for? We might have been able to tell who planted that bomb just by looking at it. We keep a file of M.O.s.

"M.O.s?"

"*Modus operandi.* People fall into habit patterns. If they do something one way the first time, chances are they'll keep doing it the same—I don't have to tell *you.*"

"No," said Judd thoughtfully. Surely Moody had known that. Had he some reason for not wanting to show the bomb to McGreavy?

"Dr. Stevens—how did you hire Moody?"

"I found him in the yellow pages." It sounded ridiculous even as he said it.

He could hear Angeli swallow. "Oh. Then you really don't know a damn thing about him."

"I know I trust him. Why?"

"Right now," Angeli said, "I don't think you should trust anybody."

"But Moody couldn't possibly be connected with any of this. My God! I picked him out of the phone book, at random."

"I don't care where you got him. Something smells fishy. Moody says he set a trap to catch whoever's after you, but he doesn't close the trap until the bait's already been taken, so we can't pin it on anyone. Then he shows you a bomb in your car that he could have put there himself. And wins your confidence. Right?"

"I suppose you could look at it that way," Judd said. "But—"

"Maybe your friend Moody is on the level, and maybe he's setting you up. I want you to play it nice and cool until we find out."

Moody *against* him? It was difficult to believe. And yet, he remembered his earlier doubts when he had thought Moody was sending him into an ambush.

"What do you want me to do?" asked Judd.

"How would you feel about leaving town? I mean *really* leaving town."

"I can't leave my patients."

"Dr. Stevens—"

"Besides," Judd added, "it really wouldn't solve anything, would it? I wouldn't even know what I'm running away from. When I came back, it would just start all over again."

There was a moment's silence. "You have a point." Angeli gave a sigh, and it turned into a wheeze. He sounded terrible. "When do you expect to hear from Moody again?"

"I don't know. He thinks he has some idea of who's behind all this."

"Has it occurred to you that whoever's behind this can pay Moody a lot more than you can?" There was an urgency in Angeli's voice. "If he asks you to meet him, call me. I'll be home in bed for the next day or two. Whatever you do, Doctor, don't meet him alone!"

"You're building up a case out of nothing," countered Judd. "just because Moody removed the bomb from my car—"

"There's more to it than that," said Angeli. "I have a hunch you picked the wrong man."

"I'll call you if I hear from him," promised Judd. He hung up, shaken. Was Angeli being overly suspicious? It was true that Moody could have been lying about the bomb in order to win Judd's confidence. Then the next step would be easy. All he would have to do would be to call Judd and ask him to meet him in some deserted place on the pretext of having some evidence for him. Then . . . Judd shuddered. Could he have been that wrong about

Moody's character? He remembered his reaction when he had first met Moody. He had thought that the man was ineffectual and not very bright. Then he had realized that his homespun cover was a facade that concealed a quick, sharp brain. But that didn't mean that Moody could be trusted. And yet . . . He heard someone at the outer reception door and looked at his watch. Anne! He quickly locked the tapes away, walked over to the private corridor door, and opened it.

Anne was standing in the corridor. She was wearing a smartly tailored navy blue suit and a small hat that framed her face. She was dreamily lost in thought, unaware that Judd was watching her. He studied her, filling himself with her beauty, trying to find some imperfection, some reason for him to tell himself that she would be wrong for him, that he would one day find someone else better suited to him. The fox and the grapes. Freud was not the father of psychiatry. Aesop was.

"Hello," he said.

She looked up, startled for an instant. Then she smiled. "Hello."

"Come in, Mrs. Blake."

She moved past him into the office, her firm body brushing his. She turned and looked at him with those incredible violet eyes. "Did they find the hit-and-run driver?" There was concern on her face, a worried, genuine interest.

He felt again the insane urge to tell her everything. But he knew he could not. At best, it would be a cheap trick to win her sympathy. At worst, it might involve her in some unknown danger.

"Not yet." He indicated a chair.

Anne was watching his face. "You look tired. Should you be back at work so soon?"

Oh, God. He didn't think he could stand any sympathy. Not just now. And not from her. He said, "I'm fine. I canceled my appointments for today. My exchange wasn't able to reach you."

An anxious expression crossed her face. She was afraid she was intruding. Anne—*intruding*. "I'm so sorry. If you'd rather I left . . ."

"Please, no," he said quickly. "I'm glad they couldn't reach you." This would be the last time he saw her. "How are you feeling?" he asked.

She hesitated, started to say something, then changed her mind. "A little confused."

She was looking at him oddly, and there was something in her look that touched a faint, long-lost chord that he could almost, but not quite, remember. He felt a warmth flowing from her, an overpowering physical longing—and he suddenly realized what he was doing. He was attributing his own emotions to her. And for an instant he had been fooled, like any first-year psychiatry student.

"When do you leave for Europe?" he asked.

"On Christmas morning."

"Just you and your husband?" He felt like a gibbering idiot, reduced to banalities. Babbitt, on an off day.

"Where will you go?"

"Stockholm—Paris—London—Rome."

I'd love to show you Rome, thought Judd. He had spent a year there interning at the American hospital. There was a fantastic old restaurant called Cybèle near the Tivoli Gardens, high on a mountaintop by an ancient pagan shrine, where you could sit in the sun and watch the hundreds of wild pigeons darken the sky over the dappled cliffs.

And Anne was on her way to Rome with her husband.

"It will be a second honeymoon," she said. There was strain in her voice, so faint that he might almost have imagined it. An untrained ear would not have caught it.

Judd looked at her more closely. On the surface she seemed calm, normal, but underneath he sensed a tension. If this was the picture of a young girl in love going to Europe on a second honeymoon, then a piece of the picture was missing.

And he suddenly realized what it was.

There was no excitement in Anne. Or if there was, it was overshadowed by a patina of some stronger emotion. Sadness? Regret?

He realized that he was staring at her. "How—how long will you be away?" Babbitt strikes again.

A small smile crossed her lips, as though she knew what he was doing. "I'm not certain," she answered gravely. "Anthony's plans are indefinite."

"I see." He looked down at the rug, miserable. He had to put an end to this. He couldn't let Anne leave, feeling that he was a complete fool. Send her away now. "Mrs. Blake . . ." he began.

"Yes?"

He tried to keep his voice light. "I really got you back here under false pretenses. It wasn't necessary for you to see me again. I just wanted to—to say good-bye.

Oddly, puzzlingly, some of the tension seemed to drain out of her. "I know," she said quietly. "I wanted to say good-bye, too." There was something in her voice that caught at him again.

She was getting to her feet. "Judd . . ." She looked up at him, holding his eyes with hers, and he saw in her eyes what she must have seen in his. It was a mirrored reflection of a current so strong that it was almost physical. He started to move toward her, then stopped. He could not let her become involved in the danger that surrounded him.

When he finally spoke, his voice was almost under control. "Drop me a card from Rome."

She looked at him for a long moment. "Please take care of yourself, Judd."

He nodded, not trusting himself to speak.

And she was gone.

The phone rang three times before Judd heard it. He picked it up.

"That you, Doc?" It was Moody. His voice practically leaped out of the telephone, crackling with excitement. "You alone?"

"Yes."

There was an odd quality in Moody's excitement that Judd could not quite identify. Caution? Fear?

"Doc—remember I told you I had a hunch who might be behind this?"

"Yes . . ."

"I was right."

Judd felt a quick chill go through him. "You know who killed Hanson and Carol?"

"Yeah. I know who. And I know why. You're next, Doctor."

"Tell me—"

"Not over the phone," said Moody. "We'd better meet somewhere and talk about it. Come alone."

Judd stared at the phone in his hand.

COME ALONE!

"Are you listening?" asked Moody's voice.

"Yes," said Judd quickly. What had Angeli said? *Whatever you do, Doctor, don't meet him alone.* "Why can't we meet here?" he asked, stalling for time.

"I think I'm being followed. I managed to shake them off. I'm calling from the Five Star Meat Packing Company. It's on Twenty-third Street, west of Tenth Avenue, near the docks."

Judd still found it impossible to believe that Moody was setting a trap for him. He decided to test him. "I'll bring Angeli."

Moody's voice was sharp. "Don't bring anyone. Come by yourself."

And there it was.

Judd thought of the fat little Buddha at the other end of the phone. His guileless friend who was charging him fifty dollars a day and expenses to set him up for his own murder.

Judd kept his voice controlled. "Very well," he said. "I'll be right over." He tried one parting shot. "Are you sure you really know who's behind this, Moody?"

"Dead sure, Doc. Have you ever heard of Don Vinton?" And Moody hung up.

Judd stood there, trying to sort out the storm of emotions that raced through him. He looked up Angeli's home number and dialed it. It rang five times, and Judd was filled with a sudden panicky fear that Angeli might not be at home. Dare he go meet Moody alone?

Then he heard Angeli's nasal voice. "Hello?"

"Judd Stevens. Moody just called."

There was a quickening in Angeli's voice. "What did he say?"

Judd hesitated, feeling a last vestige of unreasonable loyalty and—yes, affection—toward the bumbling little fat man who was plotting to cold-bloodedly murder him. "He asked me to meet him at the Five Star Meat Packing Company. It's on Twenty-third Street near Tenth Avenue. He told me to come alone."

Angeli laughed mirthlessly. "I'll bet he did. Don't budge out of that office, Doctor. I'm going to call Lieutenant McGreavy. We'll both pick you up."

"Right," said Judd. He hung up slowly. Norman Z. Moody. The jolly Buddha from the yellow pages. Judd felt a sudden, inexplicable sadness. He had liked Moody. And trusted him.

And Moody was waiting to kill him.

Twenty minutes later Judd unlocked his office door to admit Angeli and Lieutenant McGreavy. Angeli's eyes were red and teary. His voice was hoarse. Judd had a momentary pang at having dragged him out of a sickbed. McGreavy's greeting was a curt, unfriendly nod.

"I told Lieutenant McGreavy about the phone call from Norman Moody," Angeli said.

"Yeah. Let's find out what the hell this is all about," McGreavy said sourly.

Five minutes later they were in an unmarked police car speeding downtown on the West Side. Angeli was at the wheel. The light snowfall had stopped and the gruel-thin rays of the late afternoon sun had surrendered to the oppressive cover of storm clouds sweeping across the Manhattan sky. There was a loud clap of thunder in the distance and then a bright, jagged sword of lightning. Drops of rain began to spatter the windshield. As the car continued downtown, tall, soring skyscrapers gave way to small, grimy tenements huddled together as if for comfort against the biting cold.

The car turned into Twenty-third Street, going west toward the Hudson River. They moved into a land of junkyards and fix-it shops and dingy bars, then past that to blocks of garages, trucking yards and freight companies. As the car neared the corner of Tenth Avenue, McGreavy directed Angeli to pull over to the curb.

"We'll get out here." McGreavy turned to Judd. "Did Moody say whether anyone would be with him?"

"No."

McGreavy unbuttoned his overcoat and transferred his service revolver from his holster to his overcoat pocket. Angeli followed suit. "Stay in back of us," McGreavy ordered Judd.

The three men started walking, ducking their heads against the wind-lashed rain. Halfway down the block, they came to a dilapidated-looking building with a faded sign above the door that read:

FIVE STAR MEAT PACKING COMPANY

There were no cars or trucks or lights, no sign of life.

The two detectives walked up to the door, one on either side. McGreavy tested the door. It was locked. He looked around, but could see no bell. They listened. Silence, except for the sound of the rain.

"It looks closed," Angeli said.

"It probably is," McGreavy replied. "The Friday before Christmas—most companies are knocking off at noon."

"There must be a loading entrance."

Judd followed the two detectives as they moved cautiously toward the end of the building, trying to avoid the puddles in their path. They came to a service alley, and looking down it, they could discern a loading platform with deserted trucks pulled up in front of it. There was no activity. They moved forward until they reached the platform.

"OK," McGreavy said to Judd. "Sing out."

Judd hesitated, feeling unreasonably sad that he was betraying Moody. Then he lifted his voice. "Moody!" The only response was the yowling of an angry tomcat disturbed in his search for dry shelter. "Mr. Moody!"

There was a large wooden sliding door on top of the platform, used to move the deliveries from inside the warehouse to the area where the trucks were loaded. There were no steps leading onto the platform. McGreavy hoisted himself up, moving with surprising agility for such a large man. Angeli followed, then Judd. Angeli walked over to the sliding door and pushed against it. It was unlocked. The great door rolled open with a loud, high-pitched scream of protest. The tomcat answered hopefully, forgetting about shelter. Inside the warehouse it was pitch black.

"Did you bring a flashlight?" McGreavy asked Angeli.

"No."

"Shit!"

Cautiously they inched their way into the gloom. Judd called out again. "Mr. Moody! It's Judd Stevens."

There was no sound except for the creaking of the boards as the men moved across the room. McGreavy rummaged in his pockets and pulled out a book of matches. He lit one and held it up. Its feeble, sputtering light cast a wavering yellow glow in what seemed to be an enormous empty cavern. The match guttered out. "Find the goddam light switch," McGreavy said. "That was my last match."

Judd could hear Angeli groping along the walls looking for the light switch. Judd kept moving forward. He could not see the other two men. "Moody!" he called.

He heard Angeli's voice from across the room. "Here's a switch." There was a click. Nothing happened.

"The master switch must be off," McGreavy said.

Judd bumped against a wall. As he put his hands out to brace himself, his fingers closed over a doorlatch. He shoved the latch up and pulled. A massive door swung open and a blast of frigid air hit him. "I've found a door," he called out. He stepped over a sill and cautiously moved forward. He heard the door close behind him and his heart began to hammer. Impossibly, it was darker here than in the other room, as though he had stepped into a deeper blackness.

"Moody! Moody . . ."

A thick, heavy silence. Moody *had* to be here somewhere. If he weren't, Judd knew what McGreavy would think. It would be the boy who cried wolf again.

Judd took another step forward and suddenly felt cold flesh lick against his face. He jerked away in panic, feeling the short hairs on his neck rise. He became aware of the strong smell of blood and death surrounding him. There was an evil in the darkness around him, waiting to close in on him. His scalp tingled with fear and his heart was beating so rapidly that it was difficult to breathe. With trembling fingers he fumbled for a book of matches in his overcoat, found one, and scraped a match against the cover. In its light he saw a huge dead eye loom up in front of his face, and it took a shocked second before he realized that he was looking at a slaughtered cow dangling from a meat hook. He had one brief glimpse of other animal carcasses hanging from hooks, and the outline of a door in the far corner, before the match went out. The door probably led to an office. Moody could be in there, waiting for him.

Judd moved farther into the interior of the inky black cavern toward the door. He felt the cold brush of dead animal flesh again. He quickly stepped away and kept walking cautiously toward the office door. "Moody!"

He wondered what was detaining Angeli and McGreavy. He moved past the slaughtered animals, feeling as though someone with a macabre sense of humor was playing a horrible, maniacal joke. But who and why were beyond his imagining. As he neared the door, he collided with another hanging carcass.

Judd stopped to get his bearings. He lit his last remaining match. In front of him, impaled on a meat hook and grinning obscenely, was the body of Norman Z. Moody. The match went out.

T he coroner's men had finished their work and gone. Moody's
body had been taken away and everyone had departed except Judd, McGreavy, and Angeli. They were sitting in the
manager's small office, decorated with several impressive calendar
nudes, an old desk, a swivel chair, and two filing cabinets. The
lights were on and an electric heater was going.

The manager of the plant, a Mr. Paul Moretti, had been tracked
down and pulled away from a pre-Christmas party to answer some
questions. He had explained that since it was a holiday weekend,
he had let his employees off at noon. He had locked up at twelve-
thirty, and to the best of his knowledge, there had been no one on
the premises at that time. Mr. Moretti was belligerently drunk, and
when McGreavy saw that he was going to be no further help, he
had him driven home. Judd was barely conscious of what was
happening in the room. His thoughts were on Moody, how cheerful and how full of life he had been, and how cruelly he had died.
And Judd blamed himself. If he had not involved Moody, the little
detective would be alive today.

It was almost midnight. Judd had wearily reiterated the story of
Moody's phone call for the tenth time. McGreavy, hunched up in
his overcoat, sat there watching him, chewing savagely on a cigar.
Finally he spoke. "Do you read detective stories?"

Judd looked at him, surprised. "No. Why?"

"I'll tell you why. I think you're just too goddam good to be
true, Dr. Stevens. From the very beginning I've thought that you
were in this thing up to your neck. And I told you so. So what

695

happens? Suddenly you turn into the target instead of the killer. First you claim a car ran you down and—"

"A car *did* run him down," Angeli reminded him.

"A rookie could answer that one," McGreavy snapped. "It could have been arranged by someone who's in this with the doctor." He turned back to Judd. "Next, you call Detective Angeli with a wild-eyed yarn about two men breaking into your office and trying to kill you."

"They *did* break in," said Judd.

"No, they didn't," snapped McGreavy. "They used a special key." His voice hardened. "You said there were only two of those keys to that office—yours and Carol Roberts'."

"That's right. I told you—they copied Carol's key."

"I know what you told me. I had a paraffin test run. Carol's key was never copied, Doctor." He paused to let it sink in. "And since I have her key—that leaves yours, doesn't it?"

Judd looked at him, speechless.

"When I didn't buy the loose maniac theory, you hire a detective out of the yellow pages, and he conveniently finds a bomb planted in your car. Only I can't see it because it's not there anymore. Then you decide it's time to throw me another body, so you go through that rigmarole with Angeli about a phone call to meet Moody, who knows this mysterious nut who's out to kill you. But guess what? We get here and find him hanging on a meat hook."

Judd flushed angrily. "I'm not responsible for what happened."

McGreavy gave him a long, hard look. "Do you know the only reason you're not under arrest? Because I haven't found any motive to this Chinese puzzle yet. But I will, Doctor. That's a promise." He got to his feet.

Judd suddenly remembered. "Wait a minute!" he said. "What about Don Vinton?"

"What about him?"

"Moody said he was the man behind all this."

"Do you know anyone named Don Vinton?"

"No," Judd said. "I—I assumed he'd be known by the police."

"I never heard of him." McGreavy turned to Angeli. Angeli shook his head.

"OK. Send out a make on Don Vinton. FBI. Interpol. Police chiefs in all major American cities." He looked at Judd. "Satisfied?"

Judd nodded. Whoever was behind all this must have some kind of criminal record. It should not be difficult to identify him.

He thought again of Moody, with his homely aphorisms and his quick mind. He must have been followed here. It was unlikely that he would have told anyone else about the rendezvous, because he had stressed the need for secrecy. At least they now knew the name of the man they were looking for.

Praemonitus, praemunitas.

Forewarned, forearmed.

The murder of Norman Z. Moody was splashed all over the front pages of the newspapers the next morning. Judd picked up a paper on his way to the office. He was briefly mentioned as being a witness who had come across the body with the police, but McGreavy had managed to keep the full story out of the papers. McGreavy was playing his cards close to his chest. Judd wondered what Anne would think.

This was Saturday, when Judd made his morning rounds at the clinic. He had arranged for someone else to fill in for him there. He went to his office, traveling alone in the elevator and making sure that no one was lurking in the corridor. He wondered, even as he did so, how long anyone could live like this, expecting an assassin to strike at any moment.

Half a dozen times during the morning he started to pick up the phone and call Detective Angeli to ask about Don Vinton, but each time he controlled his impatience. Angeli would surely call him as soon as he knew something. Judd puzzled over what Don Vinton's motivation could be. He could have been a patient whom Judd had treated years ago, perhaps when he was an intern. Someone who felt that Judd had slighted him or injured him in some way. But he could remember no patient named Vinton.

At noon he heard someone try to open the corridor door to the reception room. It was Angeli. Judd could tell nothing from his expression except that he looked even more drawn and haggard. His nose was red, and he was sniffling. He walked into the inner office and wearily flopped into a chair.

"Have you gotten any answers yet on Don Vinton?" Judd asked eagerly.

Angeli nodded. "We got back teletypes from the FBI, the police chiefs of every big city in the United States, and Interpol."

Judd waited, afraid to breathe. "None of them ever heard of Don Vinton."

Judd looked at Angeli incredulously, a sudden sinking sensation in his stomach. "But that's impossible! I mean—*someone* must know him. A man who could do all this just didn't come out of nowhere!"

"That's what McGreavy said," replied Angeli wearily. "Doctor, my men and I spent the night checking out every Don Vinton in Manhattan and all the other boroughs. We even covered New Jersey and Connecticut." He took a ruled sheet of paper out of his pocket and showed it to Judd. "We found eleven Don Vintons in the phone book who spell their name 'ton'—four who spell it 'ten'—and two who spell it 'tin.' We even tried it as one name. We narrowed it down to five possibles and checked out every one of them. One is a paralytic. One of them is a priest. One is first vice-president of a bank. One of them is a fireman who was on duty when two of the murders occurred. I just left the last one. He runs a pet shop and he must be damn near eighty years old."

Judd's throat was dry. He was suddenly aware of how much he had counted on this. Surely Moody wouldn't have given him the name unless he was certain. And he hadn't said that Don Vinton was an accomplice; he had said he was behind the whole thing. It was inconceivable that the police would have no record of a man like that. Moody had been murdered because he had gotten onto the truth. And now that Moody was out of the way, Judd was completely alone. The web was drawing tighter.

"I'm sorry," Angeli said.

Judd looked at the detective and suddenly remembered that Angeli had not been home all night. "I appreciate your trying," he said gratefully.

Angeli leaned forward. "Are you positive you heard Moody right?"

"Yes." Judd closed his eyes in concentration. He had asked Moody if he was sure who was really behind this. He heard Moody's voice again. *Dead sure. Have you ever heard of Don Vinton? Don Vinton.* He opened his eyes. "Yes," he repeated.

Angeli sighed. "Then we're at a dead end." He laughed mirthlessly. "No pun intended." He sneezed.

"You'd better get to bed."

Angeli stood up. "Yeah. I guess so."

Judd hesitated. "How long have you been McGreavy's partner?"

"This is our first case together. Why?"

"Do you think he's capable of framing me for murder?"

Angeli sneezed again. "I think maybe you're right, doctor. I'd better get to bed." He walked over to the door.

"I may have a lead," Judd said.

Angeli stopped and turned. "Go on."

Judd told him about Teri. He added that he was also going to check out some of John Hanson's former boyfriends.

"It doesn't sound like much," Angeli said frankly, "but I guess it's better than nothing."

"I'm sick and tired of being a target. I'm going to start fighting back. I'm going after them."

Angeli looked at him. "With what? We're fighting shadows."

"When witnesses describe a suspect, the police have an artist draw up a composite picture of all the descriptions. Right?"

Angeli nodded. "An identi-kit."

Judd began to pace in restless excitement. "I'm going to give you an identi-kit of the personality of the man who's behind this."

"How can you? You've never seen him. It could be anyone."

"No it couldn't," Judd corrected. "We're looking for someone very, very special."

"Someone who's insane."

"Insanity is a catchall phrase. It has no medical meaning. Sanity is simply the ability of the mind to adjust to reality. If we can't adjust, we either hide from reality, or we put ourselves above life, where we're super-beings who don't have to follow the rules."

"Our man thinks he's a super-being."

"Exactly. In a dangerous situation we have three choices, Angeli. Flight, constructive compromise, or attack. Our man attacks."

"So he's a lunatic."

"No. Lunatics rarely kill. Their concentration span is extremely short. We're dealing with someone more complicated. He could be somatic, hypophrenic, schizoid, cycloid—or any combination of these. We could be dealing with a fugue—temporary amnesia preceded by irrational acts. But the point is, his appearance and behavior will seem perfectly normal to everyone."

"So we have nothing to go on."

"You're wrong. We have a good deal to go on. I can give you a physical description of him," said Judd. He narrowed his eyes, concentrating. "Don Vinton is above average height, well proportioned, and has the build of an athlete. He's neat in his appearance and meticulous about everything he does. He has no artistic talent. He doesn't paint or write or play the piano."

Angeli was staring at him, open-mouthed.

Judd continued, speaking more quickly now, warming up. "He doesn't belong to any social clubs or organizations. Not unless he runs them. He's a man who has to be in charge. He's ruthless, and he's impatient. He thinks big. For example, he'd never get involved in petty thefts. If he had a record, it would be for bank robbery, kidnapping, or murder." Judd's excitement was growing. The picture was growing sharper in his mind. "When you catch him, you'll find that he was probably rejected by one of his parents when he was a boy."

Angeli interrupted. "Doctor, I don't want to shoot down your balloon, but it could be some crazy, hopped-up junkie who—"

"No. The man we're looking for doesn't take drugs." Judd's voice was positive. "I'll tell you something else about him. He played contact sports in school. Football or hockey. He has no interest in chess, word games, or puzzles."

Angeli was watching him skeptically. "There was more than one man," he objected. "You said so yourself."

"I'm giving you a description of Don Vinton," said Judd. "The man who's masterminding this. I'll tell you something more about him. He's a Latin type."

"What makes you think so?"

"Because of the methods used in the murders. A knife—acid—a bomb. He's South American, Italian, or Spanish." He took a breath. "There's your identi-kit. That's the man who's committed three murders and is trying to kill me.

Angeli swallowed. "How the hell do you know all this?"

Judd sat down and leaned toward Angeli. "It's my profession."

"The mental side, sure. But how can you give a physical description of a man you've never seen?"

"I'm playing the odds. A doctor named Kretschmer found that

eighty-five percent of people suffering from paranoia have well-built, athletic bodies. Our man is an obvious paranoiac. He has delusions of grandeur. He's a megalomaniac who thinks he's above the law."

"Then why wasn't he locked up a long time ago?"

"Because he's wearing a mask."

"He's what?"

"We all wear masks, Angeli. From the time we're past infancy, we're taught to conceal our real feelings, to cover up our hatreds and fears." There was authority in his voice. "But under stress, Don Vinton is going to drop his mask and show his naked face."

"I see."

"His ego is his vulnerable point. If it's threatened—really threatened—he'll crack. He's on the thin edge now. It won't take much to send him completely over." He hesitated, then went on, speaking almost to himself. "He's a man with—mana."

"With what?"

"Mana. It's a term that the primitives use for a man who exerts influence on others because of the demons in him, a man with an overpowering personality.

"You said he doesn't paint, write, or play the piano. How do you know that?"

"The world is full of artists who are schizoids. Most of them manage to get through life without any violence because their work gives them an outlet in which to express themselves. Our man doesn't have that outlet. So he's like a volcano. The only way he can get rid of the pressure inside him is to erupt: Hanson—Carol—Moody."

"You mean these were just senseless crimes that he committed to—"

"Not senseless to him. On the contrary . . . ." His mind raced ahead swiftly. Several more pieces of the puzzle were beginning to fall into place. He cursed himself for having been too blind, or frightened, to see them. "I'm the only one Don Vinton has been after—the prime target. John Hanson was killed because he was mistaken for me. When the killer found out his mistake, he came to the office for another try. I had gone, but he found Carol there." His voice was angry.

"He killed her so she couldn't identify him?"

"No. The man we're looking for isn't a sadist. Carol was tortured because he wanted something. Say, a piece of incriminating evidence. And she wouldn't—or couldn't—give it to him."

"What kind of evidence?" probed Angeli.

"I have no idea," Judd said. "But it's the key to this whole thing. Moody found out the answer, and that's why they killed him."

"There's one thing that still doesn't make sense. If they had killed you on the street, then they couldn't have gotten the evidence. It doesn't fit with the rest of your theory," Angeli persisted.

"It could. Let's assume that the evidence is on one of my tapes. It might be perfectly harmless by itself, but if I put it together with other facts, it could threaten them. So they have two choices. Either take it away from me, or eliminate me so I can't reveal it to anyone. First they tried to eliminate me. But they made a mistake and killed Hanson. Then they went to the second alternative. They tried to get it from Carol. When that failed, they decided to concentrate on killing me. That was the car accident. I was probably followed when I went to hire Moody, and he, in turn, was followed. When he got onto the truth, they murdered him."

Angeli looked at Judd, a thoughtful frown on his face.

"That's why the killer is not going to stop until I'm dead," Judd concluded quietly. "It's become a deadly game, and the man I've described can't stand losing."

Angeli was studying him, weighing what Judd had said. "If you're right," he said finally, "you're going to need protection." He took his service revolver out, flipped the chamber open to make sure it was fully loaded.

"Thanks, Angeli, but I don't need a gun. I'm going to fight them with my own weapons."

There was the sharp click of the outer door opening. "Were you expecting anyone?"

Judd shook his head. "No. I have no patients this afternoon."

Gun still in hand, Angeli moved quietly to the door leading to the reception room. He stepped to one side and yanked the door open. Peter Hadley stood there, a bewildered expression on his face. "Who are you?" Angeli snapped.

Judd moved over to the door. "It's all right," Judd said quickly. "He's a friend of mine."

"Hey! What the hell goes?" asked Peter.

"Sorry," Angeli apologized. He put his gun away.

"This is Dr. Peter Hadley—Detective Angeli."

"What kind of nutty psychiatric clinic are you running here?" Peter asked.

"There's been a little trouble," Angeli explained. "Dr. Stevens' office has been . . . burglarized, and we thought whoever did it might be returning."

Judd picked up the cue. "Yes. They didn't find what they were looking for."

"Does this have anything to do with Carol's murder?" Peter asked.

Angeli spoke before Judd could answer. "We're not sure, Dr. Hadley. For the moment, the Department has asked Dr. Stevens not to discuss the case."

"I understand," Peter said. He looked at Judd. "Is our luncheon date still on?"

Judd realized he had forgotten about it. "Of course," he said quickly. He turned to Angeli. "I think we've covered everything."

"And then some," Angeli agreed. "You're sure you don't want . . ." He indicated his revolver.

Judd shook his head. "Thanks."

"OK. Be careful," Angeli said.

"I will," Judd promised. "I will."

Judd was preoccupied during luncheon, and Peter did not press him. They talked of mutual friends, patients that they had in common. Peter told Judd he had spoken to Harrison Burke's employer and it had been quietly arranged for Burke to have a mental examination. He was being sent to a private institution.

Over coffee Peter said, "I don't know what kind of trouble you're having, Judd, but if I can be of any help . . ."

Judd shook his head. "Thanks, Peter. This is something I have to take care of myself. I'll tell you all about it when it's over."

"I hope that's soon," Peter said lightly. He hesitated. "Judd— are you in any danger?"

"Of course not," replied Judd.

Unless you counted a homicidal maniac who had committed three murders and was determined to make Judd his fourth victim.

After lunch, Judd returned to his office. He went through the same careful routine, checking to make sure that he exposed himself to minimum vulnerability.

For whatever that was worth.

He began going through the tapes again, listening for anything that might provide some clue. It was like turning on a torrent of verbal graffiti. The gusher of sounds that spewed forth was filled with hatred . . . perversion . . . fear . . . self-pity . . . megalomania . . . loneliness . . . emptiness . . . pain . . .

At the end of three hours he had found only one new name to add to his list: Bruce Boyd, the man with whom John Hanson had last lived. He put the Hanson tape on the recorder again.

". . . I suppose I fell in love with Bruce the first time I saw him. He was the most beautiful man I had ever seen."

"Was he the passive or dominant partner, John?"

"Dominant. That's one of the things that attracted me to him. He's very strong. In fact, later, when we became lovers, we used to quarrel about that."

"Why?"

"Bruce didn't realize how strong he really was. He used to walk up behind me and hit me on the back. He meant it as a loving gesture, but one day he almost broke my spine. I wanted to kill him. When he shook hands, he would crush your fingers. He always pretended to be sorry, but Bruce enjoys hurting people. He didn't need whips. He's very strong. . . ."

Judd stopped the tape and sat there, thinking. The homosexual pattern did not fit into his concept of the killer, but on the other hand, Boyd had been involved with Hanson and was a sadist and an egotist.

He looked at the two names on his list: Teri Washburn, who had killed a man in Hollywood and had never mentioned it; and Bruce Boyd, John Hanson's last lover. If it were one of them—which one?

Teri Washburn lived in a penthouse suite on Sutton Place. The entire apartment was decorated in shocking pink: walls, furniture, drapes. There were expensive pieces scattered around the room, and the wall was covered with French impressionists. Judd recognized two Manets, two Degas, a Monet, and a Renoir before Teri walked into the room. He had phoned her to tell her that he wanted to come by. She had gotten ready for him. She was wearing a wispy pink negligee with nothing on underneath it.

"You really came," she exclaimed happily.

"I wanted to talk to you."

"Sure. A little drinkie?"

"No, thanks."

"Then I think I'll fix myself one to celebrate," Teri said. She moved toward the coral-shell bar in the corner of the large living room.

Judd watched her thoughtfully.

She returned with her drink and sat next to him on the pink couch. "So your cock finally got you up here, honey," she said. "I knew you couldn't hold out on little Teri. I'm nuts about you, Judd. I'd do anything for you. You name it. You make all the crummy pricks I've known in my life look like dirt." She put her drink down and put her hand on his trousers.

Judd took her hands in his. "Teri," he said. "I need your help."

Her mind was traveling in its own groove. "I know, baby," she moaned. "I'm going to fuck you like you've never been fucked in your life."

"Teri—listen to me! Someone is trying to murder me!"

Her eyes registered slow surprise. Acting—or real? He remembered a performance he had seen her give on one of the late late shows. Real. She was good, but not that good an actress.

"For Christ sake! Who—who'd want to murder you?"

"It could be someone connected with one of my patients."

"But—Jesus—why?"

"That's what I'm trying to find out, Teri. Have any of your friends ever talked about killing . . . or murder? Maybe as a party game, for laughs?"

Teri shook her head. "No."

"Do you know anyone named Don Vinton?" He watched her closely.

"Don Vinton? Uhn-uhn. Should I?"

"Teri—how do you feel about murder?" A small shiver went through her body. He was holding her wrists and he could feel her pulse racing. "Does murder excite you?"

"I don't know."

"Think about it," Judd insisted. "Does the thought of it excite you?"

Her pulse was beginning to skip irregularly. "No! Of course not."

"Why didn't you tell me about the man you killed in Hollywood?"

Without warning she reached out to rake his face with her long fingernails. He grabbed her wrists.

"You rotten sonofabitch! That was twenty years ago. . . . So that's why you came. Get out of here. Get out!" She collapsed in sobbing hysteria.

Judd watched her a moment. Teri was capable of being involved in a thrill murder. Her insecurity, her total lack of self-esteem, would make her easy prey to anyone who wanted to use her. She was like a piece of soft clay lying in the gutter. The person who picked her up could mold her into a beautiful statue—or into a deadly weapon. The question was, Who had picked her up last? Don Vinton?

Judd got to his feet. "I'm sorry," he said.

He walked out of the pink apartment.

Bruce Boyd occupied a house in a converted mews off the park in Greenwich Village. The door was opened by a white-jacketed Filipino butler. Judd gave his name and was invited to wait in the foyer. The butler disappeared. Ten minutes went by, then fifteen. Judd checked his irritation. Perhaps he should have told Detective

Angeli he was coming here. If Judd's theory was right, the next attempt on his life would take place very soon. And his attacker would try to make certain of his success.

The butler reappeared. "Mr. Boyd will see you now," he said. He led Judd upstairs to a tastefully decorated study, then discreetly withdrew.

Boyd was at a desk, writing. He was a beautiful man with sharp, delicate features, an aquiline nose, and a sensuous, full mouth. He had blond hair curled into ringlets. He got to his feet as Judd entered. He was about six foot three with the chest and shoulders of a football player. Judd thought about his physical identi-kit of the killer. Boyd matched it. Judd wished more than ever that he had left some word with Angeli.

Boyd's voice was soft and cultured. "Forgive me for keeping you waiting, Dr. Stevens," he said pleasantly. "I'm Bruce Boyd." He held out his hand.

Judd reached out to take it and Boyd hit him in the mouth with a granite fist. The blow was totally unexpected, and the impact of it sent Judd crashing against a standing lamp, knocking it over as his body fell to the floor.

"I'm sorry, Doctor," said Boyd, looking down at him. "You had that coming. You've been a naughty boy, haven't you? Get up and I'll fix you a drink."

Judd shook his head groggily. He started to push himself up from the floor. When he got halfway up, Boyd kicked him in the groin with the tip of his shoe and Judd fell writhing to the floor in agony. "I've been waiting for you to call," Boyd said.

Judd looked up through the blinding waves of pain at the figure that towered over him. He tried to speak, but he couldn't get the words out.

"Don't try to talk," Boyd said sympathetically. "It must hurt. I know why you're here. You want to ask me about Johnny."

Judd started to nod and Boyd kicked him in the head. Through a red blur he heard Boyd's voice coming from some distant place through a cottony filter, fading in and out. "We loved each other until he went to you. You made him feel like a freak. You made him feel our love was dirty. Do you know who made it dirty, Dr. Stevens? You."

Judd felt something hard smash into his ribs, sending an exquisite river of pain through his veins. He was seeing everything in beautiful colors now, as though his head were filled with shimmering rainbows.

"Who gave you the right to tell people how to love, Doctor? You sit there in your office like some kind of god, condemning everyone who doesn't think like you."

That's not true, Judd was answering somewhere in his mind. *Hanson had never had choices before. I gave him choices. And he didn't choose you.*

"Now Johnny's dead," said the blond giant towering over him. "You killed my Johnny. And now I'm going to kill you."

He felt another kick behind his ear, and he began to slip into unconsciousness. Some remote part of his mind watched with a detached interest as the rest of him began to die. That small isolated piece of intelligence in his cerebellum continued to function, its impulses flashing out weakening patterns of thought. He reproached himself for not having come closer to the truth. He had expected the killer to be a dark, Latin type, and he was blond. He had been sure that the killer was not a homosexual, and he had been wrong. He had found his homicidal maniac, and now he was going to die for it.

He lost consciousness.

S ome distant, remote part of his mind was trying to send him a message, trying to communicate something of cosmic importance, but the hammering deep inside his skull was so agonizing that he was unable to concentrate on anything else. Somewhere nearby, he could hear a high-pitched keening, like a wounded wild animal. Slowly, painfully, Judd opened his eyes. He was lying in a bed in a strange room. In a corner of the room, Bruce Boyd was weeping uncontrollably.

Judd started to sit up. The wracking pain in his body flooded his memory with recollection of what had happened to him, and he was suddenly filled with a wild, savage fury.

Boyd turned as he heard Judd stir. He walked over to the bed. "It's your fault," he whimpered. "If it hadn't been for you, Johnny would still be safe with me."

Without volition, propelled by some long-forgotten, deeply buried instinct for vengeance, Judd reached for Boyd's throat, his fingers closing around his windpipe, squeezing with all their strength. Boyd made no move to protect himself. He stood there, tears streaming down his face. Judd looked into his eyes, and it was like looking into a pool of hell. Slowly his hands dropped away. *My God*, he thought, *I'm a doctor. A sick man attacks me and I want to kill him.* He looked at Boyd, and he was looking at a destroyed, bewildered child.

And suddenly he realized what his subconscious had been trying to tell him: Bruce Boyd was not Don Vinton. If he had been, Judd would not be alive now. Boyd was incapable of committing murder. So he had been right about him not fitting the identi-kit of the killer. There was a certain ironic consolation in that.

"If it weren't for you, Johnny would be alive," Boyd sobbed. "He'd be here with me and I could have protected him."

"I didn't ask John Hanson to leave you," Judd said wearily. "It was his idea."

"You're a liar!"

"Things had been going wrong between you and John *before* he came to see me."

There was a long silence. Then Boyd nodded. "Yes. We—we were quarreling all the time."

"He was trying to find himself, and his instincts kept telling him that he wanted to go back to his wife and children. Deep down inside, John wanted to be heterosexual."

"Yes," whispered Boyd. "He used to talk about it all the time, and I thought it was just to punish me." He looked up at Judd. "But one day he left me. He just—moved out. He stopped loving me." There was despair in his voice.

"He didn't stop loving you," Judd said. "Not as a friend."

Boyd was looking at him now, his eyes riveted on Judd's face. "Will you help me?" His eyes were filled with desperation. "H-help me. You've got to help me!"

It was a cry of anguish. Judd looked at him a long moment. "Yes," Judd said. "I'll help you."

"Will I be normal?"

"There's no such thing as normal. Each person carries his own normality within him, and no two people are alike."

"Can you make me heterosexual?"

"That depends on how much you really want to be. We can give you psychoanalysis."

"And if it fails?"

"If we find that you're meant to be homosexual, at least you'll be better adjusted to it."

"When can we start?" Boyd asked.

And Judd was jolted back to reality. He was sitting here talking about treating a patient when, for all he knew, he was going to be murdered within the next twenty-four hours. And he was still no closer to finding out who Don Vinton was. He had eliminated Teri and Boyd, the last suspects on his list. He knew no more now than when he had started. If his analysis of the killer was correct, by now he would have worked himself up to a murderous rage. The next attack would come very, very soon.

"Call me Monday," he said.

As the taxi took him toward his apartment building, Judd tried to weigh his chances of survival. They looked bleak. What could he have that Don Vinton wanted so desperately? And who was Don Vinton? How could he have had no police record? Could he be using some other name? No. Moody had clearly said "Don Vinton."

It was difficult to concentrate. Every movement of the taxi sent spasms of excruciating pain through his bruised body. Judd thought about the murders and attempted murders that had been committed so far, looking for some kind of pattern that made sense. A knifing, murder by torture, a hit-and-run "accident," a bomb in his car, strangulation. There was no pattern that he could discern. Only a ruthless, maniacal violence. He had no way of knowing how the next attempt would be made. Or by whom. His greatest vulnerability would be the office and his apartment. He remembered Angeli's advice. He must have stronger locks put on the doors of the apartment. He would tell Mike, the doorman, and Eddie, the elevator operator, to keep their eyes open. He could trust them.

The taxi pulled up in front of his apartment house. The doorman opened the taxi door.

He was a total stranger.

H e was a large, swarthy man with a pockmarked face and deep-set black eyes. An old scar ran across his throat. He was wearing Mike's uniform coat and it was too tight for him.

The taxi pulled away and Judd was alone with the man. He was struck by a sudden wave of pain. My God, not now! He gritted his teeth. "Where's Mike?" he asked.

"On vacation, Doctor."

Doctor. So the man knew who he was. And Mike on vacation? In December?

There was a small smile of satisfaction on the man's face. Judd looked up and down the windswept street, but it was completely deserted. He could try to make a run for it, but in his condition he wouldn't stand a chance. His body was beaten and sore, and it hurt every time he took a breath.

"You look like you been in an accident." The man's voice was almost genial.

Judd turned without answering and walked into the lobby of the apartment building. He could count on Eddie to get help.

The doorman followed Judd into the lobby. Eddie was in the elevator, his back turned. Judd started walking toward the elevator, every step a separate agony. He knew he dared not falter now. The important thing was not to let the man catch him alone. He would be afraid of witnesses. "Eddie!" Judd called.

The man in the elevator turned.

Judd had never seen him before. He was a smaller version of the doorman, except that there was no scar. It was obvious that the two men were brothers.

Judd stopped, trapped between the two of them. There was no one else in the lobby.

"Goin' up," said the man in the elevator. He had the same satisfied smile as his brother.

So these, finally, were the faces of death. Judd was sure that neither of them was the brain behind what was happening. They were hired professional killers. Would they kill him in the lobby, or would they prefer to do it in his apartment? His apartment, he reasoned. That would give them more time to make their escape before his body was found.

Judd took a step toward the manager's office. "I have to see Mr. Katz about—"

The larger man blocked his way. "Mr. Katz is busy, Doc," he said softly.

The man in the elevator spoke. "I'll take you upstairs."

"No," Judd said. "I—"

"Do like he says." There was no emotion in his voice.

There was a sudden blast of cold air as the lobby door opened. Two men and two women hurried in, laughing and chattering, huddled in their coats.

"It's worse than Siberia," said one of the women.

The man holding her arm was pudgy-faced, with a Midwestern accent. "Tain't a fit night out for man nor beast."

The group was moving toward the elevator. The doorman and elevator operator looked at each other silently.

The second woman spoke. She was a tiny, platinum blonde with a heavy Southern accent. "It's been a perfectly dreamy evening. Thank you all so much." She was sending the men away.

The second man gave a howl of protest. "You're not going to let us go without a little nightcap, are you?"

"It's awfully late, George," simpered the first woman.

"But it's below zero outside. You've gotta give us a little anti-freeze."

The other man added his plea. "Just one drink and then we go."

"Well . . ."

Judd was holding his breath. Please!

The platinum blonde relented. "All right. But just one, you-all hear?"

Laughing, the group stepped into the elevator. Judd quickly moved in with them. The doorman stood there uncertainly, looking at his brother. The one in the elevator shrugged, closed the door, and started the elevator up. Judd's apartment was on the fifth floor. If the group got out before him, he was in trouble. If they got out after him, he had a chance to get into his apartment, barricade himself, and call for help.

"Floor?"

The little blonde giggled. "I don't know what my husband would say if he saw me inviting two strange men up to my apartment." She turned to the elevator operator. "Ten."

Judd exhaled and realized that he had been holding his breath. He spoke quickly. "Five."

The elevator operator gave him a patient, knowing look and opened the door at Five. Judd got out. The elevator door closed.

Judd moved toward his apartment, stumbling with pain. He took out his key, opened the door, and went in, his heart pounding. He had five minutes at the most before they came to kill him. He closed the door and started to put the chain lock in the bolt. It came off in his hand. He looked at it and saw that it had been cut through. He flung it down and moved toward the phone. A wave of dizziness swept over him. He stood there, fighting the pain, his eyes closed, while precious time passed. With an effort, he started toward the phone again, moving slowly. The only person he could think of to call was Angeli, but Angeli was at home, ill. Besides—what could he say? *We have a new doorman and elevator operator and I think they're going to kill me?* He slowly became aware that he was holding the receiver in his hand, standing there numbly, too dazed to do anything. Concussion, he thought. Boyd may have killed me, after all. They would walk in and find him like this—helpless. He remembered the look in the eyes of the big man. He had to outwit them, keep them off balance. But good God—how?

He turned on the small TV set that monitored the lobby. The lobby was deserted. The pain returned, washing over him in waves, making him feel faint. He forced his tired mind to focus on the problem. He was in an emergency. . . . Yes . . . Emergency. He had to take emergency measures. Yes . . . His vision was blurring again. His eyes focused on the phone. Emergency . . . He moved the dial close to his eyes so that he could read the numbers. Slowly, painfully, he dialed. A voice answered on the fifth ring. Judd spoke, his words slurred and indistinct. His eye was caught by a flurry of motion on the TV monitor. The two men, in street clothes, were crossing the lobby and moving toward the elevator.

His time had run out.

The two men moved soundlessly toward Judd's apartment and took positions on either side of the door. The larger of the men, Rocky, softly tried the door. It was locked. He took out a celluloid card and carefully inserted it over the lock. He nodded to his brother, and both men took out revolvers with silencers on them. Rocky slid the celluloid card against the lock and pushed the unresisting door open, slowly. They walked into the living room, guns held out in front of them. They were confronted by three closed doors. There was no sign of Judd. The smaller brother, Nick, tried the first door. It was locked. He smiled at his brother, put the muzzle of his gun against the lock, and pulled the trigger. The door noiselessly swung open into a bedroom. The two men moved inside, guns sweeping the room.

There was no one inside. Nick checked the closets while Rocky returned to the living room. They moved without haste, knowing that Judd was in the apartment hiding, helpless. There was almost deliberate enjoyment in their unhurried movements, as though they were savoring the moments before the kill.

Nick tried the second closed door. It was locked. He shot the bolt out and moved into the room. It was the den. Empty. They grinned at each other and walked toward the last closed door. As they passed the TV monitor, Rocky caught his brother's arm. On the set they could see three men hurrying into the lobby. Two of them, wearing the white jackets of interns, were pushing a wheeled stretcher. The third carried a medical bag.

"What the hell!"

"Keep your cool, Rocky. So someone's sick. There must be a hundred apartments in this building."

They watched the TV set in fascination as the two interns wheeled the stretcher into the elevator. The group disappeared inside it, and the elevator door closed.

"Give them a couple minutes." It was Nick. "It could be some kind of accident. That means there might be cops."

"Of all the fuckin' luck!"

"Don't worry. Stevens ain't goin' nowhere."

The door to the apartment burst open and the doctor and the two interns entered, pushing the stretcher ahead of them. Swiftly the two killers shoved their guns into their overcoat pockets.

The doctor walked up to the brother. "Is he dead?"

"Who?"

"The suicide victim. Is he dead or alive?"

The two killers looked at each other, bewildered. "You guys got the wrong apartment."

The doctor pushed past the two killers and tried the bedroom door. "It's locked. Help me break it down."

The two brothers watched helplessly as the doctor and the interns smashed the door open with their shoulders. The doctor stepped into the bedroom. "Bring the stretcher." He moved to the bedside where Judd lay on the bed. "Are you all right?"

Judd looked up, trying to make his eyes focus. "Hospital," mumbled Judd.

"You're on your way."

As the two killers watched in frustration, the interns wheeled the stretcher into the bedroom, skillfully slid Judd onto it, and wrapped him in blankets.

"Let's blow," said Rocky.

The doctor watched the two men leave. Then he turned to Judd, who lay on the stretcher, his face white and haggard. "Are you all right, Judd?" His voice was filled with deep concern.

Judd tried a smile that didn't come off. "Great," he said. He could scarcely hear his own voice. "Thanks, Pete."

Peter looked down at his friend, then nodded to the two interns. "Let's go!"

T he hospital room was different, but the nurse was the same. A glaring bundle of disapproval. Seated at his bedside, she was the first thing that Judd saw when he opened his eyes. "Well. We're up," she said primly. "Dr. Harris wants to see you. I'll tell him we're awake." She walked stiffly out of the room.

Judd sat up, moving carefully. Arm and leg reflexes a bit slow, but unimpaired. He tried focusing on a chair across the room, one eye at a time. His vision was a little blurred.

"Want a consultation?"

He looked up. Dr. Seymour Harris had come into the room.

"Well," Dr. Harris said cheerfully, "you're turning out to be one of our best customers. Do you know how much your stitching bill alone is? We're going to have to give you discount rates . . . How did you sleep, Judd?" He sat down on the edge of the bed.

"Like a baby. What did you give me?"

"A shot of sodium luminol."

"What time is it?"

"Noon."

"My God," Judd said. "I've got to get out of here."

Dr. Harris removed the chart from the clipboard he carried. "What would you like to talk about first? Your concussion? Lacerations? Contusions?"

"I feel fine."

The doctor put the chart aside. His voice grew serious. "Judd, your body's taken a lot of punishment. More than you realize. If you're smart, you'll stay right in this bed for a few days and rest. Then you'll take a vacation for a month."

"Thanks, Seymour," Judd said.

"You mean thanks, but—no, thanks."

"There's something I have to take care of."

Dr. Harris sighed. "Do you know who make the worst patients in the world? Doctors." He changed the subject, conceding defeat. "Peter was here all night. He's been calling every hour. He's worried about you. He thinks someone tried to kill you last night."

"You know how doctors are—overimaginative."

Harris eyed him a moment, shrugged, then said, "You're the analyst. I'm only Ben Casey. Maybe you know what you're doing—but I wouldn't bet a nickel on it. Are you sure you won't stay in bed a few days?"

"I can't."

"OK, Tiger. I'll let you leave tomorrow."

Judd started to protest, but Dr. Harris cut him off.

"Don't argue. Today's Sunday. The guys who beat you up need a rest."

"Seymour . . ."

"Another thing. I hate to sound like a Jewish mother, but have you been eating lately?"

"Not much," Judd said.

"OK. I'm giving Miss Bedpan twenty-four hours to fatten you up. And Judd . . ."

"Yes?"

"Be careful. I hate to lose such a good customer." And Dr. Harris was gone.

Judd closed his eyes to rest a moment. He heard the rattle of dishes, and when he looked up, a beautiful Irish nurse was wheeling in a dining tray.

"You're awake, Dr. Stevens." She smiled.

"What time is it?"

"Six o'clock."

He had slept the day away.

She was placing the food on his bed tray. "You're having a treat tonight—turkey. Tomorrow's Christmas Eve."

"I know." He had no appetite for dinner until he took the first bite and suddenly discovered that he was ravenous. Dr. Harris had shut off all phone calls, so he lay in bed, undisturbed, gathering his strength, marshalling the forces within him. Tomorrow he would need all the energy he could muster.

At ten o'clock the next morning Dr. Seymour Harris bustled into Judd's room. "How's my favorite patient?" He beamed. "You look almost human."

"I feel almost human," smiled Judd.

"Good. You're going to have a visitor. I wouldn't want you to scare him."

Peter. And probably Norah. They seemed to be spending most of their time lately visiting him in hospitals.

Dr. Harris went on. "It's a Lieutenant McGreavy."

Judd's heart sank.

"He's very anxious to talk to you. He's on his way over here. He wanted to be sure you were awake."

So he could arrest him. With Angeli home sick, McGreavy had been free to manufacture evidence that would convict Judd. Once McGreavy got his hands on him, there was no hope. He had to escape before McGreavy arrived.

"Would you ask the nurse to get the barber?" Judd said. "I'd like a shave." His voice must have sounded odd, because Dr. Harris was looking at him strangely. Or was that because of something McGreavy had told Dr. Harris about him?

"Certainly, Judd." He left.

The moment the door closed, Judd got out of bed and stood up. The two nights of sleep had done miracles for him. He was a little unsteady on his feet, but that would pass. Now he had to move quickly. It took him three minutes to dress.

He opened the door a crack, made sure that no one was around who would try to stop him, and headed for the service stairs. As he started down the stairs, the elevator door opened and he saw McGreavy get off and start toward the room he had just left. He was moving swiftly, and behind him were a uniformed policeman and two detectives. Quickly, Judd went down the stairs and headed for the ambulance entrance. A block away from the hospital he hailed a taxi.

McGreavy walked into the hospital room and took one look at the unoccupied bed and the empty closet. "Fan out," he said to the others. "You might still catch him." He scooped up the phone.

The operator connected him with the police switchboard. "This is McGreavy," he said rapidly. "I want an all-points bulletin put out. Urgent . . . Dr. Stevens, Judd, Male. Caucasian. Age . . ."

The taxi pulled up in front of Judd's office building. From now on, there was no safety for him anywhere. He could not go back to his apartment. He would have to check into some hotel. Returning to his office was dangerous, but it had to be done this once.

He needed a phone number.

He paid the driver and walked into the lobby. Every muscle in his body ached. He moved quickly. He knew he had very little time. It was unlikely that they would be expecting him to return to his office, but he must take no chances. It was now a question of who got him first. The police or his assassins.

When he reached his office, he opened the door and went inside, locking the door after him. The inner office seemed strange and hostile, and Judd knew that he could not treat his patients here any longer. He would be subjecting them to too much danger. He was filled with anger at what Don Vinton was doing to his life. He could visualize the scene that must have occurred when the two brothers went back and reported that they had failed to kill him. If he had read Don Vinton's character correctly, he would have been in a towering rage. The next attack would come at any moment.

Judd went across the room to get Anne's phone number. For he had remembered two things in the hospital.

Some of Anne's appointments were scheduled just ahead of John Hanson's.

And Anne and Carol had had several chats together; Carol might have innocently confided some deadly information to Anne. If so, she could be in danger.

He took his address book out of a locked drawer, looked up Anne's phone number, and dialed. There were three rings, and then a neutral voice came on.

"This is a special operator. What number are you calling, please?"

Judd gave her the number. A few moments later the operator was back on the line. "I am sorry. You are calling a wrong number. Please check your directory or consult Information."

"Thank you," Judd said. He hung up. He sat there a moment, remembering what his answering service had said a few days ago. *They had been able to reach all his patients except Anne.* The numbers could have been transposed when they were put in the book. He looked in the telephone directory, but there was no listing under her husband's name or her name. He suddenly felt that it was very important that he talk to Anne. He copied down her address: 617 Woodside Avenue, Bayonne, New Jersey.

Fifteen minutes later, he was at an Avis counter, renting a car. There was a sign behind the counter that read: "We're second, so we try harder." *We're in the same boat,* thought Judd.

A few minutes later, he drove out of the garage. He rode around the block, satisfied himself that he was not being followed, and headed over the George Washington Bridge for New Jersey.

When he reached Bayonne, he stopped at a filling station to ask directions. "Next corner and make a left—third street."

"Thanks." Judd drove off. At the thought of seeing Anne again, his heart began to quicken. What was he going to say to her without alarming her? Would her husband be there?

Judd made a left turn onto Woodside Avenue. He looked at the numbers. He was in the nine hundred block. The houses on both sides of the street were small, old, and weatherbeaten. He drove to the seven hundred block. The houses seemed to become progressively older and smaller.

Anne lived on a beautiful wooded estate. There were virtually no trees here. When Judd reached the address Anne had given him, he was almost prepared for what he saw.

617 was a weed-covered vacant lot.

He sat in the car across from the vacant lot, trying to put it all together. The wrong phone number could have been a mistake. Or the address could have been a mistake. But not both. Anne had deliberately lied to him. And if she had lied about who she was and where she lived, what else had she lied about? He forced himself to objectively examine everything he really knew about her. It came to almost nothing. She had walked into his office unannounced and insisted on becoming a patient. In the four weeks that she had been coming to him, she had carefully managed not to reveal what her problem was, and then had suddenly announced that it was solved and she was going away. After each visit she had paid him in cash so that there would be no way of tracing her. But what reason could she have had for posing as a patient and then vanishing? There was only one answer. And as it hit Judd, he became physically sick.

If someone wanted to set him up for murder—wanted to know his routine at the office—wanted to know what the inside of the office looked like—what better way than to gain access as a patient? That was what she was doing there. Don Vinton had sent her. She had learned what she needed to know and then had disappeared without a trace.

It had all been pretense, and how eager he had been to be taken in by it. How she must have laughed when she went back to report to Don Vinton about the amorous idiot who called himself an analyst and pretended to be an expert about people. He was head over heels in love with a girl whose sole interest in him was setting him up to be murdered. How was *that* for a judge of character? What an amusing paper that would make for the American Psychiatric Association.

But what if it were not true? Supposing Anne had come to him with a legitimate problem, had used a fictitious name because she was afraid of embarrassing someone? In time the problem had solved itself and she had decided that she no longer needed the help of an analyst. But Judd knew that it was too easy. There was an "x" quantity about Anne that needed to be discovered. He had a strong feeling that in that unknown quantity could lie the answer to what was happening. It was possible that she was being forced to act against her will. But even as he thought it, he knew he was being foolish. He was trying to cast her as a damsel in distress with himself as a knight in shining armor. Had she set him up for murder? Somehow, he had to find out.

An elderly woman in a torn housecoat had come out of a house across the street and was staring at him. He turned the car around and headed back for the George Washington Bridge.

There was a line of cars behind him. Any one of them could be following him. But why would they have to follow him? His enemies knew where to find him. He couldn't sit and passively wait for them to attack. He had to do the attacking himself, keep them off guard, enrage Don Vinton into making a blunder so that he could be checkmated. And he had to do it before McGreavy caught him and locked him up.

Judd drove toward Manhattan. The only possible key to all this was Anne—and she had disappeared without a trace. The day after tomorrow she would be out of the country.

And Judd suddenly realized that he had one chance of finding her.

It was Christmas Eve and the Pan-Am office was crowded with travelers and would-be travelers on standby, fighting to get space on planes flying all over the world.

Judd made his way to the counter through the waiting lines and asked to see the manager. The uniformed girl behind the counter gave him a professionally coded smile and asked him to wait; the manager was on the phone.

Judd stood there hearing a babel of phrases.

"I want to leave India on the fifth."

"Will Paris be cold?"

"I want a car to meet me in Lisbon."

He felt a desperate desire to get on a plane and run away. He suddenly realized how exhausted he was, physically and emotionally. Don Vinton seemed to have an army at his disposal, but Judd was alone. What chance did he have against him?

"Can I help you?"

Judd turned. A tall, cadaverous-looking man stood behind the counter. "I'm Friendly," he said. He waited for Judd to appreciate the joke. Judd smiled dutifully. "Charles Friendly. What can I do for you?"

"I'm Dr. Stevens. I'm trying to locate a patient of mine. She's booked on a flight leaving for Europe tomorrow."

"The name?"

"Blake. Anne Blake." He hesitated. "Possibly it's under Mr. and Mrs. Anthony Blake."

"What city is she flying to?"

"I—I'm not sure."

"Are they booked on one of our morning or afternoon flights?"

"I'm not even certain if it's with your airline," Judd said.

The friendliness dropped out of Mr. Friendly's eyes. "Then I'm afraid I can't help you."

Judd felt a sudden feeling of panic. "It's really urgent. I must find her before she goes."

"Doctor, Pan-American has one or more flights leaving every day for Amsterdam, Barcelona, Berlin, Brussels, Copenhagen, Dublin, Dusseldorf, Frankfurt, Hamburg, Lisbon, London, Munich, Paris, Rome, Shannon, Stuttgart, and Vienna. So have most of the other international airlines. You'll have to contact each one individually. And I doubt if they can help you unless you can give them the destination and time of departure." The expression on Mr. Friendly's face was one of impatience. "If you'll excuse me . . ." He turned to walk away.

"Wait!" said Judd. How could he explain that this might be his last chance to stay alive? His last link to finding out who was attempting to kill him.

Friendly was regarding him with barely concealed annoyance. "Yes?"

Judd forced a smile on his face, hating himself for it. "Don't you have some kind of central computing system," he asked, "where you can get passengers' names by . . . ?"

"Only if you know the flight number," Mr. Friendly said. He turned and was gone.

Judd stood there at the counter, feeling sick. Check and checkmate. He was defeated. There was nowhere else to move.

A group of Italian priests bustled in, dressed in long, flapping black robes and wide black hats, looking like something out of the Middle Ages. They were weighed down with cheap cardboard suitcases, boxes and gift baskets of fruit. They were speaking loudly in Italian and obviously teasing the youngest member of their group, a boy who looked no more than eighteen or nineteen. They were probably returning home to Rome after a vacation, thought Judd, as he listened to their babbling. Rome . . . where Anne would be . . . Anne again.

The priests were moving toward the counter.

"*E molto bene di ritornare a casa.*"

"*Si, d'accordo.*"

"*Signore, per piacere, guardatemi.*"

"*Tutto va bene?*"

"*Si, ma—*"

"*Dio mio, dove sono i miei biglietti?*"

"*Cretino, hai perduto i biglietti.*"

"*Ah, eccoli.*"

The priests handed their airline tickets to the youngest priest, who moved bashfully toward the girl at the counter. Judd looked toward the exit. A large man in a gray overcoat was lounging in the doorway.

The young priest was talking to the girl behind the counter. "*Dieci. Dieci.*"

The girl stared at him blankly. The priest summoned up his knowledge of English and said very carefully, "Ten. Billetta. Tee-ket." He pushed the tickets toward her.

The girl smiled happily and began to process the tickets. The priests burst into delighted cries of approval at their companion's linguistic abilities and clapped him on the back.

There was no point in staying here any longer. Sooner or later he would have to face whatever was out there. Judd slowly turned and started to move past the group of priests.

"Guardate che ha fatto il Don Vinton."

Judd stopped, the blood suddenly rushing to his face. He turned to the tubby little priest who had spoken and took his arm. "Excuse me," he said. His voice was hoarse and unsteady. "Did you say 'Don Vinton?' "

The priest looked up at him blankly, then patted him on the arm and started to move away.

Judd tightened his grip. "Wait!" he said.

The priest was looking at him nervously. Judd forced himself to speak calmly. "Don Vinton. Which one is he? Show him to me."

All the priests were now staring at Judd. The little priest looked at his companions. *"E un americano matto."*

A babble of excited Italian rose from the group. Out of the corner of his eye, Judd saw Friendly watching him from behind the counter. Friendly opened the counter gate and started to move toward him. Judd fought to control a rising panic. He let go of the priest's arm, leaned close to him, and said slowly and distinctly, "Don Vinton."

The little priest looked into Judd's face for a moment and then his own face splintered into merriment. *"Don Vinton!"*

The manager was approaching rapidly, his manner hostile. Judd nodded to the priest encouragingly. The little priest pointed to the boy. *"Don Vinton*—'big man.' "

And suddenly the puzzle fell into place.

20

"Slow down, slow down," Angeli said hoarsely. "I can't understand a word you're saying."

"Sorry" Judd said. He took a deep breath. "I've got the answer!" He was so relieved to hear Angeli's voice over the phone that he was almost babbling. "I know who's trying to kill me. I know who Don Vinton is."

There was a skeptical note in Angeli's voice. "We couldn't find any Don Vinton."

"Do you know why? Because it isn't a him—it's a *who*."

"Will you speak more slowly?"

Judd's voice was trembling with excitement. "Don Vinton isn't a name. It's an Italian expression. It means 'the big man.' That's what Moody was trying to tell me. That The Big Man was after me."

"You lost me, Doctor."

"It doesn't mean anything in English," said Judd, "but when you say it in Italian—doesn't it suggest anything to you? An organization of killers run by The Big Man?"

There was a long silence over the phone. "La Cosa Nostra?"

"Who else could assemble a group of killers and weapons like that? Acid, bombs—guns! Remember I told you the man we're looking for would be Latin? He's Italian."

"It doesn't make sense. Why would La Cosa Nostra want to kill you?"

"I have absolutely no idea. But I'm right. I know I'm right. And it fits in with something Moody said. He said there was a group of men out to kill me."

"It's the craziest theory I've ever heard," Angeli said. There was a pause, then he added, "But I suppose it could be possible."

Judd was flooded with sudden relief. If Angeli had not been willing to listen to him, he would have had no one to turn to.

"Have you discussed this with anyone?"

"No," Judd said.

"Don't!" Angeli's voice was urgent. "If you're right, your life depends on it. Don't go near your office or apartment."

"I won't," Judd promised. He suddenly remembered. "Did you know McGreavy has a warrant out for my arrest?"

"Yes." Angeli hesitated. "If McGreavy picks you up, you'll never get to the station alive."

My God! So he had been right about McGreavy. But he could not believe that McGreavy was the brain behind this. There was someone directing him . . . Don Vinton, The Big Man.

"Can you hear me?"

Judd's mouth was suddenly dry. "Yes."

A man in a gray overcoat stood outside the phone booth looking in at Judd. Was it the same man he had seen before? "Angeli . . ."

"Yes?"

"I don't know who the others are. I don't know what they look like. How do I stay alive until they're caught?"

The man outside the booth was staring at him.

Angeli's voice came over the line. "We're going straight to the FBI. I have a friend who has connections. He'll see that you're protected until you're safe. OK?" There was a note of assurance in Angeli's voice.

"OK," Judd said gratefully. His knees felt like jelly.

"Where are you?"

"In a phone booth in the lower lobby of the Pan-Am Building."

"Don't move. Keep plenty of people around you. I'm on my way." There was a click at the other end of the line as Angeli hung up.

He put the phone back on the squad-room desk, a sick feeling deep inside him. Over the years he had become accustomed to dealing with murderers, rapists, perverts of every description, and somehow, in time, a protective shell had formed, allowing him to go on believing in the basic dignity and humanity of man.

But a rogue cop was something different.

A rogue cop was a corruption that touched everyone on the force, that violated everything that decent cops fought and died for.

The squad room was filled with the passage of feet and the murmur of voices, but he heard none of it. Two uniformed patrolmen passed through the room with a giant drunk in handcuffs. One of the officers had a black eye and the other held a handkerchief to a bloody nose. The sleeve of his uniform had been ripped half off. The patrolman would have to pay for that himself. These men were ready to risk their lives every day and night of the year. But that wasn't what made headlines. A crooked cop made headlines. One crooked cop tainted them all. His own partner.

Wearily he got up and walked down the ancient corridor to the captain's office. He knocked once and went in.

Behind a battered desk pocked with the lighted cigar butts of countless years sat Captain Bertelli. Two FBI men were in the room, dressed in business suits. Captain Bertelli looked up as the door opened. "Well?"

The detective nodded. "It checks out. The property custodian said he came in and borrowed Carol Roberts' key from the evidence locker Wednesday afternoon and returned it late Wednesday night. That's why the paraffin test was negative—he got into Dr. Stevens' office by using an original key. The custodian never questioned it because he knew he was assigned to the case."

"Do you know where he is now?" asked the younger of the FBI men.

"No. We had a tail on him, but he lost him. He could be anywhere."

"He'll be hunting for Dr. Stevens," said the second FBI agent.

Captain Bertelli turned to the FBI men. "What are the chances of Dr. Stevens staying alive?"

The man shook his head. "If they find him before we do—none."

Captain Bertelli nodded. "We've got to find him first." His voice grew savage. "I want Angeli brought back, too. I don't care how you get him." He turned to the detective. "Just get him, McGreavy."

The police radio began to crackle out a staccato message: "Code Ten . . . Code Ten . . . All cars . . . pick up five . . ."

Angeli switched the radio off. "Anyone know I picked you up?" he asked.

"No one," Judd assured him.

"You haven't discussed La Cosa Nostra with anybody?"

"Only you."

Angeli nodded, satisfied.

They had crossed the George Washington Bridge and were headed for New Jersey. But everything had changed. Before, he had been filled with apprehension. Now, with Angeli at his side, he no longer felt like the hunted. He was the hunter. And the thought filled him with deep satisfaction.

At Angeli's suggestion, Judd had left his rented car in Manhattan and he was riding in Angeli's unmarked police car. Angeli had headed north on the Palisades Interstate Parkway and exited at Orangeburg. They were approaching Old Tappan.

"It was smart of you to spot what was going on, Doctor," Angeli said.

Judd shook his head. "I should have figured it out as soon as I knew there was more than one man involved. It had to be an organization using professional killers. I think Moody suspected the truth when he saw the bomb in my car. They had access to every kind of weapon."

And Anne. She was part of the operation, setting him up so that they could murder him. And yet—he couldn't hate her. No matter what she had done, he could never hate her.

Angeli had turned off the main highway. He deftly tooled the car onto a secondary road that led toward a wooded area.

"Does your friend know we're coming?" Judd asked.

"I phoned him. He's all ready for you."

A side road appeared abruptly, and Angeli turned the car into it. He drove for a mile, then braked to a stop in front of an electric gate. Judd noticed a small television camera mounted above the gate. There was a click and the gate swung open, then closed solidly behind them. They began driving up a long, curving driveway. Through the trees ahead, Judd caught a glimpse of the sprawling roof of an enormous house. High on top, flashing in the sun, was a bronze rooster.

Its tail was missing.

In the soundproofed, neon-lit communications center at Police Headquarters, a dozen shirtsleeved police officers manned the giant switchboard. Six operators sat on each side of the board. In the middle of the board was a pneumatic chute. As the calls came in, the operators wrote a message, put it in the chute, and sent it upstairs to the dispatcher, for immediate relay to a substation or patrol car. The calls never ceased. They poured in day and night, like a river of tragedy flooding in from the citizens of the huge metropolis. Men and women who were terrified . . . lonely . . . desperate . . . drunk . . . injured . . . homicidal . . . It was a scene from Hogarth, painted with vivid, anguished words instead of colors.

On this Monday afternoon there was a feeling of added tension in the air. Each telephone operator handled his job with full concentration, and yet each was aware of the number of detectives and FBI agents who kept moving in and out of the room, receiving and giving orders, working efficiently and quietly as they spread a vast electronic net for Dr. Judd Stevens and Detective Frank Angeli. The atmosphere was quickened, strangely staccato, as though the action were being staged by some grim, nervous puppeteer.

Captain Bertelli was talking to Allen Sullivan, a member of the Mayor's Crime Commission, when McGreavy walked in. McGreavy had met Sullivan before. He was tough and honest. Bertelli broke off his conversation and turned to the detective, his face a question mark.

"Things are moving," McGreavy said. "We found an eyewitness, a night watchman who works in the building across the street from Dr. Stevens' office building. On Wednesday night, when someone broke into Dr. Stevens' office, the watchman was just going on duty. He saw two men go into the building. The street door was locked and they opened it with a key. He figured they worked there."

"Did you get an ID?"

"He identified a picture of Angeli."

"Wednesday night Angeli was supposed to have been home in bed with the flu."

"Right."

"What about the second man?"

"The watchman didn't get a good look at him."

An operator plugged in one of the innumerable red lights blinking across the switchboard and turned to Captain Bertelli. "For you, Captain. New Jersey Highway Patrol."

Bertelli snatched up an extension phone. "Captain Bertelli." He listened a moment. "Are you sure? . . . Good! Will you get every unit you can in there? Set up roadblocks. I want that area covered like a blanket. Keep in close touch . . . Thanks." He hung up and turned to the two men. "It looks like we got a break. A rookie patrolman in New Jersey spotted Angeli's car on a secondary road near Orangeburg. The Highway Patrol's combing the area now."

"Dr. Stevens?"

"He was in the car with Angeli. Alive. Don't worry. They'll find them."

McGreavy pulled out two cigars. He offered one to Sullivan, who refused it, handed one to Bertelli, and put the other one between his teeth. "We've got one thing going for us. Dr. Stevens leads a charmed life." He struck a match and lit the two cigars. "I just talked to a friend of his—Dr. Peter Hadley. Dr. Hadley told me that he went to pick up Stevens in his office a few days ago and found Angeli there with a gun in his hand. Angeli told some cock-and-bull story about expecting a burglar. My guess is that Dr. Hadley's arrival saved Stevens' life."

"How did you first get on to Angeli?" Sullivan asked.

"It started with a couple of tips that he was shaking down some merchants," McGreavy said. "When I went to check them out, the victims wouldn't talk. They were scared, but I couldn't figure out why. I didn't say anything to Angeli. I just started keeping a close watch on him. When the Hanson murder broke, Angeli came and asked if he could work on the case with me. He gave me some bullshit about how much he admired me and how he had always wanted to be my partner. I knew he had to have an angle, so with Captain Bertelli's permission, I played along with him. No wonder he wanted to work on the case—he was in it up to his ass! At that time I wasn't sure whether Dr. Stevens was involved in the murders of Hanson and Carol Roberts, but I decided to use him to help set up Angeli. I built up a phony case against Stevens and told Angeli I was going to nail the doctor for the murders. I figured that if Angeli thought he was off the hook, he'd relax and get careless."

"Did it work?"

"No. Angeli surprised the hell out of me by putting up a fight to keep Stevens out of jail."

Sullivan looked up, puzzled. "But why?"

"Because he was trying to knock him off and he couldn't get to him if he were locked up."

"When McGreavy began to put the pressure on," Captain Bertelli said, "Angeli came to me hinting that McGreavy was trying to frame Dr. Stevens."

"We were sure then that we were on the right track," McGreavy said. "Stevens hired a private detective named Norman Moody. I checked Moody out and learned that he had tangled with Angeli before when a client of Moody's was picked up by Angeli on a drug rap. Moody said his client was framed. Knowing what I know now, I'd say Moody was telling the truth.

"So Moody lucked into the answer from the beginning."

"It wasn't all luck. Moody was bright. He knew Angeli was probably involved. When he found the bomb in Dr. Stevens' car, he turned it over to the FBI and asked them to check it out."

"He was afraid if Angeli got hold of it, he'd find a way to get rid of it?"

"That's my guess. But someone slipped up and a copy of the report was sent to Angeli. He knew then that Moody was on to him. The first real break we got was when Moody came up with the name 'Don Vinton.' "

"Cosa Nostra for 'The Big Man.' "

"Yeah. For some reason, someone in La Cosa Nostra was out to get Dr. Stevens."

"How did you tie up Angeli with La Cosa Nostra?"

"I went back to the merchants Angeli had been putting the squeeze on. When I mentioned La Cosa Nostra, they panicked. Angeli was working for one of the Cosa Nostra families, but he got greedy and was doing a little shakedown business of his own on the side."

"Why would La Cosa Nostra want to kill Dr. Stevens?" Sullivan asked.

"I don't know. We're working on several angles." He sighed wearily. "We got two lousy breaks. Angeli slipped the men we had tailing him, and Dr. Stevens ran away from the hospital before I could warn him about Angeli and give him protection."

The switchboard flashed. An operator plugged in the call and listened a moment. "Captain Bertelli."

Bertelli grabbed the extension phone. "Captain Bertelli." He listened, saying nothing, then slowly replaced the receiver and turned to McGreavy. "They lost them."

A nthony DeMarco had mana.

Judd could feel the burning power of his personality across the room, coming in waves that struck like a tangible force. When Anne had said her husband was handsome, she had not exaggerated.

DeMarco had a classic Roman face with a perfectly sculptured profile, coal black eyes, and attractive streaks of gray in his dark hair. He was in his middle forties, tall and athletic, and moved with a restless animal grace. His voice was deep and magnetic. "Would you care for a drink, Doctor?

Judd shook his head, fascinated by the man before him. Anyone would have sworn that DeMarco was a perfectly normal, charming man, a perfect host welcoming an honored guest.

There were five of them in the richly paneled library. Judd, DeMarco, Detective Angeli, and the two men who had tried to kill Judd at his apartment building, Rocky and Nick Vaccaro. They had formed a circle around Judd. He was looking into the faces of the enemy, and there was a grim satisfaction in it. Finally he knew whom he was fighting. If "fighting" was the right word. He had walked into Angeli's trap. Worse. He had phoned Angeli and invited him to come and get him! Angeli, the Judas goat who had led him here to the slaughter.

DeMarco was studying him with deep interest, his black eyes probing. "I've heard a great deal about you," he said.

Judd said nothing.

"Forgive me for having you brought here in this fashion, but it is necessary to ask you a few questions." He smiled apologetically, radiating warmth.

Judd knew what was coming, and his mind moved swiftly ahead.

"What did you and my wife talk about, Dr. Stevens?"

Judd put surprise into his voice. "Your wife? I don't know your wife."

DeMarco shook his head reproachfully. "She's been going to your office twice a week for the last three weeks."

Judd frowned thoughtfully. "I have no patient named DeMarco. . . ."

DeMarco nodded understandingly. "Perhaps she used another name. Maybe her maiden name. Blake—Anne Blake."

Judd carefully registered surprise. "Anne Blake?"

The two Vaccaro brothers moved in closer.

"No," DeMarco said sharply. He turned to Judd. His affable manner was gone. "Doctor, if you try to play games with me, I'm going to do things to you that you wouldn't believe."

Judd looked into his eyes and believed him. He knew that his life was hanging by a thread. He forced indignation into his voice. "You can do what you please. Until this moment I had no idea that Anne Blake was your wife."

"That could be true," Angeli said. "He—"

DeMarco ignored Angeli. "What did you and my wife talk about for three weeks?"

They had arrived at the moment of truth. From the instant Judd had seen the bronze rooster on the roof, the final pieces of the puzzle had fallen into place. Anne had not set him up for murder. She had been a victim, like himself. She had married Anthony DeMarco, successful owner of a large construction firm, without any idea of who he really was. Then something must have happened to make her suspect that her husband was not what he had seemed to be, that he was involved in something dark and terrible. With no one to talk to, she had turned for help to an analyst, a stranger, in whom she could confide. But in Judd's office her basic loyalty to her husband had kept her from discussing her fears.

"We didn't talk about much of anything," said Judd evenly. "Your wife refused to tell me what her problem was.

DeMarco's black eyes were fixed on him, probing, weighing.

"You'll have to come up with something better than that."

How DeMarco must have panicked when he learned that his wife was going to a psychoanalyst—the wife of a leader in La Cosa Nostra. No wonder DeMarco had killed, trying to get hold of Anne's file.

"All she told me," Judd said, "was that she was unhappy about something, but couldn't discuss it."

"That took ten seconds," DeMarco said. "I've got a record of every minute she spent in your office. What did she talk about for the rest of the three weeks? She must have told you who I am."

"She said you owned a construction company."

DeMarco was studying him coldly. Judd could feel beads of perspiration forming on his forehead.

"I've been reading up on analysis, Doctor. The patient talks about everything that's on his mind."

"That's part of the therapy," Judd said matter-of-factly. "That's why I wasn't getting anywhere with Mrs. Blake—with Mrs. DeMarco. I intended to dismiss her as a patient."

"But you didn't."

"I didn't have to. When she came to see me Friday, she told me that she was leaving for Europe."

"Annie's changed her mind. She doesn't want to go to Europe with me. Do you know why?"

Judd looked at him, genuinely puzzled. "No."

"Because of you, Doctor."

Judd's heart gave a little leap. He carefully kept his feelings out of his voice. "I don't understand."

"Sure you do. Annie and I had a long talk last night. She thinks she made a mistake about our marriage. She's not happy with me any more, because she thinks she goes for you." When DeMarco spoke, it was almost in a hypnotic whisper. "I want you to tell me all about what happened when you two were alone in your office and she was on your couch.

Judd steeled himself against the mixed emotions that were coursing through him. She *did* care! But what good was it going to do either of them? DeMarco was looking at him, waiting for an answer. "Nothing happened. If you read up on analysis, you'll know that every female patient goes through an emotional transference. At one time or another, they all think they're in love with their doctor. It's just a passing phase."

DeMarco was watching him intently, his black eyes probing into Judd's.

"How did you know she was coming to see me?" Judd asked, making the question casual.

DeMarco looked at Judd a moment, then walked over to a large desk and picked up a razor-sharp letter opener in the shape of a dagger. "One of my men saw her go into your building. There are a lot of baby doctors there and they figured maybe Annie was keeping back a little surprise from me. They followed her up to your office." He turned to Judd. "It was a surprise, all right. They found out she was going to a psychiatrist. The wife of Anthony DeMarco spilling my personal business to a headshrinker."

"I told you she didn't—"

DeMarco's voice was soft. "The *Commissione* held a meeting. They voted for me to kill her, like we'd kill any traitor." He was pacing now, reminding Judd of a dangerous, caged animal. "But they can't give me orders like a peasant soldier. I am Anthony DeMarco, a Capo. I promised them that if she had discussed any of our business, I would kill the man she talked to. With these two hands." He held up his fists, one of them holding the razor-edged dagger. "That's you, Doctor."

DeMarco was circling him now as he talked, and each time that DeMarco walked in back of him, Judd unconsciously braced himself.

"You're making a mistake if—" Judd started.

"No. You know who made the mistake? Annie." He looked Judd up and down. He sounded genuinely puzzled. "How could she think you're a better man than I am?"

The Vaccaro brothers snickered.

"You're nothing. A patsy who goes to an office every day and makes—what? Thirty grand a year? Fifty? A hundred? I make more than that in a week." DeMarco's mask was slipping away more quickly now, eroding under the pressure of his emotions. He was beginning to speak in short, excited bursts, a patina of ugliness warping his handsome features. Anne had only seen him behind his facade. Judd was looking into the naked face of a homicidal paranoiac. "You and that little *putana* pick each other!"

"We haven't picked each other," Judd said.

DeMarco was watching him, his eyes blazing. "She doesn't mean anything to you?"

"I told you. She's just another patient."

"OK," DeMarco said at last. "You tell her."

"Tell her what?"

"That you don't give a damn about her. I'm going to send her down here. I want you to talk to her, alone."

Judd's pulse began to race. He was going to be given a chance to save himself and Anne.

DeMarco flicked his hand and the men moved out into the hallway. DeMarco turned to Judd. His deep black eyes were hooded. He smiled gently, the mask in place again. "As long as Annie doesn't know anything, she will live. You're going to convince her that she should go to Europe with me.

Judd felt his mouth go suddenly dry. There was a triumphant glint in DeMarco's eyes. Judd knew why. He had underestimated his opponent.

Fatally.

DeMarco was not a chess player, and yet he had been clever enough to know that he held a pawn that made Judd helpless. Anne. Whatever move Judd made, she was in danger. If he sent her away to Europe with DeMarco, he was certain that her life would be in jeopardy. He did not believe that DeMarco was going to let her live. La Cosa Nostra would not allow it. In Europe DeMarco would arrange an "accident." But if Judd told Anne not to go, if she found out what was happening to him, she would try to interfere, and that would mean instant death for her. There was no escape: only a choice of two traps.

From the window of her bedroom on the second floor, Anne had watched the arrival of Judd and Angeli. For one exhilarating moment, she had believed that Judd was coming to take her away, to rescue her from the terrifying situation she was in. But then she had seen Angeli take out a gun and force Judd into the house.

She had known the truth about her husband for the last forty-eight hours. Before that, it had only been a dim, glimmering suspicion, so incredible that she had tried to brush it aside. It had begun a few months ago, when she had gone to a play in Manhattan and had come home unexpectedly early because the star was drunk and the curtain had been rung down in the middle of the second act. Anthony had told her that he was having a business meeting at the house, but that it would be over before she returned. When she had arrived, the meeting was still going on. And before her surprised husband had been able to close the library door, she had heard someone angrily shouting, "I vote that we hit the factory tonight and take care of the bastards once and for all!" The phrase, the ruthless appearance of the strangers in the room, and Anthony's agitation at seeing her had combined to unnerve Anne. She had let his glib explanations convince her because she had wanted desperately to be convinced. In the six months of their marriage, he had been a tender, considerate husband. She had seen occasional flashes of a violent temper, but he had always quickly managed to gain control of himself.

A few weeks after the theater incident, she had picked up a telephone and had overheard Anthony's voice on an extension phone. "We're taking over a shipment from Toronto tonight. You'll have to have someone handle the guard. He's not with us."

She had hung up, shaken. "Take over a shipment" . . . "handle the guard" . . . They sounded ominous, but they could have been innocent business phrases. Carefully, casually, she tried to question Anthony about his business activities. It was as though a steel wall went up. She was confronted by an angry stranger who told her to take care of his home and keep out of his business. They had quarreled bitterly, and the next evening he had given her an outrageously expensive necklace and tenderly apologized.

A month later, the third incident had occurred. Anne had been awakened at four o'clock in the morning by the slamming of a door. She had slipped into a negligee and gone downstairs to investigate. She heard voices coming from the library, raised in argument. She went toward the door, but stopped as she saw Anthony in the room talking to half a dozen strangers. Afraid that he would be angry if she interrupted, she quietly went back upstairs and returned to bed. At breakfast the next morning, she asked him how he had slept.

"Great. I fell off at ten o'clock and never opened my eyes once."

And Anne knew that she was in trouble. She had no idea what kind of trouble or how serious it was. All she knew was that her husband had lied to her for reasons that she could not fathom.

What kind of business could he be involved in that had to be conducted secretly in the middle of the night with men who looked like hoodlums? She was afraid to broach the subject again with Anthony. A panic began to build in her. There was no one with whom she could talk.

A few nights later, at a dinner party at the country club to which they belonged, someone had mentioned a psychoanalyst named Judd Stevens, and talked about how brilliant he was.

"He's a kind of analyst's analyst, if you know what I mean. He's terribly attractive, but it's wasted—he's one of those dedicated types."

Anne had carefully noted the name and the following week had gone to see him.

The first meeting with Judd had turned her life topsy-turvy. She had felt herself drawn into an emotional vortex that had left her shaken. In her confusion, she had been scarcely able to talk to him, and she had left feeling like a school girl, promising herself that she would not go back. But she had gone back to prove to herself that what had happened was a fluke, an accident. Her reaction the second time was even stronger. She had always prided herself on being sensible and realistic, and now she was acting like a seventeen-year-old girl in love for the first time. She found herself unable to discuss her husband with Judd, and so they had talked about other things, and after each session Anne found herself more in love with this warm, sensitive stranger.

She knew it was hopeless because she would never divorce Anthony. She felt there must be some terrible flaw in her that would allow her to marry a man and six months later fall in love with another man. She decided that it would be better if she never saw Judd again.

And then a series of strange things had begun to happen. Carol Roberts was killed, and Judd was knocked down by a hit-and-run driver. She read in the newspapers that Judd was there when Moody's body was found in the Five Star Warehouse. She had seen the name of the warehouse before.

On the letterhead of an invoice on Anthony's desk.

And a terrible suspicion began to form in her mind.

It seemed incredible that Anthony could be involved in any of the awful things that had been happening, and yet . . . She felt as though she was trapped in a terrifying nightmare, and there was no way out. She could not discuss her fears with Judd, and she was afraid to discuss them with Anthony. She told herself that her suspicions were groundless: Anthony did not even know of Judd's existence.

And then, forty-eight hours ago, Anthony had come into her bedroom and started questioning her about her visits to Judd. Her first reaction had been anger that he had been spying on her, but that had quickly given way to all the fears that had been preying upon her. As she looked into his twisted, enraged face, she knew that her husband was capable of anything.

Even murder.

During the questioning, she had made one terrible mistake. She had let him know how she felt about Judd. Anthony's eyes had turned deep black, and he had shaken his head as though warding off a physical blow.

It was not until she was alone again that she realized how much danger Judd was in, and that she could not leave him. She told Anthony that she would not go to Europe with him.

And now Judd was here, in this house. His life in peril, because of her.

The bedroom door opened and Anthony walked in. He stood watching her a moment.

"You have a visitor," he said.

She walked into the library wearing a yellow skirt and blouse, her hair back loosely over her shoulders. Her face was drawn and pale, but there was an air of quiet composure about her. Judd was in the room, alone.

"Hello, Dr. Stevens. Anthony told me that you were here."

Judd had the sensation that they were acting out a charade for the benefit of an unseen, deadly audience. He intuitively knew that Anne was aware of the situation and was placing herself in his hands, waiting to follow whatever lead he offered.

And there was nothing he could do except try to keep her alive a little longer. If Anne refused to go to Europe, DeMarco would certainly have her killed here.

He hesitated, choosing his words carefully. Each word could be as dangerous as the bomb planted in his car. "Mrs. DeMarco, your husband is upset because you changed your mind about going to Europe with him."

Anne waited, listening, weighing.

"I'm sorry," she said.

"So am I. I think you should go," Judd said, raising his voice.

Anne was studying his face, reading his eyes. "What if I refuse? What if I just walk out?"

Judd was filled with sudden alarm. "You mustn't do that." She would never leave this house alive. "Mrs. DeMarco," he said deliberately, "your husband is under the mistaken impression that you're in love with me."

She opened her lips to speak and he quickly went on. "I explained to him that that's a normal part of analysis—an emotional transference that all patients go through."

She picked up his lead. "I know. I'm afraid it was foolish of me to go to you in the first place. I should have tried to solve my problem myself." Her eyes told him how much she meant it, how much she regretted the danger she had placed him in. "I've been thinking it over. Perhaps a holiday in Europe would be good for me."

He breathed a quick sigh of relief. She had understood.

But there was no way he could warn her of her real danger. Or did she know? And even if she knew, was there anything she could do about it? He looked past Anne toward the library window framing the tall trees that bordered the woods. She had told him that she took long walks in them. It was possible she might be familiar with a way out. If they could get to the woods . . . He lowered his voice, urgently. "Anne—"

"Finished your little chat?"

Judd spun around. DeMarco had quietly walked into the room. Behind him came Angeli and the Vaccaro brothers.

Anne turned to her husband. "Yes," she said. "Dr. Stevens thinks I should go to Europe with you. I'm going to take his advice."

DeMarco smiled and looked at Judd. "I knew I could count on you, Doctor." He was radiating charm, beaming with the expansive satisfaction of a man who has achieved total victory. It was as though the incredible energy that flowed through DeMarco could be converted at will, switched from a dark evil to an overpowering, attractive warmth. No wonder Anne had been taken in by him. Even Judd found it hard to believe at this instant that this gracious, friendly Adonis was a cold-blooded, psychopathic murderer.

DeMarco turned to Anne. "We'll be leaving early in the morning, darling. Why don't you go upstairs and start packing?"

Anne hesitated. She did not want to leave Judd alone with these men. "I . . ." She looked at Judd helplessly. He nodded imperceptibly.

"All right." Anne held out her hand. "Goodbye, Dr. Stevens." Judd took her hand. "Good-bye."

And this time it *was* good-bye. There was no way out. Judd watched as she turned, nodded at the others, and walked out of the room.

DeMarco looked after her. "Isn't she beautiful?" There was a strange expression on his face. Love, possessiveness—and something else. Regret? For what he was about to do to Anne?

"She doesn't know anything about all this," Judd said. "Why don't you keep her out of it? Let her go away."

He watched the switch turn in DeMarco, and it was almost physical. The charm vanished, and hate began to fill the room, a current flowing from DeMarco to Judd, not touching anyone else. There was an ecstatic, almost orgiastic expression on DeMarco's face. "Let's go, Doctor."

Judd looked around the room, measuring his chances of escape. Surely DeMarco would prefer not to kill him in his home. It had to be now or never. The Vaccaro brothers were watching him hungrily, hoping he would make a move. Angeli was standing near the window, his hand near his gun holster.

"I wouldn't try it," DeMarco said softly. "You're a dead man— but we're going to do it my way."

He gave Judd a push toward the door. The others closed in on him, and they headed toward the entrance hall.

When Anne reached the upstairs hallway, she waited near the landing, watching the hall below. She drew back out of sight as she saw Judd and the others move toward the front door. She hurried into her bedroom and looked out the window. The men were pushing Judd into Angeli's car.

Quickly Anne reached for the telephone and dialed operator. It seemed an eternity before there was an answer.

"Operator, I want the police! Hurry—it's an emergency!"

And a man's hand reached in front of her and pressed down the receiver. Anne gave a little scream and whirled around. Nick Vaccaro was standing over her, grinning.

A ngeli switched on the headlights. It was four o'clock in the afternoon, but the sun was buried somewhere behind the mass of cumulus clouds that scudded overhead, pushed by the icy winds. They had been driving for over an hour.

Angeli was at the wheel. Rocky Vaccaro was seated next to him. Judd was in the back seat with Anthony DeMarco.

In the beginning Judd had kept an eye out for a passing police car, hoping that he might somehow make a desperate bid to attract attention, but Angeli was driving through little-used side roads where there was almost no traffic. They skirted the edges of Morristown, picked up Route 206 and headed south toward the sparsely populated, bleak plains of central New Jersey. The gray sky opened up and it began to pour: a cold, icy sleet that beat against the windshield like tiny drums gone mad.

"Slow down," DeMarco commanded. "We don't want to have an accident."

Angeli obediently lightened his foot on the accelerator.

DeMarco turned to Judd. "That's where most people make their mistake. They don't plan things out like me."

Judd looked at DeMarco, studying him clinically. The man was suffering from megalomania, beyond the reach of reason or logic. There was no way to appeal to him. There was some moral sense missing in him that allowed him to kill without compunction. Judd knew most of the answers now.

DeMarco had committed the murders with his own hand out of a sense of honor—a Sicilian's revenge, to erase the stain that he thought his wife had placed on him and his Cosa Nostra family. He had killed John Hanson by mistake. When Angeli had reported back to him and told him what had happened, DeMarco had gone back to the office and found Carol. Poor Carol. She could not give him the tapes of Mrs. DeMarco because she did not know Anne by that name. If DeMarco had kept his temper, he could have helped Carol figure out whom he was talking about; but it was part of his sickness that he had no tolerance for frustration and he had gone into an insane rage, and Carol had died. Horribly. It was DeMarco who had run Judd down, and later had come to kill him at his office with Angeli. Judd had been puzzled by the fact that they had not broken in and shot him. But he realized now that since McGreavy was sure Judd was guilty, they had decided to make his death look like a suicide, committed in remorse. That would stop any further police investigation.

And Moody . . . poor Moody. When Judd had told him the names of the detectives on the case, he had thought he was reacting to McGreavy—when it was really Angeli. Moody had learned that Angeli was involved with the Cosa Nostra, and when he followed up on it . . .

He looked over at DeMarco. "What's going to happen to Anne?"

"Don't worry. I'll take care of her," DeMarco said.

Angeli smiled. "Yeah."

Judd felt a helpless rage sweep over him.

"I was wrong to marry someone outside the family," brooded DeMarco. "Outsiders can never understand it like it is. Never."

They were traveling in an almost barren section of flatlands. An occasional factory dotted the sleet-blurred skyline in the distance.

"We're almost there," Angeli announced.

"You've done a good job," DeMarco said. "We're going to hide you away somewhere until the heat cools down. Where would you like to go?"

"I like Florida."

DeMarco nodded approvingly. "No problem. You'll stay with one of the *family*."

"I know some great broads down there." Angeli smiled.

DeMarco smiled back at him in the mirror. "You'll come back with a tanned ass."

"I hope that's all I come back with."

Rocky Vaccaro laughed.

In the distance, on the right, Judd saw the sprawled buildings of a factory spuming smoke into the air. They reached a small side road leading to the factory. Angeli turned into it and drove until they came to a high wall. The gate was closed. Angeli leaned on the horn and a man in a raincoat and rainhat appeared behind the gate. When he saw DeMarco, he nodded, unlocked the gate, and swung it open. Angeli drove the car inside, and the gate closed behind them. They had arrived.

At the Nineteenth Precinct, Lieutenant McGreavy was in his office, going over a list of names with three detectives, Captain Bertelli, and the two FBI men.

"This is a list of the Cosa Nostra families in the East. All the Sub-Capos and Capo Regimes. Our problem is, we don't know which one Angeli is hooked up with."

"How long would it take to get a rundown on them?" asked Bertelli.

One of the FBI men spoke. "There are over sixty names here. It would take at least twenty-four hours, but . . ." He stopped.

McGreavy finished the sentence for him. "But Dr. Stevens won't be alive twenty-four hours from now."

A young uniformed policeman hurried up to the open door. He hesitated as he saw the group of men.

"What is it?" McGreavy asked.

"New Jersey didn't know if it's important, Lieutenant, but you asked them to report anything unusual. An operator got a call from an adult female asking for Police Headquarters. She said it was an emergency, and then the line went dead. The operator waited, but there was no call back."

"Where did the call come from?"

"A town called Old Tappan."

"Did she get the number?"

"No. The caller hung up too quickly."

"Great," McGreavy said bitterly.

"Forget it," Bertelli said. "It was probably some old lady reporting a lost cat."

McGreavy's phone rang, a long, insistent peal. He picked up the phone. "Lieutenant McGreavy." The others in the room watched his face draw tight with tension. "Right! Tell them not to make a move until I get there. I'm on my way!" He slammed the receiver down. "The Highway Patrol just spotted Angeli's car going south on Route 206, just outside Millstone."

"Are they tailing it?" It was one of the FBI men.

"The patrol car was going in the opposite direction. By the time they got turned around, it had disappeared. I know that area. There's nothing out there but a few factories." He turned to one of the FBI men. "Can you get me a fast rundown on the names of the factories there and who owns them?"

"Will do." The FBI man reached for the phone.

"I'm heading out there," McGreavy said. "Call me when you get it." He turned to the men. "Let's move!" He started out the door, the three detectives and the second FBI man on his heels.

Angeli drove past the watchman's shack near the gate and continued toward a group of odd-looking structures that reached into the sky. There were high brick chimneys and giant flumes, their curved shapes rearing up out of the gray drizzle like prehistoric monsters in an ancient, timeless landscape.

The car rolled up to a complex of large pipes and conveyor belts and braked to a stop. Angeli and Vaccaro got out of the car and Vaccaro opened the rear door on Judd's side. He had a gun in his hand. "Out, Doctor."

Slowly, Judd got out of the car, followed by DeMarco. A tremendous din and wind hurtled at them. In front of them, about twenty-five feet away, was an enormous pipeline filled with roaring, compressed air, sucking in everything that came near its open, greedy lip.

"This is one of the biggest pipelines in the country," DeMarco boasted, raising his voice to make himself heard. "Do you want to see how it works?"

Judd looked at him incredulously. DeMarco was acting the part of the perfect host again, entertaining a guest. No—not acting. He *meant* it. That was what was terrifying. DeMarco was about to murder Judd, and it would be a routine business transaction, something that had to be taken care of, like disposing of a piece of useless equipment, but he wanted to impress him first.

"Come on, Doctor. It's interesting."

They moved toward the pipeline, Angeli leading the way, DeMarco at Judd's side, and Rocky Vaccaro bringing up the rear.

"This plant grosses over five million dollars a year," DeMarco said proudly. "The whole operation is automatic."

As they got closer to the pipeline, the roar increased, the noise became almost intolerable. A hundred yards from the entrance to the vacuum chamber, a large conveyor belt carried giant logs to a planing machine twenty feet long and five feet high, with half a dozen razor-sharp cutter heads. The planed logs were then carried upward to a hog, a fierce porcupine-looking rotor bristling with knives. The air was filled with flying sawdust mixed with rain, being sucked into the pipeline.

"It doesn't matter how big the logs are," DeMarco said proudly. "The machines cut them down to fit that thirty-six-inch pipe."

DeMarco took a snub-nosed .38 Colt out of his pocket and called out, "Angeli."

Angeli turned.

"Have a good trip to Florida." DeMarco squeezed the trigger, and a red hole exploded in Angeli's shirt front. Angeli stared at DeMarco with a puzzled half-smile on his face, as though waiting for the answer to a riddle he had just heard. DeMarco pulled the trigger again. Angeli crumpled to the ground. DeMarco nodded to Rocky Vaccaro, and the big man picked up Angeli's body, slung it over his shoulder, and moved toward the pipeline.

DeMarco turned to Judd. "Angeli was stupid. Every cop in the country's looking for him. If they found him, he'd lead them to me."

The cold-blooded murder of Angeli was shock enough, but what followed was even worse. Judd watched, horrified, as Vaccaro carried Angeli's body toward the lip of the giant pipeline. The tremendous pressure caught at Angeli's body, greedily sucking it in. Vaccaro had to grab a large metal handle on the lip of the pipe to keep himself from being pulled in by the deadly cyclone of air. Judd had one last glimpse of Angeli's body whirling into the pipe through the vortex of sawdust and logs, and it was gone. Vaccaro reached for the valve next to the lip of the pipe and turned it. A cover slid over the mouth of the pipe, shutting off the cyclone of air. The sudden silence was deafening.

DeMarco turned to Judd and raised his gun. There was an exalted, mystic expression on his face, and Judd realized that murder was almost a religious experience for him. It was a crucible that purified. Judd knew that his moment of death had come. He felt no fear for himself, but he was consumed by rage that this man would be allowed to live, to murder Anne, to destroy other innocent, decent people. He heard a growling, a moan of rage and frustration, and realized it was coming from his own lips. He was like a trapped animal obsessed with the desire to kill his captor.

DeMarco was smiling at him, reading his thoughts. "I'm going to give it to you in the gut, Doctor. It'll take a little longer, but you'll have more time to worry about what's going to happen to Annie."

There was one hope. One slim hope.

"Someone should worry about her," Judd said. "She's never had a man."

DeMarco stared at him blankly.

Judd was yelling now, fighting to make DeMarco listen. "Do you know what your cock is? That gun in your hand. Without a gun or a knife, you're a woman."

He saw DeMarco's face fill with slow rage.

"You have no balls, DeMarco. Without that gun, you're a joke."

A red film was filling DeMarco's eyes, like a warning flag of death. Vaccaro took a step forward. DeMarco waved him back.

"I'll kill you with these bare hands," DeMarco said as he threw the gun to the ground. "With these bare hands!" Slowly, like a powerful animal, he started toward Judd.

Judd backed away, out of reach. He knew he stood no chance against DeMarco physically. His only hope was to work on DeMarco's sick mind, making it unable to function. He had to keep striking at DeMarco's most vulnerable area—his pride in his manhood. "You're a homosexual, DeMarco!"

DeMarco laughed and lunged at him. Judd moved out of reach.

Vaccaro picked up the gun from the ground. "Chief! Let me finish him!"

"Keep out of this!" DeMarco roared.

The two men circled, feinting for position. Judd's foot slipped on a pile of soggy sawdust, and DeMarco rushed at him like a charging bull. His huge fist hit Judd on the side of the mouth, knocking him back. Judd recovered and lashed out at DeMarco, hitting him in the face. DeMarco rocked back, then lunged forward and drove his fists into Judd's stomach. Three smashing blows that knocked the breath out of Judd. He tried to speak to taunt DeMarco, but he was gasping for air. DeMarco was hovering over him like a savage bird of prey.

"Getting winded, Doctor?" he laughed. "I was a boxer. I'm going to give you lessons. I'm going to work on your kidneys and then your head and your eyes. I'm gonna put your eyes out, Doctor. Before I'm through with you, you're going to beg me to shoot you."

Judd believed him. In the eerie light that spilled from the clouded sky, DeMarco looked like an enraged animal. He rushed at Judd again and caught him with his fist, splitting his cheek open with a heavy cameo ring. Judd lashed out at DeMarco, pounding at his face with both fists. DeMarco did not even flinch.

DeMarco began hitting Judd's kidneys, his hands working like pistons. Judd pulled away, his body a sea of pain.

"You're not getting tired, are you, Doctor?" He started to close in again. Judd knew that his body could not take much more punishment. He had to keep talking. It was his only chance.

"DeMarco . . ." He gasped.

DeMarco feinted and Judd swung at him. DeMarco ducked, laughed, and slammed his fist squarely between Judd's legs. Judd doubled over, filled with an unbelievable agony, and fell to the ground. DeMarco was on top of him, his hands at his throat.

"My bare hands," DeMarco screamed. "I'm going to tear your eyes out with my bare hands." He dug his huge fists into Judd's eyes.

They were speeding past Bedminster heading south on Route 206, when the call cracked in over the radio. "Code Three . . . Code Three . . . All cars stand by . . . New York Unit Twenty-seven . . . New York Unit Twenty-seven . . ."

McGreavy grabbed the radio microphone. "New York Twenty-seven . . . Come in!"

Captain Bertelli's excited voice came over the radio. "We've got it pinned down, Mac. There's a New Jersey pipeline company two miles south of Millstone. It's owned by the Five Star Corporation—the same company that owns the meat-packing plant. It's one of the fronts Tony DeMarco uses.

"Sounds right," McGreavy said. "We're on our way."

"How far are you from there?"

"Ten miles."

"Good luck."

"Yeah."

McGreavy switched off the radio, hit the siren, and slammed the accelerator to the floorboard.

The sky was spinning in wet circles overhead and something was pounding at him, tearing his body apart. He tried to see, but his eyes were swollen shut. A fist smashed into his ribs, and he felt the agonizing splinter of bones breaking. He could feel DeMarco's hot breath on his face, coming in quick, excited gasps. He tried to see him, but he was locked in darkness. He opened his mouth and forced words past his thick, swollen tongue. "You s-see," he gasped. "I was r-right . . . You can—you can only hit a man— when he's down. . . ."

The breathing in his face stopped. He felt two hands grab him and pull him to his feet.

"You're a dead man, Doctor. And I did it with my bare hands."

Judd backed away from the voice. "You're an—an a-animal," he said, gasping for breath. "A psychopath. . . . You should be locked up . . . in an . . . insane asylum."

DeMarco's voice was thick with rage. "You're a liar!"

"It's the t-truth," Judd said, moving back. "Your . . . your brain is diseased. . . . Your mind is going to . . . snap and you'll be . . . like an idiot baby." Judd backed away, unable to see where he was going. Behind him he heard the faint hum of the closed pipeline, waiting like a sleeping giant.

DeMarco lunged at Judd, his huge hands clutching his throat. "I'm going to break your neck!" His enormous fingers closed on Judd's windpipe, squeezing.

Judd felt his head begin to swim. This was his last chance. Every instinct in him screamed out to grab DeMarco's hands and pull them away from his throat so that he could breathe. Instead, with a final tremendous effort of will, he put his hands in back of him, fumbling for the pipe valve. He felt himself beginning to slide into unconsciousness, and in that instant his hands closed on the valve. With a final, desperate burst of energy, he turned the handle and swerved his body around so that DeMarco was nearest the opening. A tremendous vacuum of air suddenly blasted at them, trying to pull them into the vortex of the pipe. Judd clung frantically to the valve with both hands, fighting the cyclonic fury of the wind. He felt DeMarco's fingers digging into his throat as DeMarco was pulled toward the pipe. DeMarco could have saved himself, but in his mindless insane fury, he refused to let go. Judd could not see DeMarco's face, but the voice was a demented animal cry, the words lost in the roar of the wind.

Judd's fingers started to slip off the valve. He was going to be pulled into the pipeline with DeMarco. He gave a quick, last prayer, and in that instant he felt DeMarco's hands slip away from his throat. There was a loud, reverberating scream, and then only the roar from the pipeline. DeMarco had vanished.

Judd stood there, bone weary, unable to move, waiting for the shot from Vaccaro.

A moment later it rang out.

He stood there, wondering why Vaccaro had missed. Through the dull haze of pain, he heard more shots, and the sound of feet running, and then his name being called. And then someone had an arm around him and McGreavy's voice was saying, "Mother of God! Look at his face!"

Strong hands gripped his arm and pulled him away from the awful roaring tug of the pipeline. Something wet was running down his cheeks and he did not know whether it was blood or rain or tears, and he did not care.

It was over.

He forced one puffed eye open and through a narrow, blood-red slit, he could dimly see McGreavy. "Anne's at the house," Judd said. "DeMarco's wife. We've got to go to her."

McGreavy was looking at him strangely, not moving, and Judd realized that no words had come out. He lifted his mouth up to McGreavy's ear and spoke slowly, in a hoarse, broken croak. "Anne DeMarco . . . She's at the . . . house . . . help."

McGreavy walked over to the police car, picked up the radio transmitter, and issued instructions. Judd stood there, unsteady, still rocking back and forth from DeMarco's blows, letting the cold, biting wind wash over him. In front of him he could see a body lying on the ground, and he knew it was Rocky Vaccaro.

We've won, he thought. *We've won*. He kept saying the phrase over and over in his mind. And even as he said it, he knew it was meaningless. What kind of victory was it? He had thought of himself as a decent, civilized human being—a doctor, a healer— and he had turned into a savage animal filled with the lust to kill. He had sent a sick man over the brink of insanity and then murdered him. It was a terrible burden he would have to live with always. Because even though he could tell himself it was in self- defense, he knew—God help him—that he had enjoyed doing it. And for that he could never forgive himself. He was no better than DeMarco, or the Vaccaro brothers, or any of the others. Civiliza- tion was a thin, dangerously fragile veneer, and when that veneer cracked, man became one with the beasts again, falling back into the slime of the primeval abyss he prided himself on having climbed up from.

Judd was too weary to think about it any longer. Now he wanted only to see that Anne was safe.

McGreavy was standing there, his manner strangely gentle.

"There's a police car on the way to her house, Dr. Stevens. OK?"

Judd nodded gratefully.

McGreavy took his arm and guided him toward a car. As he moved slowly, painfully, across the courtyard, he realized that it had stopped raining. On the far horizon the thunderheads had been swept away by the raw December wind, and the sky was clearing. In the west a small ray of light appeared as the sun began to fight its way through, growing brighter and brighter.

It was going to be a beautiful Christmas.

ABOUT THE AUTHOR

Sidney Sheldon is the author of *The Other Side of Midnight*, *A Stranger in the Mirror*, *Bloodline*, *Rage of Angels*, *Master of the Game*, *If Tomorrow Comes*, *Windmills of the Gods*, *The Sands of Time*, and *Memories of Midnight*, all international bestsellers. His first book, *The Naked Face*, was acclaimed by *The New York Times* as the "best first mystery of the year." Sheldon won a Tony Award for Broadway's *Redhead* and an Academy Award for *The Bachelor and the Bobby-Soxer*. He wrote the screenplays for twenty-three motion pictures, including *Easter Parade* (with Judy Garland) and *Annie Get Your Gun*. He created four long-running television series, including *Hart to Hart* and *I Dream of Jeannie*, which he also produced. Sidney Sheldon and his wife live in southern California and in London.